# PERILOUS ENCHANTMENT

Nicholas said a silent prayer, something he hadn't done in a long, long time. Not for himself, but for his children should he die.

He raised the water to his lips rapidly, so that he wouldn't have to think about what he was doing.

He drank—

And tasted the coldest, sweetest water he had ever had. It quenched his thirst and made him feel stronger. Without thinking, he dipped his hands again, and then again, drinking as much as he could.

Adrian reached for him, signaling him, asking him to stop, but Nicholas did not want to.

He wasn't sure if he could.

The water filled him and spread, and he drank and drank, and somewhere along the way, he realized he had been forgetting to breathe, to think, to make choices on his own.

His hands moved, his lips supped, his throat swallowed, and black spots danced in front of his eyes. He needed air. He needed—

He reached for Adrian, reached—

And felt himself slip away. . . .

Also by Kristine Kathryn Rusch

Fantasy
*The Fey: Resistance*
*The Fey: Rival*
*The Fey: The Changeling*
*The Fey: The Sacrifice*
*Traitors*
*Heart Readers*
*The White Mists of Power*

Science Fiction
*Alien Influences*
*Star Wars: The New Rebellion*
*Aliens: Rogue* (written as Sandy Schofield)
*Quantam Leap: Loch Ness Leap* (written as Sandy Schofield)

Horror
*The Devil's Churn*
*Sins of the Blood*
*Facade*
*Afterimage* (with Kevin J. Anderson)

Mystery
*Hitler's Angel* (written as Kris Rusch)

Star Trek Novels
*The Mist* (with Dean Wesley Smith)
*Echoes* (with Dean Wesley Smith & Nina Kiriki Hoffman)
*Treaty's Law* (with Dean Wesley Smith)
*Soldiers of Fear* (with Dean Wesley Smith)
*Rings of Tautee* (with Dean Wesley Smith)
*Klingon!* (with Dean Wesley Smith)
*The Long Night* (with Dean Wesley Smith)
*The Escape* (with Dean Wesley Smith)
*The Big Game* (as Sandy Schofield)

Anthologies
*The Best from Fantasy and Science Fiction* (with Edward L. Ferman)
*The Best of Pulphouse*

# VICTORY

## THE FEY

*Kristine Kathryn Rusch*

BANTAM BOOKS
NEW YORK   TORONTO   LONDON
SYDNEY   AUCKLAND

THE FEY: VICTORY

A Bantam Spectra Book / November 1998

SPECTRA and the portrayal of a boxed "s" are trademarks of Bantam
Books, a division of Bantam Doubleday Dell Publishing Group, Inc.

ISBN 0-553-57714-X

Published simultaneously in the United States and Canada

Bantam Books are published by Bantam Books, a division of Bantam
Doubleday Dell Publishing Group, Inc. Its trademark, consisting of the words
"Bantam Books" and the portrayal of a rooster, is Registered in U.S. Patent
and Trademark Office and in other countries. Marca Registrada. Bantam
Books, 1540 Broadway, New York, New York 10036.

PRINTED IN THE UNITED STATES OF AMERICA

WCD   10   9   8   7   6   5   4   3   2   1

For Chris and Steve York
with thanks for all the years of friendship

# ACKNOWLEDGMENTS

Thanks on this one go to Dean Wesley Smith for discussing the future of the Fey; Kathy Oltion for her boundless enthusiasm; Sandy Hofsommer for expecting the unexpected; Paul Higginbotham for nagging; Anne Lesley Groell for having the sturdiest desk and quickest response time in all of publishing; Matt Schwartz for keeping up the Web page (please visit @ www.horrornet.com/rusch.htm); and to all the readers who ask questions, keep me on my toes, and who've let me know how much they're enjoying the series.

# THE ATTACK

# ONE

LUKE huddled in the small trees that separated his neighbor Medes's farm from the farm the Fey had been using as a stronghold. He could barely see across the yard. The moon had set when he and his three companions had started on this mission. Luke wasn't nervous, but he could hear Jona's heavy breathing and the rustle of Medes's clothing as he moved, and could feel Totle's occasional jumps of fright.

None of them had ever done anything like this. The three men with Luke were farmers. They had tilled land, grown crops, and worked in daylight since they were tiny boys. When the Fey first invaded Blue Isle twenty years before, Totle hadn't even been born. Luke had fought, but Jona and Medes hadn't.

Luke had been captured. The Fey's treatment of him and his father had changed his entire life.

Now his father was missing, and the Fey's second invasion of Blue Isle had deposed the King, destroyed the main city of Jahn, and forced the farmers—all the Islanders—to work for Fey glory. Luke had decided that he would do that, in the daylight. At night, he would concentrate on destroying the Fey.

The others had come along because they too wanted the Fey off the Isle. They knew, as he did, that this mission was probably futile—that they could as easily die as succeed—but they also knew that the Fey had a weakness.

Their weakness was in their own arrogance, their own confidence in themselves, their own belief in their undefeatability. Luke had seen what happened to the Fey who had lost that belief. They made mistakes. They died.

He hoped to shake that confidence to its very roots tonight.

He glanced at his companions. Jona, the neighbor who had helped him set up this small resistance force, was a slender man, almost as old as Luke's father, with the thin, wiry look of a person who'd worked in the sun his whole life. His skin was naturally dark from all those years outside, but Luke had insisted in covering him with dirt anyway. Jona wore the darkest clothes he owned, and those too had been covered in the rich, black ground that gave the Islanders such healthy crops. Except for his bright eyes, he was nearly invisible in the dark.

Totle was the youngest of them. He was from a farm several miles away from Luke's. Luke had never met him before. He had come with Jona when Luke had sent out the word. Totle was in his early twenties, and had taken over his farm when his father had died the year before. He still had that leanness only the very young and the very active had. His skin had been burnt by the extra hours he had spent in the fields before the Fey forces arrived in this part of the country, and he bore a bruise on his left cheek that he had received when he had tried to guard his farm from the invaders.

They hadn't killed him. The Fey respected farmers too much. They had taken Blue Isle partly for its strategic location—halfway between the continents of Galinas, which the Fey had conquered, and Leut, which the Fey wanted next—and partly for its incredible richness. With Fey scattered over half the world, their demand for supplies and raw materials was great. They had already given the farmers in this section of Blue Isle instructions on how to improve yields and on what the Fey expectations would be for the future.

The last member of Luke's party, Medes, crouched beside Jona. Medes was a thick man, with corded muscles that ran the length of each arm. He had small, spindly legs, and he bore much of his weight in his torso, which was rounded with muscle. He too wore black dirt. His silver hair proved to be the largest problem. They had had to cake the dirt in it to hide the color, and even then Jona would occasionally glance at him, curse, and rub more dirt in his hair.

They were sitting on Medes's land. The small trees served as a windbreak between Medes's farm and the farm the Fey were now using. That farm had belonged to a man named Antoni and his family. The Fey had told Luke that Antoni and his family had gone to work for one of the southern farms, but he had learned differently last night.

He had been reconnoitering this place, searching for a first strike for his small band, when he had gone into the barn. Inside, he had discovered Fey pouches. The pouches, which contained skin and blood and sometimes bones from the victims of a battle, were used by Spell Warders to devise more magick spells. The pouches also had other uses, things Luke did not understand, but had heard of.

He had found his target.

He had also found Antoni. Luke had hit his head on a small lamp, and its illumination had flooded the barn. Inside the lamp were tiny figures composed of light: Antoni and his family. The only way their souls could have been trapped in that lamp was if their bodies were gone.

They were dead; they just hadn't realized it yet.

The Fey often captured souls and used them for light. The Fey were not wasteful conquerors. They used each part of a victim for their magick, and they used all the resources of the countries they conquered, renewing those resources whenever possible and using them to continue to build the strength of the Fey Empire. This conquering strategy was, Luke believed, one of the many things that gave the Fey their power.

Through the copse of trees, he had an imperfect view of the farmhouse. Fey were inside it, and outside. The guard on this building was not traditional for Fey. Usually, they put some kind of magick spell on the place, or they created a Shadowlands, marked by a tiny rotating circle of lights. The hoped that the fact the Fey used real soldiers as guards, instead of trusting their magick, meant that there were few magickal Fey around. The Fey guarding this place had looked, in the daylight, young. Most Fey did not come into their magick until their early twenties, forcing many of them to serve in the magickless infantry during those years.

Luke guessed that Infantry held this patch of land, not any of the higher orders. He guessed, but he did not count on it.

He was fully prepared to die in this raid.

He would do his best to make sure that Jona, Medes, and Totle did not.

Their target was not the farmhouse, but the barn, and those magick pouches. There were only two guards on the barn, both near the main entrance. It showed, Luke thought, that the Fey, for all their military knowledge, and their demands regarding yield and production, knew very little about actual farming. He had gotten into the barn the night before by crawling through an open slat in the back.

The group would do the same tonight.

And tonight, the light was with them. The moon, which had been full the night before, had set. They had very little time before dawn to conduct their raid.

Luke nodded to his companions. Totle patted his side. He had rags hanging from two pouches. Medes held up the small bottle of grain alcohol that he had brought. He had said it would help them. Jona took the wicks he had carried and held them in one hand. Luke had the flints. He didn't trust anyone else with them. He also had a few rags and a few wicks. He figured he could make do without the alcohol if he had to.

He pointed to the barn. Totle's shoulders rose and fell as he took a deep breath, then he crouched and scuttled away from the trees. Medes followed a moment later, and then Jona. Luke brought up the rear, as he had planned.

Luke had thought to go first when he set this plan into motion, but Jona had talked him out of it.

"You're the only one of us with knowledge of the Fey," Jona had said. "If they see anyone, it'll be the first. And then they'll kill him. The rest of us can get away."

Luke knew that wasn't the case; when he had been captured, he had been in the center of the attacking force, but he agreed with Jona anyway. Luke was less afraid of the Fey than he was of having his small band backing down at exactly the wrong point. By going last, he could prevent one of them from turning around, running, and calling attention to the whole group.

Totle had reached the first hay bale. Luke's biggest worry was that Totle, who was the least familiar with this field and farm, would go in the wrong direction. So far, he was following instructions to the letter.

Medes then left the hiding place at the copse of trees. He scuttled across the field as well, but his larger form was more visible, at least to Luke. Luke glanced at the farmhouse. The Fey weren't talking as they had been the night before. He couldn't see the guards very clearly at all.

But he knew they were there.

All he hoped for was that their lack of magick would help him. He hoped they would shout, or converse among themselves, before coming after Luke's small group.

But he had seen the Fey in action too many times. They always appeared silently at first and then they began their shouting. He suspected that if they saw this small band, things wouldn't be any different.

Medes made it to the first bale. Totle started for the second just as Jona left the copse of trees. Luke had set it up so that only two members of the group would move at one time. He figured that way only half of his force would get caught if the Fey weren't diligent.

If they were diligent, the whole group would die.

Jona moved the best of all of them—so low to the ground that he was almost invisible. He looked like a shadow in the darkness.

Fortunately, all of the men were farmers. They knew how to move on a cut hayfield without making any noise. They knew how to avoid the stalks that would crunch beneath their feet. They knew how to approach a bale without making it shake.

Luke was glad that these three had joined him. He had others in his small resistance movement, thanks to Jona's efforts, who would not have made as good stalkers. Indeed, Luke had been surprised: in the day since he had first spoken to Jona, Jona had gotten the word to a good dozen farmers who had, in fact, spread the word to at least a dozen more. The group had not met yet, and Luke doubted it would ever meet in full force, but they all knew of each other, and they had already developed signals and meeting places. He hoped they would have time to develop systems to fool the Fey, but he thought that might be wishful thinking. The Fey rarely gave anyone plenty of time to plan.

Jona had reached the hay bale. That was Luke's cue. He swallowed hard—his mouth was suddenly dry—and started across the field.

He moved much more like Medes, and he knew it. Upright and quick, placing his feet on the exact right places, he hurried toward the bale. As he did so, he scanned the field. The house was dark, unlike the night before, and the guards weren't as obvious. The two trees that served as a windbreak behind the house were completely still.

There wasn't even a breeze this night, which was, he thought, both good and bad. Good because the Fey couldn't smell something different on the breeze, and bad because every noise was amplified. One misstep, and they would have the guards' attention.

He reached the hay bale as Medes reached the next one. Ahead, he could see Totle pat Medes on the back.

Jona grabbed Luke's arm, pulled him close, and put a finger to his lips. Then he pointed at the barn. Luke squinted. Finally he saw what Jona did.

Three guards.

The night before they had had only two.

Well, that took care of one of his fears. With the farmhouse so dark, he had been afraid that the Fey had moved on without his knowing, that they were gone, and their pouches with them, and this entire raid had been for nothing.

But in taking care of that fear, it had given him another. Had they known about his visit the previous night?

The Fey lamp had gone on. He had made no attempt to hide the light. But he had leaned a rake against it, making it look as if the rake had fallen and jarred the light awake.

Maybe the Fey hadn't fallen for that.

Maybe they knew someone else had been in their barn.

But how?

He took a deep breath to bring down the panic. They were Fey. They had powers he did not. He shouldn't question how. He should merely accept it.

He would just have to be cautious. He hoped that Totle would be. He had tried to warn the boy. But he didn't know Totle well, and that worried him. Luke had checked for all the signs of Fey influence, the ones his father's Fey friend Scavenger had warned him about, but Luke didn't trust the Fey in any way.

There might have been one that Scavenger had left out.

Luke nodded at Jona just as Totle started for the third bale. Luke pushed Jona slightly, and he headed forward, moving as they planned.

The field wasn't very large, but this system made it feel as if it were the size of eight fields. The waiting made Luke nervous, and he checked the sky to see if there were any sign of the sun.

No. The darkness was still as complete as it had been before. There were clouds above him, and that added to the blackness. Some kind of luck was with him, just as there had been the night before. Something wanted him to get to that barn.

He only hoped that something wasn't Fey.

Totle and Jona reached their respective bales. Then Luke and Medes left their posts and moved forward. Luke felt exposed as he crossed the emptiness between bales. But he could see more of the barn. No Fey on the side closest to him. And two Fey at the door of the farmhouse.

Two Fey only.

None of the guards noticed him as he crossed the fields. They didn't notice Medes either.

So far, so good.

Totle was nearly ready to start the long trek in the open to get to the back of the barn. Luke couldn't help him with that either, couldn't warn him any more than he already had about the possibility of more guards in the back.

And about how to find that loose board. Luke didn't know how hard it would be in this darkness. He wanted to set the fire inside the barn, not outside. It would be too easy for the Fey to spot if he set it outside, and they would be able to put it out.

He wanted the fire to rage before they even noticed it existed.

He made it to his second bale. Jona clapped him on the back. Luke smiled and nodded. Then Jona left for the third bale, just as Totle crossed the field toward the barn.

Luke held his breath. He watched the boy's frame, noting the low crouch, the rapid movement. Totle was doing everything he was told, moving with complete purpose, not stopping to check his surroundings, getting to the next site and then securing it.

This was the difficult one.

This was the unknown part.

Luke wondered if this was how his father had felt when Luke had volunteered to go on that first mission against the Fey. When Luke *insisted* on going. Luke felt incredible nerves now, and he didn't even know the boy. Imagine how he would feel if the boy were his son.

Totle disappeared behind the barn.

Luke held his breath another moment—and heard nothing. No scream. No cry for help. No announcement from the Fey that they had captured one of the Islanders. Nothing.

Luke let out the breath he had been holding. He noted that Jona had made it to the third bale.

There was still no sound from behind the barn. Maybe a Fey had been there and grabbed Totle, wrapping a hand around Totle's mouth to keep him quiet.

Maybe the Fey were just waiting there, waiting to see who else would come. Maybe they hadn't noticed the four invaders at all.

Medes glanced at Luke, as if he too were uncertain about what to do next. Luke saw Medes's movement, but he didn't know if

Medes could see him clearly. Despite the uncertainty, Luke nodded, as if to tell Medes to go ahead.

Medes did.

Luke couldn't watch him because Luke had to cross to the third bale. As he moved, he saw that the three guards hadn't left their posts. Neither had the guards near the house. The sky was unchanged. Very little time had gone by, although to Luke, it felt like hours.

Days.

He hadn't been this tense in a long, long time.

Then he took a deep breath and forced himself the think of something else. Of the way his feet fell on the dying hay stalks. Of the way the bales' shadows added darkness to the already-existing darkness on the field. Of the bale looming in front of him, Jona hiding in its shadow.

Luke had the right to inform these people of the dangers. He had done that. And because he had done that, he had given them enough information to make their own decisions.

If they died, it was because they had chosen to be here this night, because they had chosen to fight the Fey.

When that thought crossed him mind, he felt better. Much better. The anxiety that had haunted him when he first reached the copse of trees fell away.

And he knew that was probably good. A leader couldn't be plagued by doubts. They would interfere with his ability to lead.

Luke reached the third hay bale.

Medes disappeared around the back of the barn.

Jona tensed beside Luke. At this close proximity, Luke could smell the scent of Jona's fear mingled with his sweat. Jona was as terrified of this as Luke had been just a moment before.

But Jona was still going forward.

There was a silence from the barn. Even though Luke squinted, he couldn't see against the darkness. He wanted to see shadows, to know if his two men struggled, to know if they needed help.

He touched Jona on the side and Jona jumped. Luke took Jona's arm, and moved it toward his side, toward the knife he had tied to his waist. Jona understood. He removed the knife. He would be prepared in case the others were in trouble.

Then he nodded once to Luke and headed across the field. Luke watched as Jona made his way, like a wraith, against the darkness of the field.

Something snapped.

Jona had snapped a hay stalk.

Jona fell flat, and that time, his movement was silent.

Luke bit his lower lip. He crawled cautiously to the edge of the bale and glanced at the guards.

They were looking around, but they didn't seem to see anything. Then one of them laughed. The others laughed with him.

A leader, then?

Or merely someone who told a good joke?

Luke turned his head toward Jona. Jona remained down, counting to fifty as they had planned. Luke looked again at the guards.

They hadn't moved.

Luke couldn't see the guards near the house.

Jona disappeared behind the barn.

Luke bit his lip so hard he tasted blood. He grabbed his knife and waited at the edge of the hay bale.

He was supposed to count to fifty too. But he couldn't concentrate. He started once, then twice, then glanced at the guards. They had moved closer to each other, but weren't talking.

Maybe they were listening.

Luke would have to be very, very careful. It all depended on him.

He started into the field.

And immediately saw why Jona had made a noise. He was amazed no one else had.

The stalks from the field trimming were short here. There were long stalks that hadn't been wrapped into bales all along the ground. It was hard to see them in the dark, and even harder to find a place to put his feet.

He went slower than he normally would have. He didn't want to make a second noise. He didn't want to draw the guards' attention if, indeed, it hadn't been drawn already.

He was breathing shallowly, his heart pounding. His ears were straining for a sound, any sound other than the hush-hush of his feet on the broken hay stalks. Every noise he made, from the rustle of his clothing to the soft exhalation of breath, sent little shivers through him. He was convinced the Fey were listening as hard as he was.

Then he made it to the side of the barn. The wood was warm and rough against his palm. He peered around the corner and saw nothing.

It was dark in the back, darker than anywhere else. His eyes, adjusted to the night, hadn't adjusted to this. He squinted, trying to see, but he couldn't. He couldn't hear anything either: no breathing, no moans, no cries.

If his friends had been captured by the Fey, they weren't outside. If they hadn't, they were inside the barn, waiting for him, him, and the flints, and the instructions.

He clenched his left fist against the barn's wood. Almost there. Almost there, and the night would be over.

The mission would be over, and he could return home.

He sensed no one else. His heart was pounding so hard, he felt that the Fey could hear the hammering. He had trouble keeping his breathing regular.

It was now, or not at all.

He kept his left hand against the side of the barn. He rounded the corner, knife out, and went to the back where the rotted board was, the board he had found the night before.

It was in the center as he remembered. He crouched down and felt the dug-out area. The board had been pulled loose, by one of his friends, he hoped, and not by the Fey.

He slid through the dug-out area, noting that the smell of dog was gone. The fur he had felt the night before was also gone, probably rubbed away by his friends.

The smell of rot remained.

He resisted the urge to sneeze. The scent got into his nostrils, invaded his body, coated him. What a difference a day made. Those pouches had a stink all their own.

And then he was inside.

The darkness was so thick he couldn't see anything. Mixed with the stink of rot was the pungent scent of the grain alcohol.

Hands touched him, pulling him up, familiar hands.

"Luke?" Jona whispered.

"Yes," he whispered back. "Everyone here?"

"Yes," Medes whispered.

"The pouches are to our right," Luke whispered. He knew that from memory.

"We have to be quick about this," Jona whispered. "They heard me on the field."

"But they haven't checked it yet," Luke whispered.

"Still," Jona whispered.

"Enough talking," Medes whispered. "Let's do this."

"All right," Totle whispered. "The rags are already soaked."

"Alcohol's poured all over those smelly pouches," Medes whispered.

"Wicks are in place," Jona whispered. "I'm holding one."

They were just waiting for him. Luke pulled the flints out of his own small pouch. He took the hand on his shoulder, put a flint in it. "Hands," he whispered. Two more touched him, and he put flints in those as well.

As if it were planned, all the flints sparked, and for a brief instant, Luke saw the pouches, the soaked rags, the wicks running to this section of the barn.

Then the sparks went out.

He crouched next to the wick Jona was holding, and lit it. It burned easily—it had been treated, as so many candle wicks had—and the flame moved quickly across it. The tiny flame looked like a large fire, banishing the darkness.

Luke's heart was trying to pound through his chest.

Totle picked up another wick and lit it, as Medes lit a third. Jona grabbed the last and lit that.

Luke's flame hit the first soaked rag and it burst into a brilliant blue flame.

"Now," he said, not whispering any more. They had to get out. He grabbed Totle, and shoved him toward the rotted board. Totle crawled through the dug-out area, followed closely by Jona, then Medes.

Luke glanced behind him. The rags were all burning, a bright high blue flame with orange on the top. He could feel the heat against his face and skin.

Then he flung himself into the dug-out area and crawled out of the barn. His companions were running across the field, not caring about the sound their feet made. Fey were shouting behind him.

Luke pulled himself to his feet, saw tendrils of white smoke emerging from cracks in the barn wall. Fire crackled inside.

"This is for Blue Isle!" he shouted.

Then he too started to run.

# TWO

CON reached the farmhouse long after the moon had set. Without that little bit of light, the darkness seemed intense. He pounded on the door, and received no answer. Then he went to the windows, and pounded on them.

The farmhouse was empty.

Or it seemed empty. Maybe someone was hiding from him, although he wasn't exactly sure why someone would. Besides, something about the way the sound echoed made the place feel deserted.

He sat on the stoop and put his face in his hands. He didn't know when he had last slept. Probably days ago. The last time he remembered eating was when he and Sebastian had been in the cavern with the Rocaanists.

So much had happened, it felt like months ago.

He still felt guilty about Sebastian. Sebastian, King Nicholas's odd son, who walked and spoke slowly, but who seemed to have an intelligence belied by his strange body. Con had rescued Sebastian from the palace, only to lose him weeks later.

He and Sebastian had gone through the tunnels and would have escaped if the rope ladder out of the catacombs hadn't burned away. They had tried to build a staircase of crates, and the Fey had caught them.

They had taken Sebastian. Con had drawn his sword—a sword with so much power, it had once killed a dozen Fey in few moments—and then Sebastian had hit the crates, burying Con under the pile, probably saving Con's life. By the time he had freed himself, Sebastian was gone.

And now Con was here, at the farm of Sebastian's friends. At least, he thought they were Sebastian's friends. Sebastian had given him instructions on how to get here long before the Fey had found them. But when Sebastian had given the instructions, he had said he was using someone else's memories. While Con was making the long walk here from the burned city of Jahn, he thought about those words often.

Someone else's memories.

Whose?

He wasn't sure he was going to find out. The field here was well tended—corn, which he remembered from his young childhood, which wasn't that long ago. He was only thirteen now, but he felt a lot older. Ten years older, in fact, most of those years gained in the last two weeks.

The Rocaan, the religious leader who was now dead, had given Con a Charge to warn the King of the Fey invasion. Con had arrived at the palace too late; the Fey had already overtaken it. There he had taken a sword, saved himself, and hid. When he set the sword down on a pile of rocks, there had been an explosion, and the rocks had re-formed into Sebastian, naked and crying. Con had taken him as a responsibility, a Charge, and had failed at that too.

The Fey had Sebastian now. The King's son. And he was such a gentle soul. They might destroy him.

Con was going to ask Sebastian's friends to help rescue him. But Sebastian's friends weren't here, and Con didn't know what to do.

He sighed and brushed his hair from his face, then adjusted his stolen shirt and trousers. He still felt odd, not wearing the robes of his office. He was an Aud, one of the few members of the Rocaanist religion left. The Fey had burned the Tabernacle and slaughtered the remaining Rocaanists in the cavern after Con and Sebastian had left.

Sebastian had saved Con's life twice. Con had to help him.

And the first thing he had to do was see what had happened in this farmhouse. The emptiness bothered Con more than he wanted to admit.

He got up and knocked again. The sound echoed through the fields, making him feel even more alone.

Con took a deep breath and tried the door. It opened easily. As he stepped inside, he noted the faint odor of baked bread. He found himself in a kitchen designed like those in the Tabernacle, with storage space and a nice-sized cooking hearth. Someone had built cabinets on the wall, things he had only heard about, and those from people who'd seen inside one of the Fey places.

Con shuddered. He ran his finger along one of the countertops. Wood, sanded smooth. It was luxurious to the touch.

Farmhouses usually weren't luxurious. Maybe these really were Sebastian's friends.

"Hello?" he shouted.

The sound fell, like sounds often did in an empty place. He was alone.

Still, he went through each room—and there were more of them than he expected: a main room, with comfortable furniture; two bedrooms, both empty; and a smaller room not much bigger than a closet, used for storage.

Sebastian's friends were gone. But they had taken nothing with them. Clothes still rested in the storage room. The beds were made. Some fresh bread was carefully wrapped and sitting inside a bread box.

Whoever had been here had planned to come back.

But why would people disappear at night?

Why would farmers?

It made no sense.

Nothing did any more.

Con's shoulders were tight, and his stomach was churning. He took some bread and dipped a cup into a bucket of water sitting on one of the counters. Then he took his meal outside, hoping the residents of the house, whoever they were—wherever they were—wouldn't mind.

He decided to sit on the stoop and wait until dawn. If no one came back to tend the fields, he would have to think up a new plan. If the Fey were tending the fields, he would run. If they chased him, he would fight.

He still had his sword.

After all the death he'd seen, he was certain the Lord would understand if Con defended himself.

He sat down on the stoop and shivered slightly in the cool night air. The days had been hot, but this night, and the night before, had been cool. Once he had gotten outside the city of Jahn—or what was left of it—the air had gotten even cooler. The fires had burned themselves out in the city, but some of the ashes still gave off heat. He suspected that in those hot areas, the fires would flare back up with very little encouragement.

If he was honest with himself, he was glad to be out. The city wasn't familiar any more. The Tabernacle, his physical and spiritual home, was gone. The south side of the city, on the Tabernacle side of Cardidas River, was in ruins. Only a handful of buildings survived on the other side, and most of those were near the palace, which was untouched.

Except for the Fey living inside.

He took a bite of bread, hoping it would quell the despair that twisted his stomach. The Fey had taken over the entire Isle. They had driven the king from the palace and recaptured Sebastian. They had destroyed Rocaanism. Con didn't know how God had allowed that.

He didn't know *why* God would allow that. He had always thought God would protect his people. The Fey didn't even acknowledge the Islanders' God. How could God be protecting the Fey?

Con made himself take another bite of bread. He washed it down with a swig of warm water.

There had to be more. There had to be. God was merely testing his people on the Isle. That was all. They had had an easy existence since the Roca had been Absorbed, but now that time was over. Now they had to show their worth again.

Con hoped.

He stood to get more bread when suddenly a loud boom rent the air. He turned toward the sound, and saw a fire burning high into the night sky. It lit up the fields. He walked toward it, trying to see what was burning, and couldn't.

The light was intense, though, and the smell as bad as the smell of the dead bodies rotting in the catacombs beneath the Tabernacle.

He had never seen flames burn so high. It was as if they were consuming the sky. Sparks flew around them, from inside them, spiraling up and disappearing into the dark.

A wave swept over him, not of heat, but of feeling. Of prickliness. Of power. It slapped him backwards and then passed over him. He turned, wondering if he could see it and for a moment, a very brief moment, he saw a ripple in the darkness.

Then it disappeared.

The fire didn't. Even from this distance, he could hear its roar. He turned back toward it, heard faint voices yelling in Fey, and watched the flames climb.

The flames weren't coming toward him. He was in no danger. Not yet.

But something had changed.

Instinctively he grabbed the filigree sword around his neck, the only symbol of his religion he still allowed himself, bowed his head, and prayed that the change was God's change.

He prayed that the change would bring only good.

# THREE

ARIANNA woke from her spot on the far corner of the cave floor. The mysterious light still glowed, and the area was as bright as daylight. She had had an arm over her eyes, blocking out the brilliance. She was ravenously hungry, but she didn't think that was what had awakened her.

Her brother by birth, Gift, sat up on his pallet on the other side of the floor. He was frowning, as if something had awakened him, too. His gaze met Arianna's. She still found his blue eyes disconcerting. She raised a finger to her lips.

He nodded.

Coulter stirred. He was sleeping near Adrian, the Islander who was close to Arianna's father's age. Arianna's father, King Nicholas, had moved his pallet behind the fountain, and as she had drifted off, she had thought she heard him laugh softly.

He had been acting strangely since she awoke from her odd exile inside herself to find herself in this cave. So much had changed since the Black King had invaded her mind. She had left the mountainside, woken up in this cave, and discovered the Shaman was dead.

Arianna felt the worst about that. She didn't understand how it had happened—her father had promised to explain later and hadn't yet—but Arianna suspected it had something to do with her. The Shaman had been supposed to rescue her, and hadn't.

Coulter had.

She glanced at him. He was sitting up too. He was pure Islander, his blond hair tousled, his eyes sleepy, and he was the most handsome man she had ever seen. Superimposed over his real image was the one he had shared with her when he had crossed her father's Link into Arianna's mind, when he had come to rescue her.

Then Coulter had looked like the perfect cross between Islander and Fey. His skin had been light, his eyes blue, and his hair blond, but he had had pointed ears and upswept cheekbones, and he had been the tallest person she had ever seen. Here, in the real world, he was shorter than she was.

They were the only three awake. Leen, the Fey woman whom Gift said had not yet come into her magick, was asleep at the foot of the stairs. The remaining member of the party, Scavenger, who was a Red Cap—a Fey with no magick—slept so soundly he snored.

Yet something had changed, something profound.

She felt a shiver run through her. Even though her father had said this place was safe for her, she wasn't sure. The Shaman, before she died, had called this a Place of Power, and had said that Gift had discovered it. What the place had turned out to be was a cave filled with the artifacts of the Islander religion: vials filled with holy water, which was poisonous to Fey and probably to her; chalices she was unwilling to touch, even though they appeared empty when Adrian looked at them: swords so sharp that Adrian had nearly cut himself on an edge; and tapestries covering more passageways, leading farther back. Arianna's father had promised they would explore the passageways, but not until she was rested.

Her ordeal on the mountainside had apparently sapped all her remaining energy. She had never been so exhausted in her life.

Her great-grandfather, the Black King, had used her brother Sebastian's Link to her to cross into her mind. Sebastian had followed and thrown the Black King out. But while the Black King was there, Arianna had kept him contained by Shifting into every form she could think of. The Black King was not a Shape-Shifter like she was, although he was a Visionary, and he did not know how to control the Shifts or even how to use a body that had Shifted.

She had held him for a time, then Sebastian had appeared, crossing the Link that she had with him. He had lured the Black King away, and in trying to kill the Black King, Sebastian had shattered again, sending her sprawling backwards into her own mind. She had gotten lost there, and Coulter had found her.

Coulter.

He smiled at her now, a bit uncertainly. None of the three of them were getting off their pallets It was as if the thing that had awakened them was not inside the cave.

It had come from elsewhere.

The hair rose on her arms, even though the cave was not cold. She pushed off the robe that she had been using as a blanket, and braced a hand behind her. Even standing was hard at this point. She had gotten so thin in the last few days that her bones were visible against her skin. Her father had been trying to stuff food into her, but she couldn't eat as fast as he wanted.

He wanted her to gain all her strength back immediately, as if he were afraid that she would need it suddenly and be unprepared.

She was afraid of that too.

Gift stood, then put a finger to his lips again. He was tall and slender, and looked something like Sebastian, who had been his Changeling, a creature that was supposed to disappear within a few days, but had somehow metamorphosed into a Golem, a creature with even more power. Sebastian had cracks and lines all over his body, and he moved slowly. Gift was all fluid movement and quicksilver thought—it was as if he changed from instant to instant.

And unlike Sebastian, Gift had blue eyes.

He looked, Coulter had said, just like a male version of Arianna.

The frightening thing was she could see it. She could see how clearly they were related, how everything they did seemed similar. She knew that when she stood, she had the same fragile grace as her brother, and she didn't like it.

But it seemed, for a moment, as if they were working together, as if they had the same thought and were acting on it. For all his posturing, for all his Feyness, he was as terrified by the changes in his life as she was.

The insight rocked her, and she shook her head, trying to toss it away. He frowned at her, apparently thinking that she was disagreeing with him. She put a finger to her lips, mimicking him, and nodded.

Then Coulter stood up. He touched Gift's arm, and Gift shook him off. The two of them had such a strange relationship. She didn't understand it. Neither of them had been in her life two days ago. Now they were such vivid presences that she couldn't imagine how she had avoided them for so long.

Coulter came over to her, stepping around Scavenger, who snorted and rolled over. He was sleeping uncovered on the marble floor. Coulter grinned at him, then crouched beside her.

"All right?" he whispered.

She nodded. He brushed his fingers against hers. Electricity ran through her. She liked the way his hands felt, so warm and strong at the same time. She like everything about him. She had mentioned that to her father that afternoon, and he had looked alarmed.

*It's probably because he rescued you, baby,* her father had said.

She had thought of that. But the explanation didn't fit. The experiences she had had with the two other people who had invaded her mind—her great-grandfather and Sebastian—had mimicked the experiences she had had with them in real life. The selves they had presented were their real selves, only more refined, purer somehow, as if they had been distilled into their truest form. Why would Coulter be any different?

"Do you know what happened?" she whispered to him.

He shook his head. "But something woke us up."

"And we're the three with magick," Arianna said.

He nodded. He'd clearly thought of that. Her stomach jumped. She wasn't ready for something new. She hadn't rested yet. She hadn't recovered her strength.

Coulter took her hand in his, then covered it with his other hand. "You'll be all right," he said. "I promise."

Could Enchanters read minds? She hadn't heard of it, but then she hadn't heard of much about any kind of magick. Her father had tried, but he had none. The Shaman hadn't tried at all, but she had answered a few of Ari's questions. And Solanda, the Shape-Shifter who had raised Arianna, had tried to tell her, but Ari had often refused to listen.

Misplaced rebellion.

She wished she had listened now.

"It's not really me I'm worried about," she said, even though that wasn't entirely true. She was worried about herself. But she was worried about her father, and his losses, and the Isle itself.

And Sebastian.

If he had shattered once, and re-formed, had he re-formed after this second time? Was he still with the Black King, or was the Black King dead?

Had Sebastian killed him?

She didn't know, and she couldn't go searching for the answers. Coulter had shown her how to shut the door to her Links, and he had requested that she keep them closed so no one could invade again. She had thought that good advice. She had closed the doors.

She was alone and protected inside her own mind.

Coulter squeezed her hand. "Stay here," he whispered. "I'm going to go with Gift."

"Be careful," she whispered.

He nodded, then smiled at her. He had a beautiful smile, one that made his entire face glow. She smiled back.

He had made the last day bearable. He had prevented the fights with her brother from getting out of hand. He had told her to give her father time, to understand that her father would explain his own strange behavior as soon as it was right.

And Coulter had held her upright, with one arm around her back, as they had given the Shaman a makeshift good-bye ceremony. They couldn't treat the body as Fey would, but her father had, on an inspiration he refused to tell her about, taken the Shaman's body and placed it deep within the cave.

When he had come back, he looked older, and more than a little frightened.

Arianna wasn't used to seeing her father frightened. She had never really thought of him as vulnerable. He had always seemed so strong. But the Shaman's death had really shaken him.

It had shaken her too.

Coulter crossed the floor silently and arrived at Gift's side. Gift glanced over his other shoulder, as if he expected to see someone there. Arianna saw no one, but she had seen Gift do that all day. Her father had done it as well.

Maybe it had something to do with the men in the Roca's line. They were the direct inheritors of the blood line from the creator of the Rocaanist religion, the man the Islanders called Beloved of God. Perhaps only the males in the family could see things having to do with the religion. It would be no stranger than all the things she had learned about Fey magick.

And she hadn't even figured out how Coulter had seized some of that magick for himself. She had asked, but everyone had told her they would explain later. They had made her sleep, and she had done that, more than she wanted.

Her body had demanded it.

Just as it demanded that she sit now, unless something serious happened. Something that made her need to respond quickly and with strength.

Coulter stayed a half step from Gift. They started up the stairs together. The opening to the cave was up there. Arianna couldn't see it from where she was sitting.

Gift was holding a knife.

She didn't know where he had gotten it from, although she had her suspicions. Scavenger had an entire cache of weapons all his own. He had brought them from outside the cave. They all agreed that no one with Fey blood should touch the weapons on the walls.

No one knew what would happen if they did.

Then she felt it, the thing that had woken her up. It was stronger than before. So strong that it almost felt like a wind, a gale. It blew in with such force that the vials on the walls tinkled together. The fountain behind her splashed suddenly, as if something had fallen in it.

The strange wind had magick in it, magick she didn't recognize. It tingled as it blew through her, and she got a vague sense of its power. The power was dissipating. It had spread out across a lot of miles, and she could—almost—sense where it had come from. She got a picture of a burning barn, of Islanders running, of an exploded Fey lamp and flaming piles of skin and bone.

And then she saw nothing.

Gift had frozen in his spot. Slowly he turned to her, as if to ask, *Did you see that too?* His face had gone gray, his eyes wide. He opened his mouth—

As Coulter tumbled backwards down the stairs.

# FOUR

THREEM hated walking when he wasn't in his horse shape. He climbed the winding path leading up the mountainside. He had left the carriage behind, and his wife to guard it. Then he, Boteen the Enchanter, the Scribe (whose name he always forgot), and Caw the Gull Rider worked their way across the river and to the mountains the Islanders called the Cliffs of Blood.

Threem understood the name. The mountains were red, and the color went deep below the surface. Their dirt slid into the Cardidas River below, making it flow red. During the daylight, the Cardidas had looked like a river filled with blood. It hadn't unnerved him—he had seen stranger sights in his years as a Fey warrior—but it had caught his attention.

Crossing the river had been difficult. It had taken most of the day for Caw to find a shallow spot in the water, and the rest of the day for the four of them to travel to it. Then Threem had had to carry Boteen and the Scribe across on his back, a humiliating thing to do. Horse Riders almost never let anyone else on their backs. First of all because it was uncomfortable—the Rider had his Fey self on the back, from torso to head—and secondly because it was demeaning. How many other Fey acted as beasts of burden? Threem had gotten used to pulling carriages in his horse shape, although he had insisted on never having a driver, but he had never gotten used to riders.

To make it worse, Threem had had to carry the Scribe and Boteen across one at a time. The water was ice-cold, and the current—even though the area was shallow—was incredibly strong. Threem had felt that if he hadn't had four legs, he would have been swept under, and possibly died.

He hadn't said anything, of course. He had carried Boteen across, then the Scribe, who had complained the entire way, and then, at Boteen's insistence, Threem had changed back to his Fey self. His horse form had shrunk until it could be absorbed into his Fey skin, and he grew a Fey pelvis, legs, and feet. He wore no clothes. He had brought none with him, thinking he would be in his horse shape for the entire trip. Fortunately, the bottoms of his feet were hard as hooves. Going barefoot across the rocks would have injured him otherwise. He also had more body hair than most Fey, and that kept him somewhat warm. But he planned to shift into his horse self as soon as he could.

Later, after they had traveled the trail for a while, Threem had understood Boteen's reason for insisting—it would have been impossible to negotiate this steep, tiny trail as a horse—but at the time, it had felt demeaning.

Threem couldn't see Boteen now. Boteen had gone on ahead, as fast as a man could go, as if there were something important waiting at the top of the mountain. The Scribe was farther back, being encouraged—or perhaps heckled—by Caw. They had been climbing in darkness because Boteen refused to stop. Threem had his theories—he thought perhaps the Islander King or his children were above—but Boteen would neither confirm nor deny them.

Threem had watched, though, when Gauze, the Wisp, had returned from her survey of the area. She had looked shocked and a bit shaken by what she had seen. Then she had insisted on talking to Boteen alone. Threem had turned his horse's head, while keeping his Fey head forward, and through his second pair of eyes, he had watched Boteen gesture with excitement, clap Gauze gently on the shoulder, and then send her away. She had flown with the currents, like Wisps were trained to do in military situations, when they had to deliver messages rapidly.

Boteen answered only to one man: the Black King.

Whatever the discovery was up this mountainside, it had disturbed Boteen for much of the previous night and all day. He had asked the others if they had seen a diamond of light, and he had sent Gauze looking for it.

Apparently she had found it.

Threem had combed his memory for anything in Fey lore that would explain a diamond of light and thought of nothing. He did know that Enchanters saw things none of the others did. Perhaps it had been a marker that only Boteen could understand.

Maybe it was a sign of the Black Throne.

Threem didn't know, and he hadn't had the opportunity to ask Gauze. After she had left, Boteen had come back, spoken sharply to the Charmer Ay'Le, and divided up their small troop. Ay'Le was to lead the Infantry to the town at the base of the Cliffs of Blood. She had protested, saying she was a Charmer—a diplomat, not a warrior—but Boteen had insisted. Then he had left Threem's wife with the carriage and sent the other carriage with its team of Horse Riders along with Ay'Le. The Scribe, a useless Fey whose only magick was an ability to parrot conversations at length, was to come with them.

Threem could have killed the Scribe a hundred times over since this last trek began. Threem had never heard so much complaining in his entire life. He never wanted to hear any again.

He had been taught, from a young age, that Fey didn't complain. Even if they had to carry other Fey on their backs, cross a river with a strong current four times, and have their fetlocks turn to ice after walking in frigid water. If he could do all that without complaint, then the Scribe could climb a mountainside. It seemed only fair.

That was one of the reasons that Threem had gone on ahead of the Scribe. The other was to keep Boteen in sight.

Unlike Boteen, who had been riding in the carriage as they had approached this part of the Isle, Threem had been watching the mountainside. The night before, he had seen fireballs being lobbed on a small plateau. The balls looked as if they were Fey-made, not natural, and they had burned a small section of ground. He had also thought he heard, over the roar of the river, shouts and cries, and a man yelling.

He knew that Boteen hadn't seen any of this, but he didn't know if Boteen had sensed it. And since Boteen led them, Threem didn't feel right asking.

He just knew this place was dangerous.

And the feeling had grown the higher he climbed. Then, not a few moments earlier, he had gotten the shudders. He hadn't had those since he was a boy and the Spell Warders had experimented with Blanket Spells that would cover an entire area with a magick haze. He remembered how it felt walking into those spells—as if he had hit a magick wall and the wall were a live thing, influencing all his behavior. He had been able to shake the feeling off because Beast Riders had powerful magick, but to do so had made him shudder uncontrollably for some time.

He had been climbing steadily on this path when a wave of cold hit him, and he had shuddered, in just that same way. It had lasted only a moment, but when it was done, he knew that something had passed through him.

Something important.

He wanted to shout ahead to Boteen, but Threem knew the magick would travel faster than his voice. The only thing he could do was climb.

Boteen had left little light markers on the trail that Enchanters often used during battle. They would fade when the rest of the troop went through. They were nice, though, because they made the darkness less intense. Threem appreciated them because he was more surefooted as a horse than as a Fey. Climbing this mountain in extreme darkness would have been deadly.

He clung to boulders on the side of the trail to help him keep his balance. Below, he heard Caw live up to her name as she goaded the Scribe forward. For a moment, and only a moment, Threem felt sorry for the man. Then he remembered how much the man had complained, and let the feeling go.

Threem climbed through a twist in the rocks and saw blackened areas where the grass had been burned. He felt the hair rise on his body. This was where the fireball battle had occurred. A faint scent of smoke still tinged the air.

He hurried around a corner and pulled himself up a steep incline. The lights, the ones that Boteen had left, still burned. So Boteen had made it this far.

Threem quickened his pace.

He got to a flat area where most of the grass and scrub had burned away. The remains of a torch were stuck in between two boulders, and the ground had been dug up slightly, as if a number of people had been in the area. Two of the light sticks were illuminating this part of the trail, but after that, they were gone.

He looked up and saw a flat rock over some natural columns. It was an obvious hiding place. But he didn't like the silence.

Or the lack of light.

He wasn't sure if he should call out. He didn't know what waited for them here.

Instead, he grabbed one of the light sticks. It felt cool to the touch.

Threem scanned the area, searching for signs of Boteen, signs of anyone else. Then he saw feet encased in Fey boots. He hurried toward them. Boteen had fallen beside two boulders, a light stick—not spelled—in his hand.

Threem held his own light stick over Boteen. The Enchanter—one of the tallest, thinnest Fey Threem had ever seen—was flat on his back, his face gray, his eyes closed.

He looked dead except for the sheen of perspiration on his skin.

"Boteen?" Threem whispered.

Boteen did not stir. Threem glance around, trying to see what had caused this. Perhaps Boteen had merely tripped. Perhaps he had fallen and hit his head. Then Threem remembered the wave of cold that had hit him.

Threem put a hand on Boteen's shoulder. Boteen stirred. At least he was alive.

"Boteen," Threem said again. He shook Boteen lightly.

Boteen moaned.

"Wake up," Threem said.

Boteen's eyes fluttered and he moaned. "Magick shift," he muttered.

Threem didn't know if that was an observation, a command, or a delirious comment. "What?" he asked.

"Didn't you feel it?" Boteen's hand went to his head. He let the light stick drop. He pushed himself into a sitting position, then moaned again and bowed his head. "By the Powers. I'm empty."

"Empty?" Threem asked.

"What was that?" Boteen asked.

"What?" Threem felt as if they were having two separate discussions.

"It was a shock wave," Boteen said, as if he were speaking to himself. "A magick wave. It had to have gone all over the Isle. But what caused it?"

"That cold?"

"You felt it too?" Boteen asked.

"It made me shudder. It was quick, though," Threem said.

"Of course," Boteen said. "You have magick. All of the Fey felt it." He scuttled backwards slightly and rested against the rock. "All of the Fey felt it, and had a reaction like yours. What did it make you think of?"

Threem told Boteen about the Blanket Spells the Warders had experimented with when he was a boy.

"Yes," Boteen said. His voice was soft. "I understand how it seemed like that. But how did it *feel?*"

"Cold," Threem said.

"No," Boteen said. "Was the memory good or bad? What was the emotion with it?"

Threem frowned. Emotion? He had been a warrior so long he had stopped thinking about emotion. It wasn't productive.

"As a child," he said slowly, "those spells made me feel out of control. Dirty, for days, as if something were wrong with me."

"With you," Boteen said. "A wave, a cold wave, bringing bad memories to all of us with magick."

"You too?"

Boteen shook his head slightly. "It took my energy," he said. "My reserves are gone. I have no magick."

"Your powers are gone?"

"For the moment." Boteen's voice crackled as he spoke. "They will return. After I rest." He glanced up the mountainside.

Threem felt the chill return. "Has this happened to you before?"

"No," Boteen said. "Not like this. I've depleted my own magicks, in the beginning of the Nye campaign, but they've never been swept from me. Not like this."

Threem remembered the Nye campaign. The Nyeians had been ready for the Fey. They had guarded their borders with everything, thinking that they might at least hold the Fey back. Rugad had asked Boteen to use all of his magick to confuse, destroy, and damage the Nyeians. The magick worked. It drove them back, and made it possible for the Fey to get a foothold into Nye. It still took a long time to conquer the country, but Boteen's actions had saved a lot of Fey lives.

He also remembered that Boteen had taken to his bed for days afterwards, and that Rugad had sent all the best Domestic Healers to him, worried about Boteen's excessive exhaustion.

"It stole your powers?"

"My *reserves*," Boteen snapped. "The powers remain. I just have no energy to draw from. Hasn't that ever happened to you, man?"

"My powers are different," Threem said. "They're a part of me, immutable. You would have to kill me to stop me from being able to use them."

"Then you are lucky," Boteen said. "Very lucky." He closed his eyes.

Threem shook him. "You can't sleep here."

"I'm not going to," Boteen said. "But let's wait for the others. I have to see what's above us."

"I don't think we should go, not with you like this," Threem said.

"I need to see it," Boteen replied. "I need to go up there." He put a hand to his face as if simply talking made him weary.

"Wait for the Black King. Let him go," Threem said.

Boteen's hand dropped. His eyes, sunken in his face, flashed with his old spark. Anger. Threem recognized it. Boteen often displayed anger.

"You listened."

"I watched," Threem said. "You wouldn't have sent Gauze away so fast if you weren't sending her to Rugad. What's up there?"

"That's what I need to find out," Boteen said.

"I can go," Threem said.

Boteen shook his head. "You're not an Enchanter."

"What's the difference?"

"I can see things you can't."

Threem knew that to be true. He also knew that sometimes Enchanters took matters into their own hands, matters better left for others.

"Maybe Rugad would want you to wait," Threem said.

"Rugad," Boteen said, "might die if I am wrong."

Threem gazed up the mountainside. He could see nothing, even in the darkness. "Did you notice all the burned grass and shrubs?"

Boteen nodded. "The light trails here are tremendous."

"What happened?"

Boteen raised his head. The movement seemed to cost him some effort. "Two Enchanters met here last night."

"Two—?" Threem had not expected that. "But I thought we killed the Failures."

The Failures were the Fey that had come in the first invasion, the ones the Islanders had conquered. Rugad had ordered them killed, afraid that they would side with the Islanders when facing the Black King. He had never even given them the opportunity to defend themselves.

"We did," Boteen said. "These are Islanders."

"It's not possible." Threem said.

"You might be surprised," Boteen said. "The answers lie above us."

Threem gazed up again. He could see nothing in the darkness. "Can you walk?" he asked.

"Maybe," Boteen said. "If I'm careful."

The answer wasn't good enough, and they both knew it. Threem sighed. "I can carry you on my back if the trail isn't too steep."

"And if it is, do we both fall to our deaths?"

"I'll go ahead of you," Threem said. "I'll see what's up there, and then I'll come back. But I need to know what I'm looking for."

Boteen sighed, as if he knew there were no other choice. "There's a cave," he said. "Guarded by giant Islander swords. That's where we're going."

"And there are Islanders inside?"

"Presumably," Boteen said.

"What's so important about the cave?" Threem asked.

"I don't know yet," Boteen said. His voice had grown faint.

"Will this light stick work away from you?" Threem asked.

Boteen nodded. The movement was small. "I'll rest while you're gone."

"Make the others wait here," Threem said.

"Of course," Boteen said. His eyes closed and his breathing became even. He had fallen asleep.

Threem gave him one last look, and shuddered. Whatever had hit them had been powerful. Add that to the two Enchanters who had fought on this mountainside, and the cave above, guarded by giant Islander swords, and he knew he was facing some powerful magick.

He took a deep breath. All he was going to do was see if the trail was too steep for a horse and rider. Then he would return. He wouldn't face anyone. With luck, he wouldn't see anyone.

He clutched his light stick ahead of him, and marched forward, into the dark.

# FIVE

MATTHIAS was lying on the floor of the kitchen. The ceiling swirled above him, the stones forming a pattern that made them seem as if they were floating in the air. The back of his head hurt. His whole body hurt.

And it was dark. Very dark.

As if in answer to that last thought, a candle illuminated the gloom. Marly carried the candle through the door and set it on the table above him.

"Are ye all right?" she asked. She had pulled a dress over her nakedness.

"I think so." His voice came out as a whisper. He felt drained, as if someone had sucked all the vitality from him.

"We should na ha done that, I know," she said. She crouched beside him. "'Twas tired from yer trip ye were, and I shoulda known better—"

He reached a trembling hand to her mouth and touched it lightly. She had put him to bed when he returned from his ordeal on the mountainside, and then she had crawled in with him, holding him. The gentleness with which she held him had turned into something more amorous, and he had allowed it to happen. That had taken all his strength, but in a good, reviving way.

Not like this.

Never like this.

"Ye've probably never forsaken yer vows before," she said against his fingers. "Maybe tis God's way a punishing ye."

"No," he said. He didn't tell her that he had made love before. There had been a woman briefly in his days after he'd left the post of Rocaan. Mostly he had been with her to see what he had missed. It had been pleasurable, but not something he really wanted to continue on a lifetime basis.

Not like this afternoon. With Marly, he had felt loved for the first time.

"God isn't punishing me," he said. "At least, not with you."

Maybe with Jewel, though. His neck still ached from the touch of her fingers. Her shade, her ghost, or something that had looked like her had tried to kill him when he reached the cave on the mountainside. The Fey's Shaman had shoved him out of the way and saved his life.

He didn't know why. He didn't have a chance to ask her. Denl, Jakib, and Tri had helped him down the mountain, and Marly had put him to bed. After he had made love with her, he had slept until a few moments ago, when he had felt something strange, got up to investigate, and then, suddenly, found himself on his back feeling weaker than he ever had.

"Then what is it?" she asked.

He didn't know. And he didn't know how to explain it to her. So much had happened to him in the last two days. He had learned he had powers he didn't expect. He had nearly died. And now this.

"Something—slammed into me," he said. "And then took . . ."

He let his voice trail off. Took what? Something essential, but something that could be replaced. It was as if he were a cup that had held water, and now the water was gone.

"Took what?" Marly asked.

"I don't know," he said. "Something important."

She put a hand on his back, helping him up. All the injuries he had gotten in the last two weeks felt as if they were brand-new. The slash marks on his face from the fight with the Fey on Jahn Bridge, the bruises in his throat, the tired muscles from the walk up the mountain, all seemed worse than they had when he had fallen asleep.

"Did ye hit anathing?" She gently touched the back of his head. He winced as her fingers found a sore spot.

"There?" she asked.

"Yes," he said.

"Ye've got a lump." She helped him into a chair. "Tis strange how much punishment ye can take. Twould knock another man off his feet. Or kill him."

But he wasn't another man. That's what the burning boy had taught him. The young Coulter, who had shown him that Islanders could sometimes have the power of the Fey. Pausho, the head of the Wise Ones, had confirmed it, saying that some Islanders had abilities, powers, that others did not. The Wise Ones killed any child that showed evidence of those powers. They had tried to kill Matthias when he was a newborn by placing him on the mountain, but his foster mother had rescued him. Any child saved from that certain death was allowed to live.

Pausho didn't like it, but she had confirmed the magick he had discovered in himself only the night before.

It seemed like days.

"What is it?" Marly asked.

"I'm different," he said.

She smiled, her features soft in the candlelight. She was one of the most beautiful women he had ever seen. She was tall, like he was, suggesting she had been born here, but she spoke as if she were raised in the Kenniland Marshes. Her auburn hair reflected the candlelight, and her green eyes held warmth and concern.

No one had ever before felt such concern for him.

"I know yer different," she said.

He shook his head, and felt a dizziness that hadn't been there before. "No," he said. "I have—abilities."

"Denl said ye had a long talk with Pausho and that strange man on the mountain."

"Yes," Matthias said.

"Maybe it explains some of the things what happened to ye," she said.

"Yes." He couldn't tell her any more. He wanted to, but he couldn't. In the past, the caring had always stopped when others learned what kind of person he was.

"Something woke me up a few moments ago," he said. "Did you feel anything?"

"I got cold." She smiled. "Musta been coz I was missing ye."

He smiled back, then caressed the side of her face. He was exhausted, hurt, and empty, somehow, but he didn't want to stop touching her.

"Ah, Marly," he said. "You don't know what you've gotten into with me."

"Twill be better'n where I was," she said.

"I hope so."

"Twill be." She spoke with such confidence. "Yer getting paler the longer ye sit. We need ta get ye back in bed."

His smile grew. "You'll be the death of me, woman."

"Ah," she said, putting her arms around him. "Tis na fer that. Ye must sleep."

He tried to stand on his own and couldn't. What had happened? It felt so strange. "I guess I must," he said.

He had hoped he would be feeling better in the morning. He needed to have Tri's help in finding the original Words Written and Unwritten. Pausho had said they were kept in a vault beneath the city of Constant. Matthias wanted to see if there was anything in them that would explain what he was, and help him.

He had to go back up that mountain eventually. He had to face the cave and whatever was inside it.

But first he had to know what his own powers were, and how to use them.

He had to know how to fight the Fey.

"Yer na thinkin a me," Marly said, a teasing tone in her voice. She had allowed him to rest his weight on her. She was half dragging him toward the bed.

"No," he said.

"Ye must rest. Ye've done all ye can," she said. Such determination. Such strength.

"No," he said. "I haven't."

"Ye do more, n it'll kill ye."

It might, he thought. But he didn't tell her that. Because she'd oppose it, and he couldn't have her disapproval. Not now. The Fey were close. He could feel them. And he was the only person he knew with the power and the strength to fight them, the only person who even had a chance of winning.

"Marly," he said softly. "You need to get Denl to check the house."

"For what?" she asked.

"Fey," he whispered. The thought had come to him just a moment before. "Maybe they're near here. Maybe that's why I feel like this."

"Ye think tis one a their magicks?"

"It might be," he said.

"I'll have him check," she said, and then helped him the rest of the way across the darkened house to his bed.

"Tell him to be careful."

"I will," Marly said. She tucked him under a blanket that still smelled of both of them. "Don't ye worry now."

But he couldn't help worrying. Everything was changing, and he didn't know if he had the strength to fight those changes.

He needed strength.

He was the Isle's only hope.

# SIX

THE palace was in chaos. The Fey were staggering through hallways, trying to determine the source of the disturbance that had awakened all of those with magick abilities.

Rugad, the Black King, ruler of the Fey Empire, climbed the stairs to the highest interior point, a glassed-in room in the North Tower. It was the room where his people had found the Islander King Nicholas, his daughter, and the Golem during the attack on Jahn. Some of the glass was broken, which was perfect for Rugad's purposes. He carried a Fey lamp, and did not answer questions from his people as he passed them. If they were old enough, they could figure out the answers for themselves. If they were not, they would simply have to wait until he had time.

He'd felt the magick wave, and known it for what it was. The Fey around him had shuddered and screamed as its power touched theirs, bringing up feelings of anger or fear or pain. He ignored them. He would have to calm them at some moment, but first he wanted to know where that wave had come from.

He knew *what* it had come from. He had felt this before. He had been a small boy during the beginning of the Histle campaign. The enemy had found a cache of Spell Warder pouches and destroyed them. The ripple through Fey magick had been profound. He had felt it, even though he had not come into his magick yet, and an Enchanter who had been near the scene had died.

Rugad took the stone steps four at a time. His new assistant, the Charmer Selia, was struggling to keep up with him. Tears had come to her eyes as the wave passed, and a look of such sadness that Rugad could almost feel it. He had said nothing about her reaction. He had merely waited until her gaze met his, and then he had commanded her to come with him.

It seemed to snap her out of the emotion. All around them, though, Fey were leaning against a wall or holding their hands against their hearts, heads, or stomachs, as if the wave had left them ill. As he had left his quarters, he had sent an Infantry guard, who was unaffected because he had not yet come into his magick, to one of the generals, to see where the pouches were being stored.

This whole thing would cost him time and energy, neither of which he had. He needed to get to the mountains in the northeast. A Wisp had arrived that morning, saying Boteen insisted Rugad come to the mountains. Rugad had gotten the Wisp to explain what Boteen hadn't said, that Rugad's great-grandson and great-granddaughter were hiding with their father in a cave there.

Rugad had had to finish his tour of the city first. He had spent the day restoring the faith of his troops in his own leadership abilities, and then spent the evening preparing for his trip to the mountains. He was taking care of last-minute plans when the wave rippled through.

It had left him boiling with anger, anger he could use. It had also inflamed his wounds. Not the one in his neck, the one King Nicholas had made with his sword, nearly killing Rugad and destroying his voice. That wound was healing well, and felt no different. Rugad still used the false voice the Healers had given him, and would always, now that his real voice had been lost.

No, the wounds that were inflamed were the cuts caused when the Golem had exploded the second time. Rugad had been standing near it, and he had fallen, shattering the jar that carried his real voice and sending in to the winds. He had bruised himself on a chair and the hard floor, and the chunks of the Golem's stone had gotten into his skin. The Healer Seger had removed the fragments, but perhaps she had not gotten all of them. After the wave had passed, Rugad noted that all the cuts looked swollen and unnaturally red. And they ached.

The stairs curved slightly, then ended in the door to the North Tower. The door stood open, and a small, cool breeze blew through it. The night was still dark, and so the room held the blackness of the sky. The Fey lamp broke through the darkness, illuminating a room that had not changed since the Fey took over the palace a little more than two weeks before.

Servants called this the Uprising Room. It was square and took up the entire top of the North Tower. There were chairs against all of the stone walls, and a stone table was built into the center of the room. The roof was supported by great pillars covered with art that Rugad had not yet examined. Glass still covered the floor from the attack that had led to the capture of the Islander King, and the broken window had not been repaired. The room was a triumph of form and design—it gave Rugad a view of the entire city, and much of the countryside beyond.

He knew what he was looking for. The only way to destroy a magick pouch was to burn it. A large fire that appeared to be consuming the heavens should be visible from one of these windows.

If, of course, the pouches had been burned nearby.

The fact that the room was still dark disturbed him. He had hoped the fire would be easy to see. There was a small cache of pouches in the cavern near the river. The Red Caps had been working on the corpses of the Black Robes and had been compiling pouches for the Warders there. They hadn't yet transported them to the sites around the Isle for storage.

He went to the windows lining the north wall. The darkness engulfed the remaining city. Even the fires he had started, the fires he had used to destroy much of Jahn, had burned themselves out. The smell of smoke, which had been pervasive ever since, remained—a faint hint on the breeze—but it had a stale odor, not the overpowering stink of a current fire.

He hung the Fey lamp on a torch hook, and continued his way around the room.

"What are you looking for?" Selia asked, sounding breathless. She had apparently just arrived in the room.

He turned slightly. Her face was gray in the thin light, but her cheeks had two dots of color. Her eyes were bright, and the sadness hadn't left them.

"Fire," he said. "I'm looking for a large fire, eating the sky."

"Is that what caused this?"

He nodded. "Somewhere."

She went to the south windows. He continued pacing across the room. Nothing to the east. He had half hoped to see something east and north of here, something he could visit and quash on his way to the mountains the Islanders called the Cliffs of Blood.

"Rugad?" Selia's voice was soft. "Could that be it?"

She pointed, her finger pressed against the bubbled glass. He squinted. From his position near the east windows, he could see nothing.

He crossed the large room, glass crunching beneath his feet. When he reached her side, he still saw nothing. "Where?" he asked.

"There's a faint light," she said. "Almost like dawn breaking. But it's not the sun."

He hadn't even seen signs of dawn to the east yet. She was right. The light on the southern horizon was faint and golden.

Fire.

Rugad clasped his hands behind his back and stared at it. The fire was no more than a glow. Something he could barely see, and then only because of the complete darkness before dawn.

It had to be two days' walk from here, maybe more.

He must have made some sort of sound of disgust—not with his fake voice, for he would have felt some pain if he had done that—but through his nose, perhaps. Or perhaps he had merely changed posture. For Selia was staring at him.

"Sir?" she said.

"Give me a moment," he said, without looking at her. He could see her, though, through the corner of his eye. She was terrified of him but tried desperately not to let that show. He had chosen her after his previous advisor, Wisdom, had betrayed him. The day before Rugad had picked Selia as his new assistant, and just before he notified her of her job, he had made her watch as one of his Foot Soldiers ripped out Wisdom's tongue. It was the worst punishment possible for a Charmer, worse than death. A Charmer's magick was based in his ability to communicate, to sway others to his opinions. Visionaries, like Rugad, were immune to a Charmer's magick, which was why Charmers made such good assistants. They could persuade others, but never their boss.

Rugad tilted his head slightly. If he squinted, he could see the fuzzy edge of the fire, showing that it truly was something burning. This time he did let out a sigh of disgust.

That wave had been powerful, more powerful than he would have expected. Islanders shouldn't have been able to find the cache, nor should they have been able to destroy it. Rugad had guards placed on each cache. It was part of his normal routine.

Guards.

Infantry guards with no magick.

He clasped his hands tighter. Of course. He had done that because he remembered from his boyhood how the destruction of the pouches hurt magick users, particularly powerful ones like Warders or Enchanters. Infantry were safe because they hadn't grown into their magick yet.

His people would be fine.

But the cache was gone.

Fortunately the Islanders didn't know what they had done. If they had, they would have been taking advantage of the chaos to attack to the palace and get to him, to try to take down the Black King.

His troops all over the Isle had to be in the same state of chaos as the palace. The wave would have gone out from the initial explosion like the ripples from a rock dropped in a still pool of water. That was what had happened the last time. The ripples had gotten fainter and wider as they covered more distance, but Fey all over the Galinas continent had felt the repercussions.

Fey all over Blue Isle would feel it now.

Whoever had caused this wave had done more damage than he realized.

Rugad cursed softly. Selia stood at even greater attention, as if by being vigilant she could change his mood.

He had planned to send all of his available troops to the Cliffs of Blood. He already had an Infantry force there, but he had instructed the Charmer who led them to attempt diplomacy first. If she failed at that, and Rugad wasn't sure she would, then the Infantry would attack. He had hoped to go into the area himself, with a massive buildup of troops behind him, and demand the surrender of the Islander King and his family.

He couldn't kill them, of course. That would bring the terror of the Blood on all of them. Black Blood killing Black Blood would cause an insanity the like of which even he couldn't imagine. It had happened once before, a long time ago, when the Fey Empire did not expand over half the world. Black Blood had fought itself, and the Fey went insane, killing everything in their path, including each other.

Only one in ten survived. Fey, non-Fey; it didn't matter. Nine died for every one who lived.

Only three thousand had died that first time. Millions would be slaughtered if it happened again.

Rugad's grip on his own hands grew tighter. He had hoped to go after Nicholas with such strength that the man had no choice but to surrender. Rugad had brought a large force to Blue Isle. It was large enough to take the place and still have troops left over, but not as large as he needed. Only yesterday he had sent one of his sea captains to notify the Fey remaining on Nye to send in the secondary force. But it wouldn't get here for some time.

Certainly not by the time he needed it.

Now, he would have to send troops to the site of that insurrection to the south and quell it. He would take an even smaller force against Nicholas than he had hoped.

He did not entirely understand how the Islanders, even though they lacked the power of the Fey, managed to control his actions. It had happened from the moment he arrived in Jahn. His troops had been routed, and although they'd rallied and captured the King, the King had nearly killed Rugad. Then, when Rugad had recovered sufficiently, he had tried to control his great-granddaughter, only to nearly die again in an attack from the Golem that the Islanders insisted was part of the royal family.

Yesterday he had regained the support and confidence of his troops, only to have it shaken tonight by this great disaster.

It had been more than eighty years since a force had managed to destroy a chache of pouches.

Eighty years.

He had not been vigilant enough. Each time he turned around, he had not been vigilant enough.

And now he was to meet Boteen at this place in the Cliffs of Blood. If Boteen survived this wave. Enchanters and Warders were most at risk because they had bits of all types of Fey magick. Those with concentrated magick, like Visionaries and Charmers, felt only a momentary disturbance.

They were safe enough.

But Rugad might not be. He could not continue to proceed as if this were a standard campaign. The Islanders had too much power for that. He needed to know what Boteen had found. He needed those Islanders captured, but he could not go himself.

He was the head of the Fey force, and this wave of disaster had reminded him just how much jeopardy he would be in.

"Get my generals," he said to Selia.

He needed a new plan of action, and he needed it quickly.

It was time to make Blue Isle his once and for all.

# SEVEN

LUKE clutched his knife and ran as fast as he could for the corn-field. His cornfield. He didn't know where else to go.

There were seven Fey behind him, running just like he was. No tricks, no magick, just running and cursing in Fey. He had not expected the Fey to have so many men to spare. Next time—if there was a next time—he would make sure he canvassed the number of troops in the area as well.

At least he had diverted them. He had wasted the time to look back once, just once, and he had seen the Fey following him. But the rest were trying to deal with the barn.

The fire had grown sky-high, and then it had exploded in a blast that had sent him reeling. He managed to catch himself be-fore falling, and that had given him a considerable head start on his pursuers. He had waited long enough, and distracted them enough, to let Medes, Totle, and Jona escape. They were going to the rendezvous. The last thing he wanted to do was lead the Fey there.

He would lead them home, and then see what happened. He had a vain hope that his father and Coulter had come back, and they would rescue him, but he knew in his heart that wouldn't happen.

So he ran and he made noise and he remained as visible as he could. No other Fey followed his friends, and they would be safe. If they chose to continue the resistance to Fey rule after he was arrested, great, but it would be their choice, not his. And they could risk their own lives, as he had done, for the things they believed in.

He careened across his neighbor's empty yard and hurtled into his own cornfield, wincing as he heard the stalks bend and break from the force of his arrival. The corn rustled and closed around him. The crop in this area would be ruined, but it didn't matter.

He had succeeded.

He had burned the pouches, the source of some of the Fey's magick, and it had had some kind of effect. He had certainly not expected that explosion. And the Fey's reaction had been more than gratifying. The anger, the cries, the shock and horror, had been worth it all.

Maybe even worth his life.

It would be worth it if they realized that the Islanders would not take this conquest lying down. The Islanders would fight, and unlike the poor souls on the Galinas continent, the Islanders had a chance to win.

The corn smelled fresh and green. It broke his run, slowed him, even though he didn't want it to. The thick leaves slapped his face, and more than one underdeveloped ear slammed him in the head. He slashed at it, cutting a path with his knife. That slowed him even more. It would be easier for the Fey to follow him here. Even though he was going between the rows he had planted, he was still trailblazing, widening them, making it possible for someone to come after him with less pain, more ease.

He didn't want them to take him alive. They had done that to his father. They had done that to Ort. They had done that to him twenty years ago, and Jewel, Jewel—the same one who had married the King—had tricked them. She had allowed Ort to die, horribly, and she had threatened the same for him. What she wanted was what she got; Luke's father Adrian as a prisoner, subject to the whim of the Fey, forced to teach them what he knew about the Isle in return for Luke's life.

But she had probably been planning to free Luke anyway. She needed a weapon in the Islander world, and she had made him into it. Someone had Charmed him, and the spell had been activated from a distance, blanking his mind and making him an assassin for the Fey. A failed assassin, fortunately.

His target had been the Fifty-first Rocaan, who had had holy water at his bedside. When the Rocaan threw the water on Luke, it had broken the spell, and Luke had come to himself. But he had never forgiven himself.

Until now.

He had gotten his revenge for that tonight.

He pushed against corn. He had forgotten how big the field was. Or maybe it just seemed that way, because he was in such a hurry, because his mind was filled with a thousand thoughts at the same time.

He finally reached the edge of the cornfield and stumbled into the open.

A young man was standing on his porch.

A man he had never seen before—apparently Islander—wearing breeches and pants and Fey boots. The young man crouched and held a sword in his right hand.

Luke stumbled toward him, brandishing his own knife. "Are you Fey?" he asked.

The man grabbed his own neck, pulled on a chain, and a filigree sword fell out of his shirt. A sword like the ones the Rocaanists wore.

No Fey would touch that.

"Are you?" the man said, and as he did, Luke realized he wasn't a man at all, but a boy. A boy whose voice shattered and rose under pressure.

"No," Luke replied, "but they're coming. Who the hell are you?"

"Con," he said. "I'm a friend of Sebastian's."

Sebastian? The King's son? The supposed Golem that Gift and Coulter had fought over?

Luke didn't have time to think about it. He could hear the Fey in the corn. They were tearing it up as they ran; the rustling was unbearably loud.

"How many of them are there?" the boy asked.

"Seven," Luke said. "For now."

"Get inside."

"No. You can't kill seven alone. They're Fey."

"Trust me," the boy said.

But Luke did not. He turned, knife out, ready to fight. Together, he and the boy would take as many as they could, and then die if they had to.

Behind the cornfield, he could see a fire burning so high that he couldn't see the top of it. A wall of flame that sparked occasionally, as if more fuel caught in the air.

What had been in those pouches?

The Fey crashed through the corn. The sky was lightening, and not just from the fire. The sun was coming up. Luke realized it when he saw the progress of the Fey. He could see, in the thin gray light, the shaking stalks, the moving leaves.

The Fey were close.

He gripped his knife, but his hands were sweating. "For the Isle," he whispered to himself.

The boy hurried past him and stopped beside the second row of corn, sword out. He held the sword like a club, and, as his sleeve fell against his arm, it became clear how very thin he was. He didn't have a real muscle on his body.

And he thought he could kill seven Fey by himself?

Then the first Fey burst out of the cornfield, and the boy brought the sword down on the Fey's arm, severing it. The arm bounced into the field, blood spraying, and the Fey cried out in shock and surprise.

Luke had to take a step backwards. He hadn't realized the boy had so much power. He had sliced through the Fey's arm as if it had been made of mud.

The injured Fey staggered toward Luke and Luke caught him with one hand, bracing him, then sticking the knife under the man's ribs, toward his heart.

The Fey cried out a second time and toppled forward as Luke pulled out the knife.

The Fey's skin was not made of mud. Luke could attest to that. He had used a lot of strength to stick that knife into the Fey's body, and as much to pull it out.

The boy didn't even look winded. He held the sword in the club position again. He was dripping blood. He had tried to wipe it off his face, but had succeeded only in smearing it.

The other Fey had to have been farther behind. The corn still moved, so they hadn't heard their leader's cries. Luke kicked him aside, feeling hopeful for the first time that night.

The next Fey burst out, and the boy attacked him. This Fey was shorter, and the boy's sword sliced into the Fey's side, opening it. Guts spilled out, and the Fey, in surprise, grabbed at them. Luke stepped forward, and shoved the Fey, letting him fall across his companion. There was no need to kill that one. He would die soon enough.

The boy hadn't move. He still held the sword in two bloody hands. Then the third Fey came through and he sliced again, chopping off another arm. Blood spurted, and as it did, Luke saw the fourth Fey and the fifth burst through the corn.

But Luke didn't have time to say anything. The third had reached him, careening forward in a berserk motion, screaming and swinging her own sword with her remaining hand. This was how he thought of Fey. Not as instant victims, but as fighting to the very death.

She swung at him, and he ducked, hearing the sword swoosh over his head. Before him, another Fey screamed, but he couldn't see what the boy had done. The woman before Luke didn't turn, didn't seem to notice the carnage around her. She swung again, and he tried to leap out of the way, but the gut-stabbed Fey grabbed his foot and he tripped.

He landed on one knee, feeling the jolt. The woman stood over him, her skin going gray with the loss of blood. He stabbed her in the leg, his arm shuddering as the knife hit muscle and bone. She brought the sword down, and he rolled onto the Fey who held him. He'd lost his grip on the knife.

Another Fey screamed, and he heard blades collide. The ring echoed through the area. The ground was saturated with blood. The first Fey was dead. The second Fey's grip loosened on Luke's ankle. He groped the body of the first Fey, wincing as he touched soft blood-covered flesh. Finally he found a sword. He kicked the second Fey, whose eyes had glazed over, and stood. The Fey woman was watching him, panting. When he stood, she held up her sword, swung, and fell backwards.

The bleeding from her stump had slowed to nearly nothing.

She had bled to death.

Another Fey lay on the ground, his head severed. Three more lay at the boy's feet.

Seven.

The boy had killed seven in a matter of moments.

He was covered in blood. He was unrecognizable as Islander, except by his height. Blood dripped off him and onto the corn.

"Are there more?" he asked.

"Not yet," Luke said, "but there's a pretty good trail to follow. When they stop battling that fire, they'll come this way. And then they'll find—this."

He looked at the mess. There was no cleaning up. No hiding the bodies. His raid had been successful, but it would cost him everything.

"Then we need to get out of here," the boy said.

Luke nodded. But go where? This was his home, had been his home since he was born. He had nowhere to go. His father might return here. Coulter might return, or Scavenger.

They had to come back at some point.

He had planned to be waiting for them.

"How did you learn that?" Luke asked the boy.

The boy shook his head. "I didn't learn anything. It's the sword. I found it in the palace. I killed more Fey than this the first time I held it, and in a smaller space."

His voice hitched toward the end of that small speech, and Luke realized that the killing had upset the boy.

"You saved my life."

"I know," the boy said. He swallowed, wiped at his bloody face with a blood-soaked arm, and then shook his head. "I know."

Luke glanced at the corn. The fire seemed to be burning even higher. The cornstalks weren't rustling.

"We have a few moments," Luke said. "We need to get cleaned up. Then we have to decide what to do."

"There isn't much to decide," the boy said. "I came to get you. Sebastian sent me."

"You said that before. But I've never met the King's son."

"He said you're a friend."

Luke shook his head. "I met his father once. He was a good man, for all his strange marriage practices."

The boy wiped his face. "You don't know Sebastian?"

That wasn't entirely true. He knew the real prince of Blue Isle. Luke knew Gift. But that would require explaining the strange situation to this boy, whom, despite his heroics, Luke still didn't know.

"You're sure he sent you here?"

"Oh, yes." The boy's entire body was shaking. He looked as if her were about to snap. "I followed the instructions exactly. He explained this place, with the corn, and everything. He said he'd seen it two weeks ago."

"He was never—" Luke stopped. Gift had been here two weeks ago. And Gift had been furious at Coulter for breaking a "link." With Sebastian? Luke hadn't understood the particulars, but he believed he was getting an inkling now. "Why'd he send you to me?"

"Because he's been captured by the Fey. I let him get captured." The boy's voice broke. He looked, for the first time, as if he were truly going to crumble.

Luke put his hand on the boy's arm. "I was captured by the Fey once. Believe me, you don't let someone get captured. It just happens. You saved the both of us."

"Well," the boy said, taking a deep breath. "He save me. That's why I'm here. We were both coming, to see if you people could hide us. But now I need your help. The Black King has him, and he's so fragile. The Black King might use him for anything. The last thing we want is for the people of the Isle to think that the Black King has won Sebastian over."

Luke frowned. He remembered Gift, remembered that ferocity of spirit. Jewel had had the same thing, and so, in a more quiet way, had King Nicholas. Did that change in a creature made of magick? "Could the Black King do that?"

"Sebastian can't talk well," the boy said. "Even if he wanted to deny something, it would take forever to get the words out. The Black King could make him appear any way he wanted."

"What do you think I can do?" Luke asked.

The boy swallowed hard. He wiped at his face again, and this time did not smear much blood. Apparently it was drying. They had to get cleaned up before they moved on, or they would be very easy for the Fey to find.

"I had thought there would be more of you. Sebastian made it sound like there was a family—"

"There was," Luke said, and left it at that. No need for this boy to know more. At least, not right now.

"I thought with a small force and this sword, we could rescue Sebastian. The Fey are easy to catch by surprise—"

"I know," Luke said, looking at the fire. But it was after the surprise that worried him. "But I suspect that won't last long. The Fey are very cunning."

The boy nodded.

Luke frowned. The light had gone from gray early-morning light to a soft white. Luke glanced at it, then at the cornfield. Still nothing. The fire raged, a wall of flame that didn't move except to burn toward the sky.

He took the boy's chin in his hand, and tilted the boy's head to the light.

"Open your eyes wide," Luke said, a bit more harshly than he intended.

The boy shivered, as if Luke's movement had frightened him, but did as he was told. His eyes were blue, the soft blue of a midmorning sky. The blue got darker toward the pupil, which was black and wide and no gold in it at all. No specks, no nothing.

Luke let go of the boy's chin.

The boy rubbed it, as if Luke had hurt him. "What was that for?"

"Sometimes Fey can look like Islanders. The only way you can tell it's a Fey is by the gold fleck in the eyes."

"I don't have gold flecks," the boy said. "I'm as Islander as you."

Luke nodded. "I know. Your appearance was just convenient, that's all."

"You think a Fey would assassinate his own kind?"

"Yes," Luke said. "If it served a purpose."

The boy let out a long sigh. He ran a hand through his hair. The hair was matted in blood. He looked frailer than he had earlier, or perhaps Luke hadn't noticed.

"When did you eat last?" Luke asked.

"This morning," the boy said. "I had some of your bread."

"I doubt it was enough," Luke said. "Let's get you cleaned up, and fed."

"We have to leave," the boy said. "Even if you won't help me with Sebastian, the Fey will come here. They'll see what I did"—again, that hitch—"and come after you."

The boy was an interesting mixture of vulnerability and strength. "How old are you?" Luke asked.

"Thirteen," the boy said.

"And who are you?"

"My name is Constantine," he said. "For that old king."

"Actually there were several old kings with that name," Luke said. "But that doesn't tell me who you really are and how you got to know the current king's son well enough to call him by his personal name."

"People call me Con," the boy said. "And I am—I was—I am an Aud. In the Tabernacle."

"You're not dressed like an Aud," Luke said.

"I know," the boy said, took a deep breath, and then, suddenly, burst into tears. Deep, racking sobs of a kind that Luke hadn't heard before. Startled, he put his arms around the boy, and Con leaned into him, crying so hard that his entire body shook. What had this boy gone through on his own? And how had he survived? He felt so frail in Luke's grasp, his body all bones and tension.

Luke glanced over Con's head at the cornfields. Still no change. That might be a good sign, but he didn't trust the Fey enough to believe there would be any good signs. He glanced up. The fire burned flat against the horizon, its top a line against the sky. No birds flew above, no sparks had floated this way.

So far they were safe.

"Come on," Luke said. "Let's take care of you, and then hit the road. Once we're walking we'll figure out what to do."

The boy took a gasping breath and eased out of Luke's arms.

Tears had formed clean patches on his cheeks, and were dripping off his chin, pale pink, the color of watery blood.

"There's only two of us," the boy said.

"For now," Luke said. And then when he saw that that did not mollify the boy, he added, "Besides, two of us might be enough. You made it here alone. We killed seven Fey. And I caused that fire with only four men. The Fey expect armies, not individuals. In situations like that, individuals can be stronger than ten men."

The boy looked at him, and there was hope on his thin, dirty face. "Really?"

"Really," Luke said, and helped the boy inside. Luke almost believed his own words. Almost. Because individuals could hold out for a long time, but armies conquered in the end. Numbers always won. In the past, the Islanders outnumbered the Fey. Now the Black King was here, and he had the resources of an entire Empire. Slaughter one army and he could send for another.

The cause was hopeless, but the boy didn't have to know that. Not this morning. This morning, Luke would give the boy clothes, and food, and hope.

Then Luke looked at the fire and smiled.

Small victories.

That was all he needed.

Small victories.

He'd had two: destroying the barn and killing his pursuers.

It was a start.

A good start.

But of what, he didn't yet know.

# EIGHT

COULTER lay at the bottom of the marble steps, his head on the floor, his hips and feet still on the stairs. His eyes were closed, his pale face an even ghostlier white.

He made an awful thump going down, but he hadn't cried out at all.

Gift stood at the center of the stairs, where he had been when that wave/Vision/magick hit. He had seen a barn, and Luke running away from it, followed by Fey. Then he felt an explosion like none he had ever felt before, and the magick shocks coming off it. Gift couldn't tell where the explosion had happened, but he did know that Luke and Adrian did not have a barn like that.

Arianna was out of her makeshift bed and running toward Coulter. She was rail-thin, so thin that Gift could see her bones. Her black hair trailed behind her. She crouched beside Coulter before Gift had moved at all.

Gift still didn't know if he wanted to help Coulter.

He still blamed Coulter for so much, even though he knew that Sebastian might not be dead.

Somehow that seemed worse—Sebastian alone and afraid in the clutches of the Black King.

"I can't wake him up," Arianna said in Islander. She was appealing to Gift. She hadn't ever appealed to him. She had barely spoken to him since Coulter rescued her.

Gift glanced up the stairs, still holding his knife.

"Come *on*," Arianna said. "He's your friend."

"No," Gift said. "No, he's not that."

"Well, he's your something," Arianna said. "And he needs you."

Even in panic, she sounded regal. So used to getting her own way. So used to being obeyed.

"I still think I should see what caused that," Gift said.

"You *know*, just like I do," she said. "It wasn't from around here."

He did know it. He also knew that going to the cave door would do no good. But it had been his course. He didn't want to change his plans. Then he would have to acknowledge that something had happened to Coulter.

And that thought terrified him.

With a soft cry, he ran down the stairs, and crouched beside Arianna. Coulter's skin was still warm—he hadn't died—but he was unresponsive. Arianna was touching him like a lover, and she hadn't even know him twenty-fours hours yet. The warmth between the two of them drove Gift crazy. It was as if Coulter was getting close to Arianna because he couldn't be close to Gift.

Leen had awakened. She was sitting up, staring at Gift as if he held answers to all the questions she hadn't asked yet.

"What's going on?" the Red Cap asked from the side. It wasn't until that moment that Gift realized that Cap's snoring had stopped.

Adrian was sitting up too. "Did Jewel do—?"

"No," Gift snapped, mostly to shut him up. They hadn't told Arianna about her mother yet. They didn't know how to tell Arianna. Nicholas, Gift's father, was afraid it would be one thing too many for her, but Gift was pretty certain that there was another reason behind Nicholas's reluctance to tell her.

He didn't want her to feel hurt.

He was protecting her, just as he always had.

As if he knew that Gift was thinking of him, Gift's father appeared from behind the fountain. His clothing was askew, and his hair was mussed. He combed it with his fingers. Without saying a word, he came to Coulter's side.

"What happened?" Gift's father asked.

"Didn't you feel it?" Gift asked. "That wave?"

"No," his father said. He started to say more, but Arianna interrupted him.

"It was magick," she said. "Something happened, something changed, and brought a wave of magick through here. As Gift and I"—she glanced at Gift as she said his name, as if to have him confirm her words—"felt it, Coulter fell backwards down the stairs. It knocked him flat."

His father glanced at Gift. Something more had happened. Something his father was unwilling to say. It was amazing to Gift that he could read this man, a man he had never really met before, a man he didn't even know.

"Did he hit his head?" his father asked.

"I don't know," Gift said.

"Of course he did," Arianna said. "He fell backwards."

"Oh, God," his father whispered, almost as if he hadn't realized he spoke. He touched Coulter lightly.

"He's alive," Gift said. "He's still breathing."

Adrian came closer. He stopped beside Arianna. Adrian was Coulter's surrogate father. He had also shown himself to be both in awe and afraid of Gift's sister and father. Adrian knew Nicholas as a King, not as a man, and Arianna as heir to the throne.

He also hated Gift's mother. That much was becoming clear. And that worried Gift.

"We have to wake him up," Adrian said.

"I want to hear more about this wave," the Cap said. "I didn't feel anything."

"Only those of us with magick did," Gift said. No sense in trying to spare their feelings. He glanced at his father, then looked over his shoulder for his mother. She wasn't visible. He looked at his father again.

His father shrugged.

"We've got to do something for him," Adrian said, putting a hand on Coulter's shoulder. The Cap slapped him.

"Don't touch him," the Cap said. "Don't move him. Don't even think of it. He might be injured. Moving can make it worse."

"I don't see how," Arianna said. "Lying like this—"

"Trust him," Gift said. "He knows things."

"Like this wave," the Cap said. "Tell me more."

"After we help him," Adrian said. He looked at Arianna. "Can't you go after him like he went after you?"

"We don't even know if that's what's wrong," the Cap said.

Leen had come over. She had put a hand on Gift's shoulder. He leaned into her warmth. She seemed to understand how he felt. If Coulter died—

If Coulter died—

Gift couldn't complete the thought. They had been fighting for weeks, but they had never been without each other.

"He's not dead," Gift said. "He can't be dead or dying, or I'd be sick."

Everyone looked at him. Both his father and Arianna looked confused. Adrian smiled. "That's right. You're Bound. No matter what he's done, you're Bound."

"Bound?" Arianna asked, and her voice had a bit of sharpness to it.

Gift stroked the side of Coulter's cheek and didn't answer her.

"Coulter saved Gift's life when they were boys," the Cap said. "When Gift's mother was dying. And Coulter Bound them to save Gift. Only he did it wrong. They're joined for life. If one dies, so will the other."

"If one is injured—?" his father asked.

"It'll drain the energy of the other," the Cap said. "This isn't physical. This is something else."

"The Black King?" Gift's father asked.

"No," Gift and Arianna said in unison. Gift glanced at her. She was staring at him as well. Her face was too much like his; her voice resonated like his, only her accent differed. She had spoken Islander as her first language. He had spoken Fey.

"Then what is it?" his father said into the silence.

"Let's find out, shall we?" the Cap said. "Tell me—"

Then Coulter moaned. He brought a hand to his head, slowly, fingers brushing his thin blond hair.

Gift felt a relief so deep that he turned away. The terror slid out of him, and he shivered. No matter how hard he tried to close his heart to Coulter, he couldn't. Coulter had been there all his life. Coulter had saved him.

Coulter had sacrificed Sebastian to save him.

The familiar old anger mixed with relief, but Gift didn't let it overwhelm him. Coulter hadn't know Sebastian. Coulter hadn't loved him.

He had loved Gift.

And Gift would have done the same thing in the same situation.

He turned.

Coulter's eyes were open, but instead of looking at Gift, he was looking at Arianna. Gift recognized the expression on Coulter's face. Coulter had used it with him often enough. There was an openness, a warmth, an affection that Gift thought Coulter only felt for him.

And now he was directing it at Gift's spoiled sister.

Coulter hadn't even looked at Gift.

Coulter reached for her face. She caught his hand in her own. Gift's father looked as if he had swallowed something sour. So the relationship seemed obvious to everyone, and Gift wasn't the only one who didn't like it.

The Cap ignored all of it. He kept his hand on Coulter's shoulder. "Stay still," the Cap said, "and tell me where you hurt."

"I hit my head," Coulter said.

"Obviously." Adrian was beside him, his face so pale that he looked sick. Gift hadn't paid a lot of attention to Adrian. He had been the full-grown adult in their troop, the voice of wisdom at times, but he hadn't really been a person to Gift until now.

Adrian loved Coulter too, enough to leave his own son and take care of this foster child. Adrian, who had also been part of Gift's childhood, but only as a curiosity, the Islander prisoner-pet of his grandfather, someone who slunk in the shadows and looked strange.

"Where else?" the Cap said. "I'm not going to let you move until you give me a full accounting."

"I'm fine," Coulter said, and as if in defiance to the Cap's words, slid down the steps and sat up. Arianna supported him with her other hand. But Gift's father didn't touch him.

Coulter moaned as he moved, then let go of Arianna, and put his hands over his face. "Oh, am I bruised," he said.

"What happened?" Adrian asked, as if he couldn't contain the question. "What happened to you?"

Coulter looked at Gift, but the look had none of the familiar warmth. It was more of a question. Did he think that Gift had pushed him? Or was he asking permission to tell about the strange magick?

"We told them about the wave," Gift said.

"Is that what it was?" Coulter asked. "It felt like a wall of voices, robbing me of every spell I've ever thought of. My magick is gone."

"Gone?" the Cap said, sounding panicked.

Coulter shook his head. "Wrong word. Drained, I guess. Depleted. Like something robbed me."

"Jewel," Adrian breathed. Gift heard hatred in his voice. Apparently, so did Gift's father.

"She wouldn't do that," Gift's father said.

"Why are we talking about my mother?" Arianna asked.

The room grew quiet. Gift glanced at his father, who shook his head ever so slightly.

"Because she's been here since we arrived," Adrian said. "They weren't willing to tell you, but I will. I don't trust her. She killed a friend of mine, imprisoned me, and nearly destroyed my son. Who knows what she's doing now?"

"This wasn't Jewel," Coulter said. "It didn't feel like it did when I touched her."

"My mother?" Arianna asked. She looked at Gift, then at her father, her gaze taking in his rumpled, hastily donned clothing, and his messy hair. "Why didn't anyone tell me?"

"It's complicated," Gift said.

"I think I have the right to know if my mother is here," Arianna said, her back straightening. Her face was so thin, the angles sharper than they would be if she hadn't lost so much weight. She looked like their mother. *He* looked like their mother, only softer, with touches of their father's round features.

"She's not here," Coulter said. He sounded exhausted. "Not now."

Gift glanced around the cave. He hadn't see his mother, but he hadn't thought anything of it. She had been with his father since his father arrived, and so Gift accepted her absence. Even though she had not left his side when he arrived.

It was odd. "How do you know?" Gift asked.

"I can't feel her," Coulter said. "I could feel her before."

"What do you mean, feel her?" Arianna asked.

"She's gone?" Gift looked at his father. Nicholas looked stricken. That was what was different about him. Besides the disarray in his clothing. He looked as if he had lost the most precious thing in the world.

"Yes," his father said. "She wavered, then vanished, like a candle in the breeze. Then I heard Coulter fall."

"My mother isn't dead?" Arianna asked.

"She's dead," Leen said from behind them all. "She's just returned."

"People don't return from the dead!" Arianna's voice went up. It was perilously close to a shriek. "They don't just reappear!"

"It's called a Mystery." Gift went to her. He felt guilty for the first time. Their mother had appeared to him and their father, but not to Arianna. He knew what it was like to be left out, abandoned. To feel unloved. And he could see in her face the disbelief, the shock and the hurt.

He reached toward her. She stared at his hand. "It's a Fey thing?" she asked, her voice trembling.

He nodded.

"Why didn't I see her?"

"Because," Gift said softly, "she could only appear to three of us."

"You, me, and Dad," Arianna said.

Gift shook his head. "Fey magick isn't that simple." He had never felt compassion for this girl before. He had never seen her vulnerable before. Even when she had been lying unconscious, when Coulter had saved her, she had seemed strong to Gift.

She did not seem strong now.

"So tell me," she said. She wasn't looking at her father. She was looking at Gift.

He took a deep breath. "She could appear to the person she loved the most," he said. "That's—" he glanced at their father, unwilling to call him anything. Gift had had a father, an adopted father, Wind, whom he had called Dad and who was now dead. Gift hadn't had a chance to mourn him yet. To call this man Dad would be wrong. Yet to call him Nicholas seemed wrong too.

"Dad, right," Arianna snapped. Even though her tone was strong, her eyes weren't. They were lined with tears. "Who else?"

"The person she hated the most. That was the man outside, the man whom the Shaman died in place of."

"My mother killed the Shaman?"

"And," Gift said, not wanting to get into how complicated it all was, "she could chose one more. She chose me."

"You?" Arianna's lower lip trembled. "You? Why you?"

He heard the rest as if she had shouted it to him. *Why not me? Didn't she love me?* And he knew if he answered this wrong, he and his sister would be enemies forever.

"Because," he said, "I think she got to chose in the moment of her death." He was making this up as he went. "And I think she thought you were going to die with her. She learned, at that moment, that I was alive."

Arianna stared at Gift for a moment, her eyes wide on her thin face. Then she looked at her father. He looked stricken, as if the loss of his wife the second time and the anger of his daughter hurt him deeply. Coulter was leaning on Adrian, color slowly returning to his face. Adrian was watching the interchange, his normally genial features set in firm lines. The Cap had his arms crossed, and was shaking his head slightly as if he could believe none of this. And Leen was watching them all, knife out, as if she expected something to appear from the top of the stairs and kill them.

Then Arianna looked back at Gift. *Is it true?*

He wasn't sure if he heard her say that or felt it. But he knew that was the thought which crossed her mind.

He nodded, even though he was lying. His mother had said she had chosen him because Arianna had Nicholas. But Arianna didn't need to know that. That was too hard a truth for her at the moment.

It would have destroyed him.

Then his sister, his angry, formidable sister, took his hand in hers. A volt of energy shot between them, suffused with warmth. It was as if he touched his other half, as if he had been waiting for this moment all his life. Her slender fingers tightened around his, and her eyes widened.

She felt it too.

For a moment, he thought she was going to pull away. Then he realized she was waiting for him, to see what he would do. He pulled her closer and then wrapped his arms around her. She was thin, thinner than he had expected. He could feel each rib, each bone. She needed food and rest and affection.

Her father was not enough.

Gift didn't know where these thoughts were coming from, but he knew they felt right. Did Arianna get a sense of him in the same way? She wasn't moving, her head resting on his shoulder. She had to bend slightly to do so as they were the same height.

Leen's eyes had narrowed, and Coulter was frowning. Gift's father, Nicholas, still looked as if he had been blindsided.

"This is all very sweet and touching," the Cap said, "but the most powerful member of our little group was just stuck down and you all decide to have a family crisis."

Arianna pulled away from Gift, keeping her head down. She wiped at her face with one hand, surreptitiously—Gift wouldn't have seen it if he hadn't been so close.

"Sorry," she said. "Sorry."

And she sounded contrite. GIft didn't know she had this range of emotion, although Sebastian had sworn that she had.

Maybe he had seen what he wanted to see.

"I still think Jewel caused this," Adrian said.

"Oh, by all the Powers, will someone silence that idiot?" The voice came from behind Gift. Both he and his father turned. His mother sat on the steps. She still wore her jerkin and breeches, her braid running down her back. But she looked older somehow, lines creasing her face, and a streak of silver marred her hair.

Gift frowned.

He could see through her.

"Mother?" he asked at the same time his father breathed, "Jewel."

"Where?" Arianna said.

"Oh, baby," Gift's mother said, looking at Arianna. "I'm so sorry."

"She can't hear you," Gift said.

His mother smiled. "I know," she said.

"She can't?" Arianna asked.

"No," Gift said. "I was talking to our mother. She was apologizing to you."

"What happened, Jewel?" His father asked, coming over to her. He tried to touch her, but his hand went through her. He looked at it in surprise.

"Tell that idiot over there to stop blaming me, and start giving credit to his son," Gift's mother said.

"Luke?" Gift said. He frowned. He had Seen Luke, briefly, running from a burning barn.

"What has she done to him this time?" Adrian snapped. He started to move, but Coulter grabbed him, and held him. The movement looked weak, as if it had caused Coulter some pain.

"She didn't do anything," Gift's father said without looking at Adrian. "She's not what you think she is."

"I could say the same to you," Adrian said.

Gift's mother made a small huff. She was glaring at Adrian. "That man does not understand the ways of war. I did him a favor.

Normally we would have killed all three prisoners, slowly and over time."

Gift's father moved closer to her, but did not touch her this time. The stricken expression had left his face, and he was watching her with an attentiveness that Gift had never seen in anyone. Apparently Arianna saw it too.

"What's going on?" she asked.

"My son," Adrian said almost at the same moment, "is he all right?"

"Yes," Gift's mother said. Gift's father said nothing. Gift sighed softly. He decided he would act as a translator for his mother.

"He's fine," Gift said.

Adrian slumped against Coulter. "Then how can she blame all this on him?"

"He burned magick pouches," Gift's mother said. Gift translated, deciding not to explain what she meant, since Adrian had lived among the Fey for five years. "He found an entire barn full of them, and burned them. That caused an explosion, which sent a ripple through the magick on the Isle. All the magick. Spell Warders and Enchanters are always affected the worst in things like this." She nodded toward Coulter. "He's lucky he was here. If he had been near that barn, he'd be dead now."

When Gift repeated that last, Coulter brought a hand to his head. "So the force was less here?" Coulter asked.

"Yes," she said.

"This is victory, then?" Adrian asked. "He hurt the Fey?"

Gift's mother nodded. "In a dozen ways," she said. "Some no one has figured out yet."

"And he's still alive?"

"Yes," Gift's mother said.

Arianna was watching this, turning her head back and forth between Gift and the other speakers. Finally, when there was a break in the conversation, she asked softly, "Can she make herself visible to me?"

"No, baby," Gift's mother said.

Gift didn't want to tell her, didn't want to break the fragile truce between them.

But he didn't have to say anything. Arianna's lower lip trembled, making the birthmark on her chin—the thing that marked her as Shape-Shifter and different from Gift—move.

"Can't she renegotiate with the Powers?" Arianna asked. "Can't she change? The one she hates isn't here any more, right?"

"He's still alive," Gift's mother said with a ferocity that made Gift shudder. His father frowned, and in his face, Gift saw a matching hatred for the man they all called the Fifty-first Rocaan.

"What?" Arianna snapped, and Gift realized he hadn't translated. He did.

"But if he's like Coulter," Gift's father said, "then—"

"He's depleted too. And so is Rugad's pet Enchanter. Those are the benefits from this," Gift's mother said. Gift repeated after her while thinking about what she said.

"How does she know all this?" Arianna whispered.

"The Mysteries and Powers bring us Visions," Gift said.

Arianna's mouth opened slightly, then closed as if the change had never occurred. She seemed to know nothing about Fey lore. Not that Gift himself knew much about the Mysteries, but he seemed to know more than she did.

Much more.

"Then what happened to you?" Gift's father asked softly. The question was meant for Gift's mother alone, but everyone seemed to hear it. Coulter sat up straighter as if he had been waiting for the answer himself.

Gift's mother took his father's face in her hands. The gesture was affectionate, and for a moment, Gift thought she was going to kiss him. Then he realized that he could still see through her, and even though she tried to touch his father, she apparently could not.

"This is hard to explain," she said. "But if you think of magick as air that surrounds all things, and enters all things—"

"Then it can leave all things," Gift's father said. "Which is what happened to Coulter."

"And it will remain so until he takes another 'breath,'" Gift's mother said. "But he needs something to breathe. Right now, the magick on the Isle, the air, was disturbed by a great wind. Great winds destroy some things and have only a temporary effect on others."

"So this is temporary?" Gift's father asked.

"For all of us," she said. "In some ways. Some parts might be permanent."

"What parts?" he asked.

"Rugad's people aren't used to losing," she said. "They aren't used to it at all. That's an advantage for you."

"We had that advantage with you," Gift's father said.

His mother smiled. "And it worked."

"A bit," Gift's father said. "We had a compromise."

"That she would have broken in a heartbeat," Adrian said. "I can't believe you trust her."

Gift had been repeating his mother's side of the conversation out loud. He stopped. Adrian was trembling. Coulter still had a hand on him, holding him in place.

"I was married to her for five years," Gift's father said. "You learn to trust in that time. You learn what a person is capable of. Jewel never lied to me. Her marriage to me put Blue Isle in the Fey Empire. We couldn't avoid that. But we were going to be autonomous. We weren't going to be invaded. My father's murder—and hers—ruined that. I'm sorry for what she did to you and your family, but that was a different time, and it was before she allied herself with me. She chose to return to me and to my family. She's willing to fight the Black King for us. You have to remember that."

Adrian shook his head. "You have to remember how cunning she is. She promised me my son's freedom. Instead she had him Charmed. He nearly killed the Fifty-first Rocaan."

"She was dead by then. That was someone else's order," Gift's father said.

Gift was listening closely. He knew none of this. Apparently Arianna didn't know much of it either, because she was staring at her father as if she had never seen him before.

"It would have been better if Matthias had died then," Gift's mother said. Gift did not repeat that sentence.

"You can't make excuses for her," Adrian said.

"I'm not," Gift's father said. "But she is still my wife. And she has come back to help us, through Fey magick, or the power of this cave, or a combination of both, I'm not entirely sure. But we need her help. We need it desperately. And I can't have you contradicting her at every turn, undermining all that she does."

"Me or her, then, is it?" Adrian asked. Gift was staring at him. Where had Adrian's awe gone? He had been proud to be near the King just a few hours ago. Had it disappeared when he thought that Jewel was trying to kill Coulter?

"If you push it that far," Gift's father said. "And frankly, I need her—we all need her—more than we need you."

"Adrian," Coulter said. His voice was little more than a whisper. "Please. Let it go."

Adrian shook his head. "Five years of imprisonment. I never saw the sun. I never felt a breeze on my face. I was a pariah, and all the time I did it for something I believed in, a lie she had told me."

"But if you hadn't been there, I wouldn't be here," Coulter said.

Adrian stared at him for a moment, as if he hadn't thought of that, then closed his eyes and bowed his head. It was an acquiescence, and they all knew it.

Gift's father sighed softly and turned his attention back to his wife. Arianna was still watching Adrian, as if he had said something that had turned her expectations upside down. What had she heard about her mother all her life? What did she know of the woman? What their father said, and little else. Where Gift had heard about his mother from all the Fey. He had heard of everything but the love his parents clearly bore each other.

How strange and unique that must have been, to find each other in the middle of a war. What Gift—and the Fey who had raised him—had assumed was a marriage of convenience had actually been a love match between equals.

And there were only two things left from that match, all that hope for peace.

Gift and Arianna.

He wondered if Arianna realized it, or if she had always known how important she was.

No wonder Gift's father fought the Black King so hard. Not only was he trying to save his land and his children, but he was trying to save a dream he had had with a wife who had been, until a few days ago, long dead.

"So that change," Gift's father said, softly this time, to Gift's mother, "that change in the air, in the magick, affected you?"

There was a vulnerability in his tone, and Gift wondered, not for the first time, what they had been doing behind that fountain. She had a physical presence in this cave. Were they—?

He shook the thought away, not willing to go farther with it.

"Yes," Gift's mother said.

Arianna poked Gift. He flushed a little, having forgotten that he had been translating, then nodded.

"But it didn't harm me," Gift's mother said. "I don't exist here. It just harmed my ability to manifest."

Gift's father nodded, as if that were all the explanation he needed. Gift needed more, but he would wait for a better time.

"You said," Gift said, feeling awkward at interrupting them even though he had been translating for them, "there were advantages to this—wind."

She turned toward him, pride gleaming on her face. Her

expression warmed him, and he felt a slight flush building in his cheeks.

"Yes," she said. "There are. I named one. Another is that all magick will be weak for a short period of time. How short, I don't know. But we can take advantage of that."

"Anything else?" Gift's father asked as Gift translated.

"There's bound to be," Gift's mother said. "We just haven't figured them out yet."

Gift was now managing to repeat and listen at the same time.

"If we figured them out," Arianna said. "won't the Black King as well?"

Gift's mother stared at her daughter for a moment. Gift could see the longing in her face. Then she looked at Nicholas and smiled sadly. Gift could see the years lost, the love lost, by his grandfather's actions.

His grandfather and Fifty-first Rocaan. The man who had killed his mother.

"The Black King might," Gift's mother said at last. "But he is operating on different principles. He know how it has hurt the Fey. Your son"—and she glanced at Adrian as she spoke; Gift did too—"has harmed the Fey. Those pouches are necessary for all types of magick."

"There are bound to be other caches of pouches," the Cap said.

Gift's mother nodded. "But the pouches are placed in strategic locations, and usually in large piles. That barn had to represent a sizable portion of your people's work since the arrival of Rugad's forces."

The Cap flinched when Gift said "your people" and he glared at Gift as if Gift had changed the phrasing. Gift shrugged, as if to say that it wasn't him.

"So," Coulter said, his voice rasping with hurt and exhaustion. "Luke destroyed a pile of weapons."

"More or less," Gift's mother said. "A little bit more, I would think."

"I hope others know this," Gift's father said. "I hope other groups can take advantage of it."

"We can't worry about that right now," Gift's mother said. "We have to make our own plans. And I don't think we have much time, since Rugad knows our children are here."

"He'll be coming for us?" Arianna asked. She apparently did not remember much of the discussion they had all had when she returned to consciousness the day before.

"Oh, yes," Gift's mother said. "In one form or another, he'll be here. And he'll find three prizes: you, your brother, and this place."

"His forces will outnumber ours," Adrian said.

"Clearly," Gift's mother said. "But your son just proved what four men and a bit of determination can do."

"No one has ever brought down the Fey Empire," the Cap said.

"And I'm not saying anyone should," Gift's mother said. Then she smiled. The look lit up her face. Gift had never realized how beautiful she was.

"We need the Empire," she continued. "The children need the Empire."

She paused for dramatic effect, even though only Gift and his father could hear her.

"If we bring down Rugad," she said, her eyes meeting Gift's, "then you and your sister will succeed them."

Gift's stomach fluttered. He didn't want to lead the Fey Empire. He hadn't been trained for it.

He wasn't ruthless enough.

He glanced at Arianna. She had gone gray.

But she was ruthless enough. She was extremely ruthless.

Maybe too ruthless.

"How?" Gift asked. "Your brothers are still alive."

"Bridge?" Gift's mother said. "He's the best of my brothers, and he's worthless. If he were able to succeed, Rugad would have him here. No. Rugad came for you and Arianna, and he made that clear to the troops. All of the Fey know that my children will succeed him on the Black Throne. We just have to make sure that happens sooner than he expects."

"But I know nothing of the Fey Empire," Arianna said.

"And I wasn't trained to lead," Gift said.

His mother shrugged. "I was," she said, and then she disappeared.

# NINE

VOICES woke him.

Boteen started, appalled that he had fallen asleep beside a boulder in a pile of burned-out grass. He could feel the residue of abused magick, the anger and the power and the fear that had gone with it.

Two Enchanters, one near him, and he had slept.

He felt no better.

He put a hand to his head and slid up slightly. That annoying Scribe and the Gull Rider whose name he could never remember were cresting the hill. The Scribe was older and a complainer, and had proven, during the night, that he had no stamina at all.

In fact, the voices that Boteen heard were the Scribe talking with the Gull Rider, hoping that they did not have much farther to go.

The Gull Rider wasn't answering.

"I could hear you for the last hour," Boteen lied, his voice coming out stronger than it had when Threem found him.

Threem. It felt as if he had been gone a long time. Had Boteen made a mistake sending him up alone?

The Scribe crossed between two boulders. He was holding a light stick that illuminated his ascetic face. He looked haggard and exhausted, moving as if every muscle in his body ached.

The Gull Rider walked behind him. She was nude, and she had a hand over her stomach. Her hair was white and feathered, and trailed down her back. She looked as nauseous as he felt.

"What happened to you?" she asked. Her voice grated. It had the harsh rasp of a gull's cry.

"The same thing that happened to you, I expect," Boteen asked. "We had a magick event."

"That wave?" she asked.

"Wave, wind, whatever you want to call it." He leaned against the boulder. Most of his magick was still gone. He could feel some of it, though, flickering at the base of himself. It also felt that if he used it, he would use himself up. "Tell me, did you return to Fey form automatically or did you chose to?"

She smiled. Even though she wasn't holding a light stick, he could see her features. Dawn was coming.

"Well, you could say I chose to do it instead of plummet into the side of this mountain."

"She swerved several times," the Scribe said. "Eight, to be exact. And she missed me all eight times, but it seemed as if she were trying to hit me. The first time I ducked—"

"I understand," Boteen said dryly. If he allowed it, the Scribe could go on forever. In precise detail. "I don't suppose you felt anything."

"For a moment," the Scribe said, "all words left my head. It was quite terrifying."

"I'll bet," Boteen said.

"It was a very brief moment," the Gull Rider added. She shivered. "I can't get into my other form. And I still ache. What was it?"

"Powerful," Boteen said. He didn't want to admit to them that he was almost completely incapacitated.

"You don't think it had something to do with the place we're going, do you?" the Gull Rider asked.

"No," Boteen said. "It came from the center of the Isle."

"You mean we still have to go farther?" the Scribe said. "I would have thought this was it." He looked around, his thin face wrinkling in disgust. "Something happened here, didn't it? It still smells of smoke."

"You'll stay here," Boteen said, not wanting to answer the question. The Scribe had become more talkative during the last day. It was as if he were using his own voice for the first time, asking questions as a stalling tactic so that he wouldn't continue to move. "Threem has gone ahead. He's gone to see how steep the trail is."

The Gull Rider sat down. A small, feather-like bit of hair floated off her skull. She sighed and hunched forward. Fine hairs, like thin feathers, covered her entire body, making her look paler than the average Fey. Her hands, in respose, bent like talons, and her feet were longer than his, with a scaly base.

"He expects to go up in horse form?" she asked. "After this?"

"He seemed less affected than you," Boteen said.

"And you, obviously," the Gull Rider said.

He wondered if a Gull Rider's magick was more powerful than a Horse Rider's. But that made no sense. They were the same type, and a horse was larger. Perhaps Threem was simply more battle-hardened, used to change and difficulty.

"Is this your first campaign?" Boteen asked.

"Fifth," she said. "But I haven't seen much fighting."

And there was his answer, just as he expected. She had never been shaken up, had not trained herself to roll with changes, with injuries, with any difficulty that might show up.

Of course, as a Gull Rider, she had very little opportunity to do so. Unlike Horse Riders, who were often in the middle of the action, Gull Riders flew above it. They managed to avoid all sorts of things, from arrows to swords, because they could remain above the melee.

"I've seen none," the Scribe said, stating the obvious.

Boteen glared at him. Behind him, he heard a scrabbling. He did not turn. The presence felt familiar, but he didn't know if it was Threem. Nor did he entirely care. There wasn't much he could do at this moment except, perhaps, talk himself out of danger.

The scrabbling grew closer, and then Threem came into view. He was still in his Fey form. When he saw the other two, he nodded.

"It's as you said it would be, Boteen," Threem said. "Except those swords are much larger than I expected. It must have taken incredible strength to place them there."

"Or incredible magick," Boteen said.

Threem smiled.

"The trail is steep," he said, "but not too steep for me. And on the last part are steps that look to be very old. The biggest risk is there. They might break beneath our combined weight."

"Are they wood?" the Gull Rider asked.

"They are a very thin stone, made even more brittle by their age," Threem said. He sounded breathless. "I'm not at full strength. We'll have to go slowly, but I'm willing to try it if you are. Someone besides me needs to see this."

Boteen normally would not have gone up a mountainside on the back of a Horse Rider, but he had no choice. He had no idea how long it would take him to recuperate.

"Did you see anyone?"

"I didn't get close enough," Threem said. "But there is no one guarding the outside. I also looked for the less obvious, Wisps and Shadowlands, and didn't see those either."

"Do you think we can get up and down without being seen?"

Threem looked at him. "I'm not sure there's anyone to see us. If there is, they're in the cave, and they would have to come out. I think we'd have time to get away."

Unless one of the Islander Enchanters still had magick, and that Enchanter was above. Boteen wasn't certain he was any safer here, in the still-smoking evidence of the other Enchanters' fight.

He nodded. "We'll try it," he said. "Help me up."

The Scribe and the Gull Rider came to his side. The Scribe's hands were bony and weak. The Gull Rider's were sharp and cold. Boteen used them mostly as support.

Threem stepped slightly away from them, clenched his fists and closed his eyes. A horse's head emerged from his stomach— more slowly than usual, almost reluctantly. For a moment, Boteen thought the head would sink back into Threem's skin, but it didn't. It grew, while the lower part of Threem's body lengthened. His two legs became hindquarters, and front legs appeared. The horse rose to full height, and shook its head, neighing. Threem himself, his Fey torso, arms, and head, looked small on the horse's back. He would have looked as if he were riding, except for the lack of legs.

His face had gone gray with effort. He too had little magick at the moment. But he had more than Boteen did, which was enough.

"There's not much room," Threem said, "and you'll have to hold on."

"I've done this before," Boteen said. Only it had been a very long time ago.

The Scribe and the Gull Rider led him to Threem's side. The black horseflesh glistened as if it had just been groomed. Threem made a large horse. Boteen could see over his back, but barely.

He didn't know if he had the energy to mount. The Scribe and Gull Rider couldn't help him. Bird Riders had no strength in their arms, and the Scribe had proven himself useless all day.

Threem leaned down, and took Boteen's wrist. The Gull Rider, without being asked, formed a stirrup with her hands. Boteen stepped in it, felt the sharpness of her fingernail-talons through his boots, and let Threem pull him on the horse's back.

Threem's torso took up most of the room. But it disappeared into the back, and Boteen's legs had space. He had to lean against Threem's upper body.

"Wrap your arms around me," Threem said. "This'll be quite a climb."

Boteen did as he was told. He had forgotten this part, sitting on a person he respected, riding him as if he were nothing more than a dumb animal. Threem tossed his horse's head as if to reestablish his own pride, then headed toward the thin path.

Boteen looked at the Scribe and Gull Rider. "You will stay until we come for you," he said.

The Scribe nodded. The Gull Rider crossed her arms. She would stay as long as she thought necessary, he knew. Then she would come for them. She had irritated him at first, when the carriages had stopped on the road, but he was gaining a growing respect for her.

"Hang on," Threem said as he started up the path. The angle was immediately uncomfortable. Boteen felt as if he would slide off Threem's back.

He squeezed Threem's waist tightly and closed his eyes, wishing he had the strength to climb by himself. He was heading toward a dangerous place unprotected. He could only console himself with the fact that whatever had hit had been a wave. Every other magick user in the area—including the other Enchanters—would feel the same way. He hoped. He was gambling on the idea that Islander magick replicated Fey magick exactly.

It wasn't a completely logical gamble, and he knew it. But he had to know what they were facing. Threem had seen nothing, and if the Islanders were going to attack, they would have attacked Threem when he was alone.

Maybe by the time they reached the cave, he would feel better. All he needed, though, was a look. A confirmation. And then, when Rugad arrived, Boteen could show him the prize above all prizes:

A Place of Power.

# TEN

LICIA sat on the stone ridge as the first light of dawn filtered through the mountains. The sky was lightening, glowing red as it had done the day before. She didn't like the sky nor the mountains known as the Cliffs of Blood, nor the reddish color of the rocks and the river threading its way through the valley. The same river, in the city of Jahn, was a brownish gray, deep and tame. Here it was red and shallow and wild as a Fey victory celebration.

She hated this country.

She had traveled all over Galinas, had helped Rugad conquer the last section of that continent, had fought in wind and dust and heat, and had not, ever, hated a place like she hated this one. It was an instinctive feeling, the same kind she got when she encountered Spell Warders or Enchanters. A hatred mixed with contempt.

Which they, of course, responded to in kind. She was an Infantry leader, a woman with small magicks, enough to get the Infantry, who hadn't grown into their magick, to follow her. She had no other real skills except for her minor Vision and her even more minor Charm.

And her abilities as a seasoned veteran of more campaigns than she cared to think about. Rugad had given her this command, knowing that it might come to attack, and she had taken it gladly.

She did not like to be idle. She would have been in the first Invasion force, the Failure force, if Rugad had allowed it. Now she understood why he had not. He wanted his son Rugar to fail. He wanted his son to die here, so that Rugad could clear the Black Throne for his granddaughter Jewel.

He had never expected Jewel to die here as well.

Neither had Licia. She had given Jewel some of her early training. The girl's mind had been comparable to that of her grandfather—cunning, swift, and sure. With practice and time, Jewel could have been one of the great leaders of the Fey.

Instead, she had died in childbirth, or so they said. Licia had a feeling there was more to the death than that, more than anyone else said.

And it had something to do with this place, with this island. She would be glad when it belonged to Fey, and she could travel with Rugad to Leut.

But this morning, her task was different. She squinted, surveying the valley below her. Rugad had warned her to judge this with wary eyes.

*Whatever looks simple*, he said, *is probably more difficult than the most difficult campaign you've ever fought.*

What was spread out before her did not look difficult. It looked like a simple campaign, especially given the level of fighting she had seen in the Kenniland Marshes. There the locals had fought sporadically—and some with great fierceness—while others had laid down their arms, declaring loyalty to anyone who took Nicholas's family off the throne.

Below her was a small town, almost a village, made entirely of stone. The houses were gray stone, even though the surrounding mountains were red. The mountains were taller than any she had ever seen, and taller than any she had ever heard of outside of the Eccrasian Mountains, birthplace of the Fey, and that thought gave her pause as well.

The Islanders did have powers the other countries she had fought in did not.

That was significant, just like the strange mountains, and the feeling she had had since shortly before the sky lightened. It had felt as if a small evil wind had blown through her, a wind that had in it seeds of destruction. It had chilled her, twinged her in an area she rarely thought of—her magick—and then had moved on.

So she had sat on this ridge line and decided to wait until dawn to make any real decisions.

To her left, across the river and away from the ridge line she sat on, someone had dug a hole in the mountain. A bowl had been carved out of it, a quarry, from which, apparently, the Islanders got the stone for their homes. The lips of the quarry were gray, like the houses, although the rest of it was red. It was almost as if the color leached out of the mountain when the stone was separated from it.

The hair rose on the back of her neck.

If that were the truth, there was even more to these mountains than she understood. Caution was the watchword. Caution and strength and cunning. And cunning was probably the most important.

She stood and brushed the dirt from the back of her pants. She wore a jerkin above them and nothing else, preferring the freedom of movement such clothing gave her. Her black hair was braided down the back, and it had gotten so long that she was thinking of wrapping the braid at the base of her skull so that it wouldn't get in her way.

She had more than enough manpower to stage a daylight attack. But she felt odd nonetheless. Rugad had insisted that Ay'Le, the Charmer, talk with the Islanders, try to get them to surrender on their own.

But Ay'Le had not talked with them. Apparently, she and Boteen had met a small force of Islanders who had warned them away, and she had allowed Boteen to do all the talking. Everyone knew that Enchanters had limited Charm and often failed to use what little bit they had. This was not as Rugad had planned it, and that was the third thing that bothered her.

She had been asked to plan their attack, and she would do that. She would do the best she could under trying circumstances.

But she didn't have to like those circumstances.

There was movement below her. The town woke early and went about its daily tasks. She could see tiny forms heading toward the center of town, where the buildings parted slightly to form a wide, flat area. She was too far away to see what was there.

She would discover soon enough.

If she had a normal enemy, the attack would be easy. She would have the Infantry come down the ridge line, the Foot Soldiers following behind, and she would use a small advance of Bird Riders to distract the Islanders from the invasion force coming at them.

But this was not a normal enemy, and, following Rugad's

strictures, she could see problems with the normal plan of attack, the first of which would be getting trapped in the small pass that led into the valley.

She would have to be more creative with her battle plan.

The troops were hidden in a pocket valley behind the ridge line. Five hundred in all, twice what Licia would have thought necessary for an area this size—more than enough proof that Rugad was being cautious. She took one last look at the small town. Stone houses would be difficult to burn. There were a lot of people below, and then there was that wind.

She shuddered again and made her way back to the troops.

The grass was thick here and a greenish blue. She had never seen grass this color before. But then, she had never seen red mountains either or a river that flowed with the color of blood. This place had a personality all its own.

She crossed embedded rocks and twists in the hillside and made her way across the road to the pocket valley. So far, none of the Islanders had seen this troop. That was always the danger of a large fighting force; it often lost a measure of surprise.

She could hear it before she saw it, the hum of voices, talking softly. That was a break in the discipline, and it made her hair stand on end. The Fey should not be talking among themselves; they should be waiting in silence for her return.

She rounded the last part of the hill into the bowl-shaped valley. Foothills rose on all sides, and the troops were in a small meadow, with scouts at the top of the hills. The scouts seemed all right—they were her people, and she knew them to be well trained. The talking, so far as she could tell, came from the Foot Soldiers, the lesser Beast Riders, and a handful of commanders, who had fallen out of their standard waiting positions. Her Infantry stood solemn, watching the procedures with faces that reflected both worry and disgust. Her stomach churned.

The Fey never lacked discipline.

Never.

She hurried down the last part of the hill and scanned the area for Ay'Le. Finally she saw her, leaning against a small boulder, hands over her stomach, eyes closed.

Licia headed straight for her. "Is this what you call leading a troop? What's wrong with you? I could hear our people at the top of the ridge line."

Ay'Le was shorter than Licia, and seemed even smaller all doubled over. Her hair had come loose from its tie, and her narrow face was gray. She looked up at Licia with wide eyes. "Didn't you feel it?" she whispered. Then she blinked, as if something cleared in her mind. "No, of course not. You're Infantry."

"Feel what?" Licia snapped, although she had an idea.

"That wave, the magick wave. It came through and—"

"I felt it," Licia said. "I'm a minor Visionary, in case you've forgotten. And it was disturbing. But that's all. Not enough to break discipline."

Ay'Le waved a hand. "It hurt," she said softly. "I felt it all the way through."

Licia took Ay'Le's hand and bent it back against the boulder until Ay'Le yelped with pain. "You will feel more pain than you've ever felt in your life if you don't gather your wits now. I'm tempted to report you to Rugad as a Failure, but that would take too long. I need you now. We have a job to do."

Ay'Le shook her head. "I—"

Licia forced Ay'Le's hand back even farther. Ay'Le's lower lip trembled. "You will gather yourself together, and then you will use every bit of that famous Charm, and you will contain your troops. My Infantry is fine."

"Your Infantry has no magick," Ay'Le said. "I felt this in my magick. I'm not sure I have any Charm left."

Licia let go of Ay'Le's arm. Ay'Le cried out slightly, gathered the arm to her protectively, and did not move. Licia spit on the ground beside Ay'Le's boots. "No wonder Boteen took over your mission. You're not worthy of being called Fey."

She left Ay'Le to her rock, went around it, and faced the force.

She had never seen so much chaos, not in all her years of commanding troops. It was as if she were facing an Islander force instead of a Fey one. Most of the Foot Soldiers had their hands hidden in their armpits—usually a sign of blood lust for them, but they did not act like they felt the lust. It seemed more as if they were moaning in pain. The Beast Riders had their hands on their stomachs if they were in Fey form, and if they were not, both heads were pressed together as if in mutual comfort. And all around, what she had first heard as conversation were really involuntary sounds, cries of pain, moans, or whimpers.

It was the whimpers that bothered her most.

They seemed to bother her Infantry as well. They were standing in the lines she had left them in, faces forward and impassive. But she could tell from the slight variations in the lines themselves that her Infantry had been shifting uncomfortably from the moment the troubles began.

All of the commanders, with the exception of the lowest

ranking Infantry leaders—the ones without magick—were as distressed as the Foot Soldiers. Only they were trying to gather themselves, trying to gather the troops, trying to stop the tide of upset, and failing.

She had felt the wind, the wave as Ay'Le had called it, and had been distressed, yes, but not like this. Was it because this troop was young and not battle-hardened? Many had fought only on the Isle. Rugad had sent them here because they were fresh and powerful. He had left some of the better fighters to guard the rest of the Isle, thinking that they could control the Islanders better.

Had that been a miscalculation as well?

It didn't matter. She had to gather these people together, and she had to do so now. It didn't matter how loud she was, because the troops were already so loud that anyone crossing that road could hear them.

She cursed Ay'Le under her breath, wishing for her Charm, and knowing that she could have none. Ay'Le would pay for this, if no one else would. Licia and Boteen would see to that.

Licia clapped her hands together.

The Infantry immediately looked toward her in perfect discipline. The Foot Soldiers brought their heads up one by one. Many of the Beast Riders did not move.

She clapped her hands again and shouted for order.

This time the voices silenced. Everyone was looking at her.

"This is how you respond to strange magick?" she shouted, loud enough for all the troops to hear. The bowl had a slight echo to it, and she used it for her own vocal advantage. "Like the people we conquer, you snivel and whine and cringe?"

The sound of her voice floated around her. Everyone was silent now.

"Foot Soldiers, crying in pain? Beast Riders acting with less courage than the Beasts you hold inside you? Are you Fey? Or has this Isle changed you into something less than Fey? Have you all become Failures?"

The Foot Soldiers were now standing at attention, arms down. The Beast Riders in Fey form still clutched their stomachs, but the other Riders stopped touching heads. They were all watching her.

"I do not care how much pain you felt," she said. "I do not care if you were hurt in your magick, a place you have never been touched before. I do not care what your personal response to this strange experience was. You are soldiers. You are Fey. And you have forgotten that."

She spat again in disgust. One of the Foot Soldiers near the front, a woman, winced.

"We had a mission and we cannot do it now because of your reaction." As she spoke, she saw Ay'Le come out from behind her boulder, still clutching her stomach. "I do not trust you to act like Fey when the time comes."

Licia took a step forward.

"I am a minor Visionary. I too felt the wave, only to me it felt like a wind. An evil wind, to be sure, but a wind just the same. It blew through me and past me and I came back here ready to do battle. Not to find sniveling cowards terrified because they had been touched in their magick."

The Foot Soldiers were now standing up straight, and the Beast Riders had let their arms drop away from their stomachs. The Infantry watched her. They were the only ones who hadn't moved.

"You were warned before you left Nye that Blue Isle would have tricks to play on you. This is a place that defeated Fey before." She put her hands on her hips, fists clenched tight. "I had thought those Fey failed because of a failure in their leadership. I had met Rugar, and while he was a mighty warrior, he was not a leader with true power. I had thought that Rugad would lead us to great victory. I see now that my view was naive."

Even the Infantry raised their heads slightly at this. She was insulting all of them, and they knew it. Ay'Le put one hand on the rock.

"Rugar was a better leader than I had thought. He might have had troubles, but I never realized that my own people, when faced with a magick force, became as weak-willed and cowardly as the peoples we used our magick to defeat."

"Licia," Ay'Le said. Her tone was curt, as if it were in reprimand.

Licia held up a hand to silence Ay'Le. The last thing Licia needed at this moment was a Charmer contradicting her.

"I am taking complete control of this force," Licia said. "I am in charge of all of you, Foot Soldiers, Beast Riders, and Infantry. Ay'Le has been as affected by this magick as you have, and thus her abilities are tainted. I was not. I was able to step past them, and move on, as all of you should have done."

Ay'Le took another step toward her. "Rugad said—"

"Rugad would kill you for your weakness," Licia snapped. "Now shut up and let me do my job."

Ay'Le brought her head up. "I am the leader of this troop."

"You did not act like it," Licia said. "And you have not

commanded a troop this size in battle. You lack Vision, which I have. You may speak as our diplomatic mouthpiece and nothing more. Even that is too much at this moment."

"You have no—"

"One more word," Licia said, "and I shall kill you myself."

She heard the strength in her own voice when the echo reached her. The valley was silent. The self-pity and fear she had seen when she arrived was gone.

The evil wind hadn't frightened her; her people's response to it had.

She turned her attention again to the small army before her. "Because I can no longer trust our magick users, our battle plan has changed. I have seen the small town waiting for us. I understand the area, and know what it will take to conquer this place. I am going to attack only with the Infantry. They are unaffected by the magick in these mountains. We shall conduct the assault."

The Foot Soldiers stirred, and slight murmurs came from the Beast Riders. This time she chose to ignore their responses.

"The Foot Soldiers shall be allowed to perform cleanup, so Infantry, do not kill each Islander you find. Leave some choice victims for the Foot Soldiers."

All the eyes in the valley were on her. The feelings churning below were powerful—anger and terror mixed. She could feel them swimming in their own responses.

"As for the Beast Riders," she said. "Your duties will differ slightly. The Bird Riders will watch from the air, and warn us of any approaching Islanders or any change in the fight below. The Beasts, those who remain on the ground, will guard the passes and the roads, preventing anyone from entering or leaving.

"Are my orders clear?"

"Aye, sir!" the troops yelled back in unison.

"And the leader of this troop is?"

"You, sir!"

"Good," she said. "Now that's clear, I have one more thing to add."

And it was the most important thing, the thing they had forgotten. She would try to make certain they would not forget it again.

"You are Fey," she said, raising her voice slightly, feeling the strain of the shout in her throat. "No matter what you see, no matter what you feel, no matter what may happen to you, you will always be Fey. We are warriors. We fight to the death. Even when we face forces more powerful than ours. Even when we face magick different from ours."

She scanned them, making certain her words were being heard.

"Should I ever see any reaction like the one I returned to today, in any Fey, ever again, I shall slaughter that Fey myself, and I shall ensure that the Fey and his family are declared Failures for all times. Is that clear?"

"Aye, sir!" The troop sounded subdued.

"Excellent," she said. "Get into battle positions. I am marching you to the ridge line. From there we shall attack the city below. Rugad wants the Cliffs of Blood secure and in Fey hands by nightfall. I intend to do it, no matter what the cost."

She stepped away from her spot and faced Ay'Le. "You will never contradict me again, and you will not speak to this troop without permission."

"You don't outrank me," Ay'Le said.

"I do now," Licia said. "I take any power you had in the name of the Fey Empire. You disgraced yourself and your Empire today. I will not stand for it."

"You are a lowly Infantry leader," Ay'Le said.

"Who can remain calm in the face of another's magick," Licia said. "You will stay here, and you will say nothing. If you make any attempt to control this troop, you will die."

"Why don't you kill me now, then?" Ay'Le asked.

"Because I might have need of your tongue," Licia said. "You can either let it save you, or you can let it kill you. But remember, the choice is yours."

"Will you report me to Rugad as a Failure?"

"If you don't listen to me," Licia said. "If you cooperate with me, I might be convinced to forget this episode."

"What about the others?" Ay'Le nodded toward the troop.

"They'll do as they are told," Licia said. "Will you?"

Ay'Le stared at her for a moment, then nodded again.

"Good," Licia said. She turned her back on Ay'Le, and prepared to go into battle. Rugad wanted the Cliffs by nightfall, and Licia would do everything in her power to do as the Black King wished.

She was Fey, and the Fey were stronger than all other races of the world.

She would prove it.

# ELEVEN

RUGAD stood with his hands clasped behind his back, facing the fire that still burned out of control miles away from him. Through the bubbled glass it looked as if it were waving at him, as if it were climbing enough to see him.

It would burn until the magick was gone, and that would take a long time. Days, maybe weeks, depending on how many pouches were there, and how fresh the layers of skin were inside them. Judging from the feeling of that initial wave, there were a lot, and the thin layers were very fresh.

He only hoped that the fire had already burned through the entire pile of pouches. When this had happened during his boyhood, there had been a second pile of pouches that had remained untouched for days, until the flames caught them.

The second wave had been less devastating, but it had done damage to already weakened Fey.

He had to prepare for that.

His generals were assembling as he watched the burning sky. He could hear the sliding chairs, the faint murmur of voices behind him.

He had decided to hold the meeting in the North Tower. He wanted to keep an eye on the fire, and he wanted to see if any force, Islander force, decided to take advantage of the chaos and attack the palace.

So far there was nothing. But it hadn't been long since the attack had happened. He suspected this was a lucky target, nothing more, but he couldn't be sure.

He couldn't be sure of anything on this accursed Isle.

The sky was lightening, not just from the fire, but with the beginning of dawn. His cuts ached down to his bones. He hadn't slept much the last two days, and he was still healing from the attach that had taken his voice. At ninety-two, he was a virile, strong man, but he wasn't recovering like he did as a young man. If here were in his thirties, he would be past all the injuries by now.

If he had known how much of a toll conquering Blue Isle would take on him personally, he wouldn't have waited twenty years to come here.

But he had needed those years to consolidate his power on Galinas. He needed to know that when he left that continent, it would remain in Fey hands. He needed to guarantee that no matter what his idiot grandson did, there would be no unrest on Nye or anywhere else.

He had guaranteed that, but at a formidable price. A price he hadn't realized he was paying until he came here.

He turned. His generals had assembled around the stone table. They looked like warriors of old, as if they belonged to this place more than they belonged to his Galinas Empire.

That was good.

Very good.

It meant that Blue Isle would be his.

He scanned them quickly. The nine of them were his major advisors and his best allies. He had met with them the day before at about this time, only then Quata, one of his ship's captains, had been with them. Quata was now on his way to the Isle's southern mountains, where he would join up with the other ships and send one to Nye for reinforcements.

Rugad clenched a fist. He could use them now.

His generals looked haggard, and Landre, his head Spell Warder, looked physically ill. He hunched, his skin so gray it looked like stone, his eyes dull. A small chunk of hair had fallen out of his scalp, and he hadn't pulled it free.

"The other Warders?" Rugad asked.

"Alive," Landre said. His voice was a whisper, nothing like the dry, almost sardonic voice Rugad was used to from this man.

Rugad nodded once. That they lived was better than he had hoped for.

"This will be a free discussion," he said, his voice raspy but strong. There was pain each time he used it, but it was pain he could tolerate. "Although I want it to be as brief as possible. The plans we drew up yesterday are moot. We have to have new action."

Slaughter, the Foot Soldier, had his hands underneath his armpits. He did not have the look of blood lust about him; he seemed to be holding them because of pain. He swiveled his chair with his feet, and the sound grated on Rugad's already frayed nerves.

He shot a glance at Slaughter, and Slaughter stopped moving.

"For those of you not old enough to remember, which I assume is all of you but Kendrad"—he nodded to his Infantry general, who seemed as unaffected as he did; she sat upright, her trim muscular body fully in her own control, the silver in her black braid catching the growing morning light—"that strange wave of magick energy you felt was an Islander attack."

Dimar, the Doppelgänger who had taken the place of a chef in the kitchen, tilted his head back. His skin was darker than it should have been, and a bit of upswept cheekbone showed in his face. "I heard nothing about it," he said.

"I doubt it had much to do with the palace," Rugad said. He pointed to the fire. "There's our problem. Some Islanders destroyed one of our pouch caches."

"And it was a large one," Kendrad said softly.

"Large enough to affect the entire Isle," Rugad said.

"You mean what we felt others will feel?" Frad'l asked. Frad'l led Rugad's Spies, and for the first time in years, Rugad saw the contours of Frad'l's real face. Frad'l had a sharp, pointed chin and penetrating eyes. It was a memorable face. Usually Frad'l's Spy talents allowed him to give off the appearance of features, but they were wholly unremarkable, even unmemorable.

"Have felt," Rugad said. "That thing moved quickly across the Isle. It may even reach Galinas."

"I hope not," Black said. He led the Dream Riders. He gripped the chair as if it were uncomfortable to him. Rugad wondered if Black could even be in shadow form at this moment. It seemed that this man, the darkest and most terrifying of the Fey, was actually reflecting light.

"It won't be as strong if it does," Rugad said. "The power dissipates as the wave travels."

"You mean we could have felt something stronger?" Ife asked, voice trembling. Ife lead the Wisps. He was suited to inside work; he had injured a wing in battle and could no longer fly. The injured wing curled against his back. The other wing, usually straight and well formed, curled slightly, as if in sympathy. Or perhaps that was where Ife had felt the pain of the wave.

"Yes," Rugad said. "When this last happened, I was a boy. We lost an Enchanter and a few Spell Warders in the attack."

"You seem so calm about that," Landre said softly.

"Eighty years have passed," Rugad said. "And I am not calm about this. We were going to concentrate our forces on the Cliffs of Blood. We cannot now. We need to divide into three separate troops."

"Do you think the troops already at the Cliffs were deeply affected by this?" Onha asked. She was the head of his Beast Riders, and had several members of her troop there. She was leaning forward, a hand covering her stomach. Her Beast form was a mastiff, and in her Fey form she had a long nose, short bristly hair, and eyes that were too close together. Her movements were powerful, but suggested, even as Fey, a bit of dog.

"Yes," Rugad said. "Although they are farther away. They didn't feel it as strongly."

"Most of the force are Infantry who haven't yet come into their magick," Kendrad said.

"Being led by a Charmer, though," Onha said. "A Charmer would feel this, wouldn't she?"

"Yes," Rugad said. "I'm sure that if there is a problem someone else will step into the breach."

He glanced at the fire, then back at his generals. They seemed slightly disturbed by the wave, but were too professional to show it.

"We need," he said again, "three forces. One to guard the palace, one to go the Cliffs as we had planned, and another to stop the insurrection in the center of the Isle."

"You have information that it's an insurrection?" Frad'l asked. He had the right to sound stunned. Usually such information would come through his network.

"Only what I can see," Rugad said, sweeping his hand toward the windows. "No Fey would touch those pouches, let alone destroy them. The taboo is too great. Besides, any magickal Fey might die if he's in that close proximity. Obviously this was an Islander attack."

"Could they have known what they did?" Ife asked. His good wing tightened against his back.

"We must assume they did," Rugad said, "I never want to underestimate these people. They defeated my son, and my granddaughter, and they have put up a good fight with us." He touched his throat for emphasis. He didn't normally like to draw attention to that injury, but he needed to right now. His generals knew what a powerful man he was. They needed to remember that even he had suffered a major defeat at the hands of the Islanders.

The Islander King.

Whom Rugad would get to in a moment.

"Whoever made that attack was smart," Rugad said. "Since the destruction of the pouches eighty years ago, we've only let Infantry or Red Caps guard the pouches."

"Except for Rugar," Slaughter mumbled.

Rugad heard the comment, and smiled tightly. "My son made many errors in judgment," he said. "And it is fortunate that he led the first force to Blue Isle."

Let them remember also that sending Rugar here had been Rugad's idea. Rugad would kill a son if he had to—as subversively as he could, to avoid Black Blood against Black Blood—in order to achieve his aims. If he would kill a son, he would not hesitate in executing a general.

"Those pouches were well guarded. Whoever attacked them might have done so with a full force, but I doubt it. Our Infantry would have seen the Islanders mobilizing and stopped it." Rugad's throat ached. He was speaking more than he had planned. "Instead, these Islanders waged a guerrilla attack."

"The Fey aren't vulnerable to guerrilla war," Dimar said. "Every country we've invaded has tried it, and we've always been able to stop them."

"The Infantry is vulnerable," Kendrad said. "They have no magick."

"And no magick can be near those pouches," Black said, as if he just realized what Rugad was getting at.

"I'm sure there are other areas in which we are equally vulnerable," Rugad said, "and as we discover them, we will protect against them. That is one of my admonitions to all of you today: Look through your areas, and see where Islanders can take advantage of us. Even though they look like a weak enemy, they are not. They are a cunning enemy, and we are not used to cunning enemies. We are used to straightforward types who do not match us in power. Expectations themselves can be weaknesses. See what you can do to educate your troops."

His generals nodded as a unit. He had given that speech to

them before, and he suspected he would have to again. But it never hurt to remind them.

It never hurt to remind himself.

Rugad clasped his hands tightly behind his back. He was standing as straight as he could. Everything had to be military this morning.

Everything.

"This is merely a side point," he said. "The main issue here is our policy toward Blue Isle. In the past, we have treated it as we treated other countries: an easy conquest which we would make cautiously while preserving the land. We can no longer be cautious. These Islanders take advantage of all of our generosity. We will have to use tactics that I have never used. If we are attacked, we respond with double our usual force. We respond with one of my grandfather's tactics. He called it full destruction, and the name describes the action. We will annihilate anyone who opposes us. Anyone at all, and his family, and his neighbors."

His words hung for a moment. Then Kendrad—because the others knew she was the only one with enough seniority to do so—leaned forward slightly.

"Forgive me, Rugad," she said. "I thought we were taking Blue Isle for its material wealth."

"We came here first for my great-grandchildren," he said. "Our second reason for taking the Isle was its location. And our third was its wealth. Wealth can be rebuilt. The Isle's wealth lies in its fertile fields, in its fresh water, in its variety of climates. Such wealth remains, even after a policy of destruction. It simply takes more time to claim it."

"I've heard of the policy," Black said, "but how do we apply it here?"

Rugad smiled at him. He had been waiting for that question. "It's quite simply, actually," he said. "We shall first apply it in the vicinity of that burning barn. We are going to destroy all the farms within walking distance, slaughter the families who have been working the land—men, women *and* children—and burn the fields. If any Islander protests, he dies. If any Islander is in the wrong area at the wrong time, he dies. Should we receive another attack like this, the perpetrators, and all those within walking distance, will die in the same way. We shall make such a policy clear only with action. Does that make it clearer?"

"Yes," Black said.

"Good," Rugad said. "Onha, I need you to coordinate this attack. Take Dream Riders. Kill Islanders in their sleep. Let them wake up to chaos. I want terror built into the hearts of any survivors, terror so extreme that the only way they can alleviate it is to never even contemplate rebellion against the Fey."

"Who do I get besides my own people and Dream Riders?" she asked.

"You don't get all of either," Rugad said. "You get half the available Dream Riders, a third of the Beast Riders—the most savage you can find—and the Infantry who are already in place."

"The Failures who lost the barn?"

"No," Rugad said. "Deal with them as you will, but judge the situation wisely. It might not be as obvious a case as you think. You will get the Infantry from the nearby garrisons and the area's Foot Soldiers. Bring some Red Caps. We need to start replenishing that pouch supply."

"Will do," Ohna said, looking satisfied. She like nothing better than a battle. She was one of his best, and most bloodthirsty, generals. She had led the attack on the Tabernacle two weeks before, and it had demoralized the Islanders on that side of Jahn. Rugad hoped she would do as well—or better—now.

"Secondly," he said. "We need guards here, a strong guard, that takes care of all entrances from the subterranean to the aerial. I want the Spell Warders here, working in this palace. I want magick users of all types. I need a solid Infantry, Foot Soldiers, and the most controllable Beast Riders. I will need a troop of Wisps. I also need most Healers and Domestics here. We will use one of the nearby buildings as a hospital for our troops only. Islanders who are injured will die."

"Doppelgängers?" Dimar asked.

"Doppelgängers and Spies will have their own separate missions. I want infiltration in all aspects of Blue Isle society. Someone planned this raid and if he's smart, he's no longer in the area of that barn. Which means that no matter how many we kill, we will not get him. I want him found. I want all others like him found. It is the duty of the Doppelgängers and Spies to locate the provocateurs, isolate them, report them, and let one of our Assassins take care of them."

Dimar nodded.

"Finally," Rugad said, "we come to the difficult area. I had planned to go the Cliffs of Blood myself. If this had been a normal campaign, I would. There is something there, something that I must investigate. But until the area is secure, I will not go. We already have a troop there, as has been pointed out, and we need more. I have reason to believe that the Islander King, Nicholas, is there. He may die, but if his children are with him, they cannot. They must be protected at all cost. Any Fey who inadvertently causes their deaths will be branded a Failure, and his death will be one of the most public ever on record. Do I make myself clear?"

His generals nodded as a unit.

"Nicholas is the most cunning enemy we have ever faced. He seduced my granddaughter and nearly killed me. He is powerful, even though he masks that power in Islander humility. Do not ever underestimate him."

Again, they nodded."

"His children will fight alongside him. You will not be able to sway them with talk of the Black Throne or glories of the Fey Empire. They have been with Nicholas too long. They must be captured, and they must be captured alive."

"Rugad," Kendrad said softly, "anyone can be killed in battle. You know what it's like. They could be mistaken for someone else. Or worse, they could be killed accidentally by their own people, mistaken for purebred Fey. I don't know if it's wise to let the responsibility for those children fall in the hands of anyone but yourself."

Rugad smiled at her. "Excellent point, Kendrad," he said, "and one I've already thought of. The chances of our people capturing those children are slim. Both are Visionaries, and the girl is also a Shifter. I think it more likely that the children will be trapped somewhere, and then we can retrieve them at our leisure."

"Have you Seen this?" Kendrad asked.

"No," Rugad said. "But I do know that I cannot go to the Cliffs of Blood at this moment. It is the expected move. Each time I have done the expected thing on this Isle, it has been a mistake."

"But the children are our first priority," Kendrad said.

Rugad shook his head. "They are our main objective. If we do not achieve that objective, then we have not lost. I simply must rethink the inheritance of the Black Throne. I am not a young man, but I am not on my deathbed. I may still father children if I must, and I will have the years to train them. I simply prefer not to."

Kendrad nodded, head down. He could tell she did not agree, but she was reserving her opinion. She obviously felt she had spoken up enough.

Rugad gazed at his generals. They were watching him, many of their expressions mirroring Kendrad's opinions. None of his people wanted to be responsible for the future of the Black Throne. Failure in that area would cause Rugad to administer the worst fate of all, and even he couldn't imagine what that would be.

"Kendrad will lead the troops in the Cliffs of Blood. I want a full fighting force to take those mountains. The Islanders there are the tallest our young Wisp Gauze has ever seen, and she has hinted at some strangeness in the area."

"I have heard stories among the Islanders," Dimar said. "There is a schism between those Islanders and the King's family. It seems odd that he would be hiding out there."

"Nicholas is shrewd. He knows we would have learned of that schism and would consider it an unlikely place," Rugad said.

"I would think," Dimar said, "that he risks his life being in that part of Blue Isle."

"Are you saying the people in the Cliffs of Blood could be our allies?" Kendrad asked.

"Possibly," Onha said. "It happened in the Marshes."

"No," Dimar said. "It sounds unlikely that these people would ally with anyone. They are considered strange by the Islanders, and their leaders, a group called the Wise Ones, are spoken of with a mixture of fear and awe."

"What else do you know?" Rugad asked. Doppelgängers were often good sources of information. They were treated as members of the race they appeared to be, and they also had access to the memories of their host bodies.

"Only that," Dimar said. "Most Islanders have not met anyone of the Cliffs of Blood. Except—" he held up a hand, frowned as if he were listening to a voice inside himself, and then nodded; Rugad had seen such behavior in a Doppelgänger before, as memories rose from the host—"except a number of people have fled the Cliffs of Blood over the years, and have refused to talk about it. The Islanders who know of the place fear it."

Rugad sighed. His instinct had been a good one, then. If Islanders feared it, then there was something there, something that he didn't understand yet.

"What kind of army am I leading?" Kendrad asked.

"You get the full contingent," Rugad said. "Whatever's left among the Infantry, Foot Soldiers, and Beast Riders. Boteen is there, so use his Enchanter's skills. Take a few Spies, but not many, and every other magick user you can find, including some Domestics. Be creative. And remember our objectives."

"Am I to understand that I'll be using full destruction?"

"You will use full destruction only after you personally have located Nicholas and his children. Then I want nothing to remain of these strange Islanders in their Cliffs."

Kendrad nodded, her mouth a thin line. She clearly didn't like the order or the responsibility but she understood it. That was why he had her lead those troops. Kendrad could be trusted. She would follow orders, and she would attain a victory.

She also understood the risks she was facing.

"Ife," Rugad said. "I need your swiftest Wisp. Send that Wisp to me, along with Gauze. I need to speak with both of them."

Ife nodded.

"I want the troops dispersed immediately. The Islanders, particularly those in the center of the Isle, need to feel our wrath as close to the event as possible. Onha, send Wisps ahead, and let the Infantry already in place know our plans. They should start full destruction immediately."

Onha's small eyes narrowed, and she smiled. She seemed to be feeling better as the plans for the attack progressed.

Rugad said, "I want the guards to set up here, the Spies and Doppelgängers deployed as soon as this meeting ends, and the troop prepared to go to the Cliffs as soon as I give the signal. Is that clear?"

His generals nodded. They moved as if they were anticipating his order for dismissal.

But he was not ready to dismiss.

"I am going to make one thing plain to you. I consider these next few days the most crucial in our battle for Blue Isle. If we do not take this Isle, if I do not have Nicholas's head on a pike, if we have not quelled all resistance within the week, we threaten the entire Empire. We cannot move to Leut without Blue Isle. It is the most critical battlefield we have fought on in all of our lives, mine and Kendrad's included. I will not tolerate failure. I will push us to complete success, whatever the cost. Is that clear?"

"Yes," Kendrad said, and she was clearly speaking for the others.

"Excellent," Rugad said. "Dismissed."

They stood. The sound of chairs scraping the floor echoed in the large room.

"Kendrad, stay. Ife, get those Wisps in here."

"Yes, sir," Ife said as he went to the door.

Kendrad stood beside her chair. Rugad waited until the others had left before approaching her. Then he glanced around. Two guards stood beside the door.

"You are dismissed as well," he said to them.

They bowed slightly and left.

"Was that wise?" Kendrad asked, her tone light. She had questioned his judgment since they were teenagers, and he had let her. Her judgment was often as good as or better than his, even though she lacked his great Vision.

He smiled. "You have no gold flecks in your eyes."

"Islanders lack that talent."

"Do they?" Rugad said. "They haven't lacked for many."

"True enough," Kendrad said.

Rugad walked to the window. The fire still burned. Occasional flares made the flames reach higher before returning to the flat level.

"There should be a battle under way when you arrive at the Cliffs of Blood," he said.

"I gathered that." She joined him, squinting as she looked at the faraway fire.

"You need to find Boteen immediately," Rugad said. "He sent a Wisp to tell me of my great-grandchildren, but she saw something and he had forbidden her to tell me."

"What do you think it is?" Kendrad said.

Rugad took a deep breath. This was the other reason he had planned to go, and, after the wave this morning, the reason he decided to stay.

"The mountains are high on that part of the Isle, and there is a wild magick in this place. My great-grandchildren have more power than any Fey before them."

'I thought that was because of the mixing of Black Blood with non-Fey blood," Kendrad said. "It always makes us stronger."

"But it does not make us different," Rugad said. "My great-granddaughter has two types of magick. She is a Visionary and a Shifter. There is an Islander—Boteen says there might be two—with the powers of Enchanter."

"Obviously," Kendrad said dryly, "I'm to make a connection that you have made."

He nodded once. "Boteen's Wisp found my great-grandchildren in a cave. She refused to say more about it, because Boteen asked her not to. The message he gave her was that he would check out the cave."

"The cave?" Kendrad's frown grew deeper.

"He also did not think that my great-grandchildren would move from there." Rugad rocked on his heels, feeling an odd pounding in his heart. To admit this aloud was difficult. If he were wrong, he would be subject to ridicule. "I believe that they hide in a Place of Power."

Kendrad turned toward him so quickly she overbalanced herself. "I thought the other two Places of Power were myths."

Rugad smiled. "Why would they be? Why would the Fey be unique? It is a conceit to think so."

"But if they have a Place of Power, then they are as strong as we are."

Rugad nodded. "Only they don't know it. They have kept much of their magick hidden. I believe the Tabernacle guarded it and we destroyed it."

"That explains the holy poison, then," she said.

"Yes," Rugad said. "Nicholas is a direct descendent of a man they call the Roca, who started their religion. I believe this Roca is the one who discovered, or learned to use, their Place of Power."

"If they're in a Place of Power, we can't get to them," Kendrad said. She had never been to the Eccrasian Mountains, but, like all great Fey military leaders, she had learned of the strengths and weaknesses of a Place of Power.

"Sure we can," Rugad said. "If they don't know what kind of powers they have."

"And if they do?"

"That's why I'm sending you," he said.

"Thanks," Kendrad said dryly. But he knew she understood. Facing a Place of Power against someone who knew how to use it was a risk he dare not take.

"Say nothing of this," Rugad said. "The raids on our Place of Power have always been unsuccessful, but this one is not guarded by Fey. We could have a splintering within our own troop."

"Do you actually think someone could steal enough power from such a place to rival the Black Family?" Kendrad asked.

Rugad did not look at her. He didn't dare. Nor did he dare answer the question honestly.

"I think the magick for that is long lost," he said.

Kendrad went silent. She mimicked his position, hands clasped behind her, staring at the fire. The growing light shone on her unlined face. She did not look like a girl any longer, but rather like a seasoned woman with a timeless beauty. Her skin was roughened by the weather, her features hardened into position. He wondered why he had never taken her to wife.

Probably because he needed her at his side, an always trusted companion. He dared not risk losing that loyalty.

"Two Places of Power," she said. "Do you believe there's a third?"

"Yes," he said.

"And once we have two, we'll be able to find the third," she said, voicing the suspicion the Fey had held for generations. "Then we would have the Triangle of Might."

"And re-form the world," Rugad said softly.

She looked at him. "You have believed in the other two Places of Power all along?" she asked.

He shrugged. "I did not disbelieve."

"And when did you suspect one might be here?"

"When I learned of my great-grandchildren. When I realized that neither Jewel nor Rugar could hold this place. When I knew the Islanders had an Enchanter with no Fey blood."

Kendrad let out a soft breath. "This changes everything."

"Yes," he said. "It does."

"We're fighting equals."

"No." Rugad smiled at her. This was why he was Black King and she was no more than a minor Visionary. For all her good advice, she could not see the larger picture. Few could. "We embraced our magick. We used it, mined it, developed it. They have tried to control theirs. They buried it, disowned it, and gave it to Black Robes, many of whom did not have the real power. Even King Nicholas, for all his physical prowess, has shown no signs of magick."

"But his children have."

"And to his credit, he's allowed it to develop. Against much disapproval from his own people. The culture even has a name for those who use unapproved magick." He unclasped his hands, unable to hold them together for the sheer delight of what he was telling her. "The phrase is *demon spawn*. In Fey, there is no exact translation, but I have heard it described as offspring of dark magick."

"Dark magick?"

"We call it warrior magick. They add an evil intent to it. They think it an abomination."

Kendrad was frowning at him. "They've buried their magick."

"It is like a child with a sword. He may have more innate skill than most around him, but if he has no practice, his skill means nothing."

"So all those attacks on us," Kendrad said, "you believe those were lucky hits?"

"No," Rugad said. "I believe the Place of Power, the magick of this place, is the reason for them. But I also believe the Islanders do not know how to harness that magick. We do."

"And we can turn their own powers against them," Kendrad said.

Rugad smiled. "Exactly."

# TWELVE

NICHOLAS would never get used to the way Jewel appeared and disappeared like that. Each time she vanished, his heart hurt anew, as if she had just died.

Again.

"Where'd she go?" Gift asked. He was standing near the stairs, looking as bereft as Nicholas felt.

"I don't know," Nicholas said. "But she'll be back."

He sounded so certain, and he wasn't. He didn't know the limits of her powers, and he hadn't asked when they were alone behind the fountain. Instead he had held her and loved her and let her know how much he missed her.

And he had missed her.

Every day of his life.

"Were you ever going to tell me?" The voice belonged to Arianna. He looked up to see her staring at him. She was still so slender, and her terrifying encounter with the Black King had left deep circles under her eyes. With her cheekbones prominent and the roundness gone from her face, she had the look of her mother.

And so did Gift.

Nicholas had never realized how much his children resembled each other. Sebastian, with his gray skin and cracked features, had been, in that way, a poor substitute.

"Tell you what?" Nicholas asked, even though he knew. He knew where her anger was coming from.

"That my mother was here? That she was visible only to you and to—to—to Gift?"

There. She had used his name. And without contempt. Gift's compassion had done something for their relationship, then.

Gift's lie.

"Yes," Nicholas said. "I was."

"When?"

"When it was time. You needed rest, Ari."

"I needed rest," she snapped. "I need to be trusted."

"I do trust you," he said. He glanced over her shoulder. The small group was watching them. Coulter's color was returning, but he still leaned against Adrian. Scavenger had his arms crossed and was shaking his head slightly. He didn't seem to like Arianna much. Leen had moved closer to the group. And Gift, Gift was watching with an intensity Nicholas had seen only in Arianna.

Nicholas wished they weren't having this fight here, in front of the others, but he couldn't easily pull her aside. There weren't many places to go. And even though he had been behind the fountain with Jewel, he didn't think he could bring Ari there. He didn't know if the water was holy water or not.

"Then you would have told me," she said.

Nicholas sighed. "Arianna, there wasn't a chance. I knew you'd be angry—"

"So you thought you could hide it from me?"

"No," Nicholas said. "But I knew I'd get this reaction. I wanted to give you a day to recuperate first."

"So, blame this on me," Arianna said. "On my reactions."

"Ari—"

"All flash and spark and fire," Jewel said from beside him. He turned his head. She was back, and she looked younger again, as if she were slowly replenishing. He could see through her, but not as clearly. "You really need to teach her some discipline, Nicholas."

"I did," Nicholas said. "Imagine what she'd be like if I hadn't."

"Where'd you go?" Gift asked, approaching his mother cautiously.

"Is she back?" Arianna asked. She looked at the spot beside Nicholas, as if she could see Jewel. "Are you here?"

"Yes," Nicholas said. "She's back."

"I wanted to check some things," Jewel said. "Rugad has not left the palace yet. I'm not sure he will. But he's angry."

Gift repeated her words for the others. Nicholas found that an annoying habit, but he knew it was necessary.

"He knows what happened?" Nicholas asked.

"I'm sure he does," Jewel said. "I didn't stay long enough to find out. I wanted to see how long we had."

"Before what?" Leen asked.

"Before his armies get here."

"There will be armies?" Arianna's voice was sharp. Her entire manner was sharp. She stood, arms crossed, eyes flashing, as if she were going to deny anything she heard.

Nicholas suppressed a sigh. She had done this from childhood, but rarely at times like these.

"He knows where we are," Coulter said gently. "We need to be able to defend this place."

As much as Nicholas didn't want to like that boy—he looked at Arianna with too much intensity, too much warmth—he couldn't help it. The boy had sense and he was kind.

"Yes," Arianna said, "the six of us. Defenders of the Isle."

"Nicholas," Jewel said. "Take me and Arianna somewhere private."

Gift looked at Nicholas, clearly asking if he should translate. Nicholas shrugged. He'd prefer to go elsewhere as well. Then he nodded at Gift.

Gift repeated Jewel's words.

"No," Arianna said. "Why would *she* want to talk to me?" And Nicholas felt the hurt behind Arianna's anger. She had understood Gift's explanation, but it had hurt her just the same. And when Arianna was hurt, she tried to hurt in return.

"Because we have to clear this anger out now," Jewel said, looking at her daughter. "It's inappropriate and it'll interfere with what's ahead of us. We need you on our side, not distracting us."

Gift looked at his mother. He bit his lower lip, then said around it, "I can't tell her that."

"Yes, you can," Arianna said. "Tell me."

Gift sighed, looked trapped, and repeated what Jewel had said.

"Inappropriate?" Arianna asked. "It's inappropriate that I don't know that my father and my so-called brother—"

Nicholas and Gift winced together. Then Nicholas looked at his son. He seemed to be even more vulnerable than Nicholas had originally thought.

"—are taking advice from someone who died fifteen years ago? If, indeed, you do exist."

"She exists," Nicholas said softly.

"Not to me, she doesn't," Arianna snapped.

"Ari, we don't have time—" Nicholas started, but she interrupted him.

"You can't take advice from this thing!" Arianna said. "I can't believe you believe in it."

"I believe it's Jewel," Coulter said, "and I can't see her."

"If you understood the Mysteries, you'd know," Scavenger said.

"As if you understand them," Arianna said. "You have no magick at all!"

Scavenger stood. "And you're no better than any other Fey I've ever seen. You let your arrogance take the place of your intelligence."

"And this is why we need to calm her, Nicholas," Jewel said. "She'll let us all spend our time catering to her."

He knew that, but he also understood how Arianna felt, how hurt she was, how exhausted she was, and how much she had lost.

He had lost it all too.

"Ari," he said.

"I won't listen to you!" she said. "You don't trust me!"

"Ari—"

"Then she'll listen to me." Jewel stood up as if Arianna could see her. "And you'll translate, Gift, just as you have been."

"All right," he said, sounding both frightened and uncertain. Then he proceeded to do as she asked.

Jewel made her way to Arianna. Gift watched her, and so did Coulter, as if he could see Jewel. He had said he could feel her energy, and that must have been what he was doing.

Nicholas sat on the steps, hands clasped, mouth dry. He had seen his wife angry. And he knew the irrational angers of his daughter. He didn't want to be anywhere near this.

"You are a disgrace to the Fey," Jewel snapped.

There was a slight delay as Gift translated.

"I am not Fey," Arianna said.

"You are Fey," Jewel said, "and it was a mistake to raise you as an Islander."

"I had a Fey teacher," Arianna said.

"Who?"

"Solanda."

"And where is she now?"

Arianna's eyes filled with tears. She looked at her father. "We don't know," he said. "We think she was killed in the second invasion."

"A Shifter," Jewel said.

"I'm a Shifter," Arianna said.

"You're also a Visionary. Visionaries are leaders. They are not disrupters. If they're upset, their troops are upset. You cannot cause this kind of discord and still be a warrior." Jewel glanced at Nicholas. "Did you teach her nothing?"

"*I'm* not Fey," he said, gently chiding.

"But you are a warrior. You should have taught her. Can you use a sword, child?"

Arianna shook her head.

"A knife?"

"Anyone can use a knife," she said.

"A bow and arrow, the Islander weapon of choice?"

"No," Arianna said. "And I don't know how it's relevant. I'm a ruler, not a soldier."

Jewel put her hands on her hips and turned to Nicholas. "So, you have fallen prey to Blue Isle's attitudes after all. Women do not fight."

"No," he said. He clenched his hands tightly. He knew he had failed in this part of Ari's training. He had done so consciously, thinking that her Shifting would help her save herself in any crisis.

"Then why did you do this? I warned you about Rugad. You knew he was going to come. Did you think you could protect this child against the greatest warrior of all the Fey?"

"No," Nicholas said. He swallowed. Everyone was watching him. His wife, his daughter, his son—whom he had just met— and the others. He would have to lead them. He couldn't look weak. "I thought her other strengths would be enough."

"He wouldn't let me out of the palace without an escort. He kept someone watching me at all times," Arianna said, looking at him. "I had to Shift to give them the slip."

Jewel's gaze softened as she looked at him. She understood. She had always understood. She knew the real reason. He had lost her. He wouldn't lose Ari, too.

"She is not a Fey warrior," Nicholas said. "She was raised Islander."

Jewel closed her eyes, shook her head once as if to clear that expectation from it, then turned back to Arianna.

"But you were raised to lead your people?" Jewel asked.

"Of course," Arianna said.

"And you are more concerned with yourself than their welfare. Have you learned nothing? Don't you know what your petty anger is doing inside this room?"

Arianna raised her chin. Her birthmark shone brightly against the pallor of her skin. She was obviously sensible enough not to answer.

Nicholas watched them. So this was what else he had missed over the years. The balance. Jewel would have given Arianna strength without allowing her willfulness to control her. He had never been able to do that.

He had never really tried.

"Our focus, until I tell you otherwise, is saving this Place of Power, keeping you and Gift from my grandfather, and keeping Blue Isle in your family's hands. Your emotions do not count. You aren't the only one whose lost things," Jewel said. "Gift has lost his adopted family, his entire world. You still have your father. And he's lost more than you can dream. You have one chance to grow up, one chance to show the kind of woman you can be, and that chance is now, Arianna. Life is full of loss. But it's also rich. You can't appreciate the richness without the loss."

"I know that," Arianna said, sounding petulant.

Nicholas gripped his hands tighter. He wanted to defend his daughter, wanted to stop Jewel from yelling at her, even though he knew that Jewel was right. Was this why Ari was so often out of control? Because he had allowed it? Because he didn't dare discipline her?

Because he was so afraid of hurting her, of losing her?

"Then you also know that a leader thinks not of herself, but of what is best for the people she leads," Jewel said.

Nicholas raised his head. She sounded like his father at that moment. This entire discussion—without some of the passion— was like the conversations he had with his father during the first Fey invasion.

"Are you saying I didn't need to know about you?" Arianna asked, her voice trembling.

"Not immediately, no," Jewel said. "Now, yes, you did. And you were right to question it, but not in front of everyone. By doing that, you undermine your father's authority."

Gift's face was flushed. He looked as if the words he were forced to repeat embarrassed him. Nicholas was certainly glad that he didn't have to do the translating.

"I wanted to know," Arianna said. "I had the right to know."

"You had no rights in this," Jewel said. "It's between Gift and Nicholas and me. It's their choice to make my presence public."

"But you're my mother." Arianna's voice ended on a wail. Her eyes were filled with tears.

"Yes," Jewel said, "and I'm so sorry about the way things turned out. I'm sorry I can't be visible to you too. I'm sorry I can't touch you. I'm sorry we never ever got to spend time together, real time, like a mother and daughter. But I think there's something your father never told you."

Arianna shot him a quick look. Nicholas felt his stomach tighten. What was Jewel going to reveal? And would he have to deal with that too?

"I suspect that if I had lived, you would not have," Jewel said. "I'd never birthed a Shifter. None of the Islander midwives had either. You probably would have died before we knew what to do."

"You're saying"—Arianna's breath hitched in her throat; it almost sounded like a sob—"we could never be alive at the same time. Why?"

"Because," Jewel said softy, "that's the way of the Powers. They give one thing and take another away. Usually the gift is better than what was lost."

"But you just said I'm not worthy of being a Fey," Arianna said.

"And I lay the blame squarely on your father for that," Jewel said. Nicholas flinched. "But then, he had no way of making you a Fey. I'm afraid you're going to have to take lessons from me. And they'll mostly require you to listen. You cannot be the center of attention here. The others might die if you are. You must work with them, and let your father lead them. Don't question him too much, at least not in public."

Gift lowered his voice on that last, to mimic Jewel's sincerity. Arianna blinked several times, then nodded. Nicholas let out a breath he hadn't even realized he was holding.

Arianna looked at him. The tears still floated in her eyes, but hadn't fallen. "Do you hate me?" she whispered, with all the melodrama he had come to associate with her. From childhood she had always gone to the most extreme emotion. He had blamed that on Solanda, but perhaps it had come from him, from the fact that he never had the courage to talk to her as Jewel just had.

"No," he said, and held out his hand. She came close, took it, and then sat beside him, burying her face in his sleeve. He eased his arm away, pulled her close, and let her huddle against him.

She was so frail. So thin. So tired.

Jewel was watching him with amusement. "Fey don't believe in coddling," she said, but he could tell she was reacting with fondness, not censure.

"I know," he said. "That's why you took great pains to coddle Sebastian."

Her smile faded just a bit, and she glanced over her shoulder at Gift. He wasn't smiling at all. He was watching her. All of them knew that Sebastian had taken his place. For good or ill, as much as they loved him, Sebastian had not been the heir. Sebastian had been their child, but not the child they had been given.

"We have to figure out how we can use this place," Nicholas said, trying to keep things on track. "How we can stop Rugad with it."

He swallowed hard after saying that. He had taken the Shaman's body deep into the cave, without light, and had felt presences there. He had knelt beside her, asked her forgiveness for his own treatment of her that last night, and said that he missed her. Then he promised her that she would be tended like a Fey, as soon as he was able to make that happen. He sat with her for some time, wishing that he had done more. That he had been able to prevent more. But he hadn't. She was gone, and it had been her choice.

But, as Jewel said, the gain was somehow greater than the loss. He had his wife back—for a short time, anyway. And that, he knew, would be enough.

At least, this time, they would be able to say good-bye.

His heart ached at the thought. He didn't want to say good-bye to her. Not ever.

But he would if he had to.

He glanced at the place he had taken the Shaman. He had thought he'd been there for a long time, but when he came back, both Scavenger and Adrian had assured him he'd only been gone a moment.

He had been warned that time would be different there.

"How is he?" Jewel asked Gift. She was looking at Coulter. Her voice startled Nicholas from his reverie.

"I don't know." Gift crouched behind him. The antipathy that had been between Gift and Coulter when Nicholas first arrived seemed to be easing. "Coulter? Any better?"

Arianna raised her head. There were tears on her face, and her skin was streaked with dirt. Her hair was matted against her cheeks. She had been crying, and Nicholas hadn't even felt it.

She had looked up at the sound of Coulter's name.

"Better," Coulter said. "But don't ask me to so much as make a spark."

"The magick is gone?" Adrian asked.

Coulter shook his head. "It'll be back. Parts are already back. Unimportant parts."

Nicholas looked away from him, even as his daughter stared. She seemed fascinated by him. With all that they had to do to prepare for the upcoming battle, she would not have time to act on that fascination.

For that, Nicholas was pleased. He was beginning to realize just how damaging sheltering his daughter had been. He didn't want her to fall in love with the first outside man she met, no matter how powerful.

Nicholas took a deep breath. He kept his arm tightly around Arianna, but now it was time to move on, as he had said he would. "Jewel, do you know the purposes of everything in this room?"

She shook her head. "This is an Islander place, with Islander religious icons. I know nothing of them."

"Yet you appeared here," Coulter said. He was looking in her direction. Even though he claimed not to be able to see her, he still found her location with amazing accuracy.

"This is a Place of Power," she said. "I would also be able to appear to my three in the Place of Power in the Eccrasian Mountains."

Gift was translating as best he could, but he couldn't quite get her inflections. Nicholas had never realized how much of Jewel was in her tones, in the strength of her voice, a strength that Gift didn't seem to have.

"So you could go to the third one," Arianna said.

"If there is a third one," Nicholas said.

"Not unless someone draws me there," Jewel said. "If your father is there, I can go."

Arianna took a deep hitching breath. "Can I ask one more question?" she said, looking at Nicholas. Her skin was blotchy and damp from the tears. "It's kind of self-serving, but kind of not."

He glanced at Jewel, who shrugged.

"Go ahead, honey," he said.

"If something happens to one of your three, like the one you hate, can you appear to someone else?" There was longing in her voice, and she flushed as she asked the question, as if it embarrassed her.

Nicholas looked at his wife. Jewel closed her eyes for a moment, as if the question hurt her in some way, and then she said, softly, "No."

Gift repeated her response as gently.

Arianna nodded, then put her head against Nicholas as if for support. Nicholas stared at Jewel for a moment longer. She raised her magnificent upswept eyebrows, as if she were signaling him in some way, and then she sighed.

If Jewel was assuming that Arianna thought like a Fey, then she couldn't answer the question any other way. If she truly desired to see her mother, a yes answer to that question would mean that Nicholas's and Gift's lives were in danger.

Not that Arianna would try anything against her father. And she had learned, now, the lesson of Black Blood. Nicholas thought she believed it now.

Nicholas kissed his daughter on the crown of her head, and slowly removed his arm. Then he stood. Their Enchanter was injured, and they had only a small force. But they had Jewel.

And these items of Rocaanism. Hundreds of them. Vials of holy water, tapestries, bowls, enough swords for an army, chalices, and the fountain. He knew the items went on, toward the back of the cave.

"What is it?" Arianna asked, her voice hoarse. She was looking up at him.

"There is a part of Rocaanism," he said, slowly, thinking as he went, "called 'the Secrets.' Only the Rocaan has them."

"The Rocaan is dead," Arianna said.

Nicholas ignored her. He knew that. He had nearly had a chance to know the Secrets, shortly after Jewel died, when he had threatened Matthias. Nicholas had threatened to control both the Tabernacle and the country. Matthias, predictably, had turned him down.

"In them," he said, "is the way to produce holy water." He was staring at the vials.

"So?" Gift asked.

"Holy water kills Fey," Arianna said. She stood beside him, then put a hand on Nicholas's arm for balance. She really was weak, although she wasn't admitting it.

"You think the others might as well?" Coulter asked.

"What does this look like?" Nicholas said. "It's not the center of the religion. There are no places to sit here, no spots for quiet contemplation. This is a place that's easily defended."

"It's an arsenal," Scavenger said. He had stood too. "You think this is an arsenal?"

"I don't know," Nicholas said. "But I do know that the Tabernacle had never heard of this place. If it had, the Rocaan, all of them, would have argued for more presence in this area. The Fiftieth Rocaan actually pulled his Auds from here after a particularly vicious encounter with the locals."

"No one would do that if he felt there was something important in these mountains," Jewel said. She had come up beside him. She turned and smiled at him. "Not even Islanders."

"That's right," Nicholas said. "Either this place was forgotten, or it had another purpose."

"Or the locals here used it," Adrian said. "I've heard of groups that aren't—weren't—fond of established Rocaanism. There've been splinters all along. Perhaps this is one of them."

"Perhaps," Nicholas said. He wasn't convinced. "Some of the things in our religion have always struck me as odd. They used to bother you, too, Jewel."

"I said that to you once and you snapped my head off," she said.

Nicholas shrugged. "The Roca was Absorbed into the Hand of God. But we never really heard what happened to the Soldiers of the Enemy. If he had been a Doppelgänger—"

"It would have looked as if he were Absorbed," Adrian said. He was still holding Coulter, who was listening intently. "And he would have been able to order the Soldiers to retreat."

"Exactly," Nicholas said.

"What's this?" Gift asked. "I know nothing of it."

"You are a descendent of the Roca," Nicholas said, without turning around. It was amazing what his children didn't know. "It's his bloodline that forms the basis for our monarchy. We have never had someone without his bloodline on the throne."

"Rocaanism teaches," Adrian said, taking this up as Nicholas paused, "that the Roca led his people against soldiers in a war he could not win. He faced the soldiers, whom the Words call the Soldiers of the Enemy, and in a ceremonial manner, cleaned his sword with holy water, turned the sword against himself, and was Absorbed into the Hand of God. It says nothing more about what happened to the Soldiers, nor, really, to the Roca. Only that he now sat at God's Hand, to better help his people."

"Or something like that," Nicholas said. It was clear none of them had been to a Tabernacle service in a long time, Nicholas since the Fey arrived, and Adrian equally as long. There was something wrong in Adrian's retelling, but Nicholas didn't know what.

It frustrated him.

"That doesn't sound like a Doppelgänger," Jewel said.

"You used to say that it seemed as if some magick were involved," Nicholas said.

"It still does," Jewel said.

"And then we have this."

"But how do we test it?" The question came from Arianna. She put her hand through her father's arm. "You never let me near the religious stuff. I'm surprised we're in here."

"The Spell Warders would use pouches and their contents to divine the magick properties," Jewel said.

"We're not Spell Warders," Nicholas said.

"We can't very well test it on us," Scavenger said, but his voice shook. Nicholas turned to him. Scavenger held his chin out, as if he were proving that he was tough, that he wasn't afraid they would use him to experiment, all the time seemingly expecting someone to suggest it.

"No one would do that," Nicholas said in his most reassuring voice. He swallowed. He couldn't believe what he was going to suggest. "Adrian, you and I need to investigate these religious artifacts."

"I don't think that's wise," Gift said. "What if they have an effect on you?"

Nicholas turned slightly. Jewel had already turned around and faced Gift. She seemed surprised that he had spoken like that. Nicholas certainly was. His son was cautious, and in that cautiousness, right.

He seemed to be the opposite of his sister.

"There's less risk of it for me than any of you," Nicholas said. "I'm Islander, and I have the Roca's blood."

"Do you think this place is associated with the Roca?" Adrian asked.

"I've heard stories about him in the Cliffs of Blood," Nicholas said, "and in the Snow Mountains. It's hard to know what to believe. But if these things come from Rocaanism, as they seem to, it is more likely that they won't affect me."

"You don't have a lot of time to check these items out," Jewel said. "The Black King and his forces will be here. As soon as they can."

"I know." Nicholas had to end this part of the conversation. He pulled Ari closer and kissed her head. "You need to lie down. Rest."

"I'm tired of resting," she said.

He looked at her and smiled softly. She wasn't changing. She glared at him, and slowly the glare turned into resignation.

"This is what you've been talking about, isn't it?" she said. "Doing what's best for the others?"

"In this case, it's also the best for you," he said.

She sighed, but let go and went back to her pallet, after shooting a longing glance at Coulter. He smiled at her and nodded encouragingly. Gift was watching from his place across from them, and an emotion flitted across his face. Jealousy? Of Coulter's attention to his sister?

Nicholas didn't know, nor did he have the time to find out. He started up the stairs. "Adrian?"

"Coming," Adrian said. He eased Coulter back down. Coulter braced himself on an elbow—already showing more energy than he'd had before—and watched. Adrian took the stairs three at a time until he caught up with Nicholas.

"Do you know exactly what we're looking for?" Adrian asked softly.

"How good is your Rocaanist training?"

"Terrible," Adrian said. "I learned enough to get by."

Nicholas sighed. He'd always been a poor student of the religion too. He could hear his father's voice, arguing with him when Nicholas used to say that his knowledge of the religion had no bearing on his future as King.

How wrong he had been. His knowledge of the religion might mean the difference between keeping Blue Isle and losing it to the Black King.

"Well, let's hope we have enough knowledge between us," Nicholas said.

"Maybe we should pray," Adrian said, and there was no sarcasm in his voice.

Nicholas shot him a startled look. Adrian's jaw was set, his eyes wide. He understood how important this was, just as Nicholas did.

"Maybe we should," Nicholas said, and wished he believed that it would do some good.

# THIRTEEN

THE meeting place was a small kirk just north of the farm. Luke had chosen it precisely because he believed the Fey would not enter it. They had checked it the day they took the area, making the Danite who worked there remove the holy water, the sword, and all the religious paraphernalia, and then they had killed him. But Luke didn't think they had ever gone inside.

Ashes from the fire coated the air. The fire had a strange smell. The smoke was acrid, as he expected, but it was tinged with the scent of burning flesh and something almost pleasant, a sharp aromatic spice that recalled some of Luke's father's best meals. The thought turned Luke's stomach, and he hurried along the roadside.

Con was following him. The boy, once he was clean, looked even younger than he initially had. Younger, and beautiful. He had round blue eyes with long lashes, the kind of perfect face that parents longed for, with its chubby cheeks and fringe of golden hair. Lack of sleep had made his eyes look sunken, and they had a haunted expression, as if the boy had seen more than he could bear.

After he had gotten cleaned up, the boy stopped his crying jag. It was as if he had had to be strong, stronger than he'd ever been, and when he finally had found someone to help him, he had lost control. Luke understood how that felt. He had felt that way many times as a young man, during his father's imprisonment. Only he hadn't cried when his father had come home. By then it had been too late.

They made their way hurriedly along the side of the road. So far the Fey hadn't followed them, and that fact disturbed Luke more than anything. The Fey seemed to have forgotten those who had conducted the raid, and that wasn't normal Fey behavior.

But the fire burned strong behind them, a wall of flames that showed no sign of burning out. Luke would never have guessed from the insides of that barn that this would have happened. He would never have guessed that the fire would continue to burn so hard and so strong for this much time.

He and Con veered off the road and cut along a field, leaving a slight trail in the dew-covered grass. Luke knew he had no time to hide it, so he didn't even try. He wasn't certain if the others were still waiting for him; he had instructed them to leave by midmorning.

With the death of the Fey and the arrival of Con, Luke had lost track of the time. He hadn't really expected to make it this far. He had been convinced that the Fey would kill him when he had diverted them from the others in his group.

He suspected they thought he was dead as well.

Con let out a soft cry of relief. Luke's eyes focused. He had walked this way so many times, he could do so without seeing anything around him. The field was grass-covered; its farmer had left it fallow this year. The Islanders had learned long ago to give a field a rest before it played out. Luke doubted the Fey would allow such luxuries now.

But it wasn't the grassy field that had caught Con's attention.

It was the kirk.

The kirk looked like so many others scattered throughout Blue Isle. It was a small single-roomed building, covered in a white wash. Its look, on the outside, was that of humble poverty. In that respect, it was the opposite sort of place from the Tabernacle, where opulence reigned.

Con hurried ahead of him, and Luke caught his arm. "They're expecting me," Luke said softly.

Con nodded. He stayed beside Luke. They reached the open doorway of the kirk—the Fey had torn off the door—and Luke peered inside.

He expected—he wasn't sure what he expected—something horrible, actually, his companions cut down the way he and Con had cut down the Fey. Blood everywhere, the retaliation instant and horrible.

But the inside was dark, and as his eyes adjusted, he saw Medes, Totle, and Jona. They were huddled as far back as they could. No one would have seen them without looking.

Luke stepped inside. The dirt floor hadn't been swept, and the wooden platform that had been the altar was bare. The religious icons were gone from the walls and the small prayer stools—this kirk had been too small for pews—were shattered like kindling and stacked in a corner.

"I brought an Islander," Luke said, careful to explain. "He's an Aud."

"Are you sure?" Jona asked.

"Yes," Luke said. "He saved my life. He killed those Fey following me."

He beckoned Con inside. Con bowed his head as he entered and murmured something that sounded like a Blessing. Then he raised his head and moaned.

"What happened here?" he whispered.

"The Fey," Totle said. "What else?"

"Have you seen the fire?" Luke asked.

"It's got magick in it," Medes said. "What did we do?"

"I'm not sure," Luke said, "but I think we did better than we expected."

"They should be combing the countryside for us."

"They will be," Luke said, "once the fire is out. I think they thought the Fey they sent after me, the ones Con killed, would be enough."

"You don't look strong enough to kill Fey," Totle said, looking at Con.

"He's very good with a sword," Luke said, not wanting to share what had happened. He didn't want them to know. He had learned long ago that the more information spread out, the easier it was for others to take advantage of things.

"Very good," Medes said, raising his eyebrows slightly as if he didn't believe Luke.

"We can't stay here much longer," Luke said.

"What's next?" Jona asked.

"Nothing," Luke said. "After this, the Fey will be expecting something else."

"We can't just sit around," Jona said. "I thought the purpose of this is to stop the Fey."

"It is to shatter their confidence, and to weaken them," Luke said. "And we have to be smart about it. It won't help any of us if we get caught."

"If that boy killed the Fey following you, they'll know who did this," Medes said.

"They'll know about me," Luke said. "But they won't know who helped me."

"What are you going to do?" Totle asked.

"Con has asked me for help. We're going to Jahn."

"Jahn?" Medes asked.

Luke nodded. "You're welcome to come if you want."

"What kind of mission?" Jona asked.

"We're going to try to rescue the King's son," Luke said. "Con knows where he is."

"The two of you?" Medes asked. "That's crazy. The Fey own Jahn now."

"I know," Luke said. "But someone has to try."

"Why you?" Jona asked.

Con started to answer, but Luke spoke quicker. "We have a common friend who sent him here." He took a deep breath. "If any of you want to help—"

"No," Jona said. "I have a family. I'll be staying."

"I don't like this," Medes said. "You said we'd all work together, that we'd be doing this for a long time."

Luke nodded. "I didn't expect the explosion this morning. I thought we'd burn the barn, hurt a few Fey guards over the next few weeks, make some other strategic hits, and worry them. I didn't expect this morning's result."

"That's no reason to abandon the plan," Totle said.

Luke's mouth was dry. He felt as if they had been in the kirk too long. He wished there were windows so that he could glance through them and see what was going on outside. "So, do one of you have a place to hide me while the Fey search for me?"

"How would they know it's you?" Jona asked. "The ones who were following you are dead."

"On my farm," Luke said.

"You could lie, say someone ran through and killed them," Totle said.

"Would you believe that?" Luke asked.

The others looked down. Con must have been feeling the same way Luke did, because he glanced at the door.

"I'm going to have to leave," Luke said. "I would love to have any of you come with me."

Jona shook his head. "I have my daughters to think of."

"I've never left my farm," Medes said.

Totle straightened, looking suddenly like a soldier. "We could continue the fight here without you," he said.

"You could," Luke said. "But you might end up in the same situation I'm in."

"Or worse," Con said.

The others looked at him. It was as if he were an outsider, a representative of the Fey, someone they didn't really trust. And he was. Luke had felt that way a short time ago. Now he felt as if he had known the boy as long as he'd known Medes.

"Worse?" Totle asked.

"The Fey could retaliate," Con said.

"They won't," Medes said. "They need the land and someone to work it. We have that much protection."

Con tilted his head slightly as if he were trying not to shake his head.

"Medes is right," Luke said. "The Fey have made it clear that they're using the Isle for its wealth. They won't ruin that."

"They want to increase the yield on the farmland," Jona said. "They can't do that by destroying existing crops."

"Or existing farmers," Totle said.

"Just be careful," Luke said. "Wait a day or so and pick your next target wisely. And don't meet, except after something to count heads, like we did here. You'll need a new leader."

"I'll do it," Medes said. "My family is used to me coming and going at odd hours."

Luke felt suddenly sad, as if a part of his life had just ended, and he hadn't even realized it. "Remember," he said. "Small strikes."

Medes nodded. "We'll do fine."

Luke took a deep breath. Con was looking out the door. Apparently he hadn't seen anything, because he said nothing.

"This is it, then," Luke said. "Good luck."

"And to you," Totle said.

Jona was watching him. "You know if you go on this mission there's a good chance you won't come back."

"I know," Luke said. He ran a hand through his hair. "Look, if my father comes back, get him away from the farm. The Fey might blame him too, especially if they know his history."

"We'll watch for him," Medes said.

That was all Luke could do, all he could hope for. In the space of a few hours, his life had changed again.

They stared at each other a moment, and Luke got the distinct impression this would be the last time he would see these men, the last time he would see the kirk, the last time he would see this part of the country. Then he waved and slipped out the door. Con followed.

They were going to Jahn to rescue a young man who was not Islander, not Fey, who looked like the King's natural son, but wasn't.

They would probably die in the process.

But they had to try. It was just another step in Luke's personal battle against the Fey. He glanced back at the fire he had caused.

He had had one victory, two if he counted the dead Fey.

Maybe God would grant him one more.

# FOURTEEN

LICIA stood on the ridge line. Her troops were filing into place. The morning sun still hadn't completely climbed over the mountains, but she could sense the day ahead. It would be warm.

The trip through the pass, at least for her unit, had been relatively easy. The Bird Riders had flown overhead, looking for Islanders or any sign of trouble. They saw neither.

Licia had led the troops to the pass, and then here. Units were still arriving and lining up along the ridge line. She hadn't participated in an attack this traditional since the last days of the Nye campaign, when the Nyeians were convinced they'd see magick attacks. So the Fey had done the unexpected, as they always did, and had given them a nonmagick one.

It had worked.

Below her, the town was conducting its morning business. More people moved about than had when she had first been here. It seemed like a busy little place; she wondered what kept all those people active. It certainly wasn't commerce with the neighboring towns.

A small group of Islanders had started up the mountainside, heading toward the rock quarry. She had decided to let them get to work, figuring that a large number of the able-bodied would be in the quarry and out of the town. A quarry was easily captured.

Its smooth sides and bowl-like shape ensured a limited battle and equally limited fighting. If the fighting got too much for the Fey, all they had to do was lay siege. There wouldn't be much food or water in such a place.

A row of troops already faced town, swords and knives at the ready. A second row was marching into place. She had enough Infantry to have seven full rows go into battle against this town.

She would send the rows in one by one, let them fight, and then, when it seemed as if the Islanders were completely engaged, she'd send in another row. She figured, based on the buildings below, that her Infantry alone probably outnumbered the town's population.

She hoped that by the fourth row, the Islanders would believe that there was no end to the troops.

Bird Riders flew overhead. They still seemed shaky from the morning attack, but her speech had shamed them. They had changed forms when she asked, even though it had been difficult. Then they had followed the plans she had laid out.

The Bird Riders stretched their wings and rode on currents into the valley, diving and gathering information for her. The Beast Riders were following the last unit of troops, and they would guard the pass. The Foot Soldiers and Ay'Le would remain in camp until Licia sent for them. She would do that only when she had won the town.

A Sparrow Rider circled above her, then eased down. Licia extended her hand. She had learned, in past battles, that Bird Riders did not like to Shift forms once they had started the fight. They said it diminished their magick.

The Sparrow Rider landed on her right forefinger. His tiny bird feet gripped hard.

Licia squinted before she recognized Shweet. He had fought with her in Nye. His name was ancient, like his family history. He came from a family of Sparrow Riders, and the males had been named Shweet since the Fey started keeping records.

"They have a built-in market in the center of town," he said with no preamble. She had to lean forward to hear him. At his small size, his Fey head and body couldn't project much. The bird's head got in the way of her vision.

She brought her hand up higher so that she could see him better. "That's where they're all going this early?"

"Yes," he said. "There are small farms and gardens at the base of the mountain. Those are the folks selling their wares. I've seen some disappear into buildings and return with wares as well. Either there's a large storage facility or there is an underground dimension to this city."

"There is in Jahn as well," Licia said.

He nodded, and his bird head moved in time to his Fey head. "I saw no weapons. The buildings are made of mountain rock. But here's the strange thing: the rock changes color when it's cut away from the mountainside. On the mountain it's red. Cut away, it's gray."

"Have you ever seen anything like that?" she asked.

"No," he said, "but my family told stories of the Eccrasian Mountains that included this detail."

"So there is magick here."

"Yes," he said. "Some of the smaller birds—but not me—said they could feel it in the air currents."

"And it's not a residual effect from that wave?"

"I can't answer that," he said.

No, of course he couldn't. He wasn't qualified.

"Some of the Hawk Riders say that there is a large group of Islanders in the quarry," he said. "They suggest you focus a portion of the troop there. The quarry has a good view of the town. They'll be able to see when the attack begins."

She nodded. She was pleased that she had already thought of that and taken care of it. "Any word about the passes?" she asked. "Any Islanders coming in? Any sign of more Fey?"

"No," he said.

The third row was marching into place. The Fey moved with remarkable silence. They had been trained well. None of her troops were old enough to have fought in the Nye campaigns. Until this moment, such a formal attack had been only theory to them.

"Anything else?" she asked.

"The Gull Riders report seeing Boteen on the mountainside. He's riding up a narrow path on a Horse Rider."

"Do they know where he's going?"

"They say there's a cave at the top of the path, but they won't guarantee that's where he's going. He left Caw and the Scribe below. Again, they didn't know why."

She pursed her lips. Boteen had been very reticent about his find, and that had disturbed her. But she didn't have time to think about it. "Thanks. Keep an eye out, keep in contact, and let me know if anything unusual happens."

He tightened his grip on her finger, their signal for a confidential comment. Not that any of the others could hear him. He was too small. "I did send a small group of Hummingbird Riders to keep an eye on the Foot Soldiers. And Ay'Le."

Licia nodded. She liked him, and had always liked working with him. He knew as well as she did that power struggles within the Fey themselves could be deadly, particularly at a time like this.

"Thank you," she said softly.

"We will let you know of any changes on the Islander—or the Fey—side."

"Excellent."

He nodded his head, then took off. The force of his launch made her hand bob. He caught a current, rode it higher, and then stretched his wings as far as he could.

He disappeared into the lightening sky.

She watched him go. He would watch things for her, but that wasn't enough. In battle, she had to be aware of everything. She had Seen nothing about this battle, not even that she would lead it. That normally wouldn't bother her—her Visions were rare and slight—but it did this time.

She felt as if she were on the edge of an important moment, a moment that would change her life, and she had no guidance.

The fourth row was marching into place. It wouldn't be long now, and her people would be ready.

The attack would begin.

She turned, shielded her eyes with her left hand, and watched a string of Infantry file up from the pass. The sixth and seventh rows would also have bows and arrows. They were more experienced, and had been taught how to use the weapons, which were more of an Islander affectation. She had to make certain that they knew how to aim. The last thing she wanted was her own people shooting each other in the back.

Then she glanced at the town. Its people still went about their business, small as insects, seemingly undisturbed. By the time the sun was straight up overhead, their lives would be over, or would be forever changed.

Licia smiled. These were the moments she lived for. The moments just before a battle, where everything hung in the balance. It gave her a feeling of power, a feeling of rightness, a feeling that the world belonged to her. And by evening, this small corner of it would.

She would conquer it, and hold it, in the name of the Black King.

Hold it for the Fey.

# FIFTEEN

PAUSHO stood at the edge of the market. Her stomach was queasy, and her head ached. She had felt ill since early morning, even though she had awakened feeling fine. Then, moments later, she had all the symptoms of a stomach illness. She didn't know what caused it, but it felt as if a wave of evil had flowed through her and beyond, leaving her entire system disturbed in its wake.

She had gotten up, dressed her early-morning clothes—two sweaters on top of layers of skirts and boots—and headed toward the market as she did every day. This morning, even going to the market felt odd because of the events two days ago. She had left Matthias on the mountain, sending him toward the Roca's Cave. She had heard that he had nearly died at its mouth, but that a tall one had saved him.

A tall one had helped him survive.

A second time.

The mountain had plans for him, then.

She had meant, this morning, to check on the legends about tall ones who survived the mountain more than once. In her training, she remembered something about that, but she couldn't remember the details. There was so much to know as a Wise One that one couldn't remember everything. Sometimes one had to check the authorities, the legends, the Words.

The Words. She needed to check those as well. Everything had changed for her two nights ago when she had seen Matthias and the burning boy exchange fire. The warnings she and the other Wise Ones of the town of Constant had been planning for, the things they were guarding against their whole lives, for the life of the town, were finally here. Demon spawn had arrived. And not one, but two. Matthias and Coulter's son, also named Coulter.

Both lay at her doorstep. She had brought Coulter to the mountain as an infant, and he had survived, later leaving the Cliffs of Blood, taking a wife, and apparently having a son who seemed to have extraordinary powers.

She had also brought Matthias to the mountainside and left him in the snow. He too had survived, and had gone on to power in the Tabernacle, then rejected that and returned here. She had tried to accept him, but he had always frightened her. His tall frame and his blond curls made him seem like a figure from myth. His anger, always on the surface, made him dangerous. And his new-found power opened his soul to the demons that controlled him.

She adjusted her sweater, wishing the nausea would retreat. The market was bustling this morning. The town had gone back to normal after its encounter, three days ago, with the tall ones. The townspeople had chanted them out, and they had gone into the mountains. Followed by Matthias, whom the townspeople couldn't compel, and a former Wise One, the one who had duped her.

Tri.

She leaned against a stall, feeling the stone against her back. Then she watched the townspeople pass her. Meeting at the market was a daily ritual, a way to keep up with the events of the week. Most bought only a few goods, enough to cook themselves food, and most used money made from the quarry. But the quarry wouldn't be able to support the town forever. Constant traded with the other Cliffs of Blood villages, but the markets were decreasing. There wasn't much need for additional items except food.

At some point, they would have to expand into the Isle. She knew it, and she'd been trying to prepare the other Wise Ones. But they were having trouble listening to her, and rightly so. The best thing about Constant, and the other towns around the mountains, was their isolation. They could almost believe they weren't part of Blue Isle at all.

The townspeople that passed her also looked a bit ill. Most of them were paler than usual, and some had very determined expressions on their faces, almost as if they were making the same kind of effort that she was. Perhaps the illness she had was catching. Perhaps the tall ones had brought it to town three days ago.

She sighed. Anything was possible. The world was changing too rapidly for her. In the past, no one would have become a Wise One, like Tri did, in order to change the Wise Ones. In the past, no one would have let him quit.

He would have died.

Her stomach turned again. The actual distress she had felt earlier this morning was gone, but it was as if that first wave had so upset her system that she couldn't get it balanced again. She had felt like this when she was pregnant, all those years ago.

Her mind shied away from the thought, but she couldn't stop the memories, suddenly and overwhelming, of the long—tall— newborn daughter she had held in her arms for a day before the Wise Ones had come to her.

She had been twenty then. Her husband left her the following day, and she remained alone, afraid to have another child for fear of its size, afraid to have it taken from her like that pretty little redheaded girl.

Her eyes filled and she blinked. That was a long, long time ago. She didn't know why she had thought of it now. She had lived her life, become a Wise One herself, and learned that it was almost harder to take a young baby from a new mother than it was for the new mother to give the child up.

But Pausho believed in the system. She had to. It was what she had been taught, what she knew. And the day she had walked into the Roca's Cave, she had known she had done the only thing she could.

"Are you feeling all right?" A woman whose name Pausho could not recall, even though she had known her for years, stopped and put her hand on Pausho's shoulder.

Pausho smiled weakly. "I've had a difficult morning."

"Many people have," the woman said. She was in her forties, and single, like so many women in Constant. "They're giving away a healing tea at one of the booths. No charge at all. I was coming to get some for a friend."

Pausho didn't ask who the friend was. She didn't have her normal curiosity. She let the woman lead her to the booth.

The booth belonged to the daughter of a former Wise One. She had a small fire going in the stone hearth behind her booth.

She was well known for cooking fresh foods, selling most of them, and giving the leftovers to those who were too sick, or too old, to get it themselves. It was almost as if she were keeping parts of Constant alive all by herself.

The woman gave Pausho a cup, then took one herself. She smiled, wished Pausho well, and disappeared into the crowd.

Few people were speaking today, and many stopped for the tea. Pausho took a sip, winced at its bitterness, and then felt a calm flow through her. The queasiness in her stomach eased but didn't entirely disappear.

She thanked the people running the booth, put a coin in their jar even though they had asked for nothing, and then tucked her basket under her arm.

She had shopping to do, people to greet, some questions to answer. And then she needed to meet with the Wise Ones.

It would be a full morning.

She finished her tea and set the cup on the back of the counter. Then she saw something out of the corner of her eye.

A flash.

She looked up and felt the breath stop in her throat.

The ridge looked different this morning. Taller. Its top moved as if it were covered with birds that shifted with the breeze. Another flash caught her eye, and she realized what she saw.

The rising sun's light hit the ridge, catching metal.

Her mouth went dry and the queasiness came back full force. She squinted and could make out shapes.

Tall shapes.

What had Matthias said? That the tall ones they saw three mornings ago were only the first. There was an entire army of tall ones on the Isle and they were called the Fey. Matthias, demon spawn, was afraid of them.

A tall one afraid of other tall ones.

He said they were powerful.

And she was feeling awful. The entire town was feeling awful. Had they done something already?

She wasn't certain. And, for the first time in her life, she didn't know what to do. Judging by the look of the ridge, there were hundreds of tall ones above. She couldn't believe that hundreds of tall ones would line up on the ridge for no good reason.

They had to be coming for the town, just as the Words had warned.

She had always thought the threat would come from within,

but it seemed that it was coming from without. She wasn't sure she was prepared for that.

Pausho took a deep breath and forced herself to think. Of course she was prepared. It didn't matter whether the tall ones came from inside Constant or outside. The arrival of the tall ones was what her people had prepared for all their lives. And all of their parents' lives, and all of their grandparents' lives.

Constant knew how to deal with the threat.

She grabbed every person that passed her, and said, "Find the other Wise Ones. Have them meet me here. Immediately."

But she never took her gaze off the ridge. The tall ones had probably been there since she felt the first wave of illness that morning.

They had almost surprised her.

Almost.

But not quite.

# SIXTEEN

MATTHIAS hated being in bed. He still felt weak, weaker than he'd ever felt. Marly had propped pillows behind him and left him to sleep. He had slept, but poorly. His dreams were filled with fire, so close and so vivid that the last awakened him.

He looked about for Marly, but she wasn't in the room. She was in the kitchen, making breakfast for the others. He could smell it, the warm scents of her porridge and her special tea. She had promised some for him when she was done. He wasn't hungry, but he didn't tell her that. She would make him eat anyway.

He had sent Denl out to see if the Fey had in some way caused this feeling. Denl had come back after searching around the house, looking up at the sky, and seeing nothing unusual. In fact, he had seen nothing at all.

But it had been dark then, just before first light. When the others finished eating, Matthias would send Denl out again.

This feeling was too strange to be an illness.

Perhaps it was a delayed reaction to his near-death on the mountain. Jewel's fingers had wrapped around his neck, stopping his air. She had nearly caused him to black out—or perhaps he had blacked out. He wasn't entirely clear on anything from the moment he saw Jewel's face until the moment he came to down the mountain. A dead woman, a woman who had died at his hands, had nearly killed him. Perhaps she had stolen his life essence. Perhaps it had traveled through his skin into her hands.

The others hadn't been able to see her. Perhaps she was some kind of spirit, something that had come just for him.

But he hadn't felt that way when he had awakened. Injured, yes; depleted, no. His neck had hurt. In fact, it was now swollen and bruised, with the marks of slim fingers on it. But he hadn't felt any part of himself leave until this morning.

He put a hand to his face and catalogued his injuries. He'd had so many since the Fey arrived this second time. He had been stabbed repeatedly, leaving wounds across his face that Marly had stitched with her needle. She had promised to remove the thread in the next few days, and had promised that would ease the itching he now felt. Those injuries, given to him by a female Fey in the Cardidas River, had left him debilitated, but he had recovered. Then Jewel had nearly strangled him. The puffiness on his neck was still tender. And now, this unnamed malady.

He hated it all.

He pushed the blankets back and eased his legs over the side. In the past, he had conquered his weaknesses. He could do so again.

Standing was easier than he had expected. Apparently the sleep had helped him. He put a hand on the wall, grabbed one of his robes, and slipped it over his head. His muscles ached from all the exertion in the days before, but the ache was a pleasant one. He had forgotten how much he liked to be mobile.

He wasn't hungry, but he made his way to the kitchen anyway. Food would help him whether his body asked for it or not.

When he reached the door, he saw Marly standing near the hearth fire, sweat on her face. It was cool near the Cliffs of Blood—summers here were never brutal—but the stone house held heat. Denl had the kitchen door open and was standing by it, sipping his tea. Denl's face had filled out, just in the few days since their arrival. His trip up the mountain with Matthias hadn't tired him at all.

Jakib, Marly's brother, was at the table, still finishing his bowl of porridge. Jakib was short where Marly was tall, and they shared only a look around the eyes. The affection between them showed them to be related more than their features.

Yasep, the supposed leader of this group when they had been thieves in Jahn, looked up from his seat at the head of the table. His cold, ice blue eyes flashed with distaste. He had never liked Matthias, but over the past two weeks, he had realized that Matthias was not only smarter, he was also a better leader. Yasep tried to keep up the pretense that he led the group, but more and more he was bowing to Matthias's wishes. Matthias suspected that one morning they would awaken and find Yasep gone. Life in Constant wasn't nearly as exciting as stealing and hiding in the tunnels beneath Jahn.

Then Marly looked up. "Ye should be sleepin," she said.

"I think I need something to eat."

Jakib stood and gave Matthias his chair. Yasep, who was done eating, hadn't moved.

Typical.

Matthias murmured his thanks to Jakib and sat down. It felt good to do so. The trek from the bedroom to the kitchen seemed as if it had taken forever.

Marly put a bowl of porridge in front of him. She had cut some fruit into it, fruit someone had to have gotten from the market. He took a spoon and ate slowly, letting the food nourish him.

This had been the right decision.

"Are ye doin better, Holy Sir?" Denl asked.

Matthias nodded. Once he started to eat, he felt the hunger that he hadn't felt earlier. He didn't even feel like chastising Denl for calling him Holy Sir.

"Tis been a normal mornin on the street, so far," Denl said. "I checked again afore we ate."

"Thank you," Matthias said. He appreciated Denl's diligence, although he wished it had born fruit.

"Do ye think what happened yestiday had somethin ta do with it?" Jakib asked.

Matthias shook his head. He didn't want them focusing more attention on him. He had had enough already.

"Tis simply his wounds catchin up with him," Yasep said, pushing away from the table. He handed Marly the dishes, then brushed Denl aside and went out.

Marly watched him go. "Tis the second morning he's been in a hurry ta leave here."

"Could he be gettin inta trouble already?" Jakib asked.

"Here?" Denl asked.

"I dinna know," Marly said. "Only that tis strange."

"Aye," Denl said. "But Yasep is na Yasep without secrets."

His truth silenced the other three. Matthias kept eating, the fruit a sweet contrast to the blandness of the porridge.

There was a knock on the other door. Marly made a move toward it, but Jakib grabbed her arm and shook his head. Jakib and Denl were always protective of her, but had been so even more in the last day, since they had gotten back from the Cliffs. On that brief trip, they had seen the horrors this area had to offer and, Matthias guessed, they didn't want Marly subjected to them.

The door squealed as it opened, then Jakib said, "Ah, tis you."

"Sorry." The voice belonged to Tri. He had known Matthias a long time, partly because they were neighbors, and had, just a few days before, ceased his short tenure as a Wise One. He had accompanied Matthias, Denl, and Jakib up the mountain, and had kept his head during all the strangeness, although, Matthias suspected, Tri had his own opinion as to what the events meant.

"I did not mean to disturb you so early," Tri said, "but I need to see Matthias. How is he?"

The question sounded less like one of concern and more like one of need. Tri's entire voice had an edge of urgency.

"I'm fine," Matthias said, his voice strong even though his throat was still raw from his encounter with Jewel. "I'm having breakfast."

Tri came in, followed by Jakib. Tri was short, like most Islanders, but he had long red hair that marked him as someone from the Cliffs. He wore a cloak against the morning chill. He seemed paler than usual, with dark circles beneath his eyes.

"Most of the town is feeling ill," he said. "It came on suddenly, with no discernible symptoms except a loss of energy."

Marly shot a startled look at Matthias. "So I'm not alone," he said.

Tri shook his head. "I've been vaguely queasy all day." He glanced at Matthias's bowl. "Although you haven't."

"He fainted," Marly said. "Twas as if someone had felled him with an ax."

"When was this?" Tri asked.

"Afore dawn," Marly said. She had her arms crossed. Matthias sensed that she didn't like Tri. Was it because she blamed him for all the things that happened to Matthias since they had arrived in Constant?

"Sounds about right," Tri said.

Matthias glanced at Marly. "And you felt nothing?"

"Concern for ye," she said.

"Jakib? Denl?"

"I felt a mite woozy," Jakib said. "Twas nothin."

"I dinna feel a thing," Denl said.

Marly frowned. "Come ta think of it, I did feel a mite dizzy, but I thought twas from getting up too fast."

"It might have been," Matthias said. And then again, it might not have been. None of them were affected as much as he was, though. Was that because he had already been in a weakened condition? Or had it been caused by something else?

Tri was leaning against the kitchen door. "Interesting as all this is," he said, "it's not why I'm here."

Matthias pushed his bowl away. He had eaten enough. He couldn't stomach any more. His entire body had become tense.

"What is it now?"

"Those tall ones you warned us about," Tri said. "Would they watch us from the ridge line?"

"The ridge line?" Matthias asked. The tension he had expected had arrived, hitting his back muscles first. He had expected the Fey to come—had, in fact, known they would—but he thought he would awaken one morning to the sounds of battle.

The ridge was on the west side of Constant. To enter the city, travelers on the roads had to go through a series of passes, one of which crossed over a ridge that was fairly flat on top. It was separated from the Cliffs on the north by the Cardidas River, which had cut a valley into the area and had once, Matthias suspected, been large enough to fill the bowl where the city was. The ridge line would give them a view of the entire city, and from a height that made such a view worthwhile.

But why would they watch and not attack?

They had attacked Jahn at dawn two weeks ago. But twenty years ago, they had spread their assault on the city over an entire morning.

He stood up so quickly he had to catch the edge of the table to keep himself from falling. Marly reached for him, but he nodded at her, to keep her back.

"Did you see anything?" he asked Denl. The back of the house faced west.

"I ha na been lookin ta the ridge line," he said, and then went out, as if he were curious.

Matthias was more than curious. A panic built in him. This

time they had found him at his weakest. He hadn't done well against them when he had been healthy, and now he had no strength at all.

He made his way to the door. Tri was beside him as much for support, Matthias felt, as to go look outside. They went out the door and stood on the stones that led to the fence. Denl was a few steps ahead of them, looking up, mouth open.

Matthias looked up as well.

The ridge looked higher, and its top moved. He wished he could see better. Marly had come up behind him, resting against him for support.

"What is that?" she asked.

"People," Tri said. "If you wait long enough, you can see glints of metal as the sun catches."

"How do ye know they're Fey?"

"What else would they be?" Tri said. "We'd know if that many people left town. You said the Isle is overrun with them, so we know these aren't Nicholas's people."

Matthias squinted. He took a few steps closer. Denl was shaking.

"How many do ye think there are?" he asked.

"Hundreds," Tri said. "That ridge is long."

"Real long," Marly said, "as I recall it. Might be more than hundreds. Might be a thousand."

A thousand. Why would the Black King send a force that large here? What could he hope to gain?

Unless this was the last place on the Isle to conquer.

Matthias shuddered too.

"'Tis na good, is it?" Marly said.

He shook his head, and ignored the subsequent dizziness. "But they haven't attacked yet. That means we have some time." He went back toward the house. He needed to sit down. Marly and Tri followed. Denl remained in his spot, staring at the ridge.

"'Tis sorry I am, Holy Sir," he said. "You asked me ta watch and I dinna see them."

Matthias sighed. He would never break Denl of the habit of calling him Holy Sir, however undeserved the title was. Nor would he ever do anything to deserve the respect and awe with which Denl treated him. Or the shame Denl felt because of Matthias, when Denl perceived that he had made a mistake.

"It's not your fault, Denl," Matthias said. "I didn't expect them to be so far away."

Had that wave of illness come from them? It made no sense. The Fey hadn't done that in either invasion. Why would they do it here? Matthias wasn't even sure they could do it. He didn't know the limits of their powers.

Or of his own.

He went back into the heat of the kitchen. It felt good after the coolness outside. He had been so absorbed looking at the ridge that he hadn't even realized he was cold.

Tri followed him and sat at the table. Marly poured them both tea. It felt remarkably domestic, given what they had just seen.

"What now?" Tri asked.

Matthias leaned forward in his chair, placing his elbows on the table to keep himself upright. "What's the procedure in town? Does Constant even have one?"

"For an attack?"

"For any kind of emergency."

"We actually have a defensive strategy," Tri said. "The Wise Ones devised it generations ago."

"Generations?" Marly repeated. "Then twould na be good now."

"Actually," Matthias said slowly, "it might." The Secrets had also been passed down from generation to generation, and one of them had been helpful in fighting the Fey. "What happens first?"

"There's several strategies," Tri said. "If there's time, the Wise Ones get together and decide which one is the most effective."

Matthias sipped his tea. In the liquid he felt strength. He would need it. "You have to get me to them."

"You know how they feel about you," Tri said.

"Yes," Matthias said.

"'Tis na safe," Marly said.

"Neither is letting the Wise Ones face the Fey without knowing what they're up against," Matthias said. He stood, carefully, waiting for the dizzy feeling.

Eventually it came.

"You're in no condition to go," Tri said.

"Exactly," Matthias said. "And that could be intentional on the part of the Fey. Get me to the Wise Ones."

"Getting you there is only part of the battle. They think you're demon spawn, Matthias. They won't listen no matter what you risk."

"Then ye can tell them," Marly said. "Ye be Matthias's spokesman."

Tri shook his head. "I burned that bridge three days go. They probably consider me to be worse than Matthias."

"Then I'll go," Marly said.

"You're too tall," Matthias said. "It's me or no one. And it can't be no one. I've seen what the Fey can do, especially in these numbers. Chances are that we're going to die. But I'd rather die fighting, and fighting properly, wouldn't you?"

Tri stared at him for a moment. "Yes," he said finally, "I guess I would."

"Do you know where they're going to meet?"

"No, that's up to the discretion of the leader."

"Pausho," Matthias said. He was resting his hands on the table, in a vain attempt to keep himself balanced. "Do you think they even know the Fey are up there?"

Tri glanced at him, then glanced away.

"You told no one but me?"

Tri shrugged. "I thought you would know what to do."

"And I do. We need to get in touch with the Wise Ones. We need to find them," Matthias said.

Tri swallowed. "A lot of people in Constant still don't know that I'm no longer a Wise One. I should be able to find them. Then I'll come back for you."

Matthias shook his head, and that brought the dizziness. "There's no time. We'll go together."

"No one will talk to you."

"They won't have to," Matthias said. "I'll stay in the background."

"If tis possible for ye ta walk that far," Marly said. "Do ye even know how ye look?"

"Probably like a man who should have been dead days ago," Matthias said. "It doesn't matter. If we don't hurry, it may not matter how I look. Or what the people of this good town think. It may not matter at all."

Tri exhaled softly. "All right," he said. For the first time since he had arrived, he looked truly frightened. "Let's go."

# SEVENTEEN

GAUZE looked tired. It seemed as if the rest she had had after arriving in Jahn the previous morning had exhausted her rather than helped her. Her narrow face had lines in it, and her eyes were sunken. Her wings were pressed against her back. She sat on the edge of the chair Rugad gave her and stared out the window at the fire, still burning out of control.

The tower room seemed empty with just the two of them inside it. Rugad knew this would be a difficult meeting and one that would test her loyalty.

He also knew he had to make it quick.

"I need you to describe something to me," he said.

She stiffened in her chair. Her wings brushed against the chair's back. She brought them even closer to her skin.

"That cave, the one in which you saw my great-grandson. I want you to describe it to me."

She stared at him, then lowered her gaze. "I already told you what I could," she said.

"You told me Boteen's message. But you've been to this cave. Describe it for me."

She kept her eyes downcast.

"He told you not to, didn't he?"

Her left wing shuddered, and she slammed it against her back as if the wing had betrayed her.

"Didn't he?"

She bit her lip.

"And you are not answering out of loyalty to Boteen? Or disloyalty to me? Or a desire for power on your own?"

At that she raised her head. Rugad kept a small smile of triumph from forming on his face. He knew how to reach his people.

"He did not want to give you a false report," she said. "He's there now, seeing what I saw."

"A false report?"

"He believes that the cave is something." Then her eyes widened. She obviously didn't like to be in this position.

Rugad liked it, though. He was interrogating her while he was waiting for Selia. He had a few other things to do before he could settle on a plan for himself. Talking with Kendrad had been good. She had helped him crystallize his thoughts. He had a direction again, and he felt in control for the first time since that fire appeared.

"Something?" he asked. "Based on what?"

"My description," she whispered. Again, she lowered her head. She knew she was trapped. And she knew her loyalty had to belong to Rugad, not Boteen. Only this time, she seemed to agree with Boteen's caution.

"Then describe it to me," Rugad said for the third time. He would say it as many times as he needed to, until she told him.

She closed her eyes and took a deep breath. Then she said, "There were great magick currents in that area. So great that I nearly got caught in one. I nearly slammed into a stone sword. They were big and stuck in the mountainside. The currents were fierce there, like eddies in a stream, and I thought I was going to die slamming into one. . . ."

Her voice trailed off.

Rugad was intrigued. Whatever happened next upset her. "Yes?" he asked.

"Then my grandmother appeared beside me. She pulled me out and by that time I was inside the cave. She kissed my cheek, told me I would be forever loved and forever remembered, and led me down stone steps."

"Your grandmother?" Rugad frowned. He didn't have Wisps on this trip old enough to be Gauze's grandmother. "What else did you see?"

"Forgive me, sir," she said. "But there's something you may not know. My grandmother is dead. She died on Nye. She was murdered."

Rugad felt the hair rise on the back of his neck. This was the confirmation he'd been waiting for. "You're certain that you saw your grandmother?"

Gauze nodded miserably.

Rugad leaned forward. "Did she love you?"

"I was her only family," Gauze whispered.

A shiver ran through him. "Who killed her?" he asked.

"I don't know," she whispered.

He sighed. That would be a problem. It could have been anyone, anyone here or in Nye or on Galinas. If it were someone here, then he would have to worry about it.

"What was her name?" he asked softly.

"Eklta," Gauze whispered, even more quietly than before.

It didn't sound familiar to him. That was a relief.

Gauze tucked a strand of hair behind one of her very pointed ears. "Then when I got inside the cave, one of the Fey with your great-grandson was explaining the Mysteries to him."

So his great-grandson had a Mystery to guard him as well. It made sense.

It made him more dangerous.

Gauze raised her head. "Boteen thought this was important."

"It is," Rugad said.

"He said he wanted to make sure of his suspicions before he told you."

Rugad nodded. He hoped that was what Boteen was doing. Places of Power were dangerous for Enchanters. They created a lure that was hard to ignore.

"You don't believe me," Gauze said.

"I do," Rugad said. "I'm just not sure I believe Boteen."

Maybe he wouldn't send the message to Boteen that he wasn't coming. Boteen might need the curb on his own ambitions. Rugad smiled at Gauze.

"I thank you for your service," he said.

"I'm dismissed?" she asked. "I thought perhaps you'd send me back to Boteen."

Rugad shook his head. He didn't want her to tell Boteen that she had disobeyed him. "Stay here. Rest. I might have need of a Wisp who can fly swiftly across country."

She frowned, just a little, as if his change in attitude made no sense. Then she nodded, and stood, understanding his dismissal. "Thank you," she said.

He smiled at her, then turned back to the window. As the sky had gotten lighter, the fire had changed. It was still tall and wide, but not as easily visible. It didn't seem as bright, and he could no longer see sparks.

How he longed for darkness.

How he longed to be in the middle of things.

How he longed to have this campaign over.

The door closed behind Gauze. He glanced over his shoulder, making certain he was alone. He had only a few moments before Selia appeared. He wanted to use them to gather himself.

Gauze's testimony confirmed that the cave was a Place of Power. He didn't need to go himself, not yet. And probably shouldn't go. Not with all that power there, not after what happened this morning.

But Nicholas was inside, if Gauze's earlier information were to be believed. She had heard that he and Rugad's great-granddaughter would be arriving shortly. He suspected Gauze was right because when he had traveled the Links, he had seen them in the mountains.

With the Shaman.

A second shiver ran through him.

The Shaman would know how to use the Place of Power, even better than Rugad would. And her loyalties were not to Rugad; they were to her own kind and, she said, to the Black Throne.

The Black Throne as ruled by his great-grandchildren, young people she could control.

Nicholas had the Shaman, a Mystery courtesy of his son, two powerful children, and the Place of Power.

Rugad had the knowledge, his armies, and the Isle itself.

Their forces might be evenly matched.

Or the odds might tip in Nicholas's favor, if he could get the Place of Power to work for him. Rugad needed something else to work for him. And Kendrad had helped him figure out what that was.

A knock on the door made him turn.

"Come," he said.

Selia entered. She was tall, even for a Fey, and her beauty was the stuff Fey legends were made of. She bowed slightly when she saw him, a habit he doubted he would break her of. "You sent for me?" she asked.

"Yes," he said. "I need a Black Robe."

She let out a small groan, as if she couldn't quite believe what he was asking. "Forgive me, Rugad," she said, "but we slaughtered the Black Robes. And if there is one alive in all of Blue Isle, do you think he'd come forward?"

"Nonetheless," Rugad said. "I need one, and I need him this afternoon. If you cannot find me one, at least get me the documents from their Tabernacle."

"The place burned," she said, her voice rising slightly. He could hear the panic in it. She felt he was asking the impossible.

"Then get me Islanders, any and all Islanders. I need to know the intricacies, the legends, and the traditions of that religion."

"Now?" she asked. "Can't it wait? We have so much to do."

He narrowed his eyes at her. She backed up a step.

"Of course," she said. To her credit, her voice did not shake even though her eyes had widened with fear. "You must have a reason for this. Forgive my presumption."

"I have a reason," he said. "And it's one of the best reasons. It will gain us Blue Isle. All of Blue Isle."

She frowned at him, as if she were trying to understand him.

"This Isle has a wild magick," he said.

"Yes," she whispered.

"They hid it in their religion. We need to know how to extract it."

"You think the Black Robes know how?" she asked.

"I think they might," he said.

"Then why didn't they use it against us?"

"They did," he said. "Their holy poison is a prime example."

"But they did nothing else. Even when we burned their Tabernacle."

"Because," he said, "I don't think most of them understand it. Now, can you find me a Black Robe?"

"I'll do my best," she said. She took a deep breath and started to turn. "I'll send you Islanders as well. But have you thought of asking Dimar and the other Doppelgängers? They might know enough to get you started."

Rugad smiled at her. "Now you're learning how to be my second," he said. "I had not yet thought of that. Send Dimar to me."

She nodded, and backed out, pulling the door closed behind her. Rugad still smiled, after she was gone. How brilliant. And he hadn't thought of it. The Doppelgänger's specialty was to absorb every aspect of the culture, sometimes so fast that the Doppelgänger didn't know what he knew.

Rugad would find out though. Even a few tidbits from the Islander religion might help him. It would be the map, the map that would lead him through the magick this Isle's Place of Power had bestowed on its natives.

It might be the deciding factor, the thing that would give him this Isle, his great-grandchildren, and send him forward toward the rest of the world.

Toward Leut, and the third Place of Power.

# EIGHTEEN

THE ride up the mountain had been treacherous. Boteen had hung on to Threem as tightly as he could, once provoking Threem to comment dryly, "If you squeeze me to death, you'll die too."

For all of Threem's confidence, the path had not been designed for horses. Only Threem's extreme balance and intelligence had allowed him to pick his way up the mountainside. Fortunately, light had broken over the top of the mountains just after they started, illuminating the way. Threem had sighed and relaxed. Boteen had been able to feel Threem's muscles loosen.

Boteen had leaned on Threem's Fey torso most of the way. The ride did nothing for his dizziness, and didn't really make him feel any better. The strength he had gained in his short, strange nap had been illusory, and vanished the moment he felt he needed it.

He could feel the cave, its magick stronger here than it had been on the other side of the river. It still called to him, feeling like the home he'd never had, making him feel wanted, giving him an urgency that he knew was artificial.

He wondered how strongly he would feel all of this if he hadn't been so weak. He doubted that it would have changed much.

Threem stopped on a narrow part of the path. There were boulders nearby and some scraggly plants. "I'm afraid I'll have to ask you to dismount here. This next part of the path is stairs, ancient, broken stairs, and I don't dare go up like this."

"Have you mounted them?" Boteen asked. His voice sounded weary, even to him.

"Yes," Threem said. "It feels odd here, doesn't it?"

Boteen didn't answer. He swung off, then staggered a little, and nearly fell. Threem watched.

"You're still not recovered, are you? Can you make it up the stairs?"

"Yes," Boteen said. It didn't matter how he felt. He needed to see this, needed to know if, indeed, they had found the prize of all prizes.

He gripped a boulder, its stone cool under his fingers. It was red, and where his fingers touched, the redness grew. He frowned. He knew something about that, but he couldn't remember what. His mind wasn't as clear as it needed to be.

Beside him, Threem changed to his Fey form. The horse shrank and absorbed into his stomach. The four legs disappeared, and two appeared in their place. Threem was naked, but not self-consciously so. Boteen didn't know how Beast Riders did that, how they faced the elements and the cultural disapproval to remain naked no matter what they did. Perhaps it came from being a Beast Rider. Beasts were never considered naked in their natural form. Perhaps Beast Riders felt the same way.

"Let me go first," Threem said.

"No," Boteen said. He didn't want Threem to spook something or someone at the top. "I don't have enough balance to feel secure going up these stairs."

The implication was clear to Threem. He nodded, knowing that he might have to catch Boteen if Boteen slipped.

Boteen started up the steps. Threem's description of them was accurate. They were broken and flat, and easy for small feet—Fey feet—but they would have been impossible for a horse, especially a horse bearing the equivalent of two riders.

He took the steps slowly, using rocks and boulders as handholds, breathing evenly to try to keep the dizziness at bay.

He hated this weakness, hated the loss of control. It made him feel unprotected at this, one of the most important moments of his life.

He was going to a Place of Power.

He reached the top and discovered a flat area that he thought was natural until he squinted at it. Then he realized it was rock mortared together so long ago that the rocks themselves had cracked. Some of the mortar had crumbled, leaving a fine dust on everything.

Footprints were in that dust, and part of the flat area had been wiped clean.

A lot of people had been up here—and recently.

Ahead of him, Boteen saw a cave opening. It was round and natural and not at all mysterious. Threem caught his arm, almost as if Threem needed the support. He was staring at the cave too.

What held them both riveted was not the cave, nor the man-made rock surface they stood on, but the swords.

Islander swords, the size of trees, stuck into the rock. Two of them were embedded into the rock, points down. Another two were sticking out of the sides of the cave's mouth. The points were also embedded into the rock, their hilts waiting to be grabbed. It would have taken incredible strength—or incredible magick—to place them there.

The fifth sword balanced above the center of the cave's mouth. It stood on its point, but its back was pressed into the stone. It didn't look as if it had been carved out of the rock; it seemed to have been carelessly left there.

"This is an Islander place," Threem whispered.

"This is a magick place," Boteen corrected. He could feel the magick pouring out of the cave mouth—and with it, something else, something he had felt a day or so ago.

Another Enchanter.

The feeling was faint, but there. Boteen gripped Threem's arm harder. He was in no condition to meet a rival. Still, he wanted to get a little closer, to see if that feeling of welcome, that feeling of home, grew.

He took a step.

Threem held him back. "It's not safe."

"Oh, but it is," Boteen lied. "It is."

# NINETEEN

NICHOLAS stood in front of the vials. They glimmered in the cave's strange light. Adrian stood beside him. Nicholas's heart was pounding. He didn't know why he was nervous here, in this place, when he would not have been nervous at all facing a wall of vials in the Tabernacle.

Perhaps it was the incongruity that unnerved him, the fact of seeing them in a cave. Or perhaps it was the way this cave constantly surprised him.

Adrian seemed to be waiting for him to make the first move. Nicholas guessed it made sense; he was still the King, no matter how little he felt like it. He had come a long way from the palace, not just in distance, but in his own mind.

He had, in some ways, ceded the leadership of Blue Isle to Rugad.

The thought made his back stiffen. He hadn't consciously thought of that before, but that was what he had done. He had fled the city with the clothes on his back and his daughter at his side, and he had not gathered a troop. He had not fought.

And now he was here, with a small group, his son and his daughter, and, surprisingly, his wife, and he was only now beginning to think of fighting.

He swallowed hard and forced himself to concentrate.

The vials rested on shelves carved out of the cave itself. The shelves were made of the same marble that covered the stairs. And the vials were full. The water formed a line near the carved glass top. The line was even in all of the bottles, as if they were all measured perfectly.

Adrian glanced at Nicholas. Nicholas gave him a small smile and then reached for a vial.

"Wait!" The voice came from Jewel. Her tone was urgent and uncomfortable. She was speaking quietly, even though no one but Nicholas and Gift could hear her. "There's someone outside."

Nicholas let his hand drop, and he turned. "Someone Fey?"

"An Enchanter," Jewel said.

"What is it?" Arianna asked.

Nicholas held up a hand for silence. "There's someone outside," he said.

"I know," Coulter said. "I can feel it."

"Let me check," Adrian said. "And see how many there are."

"And me," Scavenger said. "If Coulter can feel them, they're probably Fey."

"Or Matthias," Nicholas said.

Jewel shook her head. "I would know."

His gaze met hers. She would know. There were different things about her now, things that were part of her Mystery, that hadn't been there before.

"Go," he whispered.

Adrian hurried along the top of the steps. Scavenger stopped near the base of the stairs, grabbed two swords and two knives from his stash. Then he climbed, taking the stairs two at a time, as much as his small legs could handle. Nicholas followed Adrian, but Jewel hurried up the steps. She took his arm.

"Don't go out there," she said.

"I'm going to see," he said.

"Let them," Jewel said. "They're the least valuable. You're the most."

He smiled at her, and pulled her close. "To you, perhaps," he said so softly that he knew the people below could not hear him. "But not to your grandfather."

"Oh, you're important to him," she said. "More important than you realize. You're in his way."

Nicholas hadn't felt as if he were in the way. He felt as if he had gotten out of the way. "Come with me," he said to Jewel. "You can protect me."

"I can't protect you from yourself," she snapped.

He had forgotten this; they clashed when they disagreed.

But this time, he didn't mind.

"I'll be all right," he said to her.

Adrian and Scavenger had made it to the mouth of the cave. They were huddled toward the side, as if they could see something. Scavenger handed a knife and a sword to Adrian; Adrian strapped them around his waist. Scavenger's were already in the scabbard he wore as a belt. Scavenger whispered to Adrian, and they slipped out.

Nicholas walked to the spot where they'd been. From it, he could see two men on the stone platform. Both were Fey, and one was naked.

"Boteen," Jewel whispered, even though she didn't have to. "My grandfather's Enchanter."

"And the other?" Nicholas whispered.

"A Horse Rider. They must have ridden up here, and then he Shifted for the last part of the climb."

The Enchanter looked as woozy as Coulter. At least the effect that had hit Coulter seemed to be as universal as Jewel promised. Adrian and Scavenger hid behind one of the swords and watched.

The Horse Rider touched the Enchanter on the shoulder. The Enchanter took one more longing look at the cave, and then the two of them started down the stairs.

Adrian and Scavenger followed them, using boulders as their hiding places.

Nicholas started out, but Jewel stopped him. "No," she said.

"I can go," he said. "There's only two. They're gone."

"And one's a real Enchanter. A practicing Enchanter, not like your boy in there who only knows what he can figure out. Boteen is the most powerful Fey that you'll ever encounter."

"More powerful than the Black King?"

"In magick, yes," Jewel said.

Nicholas swallowed. "So it's safe to assume if the Enchanter's here, the Black King's not far behind."

Jewel nodded.

He put his arm around her and pulled her close. "Then it's time to gather our forces, my love. Let me know the position of the Fey all over my Isle, so I know how to defend it."

She smiled at him, kissed him on the cheek, and vanished. Suddenly he was holding empty air. He staggered slightly, then brought his arm down.

He would have to get used to that.

In the meantime, he watched Scavenger and Adrian make their way across the rocks in an attempt to see what became of the Fey's most powerful Enchanter.

# TWENTY

ADRIAN stood up and moved away from the boulder he'd been hiding behind. The two strange Fey had disappeared down the stairs. Both men were older than he was, and one of them was naked. The naked Fey had more hair on his body than Adrian had seen on a Fey outside of Shadowlands. Some of the Beast Riders were built like that, though, their hair matching their animal form.

And another Fey. A tall, thin Fey, taller and thinner than any Fey Adrian had ever seen. They had scrambled down the side of the mountain so fast it was as if they had known Adrian and Scavenger were coming.

Adrian headed across the flat rock surface. He made his way carefully, both so that he wouldn't startle the Fey and also so that he wouldn't make any noise. The rocks were loose and cracked with time, and he didn't want them to slap against each other or the ground. Scavenger followed, walking in his footsteps.

When they reached the stairs, they saw the two Fey picking their way down. For all their rapid retreat, they were moving slowly. The tall, thin Fey seemed to have trouble moving.

"Let's go after them," Scavenger whispered.

Adrian held him back for a moment. He didn't see any more

Fey, at least not near them. Then he scanned the valley below, and his heart, which was already beating rapidly, began to beat even faster.

Fey were marching up a road that came out of a sunken valley. They merged into the pass leading into the town below, and they were lining up on the ridge. The morning sun glinted off their swords. There had to be hundreds, maybe a thousand Fey along that ridge line, and even more coming up behind them.

Adrian grabbed Scavenger's arm and pointed. Scavenger's gaze followed his.

"By the Powers," Scavenger whispered, and in his voice, for the first time in a long, long time, Adrian heard fear.

"You'd think they'd come up here first," Adrian whispered.

Scavenger shook his head. "That's not how Rugad works. He thinks that the Islanders will rally around Nicholas. He wants to wipe out Nicholas's support before coming for the prize."

Scavenger's explanation made sense. Adrian felt a chill run through him that had nothing to do with the early-morning cold. "We need to warn him."

"There's nothing he can do," Scavenger whispered. He glanced back at the steps. "Funny that they aren't with Boteen. You think he's as injured as Coulter?"

Adrian shuddered. "Jewel said that every Enchanter would feel it."

"Good," Scavenger put a hand on the hilt of his sword, and started down the steps.

Adrian reached for him, and barely was able to snag his shirt. "What are you doing?"

"It may be our only chance to kill an Enchanter," Scavenger said, yanking his shoulder out of Adrian's grasp and continuing down.

"You don't know what's waiting there," Adrian said.

"That's half the fun." Scavenger's whisper was barely audible.

This wasn't part of their orders, but Scavenger was right. A Fey Enchanter, trained, would have more powers than Coulter and the ability to use them. The chance of finding such a man in a weakened condition was almost impossible.

There were only three Enchanters on the Isle, Jewel had said. Coulter, the Fifty-first Rocaan, and the Fey scrambling down the mountainside. If they killed this man, they'd take an advantage from the Black King.

Adrian took a deep breath. These were the kinds of decisions he had to make: his life versus the future of the Isle. It was not a choice. The future of the Isle, the future of his son, his family, his friends, came first.

Adrian started down the steps, hoping that he and Scavenger could catch the Fey Enchanter by surprise.

# TWENTY-ONE

BOTEEN was dizzy and exhausted. He stumbled down the last few stairs to find Threem already in his horse shape. Threem tossed his horse's head.

"I thought I heard voices above us," Threem said. "We have to hurry."

Boteen shook his had. "I can barely stand. I certainly can't mount."

"I thought of that already," Threem said. "Stand on that boulder and take my hand. I'll pull you up.."

Boteen didn't like the option, but he couldn't think of anything better. He went over to the boulder that Threem had indicated. It was half as tall as he was, and flat on top. He didn't know if he had the energy to climb it.

He glanced at the steps. He too had felt a presence, mingled with the lure of the cave. But it had been an Enchanter's presence.

"Boteen," Threem said, his voice filled with urgency.

Boteen nodded. He put his hands on the top of the boulder and pulled himself up. Threem leaned over and grabbed Boteen by the wrist.

"Wait," Boteen said, feeling his balance slip. The dizziness had returned full force. He wasn't even sure he could find a way to protect himself before he fell.

He got his feet beneath him as Threem moved as close to the boulder as possible. Then Boteen stepped across as Threem pulled.

He almost missed. He squatted hard, and slipped toward the opposite side. Threem grunted as if in pain, and then swore softly. Boteen grabbed Threem with his free hand to steady himself.

"You almost knocked us both over," Threem said.

Boteen, whose dizziness was so intense he could barely think, murmured, "What're you complaining about? You can't fall off."

"That's right," Threem said. "Too much force and you make me fall over."

The image was a terrifying one; both of them tumbling down the mountainside, Threem landing on Boteen, full horse body on a slender Fey one.

Boteen leaned his head on Threem's back. "Let's just ride," he said.

"Hang on," Threem said. "Down is harder than up."

And it was. Threem picked his way on the narrow path, leaning back toward the mountain as he went, both heads concentrating on all four hooves.

At one point, the path slid away, and Threem slid with it, only through luck and brains managing to catch himself on a string of embedded rocks.

A real horse would have fallen.

A real horse would never have tried this.

Boteen kept his eyes closed for part of the ride, but that seemed to make the dizziness worse. Then he opened them, and discovered, as he looked across the river and the valley, that he had a fear of heights that he hadn't known about before.

He tried to concentrate on the moving armies below—that was exactly what Rugad wanted—but it did no good. His stomach was queasy, his magick depleted, and his headache was growing worse.

"See what that was," Threem said.

"Huh?" Boteen asked. Threem's voice seemed to have come from a long tunnel.

"Behind us," Threem said. "Didn't you hear that noise?"

"No," Boteen said, but he turned his head anyway. He saw a faint movement along the path, but he couldn't tell if it was caused by rocks tumbling in their wake or by someone else coming down.

"See anyone?" Threem asked.

"No," Boteen said. But he kept looking. The rocks stopped sliding. Then Threem rounded a corner, and Boteen couldn't see the rocks any more.

It took less time to reach the small camp where he had left the Gull Rider and the Scribe. The place looked worse in the light. All the vegetation had been burned away, and a number of the boulders held scorch marks. The smoke stench was still strong.

The Gull Rider was sitting, in her gull form, on top of a boulder, watching their trail. The Scribe was asleep under the pillars that formed a makeshift camp. Boteen saw him only because he knew where to look.

"Wake him. We're going all the way down," Threem said to the Gull Rider. Then he turned his head slightly toward Boteen. "Unless you think we need to go back there?"

He wanted to. He wanted to desperately. But he knew it wasn't wise. Not without Rugad. Or at least a large unit of troops.

"No," he said. "Down is exactly where we need to go."

The Gull Rider flew off her perch and landed near the Scribe's head. She pecked him lightly with her beak. He called out in fear, then rolled up like a child who'd just been hit. The Gull Rider leaned back, watching him with one bird eye.

"It's just me, stupid," she said. "We're leaving."

He sat up and rubbed his eyes. "We just got here."

"Get up," Threem said. He seemed to be as tired of the Scribe's nonsense as Boteen.

And then Threem grunted.

The sound was startling, terrifying. Threem bucked. His eyes— both sets—rolled and he reared, sending Boteen sliding off his back.

Boteen tried to grab onto Threem's arms, but couldn't. Then he reached for the tail, and missed.

As he fell through the air, he tried a magick spell—any magick spell—and felt only a faint stirring within.

He landed on his own back so hard that all the air left his body. A Red Cap appeared over him. The Cap's short, squat features were relatively clean, except for the drops of fresh blood on his face.

The Cap dropped the bloody knife he held in one hand, pulled his sword out of its scabbard and held it, with both hands, beside his head.

He grinned.

"I've always wanted to do this," he said in Fey, and swung.

# TWENTY-TWO

MATTHIAS staggered through the streets of Constant, getting terrified glances from the locals, the Blooders. He must have looked hideous, with his scarred face, his puffy neck, and his uneven gait. Tri stayed a few yards ahead of him, asking everyone where the Wise Ones were meeting.

Finally, an elderly man, who clearly didn't know that Tri was no longer with the Wise Ones, told him that they were meeting in the market and even gave the precise location. Tri thanked him, then dropped the pretense of not being with Matthias. He grabbed Matthias's arm and pulled him forward with more force than Matthias believed anyone capable of.

Matthias barely had the strength to keep up. Only his knowledge of the Fey and the damage they could do kept him going. That, and the memory of the townspeople, only a few nights ago, willing him to begone, and the feeling, deep in his gut, that he should leave. A feeling they had placed in him. He had realized then that they too had magick, only they had denied it all this time.

Tri led him toward the marketplace. At the western edge, he saw Pausho and two other Wise Ones whose names he had never bothered to learn. Two more were making their way through the morning crowds.

The market was full as usual this morning. No one seemed alarmed. No one seemed to notice the Fey lining up on the ridge—no one except Pausho and the other Wise Ones. Tri kept glancing up there, and so did Matthias.

He didn't know if it was his fevered imagination or not, but it seemed as if there were more and more Fey each time he looked. The townspeople who knew that the Wise Ones were gathering thought it strange, but did not seem unduly alarmed.

Pausho looked pale and fragile this morning. She was standing beside one of the stalls, actually using it for balance. He had last seen her on the mountainside after his encounter with that Islander boy, the one who burned, who called himself Coulter. She had urged Matthias to go to the cave where Jewel had been. Pausho had told him he would touch the Hand of God. He didn't know what that meant then, and he still didn't.

Pausho was glancing around wildly, as if she were impatient for the Wise Ones to arrive. Then she would look up at the ridge.

Somehow he had expected her to be calm in situations like this. Somehow he had expected more strength.

But maybe she had never faced anything like this.

He took a deep breath and plunged into the crowd. He needed to use the last of his own strength to make her understand. Tri came with him, hand still on Matthias's arm, but now Matthias was leading him.

"Pausho," Matthias said, his voice ringing over the crowds' low murmur. "Those are the creatures I told you about. They're Fey."

She turned toward him and had to grab the stall for support. "They certainly are tall," she snapped. "Just like you."

"They're not like me," he said. "They've taken over the Isle and now they've come for Constant."

Her eyes narrowed. "You've delivered your message," she said. "Now you can go join them."

"No," he said, and pushed past the Wise Ones beside her. "You have to listen to me now. You have to trust me. They—"

"I don't have to trust anyone," she said. "And I certainly don't have to trust you."

He felt the frustration back up in his throat. He had given the last of his strength to be here, and she was still seeing him as a tall one, not as someone who had valuable information for her. For the town.

For Blue Isle.

"Please," he said softly. "You need to listen to me, or everyone in this town will die."

"Is that a threat?"

He shook his head. "It's a fact. Jahn is a charred ruin. The Fey have burned the Tabernacle. They have armies all over the Isle. There are very few places they don't own. This is one of them. You'll only get one chance. Don't do it wrong."

She glared at him. "I can't believe you'd help us."

"Why?" he asked. "Because of what you did to me? Despite that, this is my home. Blue Isle is my home. You call me demon spawn, but I'm nothing compared with those people on that ridge."

"Listen to him," Tri said. "He's never done anything to harm you. He's never done anything to harm this place, and he could have when he was Rocaan. You know it as well as I do. The Tabernacle tried to weed out the Wise Ones several times before, but it didn't try once in all the time Matthias was Rocaan."

"Pausho," a woman said. She was the Wise One who had been at Pausho's side two nights before. "Let him talk."

"We can't listen to demon spawn," she said.

Matthias let out a small breath of air. He was still dizzy and the walk hadn't helped. "Then die. I did what I could."

He started to walk away. He was weaving slightly, from the weakness, the injuries, and the beginnings of a terror he thought long buried. Somehow he would have to get Marly out of here. He would have to find a safe place for Yasep and his group, for Denl, and Jakib, and the others.

A place where the Fey couldn't find him.

He heard voices behind him, Tri's mingling with others. Someone yelled, "Matthias!"

He turned, lost his balance, and extended a hand, catching himself on the side of a stone building. Black spots danced in front of his eyes.

Pausho was looking at him. Her lips were pressed thin, her eyes narrowed. "All right," she said. "Tri and the others have convinced me to listen to you. But if you prove to be wrong, or if you go over to the side of those tall ones, I will kill you myself. Is that clear?"

He nodded. Tri came to his side and helped him back toward her.

She squinted at him, a frown creasing her forehead. "You're ill?"

"Something passed through this morning. A wave, something. It took—" he glanced at the others. They'd know soon enough. It was time to admit what had bothered him all along. "It took those powers you feared in me. I think the Fey might have caused it."

She glanced at the ridge line as if she could see the truth of his words. "I've been ill since this morning as well," she said. "Perhaps there is something to this. Will the powers come back?"

He almost smiled. It would have been a bitter one. She wanted to rely on the powers that she had nearly killed him for. "I think so. I hope so. We could use them now."

She took a deep breath. "What can we do against these tall ones?"

"I have several ideas," he said. "None guaranteed. First you need to know that they can die, just like we can, and in the same ways. A stab to the heart kills them as easily as it does us. However, they have more powers than we do."

Then he stopped, frowned, and thought. Maybe that was no longer true. He remembered the force of those whispered *begones*. "Or at least, they know how to use their powers."

She nodded.

"Gather the townspeople. Have them use their verbal force to send these creatures away, just like you tried to do to me the other night. You have a power there that the Fey might not expect."

She crossed her arms. She hadn't expected him to know how that worked.

"And then," he said, "you need to take me to the Words."

"No," she said. "No one but a Wise One goes there."

"Pausho." He leaned forward, unable to stress the urgency of this any other way. "I killed Fey with holy water. The recipe came from the Roca. We were using the recipe that had seze, from here. I suspect varin and several other things from the Cliffs might have the same effect. Who would have thought that water, blessed water, would kill them? No one. We discovered it by accident, and now they know how to counteract its effects. But there are a dozen Secrets. I know them, and know the recipes for them, and haven't had much chance to test them. The one I've tried, making a sword from varin, doesn't seem to work."

"It works," Pausho said softly.

He felt an odd elation. She *knew*. He didn't let himself smile. He didn't dare. "Then there is information in the original Words that we can use."

She closed her eyes. For a moment it looked as if she would pass out. Then she opened her eyes. Her gaze went immediately to Tri, as if she blamed him for all of this.

"I have spent my life," she said softly, "protecting my people from demon spawn like you. And now, it seems, that I will have to traffic with you in order to save my people." She swallowed visibly. "How do I know that this isn't a trick? A way to gain knowledge you couldn't get by any other method?"

Matthias's heart was pounding hard. "Do you think I'd come to you with a solution if I had invited that group up on the ridge? Don't you think I'd come in here with them and kill all the residents of Constant?" He bit his lower lip. He needed to be completely honest with her. It would be the only thing she would accept.

"If they were mine," he said, "I'd have brought them here in the dead of night, and I would have unleashed them on the town before any of you awoke. And then I would have had them kill you, Pausho, first. And the rest of the Wise Ones second."

He heard audible gasps around him. Pausho's expression didn't change. She was studying him, her mouth downturned, her eyes sad. "So you believe there is a greater evil than yourself?"

Tri took his arm. Matthias shook him off. Jewel was dead at his hand. Burden was too. And who knew how many others, if what some said was to be believed. If the Fey victory this second time was due to his stupidity, his test of Nicholas's wife fifteen years before, then he had a penance to pay.

There was only one answer he could give Pausho.

"Yes," he said softly. "I believe there is a greater evil than myself, and it stands on the ridge."

"And you believe I must join leagues with you in order to kill it."

"Yes," he said.

"And when it ends," she asked, "and if we survive, do you expect clemency from me?"

"No," he said.

"I can't take learning from your mind. I won't be able to erase anything I have shown you."

He smiled then. "Sure you can, Pausho," he said, unable to keep the sarcasm from his voice. "You know the best method. You've practiced it all along."

"Matthias," Tri whispered, as a caution.

"You can kill me," Matthias said.

Pausho smiled too. Her smile looked as cold as his must have. "So I have your permission," she said.

"No," he said. "But you would have my understanding."

She laughed, and to his surprise, held out her hand. "Allies?"

He took it. Her fingers were warm and dry. "Allies," he said.

"Until those tall ones on the ridge are defeated," she said.

"And not a moment more," he agreed.

They shook, and with that gesture, the defense of Constant began.

# TWENTY-THREE

THE last row marched into place. Licia watched as the final Fey took their spots at the end of their rows. In addition to their swords and knives, they had bows hanging over one arm and a quiver of arrows on their backs.

It was a concession to the Islander way of fighting. The Fey had been prepared for it since Nye, when the captured Nyeians had warned them that Islanders were adept with bows and arrows. It had proven true to the south. Licia had no reason to doubt the same would happen here.

She took her spot on top of a tall flat rock. From here, she would lead the attack. The view of the valley was superb. She glanced over her shoulder a final time. No more troops appeared from the pass. The sun had risen higher, sending its yellow light across the red of the Cliffs of Blood.

The mountains would be aptly named this day.

Then she held up her right hand, fist clenched. The troops, already fairly silent, grew still. No one even moved.

They were so well trained.

She wanted to smile at them, to let them know how proud she was of them, her Infantry, unaffected by the dawn's strange events. But that would only confuse them. A Fey did not praise before battle.

She opened her fist. The first row unsheathed its swords and knives. The screech of slipping metal was like music in the morning air. Then she brought her hand down hard toward her leg, slapping it with her open palm.

The sound of flesh against flesh got lost in the sudden outcry.

Fey surged forward, shouting their undulating victory cry, running down the side of the ridge toward the valley.

The row stayed even, perfectly straight, as the Infantry ran. They headed toward the town like a wave, sun glinting off the metal of the swords.

Ahead, she could see all the townspeople stop moving. They had only moments to prepare for the end of their lives.

She smiled.

Then she brought her hand back up, fist clenched, preparing to launch the second troop. Her Infantry was doing well. Not a word was uttered on the ridge line. The silence up here was a living thing. She opened her fist, and again smiled at the sound of swords being unsheathed.

Then she brought her hand down, and the second row of Infantry whooped its way off the ridge, moving in perfect unison.

Fey in their leather uniforms covered the mountainside. The battle cry caught the attention of the Islanders near the quarry. She saw them move toward the edge of their bowl. Circling gulls overhead told her the same thing.

With a snap of her fingers, she sent a small contingent of Fey toward them. She had planned to give the Islanders in the quarry some hope, a momentary thought that they would not only survive, but win a battle against these strangers.

And then she would shatter that hope, so completely, so vividly, so devastatingly, that the survivors would never think of crossing the Fey again.

Provided, of course, that there were survivors.

The first row had hit the edge of town. They looked like small toy figures scrabbling in the dirt. They cut their way through the confused Islanders around them, the blood flowing and spraying around them.

She could only see some of the details from her perch, but they were enough.

The second wave was fanning out around the first, going to sections of the town where the others weren't fighting.

She would lose some in those first two waves, but she wasn't concerned. Rows three and four would be a relief team. They would come in as the first rows were tiring, as the Islanders rallied, as they began to understand they were in a fight to the death.

Once they understood that, their fighting would change its tone. It would become desperate and vicious, and have more chance of success. The Islanders farther into town would have a chance to gather whatever weapons such people had, and they would make use of them. They would have the strength of defense, the strength of fear, the strength of right on their side.

And they would make a dent in her small army.

The third and fourth rows would repair that dent, but not entirely. The Islanders might think they were gaining a victory.

And then she would send in the fifth and sixth rows.

Any Islanders who tried to attack the ridge would be felled by arrows. And she had the Bird Riders above to give her warning.

The Foot Soldiers in the valley would only hear the sounds of war. Their blood lust would rise, but they would not be able to do anything about it, not until she was finished. Then they would be allowed to come in and clean up.

The second row had hit town. Islander screams were wafting up to the ridge, high-pitched and terrified. They were losing. They were dying.

They were beginning to realize that their perfect little lives were over.

Licia watched and waited.

She would find the exact moment, and then she would send down the next row.

Her personal prediction was right. She would send in all her troops, slaughter the townspeople, and own the town itself by the time the sun was directly above.

She smiled.

She loved her work.

# TWENTY-FOUR

SCAVENGER swung his sword at Boteen's head. The Enchanter's eyes widened, and then he rolled inward, toward the sword itself.

The blade missed his neck by inches.

Scavenger nearly lost his balance. He brought the blade back and swore. Boteen was unable to get to his feet. Behind Scavenger the Horse Rider was still bucking and screaming. When Scavenger had stabbed the knife into the horse's underbelly, he had apparently missed the heart.

He had removed the knife. He should have noticed the way the blood spurted. He should have stabbed again. It was not like him to miss a heart. A Red Cap was usually better at anatomy. He must have missed because he moved so quickly.

Then he heard a caw above, and a Gull Rider dove at him. He screamed, "Adrian!" and ducked.

Adrian was somewhere behind him, probably trying to deal with the Horse Rider. Scavenger had to keep his head down to keep the Gull Rider away from his eyes. Even so, he felt a beak peck at his skull.

He swore and stabbed blindly at it, then realized that was exactly what the Gull Rider wanted him to do. It would serve no purpose. His goal was to kill the Enchanter.

It was their only hope.

He waved his free hand at the Gull Rider, and was rewarded by a beak in the palm. He cursed it, but searched for Boteen, who was crawling on his belly down the path.

Perfect.

An Enchanter crawling, just as they always expected Red Caps to do.

Scavenger took two steps toward him, grabbed the hilt of his sword with both hands, and felt the Gull Rider pecking at his fingers. The pain was intense. He hurt from every wound the Gull Rider had made.

But he couldn't think of it.

He couldn't.

He lifted the sword as high as he could—

—and brought it down in the middle of Boteen's back.

Boteen let out a scream of pain and fury that was blood-curdling. He turned slightly, as if to see the sword pinning him to the ground. He reached for the sword, small flames growing off his fingertips. But then the flames flared and died.

They died.

The Gull Rider was going for Scavenger's eyes. He had to cover his face with the back of his left arm, and the Rider pecked at his skin, drawing blood.

Behind him the Horse Rider still screamed. Scavenger could hear it flailing, its hooves pounding on the surface. He hoped it wasn't pounding on Adrian.

Boteen was reaching for the sword, but he couldn't twist himself enough.

Scavenger pulled his knife from its haphazard position in his belt, and fell on his knees. He landed on Boteen's back near the sword, and started stabbing. The Gull Rider cried out and dove for Scavenger, getting its claws tangled in his hair, pecking at his skull with its beak, and yelling at him in Fey.

He shooed it away with his left hand, all the while stabbing with his right. Blood coated him. Boteen continued reaching, eyes wild, mouth moving as he murmured spells that didn't work.

Out of the corner of his eye, Scavenger saw Adrian slashing at the Horse Rider with his sword. The horse part of the Rider was skittish, its coat black with blood. The Fey part of the Rider was trying to control his horse self and failing. The horse kept rearing and screaming and flailing its hooves at Adrian.

Obviously Scavenger's blow had not even been close.

The Gull Rider slid slightly on Scavenger's skull, and brought its beak down in the center of his cheek. He shouted in pain, brushed the Rider off him, and felt his own blood warm on his hand. He cursed softly, and then brought his knife down as hard as he could in the middle of Boteen's back.

Boteen gasped, and a bubble of blood formed around his mouth. Scavenger stabbed one more time for good measure, and Boteen fell forward. He twitched once, twice, and then stopped moving altogether.

His eyes were open and empty, the bubble of blood still arcing over his mouth.

Scavenger grinned, and then a bird slammed into his face. White feathers, claws, wings batting the side of his head, a beak going for the crown. He couldn't even scream. He dropped the knife in sudden panic and shoved at the bird, trying to force it away.

It was stronger than he thought it was. He hadn't expected gulls to be so powerful.

It was going for his eyes, for his face, and if he didn't get control of his panic, he would die.

He would die like Boteen did.

Scavenger let himself scream, and as he did so, he grabbed the bird's feet near its breast. Then he flung it away.

That only gained him a moment as the gull caught itself and came back toward him.

Scavenger ducked, grabbed the knife he had dropped, and rolled off Boteen.

The Gull Rider followed.

Scavenger lay on his back, waiting for the Rider to drop toward him. When it did, he ignored the flapping wings, the blood-soaked beak, and he grabbed its feet a second time with his left hand, holding it, holding it, feeling the muscles in his arms ache with the strain.

In a move that seemed to take forever, he brought the knife up, and plunged it into the bird's breast.

The gull screamed, and the Rider reached down for the knife, but its Fey arms weren't long enough. Wings batted him, and the bird bucked in his hands. Blood was squirting everywhere.

Scavenger pulled the knife free, and in a swift movement, stabbed the Fey part of the Gull Rider in the torso, nearly severing it.

The bird bucked again, and then stopped, falling swiftly, its legs twisting in his grasp. He lost his grip, and it landed on his stomach. Its bird head came up and, in one final blow, slammed its beak into his chest.

He screamed in pain and shoved the bird off him.

It landed on the ground beside Boteen, a mass of blood and feathers. Both its avian eyes and its Fey eyes were open. And in that moment, Scavenger realized who he had killed.

Caw.

He had served with her in Nye.

She had been kinder than most Beast Riders, at least to a Red Cap. He was sorry the situation had forced him to kill her.

He ran a blood-soaked hand through his hair. He was bleeding from a dozen wounds. He turned to see Adrian still grappling with the Horse Rider. It was obviously tiring, its bucking not as fierce, its Fey self shouting, weakening. The horse's eyes were rolling.

Scavenger swallowed hard. The energy from the fight was still flowing through him. He gripped the hilt of his knife, and came up on the horse's side, careful to avoid the flailing legs.

He hated this, hated it, but knew it was necessary.

Legs landed around him, hooves pounding, the ground shuddering under his own feet.

But he made himself think.

*Remain calm.*

It was the only way.

He danced underneath the horse, and remembered his Fey anatomy. How many Beast Riders had he dismembered over the years? How many had he extracted the skin and bones from? The strong hearts?

A dozen?

Even though it had been fifteen years ago, a Cap didn't forget.

A Cap didn't forget.

He was whispering the words as he crouched underneath the bucking horse.

*A Cap didn't forget.*

A hoof landed close to his foot, and he nearly lost his balance.

He was too far back. That was the mistake he made. He had missed the heart by a good six inches, and probably missed other organs as well.

He gripped the hilt of the knife and asked the Powers for guidance. He had the Black Throne in his hands here; his services were for the good of the Fey, even though he was killing Fey.

He shoved the knife as hard as he could into the horse's underbelly, and felt more blood gush over him.

The horse didn't scream this time.

It reared once, and toppled sideways, grunting as it did so. Adrian stood over it, his sword bloodied. He was looking at Scavenger in surprise.

"You did that?" he asked.

Scavenger's heart was pounding and he was breathing rapidly. "Better make sure it's dead," he said.

His body was suddenly too heavy to move. His wounds ached. He was covered in blood and feathers and dirt.

But he had killed an Enchanter.

The Fey's Enchanter.

The most powerful Enchanter of all.

Scavenger smiled.

Rugad had just lost his most precious assistant—to a Red Cap.

"He's dead," Adrian said. "Now what?"

"Now we tell the others what we did," Scavenger said. "And we tell them about those troops down there."

Adrian looked. "Oh, God," he whispered.

Scavenger nodded. "That's right," he said. "This is just the beginning."

"You sound like you're enjoying this," Adrian said.

Scavenger's grin grew. "I am," he said softly. "I really am."

# TWENTY-FIVE

PAUSHO moved quickly through the marketplace, giving subtle orders. People parted when they saw her. The business of the market was interrupted, and everyone looked as disconcerted as she felt.

If she had to build an unholy alliance with Matthias to save her home, then she would. But she would make certain her home was saved.

Shortly after Pausho and Matthias had shaken hands, the Fey had left the ridge, a long line of them moving forward in the growing sunlight. They had come, without hurrying, straight toward the town. Pausho had sent Zak to the outskirts; he was the only Wise One she could spare. Tri had gone back, on Matthias's instructions, to Matthias's home to get his friends and, Pausho understood, a woman.

She couldn't picture Matthias with a woman. It was the antithesis of the Tabernacle's ideals. But Matthias had made it clear that he was no longer with the Tabernacle.

The woman proved it.

Pausho was getting her people to move forward, to form a half circle around the marketplace. They were frightened—they all saw the forces coming off the ridge. A second line had come, and then the first had disappeared into the outskirts of town.

Then the sound of metal ringing against metal pierced the early-morning quiet, followed by screams. The screams were often words, in Islander, and Pausho knew that if she concentrated, she would be able to identify individual voices.

Why did Matthias have to be right?

She stopped, put a hand on a stall, and caught her breath. One of the townspeople, a young man she didn't really know, put his arm around her waist. "I'll get the rest, Old Mother," he said.

And she knew what he meant. He'd go through the streets, rounding up as many people as he could.

"Get them to do the same," she said.

He nodded, then hurried off.

There was so little time, and she had no energy. She stood upright in time to see another row of tall ones hurry off the ridge. And still, more waited beyond it.

The chant would have to be the most powerful they could summon. The rest of the town wasn't as sick as she was. Perhaps they could do it.

The faces around her had more color than they had around dawn. The people seemed to have more strength. Even a bit of strength would work.

Just as long as it combined into the right chant.

She waved her arms, pulling everyone into the half circle. She made them face outward, even though they didn't want to. Half the town must have been there: five hundred people in rows six deep, maybe more.

"We chant until they go away," she yelled, feeling the effort throughout her body. "We put everything we have into it. We only get one chance."

Matthias had told the others to get the children to find weapons and bring them to this section of town. Already some of the people in line held bows and arrows, knives, and clubs made from everything from sticks of wood to bits of stone.

Her people had never looked like this before. She had never seen them so fierce, so strong.

They would give her the power she needed.

She climbed on top of the stall she had been using for support. From there, she had a great view of the approaching tall ones.

They were stopped at the edge of town, their swords flashing in the sunlight as they cut down Blooders.

Dozens of Blooders.

With more passion than she had ever felt in her life, she thrust her fist toward the heavens.

"Begone," she said.

The entire group picked up the cry.

*Begone.*

*Begone.*

*Begone.*

The words were fierce. They were strong. They shook the very stall she stood on. Other fists rose in the air.

*Begone.*

She had never heard her people's voices sound so powerful. Never felt such a wave of energy move forward before. Her dizziness was growing worse, but she didn't care. She would get these tall ones out of her town if it killed her.

And it very well might.

*Begone.*

The first wave of tall ones stopped in the middle of their fighting. Some were cut down as her people grabbed the tall ones' weapons and fought back. Others simply stood in place, as if they heard a music they had never heard before.

*Begone.*

The second row of tall ones coming down the hill stopped. The line they formed was perfect; it almost looked as if they had hit a wall.

*Begone.*

The third row also stopped suddenly, as if it too had hit something. The tall ones didn't move, didn't fight back. She knew what their expressions would look like. They would have looks of stunned surprise, and then they would slowly back up.

She raised her other fist, as if having both hands in the air gave the chant more power. Others saw her and did the same thing.

*Begone.*

The tall ones looked around in confusion, as if trying to find the source of the voices. On the ridge, another group started down, only to stop where the third row had.

Birds flew overhead, their patterns getting more and more frenzied. A large group of them flew off to the ridge.

Pausho wondered if they were affiliated with the tall ones

somehow. Did they have so much power that they could tame birds?

*Begone.*

More and more of her people at the outskirts snatched weapons from the tall ones and killed them where they stood. Her people there didn't join the chant; instead they took advantage of it, killing as they moved forward.

She blessed their learning, blessed their courage. They saw tall ones and understood the threat.

She didn't even have to tell them.

Her own strength was fading. She could feel it, leaving her. She had almost nothing left.

But it didn't matter.

It didn't matter at all.

Her people were winning.

They were driving back the tall ones, even though Matthias said it might be impossible, even though Matthias said they would need the Words to help them.

The tall ones were milling around in confusion, heads tilted as if listening for Blooder voices.

*Begone.*

She was losing the last of her strength now, and she knew it. Black spots danced in front of her eyes.

"Keep chanting," she called, "until they are gone. Keep chanting—"

A few people turned and looked at her. A few others nodded. The chant continued, deep and firm and hard.

*Begone.*

*Begone.*

*Begone.*

It was the last thing she heard as her body crumpled beneath her, the last thing she felt as the blackness approached.

"Begone," she whispered, and passed out.

# TWENTY-SIX

WHAT were they doing?

Licia stared at her troops below. They had stopped moving, stopped shouting, stopped fighting at all. The first row was dying as the Islanders took the weapons out of Fey hands and killed them.

She had never seen anything like it in all her years in Infantry.

She had sent another row forward, and it had stopped where the third row had stopped. Stopped hard, as if it were hitting an invisible wall.

The Fey on the ridge were losing their perfect form. They were milling around, muttering, a fear that was foreign to Fey rising from them.

She could smell it.

She didn't think Fey ever smelled of fear.

She put a hand over her face and looked down from her flat rock, unable to see exactly what was causing the problem. No magick shimmers, no strange lights.

Whatever was happening was new.

The first row had gone through it, had started killing the Islanders as ordered, and then had suddenly stopped on the outskirts of town.

As if they were Compelled.

She frowned and squinted. In the center of town a large group of Islanders had formed a half circle facing the ridge. They were standing in the circle, fists raised. They hadn't been there before.

That was what was different.

They did have magick.

She cursed. Her people were getting slaughtered below. Slaughtered because they weren't used to being Compelled. Their orders were conflicting with their common sense. They knew they couldn't turn and run, but the Compelling wouldn't allow them to move forward either.

They were Infantry. They didn't have the power to break a through a spell like this.

She had to solve it. She had no choice—except to let her troop die on the field. She had to solve it, and she didn't want to.

Not after the speech she had made this morning to Ay'Le, the Beast Riders, the Foot Soldiers, and all the others who had magick.

What was holding her mouth closed was pride. She would let an entire troop die because of her pride? Then she wasn't a worthy commander.

She cursed again.

"Retreat!" she cried. "Call a retreat!"

The troops on the top of the ridge stared at her in complete shock. She had never done anything like that before. The Fey had rarely done it, and often that had been a tactic planned beforehand.

The troops knew this was no plan. This was a true retreat.

Bird Riders swarmed above her. Shweet landed on her shoulder. "It's a Compelling," he said, his voice small in her ear.

"I know," she snapped.

"It's powerful."

She didn't want to hear it. She didn't want to face this retreat, the meaning of it, the humiliation of it.

"Can the Foot Soldiers get by it? Beast Riders?" she asked.

"Bird Riders can't," he said. "I've never felt anything like this. The entire town is united."

"A good quarter of the town is dead," she said.

"No," he said. "The killing had just started. Maybe fifty dead. And that's being optimistic."

"Is it happening at the quarry?"

"Strangely, no. The troops have the workers trapped there. I would wager the dying will start soon, if it isn't already underway."

It was a start, at least. A small victory to cling to in the face of this hideous defeat.

"I called a retreat," she said.

"What else could you do?" he asked. "No Fey would Compel like that. Not as a group. This is a new magick. Something we haven't encountered before."

Rugad had warned her. He had warned all of them. Whenever it seemed too easy on Blue Isle, it was.

As it was here.

This afternoon, instead of celebrating a victory, she would have to protect her people, inspire them to attack again—if she could figure out a battle plan—and keep them from each other's throats.

For failing.

She swallowed hard.

The fourth row, the last row she had sent, was climbing up the ridge. Heads down, shoulders slumped, bodies hunched, they looked as if they had been defeated in hand-to-hand combat, but they had no blood on them, no wounds.

Only emotional scars.

She had seen armies look like that.

Armies that had gone against the Fey.

Licia took a deep breath. "Shweet," she said, "go inform Ay'Le that we've met magick users more powerful than we've ever dreamed."

"Have we?" he asked.

"What do you think?" she snapped.

He inclined his head—his Fey head—toward her, then glanced at the battlefield. The third row was scrambling up the ridge, out of formation, hurrying as quickly as it could. The first and second rows were still trapped there, as if they hadn't heard the retreat at all.

"And get them," she said. "Get them out of there."

"If I can send someone into that mess," he said.

She felt her breath catch in her throat. "Someone has to go."

A slaughter. That's what she was facing. A slaughter.

"Suggestions?" she snapped.

He shook his head. She was on her own.

"Get Ay'Le. *Now*," Licia said. Sending more Infantry down there would be sending them to their deaths. If Ay'Le got here, and fast, perhaps her ability to Charm would counteract the Compelling.

She would speak the retreat, and the ones closest to the Compelling might hear her.

If they still lived.

"Have her come on a Horse Rider," Licia said. "We need her immediately."

Shweet didn't need to be told again. He took off, his wings flapping hard as he headed toward the valley.

No matter how quickly he got there, it wouldn't be fast enough.

Dead would litter the ground below.

*Fey* dead.

It would be hard, Rugad had said. But he hadn't said how hard. He hadn't ever trained any of the leaders to deal with failure of this kind.

She watched, hand shielding her eyes, as most of her first row got cut down by Islanders. The second row still stood, frozen, waiting for their own death, despite the calls of retreat echoing down the ridge.

Rugad's son, Rugar, had been defeated and trapped here for twenty years. Perhaps Rugad overestimated his abilities to defeat these people, these Islanders.

Perhaps the Fey had finally met their match.

# THE SECRETS
## [AFTERNOON]

# TWENTY-SEVEN

RUGAD stood before the southern windows of the tower room, hands clasped behind his back. The city spread before him— small buildings on this side of the Cardidas River and ruined hulks on the other. The Tabernacle still looked as if it functioned, except that the once-white towers were scorched and the windows were empty. He knew, up close, that most of the building had fallen in. But that wasn't visible from this side.

Beyond it, and as far as the eye could see, a wall of smoke rose like a cloud bank before a particularly severe storm. The afternoon sunlight had a misty, almost grayish tint to it, as ash slowly made its way north.

He hated this type of retaliation. He knew what it would look like by the time he was done with the center part of the Isle. Bodies everywhere. Innocent Islanders dead because some fools got it into their heads to form a resistance cell against the Fey.

Hadn't those fools realized that the Fey had fought for centuries? Had conquered for centuries? Hadn't the fools realized that in the past, other groups had tried secret warfare, had tried attacking the Fey by night? Wouldn't it be obvious that the Fey knew how to deal with such people?

It would be so to Rugad.

But then, he was a warrior.

Although he didn't feel like one at the moment. It wasn't his normal practice to hole up in a fortified building while his people fought. Even the morning's work of interviewing Islanders— pathetic, terrified Islanders—hadn't made him feel useful.

It had made his frustration worse.

Selia had brought Dimar, the Doppelgänger, to Rugad first. Dimar was looking better. His Fey features had almost receded into his Islander ones. But if one knew how to look, one could find the Fey inside the Doppelgänger.

He had quizzed Dimar about the religion. Dimar had known many things: He had known that the swords were a symbol of worship; that the historical religious leader, the Roca, had used one in an "absorption"; that holy water had been used for Blessings and for Midnight Sacrament. But his knowledge beyond that had been filled with "I thinks" and "I supposes," and that had done Rugad no good. So he had sent Dimar away and had Selia's Islanders enter.

None were Black Robes. The Black Robes indeed seemed to be dead, an act that Rugad now regretted. He should have saved one, just one, to tell him of the customs and the history of that Tabernacle.

Still, what he had learned from the succession of religious and nonreligious Islanders was fascinating.

The religion had formed, as he knew, centuries before. The Roca, the religious leader, had come down from the mountains (but most did not know which mountains) to save the Islanders from the Soldiers of the Enemy. No one seemed to know who those Soldiers were, but one elderly man claimed that the Rocaan, the man who had been religious leader when Rugar arrived, had believed the Fey were the Soldiers of the Enemy, and had gone to face them as the Roca had centuries before.

His holy bid had failed.

And yet, there was wild magick on the Isle. Nicholas himself was a direct descendent of that Roca. The line had been unbroken throughout all those centuries. So Rugad's great-grandchildren had descended from a holy man who had come from the mountains to save a people.

Mountains where a Place of Power was?

It seemed likely.

And the more he heard, the more likely it seemed.

Although he was missing answers, answers to questions that seemed obvious: How did the Islanders come to use holy poison in their religious ceremonies? And how did that young Black

Robe kill so many Fey on the day Rugad nearly died? He had used a sword, but Black Robes had used swords before without such an effect.

A knock sounded on the tower door, and then it creaked open. Selia. Rugad had told her to enter whenever she needed to.

"I bring you one last," Selia said. "I have several guards with him, as he seemed quite reluctant."

Rugad turned.

She stood, hands clasped behind her in an unconscious imitation of him. She was frowning, her beautiful face marred slightly by the look.

"Is there something else?" he asked.

"He is not immune to Charm," she said, "but he is familiar with it."

"From all those years around my son's Failures?"

She started to shake her head, and then stopped. "The Islanders seem fairly oblivious to our magick tricks. He seemed familiar with them. It's unusual."

Rugad nodded. It was unusual, come to think of it. "And who is this one?"

"His name is Ejil. He is one of the grooms you decided to keep."

Rugad took a soft breath. The grooms. He had forgotten about them. He had placed them under Fey watch, and thought of it no more. The Fey didn't need grooms. They hadn't brought their own horses, only Horse Riders. So, when Rugad took over the palace, the only people who could care for the King's stable were the King's grooms.

They had added to the stable as well over the last few weeks, as the Infantry and guards found other horses wandering free. Many had come from other high-ranking Islanders' properties, and some had come from a small stable near the Tabernacle. The grooms had been very busy since the Fey had come, finding space for the horses and caring for them.

Rugad had sent for a few Fey grooms from Nye. The sooner he could use the horses himself without burdening his own Horse Riders, the happier he would be. But he did not trust the Islanders enough to use the horses, no matter how well guarded all of them were.

Not until he learned the extent of Islander magick.

"Send him in," Rugad said. The groom would probably know as little as the other Islanders had. It amazed him the way that magick had developed here. It had been kept in the hands of a select few, and those few had lost knowledge of it. Nicholas probably did not know that he had within him the wild magick of the Isle. Or had not known until his children were born.

Even if Nicholas had talents of his own—and Rugad suspected he did, or he would not have been as effective with a sword as he was—he would not be able to use them. Not unless someone ferreted out the talents and trained him.

But his children—his children were another matter.

Selia had turned and beckoned someone to enter. First three guards came in, and then they were followed by an Islander with his hands tied before him. Three more guards followed. Selia and Rugad had agreed that no one saw the Black King without adequate precautions. The lax way they had handled prisoners on Nye would not do here.

Selia nodded at Rugad and then left. He had not asked her to stay and had, indeed, asked her to bring in different guards with each Islander. The Islanders weren't normally prisoners—they were allowed to go about their own lives, such as they were now—but they were prisoners once they came into the palace.

The groom's lower lip trembled. His eyes were downcast, and his right hand was clenched into a fist. Slowly he relaxed it, as if it gave away too much.

With a sideways motion of his head, Rugad indicated to the guards to move away from the Islander. He was typical of all Islanders: short, squat and blond, but something about him made Rugad wary.

"You are?" he asked, even though Selia had named the groom for him.

"Ejil, sir," the groom said.

Sir. Not "sire" as so many of the Islanders had done, believing him to be a king on par with theirs. But "sir."

Like the Fey did.

Rugad took a step closer. The groom, this Ejil, did not look up at him. "I want you to tell me about the Tabernacle. Can you do that?"

"Aye, sir," the groom said. "Twas me, you know, what found the man done killed her ladyship."

Rugad frowned. Whatever he expected this groom to say, it had not been that.

"Her ladyship?"

"Aye, sir. The Fey woman. King Nicholas's wife."

Jewel. And the Tabernacle. Rugad had known—he had Seen—

when Jewel died at the hand of the religious leader. But he had not realized it needed to be discovered.

"I done saw him put the cloth with the holy water, sir. Twas a purposeful thing."

"You believe that's why I brought you here?"

The groom shrugged. "I dinna know. But I thought, when you said Tabernacle—"

"That you'd ingratiate yourself with the Fey. How un-Islander of you." Rugad smiled.

The groom flinched. The movement, again, was slight, almost invisible. But Rugad saw it.

"Why won't you look at me, Ejil?"

The groom swallowed, then tilted his head toward Rugad, keeping his eyes hooded. A small shiver ran down Rugad's back. How interesting. How very interesting. He would play this as long as he needed to.

"What you've said about my granddaughter is important," Rugad said, "but it's not why I called you here. I want you to tell me about your religion."

"Sir?"

"I want to know what you know." Rugad extended a hand toward one of the chairs. "Sit. Be comfortable. Tell me about the ceremonies and the holy waters, the swords and the icons."

The groom slid toward the chair, moving as little as possible, as if his own body would give him away. He sank into the chair gratefully, keeping his head bowed.

"I dinna know what it is ye want," he said.

"Tell me about—the Roca's Absorption," Rugad said.

"Surely others ha told ye—"

"They have," Rugad said. "But they didn't tell me the story behind the Absorption. Only a short explanation."

The groom licked his lips. He did not question Rugad as the others had. They wanted to know why he was gathering this information. They wanted to know what good it would do. And when he said he was learning about their culture, they did not relax. They told him as little as possible.

"I can quote Midnight Sacraments," the groom said. "I used ta go ever night."

"Did you?" Rugad asked. The groom didn't look the type. He didn't even wear the small sword some of the others had, nor did he have the instinctive loathing they seemed to have for the Fey. He seemed calmer than he should have been when faced with the Black King.

"Aye, sir."

"And you memorized the service?"

"Aye, sir. When ye go ever night, it gets inta yer blood, it does." The groom lifted his gaze slightly. His eyes were Islander blue, with a hint of gold.

"I'm certain that's made easier when you've actually worked in the Tabernacle."

"Oh, aye, sir. But I dinna. I been with the palace all the time I been a groom."

"I believe that," Rugad said. "It's the time before you were a groom that I'm curious about." He frowned, trying to remember. He had never been the best with names, but the ones he did remember might be good enough.

The groom had dropped his gaze again. A small, almost invisible, shudder ran through him.

"Let's see," Rugad said. "My son was particularly fond of Doppelgängers, and he always had several. We found none in Shadowlands, which I had thought curious. You're either Quest or Silence or—"

"I dinna know what yer talking about," the groom said.

"Oh, but you do." Rugad took two quick steps toward him. The guards closed in as well. Rugad bent down, grabbed the groom's square chin, and pulled it up. Even then, the groom kept his gaze down, his lids over his blue eyes.

Rugad's fingers dug into the skin. "Open your eyes," he said in Fey, "or I'll pluck one out to prove my point."

The groom opened his eyes wide. That action, more than the gold flecks around the eyes themselves, proved him to be Fey. Most Islanders did not speak Fey. Even if they did, an Islander wouldn't know that Rugad was not using a figure of speech.

"Tel," the groom whispered in the same language. "My name is Tel."

Tel. Rugad didn't remember that one, but it meant nothing. He didn't know the name of every Fey, certainly not of Fey that had come here twenty years before.

"You're quite an interesting Doppelgänger," Rugad said. "Living among the enemy for twenty years." His grip on Tel's chin remained firm. Another shudder, this one deeper, ran through Tel.

"I was sending information to Rugar. I got the man who killed Jewel run out of the Tabernacle. I thought they would kill him, but these Islanders are not very bloodthirsty. Then when Rugar died, I had no one to report to. I did not want to return to Shadowlands, so I stayed here, gathering information. I knew you would come eventually, sir."

"Then why didn't you come to me immediately, Tel?" Rugad asked.

"I had heard, sir, that you killed the others for Failures."

"And you were afraid for your life?"

Tel nodded, just once. The last part was honest, the rest self-serving. It didn't matter. Tel was a traitor, a coward, and a failure who chose to live among the Islanders because he was afraid to do anything else.

Rugad nearly spit at his feet.

Apparently, Tel saw the change in Rugad's face. Tel's hands clenched. "I—uh—I can help you in your quest for information from the Tabernacle," Tel said.

"Can you?" Rugad kept his voice cold. He didn't want the Failure to lie to him any more.

"Yes, sir," Tel said. "Before I became a groom, I was an Elder. I held the highest rank in the Tabernacle behind the Rocaan. I performed their ceremonies, and I was in their secret meetings."

"Near the holy poison, and you did not die?"

"No, sir, I did not," Tel said. "Rugar ordered me to that place, and I stayed until they started searching the entire staff using holy water."

The last sentence, too, was a lie. Tel did not lie effectively. He turned his eyes slightly, increased the tension in his shoulders, and jutted out his chin as he did so. Rugad nearly smiled. The Doppelgänger was aptly named.

"How did you perform the ceremonies without dying yourself?"

"I was cautious," Tel said. "I switched the holy poison with river water."

So that was truth as well. Interesting. "What can you tell me, then?" Rugad asked.

Tel smiled. "I can recite the ceremonies. I can tell you the history."

"What of the magick?"

"Sir?" Tel had clearly not thought of any of the Tabernacle as magick.

"The things that allowed the Tabernacle to produce its holy poison. The reasons for the swords the godly hang about their necks. That magick."

"The Secrets?" Tel asked.

The hair rose on the back of Rugad's neck. Finally, finally he was getting somewhere. "Is that what they're called?"

"Yes," Tel said. "But only the Rocaan knows them. They are passed from Rocaan to Rocaan in an unbroken line. I was going to kill the Fiftieth Rocaan to gain them, but I never got close enough. Quest did. He had just become the Fiftieth Rocaan when Islanders poured holy water on him and he died."

Another failure. But Rugad couldn't toll those up at the moment. He had to concentrate on what the Doppelgänger was saying.

"The Rocaan knows the Secrets? But we have killed the Rocaan." Perhaps that would bring out the knowledge, if Tel had any.

"You killed the Fifty-second Rocaan," Tel said. "The Fifty-first Rocaan is still alive."

"I thought the position was inherited after the death of the predecessor," Rugad said.

"It is," Tel said. "But Matthias, the Fifty-first Rocaan, the one who killed Jewel, is still alive. He fled the Tabernacle after murdering another Fey a few days after he killed Jewel."

"So where is he now?"

"I don't know," Tel said. "I'd heard he was in Jahn just before the Fey—before you—arrived, but that was all. I had not seen him, nor do I know if I'd recognize him. It's been fifteen years."

"And he knows the Secrets?"

"He's the only one who does."

"What are these Secrets?" Rugad asked.

Tel shrugged. "There are two dozen of them. I've only heard of a few. Most are not in use. The ones that are in use have to do with ceremonies still practiced. One has to do with the making of holy water. Another has to do with the Feast of the Living. A third deals with the Lights of Midday."

"And the rest?"

"I don't know much about the rest," Tel said. "I was an Elder, not Rocaan. The Secrets were jealously guarded. Even though they weren't in use, they were considered important."

Important. Secrets. Held by the man who was supposed to be God's beloved on Earth. A position once held by the Roca's second son. An Enchanter? Whose power complemented that of his brother, a Visionary?

The Roca went into the Place of Power, and emerged changed. He had two sons, one who founded a line of hereditary rulers on

Blue Isle and another who was supposed to lead a line of religious leaders.

But the religious leaders were chosen from second sons throughout the kingdom. It seemed like an odd thing.

Unless the first Rocaan, the Roca's son, was truly an Enchanter, who ruled until he died—insane, like most Enchanters.

Then the religious, afraid of that side of the line, might not have let his children rule.

What happened then? The schisms that a few of the religious Islanders had referred to? Had the Roca's grandchildren separated from the "official" religion? And if so, why had the hereditary ruler allowed it? Fear of the powers the religion had? An Enchanter, not properly controlled, could wreak havoc on everything around him.

Rugad was only guessing, but the guesses seemed to make sense. The feeling he had had earlier, the feeling that he was on to something, had grown stronger.

Tel was watching him closely, golden-flecked eyes glistening with fear.

Rugad snapped a finger. One of the guards nodded to him. "Get Selia," he said.

The guard bowed once, then left. Rugad walked close to Tel, but not too close. A Doppelgänger who had lived on his own for a long time might take advantage of any situation.

"I want to know everything you know of this religion," Rugad said. "Everything you remember. Customs, no matter how small. Artwork, no matter how insignificant. Gestures, no matter how rarely performed."

"Yes, sir," Tel said.

The door opened, and Selia entered. Rugad turned to her with a smile. "Selia," he said gently. "Meet Tel. He's one of Rugar's Doppelgängers."

Her eyes widened slightly, but nothing else about her changed. She did not even look at Tel. He was a Failure, and for all she knew, Rugad was testing her responses.

"I want you to put that dungeon below to use. Put him in there. Do not let anyone—and I mean anyone, Islander or Fey—get within touching distance of him. No one goes into the cell area alone. Send people in groups of two or more. I want him fed with a tray slid under the cell door."

"I'm not going to go anywhere," Tel said.

Rugad glared at him.

Tel bowed his head.

"I want the eyes of each person who goes near that cell checked, and that includes mine."

"Yours, sir?" Selia asked.

"Mine," Rugad said.

"And what," she asked, keeping her voice level, "should we do if we see gold flecks in your eyes?"

He grinned. He understood the difficulty as well as she did. No one could kill him—or a Doppelgänger resembling him—as easily as any other Fey.

"Find my great-grandchildren," he said, "and look for bones in the Doppelgänger's cell."

She nodded, a smile playing on her lips. She was beginning to relax around him. "Just don't put yourself in that position," she said.

"I will do what I have to," he said. "Our friend Tel has some information I need. Seems he was a Black Robe in a previous incarnation—one of the high-ranking Black Robes—and he knows a few things I need to know."

Selia put a hand on Rugad's arm, then turned to Tel, and flashed a full smile on him. One of the guards stepped back slightly, as if the impact of Selia's beauty had hit him physically.

Tel looked up at her.

"Your Islander form suits you," she said in a soft voice, a voice that grated on Rugad's ear. It must have been her Charm voice. "No wonder you kept it as long as you did."

"Thank you," Tel said, and he sounded as if she had really complimented him.

"You've heard Rugad's orders?"

Tel nodded.

"You're not going to cause us any trouble, are you?" she asked.

Tel shook his head. His eyes were glazed slightly.

"You've missed being Fey. You'll cooperate in any way you can."

"Yes," he said. "I will."

"You will remember everything you can about the Tabernacle, Rocaanism, and the Islander's magick, won't you?"

"Of course," he said.

She let go of Rugad's arm and walked close to Tel. She crouched before him. "You poor thing," she said huskily. "I've never seen a Doppelgänger who hates being touched. Physical contact makes you ill, doesn't it? The idea of using your hands to touch a person's face fills you with such self-loathing that you would rather die than do so. How hard it is for you."

A tear ran down Tel's face. His skin was blotchy. She reached a hand toward him, and he screamed, leaning back to avoid her touch.

"Tel," she whispered, and he calmed immediately. "Tel, do you remember what I just said?"

His lower lip trembled. "Please don't touch me," he said. "I can't think when anyone touches me." There were more tears in his eyes, but his vision was no longer glazed.

"I've been talking to you for a few moments," she said. "Don't you remember?"

The trembling on his lower lip had grown severe. "I can't think when someone's so close," he said.

"So you don't remember?"

"No!" He glanced up at Rugad, as if Rugad would punish him for forgetting what Selia had said. "Please! I can't—"

"It's all right," Rugad said, half-disgusted and half-pleased. He had never seen Selia in action, hadn't realized what a wonderful Charmer she really was. He had seen the results of her work, but never seen the smoothness with which she seduced and changed her victims.

He was glad the Charm magick would not work on him. Her victims had no idea they had been spelled.

"I don't think you'll have a problem," she said as she stood and came toward Rugad.

"Unless I want to use his Doppelgänging skills someday," Rugad said.

She shrugged. "That's doubtful, isn't it?"

Rugad looked at the guards. "Take him to the dungeons," he said.

"Sir, can't I go back to the stables?" Tel asked.

"You miss the feel of horseflesh beneath your fingers?" he asked.

Tel shuddered visibly, and then looked confused. "No, I—"

"Take him," Rugad said.

The guards reached for him, and he shrank away from them. "I can move on my own," he said. He struggled out of the chair, and hurried forward, the guards walking quickly to keep up with him.

Selia's smile grew as she watched him leave.

"Enjoyed that, didn't you?" Rugad asked.

Her smile faded. "Doppelgängers are easy because their minds are so malleable." Then she turned to Rugad. "Are you sure I can't just pull the information from him and then let the Foot Soldiers have him?"

"It would seem logical," Rugad said. "But I need to do it. I know more about Fey magick than most everyone else."

She nodded. "Still," she said. "To leave a Failure alive might hurt morale."

"I doubt it," Rugad said. "Besides, he won't live long."

"You'll kill him when you have the information?"

"I'd kill him now if I had a Doppelgänger to spare."

"This is so important?" Selia asked.

He looked at her. Her beautiful face was guileless. She truly didn't understand, and yet she had served him well. Protecting him, and his people, with her great Charm.

"Yes," he said. "It's extremely important. I think the knowledge he carries is at the heart of conquering Blue Isle."

"And if he has none?"

Rugad studied her for a moment. It was possible. His knowledge might be superficial and old. That was always a risk with Doppelgängers.

"If he has no knowledge," Rugad said, "then we search for an Islander named Matthias."

"Matthias," she repeated.

Rugad nodded. "I understand he holds all Blue Isle's Secrets."

# TWENTY-EIGHT

PAUSHO opened her eyes. Her head hurt, and her limbs felt strangely numb. She was hungry and thirsty and oh, so tired.

The nausea was gone, though.

The room was dark and shadowy. No one had opened the curtains. She saw other forms near her, dark forms, three of them, sitting on the chairs around the table. Which she was lying on.

In the Meeting Hall.

She moaned, and all three heads swiveled toward her. Zak, and Tri, and Matthias.

Matthias.

She shivered, remembering the deal she had made with him.

A party with demon spawn, renouncing everything she had ever done. Every belief she had ever had.

To save her home.

"Pausho?" Zak asked. His voice sounded shaky.

"I'm all right," she said, even though she was uncertain of it. "What's happened?"

"They're gone," Zak said.

"For the moment." Matthias sounded exhausted.

Tri had stood. He had a cup of water, and he was holding it for her. She reached for it, took it, and sipped. The water was warm and brackish. They had probably taken it from the well outside just after they had come in here.

"How long was I out?" she asked.

"It's past lunch," Zak said.

"They've retreated," Tri said. "It took some time to get all their forces away from Constant."

"The ones that didn't leave died," Matthias said.

She shuddered. He sounded almost joyful, as if the deaths pleased him. All the deaths she had caused, all the things she had done, had never caused her joy.

"How many?" she whispered.

"We don't know," Zak said. "A hundred, maybe more."

"They're taking the bodies and placing them outside the town, like a wall," Tri said. "It was Matthias's idea."

Pausho put a hand to her head. She wasn't feverish. "Why?" she whispered.

"Because," he said, "they have no respect for our dead. We need to show them that we have no respect for theirs."

"Surely there's another way," she said.

"Oh, there is," he said. "Their way. They mutilate the bodies, cut them up like we would sheep after they've been slaughtered. It's a hideous practice, made even more hideous by the glee they show in doing it."

She shuddered. How had she walked into this nightmare?

"A number of others have passed out as well," Tri said. "We think it has to do with that wave."

"Yes," she said.

"I'm the only Wise One who didn't," Zak said. "But then, we all know—"

"Yes," she said again, not wanting him to go farther. The other Wise Ones didn't appear to be in the room. "How many dead do we have?"

"Only the ones we saw at the start," Matthias said. "Your chant worked. There's power here, Pausho."

"I know," she whispered.

"The Fey would call it magick."

"And you?"

"I think it's similar to the power I have," he said. But he didn't look at her as he spoke, and there was a note of hope in his tone. Did he think she would accept him after all these years? He didn't understand, didn't understand at all. All his years in the Tabernacle had taught him to close his mind, not open it. They had done nothing more than confirm him in his demon spawn status.

She sat up and took the last sip from her cup, then set it on the table beside her. "Now what will happen?" she asked. "Are they gone for good?"

"They disappeared over the ridge," Tri said.

"They ran over the ridge, taking their trained birds with them," Zak said.

"Those birds aren't trained," Matthias said. "They're Fey also."

"Sounds like a fancy to me," Zak said.

Matthias merely snorted. Grimly.

"Matthias," she said even though she didn't want to. "You seem to know what these tall creatures are. These Fey. Are they gone?"

"They've conquered half the world," Matthias said softly. "Half, Pausho. Creatures like that don't have such success by running from one battle. They'll go to their base, and plan another attack. Maybe they'll get recruits. These weren't magick Fey, so far as I could tell. These were the ones without magick. We're in trouble when the magick ones arrive. A chant won't work forever."

"We have swords," Zak said before Pausho could silence him.

"Weapons are good," Matthias said. "But there were swords in Jahn, and that wasn't enough."

"Not these swords," Zak said.

Matthias turned to him, his entire posture different. Pausho closed her eyes for a moment, wishing this day would end. It had already gone on too long.

"Varin swords?" he asked. "You have varin swords?"

"Of course," Zak said. "It's an Old Stricture that swords made of varin are the best. Didn't they teach you that in the Tabernacle?"

Matthias frowned at Tri. "You didn't tell me."

"I didn't know," Tri said. "I wasn't a Wise One long."

"Most people don't use swords for hunting," Pausho said, wishing the conversation had not gone this way. "They use bow and arrow."

"We have those too," Zak said.

"I don't care what you have," Matthias said. "It's not enough."

"How do you know?" Pausho snapped. She had grown tired of his warnings, tired of his attitude.

"There are thousands of Fey on Blue Isle. Most of the Isle is theirs. Eventually, if we don't surrender, all of the Fey will come here. Do you have enough arrows for thousands of Fey? And even more for the birds and the beasts they control? Can your people swing their varin swords for days nonstop? Because that's what it will take, Pausho. It'll take more effort than we're capable of."

He sounded so certain. And he had been right about the morning. She hated this. Hated it. She had no idea her life would end up this way.

"What do you suggest?" she asked.

"The varin swords," he said to Zak, "do they cut bone like it's water?"

"The older ones," Zak said. "The ones from—"

"The older they are," Pausho interrupted, "the better they work. It's as if we've lost something in the making of them."

Matthias nodded, as if he expected that. He turned to Pausho. Her eyes had adjusted to the dim light. She could see the swelling on his neck, the bandages on his face, the lines around his mouth. His curls were more gray than blond now, and he hunched forward whenever he wasn't paying attention.

She turned away from him, the compassion she felt twisting in her heart. She couldn't, couldn't, couldn't allow herself to feel anything for this man.

This demon spawn.

"You know the Secrets of the Tabernacle include a formula for making a varin sword," Matthias said. "I've been attempting it for over a year now. It explodes when heated."

"You've been using a traditional forge," Zak said.

"Zak," Pausho cautioned. She had agreed to work with Matthias, but that didn't mean telling him everything.

Matthias touched his bandages lightly. It seemed to be an unconscious movement, one he did as he went deeply into thought. "So there are bits missing to the Secrets," he said. "I wondered."

"The Secrets," Zak said, and snorted slightly.

"Zak," Pausho said again.

Matthias looked at her. His eyes were watery, sad. He seemed as tired as she was. "There's no sense keeping it from me, Pausho," he said. "The Secrets and the Words might be our last hope. You already agreed. Don't go back on that agreement now."

She wanted to. How did he know? She couldn't bear to have a man like him in the Vault, touching the ancient documents, seeing the real history of the Isle.

"Pausho," Matthias said softly.

She put a hand to her head in an unconscious imitation of his movement. Her head still ached, although she felt a bit of her strength returning. What had she been taught? That the Soldiers of the Enemy would return in full force.

That the old ways would save the Islanders—and ruin them.

Those words were the oldest they had. They dated from the Roca's first return, long before he told them about the demon spawn. Before the splits and the schisms. Before the Roca's son was removed from his position as head of the Rocaanists.

"Pausho, please," Matthias said. "Trust me on this. Only you and I can do this."

"Not so, lad," Zak said. "I can do it too. Pausho, she has reasons for her reluctance."

Pausho swallowed, then pushed a strand of hair away. She slid off the table. Her legs were shaky, her body weaker than she wanted.

"No," she said to Zak. "I need to go. Matthias is right."

"Why?" Zak asked. "I can show him well enough. I know the history."

But he didn't lead the Wise Ones. He didn't have the complete authority. The Wise Ones had no secrets from each other, not like the Tabernacle had, but they did have rules to prevent schisms. And one of those rules was that Wise Ones took orders only from their leaders.

Even if Zak took Matthias to the vault, and Matthias learned all there was to learn, the two of them could do nothing. They needed Pausho.

They needed her.

She sighed. "I have to do it," she said. She took her hand off his shoulder, and turned to Matthias. "You must swear not to reveal what you've seen."

"Swear on what?" he asked. "What do we both hold sacred?"

It was a good point, and not one she really wanted to think about. "Your life," she said. "Swear on your life."

His mouth turned up in a half smile. "You do not hold my life sacred," he said.

"No," she said. "But you do."

He took her hand in his. She started to pull away, but he tilted his head in her direction, warning her not to. He took her hand and placed it, under his own, over his heart.

"I swear," he said in that soft, calm voice of his, "on all that I believe is sacred, all that I hold holy, that I will not reveal what I will see to anyone—unless it must be revealed to save the town of Constant, the Islanders, or Blue Isle itself. I make this a holy oath, with the Roca's Blessing, on the soul of my dearest friend, the Fiftieth Rocaan. I make this a personal oath, by swearing on my life that I will reveal none of this. Should I break the personal oath, I will die."

Then he repeated softly, "I will die."

His words sounded right, but they felt hollow. She had no proof that he would keep the oath, no proof that he would do as he said.

He seemed to sense her hesitation. He was about to speak when the door to the Meeting Hall opened.

A tall, red-haired woman entered, a basket over her arm. She flowed forward, her skirts covering her legs as she moved. She did not dress like someone from Constant, nor did she move like one. And she was tall, nearly as tall as Matthias.

"Tis sorry I am I dinna come sooner," she said. "But there is much ta do. Many are down, na jus with wounds, but with some faintin disorder. N a few of them Fey are na dead. The healers dinna know what ta do with em. I said I was comin here, n I'd ask."

Pausho stared at her. She had left the door open, and the outside light flooded the room, making her eyes hurt. The woman was lovely in a Blooders way. Even though her speech came from the Marshes, her look belonged to the Cliffs.

One of the many who had escaped.

One of the many tall ones.

Like Matthias.

And now they were together, like the prophecies said.

"Is this your woman?" Pausho asked softly.

Matthias shrugged. "This is Marly," he said. "She's a healer. I asked her to come check you."

"I been workin with some a yer others. Can ye get them ta trust me?" she asked. "I been healin longer'n most a them, and I am good at what I do."

"I believe you probably are," Pausho said. "But their distrust is natural."

"You're tall," Matthias said.

"But they dinna ha a problem with Jakib."

"He's not tall," Matthias said. "And he's not trying to heal them."

Marly made a soft sound of disgust.

"Jakib?" Pausho asked.

"Her brother," Matthias said. And then he added, "You know how that is."

Pausho looked away. She did know. Height ran in families, yes, but the ones it skipped were allowed to live. Her predecessor had argued against it, had once said that perhaps the whole family should go if a tall one was born into it. That had been one of Pausho's first days as a Wise One, and it had caused her first argument. *If you were to do that*, she had said, *then there'd be no one left in Constant.*

No one at all.

She put a hand to her face. Marly came to her side. "Let me see how ye are."

Pausho shook her head, shook Marly away. It wasn't the strange weakness this time. It was memory, memory of a day-old baby girl, naked on a mountainside—

Pausho made herself take a deep breath. She could do no more. She had served the Roca her entire life. She had given up everything and more for her duties as a Wise One, and if Matthias was right, if the evidence was right, she would lose it all in an afternoon.

"Zak," she said. "Come with us. You can act as my second."

Zak raised his head. His look was leveling. He understood. If anything went wrong, his job would be to kill Matthias.

"You'll never trust me, will you?" Matthias asked her.

She didn't answer. She took Zak's hand, and used it for balance.

"Afore ye go, let me look at ye," Marly said.

"No," Pausho said. "We haven't time."

"Ye sound like Matthias," Marly said.

Pausho started. Matthias grinned. "And for good reason," he said to Marly. "We haven't much time. The Fey will be back."

"I dinna believe ye when ye said they'd be here, and yet ye were right. I dinna understand yer fear when we hurried across the Isle, and ye were right. I suppose yer right this time too." Marly sighed. "I dinna want ye to be."

"I don't want to be either," he said.

Pausho heard the sincerity behind his words. He hated those

Fey. War among the tall ones. She didn't like it. She didn't like any of it.

"Come on," she said to Matthias. "We can get to the vault from here."

And then, against all her training, against all her beliefs, she led a tall one into the most sacred place on Blue Isle.

# TWENTY-NINE

THEY had managed to get some of the injured to the valley.

Licia sat near her boulder, watching the troops mingle. She and Ay'Le had agreed that the troops would need a bit of time to respond to the retreat, to get their bearings.

To get angry, as Fey should.

The few Domestics they had brought with them were doing temporary healing spells near the base of one of the mountains. Licia did not have the power to create a Shadowlands—she wasn't a great enough Visionary—so the Bird Riders were doing patterns over the area, searching for Islanders coming to finish what they started.

Apparently Ay'Le had been right; the Islanders weren't experienced in war, only in defense.

So far no one had come, and it had been hours since the retreat.

The surviving troops were mostly silent. Some sat on stones, others dealt with the wounded. The Foot Soldiers hovered near the road into the valley, hoping for permission to return to the ridge, to fight on their own.

The afternoon sun held little warmth. Even though they were in a valley, they were still high above sea level, and the air had a chill at midday. Part of the chill that Licia felt had nothing to do with the weather.

At least, the battle for the quarry had gone well. The Fey had captured, and imprisoned, over a hundred men in the quarry itself. Licia had the quarry owner brought to the Fey camp. She wanted to interrogate him about the change in rock color when the rock was cut from the mountainside. She had heard that the same thing happened in the Eccrasian Mountains, and that there it had a magickal property.

She suspected it did here too.

Only she couldn't get up the energy to speak with him. Her throat was hoarse from shouting the retreat. Her body ached from the terror of it all, and her mind was clouded.

She had seen this happen to other commanders and couldn't believe it had happened to her. A defeat had led them to inaction. Rugad usually replaced them immediately. She had always laughed at them, at their lack of resiliency, at their inability to overcome failure.

None of those commanders had failed like she had.

One unit slaughtered. Another half gone. The dead left on the battle site, hundreds of lives wasted. Hundreds of bodies wasted, unless she could get Red Caps down there to work.

She didn't dare send anyone to the ridge, let alone the town. Not until she had a plan.

"Licia." Shweet had landed beside her. His feathers ruffled slightly in the chill breeze. He lifted his wings a little, and settled them down again, as if adjusting to the wind. "You must see what we found."

She didn't want to see anything, but she knew he was right. If she thought she had failed before, imagine what would happen to her if Rugad discovered that she had hidden in this valley and waited for the Islanders' attack.

"Are they coming?" she whispered.

"No," Shweet said. "I think they're expecting another attack on their little town."

His tone implied there was more, but she didn't ask for it. Not yet. "What did you want me to see?"

"At the edge of camp. I'll meet you there." And then he flew off.

She watched him head directly toward the pass that led into the valley. Then she sighed and got up.

It was a maneuver on his part, a way to get her to move. Because if she moved, she would have to see the Infantry members who were sitting on bare grass, hands covering their faces; the seasoned warriors trying to figure out what had stopped them from charging; the wounded whose injuries weren't serious, who didn't know how they let their weapons get pulled from their hands.

Ay'Le was walking among them, finally putting her Charm to good use. She was speaking to each one, reminding them they were soldiers. Perhaps Licia would let Ay'Le call the next attack. Licia would draw up the battle plan, and Ay'Le would execute it.

The Fey had orders—standing orders—to fight to the death. Licia shivered. But that did not mean senseless slaughter. Even Rugad would have called a retreat in that circumstance.

But he would have come back harder, stronger.

Prepared.

She stepped around her own people. They ignored her, feeling the same shame that she did. That was what she had forgotten. How to turn defeat into victory. She knew now that the Islanders had powers no other army the Fey had faced had.

If she thought of them as Fey, perhaps she could fight them better. She had done it before, with the Failures.

She shuddered a little, remembering the quick work they had made of the Shadowlands Rugad's son had built. She had gone in, taken the lives of unsuspecting Fey, many of whom had already been spelled by Dream Riders. Those had been easy deaths, comparatively speaking, and difficult only when she looked at the faces.

Faces of people she had known, of people she might have known.

Faces of people who had believed in the same things she had, and failed.

She shuddered a third time. She had to get the thoughts of failure from her mind. That was the only thing that would save her. She had to think of winning. Rugad didn't care how a victory happened, only that it did.

Licia had reached the pass. Shweet was still in his bird form. He flew to her side, perched on her shoulder, and murmured to her, his soft voice almost a song, as he gave her directions to the spot where he wanted her.

Two Horse Riders stood near a man leaning against a boulder. One of the Horse Riders, a woman, had tears running down her cheeks. She was watching the man as if something would change, as if he would speak to her and make her feel better.

But Licia doubted that the man could make anyone feel better. He was covered in blood. His boots were nearly ruined, and through the cracks in the leather she could see his feet.

They were bleeding too. His hands were long and thin, not warrior's hands at all. His face was windburned, his skin peeling on his cheeks.

He didn't seem to notice.

"Licia," Shweet said, "this is the Scribe that was traveling with Boteen."

Her heart did a double flip. She wasn't sure she wanted this news. "His name?"

"He hasn't given it. You know Scribes. They prefer to be forgotten."

She did know Scribes. She had spoken to many of them after battles, allowing them to record Fey triumphs. She had been trained in how to tell stories to them, because the Scribes took down every word, picked up every doubt, made no changes at all in the way the stories were told.

"Why am I here?"

"Because you need to listen to him," Shweet said.

She sighed, wishing the bird would get off her shoulder. His small weight was almost more than she could bear. She passed the Horse Riders, not looking at the woman, and crouched beside the Scribe.

He stank of blood and sweat and fear. The blood smelled old, as if it were already rotting. It was black against his clothes, and beneath it, she could see scratches. But she doubted the blood was his. He didn't look ill. Only exhausted.

"Scribe," she said. "I'm Licia. I head this troop."

He nodded.

"Tell me what happened."

"Nooo," Shweet whispered, but it was too late. The Scribe leaned forward.

"It began before we arrived at the ridge," the Scribe said. "Boteen saw a diamond glinting high on the mountainside. He called me out of my carriage. I got out. When I saw him, I bowed. He said, 'I'm not someone to bow to, Scribe.'

" 'I'm sorry, sir,' I replied—"

"I don't have time for the entire story," Licia said. The entire story could take two days or more, depending on how long it took to happen. "I don't want you to practice your craft. I need you to tell me, as others would, why you're covered in blood."

"Because I checked them all to see if they were dead."

She froze. "Who?"

"Threem," the female Horse Rider said, her voice rising into a whinny that sounded like a wail.

"Caw," Shweet said.

"And Boteen," the Scribe said.

"Boteen," Licia whispered. "Who could have killed him?"

"A Red Cap," the Scribe said.

Licia frowned. It made no sense. Boteen wasn't traveling with a Red Cap.

"And an Islander," the Scribe said.

"Tell me—but condense where you can. I need to do other things this day," she said and steeled herself for a long version. The Scribe, in torturous detail, told her of traveling up the mountain to examine the "diamond of light" and of the wave hitting Boteen so hard that he nearly lost consciousness. Of sending Threem ahead to see if the mountainside were crossible, and of the hiding place where the Scribe and the Gull Rider waited. How Threem and Boteen returned, followed moments later by a Red Cap and a short, blond Islander. How the Red Cap snuck between Threem's legs and stabbed him in the belly. How Threem bucked and kicked, and how Caw had attacked, only to die at the hands of the Cap. How the Red Cap savagely murdered an Enchanter.

An Enchanter.

The only one the Fey had.

Licia felt her hands grow cold in the retelling. She hadn't thought things could get worse, but they just had. She didn't need to hear any more. "The Islander and the Red Cap came from the same place Boteen had gone?"

The Scribe nodded.

"This place he claimed had magick. This place he wanted to see before he let Rugad go."

The Scribe nodded again.

"Did Boteen give any indication that the place was what he thought?"

"Threem thought so, when he came down the first time. But Boteen didn't live long enough to speak to me. I gave it to you word for word. I didn't leave anything out." How a man who was covered in dried blood managed to sound both aggrieved and arrogant at the same time, she didn't know.

"Did you get a sense how many 'others' there were?" she asked.

"No," the Scribe said. "I had no idea there was anyone above us. I don't think Boteen did either."

"That doesn't make sense," Licia said. She frowned. The Scribe had told her everything in so much detail she was having trouble sorting through the facts. "Not if he mentioned the Islander King and his children. No. He knew that someone was above. He knew exactly what he was going for. He found it and they murdered him."

Licia took a deep breath. Shweet was unusually silent on her shoulder. "Are you sure that was a Red Cap?"

"Yes," the Scribe said.

"How do you know?" she asked.

He frowned at her, as if she were impugning his intelligence. "He was Fey, and short, but not dirty until he attacked Threem."

"Good with a knife?"

"And a sword."

"Red Caps aren't good with swords," the other Horse Rider, a male, said.

"Our Red Caps," the Scribe said.

"What other kind is there?" Licia asked. "If the Islanders had Red Caps, they would be blond and blue-eyed. Right? Are you sure this one wasn't? Are you sure he was Fey?"

"*Yes,*" the Scribe said.

"What would a Fey be doing with an Islander?" the Horse Rider asked.

"It's one of Rugar's people," the Scribe said. "Who knows?"

Licia frowned. That was a safe assumption, although she hadn't heard of any unity between Fey and Islander, Rugar's people or not.

Except for Jewel's marriage.

Except for Jewel's children, one of whom was a Shifter.

Why would a Shifter make herself look like a Red Cap? So that she wouldn't be captured?

"Did the Red Cap have a birthmark on his chin?" she asked.

The Scribe looked at her, his frown increasing. This time, he seemed to understand the reason for the question. "I was too far away," he said. "I couldn't see."

"They never searched for you, did they?" Licia said.

"They didn't know I was there," the Scribe said.

"But after the Red Cap admitted enjoying killing, they left. They didn't search the area."

"No," the Scribe said. "I was lucky."

"Very lucky," Licia said. She peered at him. He had no birthmark on his chin either, and he had acted like a Scribe—with annoying accuracy. She took a step closer and checked his eyes. They were dark, with no gold in them. He wasn't a Doppelgänger either.

Shweet shifted his small weight on her shoulder, one foot moving to a sore spot on her flesh. She picked him up and transferred him to the other side, ignoring his squawk of protest.

"We must assume, then, if this is a Fey that it is one of Rugar's.

We've had no news of desertion from our ranks, nor from anywhere else on the Isle, have we?"

The Horse Rider shook both of his heads. The Scribe just watched her.

"I'm sure we would have heard," Shweet said.

"If a lowly Red Cap survived, then we might have missed other Failures, and they're blending in with our people. We must be careful. The Islanders seemed to have worked some sort of magick on them as well, and they might be serving our enemies." Licia sighed. This was getting too complicated for her. She turned to the Scribe. "We have healers in the valley. They'll clean you off, tend your wounds, and help you feel better. Take your time getting there. They're a bit overburdened at the moment."

She moved away from him and the Horse Rider. The female Horse Rider was standing near the opening to the pass, staring at the red mountains beyond. Her Fey face was blotchy with tears. Apparently Threem had been part of a mated team. Licia left the Horse Rider alone to deal with her grief.

"Shweet," Licia said as soon as she was out of earshot from the group, "we need to send word to Rugad. Get me two Wisps and the fastest Bird Rider you have."

"Ay'Le already sent word of the defeat," Shweet said. His voice was soft, apologetic against her ear.

Licia felt all her muscles tighten. She was supposed to send word. She was supposed to be in charge. But Ay'Le knew how to play political games better than Licia did. Obviously the blame for the failure would not fall on Ay'Le, but on Licia.

She had to turn it around. Now more than ever. Rugad would forget the notification—perhaps even punish Ay'Le for acknowledging defeat prematurely—if Licia could conquer this section of Blue Isle.

"I still need the Wisps and the Bird Rider," she said. "We'll need reinforcements. I want Dream Riders, and Doppelgängers, and Rat Riders. I'll need Hawk Riders and Bear Riders, and anything else that might strike terror into those Islanders below."

"All right," Shweet said.

"And I need to let Rugad know about Boteen. He can't be making plans based on Boteen's continued existence."

"Will you tell him of Boteen's discovery?"

"I'll tell him of the Red Cap and the Islander, and the murders," she said. "And of the possibility that there's something up there, something that the Islanders need to protect."

She held out her left forefinger. Shweet hopped from her shoulder onto her knuckles. He tilted his bird head to one side, so his Fey head could see her better.

"I don't want anyone to use the word 'defeat.' Let that be Ay'Le's call. Two can play this kind of politics. I want her acceptance of failure to be premature."

"The Islanders have magick," Shweet said.

"They do," Licia said, "and so do we. We have to stop acting like naïfs who've never fought before, and we have to start thinking about our fight plan."

"What about Ay'Le?" Shweet asked.

Licia smiled. "I'll deal with her. Just get me the fastest Wisps and Rider you can find. We'll give them all the same message, and see who reaches Rugad first."

"He might come here," Shweet said.

"He might," Licia said. "But it wouldn't be wise. Although I wouldn't mind the assistance of someone more experienced. Kendrad, perhaps, or Onha, or whoever masterminded the attack on Shadowlands."

Shweet flapped his wings and rose above her hand, fluttering before her. She looked at him.

"Go," she said. "We can't waste any more time."

He nodded, turned in the air, and flew away from her. As he did, she realized she was feeling better. Even with the retreat. Even with Boteen's death.

She now had the beginnings of a plan.

# THIRTY

THEY made their way cautiously over the countryside, going, Con said, as the crow flies, an expression that made Luke nervous. He constantly looked above him, expecting to see Fey, but so far as he knew, they had no idea where he was.

He wasn't even certain if they had found the bodies of their companions yet.

He and Con had gone several miles directly north. They were heading toward Jahn. Behind them, the fire still burned, orange against a white sky. The stench followed them as well—the co-mingled smells of burned flesh, cooking food, and something stark and tangy, rather like the smell he had once encountered when he went to investigate a tree that had been struck by lightning. Con described that odor as the scent of burning magick, and it stuck in Luke's mind.

Magick was the only reason he could think of for that fire to burn as long as it had. Scavenger had told him that those pouches were used for magick, but Luke had never known exactly how. He had always seen them as the abominations they were—sacks filled with harvested skin and organs from Islanders and, in this case, friends.

He and Con were crossing a small creek that separated two farms. The crops here looked as healthy as the crops on Luke's farm, not that he would ever see them again. He and Con were careful to stay out of the fields. Farmers would note damage to their carefully tended rows more than they would notice two Islanders walking north.

Traveling this way was slow, though, because—for all Con's optimism—the two men weren't going in a straight line. Luke was navigating by the sun and worrying about how he would continue that navigation at night. He led them around planted fields, behind farmhouses, and down knolls. He kept them away from the road.

The extent of the fire worried Luke. He had planned small strikes on purpose; he hadn't wanted to call attention to himself or his men. Now the entire area knew that something had happened. Those bodies on his farm would make matters worse. He said nothing to Con, but he was worried that the Fey would try something—probably a countrywide search for the people who had destroyed the barn and murdered the guards. Two Islanders walking north would immediately be suspicious.

Con had said little since they left the kirk. The building itself seemed to have subdued him even more. He looked exhausted, and this long walk would not help him. Only his desire to rescue Sebastian, whom he believed to be the King's son, kept him going.

Luke wondered what his father would think of this, his father who had left with the King's real son. His father, who believed that his adopted son Coulter needed more protection than his real son.

No matter how much Luke tried to deny the feelings, they still rose every now and then. The bond his father had with Coulter seemed like the bond Luke and his father had had before the Fey arrived. Luke had never been able to reestablish that bond; he felt that Coulter was in the way.

And then Coulter had taken his father from him. Maybe this time for good.

Luke ran a hand through his matted hair, trying to tell himself that such things didn't matter. His father and Coulter were probably dead. Luke himself probably wouldn't survive this trip. Even if he made it across the countryside and through the city of Jahn, he would have to survive the palace, and he didn't believe that possible, no matter what he told Con.

Luke was hoping that he would come up with something else before that.

The creek was shallow, a thin trickle. It would be dried up by the end of the summer. Luke was able to cross without getting his boots wet. He toyed with the idea of walking along the creek for a few miles, but changed his mind. The creek ran east to west, and while it would hide their tracks, it would also take them even farther from their goal.

Con started to cross, slipped on a rock, and splashed himself. He didn't curse, as Luke would have done, merely continued straight ahead.

"We need to eat something," Luke said.

Con shook his head. "We have to hurry."

"Hurrying will do us no good if you collapse." Luke looked around for a place to sit where they would be unnoticed. The remains of a stone chimney sat at the edge of the nearest cornfield. The road wasn't far from that area, but if Luke and Con were careful, no one would be able to see them. The chimney was behind the current farmhouse; judging by the blackened sides of the stone, the previous farmhouse had burned down.

Luke led Con to the area. The chimney was larger than it had looked from the creek. Luke sat on a fallen stone, and Con sat on another. Luke opened the pouch he was carrying, and took some of the dried meat his father had cured in the Fey manner. He split it between both of them—a meager piece, since the food might have to last them for days—and then slowly chewed his.

Meat prepared this way was salty and almost inedible. He figured they could use the water from the creek to wash the meal down.

Con looked as if he needed the rest. He ate quickly, and then closed his eyes, as if he couldn't keep them open. He had one hand on the hilt of his sword. Luke wondered how many nights Con had catnapped like that.

The day was glorious—cooler than it had been in nearly a week. A slight breeze caressed his hair, and for a moment, he wished none of this had happened. He would be at his own farm, listening to his own corn rustle, working his own land.

He sighed, finished the small meal, and was about to get off the rock when he heard voices. He froze, glancing slowly at the farmhouse. He saw nothing there.

Slowly he looked around the chimney. Fey filled the road. They were all Infantry, and they were all heading in the direction that he had just come from. They didn't look tired, either; they had probably come from the many garrisons that the Fey had established around the countryside.

They were heading toward the fire. When they got there, what would they do? Search for the ones who caused it? And what would they do if they couldn't find anyone?

He shuddered. He hadn't expected this sort of response, at least not this quickly. He glanced up. No birds flew overhead; no small points of light reflected against the sun. So far, so good. No one had seen him.

With his left hand, he shook Con awake. The boy sat upright, clenching the hilt of his sword. Luke put a finger to his lips, then pointed at the road. Con turned and slowly eased back into position, his face so white that it seemed bloodless.

Luke's heart pounded to the rhythm of the Fey's march. He leaned against the chimney and tried to make himself as small and motionless as possible. They were trapped, trapped in the open, until the Fey passed by.

# THIRTY-ONE

NICHOLAS sat near the fountain, his head leaning against its base. The stone was cool, and the sound of running water above him was soothing.

He was waiting for Jewel to return. She had been gone a long time now, and he didn't know what that meant. He was afraid, deep down, that once she disappeared, she would never return again.

Arianna was asleep, curled on her makeshift bed, her cloak a pillow. Coulter sat near her as if he were guarding her. Nicholas was watching the boy, still not sure how he felt. He suspected he would like Coulter if the boy weren't so interested in Arianna.

Did all fathers feel that way? If so, it explained a lot about Rugar's reaction to Jewel's marriage.

Nicholas smiled. Rugar wasn't a typical father. Nothing about the Black Family was typical, not even Nicholas's children. Gift was sitting on the steps, talking with Adrian. Scavenger was cleaning off his weapons. Leen was helping. He wouldn't let her touch his wounds. They weren't serious—mostly scratches and cuts—but he had looked terrible when he returned.

*The price of victory*, he had said. The price of victory. Against an Enchanter.

A Fey Enchanter, outside this Place of Power. Nicholas had been mulling that over since he learned of it. It unnerved him a bit, made him realize just how precarious their situation was. Adrian and Scavenger had saved them this time, but what of future times? If the Enchanter had come in, had gone after the group, what then? Coulter had similar powers, but he was younger and untrained. He wouldn't have been the necessary match for an older, wiser man.

While they were gone, Nicholas had taken stock of the materials inside the cave. The vials were filled with holy water, and there were hundreds of them, all useless now that the Fey knew how to counteract it. The swords were ancient but exceedingly sharp. He had a slight cut beside the nail on his index finger from brushing against the business end of one of the blades. They would help, but the swords weren't enough in and of themselves. If Nicholas had an army in here, then the swords would be perfect. But with only seven people, and four of them Fey, Nicholas doubted the swords would be of much use at all.

The rest of the items belonged in Tabernacle ceremonies. Hundreds of bowls used in the Feast of the Living; the glass globes made for the Lights of Midday. There were several other items he was completely unfamiliar with: great balls of string that had their own shelves; sealed jars of reddish liquid, possibly blood; tapestries that covered one stretch of wall. Behind them were words in Islander so old that he didn't recognize them. If he could read them, then perhaps he would know what the tapestries were for. And despite centuries of exposure to the air in the cavern, the tapestries were in excellent condition. They hadn't molded or rotted or even become dusty.

That disturbed him.

But what disturbed him most of all were the jewels. A hundred diamonds, cut into the same shape, all the size of his thumb, rested on one shelf. The shelf below held rubies, and the shelf below that, emeralds. Then, strangely, there were bits of black stone that when he picked them up sparkled with the same radiance the diamonds had. Below those were sapphires, and below them, sparkling gray stones he had never seen either.

He had stopped his inventory there, even though there were more shelves and more items. Scavenger and Adrian had come running into the cave, and had told their story—Scavenger with triumph, Adrian with fear. Adrian was worried about the armies below.

So was Nicholas.

He retreated to the fountain. It was his next chore, to see if the water in it was holy or was something else. But he still didn't know what to do with all of this. He wondered if he would have known had Matthias told him the Secrets fifteen years before.

Arianna stirred slightly. She hadn't wanted to sleep, but he had made her after Adrian and Scavenger left. Their return hadn't awakened her. Nicholas let her continue to sleep. He doubted she would get another chance.

Coulter caught Nicholas watching her. He smiled faintly at Nicholas, who nodded in return. Coulter apparently saw that as an invitation. He left Arianna's side and approached Nicholas, bowing slightly when he stopped.

"Forgive me, sire," he said softly. "I don't know the etiquette of being around a king."

Nicholas smiled. As if etiquette mattered. "You've traveled a Link of mine, and saved my daughter," he said. "I doubt I should stand on ceremony with you or anyone."

"Still," Coulter said, and Nicholas finally understood. Coulter wasn't coming to him as a man whose daughter he liked. He was coming to him as the King, as the commander of this small force.

"Sit," Nicholas said. "Speak your mind."

Coulter nodded. He sat cross-legged across from Nicholas. "If Adrian's tale of the army is true, it's only a matter of time before they come here."

"They might not know we're here," Nicholas said.

"Maybe," Coulter said. "But Gift and I saw this place and we have magick. So, apparently, did the Fey Enchanter, and so did Matthias. This is a great draw for those who can feel it. They'll be here."

"And we need to defend it," Nicholas said. "And we need to start soon. I know. I just have no idea how."

"I've been thinking about it," Coulter said. "They'll want Gift and Arianna alive. The rest of us will probably die."

"I've thought of that too," Nicholas said.

"They'll go through us to get to the others, unless we figure out a way to keep them from here."

"I know," Nicholas said. "I just haven't figured out what the six of us can do. I don't want to risk Gift or Ari."

"There is nothing among all this stuff?" Coulter waved his hand toward the walls.

"The swords," Nicholas said. "The rest of it has to remain

untested until the Fey arrive. And even then, I'm not sure if we should use it. It might hurt my children, and Scavenger and Leen."

"What's down these other passages?" Coulter asked.

Nicholas shuddered despite himself. The passage where he had left the Shaman's body was dark and had a feeling of timelessness to it. He had felt bigger in there, but lost as well, as if he had entered another place, a place he might never return from.

"There's more magick in there, I'll wager," he said, "but it's not something I'm familiar with. I think it's very powerful, and may not be a solution to our current situation."

Coulter glanced at Ari. Nicholas did too. She hadn't moved. "I know a lot about Fey magick," he said. "I was raised among them. I have some ideas about what we can do."

He waited. Nicholas understood. Coulter wanted his permission before going on.

"Anything will help," Nicholas said.

Coulter nodded. "When I was a boy, Gift showed that he had the ability to create a Shadowlands by saving the Fey Shadowlands when his grandfather died. I don't know if you're familiar with a Shadowlands—"

"I am, in principle," Nicholas said. "I've never been in one."

"They're all surrounded by a Circle Door," Coulter said, "a door that requires magick to allow a person to enter. I think Gift should make a Circle Door at the mouth of the cave."

"And a Shadowlands?"

"No," Coulter said. "The Fey will expect that. They'll know what to do with a Shadowlands. But they won't expect a Circle Door with no Shadowlands. And they won't be able to enter if he keys it only to us."

"Is that possible?"

"Yes," Coulter said. "But I don't know if Gift can do it."

Nicholas sighed. It seemed like a good start. "What else?"

"Arianna has seen her great-grandfather, hasn't she?" Coulter asked. "If she could Shift into him, she could order about his armies. They wouldn't know the difference, and when he arrived—"

"No." The voice belonged to Jewel. Only Nicholas heard it. Coulter had continued speaking.

Nicholas held up a hand. Jewel was standing behind them, leaning against the fountain. Coulter turned as if he had suddenly felt her magick.

"Why not?" Nicholas asked.

"That's too powerful a magick," Jewel said.

"It seems like we might want to take the risk, Jewel."

"Do you want her to get stuck in his form?" Jewel asked. "He's already invaded her mind. We don't know what he's done there. If she Shifts into him, then that might be exactly what he wants."

"What do you mean, what he's done there?"

Coulter sat up straight at Nicholas's words, frowning as he did so. It was hard to understand a conversation when only hearing half of it.

"A great Visionary has powers beyond creating Shadowlands and seeing parts of the future, Nicholas," Jewel said. "There's a reason he went after our children's minds."

"Jewel," he said. "Be clear."

"Because," she said, "a great Visionary can control them."

"Control them? Do you think he has?"

"No," she said. "I see no evidence of it. But there are a dozen different ways he could do so. He might set it up to trigger at a particular time, or he might not have been able to finish. It doesn't matter. But my grandfather is cunning. He learned when he was trapped in Arianna that she can become anything. If he thought about it, he would know she could become him. And if he had time, he might have made sure that any time she took on his form, she came under his spell. Completely."

Nicholas's mouth went dry. Jewel's words so unnerved him that he lost all the joy at seeing her again. He brushed his hair out of his face. "Adrian says there are armies nearby."

"Oh, yes," Jewel said. "I have much news."

"You said you would help us figure out a strategy."

"I've never seen you at a loss before, Nicholas."

"I've never faced an army with seven people before, Jewel." He snapped at her. He had not snapped at her in years. He hadn't thought it possible, because he was so happy to see her, so pleased to have her back.

"You have eight people, Nicholas," Jewel said softly, as if that made a difference.

He sighed. "Coulter, get Gift. Wake Arianna. We need to hear what Jewel has to say."

Coulter nodded, then crossed the floor. He stopped beside Ari first, touched her shoulder, and crooned her awake.

"So interesting, that," Jewel said.

"Too interesting," Nicholas said.

"He's perfect for her," Jewel said. "It's the perfect alliance. An

Enchanter mating with a Visionary Shifter. What kind of children will they have?"

Nicholas shivered. He didn't want to think of his daughter mating with anyone. "An alliance, Jewel?"

She smiled. "Sometimes they turn out all right, Nicky."

He smiled back, the anger suddenly forgotten. "Sometimes they do," he said. Then he sighed. He had to keep to the matter at hand. "What do you have?"

"It's grim," she said. "I'm not sure they should hear it."

"I'm not sure protecting them is the best thing," he said.

She nodded, then took his hand and helped him up. She led him to the center of the floor. Arianna was awake and rubbing her eyes. She seemed more rested. Leen was giving her some water, and Adrian had found more tak. Gift was watching his parents, as if waiting for a signal before beginning to translate his mother's words.

Nicholas nodded at him.

"Jewel's back," he said. "And she says she has news."

"It's not pretty," she said. She sat on the edge of one of the marble steps and wound her arms around her legs. Gift sat beside her, mimicking her position as he repeated her words. Nicholas wondered if Gift knew he had done that. "Adrian's son Luke and several other Islanders destroyed Spell Warder pouches, as I told you."

"Near my farm?" Adrian asked.

Jewel looked at him, her gaze level. "Yes. The result enabled Scavenger to murder Boteen . . ."

Nicholas noted that she now called Scavenger by his name instead of calling him "the Red Cap."

". . . and debilitated most of the magickal Fey on the Isle, in one way or another. It was one of the most successful resistance actions ever performed against the Fey." She took a deep breath, glanced at Adrian, then glanced away.

Nicholas felt a sudden chill.

"But success always has its consequences when dealing with my grandfather."

Adrian sat on one of the steps as if his legs could no longer hold him. Gift's voice wavered as he spoke. Coulter's face had gone pale.

"Luke?" he whispered.

"Is alive and is traveling to Jahn in the company of my Golem's friend Con. I wish I could say the same of the other members of his resistance cell."

Her words were powerful enough. Echoed by Gift, they seemed to have even more weight. Nicholas felt the muscles in his shoulders tighten.

"Rugad burned every farm nearby. He slaughtered every man, woman, and child in the same area, took their souls for lamps and their bodies for pouches. He said he was determined to replace the pouches lost. He hasn't come close yet."

"When did this happen?" Nicholas asked.

"This morning. He sent word to the Infantry in the area. They started his dirty work, but it's clear he's not finished. He's mobilized other troops, and they're coming down from Jahn. I doubt there will be much countryside left when he gets done."

"I thought Rugad didn't believe in destroying land," Scavenger said.

"He does," Jewel said, "when he has no other choice. Luke was successful. He had discovered a way to remove the Fey's greatest asset, their magick. I don't know if he knows that, but Rugad did. The threat was great enough to make this sort of retaliation necessary."

"And Luke is all right?" Adrian asked. Then he looked at the others. "I'm sorry. I know a lot of people died, but he's my son—"

"Don't apologize," Nicholas said. His concern would have been the same.

"He's alive so far." Jewel shrugged. "I don't know how long he'll last. Rugad is determined to destroy the resistance."

Adrian winced, and looked away. Nicholas swallowed. "Will he destroy it?"

Jewel was watching him. "He cannot destroy the resistance as long as you're alive," she said.

"The resistance is made up of my people," he said. "And they're dying while I'm sitting in this cave."

Her smile was gentle. "I know. It's time to take a stand."

"With seven of us?"

"Eight," she said.

Gift had stopped translating. The others were frowning in confusion.

"Daddy," Arianna said, "Don't you think Blue Isle is worth dying for?"

He looked at her, his too-thin, sharp-faced daughter. Her skin was still ashen, and the birthmark stood out on her chin.

"That shouldn't be so hard to answer, Nicky," Jewel said.

He leaned his head back and sighed. "It's worth dying for. I've been raised to die for it, and to live for it," he said. "But those people who are dying now have done nothing. They don't know, and they are probably suffering. Children—"

"They probably are," Jewel said. Gift began translating again. Nicholas wondered what had made his son stop in the first place. "They are all probably suffering, including the children. That sort of thing has happened since the Fey came down from the Ecrasian Mountains from our Place of Power. Your people created a religion with your magick, at least that's how it seems. Mine created war. We've slaughtered children since we took our first country, and we're raised from birth to think such a thing natural."

She raised her head, her dark eyes flashing. "People will continue to die as the Fey move on to Leut. Children will die. You cannot give up now, Nicky."

"I'm not giving up," he said.

"Ah, but you are. You're sounding like your father."

He shook his head, even though he felt the truth of her statement. He was saying things that his father had said. He remembered coming in on his father in the war room, going over the lists of the dead.

*I don't know why you're torturing yourself with that,* Nicholas had said to his father. *We're at war.*

We're at war.

Nicholas sighed. He *was* sounding like his father. But now he was his father's age and had his father's responsibilities.

And understood them.

The people who were dying this day were his responsibility. Their lives were entrusted to him. It was part of the compact between King and country, magnified by the Roca's blood running through his veins.

"She's right, Daddy," Arianna said. "You have to look at the lives you'll save, not the ones taken."

"My father died for Blue Isle," Nicholas said. "And I'm willing to as well." He stood. "I just don't want any more senseless deaths."

Jewel watched him.

"We'll do what we can to prevent them," Adrian said. Adrian, who still had the blood of the Fey on his clothing.

"There will be more," Jewel said. "Until my grandfather is dead, there will be more deaths. And if the Fey Empire isn't in the hands of our children, my brothers will—in their own inept way—attempt to follow my grandfather's schemes."

Nicholas knew her well. All the years hadn't diminished that. As she had said that last, she hadn't looked at him. She had stared at her hands, clasped around the front of her knees.

"What else, Jewel?" he asked. "There's something you're not telling me."

She raised her eyes. She looked impossibly young. The same age as Gift, maybe, a few years older than Arianna. She didn't look like their mother. She looked like their full-Fey sister.

"There have been other deaths," she said, "besides the center of the Isle."

He closed his eyes. Why had this news been easier to take as a boy? Because he hadn't lived like this before? Because he hadn't been responsible?

Or because he hadn't understood then how precious life really was?

"Where?"

"In Constant, the village just below."

"That army," Scavenger said.

Jewel nodded. Gift repeated her affirmative.

"They attacked the village," she said. "Your Islanders drove them back."

Nicholas opened his eyes. He was certain he hadn't heard that correctly. "What?"

She smiled at him. The smile was small and mean and slightly sad. "They drove the Fey back."

"How?"

"Matthias," she said, and he could see how the word cost her. It was filled with bitterness and hatred, and a reluctance to admit that Matthias could do anything well, anything right. "Matthias and the people called the Wise Ones. They used something they called a Chant. The Fey call it a Compelling. Your people died today, but so did a lot of Fey. And each Fey loss shatters their confidence even more."

Nicholas felt a shiver run down his back. "Matthias?"

The Shaman had said Matthias was the key. She had said more when she died, but that was how he preferred to remember it. Matthias was the solution to Black Blood against Black Blood.

"So," Jewel said, obviously not wanting to say anything else about the man she had tried to kill, the man the Powers had given her revenge over, "today you have won two battles and lost one. All without fighting, good King Nicholas. Your people believe your Isle is worth dying for." She unclasped her hands, and lowered her legs. "And obviously, so do I."

He stood. "You think I'm doing something wrong."

"No," she said. "I think you will be if you do not take action now."

"I don't know how to use"—he glanced at her—"*eight* people to fight an army."

"That's my job," she said. "I'm the one who was raised from birth to think in military strategy. Eight people, in a Place of Power. We may even have the advantage."

"I don't know how," Scavenger said. "I was raised to think of battles too, and I have no idea."

"Me, either," Leen said.

Jewel shook her head slightly. Gift did not mention that. Nicholas watched him, marveling at him. His son was a diplomat, an easy, natural diplomat.

"You were not raised for the Black Throne," Jewel said. "There is a bit of a difference."

Scavenger's eyes narrowed. He glared at Gift, who had spoken the words, not Jewel, whom he couldn't see. Gift held out his hands, as if in apology.

Jewel grinned at Scavenger. Then she raised her eyebrows playfully at Nicholas. She had always know how arrogant she was; she had once said to him that her arrogance didn't matter. It was her birthright.

He had replied that the world took care of the falsely arrogant.

And she had grinned at him then. *Is my arrogance false?* she had asked.

They both knew it was not.

"We have," she said, moving as she spoke, "an army in this cave."

"Seven people," Arianna said.

"Eight," Nicholas added, smiling a bit. He had made that mistake too many times.

"An army," Jewel said, looking at her daughter. Nicholas caught his breath. *Sisters,* he thought again. One Fey and one half-Fey. One trained, and the other not.

He hoped, if they won, that Jewel could remain, and help him train his daughter. She so needed someone with both magick and discipline. Solanda had had the magick and not the discipline, at least not the kind that Arianna had needed.

Although Solanda had been there.

Nicholas's heart twisted. So many were lost. So many had died. Islanders, Fey, it made no difference. Each loss was a great one.

He had learned that from his father.

"Nicholas?" Jewel said. She had stopped moving. She was watching him. "Are you with us?"

He nodded.

"Good," she said, "because this is important. We have the makings of an army here. We have a Red Cap." She touched Scavenger's shoulder. He flinched as if he could feel it.

"I can fight," Scavenger said after Gift translated.

"Of course you can," Jewel said. "All Red Caps can."

"I've killed an Enchanter."

She peered around him, looking at his face even though he couldn't see hers. "Don't let it go to your head. He was weakened."

"And a Spell Warder."

"That is one to be proud of."

"And maybe I'll take a few others."

"Maybe," Jewel said. "But you won't be doing this alone." She moved behind Leen and touched her too. Leen looked over her shoulder at Jewel's hand, staring at the spot where Jewel had touched her as if she could see it. "We have Infantry."

Leen nodded once, as if Jewel's closeness made her nervous. But Jewel had already walked past her, to Adrian.

"We have"—and Jewel put both hands on Adrian's shoulders, as if she were holding him in place; he stood straighter, as if she had given him strength—"an Islander who is good with a sword."

"I can hold my own," Adrian said. He sounded a bit formal, as if he still weren't comfortable with Jewel around.

"Better than hold your own. You can outthink your opponents, just as your son did." She leaned closer to Adrian. Gift had to move nearer in order to hear her. She bent her head near his, her lips by his ear. "Your son is a great warrior."

"My son has a great hatred for the Fey."

"I really don't think that's true," Scavenger said.

But Jewel seemed unperturbed. She moved past Adrian, stopping behind Coulter. But she did not touch him. She held her hands near his arms. He turned, and it looked as if she were trying to hug him, but a barrier blocked the movement. He had tilted his head slightly, so that his eyes were level with hers. If Nicholas hadn't known better, he would have thought that Coulter could see her.

"We have an Enchanter," she said. "A powerful one, if untrained."

Coulter's spine straightened as Gift repeated the part about being untrained.

"So train me, then," he said.

"I will do my best," Jewel said, "in the time we have."

Then she walked to Arianna and slipped her arm around Arianna's waist. Ari glanced at Gift, then at Nicholas, clearly not sure where her mother was.

"Then we have something unique among all the Fey," Jewel said, drawing closer to Arianna. Their hips touched, but Ari didn't seem to feel it. Her arm remained at her side and she did not lean into her mother as the others had. "We have a Shifter and a Visionary, both sides untrained."

"I'm trained as a Shifter," Arianna said. "I can Shift more than anyone else has ever been able to."

"A Shifter who does not know the limits of her powers, then," Jewel said, "and a Visionary who has just begun to discover hers."

"Like you were when I met you," Nicholas said.

Jewel glanced up at him. Her eyes flashed with amusement—she knew he was protective of Arianna, but the level of his protectiveness surprised even himself—and then the amusement vanished.

"No," Jewel said. "Arianna is a more powerful Visionary. Her Visions are strong, although they're not as strong as yours, Gift."

She let go of her daughter and went to her son. She took his hands. He let her. "You," she said, "were a more powerful Visionary than your great-grandfather when you were a boy of three. You're even more powerful now. Although I hesitate in using your Vision."

"Why?" Gift asked, forgetting to translate. Nicholas took up the task, softly, speaking rapidly so that the others wouldn't get lost.

"Because there is such gentleness in you. That's Domestic magick, not Warrior Magick."

"Shamans can't make Shadowlands," Scavenger said.

"Shamans don't make Shadowlands," Jewel said. "There's a difference."

"I will fight for this place," Gift said. "My home is here. My family"—and at that, he looked at Leen, then shyly at Coulter, before glancing at Nicholas—"is here. I will fight if I have to."

"And if you do, you may lose us our greatest advantage of all," Jewel said. "The Shamans guard the Place of Power in the Eccrasian Mountains. The only Shaman on Blue Isle is now dead."

"I don't understand," Gift said.

"You aren't meant to. Not yet," Jewel said. "But you fight only as a last resort. Until then, you help your sister. We only need one Visionary."

"And we have three," Nicholas said.

Jewel smiled. "I am no longer technically a Visionary. I am a Mystery."

"You were always a mystery, Jewel," he said softly.

She inclined her head toward him, acknowledging the warmth between them.

"And me," he said. "How do I fit into your army?"

"You too are good with a sword," she said. Gift took over the translating again. She let go of his hands and came to Nicholas. "I remember that."

"I can fight," Nicholas said.

"In the Fey armies, the King leads," Jewel said.

"You're doing an admirable job of that," he said.

"I am merely your advisor, Nicky. The orders come from you." She came up beside him and threaded her arm through his. She felt warm and real and soft. He wondered why the others couldn't feel her when she seemed so vibrant to him.

"That's not enough," he said.

"No, it's not," she said. "I am hoping that your heritage will help."

He frowned at her. "My heritage?"

"Your Roca," she said. "His blood sings in you."

"And thrives in Gift and Arianna."

"Magick is not always visible, Nicholas," Jewel said. "Sometimes it exists in small ways. Such as the ability to awaken powers that have lain dormant."

"I have seen no evidence of that," Nicholas said. He felt uncomfortable discussing his own abilities, or lack of them, in front of the others. But for once, Jewel was not sensitive to his moods.

"You wouldn't see it," she said. "It's not readily noticeable. But Arianna—"

"The Shaman said our children's powers came from the mingling of the bloodlines," Nicholas said, not wanting Jewel to go much further—especially since Gift was still translating.

"They did," Jewel said. "But the fact that they exist at this great extent shows the power in your bloodline."

"Latent power," he said.

"Invisible power," she said. She glanced at the objects in the cavern. "We're in a Place of Power, Nicholas."

He wasn't following her shift. "Yes," he said, a bit cautiously.

"The items here are magick items."

"They're religious items," he said.

"They've become religious items." She clasped her hand behind her back. "Your people have worshipped the sword but not used it. You worshipped holy poison"—she shuddered slightly as she spoke those words—"but didn't use it properly until the Fey came. Matthias"—and that distaste dripped from her mouth—"Matthias and his magick ignited the holy poison. I'll wager, if you go back far enough, he has some of your Roca's blood too."

"You're saying that we're related?" Nicholas couldn't fathom that.

She shrugged. "When a bit of the veil is lifted, Mysteries can see the truth. He comes from the second son, you from the elder. He was in the right place when the Fey came. Only he squandered his ability. Magick does not make a person wise, Nicky."

"I'm not an Enchanter," Nicholas said.

"No," she said, "you're not. But you might have an ability that is natural to those whose families discover a Place of Power. You might be able to ignite the magick."

"You don't know?" Arianna asked.

Nicholas turned to her. He had forgotten she was listening. In the last few moments, he had forgotten that all of them were listening. He felt a slight flush warm his cheeks.

"You said," Arianna continued, "when the veil was lifted, you could see clearly."

"But not everything," Jewel said gently. "It's like Vision. Unpredictable."

"You must hate it that Matthias is as much a child of the Roca as King Nicholas is," Adrian said. Even though he seemed to understand the need to work with Jewel, he still did not seem to care for her. And why should he? She had done things, in war, to his family that could never be undone.

"Who we are born to is not who we are," Jewel said. "If that were the case, any of my brothers could take the Black Throne."

"So what you're saying is that we need Matthias?" Nicholas asked. He had heard this from the Shaman. Now he was hearing it from Jewel. And he didn't like it. "You tried to kill him."

"I will still kill him if I see him," she said.

"But we need him, you say."

She shrugged. "It is my nature now. I made my request before I became a Mystery. How was I to know what was necessary and what wasn't?"

"You'd kill someone we need?" Arianna asked. "How can you?"

"How can you Shift?" Jewel asked.

"I just do," Arianna answered.

Jewel nodded. "I too will just do." Then she looked at Nicholas. "This is why you lead."

"If you know where Matthias is, why don't you go to him, get him there?"

"Because I only have physicality here," she said. "And I need the physicality to kill him."

"If he doesn't come here, he's safe," Nicholas said, not sure if he wanted Matthias to be safe. Not sure how he felt about any of this.

"But he will come here," Jewel said. "The question is when."

He gazed at her. She gazed back, unblinking. She knew that there was a contradiction, a problem with what she had to do. She knew, and was unable to change it. Without it, she would not be here. Without her vow to Gift, to Nicholas, or to Matthias. She would protect Gift, love Nicholas, and kill Matthias.

She no longer had a choice.

But Nicholas did.

"You believe," he said slowly, "that I have the ability to make these religious items become magick items."

Jewel nodded.

"If he has it, Gift and I do too," Arianna said. "We have the same blood."

"But you're Fey," Jewel said. "You might not be able to use these things. Your father can."

"But I don't know what those items do," Nicholas said.

"Some of it will be buried in your traditions," she said. "And others you will have to learn as you use them."

He put a hand to his head, running his fingers through his hair. "That's not a strategy, General," he said, attempting to lighten the tone.

"No," she said, "it's not. The strategy comes from what we already know we have. Our army."

She looked at all of them.

They looked back, even though most of them couldn't see her.

"Coulter," she said. "How are your powers?"

He glanced at Gift when Gift repeated the question. "Still weak," Coulter said. "But improving."

"When do you think you'll be back to full strength?"

"I don't know," he said. "Why?"

"Have you ever performed a Duplication?"

He shook his head slowly. "I've never even heard of one."

"Only great Enchanters can do that," Scavenger said. "It hasn't been done for centuries. It might be a myth."

Jewel waved a hand at him, a gesture that Gift did not repeat. Nicholas crossed his arms. He wanted to hear this, but he wasn't sure where it was going.

"It hasn't been needed for centuries," Jewel said. She approached Coulter. "You will take Leen, and use her as a template for an army of Infantry. They will move as she moves, so you must have care in deploying them. They will not die unless she dies."

"But they won't fight unless she does either," Scavenger said. "And they can't kill unless she does."

Nicholas suddenly understood what Jewel was doing. She was buying them time. Time to learn the secrets of this place.

"They may not need to fight," he said. "If it looks like we have an army up here, the Fey might think we do."

"And if they believe it's a Fey army, they'll hesitate," Leen said.

"Even if they believe the army is composed of Failures?" Gift asked.

His question silenced them. They all knew of the loss Gift and Leen had suffered, how all the Fey from the first invasion had died at Rugad's hands. In Shadowlands.

"Failures who know how to fight would be much more threatening than Islanders who don't'," Jewel said.

"Some Islanders can fight," Adrian said.

She nodded. "Which is why we'll have Coulter duplicate you as well. We'll have you and Leen do separate shifts. That way you can get some sleep."

"Do you think there'll be time for sleep?" Leen said.

Jewel turned to her. Leen probably would have taken a step back if she had seen the intensity of Jewel's glare. Nicholas knew the look; it was Jewel's incredulous, I-can't-believe-you-said-that look. Directed at Leen, it meant that she might not really be Fey, or be worthy of the name Fey.

"Most of us weren't trained," Gift said to his mother, as if to placate her. So he understood the look too, and he hadn't spent hardly any time with her.

"Were you trained to fight?"

"Leen was," Gift said.

"Trained to wage war?"

"There was no war to wage," Gift said.

Jewel turned away then. Her gaze met Nicholas's. There was no war to wage because of their marriage, because the Fey were supposed to blend into Islander society. Because the marriage was supposed to make Islanders and Fey into one race. A race that belonged in the Fey Empire, but one that was not conquered.

One that was brought in as an alliance.

An alliance, ruined by Matthias and Jewel's father.

She sighed. Nicholas felt a sadness from her, a sadness he always felt when he thought of the possibilities of those days.

"There is always a war to wage," Jewel said. "At least to the Fey." She brushed a strand of hair from her face. "You can tell her what I've said," she said to Gift.

He nodded and translated.

Leen crossed her arms. "I don't understand why my question was so hard," she said. "Why it deserved such a response."

Nicholas wasn't sure either.

But apparently Jewel was.

"Battles," she said, "are fought in their own time. We have a defensible position here. And we have a Place of Power. We've killed an Enchanter. My grandfather isn't going to send just anyone against us. He can't afford to. He'll know that Nicholas is here, that his great-grandchildren are here. He'll think the Shaman is here too. He'll know he'll have to wage quite a battle for this place, and he'll have to do it delicately. A battle like that isn't dreamed up in a day."

"You mean he won't be here soon?" Scavenger asked, as if he found that inconceivable.

"He might," Jewel said, "and then, he might not."

"But the longer he takes, the stronger we get," Adrian said.

Jewel smiled. "It doesn't always work that way. People are bad at waiting, especially if they're in a situation where they're prepared for battle. After a few days, they lose their drive to fight. They become restless and careless. Also, a place like this might not have enough food stores, so they become weak as well. He could lay in a siege, and then where would we be?"

"We have enough food," Scavenger said.

"For weeks, maybe," Jewel said. "But what about months? What about a year?"

"It won't take him a year to come here," Coulter said.

"It might," Jewel said. "Just because we do not expect it. Because by then we'll be weakened from waiting, ready for action, and reckless with the thought of it."

Her fantasies were good; her points very good. But Nicholas knew they were wrong. "He won't wait a year," he said.

"Why not?" she asked.

He remembered the look in the Black King's eyes when he re-alized how smart Arianna was. How intense the Black King had become, how greedy, even in that moment, frozen in time, when Arianna threw the sword at Nicholas and Nicholas proceeded to stab the Black King. The Black King's gaze had been on Arianna, his eyes full of surprise, yes, and pleasure too. He thought she was worthy of his line.

He wanted to train her.

"His great-grandchildren are here," Nicholas said.

"And they have no place to go from here. He'll know where they are. They'll be trapped."

"And," Nicholas said. "This is a Place of Power, a place your people have been searching for for generations. He won't let us learn its secrets."

She smiled at him. "I like how you think, Nicky," she said. "You're right. He won't. If he thinks us capable of learning them."

"He doesn't know about you," Adrian said softly.

She nodded.

"But he knows about Arianna and Gift," Nicholas said, "and he knows they have amazing abilities. He'll come, and soon. He won't want his great-grandchildren to have control of this place before he has control of them."

"Can we control this place, Daddy?" Ari asked.

"I don't know," he said to her.

"Of course we can," Jewel said. "If we have enough time."

"That is the key, isn't it?" Nicholas said. "Time."

"Only if we waste it," Adrian said. He glanced at Nicholas as if to see if Nicholas found his attitude insubordinate. Nicholas didn't.

"So," Leen said, as if she understood. "Adrian and I will take shifts outside. Then what?"

"Gift builds a Circle Door, just as Coulter suggested," Jewel said.

"Will Adrian and Leen have to remain outside of it?" Coulter asked.

"I'm afraid so," Jewel said. "But only one of them at a time. And, if Gift builds it right, it will be keyed to them, so they can enter but my grandfather's people can't."

"Immediately, anyway," Scavenger said.

Jewel nodded. "Immediately."

"Then what?" Nicholas asked.

"Then we learn the secrets of this place, and use it as our third line of defense."

Nicholas's palms were sweating. It had grown warmer in the cave, or perhaps the ideas he was considering had made him nervous.

It all came down to here, to this place, to this time.

"There's no offense in this plan, Jewel," Nicholas said.

"The offense is more difficult," she said.

"I know," he said. "But it's necessary."

She looked at him. "The offense is based on one thing we cannot control."

He waited. But the others couldn't. Coulter seemed to understand the fastest. "The Black King?" he asked.

"Yes," Jewel said. "We need to entice him here. If his troops can't get in without a major fight, he'll have to supervise."

"And if they can?"

"Then we'll have to revise our plan," she said.

"If we live long enough," Scavenger said.

She got an amused smile on her face as she looked at him. "I could put you outside as well, Red Cap."

"Why don't you?" he asked. "I'm a good fighter."

"I know," she said. "We'll keep you and your sword behind the Circle Door in case the wrong element gets inside."

He grinned. "Imagine if a Red Cap kills the Black King."

Nicholas looked at her. "That's your plan, isn't it?" he said. "Killing Rugad?"

"It's our only option," she said.

"So what if we do kill him?" Adrian asked. "There will still be a Fey army outside."

"Solanda killed Rugar," Arianna said. "The Black King still came here."

Nicholas looked at her, feeling startled. Apparently Solanda had told her that story. He hadn't.

"The Black King did, yes," Jewel said. "My father was not the Black King, nor would he ever have been. I didn't realize it until I came here; my grandfather wanted him dead. I would have inherited. But instead I went with my father. And I died."

Nicholas felt his heart twist again. He would never get over her death. Not even with her standing before him, as young as she had been when they met. All those years apart, all those years when he had needed her, when Blue Isle had needed her, stolen by Matthias.

"I don't understand," Arianna said.

"The Black King rules the Fey," Jewel said. "He's here because he wants you or your brother to do so when he's dead. But he has to train you first. If he dies . . ."

Her voice trailed off. Gift finished for her. "The Fey will follow us?"

She shook her head. "The Fey will follow the Black Family," she said. "I still have living brothers."

"So the Fey will listen to them?" Arianna asked.

"The Fey will follow whoever is the strongest," Jewel said. "And one way to prove strength is to kill the Black King."

"But our children can't do that," Nicholas said, "or it'll cause Black Blood to face Black Blood."

"That's right," Jewel said. "And I can't, and you might not even be able to."

"Which leaves me," Coulter said.

"And me," said Adrian.

"And me," Leen said.

"Yet you put them all outside," Scavenger said. "Or you use up their powers like you will Coulter's. It's not a good plan, oh great Mysterious one."

"You could kill him too," Jewel said. "Just like you said."

"And what happens to the person who kills the Black King?" Scavenger asked. "What usually happens?"

Jewel looked away.

"He gets killed too, doesn't he? You've planned for that as well."

"I haven't planned for anything yet," she said. "I can't, entirely. If you kill him at my behest, it may bring the curse of Black Blood on all of us."

"So you leave it up to us," Scavenger said.

She nodded.

"How do we know we'll be better off after he's dead?"

"You're a Failure, Scavenger," she said. "A Failure who's murdered an Enchanter and a Spell Warder. Do you really not know the answer to your question?"

This time it was his turn to look away.

Nicholas couldn't let this continue. Jewel was right about the tensions; the longer they waited the less unified they would become.

"So our ultimate goal is the one Arianna and I strove for from the beginning," Nicholas said. "We get rid of the Black King."

Jewel smiled. "Actually, no," she said. "Our real goal is the same as his."

"What?" Gift said, unable to translate.

"Just repeat it," Nicholas said softly.

"It is," Jewel said, looking at her son. "Our goal is the same as the Black King's. We want you or Arianna to rule the Fey after my grandfather is dead."

"Only we want to train you," Nicholas said.

Jewel smiled at him. Her beauty was incandescent. He had forgotten its power. "That's right," she said. "We've wanted our children to head the Fey Empire from the beginning. And we're finally getting our chance."

# THIRTY-TWO

RUGAD stood in the Tower Room, staring at the smoke that loomed like a black cloud on the southern horizon. Below him the city was beginning to look empty. Many of his troops were heading to the center of the Isle or to the Cliffs of Blood. Those that remained guarded him and were mostly invisible to the naked eye. As they should have been. He didn't want any intruders to know how to destroy his troops.

He was expecting intruders now. The morning's attack, coupled with King Nicholas's defiance and his daughter's courage, showed a side of the Islanders that even Rugad had not expected. He had not expected the suicidal willingness to take on the Fey at all costs.

He should have expected it. After all, the Islanders had won against Rugar. They had forced Jewel into an alliance that she later claimed was a love-tie.

They had more power than he expected.

He would have to speak to the Doppelgänger. He needed this Matthias. Rugad had sent word through his generals that any Islander named Matthias was to be taken alive and treated as if he were as dangerous as a rogue Enchanter. This Matthias held the Secrets to the Islander magick, and Rugad was determined to learn them any way he could, even if it meant facing someone who would cause a danger to him and to his kind.

A knock sounded on the door. Rugad didn't answer. As he turned, the door opened, and Selia entered. "Forgive me, sir," she said. "You said to interrupt when there's news. . . ."

She let her words trail off, as if she were expecting him to contradict her. She wasn't interrupting anything, except his own silent worries, his own hatred of waiting. But she didn't have to know that.

"Proceed, Selia," he said.

"You have a messenger, sir," Selia said.

"Who is this?"

"A Wisp," Selia said. "Her name is Swirl. She's from Ay'Le."

"Ay'Le." Rugad didn't like the sound of that. Gauze had already arrived from there. He had sent a Wisp back with a message and had sent Kendrad with a large force.

Kendrad couldn't have gotten far, not far enough to have made any difference. Ay'Le wouldn't have sent anyone without a good reason. A reason Rugad wasn't sure he liked. "Do you know what this is?"

She shook her head. "Swirl said she must speak directly to you."

He nodded. "Send her in."

Selia left. He walked over to the window. The bubbled glass distorted the view slightly. He put his fingers on it. It was warm. He hadn't been outside in some time. He would have to soon, just to keep himself from going crazy. Just to keep himself under some kind of control.

What he had to do was think of this place, this palace, this city as his battlefield Shadowlands, and he had to treat it that way. When he was a young commander, he had gotten impatient conducting a war from Shadowlands until his own father had reminded him that even if he were in battle, he couldn't be everywhere.

"Rugad," Selia said from behind him.

He turned. She stood beside a Wisp who made Gauze look as if she hadn't flown at all. This Wisp was windblown, her wings hanging off her back as if they wouldn't work any more. She was visibly exhausted. Her skin was ashen, her eyes black points in her face, her mouth a single grim line.

"Rugad," she said, and bowed her head slightly. The movement made her stagger, but she caught herself on the doorjamb.

He nodded to Selia to help her, and Selia moved toward the Wisp, but the Wisp held up a hand. She had made it this far, the movement said. She would make it the rest of the way.

"I bring you a message from Ay'Le."

He clasped his hands behind his back, resisting the urge to

offer her a chair. The Wisp was right; if she rested, she might not move again. He'd been that exhausted. He knew how it felt.

"There has been a grievous defeat in the Cliffs of Blood."

He had known it from the moment he saw her, but he had been unwilling to admit it to himself. "A defeat?" he asked.

"The Islanders have a wild magick," she said. "It is strong there."

He waited. He had not expected a defeat. He had expected to send Ay'Le in, have her Charm them, and then bring in his troops to take over the village.

"I thought there was to be no attack," he said.

Swirl bowed her head slightly. "Plans had to change," she said. "Boteen the Enchanter did not allow Ay'Le to do her work. He spoke to the villagers and alienated them. And then there was this—thing—this morning. A universal loss of magick."

"I know," Rugad said. "We felt it too."

And he suddenly realized why she was so drained. In addition to her flight here, an exhausting trip when done quickly, one that had nearly destroyed Gauze, Swirl had done with no magick reserves.

He would make sure the Domestics cared for her well, and that she was well rewarded. She was a valuable Wisp.

She raised her eyes to his. "It was not caused by the Islanders?"

"Oh, it was caused by the Islanders," he said. "But south of here. Not in the Cliffs of Blood."

"They destroyed a cache of pouches," Selia added.

"Ohhh." There was relief in the word. He didn't like the sound of it. It meant that the Fey were already assigning to the Islanders more powers than they already had.

Rugad continued looking at her. She took a deep breath, and went even paler. She put out a hand, and this time Selia took it, giving her balance. Swirl's wings fluttered weakly.

"Come," Selia said. "Let's get you a chair."

"No," Swirl whispered. "I will finish." She continued to clutch Selia's hand, but did not otherwise move. "There is a place in the Cliffs, a magick place. Boteen went to it."

"I know," Rugad said.

"Leaving Ay'Le with a ruined mission. She was to fight only if she had no other choice."

"I understand," Rugad said.

"But the—thing—this morning, left the troops devastated. The Infantry leader, Licia, took control from Ay'Le, and mounted an attack at dawn. She used the Infantry only, leaving the others to recover. The attack was going well, and then—"

Her voice broke. Selia moved closer, offering comfort. Swirl did not seem to want it. Rugad did not alter his position.

"And then?" he asked.

"The Islanders did some sort of Compelling. The Infantry stopped as it moved, and those caught up in it were slaughtered where they stood. When it became clear that all the Fey would be slaughtered, that the Infantry had no way around it, Licia called a retreat. Still, we lost nearly one full unit."

One full unit. Against a Compelling. There had to be a lot of magickal strength among the Islanders to affect that many Fey, even Infantry, who had not yet come into their magick.

"Ay'Le dispatched me immediately. She asks for magickal reinforcements, as many as you can spare. She believes there will be a pitched battle for the site, and it will be difficult for the Fey to win it."

"What do you believe?" Rugad asked.

The Wisp blinked at him. "Me, sir?"

He nodded once, a crisp military movement that he found usually worked well with flustered troops.

"I believe that we were caught by surprise. The Infantry have few defenses against such things. Our people are not used to magickal attack. I think perhaps now that we know the extent of their magick—"

"Do we?" Rugad asked.

"Do we what, sir?"

"Do we know the extent of their magick?"

Her mouth opened, then closed again. Obviously she had not thought of that.

"A Compelling is a simple spell. It sounds like something a surprised people would do. But they have not yet organized. We don't know what they're capable of, now do we?" Rugad asked.

"Ay'Le—"

"Ay'Le is a Charmer, not a military leader. I am more interested in Licia. I know of her record. It is strong. She is a good minor Visionary, an excellent leader. The situation had to be extreme for her to call a retreat."

"She attacked only with Infantry."

"A smart move, I would think, given the condition of the magickal troops."

"The Infantry was unable to fight the magick," Swirl said. She was repeating the words that Ay'Le had obviously given her.

Ay'Le had Charmed her into speaking Ay'Le's words directly to Rugad.

"And you believe that magickal troops would have been able to fight the magick?"

"Sir?"

He turned to Selia. "Take this woman to the Domestics. She's been Charmed, which is why she will not get off her feet. It's lucky she survived the trip here. I want a fresh Wisp sent to Kendrad. Have her relieve Ay'Le immediately."

"Forgive me, sir," Selia said, "but Ay'Le is a good Charmer. She's one of the best."

"That may be," Rugad said. "But a diplomat has no place in the middle of this kind of war, and no understanding of what she faces. I trust Licia here. It takes an incredible force to get a tested military leader to call a retreat."

"Wouldn't that be a mistake, sir?"

"She'd lost one unit to magick she had not expected. The mistake would have been to lose her entire troop. No," he said. "It was not a mistake."

"Sir," the Wisp said. "Ay'Le has asked for reinforcements—"

"They're already on their way," he said. Then he turned to Selia. "Make sure the Wisp you send informs Kendrad about the extent of the magick in that area."

"Yes, sir," she said.

"And return to me when Swirl is in the hands of the Domestics."

"Yes, sir." She turned and helped Swirl out of the room. Swirl looked back over her shoulder at him. Her face was haggard, and he could see the Charm working its way through it. She had more excuses. More complaints. Boteen had gotten in the way. Licia had taken over. But nowhere had Ay'Le admitted any mistakes of her own.

He was disappointed. Like Selia, he had thought Ay'Le was a good person for the job. But she was not. He couldn't have leaders who did not take responsibility for their own actions, who could not handle mistakes, or admit to them. And he worried about the underlying tone of Swirl's words.

Panic.

The panic he had tried to quash when he had visited the troops here in Jahn. A growing fear of the Islanders and their power.

He had to quash it now.

# THIRTY-THREE

THE Domestics had taken over much of the second floor of the palace. There was, as one of them said, a good energy here. The feelings of warmth and kindness were overwhelming. Some of the King's former rooms were here, as were the suites of his family. They were lovely areas, most with views of the garden, and all of the children's suites had that warmth.

Seger liked the warmth. She was Rugad's personal Healer, but she also did other Domestic work. Her hands were usually busy with stitching or mending tasks. She did those to relax. Her healing was her gift, and she guarded it jealously. It had taken her decades to be good enough to be the Black King's personal Healer. She didn't let anyone else close to him.

Although tending him had been trying of late. His health was directly related to hers. If he died of wounds or illness, she would most likely be killed by his successor. She knew the risks. The members of the Black Throne weren't immortal, but they were treated as such. Therefore their deaths could not be their own fault. Although Rugad seemed to be working toward it.

Seger had the suite of rooms that had once been the nursery. There was a fireplace in the main area, and a bed in the second room. She had converted the room with the fireplace into her workshop. She, and several lesser Healers, mixed potions and did minor treatments from that space. But she let no one in the bedroom. It was her hideaway, her haven. Her place to call all her own.

That was the thing she liked best about being the Black King's Healer. She could take a room just for herself instead of sleeping with the other Domestics. She was treated as a leader in her own right, which made her wonder, once more, if she were abusing the privilege.

It was a slow afternoon. Most of the wounds that the soldiers had received during the battle for Jahn had been treated. A few soldiers were still in the infirmary, which had been made from converted guard barracks on palace lands. She saw those few regularly even though she wasn't their primary Healer. She also kept up with the small illnesses, the cuts and bruises, the accidents. Because those folks told her things, either with their wounds or with their mouths, that no one usually spoke of.

She knew the state of the Fey, and she had warned Rugad about it. The Fey were restless. The Fey were frightened.

And so was she.

That was why she spent so much time in her rooms, hiding away from the others. Why she spent even more time in her bedroom. She was there now, standing in the window overlooking the gardens. In the few short weeks that the Fey had run the palace, the gardens had gone from controlled beauty to overgrown chaos. Many of the birds had left. Those that remained seemed to be searching for something in the garden ruins. They burrowed and dug with their beaks; they worked the land as if they were trying to rebuild.

In a sense, she was too. She had never felt so rootless before. This place's wild magick made her uneasy. Its ability to defeat the Fey frightened her. And she didn't like the injuries she had seen on the Black King.

They seemed, to her, a sign of bad things to come.

His injuries were severe, the worst she had ever seen in her years of treating him. The cut to the neck, given to him by the Islander King Nicholas, would have killed a lesser man. Rugad had remained conscious, though unable to speak. It had taken her, with a team of six Healers, nearly a day to repair all the damage. And even then, the repair work couldn't be completed. His voice box was so ruined that he couldn't speak. It would have to heal naturally. When he found that untenable, he demanded a way to speak. She had to remove the voice box and rework the muscles. The new voice was a pale imitation of his own, and she knew it pained him to use it. But use it he did. And each time he did, she winced. With each word he spoke now, he destroyed the chances of ever using his own voice again.

Although she wasn't sure if he still had the voice. She had given it to him in a small jar, and he had worn it around his waist so that no one would steal it. When she treated him for the wounds given him by the Golem, the jar was gone, and the Black King had several cuts around his right hip, where the jar had rested.

She shook her head. The Golem. It was the source of her unease, and had been for the past few days. She had pieces of it, the pieces she had pulled from Rugad, on a small table beside her bed. The first night she had left them piled in a small triangular formation, the smallest on top. When she awoke in the morning, they were flat, forming a perfect square on the wooden surface.

Golems made her uneasy, probably because she knew more about them than most Healers. There was a history of Golems around the Black Throne. She had learned that history, and all the esoteric healings that went with it so that she could get this position, this position she was no longer sure she wanted.

Maybe she believed that Rugad was going to die.

He had nearly died from the neck wound, and this Golem attack was also serious, more serious than she had led him to believe. Rugad had two broken ribs and many bruises. But those worried her less than the cuts.

From those cuts she had pulled bits of the Golem. And those bits could have sent a poisoned magick through Rugad's system. She knew that had happened before, to others who'd been around Golems when they exploded, but she didn't know how to treat it. She wasn't even sure of the symptoms. And that, she had told Rugad, was why she kept the stones.

But she wasn't being truthful.

She left the window and walked to the bed. She sat on its soft side, and looked at the table. She had taken everything off of it except the Golem stones. They were still flat as they had been from the morning, the square perfect even though the stones were different sizes. If she had done the work, it would have taken her house. It looked as if someone had put together a puzzle, a puzzle designed to be a square.

But it felt as if someone had left her a message.

She knew the message hadn't come from the Fey. No one would come into her room unbidden. She was a Domestic, and to do so was a great risk. Disturbing the comfort of a Domestic's abode often meant that the person who did so, if not forgiven by the Domestic, would never be comfortable again. Even though the Fey had a high tolerance for discomfort, it gave them an even higher appreciation for real comfort.

No. The message, if that's what it was, had not come from the Fey. Although it could have come from the Mysteries.

It was said that the Golems were of the Mysteries. She did not believe it. Golems were easily made, and just as easily destroyed. Any Visionary could imbue a Domestic's stone with the Visionary's essence. It was giving that essence a life of its own that was nearly impossible.

Only a handful of Golems in all the history of the Fey had lives of their own. One of them had belonged to Rugad's grandfather. That Golem had been strong enough to create a Golem of its own. The original Golem had lived for three decades after Rugad's grandfather died, and it finally had to be destroyed. Destroying it had been difficult and, for a time, the Black Family had thought it impossible. But after the last attempt, it did not re-form, and everyone considered it gone.

This Golem had been re-formed once that she knew of, although reports said its face was cracked long before its first shattering two weeks before. It disturbed her that the Lamplighter had been unable to capture the Golem's essence in the room where it had met with Rugad, and this re-forming of the stones bothered her even more.

Most Golems, when shattered, never re-formed. The ones that re-formed often did so only once, and then when they shattered again, their stones were scattered to the four winds and their essence was captured for a Fey lamp.

This Golem's stones were scattered, all except for these small pieces, and its essence was missing.

It had, in concert with its Islander keepers, taken on a Black King once and nearly destroyed him. Then it had taken on the Black King alone and nearly destroyed him again.

This Golem, which had lived almost two decades longer than a normal Golem, was one of the rare few that had powers which were undefined. That made it a part of the Mysteries. This movement of the tiny stones into a square confirmed it.

She brought her hand over them, but couldn't bring herself to touch them. She'd only touched them the once, when she had taken them from Rugad's body and placed them on this table. She wasn't sure she wanted to touch them again.

But she was fascinated by them. They were gray and had many

different shapes, all with jagged edges from the sudden explosion that had cause the Golem's shattering. She remembered how they had felt against her hand. They had been warm. She had thought that was because she had removed them from Rugad's body, but now she wasn't sure.

She wondered whether, if she touched them, they would still be warm.

Her hand was shaking. She brought it back to her side, letting it rest on the soft bedcovers.

She should tell Rugad her suspicions, but she couldn't bring herself to do so. She had mentioned them to him that evening when she had removed them, but he hadn't paid much attention. And, to be fair, his attention had been taken by other things: the betrayal of Wisdom—and his grisly punishment—and the unease among the Fey. All of those were more important than these bits of a Golem.

Weren't they?

She didn't know. All she did know was that if she did tell him about these stones, he would make her throw them away. And she couldn't do that.

But she couldn't bring herself to tell him. She couldn't bring herself to tell anyone. And that indecisiveness was unlike her. She found herself wondering if it truly was her indecisiveness or if it was the Mysteries guiding her hand.

The Mysteries and the Powers had their own schemes, their own reason for doing things.

*I want it destroyed*, Rugad had said to her.

She had closed her fist over the shards. *It might be a tool of the Powers, Rugad.*

*I don't care*, he had said. *It tried to kill me.*

*Perhaps*, she had said slowly, afraid of what he would do to her for speaking her mind, *it thought you were violating a magick law.*

In the end, he had done nothing to her. He hadn't even responded to her comment. She didn't know if he'd actually heard it, if it had actually made an impact on him. Perhaps that was where her fear was coming from. Perhaps she did think he had violated a magick law. Or several magick laws.

Since he had come here, he had become different. His objectives were different. He had burned land, slaughtered people in a way that Fey rarely did. He had done so because of his great-grandchildren. He claimed they were the reason he was here, not because Blue Isle was the only stop in the Infrin Sea on the way to Leut.

He had made choices that she found more and more difficult to support. Not, she reminded herself, that it was an option to support him. He was the Black King. She owed him her loyalty unto death.

Almost without thinking, she brought her hand back up. Her fingers were shaking. Slowly she put her hand above the stones. Then, just as slowly, she bent her forefinger and let its tip touch the center shard.

It was warm, almost hot.

She pulled her hand away and cradled it against her chest. "Powers and Mysteries, give me guidance," she whispered.

But she knew they were already guiding her. And she didn't like the direction they were forcing her to take.

# THIRTY-FOUR

THEY started in the back of the cave. It was darker there. The strange luminescent rock seemed to have less power. The darkness brought with it more dirt, and spiderwebs.

Nicholas didn't like working in the thin light, but he saw no choice. He sat on the stone floor, Adrian beside him, staring at the tapestries. They were lovely, intricate. He remembered the tapestries his grandmother had done, the tapestries that covered the windows all over the palace. He had rarely looked at the stitching on them, only at the images. His grandmother's images were better designed than some of the other tapestries. There were older ones, to be sure, and newer ones, done by his stepmother, his father's second wife. Jewel hadn't done any. When the ladies of the court had asked her about her stitching, she had laughed at them.

*I have a warrior's hands*, she had told them. *They aren't made for delicate work.*

But there had to be something in this delicate work. Something important. First of all, he couldn't tell how old it was. The ancient tapestries at the palace were falling apart. One of the ladies had finally asked for her own needle artists to come in, to repair the older work before it was gone forever. Nicholas remembered the rotting smell of it, the way the canvas had crumbled beneath his fingers. Years of rain and bad weather had ruined the fabric. Years of sunlight had faded the colors.

Many of the images weren't worth remembering anyway; battle scenes from the Peasant Uprising. Wedding tapestry after wedding tapestry after wedding tapestry. Birth tapestries for each future King—except Sebastian, because his mother had a warrior's hands.

He frowned. He was doing the tapestries because Adrian was completely unfamiliar with them. Adrian had grown up on a farm, tutored by a local Danite. His religious education had been completely different from Nicholas's. Nicholas had studied the religion as if it were mathematics. His father had believed it essential to running the country.

But that had been two decades before. After Nicholas had married Jewel, he hadn't gone into the Tabernacle, and after Matthias killed her, Nicholas had forbidden all mention of Rocaanism within the palace walls.

He had forgotten so much, and it could be so important.

He was sitting in a corridor that went on down several flights of steps. The steps were dark, and a coldness came up from them. He didn't want to go down them alone, and wouldn't, if he could find a way to avoid it. This cavern was spectacular. It had openings and corridors and other rooms that seemed to go on forever. He and his small band had only spent time in the main area—except for that brief visit he had paid down another corridor to place the Shaman's body out of harm's way.

He wished for her guidance now. She had an easier presence than Jewel, and even though the Shaman had always been mysterious, he had trusted her on a deeper level than he had trusted anyone else. He could trust Jewel and her knowledge of war, but he knew her too well. He knew that she wouldn't understand some things about the Islanders, that she would operate from her own prejudices and her own needs as often as she would operate from his. As long as they coincided, everything would be all right. But if they didn't—

He didn't want to think about it. Not when he should be concentrating on the tapestries. He glanced around the cavern. He and Adrian were working on discovering the Secrets of this cavern because they were the only ones who couldn't be harmed by the items from Rocaanism. Arianna was resting, although she wasn't sleeping as Nicholas had wanted. Gift was showing her how to make Shadowlands. They were forming tiny boxes in the palms of their hands. When Jewel had questioned Gift about it, he had said he was practicing.

Gift had never made a Circle Door that stood alone before. And while he practiced, he felt that he may as well teach his sister the necessary skill.

At least they had stopped fighting.

Coulter was leaning against the steps, watching Arianna and Gift. Coulter was supposed to be resting as well; so much of this plan required that he be back at full strength, but he seemed more interested in Arianna's doings than his own.

Leen and Scavenger were patrolling outside. Jewel had disappeared; she was supposedly keeping an eye on the armies below. She would return with word if they needed to set the plan in action immediately.

Nicholas was hoping for time, time enough to figure out what exactly these tools were. He could barely remember some of the ceremonies. Adrian confessed to the same problem. They were both lapsed Rocaanists whose religion had finally become important.

Nicholas stared at the tapestry before him. The colors were richer than those in the other tapestries he had seen. It was as if the dye were better, as if the Islanders of old knew more about color than his stepmother and his grandmother. The vibrancy surprised him, as did the delicacy of the work itself.

The image was one he was unfamiliar with. It didn't grace the Tabernacle or the palace. It was a portrait of the Roca, with goblets surrounding him. He was sitting cross-legged on a white floor. The goblets were full, and he was alone.

It appeared to be a night scene, for all around him was black, representing darkness. The goblets were gold like the bowls that were used in the Feast of Living. But the tapestry had to have been done after the Roca's death, because all of the goblets were decorated with a small unsheathed sword.

Nicholas understood nothing about that tapestry. He looked at the next, the one Adrian had been staring at for some time. It was a busy tapestry, busier than any he had ever seen.

This tapestry had small swords in all four corners. In the center was a kirk of the old style, a single white building with no windows and a square door. Through the entire tapestry, the Cardidas flowed—at least, Nicholas thought the river was the Cardidas. In the upper right-hand corner, a diamond glittered. In the lower right were tufts of green yarn, apparently representing something that grew there. A few more tufts of yarn appeared around the diamond.

There were words in Ancient Islander under several of the items. Nicholas recognized the language, but he had never learned it. Matthias would know what they said. Matthias the scholar, Matthias the man who understood the importance of languages. Nicholas had struggled with Nyeian language as a boy but learned it only because he would one day be King. In those days, he thought—everyone thought—that the trade with Nye would continue, and that somehow the Fey would remain on Galinas.

How wrong they all were.

There were other symbols on that tapestry. Globes of light floating across the river, more goblets and bowls, and a vial that looked as if it contained holy water. The river seemed to flow in two directions from the kirk in the center.

"Do you understand any of this?" Nicholas asked Adrian.

Adrian squinted. "I was wondering if it was a map," he said.

Nicholas frowned at it again. "A map?"

Adrian nodded. "The only thing that tells me that is the river."

"I thought it was the Cardidas, but that's the only maplike element to me."

"And to me," Adrian said. "But if you accept that as the Cardidas, then the diamond represents this place, and the kirk is the Tabernacle."

"But it's in the wrong place for the Tabernacle," Nicholas said. "The Tabernacle is farther west than that."

"Now," Adrian said. "But wasn't there something in the beginnings of Rocaanism? Some sort of split? And wasn't the original Tabernacle in the exact center of the country?"

Bits of memory rose in Nicholas's mind. Adrian was right. There had been a split. There had been several splits, but the worst came early, between the Roca's son and other members of the budding religion. The Roca's other son, the King, had taken the side of the other members, because the Roca's second son, the original leader of the Tabernacle, was said to be mad. His children had to flee the Tabernacle, and were never heard from again.

"I wonder how old this is," Nicholas said.

"There's no way to tell," Adrian said.

"Except the words." Nicholas cursed softly. He wished now he hadn't talked his tutor out of those lessons in Old Islander. "And the one of the Roca with the goblets?"

"Makes no sense to me at all," Adrian said. "Although this

one"—and he pointed at the third tapestry—"shows the Lights of Midday, although in a way I've never seen before."

Nicholas looked at it. The Roca stood on a cliffside, apparently here in the Cliffs of Blood because the rocks were red (except for the ones tumbling past him, over the precipice into a frothing sea). A yellow sun was directly overhead, but in the Roca's hands were smaller suns, all being thrown inland.

Nicholas frowned. The Lights of Midday had been one of his favorite ceremonies as a child. It was always performed on the darkest day of the year, chosen during the middle of winter by the Rocaan. The ceremony was heralded by bells that called everyone to the Tabernacle (although, he supposed, in the countrysides they went to kirks) and as people entered, they were given glass globes. The sanctuary was dark; the Roca's sword always looked ominous hanging down in the center of it, larger than life. Nicholas had taken the King's box with his father, and their globes were always slightly bigger.

The Rocaan would tell the story, an uplifting tale, Nicholas used to think, of the Roca bringing light to his people on a day when the sun had disappeared, saving them all from eternal darkness. And as the end of the story neared, the globes in the hands of the congregation would fill with light.

Nicholas used to ask his father how that worked, and his father wouldn't tell him.

*Let the Tabernacle have some Secrets, son,* he would say. *The ceremony is richer for it.*

And that response always made Nicholas think that his father didn't know how the lights worked. As he got older, Nicholas used to turn the globe over and over in his hand, hoping to activate it without the words of the Rocaan. Sometimes he would utter part of the story himself, but the globe never lit without the Rocaan, no matter how hard Nicholas tried.

"I never imagined the Roca standing on a cliff," Nicholas said.

"Me, either," Adrian said. "I had always thought he spoke some words and lights came on all over the country." He reached out a shaking hand, and lightly touched the balls that the Roca was throwing.

"Notice too, that the Roca looks different here than in the other tapestry," Nicholas said.

Adrian looked at that one, then at the other one, then at the rows of tapestries that covered the wall. "He doesn't look the same in any of them," he said.

"Except that he's tall," Nicholas said.

Adrian shook his head. "He's not tall in all of them. In some you can't tell."

He was right. In some of the tapestries, the Roca was sitting alone, or standing alone, with nothing behind him to show his actual height. In all of them, though, he seemed abnormally thin, even bony, rather like Arianna looked at the moment.

Nicholas stood. He walked over toward the shelves holding the globes and frowned at them. They weren't like the globes he had held in the Tabernacle. Those were blown glass, smooth and perfectly round, with the bubbles smoothed out. They were light and delicate, but they seemed unbreakable.

These were cruder. They had bubbles, and the glass, if it was glass, appeared to be thick. The roundness wasn't perfect. Some of the globes almost seemed oblong.

He picked one up.

Light flared against his hand. It shot around the cavern, filling it with the intensity of a hundred suns. Screams rang out behind him. He turned—

—and saw his children ducking, hands over their eyes.

"Let it go!" Coulter shouted. "Let it go!"

Nicholas did. He nearly dropped the globe, then worried that in doing so, he would make the light worse. So he carefully, very carefully, set it back in its place.

The light faded slowly. It stayed in the center of the globe for a long moment, like the shadow of light, and then it finally disappeared.

Nicholas wiped his hands on his pants. He hurried down the steps to his children.

Jewel had reappeared. She held out a hand, as if to stop him. "Let me see your palms first," she said.

He held them out. Gift and Arianna had their heads bowed, but they had stopped screaming.

They hadn't moved.

Jewel inspect his hands, her fingertips running over them slightly. "There's nothing on them," she said.

He pulled his hands away from her, and wiped them again just in case, then he crouched in front of his children.

Coulter had his hands on Arianna's shoulders. She seemed frozen in place. Nicholas took Ari's left arm in his right hand, and Gift's right arm in his left hand.

"I'm sorry," he said. "Let me see what happened."

They raised their heads together, slowly, and his heart nearly stopped. In his mind's eye he had envisioned them eyeless, with only sockets remaining. But their eyes were fine. Tear-filled, red-dened, and slightly swollen, but fine.

"Can you see?" he whispered.

Arianna nodded. "It hurt, Daddy," she said.

"Yeah," Gift said, only he looked to his mother. Jewel was crouched beside him.

"Can you really see?" she asked.

And then Nicholas understood the question. *Can you really See?*

"I don't know," Gift said. He touched his eye with his left hand. "I don't have any way of knowing."

"Sure you do," Jewel said. "Make a Shadowlands, just as you were doing."

Gift glanced at Arianna. She swallowed. "You first," she said.

He held out his hand, palm up, and closed his eyes. After a moment, a tiny box formed in his palm.

Jewel let out a sigh of air. Then she turned to Nicholas. "Now have Arianna do it."

"Ari," he said. "Can you do that?"

"I'm not very good at it," she said.

"It doesn't matter. Just try."

Gift opened his eyes. He held the box on his hand as if he couldn't quite believe it was there.

Arianna took a deep breath, then closed her eyes. She put her left hand out, palm up, and frowned.

"Relax," Gift whispered. "Remember what I told you."

Ari swallowed, and her frown grew deeper. Her eyes flew open. "I can't—"

And as she said the words, a tiny box formed on her palm.

"I did it!" she said.

"The moment you gave up," Gift said. He smiled at her. She smiled back. Coulter watched from above as if he were Bless-ing them.

"They're not injured," Nicholas said to Jewel. Then he saw Adrian out of the corner of his eye. Adrian was standing at the top of the stairs, looking down.

"We can't test these things with anyone Fey inside," he said.

"One problem at a time," Nicholas said. "I want to know what you felt, what you saw."

Arianna and Gift glanced at each other. Their similarities made the hair on the back of Nicholas's neck rise.

"It was like—"

"—something burned into my eye—"

"—and it was so bright—"

"All I could see was light."

"And then nothing."

"That's right. Nothing."

"And when it stopped—"

"The burning continued for a moment—"

"And that stopped too."

"But I didn't want to move. The pain was still there—"

"Like I had stared into the sun on a hot day—"

"The sun reflected on water—"

"And I was afraid . . ."

"I would never . . ."

"See again."

They spoke the last two words together. The rest of the description they had alternated, as if they had known what the other one was going to say. Coulter had taken his hands off Arianna's shoulders and was watching her in a stunned amazement. Jewel had her mouth open as well. Adrian sat down on the top of the stairs as if it were too much for him.

Nicholas didn't believe they knew what they had done, how they had spoken, how attuned they were. He wasn't sure he would call attention to it yet.

"The pain is gone now?"

"Yes," Arianna said.

"If I had held on to that globe a moment longer," he said, "what do you think would have happened?"

"We would have gone blind," Gift said.

"Which sight would you lose?" Jewel asked.

"I don't know," Gift said. "Maybe only the physical."

"Was she asking about Vision again?" Arianna asked.

Gift nodded.

"It felt like the burning went behind my eyes, into my brain. The pain was something else," Arianna said.

Jewel bit her lower lip. She reached for Arianna's face, and then stopped. "Gift," she said, "ask your sister if she can still Shift."

"Of course she can."

"Ask her."

He did.

"I don't know if you should even try," Nicholas said to Ari before she could respond. "Given how very tired you are."

She looked at him. "I want to know," she said.

"Then be careful," Coulter said.

She looked at the hand still holding the box. It Shifted, became a tiny claw. The box tumbled and shattered on the marble floor. Then the hand Shifted back.

"I'm all right," Arianna said softly. "I am."

Nicholas let out a sigh of relief and pulled her close. She felt so frail. He hated that. Over her shoulder, he saw Gift watching them, and Nicholas reached out with his left arm. Gift slid uncertainly into the embrace. Arianna moved slightly to make room for him, and for the first time in his life, Nicholas held both of his children together.

Then he let them go, smiled at them both, and glanced at Jewel. She was watching, a wistful expression on her face. She couldn't hold them both. She couldn't even try.

"I'm sorry," he said, but whether it was to her or his children he didn't know. "I had no idea this would happen."

"You couldn't have known," Adrian said from above. "I would have done the same thing. But I mean what I said before. We can't do this while anyone even partially Fey is here."

Nicholas shuddered. He wondered what would have happened to the two full Fey in their troop: Scavenger and Leen. He didn't want to find out.

"That's right," Jewel said, "but I am encouraged by this."

Gift shot her a look that was filled with shock. Nicholas frowned. He was behind her again. He wasn't sure quite how.

She noted his confusion.

"If you had continued to hold that globe, imagine the power you would have controlled," she said. "That gives us an advantage over the Fey. It didn't hurt your eyes, did it?"

"It was bright," Nicholas said. He looked at Coulter, then at Adrian. They both shrugged.

"It seemed bright to me," Coulter said, "like a hearth fire flaring, but nothing more."

"That describes it," Adrian said.

"This is another weapon," Jewel said, almost breathlessly. "One that harms Fey and does not harm Islanders. Oh, Nicholas, you know what that means, don't you?"

He shook his head, still rattled by her change of mood. He was still shaken by the near-harm he had caused his children. She was almost jubilant.

"It means," she said, "that I was right. Everything in this place is a weapon. Everything. We just have to figure out how to use it."

"And to keep it from harming us," Gift said. His eyes were still red, and his skin had become pale, although whether that was an aftereffect of the pain or whether it was because of his mother's words, Nicholas didn't know.

"That's the main thing," Nicholas said. "We can't have it harm our own Fey."

Jewel nodded. "But we have what I thought we had. A chance."

So that was the nature of her jubilation. For all her big talk, she had been as worried as he about their small force, about their chances.

"We need to find out about the other items. We need to know—"

"It may not be as simple as you think, Jewel," Nicholas said. "Forgive me, but the only way we learned about holy water was through its use on the Fey."

She shuddered and raised a hand seemingly involuntarily to the top of her head. "I know," she said. "Some things we may not learn until we're in the middle of battle. But I'll wager that light would flare whether or not there's a Fey in the room."

That was probably true, and it would be easy to check. "Still," Nicholas said, "I want to be cautious."

"You can't be cautious," Jewel said, "and win a war."

"You can win a war," Nicholas said, "and lose everything."

They stared at each other for a moment, both breathing hard. It made him remember what it had been like during that first meeting, across the kitchen where she later died, swords crossed, exchanging words in various languages, the attraction already flaring between them.

"All right." Scavenger's voice echoed from above. "I know we weren't supposed to come in, but I had to know about that light."

They had seen it too. Nicholas felt a chill. Even outside the cave they weren't protected.

"Are you all right?" Adrian asked.

"We both are, but I'll have you know, it startled us. What was it?"

"Another weapon, my mother says," Gift said. Scavenger reached the top of the stairs and looked down.

Nicholas looked up at him. "Another part of Islander religion that has a bad effect on Fey. Are your eyes all right?"

"We didn't see it directly." This time the speaker was Leen. She came to Scavenger's side, towering over him, looking ridiculously thin at that strange angle. "It hit the exposed jewel on one of the swords and then flared like a prism."

"Flared?" Adrian asked.

"Flared," Nicholas repeated. The jewels. He glanced at Jewel. She smiled. He took a deep breath. "Arianna, Gift, go outside with Leen and Scavenger, and keep watch until we send for you. Coulter—"

"We can't do that," Coulter said. "We can't test anything with them nearby. If the light escaped the cave, imagine what else might happen. They could die."

"Risks," Jewel said.

"We need to take risks," Gift repeated.

"But not with the two of you," Coulter said.

"I'm so tired of that!" Arianna said. "You all sound like my father. It's my life and I'll risk it if I choose."

"It's not your life," Jewel said. "Tell her, Gift. It's not her life."

"Then whose is it?" Gift asked.

"It belongs to her country, to her people," Jewel said. "Just like yours."

"And yours?" Gift asked. "Did you think of that when you went to my father's coronation?"

Jewel took a step backward as if she had been slapped. Nicholas went to her and put his arm around her, pulling her close. "She had," Nicholas said. "The one who wasn't thinking of others at that moment was Matthias. Jewel was being a diplomat. It was the only role she could play at the time."

"But she took a risk," Arianna said. "And not just with herself. With me, too."

Nicholas sighed. Jewel's body tightened against him.

"She's right," Jewel said. "She's right. We have to take some risks. But we'll do what we can to minimize them. Maybe Gift should make a Shadowlands outside. It should protect them."

Nicholas nodded. "Good idea."

"Won't the Fey see it?"

"Only the Circle Door," Gift said, "and they'll see another soon enough. They know where we are. It's only a matter of time anyway."

"Then we'll go outside and wait in one of those empty places?" Arianna said.

"It'll be all right," Coulter said. "At least you won't spend years in it."

No one spoke for a moment. Then Nicholas let Jewel go. "That's right," he said. "This is the thing to do. Arianna, Gift, please leave with Scavenger and Leen."

"I'll go too," Coulter said. "Scavenger and Leen'll have to be in that Shadowlands as well, and someone will have to keep an eye on the army below."

"As long as you rest," Jewel said. She turned to Gift. "Tell him that. As long as he rests."

Gift did.

Coulter nodded. "I will. Waiting out there will be as good as waiting in here."

Jewel put a hand on Nicholas's arm. "You'll have to hurry. We don't have much time."

"I know," he said.

"You'll be all right, Daddy?" Arianna asked, and even though she tried to sound brave, he could hear the fear in her voice.

"I'm probably the safest of all of us," he said. "I'm the one who is the direct descendent."

"So am I," Ari said.

"And I have no Fey blood," Nicholas said. "I'll be fine."

Coulter glanced at Adrian, who smiled. "So will I," he said. "The Tabernacle has never injured me, although some of its teachings may have."

Jewel ran a hand over Nicholas's face. Her fingers were cool and soothing. "I won't stay either," she said.

He leaned into her touch. "I wouldn't want you to. I don't know what can harm Mysteries."

"Nothing," she said. "Except Powers. And this is a Place of Power. I don't want to be surprised. I'll keep an eye on the armies below, and then I'll warn you. I'll also let you know Rugad's plans if I can learn them."

"Be careful," Nicholas said.

She smiled. "I should be saying that to you."

"Arianna already did."

She kissed him, gently, her lips warm against his. "Just don't let anything happen to you."

He nodded against her, but did not speak. Gift was right; they needed to take risks. And he would. He would discover what treasures lay within here. The globes would help, but they would not be enough, just as the swords would not be enough. The holy water was useless. But the jewels might help him. And if he could figure out the tapestries, he might find even more help.

"I'll do what I can," he said to her, but he wasn't certain if he was speaking of his work in the cavern, or if he was talking of his own survival.

He hoped he could discover all the secrets of this place

without harming himself; but he doubted that would happen. And he was the logical sacrifice this time. Arianna and Gift could make it without him, especially with Jewel's help.

He only hoped it wouldn't come to this.

But he suspected it might.

# THIRTY-FIVE

PAUSHO looked like an old woman. She huddled near Zak, walking as if movement hurt her, and she kept her head bowed, as if she had been defeated.

As if he had defeated her.

Matthias walked behind her. He refused to feel guilty. He also was keeping the elation down. He had wanted to see the original copy of the Words since he learned of it a few days ago, but he hadn't been able to. He had thought that the Wise Ones would never let him see their Vault.

And now they were.

Because of the Fey.

Zak had opened a hidden doorway built into the wall of the Meeting Hall. Stairs went down into a great darkness. Zak lit a torch and carried it before him, but it did little to dispel the gloom.

The stairs ended in a wide corridor. It was built of the mountain stone and it was well kept. It was clean and dust-free. No cobwebs here, no rotted wood. This place was used, and cared for. It reminded Matthias of the catacombs beneath the Tabernacle and made him wonder what they had held at one time.

This seemed older, though. The stones were uneven and held in place with generations of mortar. Some of it had flaked off, and he could see the older material beneath.

The Wise Ones of Constant had sat on this information for centuries. And now they were sharing it with a tall one.

The elation flared again, and he tamped it down. He couldn't let Pausho see any of it. If she did, she would stop this immediately, and she couldn't. He needed to see this information. He hadn't lied to her about that. He needed to see what was here, to see if it gave them any answers. They needed a way to fight the Fey. This seemed to him like a last stand.

If they didn't defeat the Fey here, the Isle would be lost.

The corridor stretched for some distance as well. The single torch illuminated an area in a circle around Zak. The air got colder and damper, and bits of water glistened on some of the stone. They had gone for several moments before Matthias realized that the floor had changed color.

Now it was red like the mountains, like the mountain stone before it was cut away.

They were in the Cliffs of the Blood, going back to a place that had existed before the town, before the Meeting Hall. Maybe even before the Wise Ones.

He felt the hair rise on the back of his neck. Some of that reaction, he knew, was due to the chill, but not all of it. There was a feeling here, a feeling not unlike the one he had felt on the mountainside, a feeling of great power.

Only he wasn't at the center of it.

Pausho didn't look at him. She didn't speak at all. She clung to Zak and made her way ahead of him, shuffling her feet as she did so. She had given her all in that fight with the Fey. Matthias had seen it, and it had surprised him, even though it shouldn't have.

Everything she did was for Constant. If Constant were threatened, of course she would respond the way she did. It was consistent with who she was.

He had never thought, though, that she would be on his side, even reluctantly. He had seen her as pure evil.

She was not.

And that, in some ways, disappointed him. It was easier to believe in her evilness, easier to believe she had done all that she had done, including trying to kill him, because it was her nature, not because it was, to her mind, a rational choice.

He was tired. And his body still hurt. His neck still hurt. The energy he had felt as a part of him was still depleted. This long walk, a walk he hadn't prepared for, was exhausting him even more.

The corridor stopped tilting downwards, but the chill grew. They were underground. The ceiling was no longer made of cut stone, but was all a single piece, carved open by hand, or maybe by the elements. This too was red, as were the walls.

He was in a cave.

He wondered if it was related to the cavern that Jewel had

guarded. He knew they were both in the same mountain range. But the one Jewel had guarded was quite a walk in the other direction. Here he was walking toward the sunrise. The other cave had been farther north.

He had heard, though, as a child that the Cliffs of Blood were riddled with caves, and he had been warned away from them. Which made sense, since he was also warned away from the Cliffs themselves, even though they sang to him.

Still sang to him.

Pausho turned to him, her face only half-lit by Zak's torch. She studied Matthias's face for a moment, and then sighed. "You feel it."

He didn't respond. The statement wasn't a question. It was obviously some kind of test.

"He feels it, Zak."

"Why does that surprise you?" Zak said, so low that Matthias had to strain to hear it.

Pausho shook her head. "I had hoped differently."

"You had hoped that I wouldn't be like you," Matthias said. "Every time I'm like you, it upsets you."

But Pausho didn't answer him. She leaned on Zak and continued forward as if she hadn't spoken.

Matthias was trembling. An anger he hadn't realized he felt was building inside him. Pausho, no matter how much he fought her, always managed to upset him.

Then they turned a corner. Before them was a large stone door. It was gray, and looked dead next to the red stone. The door had been carved of a single block of stone and made to fit the area. A wooden bar held it closed, as if it were holding something inside, and the bar was held in place by a large lock.

Pausho fumbled with the pocket of her skirt and finally removed a key. She opened the lock and tugged on it.

It fell to the floor with a clang.

Then she struggled with the bar, pulling it up, and then pulling it out, setting it on the floor beside the door. Matthias moved to help her, but Zak held him back with a single hand.

The torch created bloody shadows on the walls. The clanging of the lock and the banging of the bar against the floor echoed in the small space. Matthias suddenly decided that he didn't like it here.

Pausho swung the door open. It narrowly missed the bar, and slammed against the stone wall. The stone turned pink for a moment, then went back to its original deep red. It was as if the stone could be injured.

Matthias stared at it, and took a deep breath. They could just as easily be bringing him down here to kill him as they could to be working with him.

He swallowed, trying to force down the nervousness that had arisen inside him. He had learned long ago that if he showed Pausho a weakness, she would pounce on it.

And then he remembered how it felt to have all that energy flow through him, and he wondered if enough of it had come back for him to command fire with his fingertips again.

He couldn't test that here, in this corridor, with Zak and Pausho so close. But he wouldn't hesitate to use the power if he had to.

Zak had a hand on Pausho's shoulder. He was speaking softly to her, and even without hearing him, Matthias knew what he was saying. Zak was telling her this was her last chance to turn back, her last chance to deal with Matthias as Matthias, not as someone who knew the Secrets of their Vault.

Pausho took the torch from Zak and stepped inside. She paused to light torches on either side. Then she looked at Matthias.

"This goes against everything I've been taught," she said.

"Showing a tall one the insides of this place?"

"Yes," she said.

"I've sworn to you—"

"I don't care what you've sworn," she said. "All I care about is that you're right, that there is a way to stop those invaders, a way hidden in here."

"And if I don't find it?" he asked.

She stared at him for a moment, and then she turned her back on him, going inside. Zak stood at the door watching him, a slight smile on his face.

They could kill him. He could die as easily as a Fey surprised by a sword. Or maybe they had other ways of killing tall ones, ways not used against babies.

Gooseflesh had risen on his arms. He rubbed it absently. He had made this choice. It was the only way to defeat the Fey.

He took a deep breath, and walked past Zak, not looking at him as he did so.

The inside of the vault was surprisingly warm, as if it had an internal heat source. Pausho was lighting more torches that were built into the red walls of the room. And it was a room, complete with chairs and tables and lamps. A bed stood in the corner, and off to the far side, another doorway beckoned.

"Wise Ones are encouraged to live down here while they study," Pausho said, as if he were an initiate.

A number of people could stay here at one time, if they wanted to sleep on daybeds or chairs. With the torches lit, the place was pleasant, albeit a bit warm. Even the red walls, floor, and ceiling had a homey glow.

He saw nothing that could be the Words. Nor anything that indicated religious items nearby.

"You'll wait here," Pausho said to Zak.

Zak sighed and sank into one of the beds, arms crossed. He stared at the far door, as if he could see through it. Matthias understood. He and Pausho would go through that door, and Zak would remain in that position until they returned.

"Come on," Pausho said to Matthias.

She wound her way around the furniture and headed toward that door, still holding her original torch.

The door was small and wooden. It looked unprepossessing, as if it were merely the door to a storage closet. It had no lock, merely a handle, which Pausho pulled down on. The door swung inward, and as it did, Matthias had to frown at the light.

The light.

At first he thought someone had left torches burning, but that made no sense. Torches burned down into nothing. Besides, it was dangerous to leave them burning. Sparks could ignite or an errant flame could touch the torch holder, setting it afire. Beside, the light wasn't a wavery torch sort of light. It was an even light, like daylight only not quite as bright, like moonlight only not quite as dim.

He had never really seen any light like it before.

And it seemed to be coming from the floor.

The floor was all white with its own glow. Pausho stuck the torch in an empty torch holder beside the door, and stepped onto that floor.

Nothing changed beneath her feet.

She tilted her head at him. "If you want to see the Words," she said, "they're inside."

She seemed unharmed, and she was no different from him. Was she? He didn't know. He had never really stopped to think if there was something physical behind the name of demon spawn, something that had to do with more than just height.

He didn't want to think about it.

Besides, it was too late.

He followed her.

When his feet touched the white floor, he winced, expecting heat. But there was none. The floor felt the same through his boots as the floor he had just left.

Once inside the room, the light seemed more appropriate, almost as if Pausho had made it dim. He stepped all the way inside, and the door closed behind him, clicking shut.

Pausho hadn't touched it.

His heart was pounding. The room was silent. He couldn't even hear Pausho breathe. It was silent, and it felt holy.

He had never been in a place that felt holy before.

It felt more like a sanctuary than the Sanctuaries in the Tabernacle. For the first time in his entire life, he felt as if he were in the presence of God.

Pausho watched him, her faded blue eyes taking in everything. A slight frown creased her forehead, and she was too pale. But she hadn't moved. She said nothing, letting him look at the room.

It wasn't vast, even though it felt vast. The ceiling was carved out of stone just as the rest of this cavern had been, only it too was white. He couldn't tell once again if the carving had been done by Islanders or if it had been done by waters generations ago. The walls were also white, and covered with tapestries whose work was exquisite. The strange light made the fabrics shine. The golds seemed golder, the reds vibrant, the greens—he had never seen green on a tapestry before—as brilliant as damp grass on a sunny day. The tapestries were hung evenly, like curtains, around the room, and ending only where the room branched off into a series of corridors.

Down one of those corridors, he felt the pull.

He looked at it, but could see nothing different about the corridor. He could only feel the urge to move toward that feeling, to go where he had always wanted to be.

Would Jewel be down there as well?

He didn't know.

Pausho bit her lower lip. She knew well where he was looking.

Then he forced his gaze away from the corridors. In front of him was a stone altar, and on it was a large book filled with loose papers.

The Words.

He was amazed they were open like that, that the papers, fragile even after a few years, seemed undamaged. Perhaps it was a ploy for the unbeliever. Perhaps the Words were elsewhere, and this was only something to attract someone who was looking for symbolism.

He made himself look at everything else first: the table, set up for the Feast of the Living, the silver bowls in the center of the table sparkling as if they had just been polished. Vials of holy water sat on freestanding shelves, and swords lay between them. Suspended from the ceiling in an arching pattern were the globes for the Lights of Midday. He felt if he touched one, it would flare into light.

Several small dolls made of hand-blown glass sat on tiny chairs, and he shuddered. He'd never seen physical representations of the Soul Repositories. That was one of the Secrets the Fiftieth Rocaan had simply given him, not even trying to explain its history or its purpose. The dolls appeared empty, but he was afraid to touch them, afraid of seeing eyes form in the glass emptiness, of seeing faces within that he would recognize.

Bottles lined one wall, and he knew that inside them was a substance that should be the Blood of the Roca. They glowed redly as he looked at them. Each Rocaan was supposed to bottle his own blood and store it in case "the religion lost its power," but none had done so—at least that was what the Fiftieth Rocaan had told Matthias.

None had done so because it was the Roca's blood that had special properties and no other.

Likewise the skin drums that hung from one pillar. The skin had been pulled tightly across them, and he supposed the Wise Ones believed it was the skin of the Roca, and the bones crossed in front of it his bones. Matthias had always had trouble reconciling that Secret with the entire idea of the Absorption: If the Roca had been Absorbed and now sat on the hand of God, why had his body remained? And who had thought of using its parts in sacred services?

"You promised you would hurry," Pausho said.

"I am hurrying," he said, realizing he hadn't moved. All of the Secrets had to be represented here. All of them, even though he couldn't see each one. Although he wouldn't know some of them if he saw them. The Fiftieth Rocaan had gone through several so quickly that all Matthias had was a single sentence, sometimes a fragment, and when he had questioned the Fiftieth Rocaan, the man had said simply: "There is no more."

*There is no more.*

But this room, this Vault, was proof that there was more. Much more.

"The Words," she said, and looked at the altar.

"I thought there would be histories here too," he said.

She sneered. He had never actually seen that expression on her face before—such full and utter contempt.

"There are several histories," she said. "Most are not written, and some we carry by oral tradition."

She didn't have to bring him here to tell him stories. He almost said that, and then he saw what she was looking at.

The tapestries.

One of the forms of history came from the tapestries.

"You will help me?" he asked, looking at them.

"If it benefits us," she said.

"How will you know?"

She shrugged. She wouldn't know any more than he would. How could she? She didn't know what they all were up against.

He did.

He would start with the Words. He had the other Words memorized, but he expected these to be different. Perhaps they would even explain the Secrets.

He took a step toward them, and as he did, his foot brushed against something. He looked down.

A ruby glimmered in the strange light. Odd that he hadn't seen it before, along the white, white floor. The ruby was the size of his fist and embedded deep into the floor's material.

He frowned. Somehow the touch of his boot had revealed the jewel to him. There were other jewels as well, set about a foot apart from each other, and all the same size. To his right was an emerald that seemed to have a green glow as he looked at it. Beyond that, a sapphire, and farther along, a diamond that seemed like a clear hole in the floor. The jewels continued to form a large ring around the alter. To his left there were two stones he had never seen before: a black stone that had a diamondlike brilliance and clarity, and a gray stone that also had a gem's brilliance. Then there was another diamond, and he realized that he was looking at a pattern: ruby, emerald, sapphire, diamond, gray stone, black stone. He wagered that there was another ruby on the other side of the altar.

He took another step forward, and more jewels revealed themselves. Only the pattern had shifted slightly. This jewel, smaller and rounder, was an emerald. The ruby was to his left, the sapphire to his right.

He glanced at Pausho who was watching him intently. Were

the stones guardians, somehow? Did they do something to the unwary?

They weren't doing anything to him, at least, nothing obvious.

He took another step forward, this time igniting a sapphire. The jewels that appeared closer and closer to the alter were smaller and smaller, but he realized that again, the pattern was repeating.

Everything worked its way out from the alter at the center.

He stepped on the black jewel, and then the gray jewel, and then he was at the altar itself.

It took him a moment to realize that the altar was made of stone as well. It wasn't the glowing white stone of the floor, nor was it the clear crystal brilliance of the jewels. It wasn't the living red rock that made up the mountain either, nor was it the shattered dull gray of the rock when it had been removed from the mountainside.

This rock was gray threaded with pink, like veins, running through it. Gold intermingled with the pink, and a touch of silver glinted. The stone had not been carved, at least that he could see. It seemed to have risen from the floor in the shape of an altar. A natural formation mimicked by the people around it? Or did the people somehow carve this and make it look natural?

He couldn't tell, but he was afraid to touch it.

"Who found this place?" he asked Pausho.

She crossed her arms. She looked even paler than she had before in the strange light. "The Roca left it for his second son."

The one who led the Tabernacle. The one who started Rocaanism. The one who caused the first big split.

"Have you changed anything?" he asked.

"We have added nothing," she said. "Not in all the years the Wise Ones have guarded this place."

"What are the jewels for?" he asked.

"I thought you came to see the Words," she said.

"I've come to see what'll help," he said.

"They won't." Her words were sharp and final, and he wasn't sure he believed them. But for the moment, he would take what he could. And what he could take was the Words.

He was the greatest scholar of Rocaanism alive, and had been even when the Tabernacle was filled with scholars. He had memorized the Words Written as well as the ones Unwritten. He could recite every ceremony from memory, and he knew the entire oral tradition—the sanctified oral tradition—that was approved by the Tabernacle.

It wasn't until he left the Tabernacle that he realized the countryside had a whole other oral tradition, one that he, and most of the scholars, had never heard of. Combine that with the Secrets, and he was the greatest living expert on Rocaanism.

But since he'd entered this room, he felt as if he knew nothing.

It would take years of scholarship to learn all of the room's Secrets. That bothered him. He had thought, when he had heard of the Vault, that he would see a small room filled with a copy of the Words and nothing else.

No tapestries and jewels and physical manifestations of the Secrets. Not even the Tabernacle had kept physical manifestations of the Secrets just lying around. Not even in the Rocaan's secret places or in the catacombs below.

It wasn't done.

The Secrets were the Secrets, and they had been jealously guarded from the beginning of Rocaanism itself.

He had always thought it was because they were the secret to power within the religion, but now he was beginning to wonder.

Could they have become Secrets to *prevent* their use?

"Are you going to read the Words, or merely stare at them from a distance?" Pausho asked.

He didn't want to answer her yet. The room itself was a revelation. His mind was working on it too hard.

"What do you use this room for?" he asked.

"Study," she said.

"And why do only the Wise Ones use it?"

"Because we are in charge of maintaining the Roca's legacy."

"The Roca's legacy," he said slowly. "That includes murdering babies?"

Red suffused her face, and then faded just as quickly. "Why does it always come back to that?"

"Because I was taught to believe in a beneficent Roca, not a man who slaughtered innocents."

"There are no innocents," she said, and her voice trembled. "If you do not believe me, read the Words."

"The Words say nothing—"

"Your Words," she said. "Read the Words of the man who was called the Roca. See how wrong your pathetic religion was."

He wasn't sure he wanted to. His hands were shaking. "You would follow the teachings of a man you do not consider wholly good?"

"No man is wholly good," Pausho said. "A man is just a man. It is for God to decide what is right and what is wrong."

"Is it?" Matthias asked.

"Just read," she said.

He couldn't delay this any longer, not even by arguing with her. He had reached the moment he wanted and it terrified him. The Fiftieth Rocaan had been right; what Matthias had seen in himself as unbelief was not. It was merely an intellectual refusal to take everything at face value. Underneath that refusal, he had believed.

And he was afraid the belief would be shattered.

He took a step closer, stopping in front of the altar. He put his hands on its sides, as if he were going to preach from it. The stone was warm, almost hot to the touch. There was more gold in it than he had thought.

Pausho moaned slightly and sank to the floor.

He looked at her. "Are you all right?"

She nodded, then bent her head and covered it with her left hand, as if she were not willing to watch him touch the most sacred document of her world.

The book in front of him was closed. It was made of leather and was very old. It wasn't a book in the formal sense—the pages weren't stitched together. It was more of a notebook, something in which to keep loose papers and protect them from loss.

He ran his hand along the cover. The leather felt soft beneath his fingers, well used, even though it looked new. Pausho had stopped watching him. She remained, huddled, as if she were protecting herself.

But he was all right. The gold in the altar had become the dominant color. It shone throughout the room. What a strange effect, he though. He had never known that stone could do such a thing.

He fingered the edge of the leather, felt the workmanship, then took a deep breath, and thought of the opening line of the Words:

*Blessings to all who gaze upon this page.*

He opened the leather cover, smoothed it back, and looked at the paper before him without actually reading it.

The paper was art in and of itself. Thick and textured, it felt good against his fingers. The Words were written in a distinctive hand, not copied meticulously, like the ones he had seen. Not made with an attention to each letter. No, these Words belonged to the writer. They were scrawled as if in haste, and they had smudges, blurs, that came from the writer's hand.

The writer had used his right hand, and had written from right to left, as was customary in Ancient Islander. Such a writer had to be very careful of his work or he would smear the words, as the writer had done in a few places.

Haste.

Not copies.

The hair rose on the back of his neck.

But the writing looked fresh. It almost seemed as if he could touch the ink and smear it himself.

But he didn't. He didn't touch more than the edge of the page. And he stared at it, realizing for the first time in his scholarly career that the Words he had studied had been in Islander, not Ancient Islander.

He felt like a fool.

It should have seemed so obvious.

But he had always known those Words were copies. He just hadn't realized that the shift in language, even if it was from one language that evolved into the next, would cause a shift in meaning. And he should have realized it, since he was fluent in both languages, the current and the dead.

He leaned forward, expecting to read the Ancient Islander version of the opening, which should have gone something like:

| *eral osselg a sail htecul ee furhsO*

He had so expected to see those words that it took him a moment to realize what he was reading.

| . . . *enitantsnoC ta/ irtimiD ta/ salohciN ta/ retluoC/ eN*

He stopped and translated it like a boy learning his first written language, and it changed nothing. The Words were still nothing like what he had expected.

I, Coulter, son of Nicholas, son of Dimitri, son of Constantine, do write this freely and of my own hand. I have learned the price of these powers which face me, and the price is not one which I would like my sons to pay.

But, it seems, I have bargained with the demons of this place, and for the riches they have given me, for the riches they have given the Isle, I will soon pay—not with my life, but with the mind of my son.

Would that I could change this path, but I cannot. My

sons, Alexander and Matthias, have already left this place, and I cannot reach them. They have embarked on a new journey for the Isle. I can only hope that when they receive these documents, they rethink my bargain with the souls of the mountain, and they turn away from it, pursuing life with their own wisdom, under their own guidance, forsaking this simplistic offer of power and return to the world as we knew it before the war.

Should my messenger, for whatever reason, be unable to deliver these papers to my sons, I implore whomever finds these documents to finish the messenger's task. For this, I sent you my Blessings, if one such as me can still voice Blessings.

For I am the man they call the Savior, be it for good or ill, and although it is widely believed that I died twenty summers ago, the demons have allowed me to live here in this cave ever since. . . .

Matthias stared at the beginning of that last section for a long moment, tears blurring his eyes. He had called himself a scholar, but he had never thought. He had always gone from the Tabernacle's teaching, and never from his own reason. And he should have seen the connection the very day he learned Ancient Islander.

. . ./acoR iii osselg moh en A

*For I am the man they call "Roca."*

"Savior" in Ancient Islander.

Roca.

He had always thought it a name, like Matthias, not a designation that had been given after the fact. The Roca had a real name, and it was Coulter, like the boy who had burned before Matthias on the mountainside. And this Coulter, the Roca, had named his son Matthias.

Good old names, Pausho had once said.

From the Cliffs of Blood.

Family names.

Found beneath a town once named Constantine, now called Constant.

And the Blessings were in there. Misquoted and changed. Ancient Islander was more delicate than Islander. Changing the order of words altered their meaning. A simple deletion of some words, a reordering of some others, and the phrase *I implore whomever finds these documents to finish the messenger's task. For this, I send you my Blessings . . .* became *Blessings to all who gaze upon this page.*

Pausho had not lied about the Words.

On one level, he had wanted her to. For if she had told the truth about the Words, perhaps she had told the truth about everything else.

Perhaps he should not have lived.

Perhaps he was the demon spawn after all.

But if he was evil, then what were the Fey?

He did not know yet, but he suspected he held the answer in his hands.

# THIRTY-SIX

THE guards walked ahead of him as Rugad made his way up the stairs. There were so many hidden passages through the oldest part of this palace, so many back ways from one area to another. There was war in the history of the Islanders, or at least an intrigue they were not admitting to.

There were many things these people were not admitting, and it irritated him. He had spent a long time with Tel, the Doppelgänger. Rugad had been good; he had stayed away from the bars of the cell, out of Tel's reach. Not that the Doppelgänger would have tried anything. Selia had made Tel terrified of touch, so much that Rugad might have to have her work on him again. Tel didn't even like the feel of the wall against his back, or the chair beneath his legs. Her Charm spell had been too potent; Rugad suspected that Tel might not like the feel of food against the inside of his mouth, and that would not be good. For right now, Rugad still needed Tel.

Tel had told him all the Tabernacle rituals. He had also told Rugad as much as he could remember about the religious history, and he quoted the religious text to him. It had seemed to Rugad to be a lot of gibberish that made sense only to the practitioners, but he had promised himself that he would mull over its information and see what he could learn.

But it wasn't easy. None of it was. He had thought to interview someone who knew something about the Islanders' religion, and then he would understand their magick.

He understood only that most of them were unaware they had any, and that the religious system seemed to be based on the idea that magick belonged to a select few, who chose not to use it—except, it seemed, in some sort of emergency: the kind that hadn't occurred in hundreds of years.

With his head, he indicated a passage for the guards to take. A few waited so that they could slip behind him, now that they were far from the Doppelgänger. Rugad had kept the guards at a distance during his conversation so that they wouldn't hear what the Doppelgänger had to tell him.

Not that it mattered.

The Doppelgänger's information had been oblique at best. Rugad suspected most of it was worthless.

His problem was that very little of what Tel had told him sounded like magick, at least as Rugad understood it. The Lights of Midday story sounded vaguely like an Enchanter's use of fire, but the way the ritual was celebrated suggested a more formal approach. Globes and lights did not apply to an Enchanter's magick, at least, not any that Rugad was familiar with.

No one had known the holy water's properties until one of their religious leaders had accidentally discovered it. There was nothing, at least in all the things that Tel had told Rugad, to suggest that holy water killed like poison. It had been used only to clean a sword, and that sword had been used to kill the first religious leader: the Roca.

Rugad slipped through the door and into the Great Hall. It was empty except for him and his guards. Sunlight streamed in from the southwest corner of the tall windows, even though the view through them showed the blackness from the fires in the central part of the Isle. He found it refreshing after the cobwebby dankness of the dungeons. They had an ancient smell of waste and blood, suggesting a use so heavy that not even time could dispel its memory.

But there was nothing in Islander history to suggest such use, not in the history that his Doppelgängers had discovered, nor in the history he had studied on Nye.

This place was a mystery to him, and the longer he was here, the more of a mystery it became.

He turned his back on the sun and stared at the wall of weapons. Swords lined this stone wall, swords from every period of Islander history. The oldest ones were nearest this door. There was even a space on the wall, burned in by centuries of light, that showed where the sword the Black Robe had stolen had come from. Rugad ran a finger along the emptiness. The stone was cool against his fingers. There were other swords nearby. He wondered if they were as sharp, as magickal.

There was only one way to see.

He turned to one of his guards. "I need a Red Cap," he said.

The guard bowed his head slightly, then turned sharply and left the hall. Rugad put his hands behind his back and studied the swords. Some were still rusty with blood. Others gleamed. All of them would have suggested a warlike people to him, if it weren't for the cursed religion. The religion that worshipped the sword.

He found it curious. The swords were everywhere in the Tabernacle and in the religion, yet only one place did it show up in the ritual. And that was the ritual of the Absorption.

That Absorption bothered Rugad. He had had Tel repeat the story several times. Rugad could almost recite the words himself. The Roca had faced "Soldiers of the Enemy" in the holiest of places, cleaned his sword with holy water, and then plunged it into his own stomach. He was Absorbed into the hand of God.

The wording of it all was curious, which was why he had Tel repeat the thing until Rugad had it memorized. He believed that there was something important in the details, something he needed to know.

When the Roca asked for God's ear, he begged for
safety for his people. Yet they were besieged by enemies,
and it appeared that God did not listen.

So that was the war that Rugad had noted, but what kind of war, who the enemies were, and what happened to them was unclear. Also the date of this Roca was unclear. Tel had an idea of how many generations had passed since the Roca lived, but those generations were marked by the religious leader, the Rocaan, and as Tel pointed out, a few of those leaders had died within a year of getting their term, while others had been Rocaan for more than forty years. So even though the Fey had killed the Fifty-second Rocaan, it wasn't quite accurate to say that fifty-two generations had passed.

Rugad doubted this palace was fifty-two generations old,

although some of the swords looked that old. For the first time since leaving Galinas, he felt out of his depth. He knew the history of the Galinas continent, of its lands and its peoples. He even knew Blue Isle's history for the past two hundred years or so, but that gave no real clue to the Blue Isle he needed to understand.

That Blue Isle was lost to the mists of time.

The Roca brought the enemies to the holiest of places and there he asked God to strike them down. When God did not, the Roca thought to strike them down himself, but he thought, "Would that mean that I believe I am better than God? For if God is not willing to do this thing, He in his wisdom must have a reason. And I am but a lowly creation, not a creator. I do not have the ability to see more than my small corner of the Isle. I cannot even see what is across the water. I cannot see God in his holy place. I cannot see the beasts in the trees, I am lowly, unworthy of making decisions for my God."

Some of this seemed added. It had the feel of ritual to Rugad, the feel of mythmaking for the sake of mythmaking. He had heard so much of it from other cultures, although none of the stories were quite this strange.

Would a man actually have those thoughts? And how would posterity know of it?

So the Roca ordered his men to stand at his side, their blades out but useless. And when he was approached by his enemies in that holy place, he welcomed them and bid them to wait until he cleaned his sword. Then he took the water left him by a fallen comrade and cleaned the blade.

Rugad had queried Tel repeatedly on that point. The water that the Roca had used to clean the blade had been holy water, at least that was what the Tabernacle said. Yet the holy water, the thing that had killed an entire invasion force of Fey, had come not from this Roca, but from his fallen comrade.

Rugad found this curious.

As he cleaned his blade, the Roca told this to his men. He said, "Without water, a man dies. A man's body makes

water. His blood is water. A child is born in a rush of
water. Water keeps us clean. It keeps us healthy. It keeps
us alive. It is when we are in water that we are closest to
God."

A man in danger did not stop to explain his actions in cryptic
terms to his followers. A man in danger did not have time to stop,
clean his sword, and then ram it into his abdomen.

Rugad frowned, and peered at the swords in front of him. The
whole thing made no sense. This was what had disturbed him as
he spoke to Tel.

And then there was that statement about water: *Without water, a man dies.* But here, on Blue Isle, water killed.

At least it killed the Fey.

And there was nothing in this ceremony that explained such a
phenomenon. If holy water killed the enemy, then why didn't the
great Roca turn the water on the enemy?

Rugad swore softly. He hated Islander magick. It was based
on subtlety and denial. The Fey had embraced their magick.
The Islanders had suppressed theirs, making each statement cryptic, each action fraught with meaning that no one seemed to
understand.

He walked to the floor-to-ceiling windows, hands clasped behind his back. The light was pouring in, catching the bubbles in
the glass.

He continued to review the Absorption ceremony, wishing
that insight he had just had would come to the forefront of his
brain. There was so much to understand.

But his men said, "Holy Sir, when a man stays too long
in water, he dies."

There was death in the water, but that wasn't about holy water. That described drowning. As Rugad understood holy water,
even a simple touch killed. So therefore, a man could not stay
"too long in water."

And the Roca looked at them all with great pity
in his eyes. "A man dies only when he is not pure
enough to sit at the feet of God. When you touch
water," the Roca said to them all, "you touch the
Essence of God."

That was the key. There, a clear announcement of magick. But Rugad did not understand exactly what it meant. The Fey, in the eyes of the Islanders, were not pure enough to sit at the feet of God. Yet the Roca had died with a holy-water-cleaned sword.

Wasn't he pure enough?

The Islanders said he was Absorbed into the Hand of God, not the Feet of God.

Was that a crucial detail?

Rugad felt a slight headache build between his eyes. This was so convoluted. He would have to hand Tel and his descriptions to the Spell Warders, and see what they could come up with.

He would ask them to focus on that last phrase: *When you touch water, you touch the Essence of God.*

The Essence of God.

Did water grant power? And if so, what kind of power? And was it all water or merely one type of water? Was he making a mistake thinking it was just holy water?

He didn't know. That was the difficulty of it all. He didn't know. And he needed to.

Tel told him that phrase was the end of the direct quotes. The rest was a tacked-on section of the service, added by a Rocaan years down the road. But Tel didn't know which Rocaan or how much later these last words were added:

We allow no enemies here. The Roca has protected us from all that would threaten us. We shall not die by the Sword. Instead, we live by it.

And a sword had killed Fey as efficiently as the holy poison had. Water and swords were both mentioned in this service, and Rugad knew both had a magickal property.

He wondered how many other magickal properties were named in the service, and he simply did not understand them. Or if there were other properties in the other services, the ones he had not memorized.

He snapped his fingers without turning from the window. Another guard appeared at his side.

"Tell Landre that I want him and his Spell Warders to meet me here," Rugad said.

The guard nodded and then left. Rugad frowned at the window. Maybe the Warders could parse out this convoluted system. They thought in magickal terms much more theoretical than his own.

He could pick out the magick phrases, but not their meanings. The Warders might be able to figure it all out.

He hoped.

They didn't have a lot of time.

# THIRTY-SEVEN

THEY hadn't gotten very far.

Luke sprawled facedown in the rich dirt of some poor farmer's cornfield. The ground smelled loamy and fertile, and the corn rustled faintly above him.

Corn sprawled one row over. He faced the opposite direction, and he slowly turned his head from side to side as if he expected to see something.

Neither of them looked up. Not any more. Once had been enough.

Con had spotted the birds first, coming from the north in one dark clump. He had pointed at them, and Luke's heart had stopped. They were still sitting behind the ruined chimney, as exposed as two people got, and they had nowhere to go. The birds would see them as soon as the flock was directly overhead.

The Fey Infantry still marched down the road. Only this was a later group, and not as well organized. Obviously they had orders about where to report, but several were veering toward the sides of the road, as if taking stock.

Luke had nodded toward the corn, and they both dove into it. Luke landed on his back, and he watched through the long green leaves as the sky darkened with birds. Gulls and sparrows and robins all flying together. Birds—real birds—never did that.

These were Fey.

They were flying toward the fire.

He had closed his eyes in horror, and Con had hit him. "They'll see us if they look."

Luke made himself concentrate. He grabbed dirt, rubbed it in his hair, and made Con do the same. Then they rolled over to hide their skin and shiny faces. Luke had put more dirt on his for good measure. Con had done the same. Then, somehow, Con had turned, so that he would be able to see any small Fey creature that snuck up on them from behind.

And there the two of them remained for what seemed like hours. The sun had moved across the sky, and the shadows were growing long. The Fey continued to march past, only now they were rowdy, laughing, all discipline gone.

Luke didn't know what that meant. He had never encountered undisciplined Fey before.

The air was thick and warmer than it had been before. Small whitish gray flakes were falling from the sky.

Ash.

Something was burning, and he suspected it was closer than the fire he had started.

The Fey shouts were growing louder. There were screams nearby—female screams. Con started to move, and Luke grabbed his leg.

"We can't do anything," Luke whispered. He knew what was going on. The Fey had the farm family. The woman's screams were repetitive, hideous. A man shouted, hoarse, in protest. "They'll kill us too."

"Those people aren't dead," Con whispered.

"They will be."

The woman's scream rose and broke off into a sob. A child started to cry. Then another woman's voice broke the silence, and it sounded older, more resigned.

Luke buried his face in the dirt. Laughter echoed around him, and he tried to block it out, the laughter mingled with the screams. The man was still shouting: "Leave them alone! Leave them! Take me."

*Take me.*

Luke's father had said the same thing once.

The man repeated it over and over, and finally stopped, mid-word, as if someone had shut him up. Or killed him.

Con shifted. Luke tightened his grasp. Fey were nearby. Luke could hear their boots on the soft ground.

"He wants us to burn it all?" one of the Fey asked, in his native language.

Con froze. Luke didn't know if he understood Fey or not.

"All of it. Every last bit," another Fey answered.

"We've never done this before."

"No one's ever destroyed a cache before."

"That's not true," a third voice said. "My grandfather told me—"
And the voices faded away.

"They're going to burn what?" Con whispered.

"Where did you learn Fey?" Luke asked.

"Tabernacle requires—required—it," Con said. "I'm not real good."

"They're going to burn everything."

"Even the crops?"

Luke didn't know how to answer. Scavenger had told him it would never come to this. But Luke had to assume the worst.

Con heard the answer in Luke's silence. "We have to get out of here."

"They'll see us."

"We have the sword."

"Against an army?" Luke asked.

"We have no other choice," Con whispered.

They didn't. It was either burn to death in this cornfield or flee for their lives. There weren't any more birds overhead. They could try it. Maybe the Fey were so preoccupied with the farm family and the fires that they wouldn't see Luke and Con.

"Turn around," Luke whispered, "and on my signal, we head for the creek."

The woman screamed again, a sharp piercing wail. They didn't have much time. Con turned slowly, careful not to hit any plants. He rose to a crouch, and so did Luke.

Their gazes met and held for a moment. Then Luke nodded, and they ran.

# THIRTY-EIGHT

ARIANNA stepped outside, and blinked at the light. It was so bright that her eyes teared. Maybe there had been a bit of damage from the globe, or maybe it had simply made her eyes sensitive. She resisted the urge to rub them.

Coulter was beside her. He had taken her arm to help her up the long flight of stairs to the mouth of the cave. His hand had been gentle on her elbow, and he removed it the moment they stepped outside. She wished he hadn't. She didn't know how to ask him to touch her again.

Gift was slightly ahead of her, looking at the sky as if it gave him answers. Scavenger had gone to the edge of the platform and was looking down. Leen remained beside Gift, as if she could give him support just by standing next to him.

"Ari." Gift's voice had command in it, something she had never heard from him before. "Come here."

She glanced at Coulter. He was frowning at Gift. She took a deep breath, about to say something rude—no one had ever spoken to her that way before, except maybe her father—when she thought the better of it.

"What are you thinking about?" Coulter asked softly.

She smiled at him, and shook her head. Gift turned to her.

"Ari?" he asked, the note of command gone from his voice.

"Coming," she said.

There was a breeze, and it felt good against her face. She hadn't realized how much she disliked being in that cave. She took a few steps and stopped beside her brother, away from the swords, on the center of the platform.

"Shadowlands come out of Vision," Gift said. "Anyone with Vision can make them, and they grow better with practice. The stronger your Vision, the stronger the Shadowlands."

"Like our grandfather's?" Ari asked. It was the only one she had heard of, the Shadowlands in which all the Fey had lived on Blue Isle for decades.

"Actually," Coulter said from behind her, "it was nearly destroyed when your grandfather died. Gift rebuilt it."

She looked at Gift. A slight color stained his cheeks. He shrugged, and seemed to pretend that it didn't matter. "You know how Vision works," he said. "No one else can really see the magick. It's the same with a Shadowlands. But you can watch the formation. It'll show you a few things."

"All right," she said, uncertain how she would ever use a Shadowlands. Then she remembered one of the first rules Solanda had ever taught her: learn everything. You never knew when something might come in handy.

Gift closed his eyes and extended his left hand. Then he raised his right. Between his fingers a small box formed out of air. It rose from his hands and expanded as it did so, flying away from them, and growing until its black edges looked big enough to hold living beings. Then it vanished.

Gift raised his left hand next to his right, and tiny lights, almost invisible in the bright sun, formed near his fingertips. The lights blinked and rose, spinning in a circle. He opened his eyes slightly and stuck a hand through.

His hand vanished.

Then he pulled his hand back out, and smiled at her. "Done," he said.

"That looked easy," she said.

He shrugged.

"But how did you make it vanish?"

"Shadowlands are supposed to be invisible," he said.

"It wasn't at first."

"I made it that way so you could see it," he said. "That's how you should practice. Then, when you're sure of what you're doing, make them invisible from the start."

She frowned at him, still uncomfortable with the whole idea. Shadowlands. She had heard of it all her life, and never really understood it. Her father had said that most Fey used it as a bivouac while fighting on foreign battlefields, but that the Fey on Blue Isle had settled in theirs, living there when Fey never had before.

Her mother, according to his father, had not respected the decision to live in Shadowlands.

"We need to go in the Shadowlands before they start those experiments again," Leen said.

Gift smiled at her. His face seemed both foreign and familiar when he did that, as if it became more Fey. Yet Arianna saw bits of herself in it. She had never had this odd feeling with Sebastian. They had always been two separate beings.

"You go first," Gift said.

"You don't need a guard to go first in a Shadowlands you created," Leen said, and it took a moment for Arianna to realize that she was joking.

She reached her hand forward, placing it in the exact center of the circle of lights. For a moment, the lights flared, then the circle moved faster.

"I don't think—" she started, and then the circle opened. "There we go," she said and stepped inside.

The lights continued to whirl rapidly for a moment and then stopped.

Leen had completely disappeared.

"How does that work?" Arianna asked.

Gift smiled. "It's rather like we carve a place out of the sky. You can't make a Shadowlands inside something solid, like inside a rock. It must be near air. But even if you have a little bit of space, you can house an entire army."

"I don't understand," she said.

"And I don't understand why you Shift and I don't," Gift said. "Do you?"

No, of course she didn't understand. She wasn't raised Fey. Couldn't he remember that?

A bit of her irritation must have shown in her eyes, because Gift shook his head. "You'll understand after you do it," he said.

"Are you so sure I can?" she asked.

"You're a Visionary," he said. "All Visionaries can, even the least of them. Some just can't make them big enough to use."

"And you think I'm one of the least," she said.

He rolled his eyes. "I didn't say that."

"You didn't have to," she said.

He sighed. "I'm not trying to pick a fight with you, Arianna."

"Really?" she said. "It seems like you are."

Scavenger came over. He was standing beside her, arms crossed. "You're the one with the uncontrollable temper," he said to Arianna. He reached toward the circle of lights, then pulled his hand back. "I hope you made this for nonmagickal beings," he said to Gift.

"Leen went in."

"She's Infantry. She'll have magick some day."

Gift took a deep breath, as if he were trying to control his own temper. "Try it," he said.

Scavenger put a fist through the lights. They rotated quickly, just as they had done for Leen. Before he went inside, he turned to Coulter.

"The armies haven't moved," he said.

Arianna glanced behind her. Coulter was close, leaning against the edge of the rocks. She got the distinct impression that he had been watching her. Her heart gave a slight lurch.

"Thanks," he said to Scavenger. Scavenger went inside.

Gift glared at Arianna, then shook his head, as if he had thought better of fighting with her. He followed Scavenger into Shadowlands. Arianna looked at the circle of lights. The Circle Door, they called it. Except for that small rotating circle of light, the Shadowlands were invisible. It was impossible to tell that three Fey were inside.

"Why are you so hard on him?" Coulter asked softly. "He was trying to help you."

"I don't need help," Arianna said.

"He knows things you don't."

"And I know things he doesn't."

Coulter nodded. He pushed off from the rock and came toward her. It startled her, as it did each time, to look down at him.

He stopped within inches of her, and ran a hand along her cheek. His fingers were warm. "I think you get angry at him whenever he tries to get close to you."

Her skin burned where his fingers touched. "That's not true."

"Then why do you fight him so?"

She took a step back, and put her hand where his had been just a moment before. "I don't."

"You do," Coulter said. "You're the only family he's got. You and your father. He doesn't have anyone else."

"Is that my fault?" Arianna asked.

"You could have some compassion for him," Coulter said.

"I'm not good at compassion."

He smiled. "Sure you are. You've just never been taught to value it, which is odd, since your father seems to have a lot of it."

"Solanda said that compassion was for the weak."

He nodded once, smile gone. "The Shape-Shifter."

"Yes," she said.

"Well, that Shape-Shifter kidnapped me and brought me to the Fey Shadowlands, then abandoned me there. I spent the first five years of my life unsupervised and unloved. That's where lack of compassion gets you." He spit out those last words. She had never heard him so harsh. She wasn't sure she liked it.

"That's where it got you," she said. "What did it get Solanda?"

"Nothing that I can see," he said. "No one listened to her about my abilities, and she didn't take the time to raise me, not like she did you."

"Are you jealous of that?" Ari asked.

He shook his head. "Jealous that I wasn't raised by the most coldhearted of the Fey? That's what they call Shifters. Is it true?"

Her lower lip trembled. She didn't want Coulter to be angry at her. She didn't like it. "Is that what you think?" she whispered.

"I think that of Solanda," he said. "I think it could become true of you if you're not careful. She trained you well."

She bit her lower lip. It still trembled. She whirled away from him, not wanting him to see how upset he made her. She flailed for the Circle Door, found it, and stuck her hand in.

The interior was the same temperature as outside. Somehow she had thought it would be colder.

Then Coulter grabbed her arm, and pulled it from the door. He turned her around. "I don't think you're like Solanda, Ari," he said softly and caressed her face again. He moved her hair back, stroked her cheek, then touched a thumb to her chin, bringing her head down.

He stared at her for a moment, then, gently, he kissed her.

It was nothing like the kiss he'd given her when he had traveled her father's Link and found her, trapped inside herself. That kiss had felt real.

This one was.

He explored her mouth for a moment, then pulled her close, cradling the back of her skull with his left hand, his right arm wrapped around her waist. He felt wonderful, warm and good, strong, even though she knew the events of the morning had left him weak.

She tilted her head toward his, tasting him—

"How very interesting."

The voice belonged to Gift.

Coulter jumped back, looking up at a point over Ari's head. Ari didn't move that quickly. She didn't want anyone to know how flustered she felt. But her heart was pounding hard, and she didn't think it was because her brother surprised her.

"Gift," Coulter said, and then stopped. His face was bright red.

Arianna turned. Her brother's head appeared to be floating in the air. The circle of lights rotated rapidly around him.

"You don't approve?" she asked, her voice flat.

He looked from her to Coulter, then back to her. "I thought peasants weren't supposed to do that to royalty in this country," Gift said.

Coulter's flush deepened.

That, more than anything, upset Arianna. "How would you know?" she snapped. "You were raised in a little box, among people known for their incompetence."

"Ari—" Coulter started.

"Don't chastise me," she said. "It's time someone stood up for you. Gift treats you like dirt, and you treat him like the most precious thing in the world." She turned her head and glared at Gift. "Our parents think you're gentle. They haven't seen how mean you really can be."

The color leached from Gift's face. She suppressed a smile. A point for her side.

"Now get out of my way. I want to see what your precious Shadowlands looks like."

He disappeared into the circle of light. Before she followed him, she turned to Coulter, and this time it was her fingers that brushed his cheek.

Then she let herself smile. "I think you're tremendous," she said.

His cheeks were still bright red. "I'm sorry—"

"Don't be," she said. "Gift's just jealous." And then she realized what the problem was, what the fighting was all about.

Gift was jealous.

And so was she.

She was afraid she'd lose her father to her brother. How petty and small. She should trust her father more than that. And her brother, too. Gift had been trying to help her, to teach her, and she had snapped at him.

She would never learn.

"You all right?" Coulter asked softly.

She nodded. "I've got to go inside now."

"I know," he said.

She smiled at him one last time, then stuck her hand in the Circle Door again. The lights rotated and flared, and she saw an opening before her. Behind it was grayness. She stepped inside, and the door closed behind her.

She was standing on nothing. At least, that's what it looked like. Leen was sitting on the same nothingness, her arms wrapped around her knees. Scavenger was leaning against something— apparently a wall—and had his eyes closed. He was snoring softly.

Gift was glaring at Arianna.

She ignored him for a moment. This place was nothing like what she had imagined it to be. She had always thought of Shadowlands as a vibrant place—after all, the Fey were vibrant people— but it wasn't. It was as it had seemed in Gift's hand, a box made out of air.

Arianna crouched and touched the floor. It felt solid. It wasn't really invisible; it was gray, the kind of gray the sky got on stubbornly overcast days. No rain, but no sun either. And the gray was almost white, almost clear, but not quite.

Then she looked at her hand. It looked pale in here, not the brown color that had so irritated her, but not the light color of her father's skin either. It was as if the brown had been leached out of her. Her clothes were the same, a monotone version of themselves.

Everything external felt muted. The floor wasn't hot or cold, but the same temperature as the air around her. The slight wind she had felt outside was gone. And the light seemed fake, not like the light from candles, but more like the light inside the cavern she had just left, a light that came from a source she couldn't identify.

"You lived here?" she blurted at all three of them.

Leen just nodded wearily.

"It wasn't here," Gift said. "It was a different Shadowlands."

"But are they all like this? Such dead places?"

"We had buildings," Leen said, her voice flat. "And the Domestics always tried to have gardens."

"And colors." Gift looked at her. Leen's eyes filled with tears. She bowed her head, so that her forehead touched the top of her knees.

Ari felt her heart lurch. "I'm sorry," she said. "I didn't mean to bring back bad memories."

"They weren't all bad," Gift said. "Shadowlands was all I knew for a long, long time."

"Coulter got the Overs when he left," Scavenger said. He hadn't been asleep after all. He was watching her.

"The Overs?"

"He couldn't take all the colors and the smells and the sensations of the real world. It drives some Fey insane after too long in a Shadowlands. Shows how strong he really is that he recovered."

No smells. That was what was bothering her. The air had no smell.

What an awful, awful place.

"Sit down," Gift said. "We're going to be here a while."

"You think this'll protect us?" Arianna asked.

"Shadowlands is supposed to protect you from everything," Scavenger said.

"Everything from the outside," Gift said.

"Except the death of Shadowlands' creator," Scavenger said.

"Except that," Gift said, and his face looked haunted.

"You think I can make one of these?" Arianna asked. She sat down beside her brother. He didn't move away. That she saw as a good sign.

"Yes," he said, but added nothing else.

"Look," she said, "I'm sorry. I don't know that comes over me sometimes."

He glanced at her sideways, his blue eyes measuring her. "Coulter is very vulnerable."

The change of subject surprised her. "Coulter?"

"Don't take any advantage of him. His emotions have always been fragile, even though he would deny it."

"You think I kissed him?" Arianna asked, voice rising.

"That's what I saw."

"He kissed me," she said. "Twice."

"Twice?"

"No one's taking advantage of anyone," Arianna said.

"I would hope not."

She let out a deep sigh. "My father wants us to get along. Can't we put all of this aside?"

"I won't let anyone hurt Coulter," Gift said.

"Except you," Arianna snapped.

Gift glared at her. "You wouldn't understand."

"Oh, I think I do."

"He let Sebastian get hurt."

"By closing your Link?" Arianna asked.

Gift nodded.

"And you're so all-powerful that you could have saved him?"

"I would have."

"And let my father die."

Her words echoed in the silence. Gift hadn't been there. She had. The Black King's guards were going after her father, swords out. He wouldn't have lived through that attack. Sebastian had saved his life, just as he had saved hers on the mountainside.

"No," Gift said, softly. "I'd have found some other way."

"There wasn't time to find another way," she said. "I was there. You do a discredit to Sebastian, thinking he couldn't survive without you. He did just fine, and I suspect he's still doing fine."

"You don't know either?"

"I closed my Links too," she said, not willing to tell him it was on Coulter's advice. He was angry enough at Coulter. "Being invaded that way once was plenty, thank you."

Gift shuddered, and she remembered someone telling her he had experienced the same thing.

"It's not me you're mad at, is it?" she asked. "You're just mad, at everyone, for what's happened."

Gift didn't answer her.

"It's the Black King you should be mad at," she said. "He's the one that caused everything. If he hadn't arrived, your adopted family would still be alive, Sebastian would be with me, and Coulter would never have kissed me."

"Can't change the past," Gift said.

"No," she said softly. "We can't. But we can change the future."

He was silent for a long moment. Scavenger had his eyes partly closed, but Arianna knew he was watching them both. Leen hadn't moved from her position, and Ari wondered if she was crying.

Strange to think of someone as strong as Leen crying.

"I guess we can," Gift said. He looked at Ari and nodded. "I guess we can." He took a deep breath. "So, do you think my mother's plan will work?"

"It might," Ari said, glad they were turning their attention to something useful, something that would help them survive, something that would keep her mind off Coulter and that gentle kiss. "But let's see if we can come up with something else, just in case hers fails. What do you think?"

"I think that's a good idea," Gift said, and smiled at her.

She smiled back. They would keep fighting, she knew it. But that was because they were both strong, and their emotions seemed to mirror each other's. But as long as they could keep coming back to this place, and learn to work together, they would be fine.

They needed each other. Even she could see that.

Maybe her mother was right; maybe there was enough strength in this group—if they all worked together.

It was time they found out.

# THIRTY-NINE

NICHOLAS stood in front of the globes. There were dozens, maybe a hundred of them, sitting on shelves. The globes were all sizes, but they all looked different from the ones used in the Tabernacle. They all looked like the ones that had nearly blinded his children.

"Are they inside Shadowlands yet?" he asked Adrian, without turning. Adrian was standing at the mouth of the cave, watching everything.

"Everyone except Coulter. He's gone to the edge of the platform."

"Good," Nicholas said. He reached for the globe he had touched before. His hand hovered over it, and then he pulled back. "Is the door closed?"

"Yes," Adrian said. This time Nicholas looked. Adrian was walking away from the mouth of the cave.

Nicholas ran a hand through his hair. Adrian stopped beside him. "Where do you want me to start?"

"I don't," Nicholas said. "I've been thinking. We know that the globe affects those with Fey blood. But what if one of these things affects its user?"

Adrian stared at the walls, at the shelves, at all the items on them. "Then we die," he said softly.

"That's right," Nicholas said. "We do. And our side gains nothing. No knowledge, no idea what happened. They'll come back in here, and you and I will be dead."

"Our bodies might even be gone," Adrian said.

Nicholas smiled grimly. "I thought of that too."

"But we have to try. We have to see what's here," Adrian said.

"Yes." Nicholas took a deep breath. "Only, I'm going to try. You're going to watch. You'll be the witness."

"I think it would be wiser, sire," Adrian said with his head bowed, "if I tried each of these things. Then I would die, and you would continue to live. My life is more expendable than yours."

Nicholas grinned at him. That was how they had both been raised. The King before all else. Long live the King. Only that wasn't true any more. The King was the king of nothing. If he could keep his children alive, they had a chance of ruling Blue Isle and half the world.

"Actually," Nicholas said, "both of us are expendable. Forgive me, Adrian, but it's true. And that's why we're here."

"Sire—"

"Stop," Nicholas said. "We're comrades right now. My title matters only in one thing: I am a direct descendent of the Roca. Are you?"

'Adrian stared at him. "My family goes back generations."

"All families do," Nicholas said. "But how many can you trace?"

"Not that many," Adrian said softly.

Nicholas crouched in front of the shelves and stared at the slightly larger globes. He could see his own face reflected in them, distorted and changed by the globe's outer side. Blue eyes, blond hair turning gray, cheeks that once were round and now had become thin with constant exercise and insufficient food. Had the Roca looked like this? It was impossible to tell from the tapestries. Although, in those, he had had long flowing blond locks.

Nicholas's silence seemed to unnerve Adrian. "Sire, if you're thinking that you should do this, you're wrong. I'm the logical one—"

"I'm the logical one," Nicholas said. "If our understanding of this place is correct, these items were left by the Roca. And if they were his, they probably required some sort of power on his part. There has to be a reason that he made the admonition to his sons: one to head the country and the other to head the religion."

"Yes, but the Rocaan never was a direct descendent of the Roca. The Rocaan couldn't have a wife, couldn't have children."

"Later," Nicholas said. "Not at first. So much changed, Adrian. That I do know. What if the Secrets, what if Rocaanism, was supposed to be like the monarchy, led only by someone with the Roca's blood?"

"We can't know that," Adrian said.

"Not with any certainty," Nicholas said. "But it seems logical."

Adrian frowned. "I don't remember anything like that in the Words."

"Neither do I," Nicholas said. "Except for the admonition about the jobs for his sons. That's enough for me."

"I disagree," Adrian said.

Nicholas smiled at him. "It doesn't matter," he said. "I'm going to be the one to handle these items. You're going to be the one who watches. And we're not going to argue further about it."

"I thought you said we were comrades."

"We are," Nicholas said. "But if you were more proficient with a knife and I was more proficient with a sword, you would handle the knife fights and I would handle the sword fights and we wouldn't disagree."

"This isn't the same thing," Adrian said.

"Isn't it?" Nicholas asked.

Adrian stared at him for a moment. Nicholas stared right back. This one was too important to budge on. This one could mean the survival of the entire troop.

"All right," Adrian said. "But after you've manipulated the object, give it to me. We need to know if those of us whose heritage isn't as lustrous can work these items as well."

Nicholas nearly disagreed. But that point was as logical as his.

And if he were arguing logic, which he was, he couldn't change simply because it didn't suit him. He had meant what he said. He wasn't trying to be King here. He wanted to work beside Adrian, not command him.

"All right," Nicholas said. "I'm going to start with the globes because we know what they do, sort of. But I'm curious as to whether the longer I hold it, more things happen."

"And I want to know if I touch it, I'll get the same result."

Nicholas grinned at him. He liked Adrian. The man had good sense.

Then Nicholas took a deep breath and grabbed the globe he had picked up before. Light flared against his hand, then shot around the cavern. The light of a hundred suns, so bright that it should have been blinding, but it was not. It seemed to fill him, become him, shot from him, and not just from his hand. Adrian watched the light, his skin almost white, reflecting the light back, but he made no attempt to cover his eyes.

After a moment, he pointed toward the jewels.

They sparkled. All of them, even the black ones, and the light broke off into a thousand tiny pinpoints, all of which shot into an individual jewel which then absorbed the light, and dispersed it into a spectrum. The colors of the lights differed according to the colors of the jewels, and not logically either. The ruby did not create a series of red lights.

The globe in Nicholas's hand grew warm. The light continued to flow from it, and he felt the power of it. It felt as if it were flowing from him, as if it were pulling something from him, but it wasn't exhausting him. Instead, it seemed to be filling him with the same light.

He tightened his grip on the globe, and the light narrowed. It flowed in a steady stream toward the wall of the cavern. A small hole burned in the place where the light touched.

Then Nicholas loosened his grip and the light widened. The hole smoked, but grew no deeper. Adrian stared at it, then went over to it, touched it, and moved his finger away as if he'd been burned.

The globe flared bright, brighter, and brighter still, and then went out. The heat slowly dissipated.

Nicholas was shaking as he set the globe back in its place.

"Wait," Adrian said. "Let's see what happened to it."

It took Nicholas's eyes a moment to adjust to normal light. The globe looked different from its fellows. It was darker, and it looked scorched inside, as if something had burned up. But as much as Nicholas peered at the other globes, he couldn't see anything that looked as if it could burn. He couldn't see anything inside the globes at all.

"Now me," Adrian said.

"Wait," Nicholas said.

He went over to the jewels. The strange lights they had given off were gone, but the jewels seemed brighter somehow, cleaner, as if the light had polished them and given them brilliance.

He didn't touch them. Not yet. He wasn't ready to.

"All right," he said to Adrian.

Adrian picked up one of the globes. Light flared from it as well. It lit the cave, but didn't seem as bright to Nicholas, although he wondered if that was because he wasn't holding the globe. Maybe it didn't seem as bright to an Islander who wasn't near it.

"Wow," Adrian said.

The light touched the jewels, and they absorbed it again. The entire scenario played out, just as it had for Nicholas, and then the light faded. The second globe also looked dark and scorched.

They looked ruined.

Nicholas picked up his globe. It didn't flare again. Somehow he had expected that. The globes could be used only once, and he had no idea how to make new ones.

Weapons, yes, but a limited supply. And not something that could be used with his children around.

Adrian stared at it for a moment, then looked at Nicholas. "Swords?"

Nicholas shook his head. He wasn't ready for those yet, the weapon that looked like a weapon, the holy symbol that represented precisely what it was. Instead, he went to the silver bowls for the Feast of the Living.

They were as old as the globes, older perhaps, judging from the quality of the silver work. But strangely, they weren't tarnished. They gleamed as brightly as they would have if they had just been polished.

It had been decades since he had experienced a Feast. He could barely remember it. Something served with green ota leaves and blessed with holy water. The Danite conducting the service had picked up the full bowl and spoken a Blessing over it, but it had been a special Blessing, the wording of which was lost to Nicholas's memory.

"Have you ever participated in a Feast of the Living?" he asked Adrian.

Adrian came up beside him. His right hand, the one in which

he had held the globe, was tightened into a fist. "No," he said. "I hadn't heard of it until you mentioned it."

Nicholas nodded. No help there. All he could hope for was that his traitorous memory would come up with the words.

He picked up the bowl as the Danite had done so many years ago, cupping it in both hands and raising it above his head. He cringed as he did so, expecting something to happen.

But nothing did.

He lowered the bowl. "I don't suppose you see any ota leaves here, do you?" he asked.

Adrian shook his head. "I don't even know what they are," he said.

Nicholas had never seen the plant, but the leaves were distinctive. Cooked, they shrank to one-eighth their size and had a slightly sweet taste. Uncooked, they were tangy and made him think that if the color green had a taste, that would be it.

They were considered a delicacy at the palace, and they were brought in from the Cliffs of Blood every spring, to be served with a special sweet sauce. Their season was short, only a week or so, and they were one of his favorites.

Strange that he would remember that part. The fact that ota leaves were used in the ceremony. Green ota leaves. There were purple ota leaves as well, but they were from later in the season and weren't nearly as flavorful.

He wondered if the bowl needed its leaves to make the magick work. Just as the vials were nothing without holy water.

He set the bowl back down. Then sighed and looked at the shelves. The small bottles filled with the reddish liquid unnerved him. The closer he got, the more it looked like blood.

He wasn't ready to touch the jewels. Their brilliance hadn't faded. It seemed as if the light from the globe had enhanced them permanently.

He went farther back, past the tapestries. The air was cooler here and damper. It almost felt like a cave. Leaning in a corner, not on a shelf, was a group of small dolls. He crouched. They appeared to be made of glass, only this glass did not have the flaws the other glass had. The dolls' glass was clear and perfectly formed, although he couldn't tell if the dolls were meant to be male or female. They was very small, about the size of his hand. And they didn't correspond with any part of the religion that he knew of.

He picked the nearest one up, wondering if a child had left it here, centuries ago. Then the doll stirred within his hand. Its eyes blinked and it smiled at him.

He dropped it. It cried out—at least he thought it cried out—and he moved swiftly, catching it before it hit the stone floor.

It would have shattered then, and he would have lost all he could have learned from it.

Its tiny hand clutched his little finger.

His mouth was dry. "What are you?"

It didn't answer, but its face, which had been clear glass a moment before, was now a light gold, like skin too long in the sun. Its lips were pink, its nose well formed, and its eyes as blue as his. It had blond hair and round cheeks.

The mouth was moving. It was speaking, but he couldn't hear it.

And then he realized that what he was seeing was *behind* the glass, not part of the glass itself. It was trapped inside the glass, just as those poor souls who got trapped in the lights that the Fey used.

Only this creature did not give off light. It gave off nothing at all. But it seemed to have some control of its glass prison.

Adrian had come up behind him silently. Nicholas felt, rather than heard, him arrive.

"What is that?" Adrian asked.

"I don't know," Nicholas said. It twisted in his hand to look up at him. Could it hear him although he couldn't hear it?

He didn't know that either.

"What are you?" he asked again.

It gazed at him solemnly for a moment, then let go of his little finger and pointed at the jars filled with red liquid. Nicholas glanced at Adrian. "You're part of that?"

It shook its head and pointed harder, as if they were not understanding it.

Adrian walked toward the jars. The creature inside the doll nodded. Adrian touched one, gingerly, as if he expected it to bite him.

Nothing happened. The creature watched. Adrian held the jar and looked at Nicholas. He shrugged. The creature mimed bringing the jar toward it.

Nicholas wasn't so sure it was a good idea, but he and Adrian had agreed they would test everything.

Adrian brought the jar closer. It didn't seem to have any relationship to the glass doll in Nicholas's hand. The glass on the jar was like the glass in the globes, filled with imperfections, thick and almost rough to the touch.

It was sealed with a glass stopper, and around the stopper, someone had placed a layer of wax.

Adrian shook the jar. The red liquid inside had black sediment, like blood that had partly congealed.

Nicholas swallowed hard. He took the jar from Adrian, half expecting the jar to erupt into light as the globe had.

Nothing happened.

Except the creature in his other hand reached for the jar. The jar was nearly as big as it was.

The creature stood on Nicholas's palms. Its glass feet were warm, but whether that was from his warmth or the creature inside, he couldn't tell. It braced itself against the side of his fist, between his forefinger and his thumb, and grasped the stopper, attempting to pull it free.

Adrian looked at Nicholas, as if expecting Nicholas to give some kind of order, make some kind of choice. Nicholas did nothing. He could feel some sort of danger in this, but he didn't know what kind. Or to whom the danger would be directed.

He moved the jar away from the creature and tilted its top toward Adrian. "Remove the stopper."

"I don't think that would be wise," Adrian said.

"I'm not sure any of this is wise," Nicholas said, "but it's necessary."

Adrian picked at the wax seal. As he did so, the creature rested its glass hands against the top knuckle of Nicholas's forefinger. It leaned forward to watch, as if it didn't dare miss what Adrian was doing.

After Adrian picked a corner of the wax, the rest came off in one large lump. He raised his eyes for just a moment. They met Nicholas's, and Nicholas saw fear in Adrian's eyes.

Nicholas nodded.

Adrian pulled the stopper free, and held it up.

Nothing happened.

Nothing at all.

Except a huge stench filled the room.

Nicholas's eyes watered. He recognized the smell from his days as a warrior against the Fey.

Old blood, beginning to rot.

"Phew," he said.

The creature took its hands off his finger and mimed bringing the jar toward him. Adrian again waited for Nicholas to give the order. Nicholas nodded.

Adrian tilted the jar toward the creature. The creature signaled with its right hand to bring the jar down farther, farther, farther, until the jar's mouth was near its face. It didn't seem disturbed by the smell.

It grinned, leaned forward as far as it could, and plunged both hands into the mouth of the jar. It bathed itself in blood to the elbows.

Pink shot through the glass doll, webbing it like blood veins. Then the pink grew into a fierce red, appearing to flow into the creature inside. Nicholas wanted to let go, but he didn't. The doll would shatter, and he didn't know what would happen to the creature.

The red coated everything, obscuring his view of the creature. Adrian started to lean forward when the glass doll shattered.

Shards of glass went everywhere. Into Nicholas's hand, into Adrian's face—narrowly missing his eyes—into their clothing. Glass shot through the air, and landed with a light tinkling sound, all around them. The jar tilted but didn't fall. Somehow Adrian managed to maintain his grip on it. Pieces of the glass doll went inside the blood, and the blood started to boil.

A red haze flew off Nicholas's hand. It landed beside him and grew until it reached his height. Then the haze coalesced not into a creature, but into a man.

A naked man. A man whose face was slightly pink, as if he had exerted himself. He was clearly an Islander, his skin light, his eyes blue, and his hair a white-blond that was rarely seen any more in adult Islanders, but was common in the children.

He grinned at Nicholas, and spoke, but Nicholas couldn't understand the words.

"I'm sorry," Nicholas said. "Do you speak Islander?"

The man spoke again, and this time Nicholas picked out a few phrases. The man was speaking Islander. Old Islander.

"I'm afraid I don't understand you," Nicholas said.

The man made a slight sound of disgust, then grabbed Nicholas's face with his left hand. His hand was warm, his flesh firm. Adrian reached for the man's wrist, but by the time he had done that, the man pulled away.

"Bastardized," the man said. At least, that's what it sounded like he said.

"What?" Nicholas managed.

"Bastardized," the man said again. "You have ruined the language."

"What just happened here?" Adrian asked.

"You are not of us," the man said and turned his back on Adrian. "But you are." He directed this last at Nicholas. The man tilted his head back and raised his arms to the ceiling. "This is very freeing!"

"How long were you in there?" Nicholas asked.

The man brought his arms down, as if the question disappointed him somehow. "It seemed like forever."

"How did you learn the language, then?" Adrian asked.

The man frowned, raised his chin slightly, and said to Nicholas, "Can you have that man stop talking?"

"He's a friend of mine," Nicholas said. "And he has a good question. That was Old Islander you spoke a moment ago. Now you're speaking my language."

The man sighed. Then he tucked a strand of that white blond hair behind his ear. "Already the questions," he said. "All right. Language is everywhere. Didn't they teach you this? It is an invisible matrix, just like the power in this place is. It may be plucked out of the air."

"And learned, that fast?" Adrian asked.

The man glanced over his shoulder. "Do you let this man speak for you?"

"He speaks for himself," Nicholas said. "But I share his interest."

"It is absorbed," the man said. "Like everything in this place."

"Absorbed?" Nicholas repeated. He had not thought of language as something absorbed, but it was, by infants. Only not as rapidly as this man—this creature—had.

"Things are quite different here," the man said, and sighed again. He touched his hands, his arms, and then his face. "This feels so good."

"What are you?" Adrian asked.

"Was everything lost?" the man asked. "How can you not know what I am? Who I am? Surely you of all people know." This last he spoke again to Nicholas.

"You seem to think I'm someone else," Nicholas said.

"You are Coulter," the man said.

Nicholas started. How did this strange man know of Coulter? How could he mistake Nicholas for him?

"No," Nicholas said. "Coulter is outside."

The man's eyes narrowed. "If you are not Coulter, then you are Alexander."

A shiver ran down Nicholas's back. "No," he said. "I am Alexander's son."

"Well then," the man said. "That explains it. So he did not believe the admonition after all that having children was not wise."

"I don't think you're talking about the same people," Adrian said softly.

Nicholas didn't think so either. He swallowed. "I am Nicholas the Fifth, King of Blue Isle, son of Alexander the Sixteenth, son of Dimitri, son of Sebastian, son of Constantine the Twelfth."

The man was staring at him in awe. "But you are of Coulter's line?"

"The Roca's line," Adrian said.

The man seemed to forget himself for a moment and glanced at Adrian, then murmured something in Old Islander. It ended with the word "roca," which Nicholas recognized.

The man put a hand to his head. "Surely it hasn't been that long."

"How long?" Nicholas asked.

"I helped Coulter find this cave. We stocked it. You must know that."

Nicholas shook his head. "We don't know what most of this is. We don't know what you are."

The man smiled, but the smile was sad. "I am an old soul," he said, and vanished.

Nicholas reached for him, but his hand closed on nothingness. His fingers slid across the glass shards sticking out of his palm. He hadn't felt any pain until that moment.

He cursed softly and cradled his hand against his chest. Adrian put a hand to his face.

"We were supposed to understand that," Adrian said.

Nicholas nodded. He wasn't done yet. He looked up. "Come back. We need your help."

There was no response. The hair rose on the back of his neck. He felt as if someone were listening, whether it was the man or someone else. Was this place filled with people like Jewel? People who were dead and not dead? People who could vanish at will and yet had the warm flesh of the living?

"Please," Nicholas said.

Adrian shook his head. "He won't come back," Adrian said. He crouched. An intact piece of the doll's head, part of its skull, lay against the stone floor. He still clutched the jar of blood.

"What is this, do you think?"

"Something else," Nicholas said. "One of the Secrets we don't understand. And I don't see how it can be of use to us now."

"We could try one of the other dolls," Adrian said.

"I'm not sure I want to." Nicholas looked at them. The strange man had vanished, but Nicholas didn't know if he was gone. Even if the man had stayed, would he have helped them or hurt them?

Nicholas didn't know.

Adrian nodded. His hand hovered over the broken glass. "Do you believe what he said about language?"

"I've heard stranger things from the Fey," Nicholas said.

"And that bit about Coulter? And your father?"

Nicholas shook his head. "I didn't understand that at all. But he seemed to understand the term 'roca.' "

"And he didn't like it," Adrian said.

Nicholas had noted that too. The man had been imprisoned, it seemed, within that doll, and very glad to be free. How long?

*Forever,* he had said.

Forever.

How long was that?

"He said he discovered the cave with Coulter. Could that have been the Roca?"

Nicholas looked at Adrian, startled. He had never thought of the Roca as having a name before. But he must have. The Roca was just a regular man. That was part of the religion, that a man had found the courage to stand up to the Soldiers of the Enemy, had found the strength to sacrifice himself to save others.

Coulter?

Like their Coulter?

Only he said Nicholas looked just like him.

Nicholas crouched, then picked the shards of glass from his hand, and placed them beside the doll's crushed head. Then he removed more shards from Adrian's face. The cuts were small and bled only slightly.

"Does it hurt?" Nicholas asked.

Adrian shook his head.

"Mine really doesn't either." And Nicholas found that curious too. The glass doll was obviously some kind of magick. But was it the kind that had created Sebastian? Or was it something unfamiliar?

He took the jar from Adrian's hand. The smell of decaying blood was still strong. The jar was warm from Adrian's touch, but otherwise there was nothing unusual about it.

Nicholas glanced at Adrian, then lowered the jar slightly. Holding it in his right hand, he dipped his left forefinger in the liquid.

A tingle ran from his finger through his spine and then spread through him, much as the color pink had spread through the doll. He shuddered once, and the feeling went away.

"What was that?" Adrian asked.

Nicholas shook his head. He didn't know if it was anything at all. He wasn't sure if that shudder was just his own reaction or if it was something more.

Or something less.

Too many questions, and no real answers.

He sat down, careful to avoid the glass. Adrian began scooping up the remaining pieces and placing them near the doll's head. The glass was clear again. All of its red lines had vanished when it shattered.

"Adrian," Nicholas said, "we've been going about this wrong."

"Sire?" Adrian did not stop working.

"We've been assuming that our religion is in contrast to the Fey's magick. But what if it's the same thing?"

"I don't follow," Adrian said.

"We know that Coulter has the same powers as a Fey Enchanter, only without the training. Jewel says that my family probably has magick in its line. Matthias is also an Enchanter. That's very Fey. And now both races come from a Place of Power."

"Yes," Adrian said, but he sounded cautious, as if he were uncertain where Nicholas was going.

"That glass doll is similar to Fey magick I've seen, and those globes of light are like the fireballs that Coulter can make with his hands."

"Yes," Adrian said again. He seemed to be waiting for Nicholas to reach a sort of conclusion.

"And this," Nicholas said. "This blood. It had the power to shatter that glass shell, to free that man or old soul or whatever he was, and to allow him to vanish. What if it has other properties as well?"

"Like what?"

"Why do the Fey flay their victims and store the skin in pouches?"

"I don't know." Adrian sat beside him. "No one would ever tell me. Not even Scavenger. I'm not sure he knows."

"Yet you know it has a magickal purpose."

"I've seen it," Adrian said. "When Coulter was a little boy, the Fey tried to find out what kind of magick he had. He made a bubble around himself, only it was invisible. No magick could touch him through that bubble. And then the Fey used some of their skin on it, and made the bubble visible. They found an opening, and nearly killed him."

Nicholas looked at Adrian. The image was disgusting, but it made him think. A bubble of magick. The pouches made the magick visible. He'd also heard, from Jewel, that they used the skin to test holy water, to see what its properties were.

"What if," he said, "the skin, when removed the way the Fey do it, has magickal properties of its own? What if it becomes a magick item?"

"I figure it does," Adrian said, "or they wouldn't guard it so closely."

"And the magickal people around us wouldn't have felt such an impact when your son destroyed a cache of pouches."

Adrian looked at him. Nicholas could feel the pride Adrian had for his son; pride mixed with worry. Exactly as Nicholas would have felt for his children. "Are you saying this blood might have the same properties?"

Nicholas nodded. "Or similar ones. Why store blood? Why save it?"

"I don't know," Adrian said. "This whole place frustrates me. It shows me how much I don't know."

He ran a hand over his face, then looked at the fountain. "Even that," he said. "We're afraid of a source of water because we don't know what it is."

"We know what we think it is," Nicholas said.

"But we don't know, not really," Adrian said. "And even if it were holy water, which I'm not sure it is, it wouldn't harm us. You and me."

Nicholas nodded. "I'd been thinking the same thing." He took the stopper for the blood jar from Adrian and closed the jar. They didn't have any wax to complete the seal, but he didn't think that mattered, at least, not at the moment. He put the jar back on its shelf, then rubbed the remaining blood off his fingers onto his pants.

Then he went down the stairs to the fountain. Adrian followed.

Nicholas had been close to it several times, but he had never really looked at it. He had always guarded Jewel from it, afraid that it would melt her somehow or make her disappear forever. His children hadn't gotten near it, and neither had Leen and Scavenger.

The fountain bubbled. He was so used to the sound now that

he heard only it when he concentrated on it. It was a soothing sound, a comforting sound, one of the reasons this place felt as safe as it did.

The fountain's pedestal rose from the floor, and where it did, the corridors split off. It was as if the fountain itself was a nexus, and everything flowed from it.

Nicholas crouched beside the pedestal. It had been carved from an existing rock. No one had moved the rock to carve it, but had instead made its design in that very spot. The rock flowed naturally from the floor, and its base was as wide as his shoulders. It tapered into an area the size of his wrist before expanding again to hold the bowl.

The bowl was obviously carved and added later. Its design matched that of the bowls for the Feast of the Living, except at the bottom. There it had been left open in a square big enough to put his fist through. The water flowed into it, and through the base, through the rock, into the floor below.

Natural water.

Nicholas swallowed. Something tickled his memory. The Absorption service. Something about water.

He waited and let it come.

It didn't.

Then he looked at the source of the water itself.

He had thought it bubbled up from the base of the fountain, and back through it, but as he studied it, he realized that the water came down a crack in the rocks that formed part of the wall. It ran through the wall, over some more carvings that were, like the base, attached, and opened onto the basin.

Then the water bubbled into the opening below.

It was a closed system that came from the mountain itself.

"Adrian," Nicholas said as he turned. Adrian was standing beside him, hands clasped behind his back, staring at the same things Nicholas was. The small cuts on Adrian's face had bled more. A drop of blood smeared his right cheek, just below his eye.

"It's not what I thought," Adrian said.

"Me either," Nicholas said. "Do you remember the Midnight Sacraments? What was the line from the Absorption about water?"

" 'A man cannot live without water,' " Adrian said, frowning as he did so. "Something about he's born in a rush of water, and something else I can't remember. And then it ends with a phrase like this: Water is the Essence of God."

"Water is the Essence of God," Nicholas said. He brushed

himself off, then took the stairs two at a time. He stopped in front of the tapestries. One of the ones toward the back depicted two scenes. The first was of a small frail man entering a cave. The second was of him emerging in a storm of wind and light and brightness. The man looked larger somehow, and in his right hand he carried a sword.

"Did you ever hear that the Roca came from the Cliffs of Blood?" Nicholas asked.

"And the Snow Mountains," Adrian said, "and the Kenniland Marshes. Every area claims him."

"But only one can be right." Nicholas walked down the stairs again. "Water is the Essence of God. The Tabernacle always took that to mean holy water, didn't it?"

"I don't know," Adrian said. "My local Danite did. But he rarely dwelt on that passage. I remember Luke, my son, being angry at him once for failing to discuss it with him. Luke always believed there were too many references to water in the passage for it to mean one thing."

"I think I like your son," Nicholas said.

Adrian grinned at him, then leaned forward and sniffed the air above the splashing water. "You know," he said, "this doesn't even smell like holy water."

Nicholas looked at him, feeling a bit of a shock running through him. He had been thinking that for days, but not consciously. No wonder the fountain had always bothered him. Holy water had a distinctive, bitter odor. This water smelled fresh, fresher than anything he had ever smelled before. Even the tiny streams he had encountered north of Jahn didn't have this sweet an odor.

"It's not holy water, is it?" Adrian said.

"Holy water is made," Nicholas said. "I know it is. We had to get the Rocaan to make more in those first battles against the Fey. I know he didn't send anyone to get more. We were under siege. There was no getting out of Jahn."

"Besides," Adrian said, "there haven't been Rocaanists here for a long, long time."

They looked at each other. Nicholas felt his heart pound, hard. He hadn't thought of that. He hadn't thought of it at all.

In all the events of the past few days, he had missed so much. Right now, he had to pay attention to everything.

"I think this time, I should be the one to test it," Adrian said.

Nicholas frowned. "I'm the Roca's descendent. I thought we agreed—"

"We did," Adrian said. "But we agreed for the items on the shelves above. Not for this. Those were placed by Rocaanists, or so it seems, or by the Roca himself. This one wasn't."

It clearly wasn't. Even though the base was manmade, the water came from the mountain itself.

*Water is the Essence of God.*

Did that mean this water? And if so, what was Nicholas allowing Adrian to do? Touch the Essence of God?

"We don't know what this is," Nicholas said.

"It might just be water," Adrian said.

"It might be more."

"What, exactly, are you afraid of, sire?" Adrian asked.

And Nicholas couldn't answer him. The fear was undefined, hard to quantify, even harder to explain. It was a sensation at the base of his stomach, something that warned him that this, not the globes, not the swords, not the tapestries, held the key to the cavern.

"Everything," Nicholas said. "And nothing." He swallowed. "I am willing—in fact, I would prefer—to taste this myself."

Adrian was silent for a moment. Then he nodded. "I cannot argue with you, sire," he said, even though that was exactly what he had been doing. Nicholas noted that Adrian had been using the word "sire" whenever he felt that Nicholas was pulling rank or when Nicholas had to make a decision that Adrian did not agree with.

"No," Nicholas said. "You can't."

He moved closer to the basin. The fresh scent of the water filled the air. It was wonderous, tempting, sweet. He wiped his hands on his robe, then stuck them into the water swirling through the bowl.

It was icy cold. He gasped with the shock of it. Adrian stared at him.

"Cold," Nicholas said.

And bracing. It chilled his entire body, but felt good at the same time. He hadn't realized how warm he was.

The water steeped into his cuts, stinging, then numbing them. He leaned over and splashed some on his face. The cold felt wonderful. It awakened him. He felt alive again for the first time since the Shaman died.

He hadn't realized how cut off he had been feeling, even with Jewel's arrival.

The water tingled against his skin. Adrian was watching him

closely. Nicholas smiled at him in reassurance. Adrian did not smile back.

Nicholas raised his dripping face slightly, and cupped water with his hands. He swallowed hard. His heart's pounding grew. He was shaking slightly.

Here was the test.

He said a silent prayer, something he hadn't done in a long, long time. The prayer was not for himself, but for his children should he die. They would need guidance. He hoped they would find it from someone who would give them good advice.

He raised his hands to his lips rapidly, so that he wouldn't have to think about what he was doing.

He drank—

And tasted the coldest, sweetest water he had ever had. It quenched his thirst and made him feel stronger. Without thinking, he dipped his hands again, and then again, drinking as much as he could.

Adrian reached for him, signaling him, asking him to stop, but Nicholas did not want to. He wasn't sure if he could.

The water filled him and spread, and he drank and drank, and somewhere along the way, he realized he had been forgetting to breathe, to think, to make choices on his own.

His hands moved, his lips supped, his throat swallowed, and black spots danced in front of his eyes.

Adrian took his wrists, trying to make him stop, but Nicholas didn't stop. He didn't—

The black spots grew. He let his hands fall. He needed air. He needed—

He reached for Adrian, reached—

And felt himself slip away.

# FORTY

PAUSHO huddled on the floor of the Vault, left hand cradling her head, legs crossed. She was still slightly dizzy from the morning's event, and she was exhausted, although she didn't entirely know why. She suspected it had to do with Matthias.

And the golden glow.

The entire room glowed. He didn't seem to notice. The glow was increasing. It flowed from the altar, where his hands were clutching the sides, except when he occasionally raised one to turn a page.

He looked devastated, although he shouldn't have hit anything yet. Nothing that should cause that look. Except, perhaps, that what she had told him was right: she had guarded the Words. The real Words.

She let out a sigh, and let her hand drop. Matthias didn't even seem to hear. He was so engrossed in the Words, his lips moving as he parsed out the Ancient Islander.

The glow kept increasing.

She wanted to curse it. She bit back a phrase, then shook her head. Her failure was absolute. Her failure, and the failure of her entire kind.

The fact that Matthias was alive proved that.

Tears stung her eyes, and she stood, blindly reaching for the door. She wouldn't wait here. She couldn't. But she had to. It was her duty.

Even if Matthias was of the Roca's blood, he was not one of the Wise Ones. He could not be here without supervision.

She had failed everything else. Herself, her unnamed daughter. She could not fail this.

She took a pillow from the far wall and laid it on the floor, sinking into it. The golden light was almost unbearable. She had never seen anything like it, had never thought she would see anything like it, indeed, hadn't thought anything like it was even possible.

She leaned her head against the wall, wondering what she would tell the others. Wondering if she could tell the others. Generations of Wise Ones had failed. She wondered if they had failed as she had done, by bending the rules just slightly, by allowing the mountain to choose for them.

Of course the mountain had chosen. It had chosen one of its own. It had chosen a descendent of the Roca. She wondered how many others were out there, how many others she had let live because the mountain helped them survive as infants.

She carried none of that blood in her. If she had, her own daughter would have survived. She couldn't think about that, not now. Not so many decades later, when there was nothing to do to change it. But it broke her heart. It had that day, and it did now.

*You will know my blood by the touch of skin against this barrier. It will create a golden light that bathes all thing.*

*Do not allow my blood to live.*

The Wise Ones had lived with that admonition since the Roca had returned. He had seen, after decades away, what the power had done to his sons. The eldest, Alexander, had used the subtler powers, persuasion and warmth, a sort of camaraderie where there had been none. He had developed those, and so had his children, and his children beyond that.

It was said King Nicholas was the most charming of all. He could capture the hearts of his enemies without speaking a word.

But the Roca's younger son, Matthias, he had done everything that Alexander had not. He had tested each power, developed more, and found ways of persevering them. He had codified them and ritualized them, and given them credence among the Islanders. By the time the Roca returned, Matthias had gone insane. He had been removed from the leadership of the budding religion, and so had his children because, the others believed, such insanity was hereditary.

The Roca believed it was as well—not because of his family's lines, but because of the way it used the powers he had discovered in the cave. That was why Alexander's line had never lost its grip on sanity, and Matthias's did all too often.

*A man cannot have the powers of God*, the Roca had written. *It will ultimately destroy him.*

And the Roca ordered that all of those who manifested such power should be destroyed. The opening to the Roca's cave was closed, but it never remained that way. Explorers would always find it—and it would always be open. Finally Wise Ones placed the Holy Swords in its place as a warning, and the directions to it were lost. Those who went inside often never returned. Or if they did, they were killed by the Wise Ones.

The Wise Ones were supposed to eradicate the powers that the Roca had unleashed on the Isle. Generation after generation removed, innocents slaughtered, according to the Roca's plan.

*Let us hope it never reaches the day when my descendants, the children of my children, Alexander and Matthias, again rule the Isle*, the Roca had said in the Words Unwritten. *Let us hope that by ending this curse now, we save our home.*

Matthias hadn't moved. Pausho looked at him and shook her

head. Should she have known, when Matthias headed the Tabernacle and Alexander the country, that the Roca's words were coming to pass? It didn't seem likely to her. There had been fifteen Alexanders since the first, and countless Matthiases, particularly in the Tabernacle. She had never thought that the descendants the Roca was referring to would be so easily identifiable, so much a part of the present.

And now it was too late. Matthias was here. He no longer ruled. The Fey—those strange murderous creatures that had descended on Constant that morning—owned the Isle. The descendants of Alexander—Nicholas and his children—had been dethroned, and the Isle did not know peace.

The moment the Roca had warned them against had already passed.

And she had allowed it.

She let out a small moan, and leaned back. Now a descendent of the Roca stood in the Vault, a place the Roca had once built for his sons and then had decreed they should not enter. Matthias was learning the Secrets, learning everything that had been lost to all outside the Cliffs of Blood.

And she was allowing it because she had no choice, just as she had had no choice when she had let the Wise Ones carry her newborn daughter up the mountainside, and left her, naked and squalling, in the cold.

What merciful God would allow a woman a life like this?

She already knew the answer. It had been repeated to her countless times, and it filled the Roca's writings. God was not merciful. It was only human assumption that made him so.

God was God, both good and evil, strong and weak, powerful. Always powerful.

And generous.

Willing to share his power.

To anyone willing to pay the price.

# FORTY-ONE

Hε smelled the Red Cap before he saw him.

Rugad remained at his post by the floor-to-ceiling windows, mulling the intricacies of Islander magick. And then the smell overwhelmed him—that special mixture of decay and rot that only seemed to travel on Red Caps. They rarely washed, apparently seeing no point to it, and the stench they carried with them was palpable.

Rugad turned.

The Red Cap was standing with the guard near the door to the Great Hall. The Cap was male, as old as Rugad, with dirt encrusted in his face and on his clothes. His hands were black. He hadn't cleaned up when he left whatever site he had been working on.

Rugad kept an expression of distaste off his face. He crossed the room, willing himself to handle the smell, which he knew would get worse the closer he got.

It did.

He wanted to breathe shallowly, but he wouldn't allow any portion of his army, even its lowest members, to know that he could not tolerate something—even something as abominable as this.

"Come with me," he said to the Cap.

The Cap nodded once. The guard stepped back—gratefully, it seemed—and watched. Rugad walked to the wall of swords. He stopped in front of the oldest ones.

"Touch the blade," Rugad said.

The Cap frowned at him, but raised his hand. As he reached toward the wall, Rugad added, "Use pressure."

The Cap's eyes narrowed, but he continued to move. He touched the edge of the blade, and nothing happened. He looked up at Rugad, questioningly.

Rugad placed his own hands behind his back. "Continue," he said.

"What are we looking for?" the Cap asked.

Rugad was not about to tell him. Most Fey were rarely in a need-to-know position. A Red Cap never was. "Just keep working."

The Cap frowned, but touched another blade, and then another. Their edges were so dull they did no more than dent the skin. The Cap obviously was beginning to think of this as a waste of time. He pressed a blade and then another and then another. He continued to do so, going across one whole row before he yelped.

Rugad stepped closer.

The Cap was cradling his hand near his chest. He was bleeding. "Sharp?" Rugad asked.

The Cap said nothing. He held out his hand. The finger he had been using to touch the blades was gone.

It was on the floor.

"Pick it up," Rugad said.

The Cap bent slowly and picked up his finger, holding it in his other hand.

"Now, show me which blade you touched."

The Cap nodded toward a blade shaped like the ones that had decorated the Tabernacle. Rugad felt a slight elation. So it was the blade and not the Black Robe that had caused the slaughter of his people in this very room.

It was as he had hoped.

"Hold out your hand," Rugad said.

The Cap did so. Rugad ripped off a piece of his own shirt and tied it around the finger-stump, cutting off the flow of blood.

"There," he said. "Put your finger in your pocket. You can take it to the Domestics when you're through."

"I would like to be excused now, sir," the Red Cap said tightly.

"You're not done," Rugad said. "You may leave when I tell you to."

The Cap nodded. His skin had become ashen, his eyes tiny points in his face.

"I want you to touch the other blades that resemble this one," Rugad said. "Do so with less enthusiasm, and you probably won't lose another finger."

Although he couldn't guarantee it. The blade had some sort of property that made it extra sharp. He grabbed the hilt and took the sword off the wall, all the while watching the Cap move gingerly from sword to sword.

The blade was thinner than any Fey-made blade, thinner than any working blade he had ever seen. He peered at it, looking at the workmanship. It glinted, and the blood left by the Red Cap had disappeared.

The Cap yelped again. This time the sound was muted, almost as if he didn't want anyone to know about his pain. His second finger still remained attached, but had been sliced cleanly between the first and second knuckles. It would take the Healers some work to save that as well.

Rugad removed that blade. And the next that made the Cap cry out. And the next. He set them in a pile on the floor. Amazing how many blades had been camouflaged in this wall.

These could destroy his people. Now all he needed to know was whether or not they could also hurt Islanders.

The Red Cap was swaying on his feet. He had lost a lot of blood, probably too much for him to continue.

Rugad put a hand on the Cap's filthy shirt, holding him up. He looked at the guard who had brought the Cap to the Great Hall. "Take him to Seger. Tell her that she should treat him as if he were a member of the Black Family. Allow him healing time before he returns to work."

The guard's features crinkled in disgust, but he nodded anyway. "Yes, sir," he said. He frowned at the Cap. "Come along."

The Cap wrenched his shoulder out of Rugad's grip and staggered after the guard. Rugad wondered if the Cap would make it to Seger's quarters. He turned away. It was no longer any of his concern.

The Cap had shown him what he needed to know. There were swords here, mingled with the others, that had the properties which would slaughter Fey in an instant. The question was whether they would do so to all peoples, including Islanders.

Rugad snapped his fingers again. Another guard came forward. She nodded at him. "Get me an Islander."

"Any Islander?" she asked.

"Any Islander, preferably one that was uninjured."

"Yes, sir." She disappeared through the far doors, just as the previous guard had.

Rugad crouched by the pile of swords but did not touch them. They all had that impossibly thin blade and looked as if the slightest pressure would break them.

But it did not. They were masterwords of craftsmanship, a craftsmanship that had clearly been lost. Which was fortunate for the Fey, or the Islanders would have slaughtered them this second time around as well.

"You wanted to see me, Rugad?"

Rugad recognized Landre's dry tones, and wondered how the Spell Warder after all these years could still sneak up on him.

"Come see this," Rugad said. "But don't touch."

Landre crouched beside him. The Spell Warder was a thin man, not as thin as Boteen, but still he had that gauntness that came with too much magick. He was also slightly taller than Rugad, even when he crouched.

Landre was wearing breeches that went to midcalf, and a robe-like garment on top that Rugad had never seen before. He smelled faintly of decay.

Rugad had obviously disturbed his work.

"Swords?" Landre asked.

"Not just any swords," Rugad said. "These swords are like the one the Black Robe used to kill so many of our people a few weeks ago. I just tested them on a Red Cap. He lost a finger just by touching one."

"Hmmm," Landre said, peering down. "I don't recognize the material."

"Neither do I," Rugad said. "But I want you to take one and see what you can learn from it. I just sent a guard for an Islander to see if this blade cuts their skin as easily as it cuts ours."

"If it does," Landre said, "we may have a new weapon for the Fey arsenal. It will serve us well on Leut."

"If we can figure out how to make it," Rugad said.

Landre smiled. "Given time, I can learn anything."

"I'm counting on it," Rugad said. He put his hands on his knees and pushed up. He wiped his palms on his pants. His skin still crawled from touching the Red Cap.

Landre stood as well, his long body cracking and popping as he rose. "You did not bring me just for the magickal sword."

"No," Rugad said. "You know the Doppelgänger we have in the dungeon."

"Yes," Landre said and smiled without mirth. Rugad did not entirely understand what the smile was for.

"He knows of the Islander's religious rituals. I believe within them is buried the key to their magick. Only I don't have time to parse it all out. I want you and the other Warders to work on it."

"It means we have to get close to the Doppelgänger."

"Yes, but only with guards present. I don't trust him."

"For obvious reasons," Landre said. "A Doppelgänger who had kept his shape that long has, in essence, converted."

Rugad nodded. "Selia Charmed him. He abhors touch. She's quite good."

"Better," Landre said, "than any Charmer I've known."

Rugad let out a small sigh. Landre had been with him for a long, long time. Like most Warders, Landre was arrogant, but brilliant. He could get results when he tried.

"You've had time to study the Islander magick," Rugad said. "I believe turning it against the Islanders is one of the few tools we'll have in their rapid defeat."

"If you insist on calling what they have magick," Landre said. "I am not so certain."

"It seems like magick to me," Rugad said.

"Yes," Landre said. "But it is so slight."

"It leaks," Rugad said. "They don't use it properly."

Landre dipped his head forward as if in acknowledgment. "But what you must ask yourself is: At what point does it cease to be magick?"

"What do you mean?" Rugad asked.

"Magick involves control," Landre said. "It is not about power, but about manipulating power. I believe these Islanders have a lot of raw talent, a lot of what we have been calling wild magick, when in reality it is wild power, vast and untamed. In the taming of this wild power, we gain magick. The more we control the wild power, the more magickal we become."

Landre was right, although Rugad had never thought of it that way.

"My job," Landre said, "is to make the Fey the most magickal race. Not the most powerful. These Islanders may be more powerful. We may encounter a country on Leut with even more power than that. But the questions is, how much control do they have?"

Rugad nodded. "So you sense a vast amount of power here?"

Landre smiled. "It feels limitless, although I am sure it is not."

"But no magick."

"Oh, there is magick, but it is weak," Landre said. "We destroyed most of it when we destroyed their holy place. The rest of it they seemed to have forgotten."

"Not entirely," Rugad said, and told him of the rout that morning.

Landre shook his head. "It is child's play to turn an army like that. You know it, Rugad. The problem is that our people, particularly our Infantry, are not trained to face magickal opponents. It is surprise that is defeating us, not the Islanders' magickal abilities."

For the first time since they had known each other, Landre was calming Rugad. Usually Landre's observations made him tense. But Landre was right. It was so elementary, and Rugad had known it for other disciplines. He had trained his own people in those arts, and he watched as they learned their magicks. The ones who rose to positions of leadership, like Landre, often had the greatest control.

That was where his grandchildren, Jewel's brothers, had failed. They had never bothered with control. They had wasted their powers, what they had of them, and expected leadership as a right of birth.

Expectations did not create Black Kings.

He led the Fey not because he was the best Visionary, but because he had combined his Vision with his military acumen. He had spent every waking moment of his life from childhood forward learning everything he could about military techniques, strategies, and thinking. He had augmented that by learning all the various Fey magicks and the histories of the countries he wanted to conquer. He had learned languages and art forms and weapons creation.

Each moment of his life, he had struggled to control something new, just as he was struggling now to control Blue Isle.

"Raw power," Rugad said. He mulled it over, enjoyed the sound of it. Landre was watching him from beside the small pile of swords. "So we do not need to learn their magick techniques?"

"We should learn them," Landre said. "We should learn as much control as they have. But it's not necessary, and it's certainly not something we can learn quickly enough."

"Maybe," Rugad said. He wasn't sure he agreed with that last part. "Maybe. I still think those techniques hold some clues to defeating the Islanders."

"I think removing the element of surprise, being ready for anything, will defeat the Islanders."

"It sounds so easy," Rugad said. "But I have tried to warn this entire troop of that, and it has not worked. Telling our people to expect the unexpected is one thing; actually getting them to do so is another."

"They believe that no one is as powerful as the Fey."

"That's true," Rugad said.

"That was true until we came here."

Rugad stared at him, feeling exasperation grow. "You just said that—"

"I said that the Islanders are powerful. They have no control. Their magick leaks, Rugad. Think of it. Think of those Shifting children who aren't guided by older Shifters. Think of the young Charmers who haven't learned how to mold their powers. Think of teenage Enchanters who allow their rage to fuel their magick."

Rugad knew all those examples. He had seen such things hundreds of times. Fey who could not or did not control their own magick died. The Shifters got stuck in a position, often accidentally, and killed themselves. The Charmers would convince someone to do something unintentionally, often leading to that person's death days later. And the young Enchanters, filled with rage, usually lost their temper and sent a fireball shooting into a building before they could stop it.

The Fey had rules to control such things, but events still got away from them. Fey died all the time due to carelessness, to lack of control.

"So we harness their power," Rugad said.

"As if they were unruly teenagers," Landre said.

"As is they were young Shifters needing our guidance."

"As if," Landre said, "their power funneled into our own."

Rugad smiled, truly smiled, for the first time in days. "Landre," he said. "You are brilliant."

"Of course I am," Landre said. "You wouldn't work with me if I weren't."

"No," Rugad said. "It is more than that. You have probably just won the war for Blue Isle."

Landre shook his head. "I have done more than that," he said. "I have just increased the power of the Fey a hundredfold."

"Their power is our magick," Rugad said.

"And our magick," Landre said softly, "is our strength."

# FORTY-TWO

THE afternoon crawled past. Licia had gone from wounded soldier to wounded soldier, comforting as she did so. She had spoken to her uninjured troops, trying to revive their spirits.

And she had finally worked her way to Ay'Le.

Ay'Le, who was sitting on a boulder in the center of the valley, talking to a small group of Beast Riders. Ay'Le, who sat cross-legged, arms back, looking like someone who had not just seen the worst defeat of her lifetime.

One of the Beast Riders made a small movement with her hand as Licia approached. She wouldn't have seen it if she weren't watching for just that thing.

Ay'Le was still playing politics, and playing it against Licia.

Licia stopped beside the boulder, feeling the thin warmth of the valley's sun. Apparently it never got hot here, and she found she didn't miss it. But the constant chill was beginning to get to her as well.

Licia was about to speak, when Ay'Le looked down at her. Ay'Le's dark eyes glittered. "I have sent a message to Rugad that you have Failed."

The Beast Riders were watching, all of them seemingly on Ay'Le's side. And why wouldn't they be? She had Charm. Charmers often had supporters, whether logic dictated it or not. But Visionaries, even minor ones like Licia, were immune to Charmers.

And she never felt it so much as at that moment.

"Did you?" Licia asked coolly.

"I am awaiting instructions from him. I am quite sure that he will relieve you. If, of course, he doesn't order you killed."

"You don't need his permission to kill a Failure," Licia said softly. "Or is that something else you don't know, Ay'Le?"

Ay'Le's eyes narrowed. "Criticize me all you want. But I am doing you a favor by asking permission."

"Are you?" Licia asked. "Or are you hoping that I will squirm?"

"No one likes seeing Failure," Ay'Le said.

"Especially when you caused it," Licia said.

"Are you blaming me for your mistake?" Ay'Le asked.

Licia shook her head. "Only for your own."

"You'll get nowhere fighting with her, Failure," one of the Beast Riders said.

Licia didn't even look to see which one spoke. She didn't care. She would deal with them later. Right now, she had to deal with Ay'Le.

"You really are pathetic if you don't see how badly you lost today," Ay'Le said.

Licia leaned on the boulder, very close to Ay'Le's knee. "I know how badly we lost. I know the circumstances that led to it. The wave that went through that harmed all of you magickal ones. The abilities of the Islanders, abilities we weren't equipped to handle. I understood what happened."

"Then you understood how you've Failed," Ay'Le said.

"I find it amazing you call such an event a Failure."

"A retreat? For the Fey? That is nothing but a Failure," Ay'Le said. "There is nothing else you can call it."

"I call it a battle. A battle lost, true enough, but a battle all the same." Through the corner of her eye, Licia saw the Beast Riders shift slightly. Logic did fight Charm, when the logic came from a leader. It rarely worked at any other time. "We have not yet finished the war, Ay'Le."

Ay'Le leaned toward her. "You mean you're going to risk more of our people?"

"Of course," Licia said. "We're Fey. We're a fighting people. I'll risk us all if I have to. I don't admit defeat." She paused for effect. "Unlike you."

There was slight growling from the Beast Riders.

"Hush!" Ay'Le said to them.

Licia smiled at them. "She doesn't want you to think for yourselves. She doesn't want you to know that our Failure, as she puts it, was partly her fault. She was supposed to negotiate a peace without any fighting at all. And she did nothing."

"Boteen did not follow orders. He made it impossible—"

"So you blame a dead man for your failure in achieving your mission?"

Ay'Le's face lost color. "Boteen's dead?"

"Murdered by the Islanders on the mountain," Licia said, deciding not to tell them the part about the Red Cap.

"You lie."

"I heard it from Boteen's Scribe. Your Scribe. The Scribe you brought along to sing your praises, to let everyone know how brilliant you are. Scribes don't lie."

The Beast Riders shifted, as if the news disturbed them.

"The Islanders are even more powerful than we thought, if they can kill an Enchanter," Ay'Le said.

"An Enchanter weakened by the same wave that struck our people," Licia said. "You allow everything to defeat you, don't you, Ay'Le?"

Ay'Le frowned. She obviously sensed a trap but did not know how to get around it. "I think the loss of an Enchanter is important."

"It is," Licia said. "Just as the loss this morning was important. But it was not a Failure. A Failure is a refusal to believe in yourself. A Failure is the inability to rise from a defeat and to turn it into a victory."

"And you think you can do that?" Ay'Le asked.

"I know I can. I've already sent to Rugad for reinforcements, telling him of our defeat, but also giving him my plan to turn this into one of the Fey's biggest successes."

Now color flooded back into Ay'Le's cheeks. She obviously understood what Licia had done. Licia had outmaneuvered her, turned Ay'Le's moral superiority into a weakness, and she had done it before the Black King.

"Good," a different Beast Rider said. "It is better than sitting in this stinking valley until they find us and slaughter us."

"They won't," Licia said. She glanced at them. They were all watching her now, instead of Ay'Le.

"Ay'Le," Licia said, "get down."

"I don't have to listen to you," Ay'Le said.

"Actually," Licia said, "you do. I am still the leader of this group."

"The leader of a Failed Infantry," Ay'Le said.

"Don't push me," Licia said. She felt the muscles in her back tighten.

"You have no right to order me about."

"I have every right," Licia said.

"She does," the second Beast Rider said. Licia looked. It was a small Cat Rider, still in her cat form, with a woman astride her back. "She is our leader."

"You all recognized me as the leader," Ay'Le said.

"And how much Charm was involved?" a Horse Rider asked.

Ay'Le raised her chin. "You don't trust me—"

"And with good reason," Licia said. "Get down."

This time Ay'Le realized that she had no choice. She slid off the boulder and stopped between the Beast Riders and Licia.

Licia let her hands slip to her waist. She rested them on her hips, feeling her belt. The hilt of her sword brushed against her left wrist, and the hilt of her knife brushed against her right.

"What are you going to do to me?" Ay'Le asked.

"What you should have done when you believed that I had Failed," Licia said.

"I will go to Rugad," Ay'Le said, obviously misunderstanding.

But the Beast Riders did not. They craned their necks to see, many moving Fey heads around animals heads so that both pairs of eyes could see what would happen next.

"No, you won't." Licia's mouth was dry. She knew the drill. It had been drummed into her, along with other leadership training. She knew. She had just never done it before.

"Ay'Le," she said softly.

Ay'Le turned, her long angular features still caught up in a frown.

"You have Failed in your mission to convert the Islanders to the Fey side."

"Boteen gave me no chance."

"You Failed in your first attempt to lead this troop."

"You got in my way."

"You subverted my authority by going to the Black King and telling him that we had lost."

"We had." Ay'Le's voice was rising.

"You have done everything you can to aggrandize yourself at the expense of this mission. Do you know what that means?"

"It means you misunderstand," Ay'Le said. "I want only the best—"

"It means," Licia said, unable to stand the rationalizations any longer, "that you have Failed in at least three different ways. And because you will not succumb to my authority, you leave me no other choice."

With a single, swift movement she grabbed her knife and plunged it into Ay'Le's chest.

Ay'Le let out a *whump* of air, reached for the knife, and held it for a moment. "You can't do this," she said, but her voice came out in a whisper.

"I just did," Licia said.

Ay'Le tugged on the hilt, but obviously didn't have the strength to pull it free. She looked at the Beast Riders. "Help me," she said.

But none of them moved. They all watched, some with hungry expressions on their animal faces. She stood for several long moments, then slumped to her knees.

"You have no right," she said, and fell forward, landing on the knife.

Licia stood over her. Ay'Le didn't move. Licia toed her arm, then nodded at the Beast Riders. A few of them were ashen, but she couldn't tell if it was because of her action, because they had sided with Ay'Le, or because of blood lust.

She didn't care. The message was clear now.

Licia led the troop.

And she would let no one take her authority from her.

# FORTY-THREE

LUKE burst out of the cornfield, Con at his side. There were no Fey at this end, although the road was filled with them. Behind him, the second woman screamed, and a child wailed. The farmhouse was in flames.

He stumbled across the destroyed chimney. Con was now ahead of him, running down the embankment. Luke had no plan; all he knew was that they had to get out of there.

The air smelled of smoke, and was growing warmer. He reached the embankment and slid down it, his feet hitting the rocks of the creek.

"Now what?" Con whispered.

Luke pointed north. "We have no choice," he said.

He glanced behind him and saw no Fey. For the moment, they were protected. No Fey flew above either; the Bird Riders he and Con had seen had probably been the only ones.

Con crossed the creek and started up the slope. He paused halfway, and Luke's heart sank. He knew. More Fey ahead.

He reached Con's side. Two Fey were trying to set fire to green cornstalks. The ground was wet from recent rains and the weather, though it had been hot, hadn't been arid. The plants were healthy and vibrant. It would take a lot to burn them.

The Fey were standing side by side, contemplating their failed attempt.

Con crawled closer.

"If we go through the corn," Luke said, "we risk getting burned out."

"And if we go around it, we'll get seen."

There was no hiding their Islander features or builds. They couldn't just go up the road. They had to continue in the way they had been going.

Luke glanced around for more Fey. The ones on the road were scattering, obviously having received orders to destroy everything around them. The Fey were moving in parties of five or fewer; that made things easier.

But he and Con still had to deal with the two Fey in front of them.

"I can get them," Con whispered, and without waiting for Luke's permission, scurried up the slope, sword out. Luke hurried after him, reaching the edge of the field as Con sliced through both Fey with one swing. He caught them both in the torso, allowing them to scream as they fell.

Luke cursed, grabbed Con, and headed into the corn. The Fey would see them move, but wouldn't be able to catch them, and certainly couldn't light the corn on fire.

But as Luke shoved his way through the tight rows, he knew there could be someone waiting on the other end.

He hurried to Con's side and grabbed his arm. Con was splattered in fresh blood. Luke tugged him left, trying to get him to go west.

"But you said—"

"I know," Luke said. "They'll be waiting for us."

They had been on the eastern edge of the cornfield. They had an entire field to run through. He hoped he was right about the Bird Riders. The Fey wouldn't be able to see the change in direction from the ground. They would have to either guard the field or send their own people charging into it. Or continue to attempt to burn it.

No matter what, Luke wanted to be gone.

Con managed to switch direction, and they hurried through the corn. Long flat leaves cut at Luke's face, and the hardening corn slapped him as he ran. His breath was ragged, and his heart pounding. This was the second time in a day he had run through a cornfield. Corn simply wasn't made for that. And this farmer seemed to like wide fields.

Just when Luke thought the field couldn't go on any farther, he staggered out of it, into a wide patch between this field and the next. A moment later, Con staggered out beside him. The boy's face was streaked with dirt and sweat and blood. Bits of leaves were in his hair and all over his clothing.

There was no sound except for their heavy breathing. The Fey hadn't come this far west yet.

But they would be here soon, if what Luke had overheard was any indication.

Burn it all, they had said.

All.

He had forced them to perform this sort of retaliation. It was his fault.

Con grabbed his arm. "Come on," Con whispered. "We only have a moment."

Con was right. They ran through the wide space between the fields, ran north, toward Jahn.

Luke wondered how far they would get before the Fey found them again.

# FORTY-FOUR

NICHOLAS hadn't really blacked out.

Adrian was reacting as if he had, crouching over him, patting his face. But Nicholas was conscious. He simply couldn't move. He could feel the cool marble beneath his back, a slight throb where his head had hit too hard, the discomfort of his right hand resting against the fountain's pedestal. The pedestal was cold and beaded with moisture. He could feel the water running through it, and that made him crave the wetness again.

He still taste the sweetness of the water on his tongue, the best water he'd ever had.

He had forgotten to breathe, that was all. And if he could remember again, he would tell Adrian.

Adrian, who was beginning to panic.

Nicholas wanted to tell him not to, and then wondered at the impulse. He would worry if it had been Adrian who had fallen, Adrian who had seemingly blacked out. And it had seemed as if he had blacked out. He saw the darkness coming. He lost his fight with it.

He fell.

And now he was here, inside himself, but unable to move his body.

His insides tingled. That was what felt different. They tingled, as if he could feel the water flowing through him instead of his own blood.

Was that what happened?

Had he hurt himself in some way? And if so, why wasn't he worried about it? Why wasn't there that small thread of panic that came when the body was immobile, when the commands from the brain did not reach the limbs?

Adrian stood and called out. Nicholas couldn't make out the words. But he wasn't really trying to hear.

Something was distracting him. Something that he sensed but didn't yet see. He squinted—or at least, it felt as if he squinted, except that his eyes didn't move.

Then he felt the mental equivalent of a frown.

His eyes were closed, yet he could see Adrian.

What was going on?

Had he died?

Adrian started up the stairs, glancing once at Nicholas, as if looking to see if things had changed. Then he ran, taking the stairs four at a time. Agile man. Nicholas wished he could move like that.

—Ah. *Wishes.*

He heard the voice and didn't hear it. It was male and raspy, and seemed to echo in the cavern. But it felt as if he had heard it with his mind, not his ears. Just as he had squinted without moving his eyes.

—*Not yet.*

That voice was female and soft. He looked toward the roof of the cavern. It was vaulted. He hadn't realized that. Vaulted and studded with jewels and threaded with gold.

—*I think it's time.*

Another male voice said that, old and querulous, and vaguely familiar, like a voice from Nicholas's childhood. Swirls of mist circled the vaulted ceiling. He could have sworn they hadn't been there before. Swirls of mist.

Individual swirls of mist.

—*What of the others?* the first voice asked.

—*Stall them,* the female voice said.

—*Isn't that direct interference?* the second male voice asked.

—*Does it matter?* the female voice said.

And then there was silence. A profound silence. And end-of-the-world silence.

Was he dead?

The swirls of mist had grown more numerous. They were descending toward him. A chill dampness touched his face, then another and another, until he was enveloped in fog.

Outside, Nicholas suddenly knew, Adrian couldn't find Coulter. He couldn't find the opening to the Shadowlands. He felt lost.

Was this the interference the voices were talking about?

What was wrong with it?

The fog lifted off of him, leaving a slight dampness, a slight chill. The kind that could be dispelled only before a large, warm fire.

But he still couldn't move.

—*I should have realized,* another voice said. Female again, but young and vibrant. *Look at his face.*

—*Face? The entire body. How history repeats itself,* the other female voice said.

—*Well, it is wasted on him. Have you checked the blood?* the first male asked.

—*Already marked,* the second male said. *And centuries ago. This is the direct descendent.*

—*I thought they killed the descendent,* a new female voice said.

—*One of them,* a different male voice said. *But the eldest lived.*

—*He used none of his talents.*

—*He was wise.*

—*Was that wise?*

—*Perhaps.*

There were now countless voices participating in the discussion; male, female, and some whose gender he couldn't identify. The individual swirls of mist still floated around the ceiling of the cavern. They were floating faster and faster, their movements as agitated as the conversation.

—*If he is already marked, why did we let him drink?*

—*Haven't you learned? We don't let them do anything. He chose to drink.*

—*But now what do we do? Expand what is there?*

—*It would create a new form.*

—*The last time we created a new form within the old bodies, it created problems among the people.*

—*And those problems were eventually settled.*

—*Not all of them.*

Nicholas wanted to reach to the shapes. He wanted to ask questions, but he didn't know how.

—*No,* one of the first voice said. *Not all of them.*

—*I still say it is a gift they are not ready for.*

—*And one we have no choice in giving.*

—*It is said others have made use of it.*

—*And it has corrupted them.*

—*You think there was no corruption here?*

—*Stopped. I think.*

—*So we start it again?*

Nicholas frowned again. If he could squint without moving his eyes, and hear without using his ears, surely he could speak without moving his mouth.

"Hey," he said.

The swirls stopped moving. They hovered above him and bent in half, as if something were pushing against their middles.

—*It spoke?*

—*He did.*

He thought he heard awe in their tones.

"You're talking about me," he said. "What has happened to me? Am I dead?"

—*Not yet,* one of the voices said.

—*Would you like to be?* another asked.

He ignored the question. "Are you real?"

—*It depends on what you call real, lad,* a completely different voice answered.

"What's happened to me?"

—*You have drunk from the Well of Life,* a new voice said.

"What does that mean?"

—*Whatever you want it to*, one of the first female voices said.

—*No*, a second female voice said. *You cannot give him that power. His family already has it. To expand it is not fair.*

—*Fair to whom?*

—*Power is not fair.*

—*The further mutations of his being could kill him.*

—*Or it could make him stronger.*

"Are you talking about giving me magick?" Nicholas asked.

—*We speak of power.*

—*Power like your Roca.*

—*Power of old.*

—*(He has power like this Roca)*, someone whispered as if to the others, as if he couldn't hear. *(He just hasn't developed it yet.)*

—*And never will. Can't you see he comes from a line that has denied its power?*

"My daughter has power," Nicholas said. "My son too. Is that from the Roca?"

—*Yes*, the first female voice said.

"And you wish to give similar power to me?"

—*You requested it.*

—*You drank.*

"The fountain gives a person magick?"

—*It gives one power.*

—*Not magick.*

"What is the difference?" Nicholas asked.

—*You already have power.*

—*You have never learned magick.*

—*If we give him more power*, yet another new voice said, *he will insist upon wasting it, as he has done before. As all from his line have done.*

—*He has used some of the power.*

—*He has converted some of it into magick.*

—*Such great Charm.*

—*There have been few with that ability.*

—*But that is it.*

—*Except for saving the child.*

—*That doesn't count. Power used in panic is not controlled.*

—*Still, the daughter lived.*

—*More than once.*

Nicholas was having trouble following the conversation. The voices were speaking all at once, and he couldn't tell where they

came from and in what order they went. What he was able to
parse together seemed to make sense.

But they seemed to be discussing his magick.

He had none.

Or did he?

Had it always been so subtle?

"What did I request?" he asked.

—*More power,* one of the voices said.

—*But we cannot give it to you.*

—*We can, but you would squander it.*

—*Unless you had more children. Then the power would be theirs.*

—*Great power.*

—*Which would kill them.*

The last voice was shushed by several other voices. Nicholas
wished he could tell where they were coming from. What these
voices actually were.

—*It would not,* a different voice said.

—*Full use already drives them insane. Imagine the augmented
power. Even casual use would be dangerous. Their minds could not
control it.*

—*Unless they grew into it.*

—*His would not.*

—*Will you have more children?*

It took Nicholas a moment to realize that they were speaking
to him.

"No," he said.

There was suddenly a great silence around him. Greater than
he had ever heard before. He couldn't even hear himself breathe.

"My wife is dead," he said into that silence.

—*People take other wives.*

"I do not want another wife."

—*Not even for children?*

"I have children," he said.

—*See?* one of the earlier dissenting voices said. *The power
would be wasted.*

The silence grew again.

This time he did not speak. He wasn't sure what they were offering him, what they seemed so agitated about.

He decided to gamble. "I would have more children," he said,
"if you brought my wife back. If you made her live again, outside
his cave."

—*We cannot do that.*

"Why not?"

—Her life cannot be beholden to yours.

—We have denied this request before. We cannot give you what we denied your ancestors.

"I thought you could do anything," Nicholas said.

—We can. We will choose what we will and will not do. We will not do this.

The voices seemed to be speaking in unison.

—You may have more children with another wife. Or another woman. It is a simple matter. A biological matter. It has nothing to do with love.

"For me, it does," Nicholas said.

—Principles, a male voice sneered. Just like the ancestor.

—The ancestor gained principles after death.

—Inconvenient, that.

—What's past is past. What's present is important. He will not have more children.

—Then giving more power to him would not matter.

—Except that he is the descendent. We need him to live.

—We need nothing. It is merely a game.

—To us, perhaps. But not to them.

—And then what? When they finish the game?

—They put the pieces together as we have promised.

—And get full power.

—Which kills them.

—It is not a reward.

—Or is it?

—Perhaps we will give them ways to survive it.

—Perhaps.

—We already have.

—But they have forgotten.

—Surely one remembers.

—Not everything.

—Perhaps we could give him a teacher.

—That is interference.

—Is it? He has power, and chooses not to use it. Interference means he does not have a choice.

—That is debatable.

—But if we do not augment him, we must give him something.

—Why?

—Because he asked.

They were no longer making any sense to him, if, indeed, they made sense before. And they were no longer speaking to him.

*—He gave us the Useless One.*

*—The Useless One is free.*

*—We could—*

"What are you?" he asked.

They lowered, coming so close he could almost touch them. If he could figure out a way to move.

*—We are many things,* one of them said.

*—We are Powers,* said another.

*—We are Ancestors,* said a third.

*—We are God,* and that seemed to have been spoken by all of them at once.

*—At least,* a single male voice said, *that is what your people have called us from the beginning of time.*

"So there is no God as taught by the Words?"

*—Which Words?* one of the voices asked.

*—We are taught,* another said, *but not remembered.*

*—Time loses things,* a third said.

*—You come from the Roca,* a fourth said. *He is your ancestor.*

"Is he with you?" Nicholas asked, remembering what they had just said.

*—The Right Hand,* one said.

*—Of course,* said another voice.

*—No,* said a third.

The silence again. Not only could he not hear his own breathing, he couldn't hear his own heartbeat.

*—Do not lie to the boy,* said a different voice.

*—We are not lying,* said one of the earlier voices. *He is not being specific.*

*—He does not know what to ask. So much has been lost.*

*—And whose fault is that?*

*—Not his.*

*—His family's.*

*—His family is not responsible.*

*—He is a descendent.*

*—Of the elder. Only the elder.*

The swirls of mist lowered still. One of them stopped above his face. He could feel the dampness, the chill, growing around him.

*—We will not enhance you,* a voice said, and it sounded as if it was reverberating through him, *even though you asked. You did not use what you have already been given.*

*—(Not fair),* another voice said, the one that had whispered to the others earlier. *(His children use it. He did not know.)*

*—(Ignorance is not an excuse.)*

"At least let me know what you're denying me."

The voices erupted around him. The cacophony was so great he wondered if they would shatter his eardrums, even though he wasn't listening through them.

—*He did not know what he was asking for.*

—*It was all lost.*

—*All.*

—*He is unworthy.*

—*He is perfect.*

—*He will lead them to the wrong place.*

—*He will not lead them. You know that.*

—*He did not know what he was asking for.*

—*He had an idea.*

—*He had to. He is a descendent.*

"Stop!" he said, and his single voice made all others quit. "Tell me what you told him. The Roca. When he asked."

The swirls floated back toward the vaulted ceiling. The chill left him, and the damp, and the strange mist.

For a moment, he thought they weren't going to answer him.

—*We told him,* they finally said as one voice, *that he has touched the Essence of God.*


# FORTY-FIVE


THE golden glow was so bright that Matthias's eyes hurt.

He looked up from the Words, wondering where the light was coming from. Then he looked down at his hands, and saw that it was coming from the altar. From his touch.

He pulled away, and the light went out.

Pausho was still watching him. She had moved to a cushion near the door. She looked older than she ever had before.

"What was that?" he asked.

"Your heritage," she said, and in her voice, he heard defeat.

He felt a shiver run through him. He thought he understood her, but knew he didn't want to.

"The Roca," he said.

She nodded. "You come from him."

"You tried to wipe out his bloodline."

"Here," she said softly. "In the mountain. We never tried to touch the King."

"Because of the insanity?"

"Because he did not use his power. None of them did."

Matthias was shaking. His hands tingled from their touch on the altar. The jewels on the floor still glowed with an interior golden light. He hadn't realized that they had been both deflecting and absorbing his glow.

"I didn't know," he said.

"It doesn't matter," she said. "You come from the younger. He made the choice for you and all of your ancestors. The power runs through you. And you have used it."

"Accidentally."

"At first," she said, and he heard the truth in her words.

He ran a shaking hand over his face. So the Fiftieth Rocaan had been right all along. Matthias was supposed to be Rocaan. By the original design, because he was a descendent of the second son. He was the most natural Rocaan of all.

And Nicholas was right too. They should have worked together, not separately.

Together.

Except that the Roca himself denounced the plan he had set in motion before his original death. He had tried to reverse it.

Hence the Words.

"They are not your Words, are they?" she asked softly, with no sarcasm at all.

He shook his head. The Words Written, the ones he knew, had only a fraction of the information in this document. They followed the path originally set by the Roca before his death. He understood the initial split now: When the second son went insane, and his family was deposed by those who later led the Tabernacle, they ignored the return of the Roca as much as they could, probably thinking it irrelevant or maybe even impossible. They chopped up the Words, destroying their purpose as a document of history and warning, and they transformed the Words into a document of myth.

"You don't follow the Words Unwritten, do you?" he asked.

Pausho shook her head. "They were added by the Tabernacle. We do not believe in them."

He was shaking. "This power I have will make me insane."

"If it hasn't already," she said.

He glanced at the jewels, still glowing at his feet.

*If it hasn't already.*

The coldness within him, the thing everyone had remarked upon, the feeling at times when emotions overwhelmed him, emotions he could not control. Something else took him over, as it had when he killed Burden, all those years ago.

He closed his eyes, remembering the emotion.

Remembering the trigger:

*"You have a great magick, holy man,"* Burden said. *He shook his head. "Aren't you ashamed of killing the very thing you are? Or is that why you did it?"*

*"I'm not like you,"* Matthias said.

*"You're just like me,"* Burden said.

And then Matthias had used his own power, only he had not know what it was. A screen he had made of energy had gone up before his face, as if he were lifting a shield.

And he remembered the emotion that had welled within him, the thought—

*He wasn't a demon spawn. He was a good man. All his life he had worked to be a good man. He was Rocaan. The Holy Sir.*

*Beloved of God.*

*"I'm not like you,"* he whispered.

*"That's probably true,"* Burden said. *"Your power is reckless, out of control. You have no idea why you hate as intensely as you do. You hate us because we remind you of yourself."*

He waited for the anger to return, the emotion to overwhelm him, just as it had every time he had that thought, and it did not return. Perhaps, with his confrontation with the younger boy, Coulter, and now, with the real Words before him, the anger had been quelled.

Maybe what he felt hadn't been the insanity at all.

Maybe it had just been fear.

"Matthias?" Pausho still spoke softly to him, as if she were afraid of him.

Maybe everyone was afraid of him.

Maybe they had a right to be.

"You said you would find a way to defeat those invaders."

He opened his eyes.

She was still sitting on her cushion, watching him warily. The jewels weren't as bright any longer, and the vault's light seemed to be coming mostly from the torches.

Had he changed that?

He sighed. "I don't know if we can defeat the Fey. But we can fight them on their own terms."

He crossed the jewels and stopped before her. She cringed against the wall. She *was* afraid of him. He wanted to reassure her, but he didn't think he could.

He was afraid of himself.

"In here are your weapons, the swords, the globes." He smiled without mirth. "If you could get them to eat ota leaves, you'd kill them as well."

"I don't think we can do that," she said.

"Me, either." He took a deep breath. He had been right, just as he had always thought. The Secrets held the way to kill the Fey. Only they hadn't been designed for that.

They had been designed to kill others like him. They were tools created for a civil war, a war among those who continued to use the magick power granted in the cave and those who did not or no longer did. Somehow, the greater the magick within a person, the more deadly the weapons were.

But their design was even more insidious than that of a usual weapon. They could be targeted—directed—guided—by the user, if the user had magical ability. They could be directed against a family, and all the members of that family who were touched by the item would die. They could be targeted against men and all men who came in contact with the weapon would die. Or they could be targeted against a race, as he had done with holy water. And then the race, when attacked with the item, would die.

The weapons were also dangerous to their users: If the user shared a characteristic with the target—if a family were targeted, and the user was distantly related—he would die. The weapons were ugly, ugly remnants of what must have been an ugly time.

*These tools do not harm those who use them,* the Roca had written in the Words, *only those against whom the tools are used.*

So if the Fey had picked up the holy water on that fateful day during that first invasion when they had trapped Matthias in the Servant's Chapel—and had targeted him as he had targeted them, by throwing the vials of holy water at them hoping the Fey would be killed—then he would have died. And so would all Islanders.

It was a cunning magick that the Roca had invented after his return. He tried to use it to wipe out the magick he had brought to Blue Isle. He used it against his friends—in the Soul Repositories were some of his closest friends, those who did not agree with his change of heart—but he could not bring himself to use it against his own family.

He left that task for others, for the Wise Ones, who ultimately failed.

"What else can we do?" she asked.

"There are many other things we can do," Matthias said. "although some of it is not useful in battle."

"We'll have to remove the jewels from the floor. I don't think we'll have time."

He glanced at them again. They were dark. They looked as they had before he touched the altar. When one combined the knowledge in the Words and the Secrets, it became clear that the jewels had more properties than all the other items. The jewels focused everything. With one jewel, a man like Matthias had an arsenal, if he knew how to use it.

"We'll leave them," he said with reluctance. "The Roca initially put them here to guard the way to the cavern."

As he spoke those words, he felt the pull once more.

"There are more weapons in the cavern," Pausho said. "I will get them."

"Are there jewels?" he asked.

"And orbs and soul repositories and swords. Most of our items are stored there."

He glanced at the opening, felt the pull again. He couldn't carry all the weapons, but he could carry some. A pocketful of jewels would be enough to save the town.

But he didn't want Pausho to touch them. She destroyed everything she touched.

"I'll go," he said.

"You nearly died the last time you went there," she said.

"I know."

"Then what makes you think you can go again?"

The Words sat open on their pedestal. He wished he could touch them again, read them again. They had changed everything for him.

His whole life was now different.

And he had been so wrong.

"I may die there," he said to her. "But what happens to me is not the point."

"What is the point?" she asked.

He extended his hand to her to help her up. She stared at it for a long time. He wasn't going to move his hand, nor was he going to answer her question, until she stood beside him.

She seemed to sense that. Finally she put her hand in his.

Her skin was leathery, tough, and slightly cool. He wondered if she had regained any of her strength at all. He couldn't tell from her touch. It seemed almost passive, a word he had never associated with her before.

"You have to lead them," he said, covering her hand with his other hand. "They won't listen to me. You'll have to be bold and courageous, and willing to sacrifice."

"Lives," she said.

He nodded.

"You can lead," she said. "I'll tell them to listen—"

"It won't work and we both know it," he said. "That might last for a while, but when the fighting gets intense, they'll turn to you anyway. You have the knowledge. You know what the choices are."

"But I'm not the one who understood the Secrets," she said.

"You knew of them," he said. "You know more about them than I do."

She stared at him, and he wondered, for a moment, if he was wrong. She did know about them, didn't she? She'd been in here enough. Zak had told him that the forge they'd been using for varin swords was wrong. Surely they knew enough.

He was counting on it.

They all were.

"Still," she said, "you were the one who knew to use them against these creatures."

"And you were the one who drove them back."

Her gaze didn't meet his. And he knew why. He knew, just as she did, what they had used to hold the Fey back.

"There is no eradicating the Roca, is there?" he asked. "There is no destruction of that bloodline."

She bowed her head. Her gray hair was thinning on top. For so many years she had been the nemesis in his life, and now he was seeing her for what she was: an old woman who had failed at everything she had tried to do.

"It's not that," she said. "There are very few of you. And we saw most of them. It's the others."

"Others?" he asked.

"The Roca's cave is still open. No matter how many times we try to close it, it does not stay closed. It cannot stay closed. The swords should have kept people away. But they did not. Not entirely."

"You're saying others have the power of the Roca."

She shook her head. "It's not as simple as that. What the cave gives to one is not the same as what it gives to another."

"And what did it give to you?"

She raised her head. Her cheeks were flushed.

"You told me on the mountain," he said. "You said you were there as a girl. You said that was why you had become a Wise One. You said it was a holy place, and you said no one should be discouraged from touching the Hand of God."

"The Right Hand of God," she whispered, and pulled her hand from his. "Did you go inside?"

He shook his head.

"Then you do not yet know." She closed her eyes. "I asked for this. And I vowed not to use it."

"What?"

"The power," she said. "The same power you have. Only it changes from person to person, line to line."

"How does it change?"

"By how you use it," she said. "By what you want it to be. Your wants are its limitations. The Roca said his wants had no limits. He limited his sons, by limiting their minds."

"But not enough," Matthias said.

"Enough for the King's family." She smiled sadly. "Not enough for yours."

"And that's what you used to drive the Fey back," Matthias said.

She ran a hand through her thinning hair. "I promised never to use the power," she said. "When I returned, frightened and dizzy, I promised never to use it, and the Wise Ones took me in."

"They had gone to the cavern?"

"We guard it. This is the main entrance, not the one above. So few go that high in the mountains. We know when they do."

"And make them Wise Ones."

"If we can."

"So why are you so dedicated to stopping the use of the power?" he asked. "Why did you call the rest of us demon spawn? Why didn't you use what had been given to you?"

Her eyes held tears and he didn't know why. She opened her mouth to answer him, then closed it, as if words were not enough.

"Because of the insanity?" he whispered.

She nodded. "The Roca is so clear on that point. He knew that too much power destroyed the mind."

Matthias's mouth had gone dry. He glanced at the Words. "Then how do you know that isn't the raving of a madman?"

"Because he had died before the insanity took him," she said

"He was no longer of this place. He had gone to another, and yet he still cared about this place."

Like Jewel. She was dead and not dead.

Matthias could still feel her hands around his throat.

He touched it, felt the swelling and the bruises.

The insanity. He shuddered. He would have to face it, was already facing it. Already questioning it. He wondered how subtle it could be.

And then he knew.

"You're wrong," he said softly. He had his back to her. He was looking at the tapestries, seeing the images, even from this distance. "The insanity will come anyway."

"There's none in the King's family."

"That we know of," Matthias said.

"You're coming back to the children, aren't you?" she said, and her voice was trembling. "It's not fair. That practice has existed—"

"For generations, I know," he said. "But it's not mentioned in the Words."

"It is too!" She had come up beside him. "You saw it. The Roca admonished us to give his line to the mountain."

"That's not what it said," Matthias said. "The Old Islander was quite specific. 'Bring my children to the cavern. And failing that, bring their children, and their children's children.' "

" 'So that my line might end here,' " she added.

" 'So that my line might end here,' " Matthias said. "Not 'die here.' It's different, Pausho. A man could live out his life in that place and harm no one. That was the context, that was what the Roca was saying."

"But he said his line couldn't continue."

"He said the magick couldn't continue, that the power should not be set free from the cave, that all who take it outside have not the power of God within them but the power of the demons above. Those who take it *outside*, Pausho. That means someone has it inside. The Roca meant for his line to live in the cavern, perhaps to guard it, until his line died out."

She gave a cry like none he'd ever heard, and fell to her knees clutching her stomach, her head bent.

He had always wanted to see her defeated. His entire life, he had wanted an acknowledgment of her mistakes, of the mistakes of the Wise Ones. But now that he had it, now that she had shattered before him, he felt empty.

He crouched beside her, and put a hand on her shoulder. She flinched away from him. "You were taught that," he said. "You were taught by the other Wise Ones."

She nodded, not looking up, not moving her hands. "I took— I took—"

"Countless babies to the snow line, I know," he said. "I know. You were taught it was right."

She raised her face to his. He had never seen such anguish, not ever, not in all his years in the Tabernacle or in his years since.

"What have I done?" she whispered.

Sympathy would not work now. He knew it, and so did she. He kept his voice gentle, even though his words were not. "You committed murder in the name of God because you were taught to believe it was right."

"But I should have known . . ."

"What is obvious," he said, "isn't always easiest."

As he well knew, since he had done the same thing.

He helped her to her feet, and she leaned against him so hard that he nearly staggered under her weight.

"Come on," he said. "You can't quit now."

"But what if I'm wrong again?" she asked. "What if you're wrong?"

"We will live with it," he said. "As we live with the rest of it."

She stood. Her tears were drying. "That's not good enough," she said.

He knew. He closed his eyes.

"It's all we have," he whispered. "It's all we have."

# FORTY-SIX

RUGAD was not going to wait for his people to find an Islander to experiment on, not after his conversation with Landre. He had explained the procedure to Landre, and Landre would oversee the touching of the swords.

Rugad was excited by Landre's words.

Power.

Control.

Magick.

The Islanders had power, but the Fey had allowed their surprise at the Islanders' abilities to give the Islanders control. The Islanders did not normally have control, or if they did, it was ancient and misunderstood.

The Islanders had power.

The Fey could turn that power into magick.

Rugad had been a warrior for so long that he sometimes missed the subtleties.

He was headed out of the Great Hall in search of Selia when she nearly collided with him. She was followed by yet another Wisp, this one looking as if he had flown through flames and floods and hurricane winds to get to Jahn. His wings were torn, and his face was covered with dirt. He had a long scratch beneath one eye where something had hit him as he flew, and he appeared to be favoring his right arm.

"A moment," Selia said to Rugad. She looked pale, drawn, much as she had when he had first seen her, only days ago.

"A private moment, it seems," Rugad said, and led them to the former King's Audience Chamber.

He hated this room. He had nearly died here, and even though his people had wiped his blood off the floor, he could still feel it, like a stain on his entire being. The pain in his throat, which he had grown accustomed to when he spoke, seemed worse here, and so did the bruises the Golem had given him when it had tried to kill him.

Still, he had used it several times because it was large, and because it was close to many important areas of the palace.

The table that Rugad had used for his meeting with the generals had been moved to the North Tower before dawn. Someone had placed other furniture here, probably to store it. Several chairs, most of them from more comfortable areas of the palace, littered the floor, looking small and out of place in this formal area. Still, he sat in one and pushed a cushioned footstool toward the Wisp.

The Wisp sat on it gingerly, as if the very movement of sitting hurt him.

Selia remained standing until Rugad motioned for her to sit.

"The worst first," Rugad said to the Wisp.

"I am instructed, sir, to tell you in a particular order." The Wisp's voice was raspy and raw, as if exhaustion had taken everything from it.

"I don't care," Rugad said. "I want the worst. Then you can tell me the rest."

The Wisp closed his eyes. His brows met over his nose, forming a winged creature on the upper half of his face. The Wisp had unique features for a Fey, all angular and lined, like the rest of the Fey, only molded to make him look slightly birdlike, and less delicate than most Wisps.

"Forgive me," he whispered.

"I will not blame you for the news," Rugad said, already knowing it was bad. Very bad. He had only seen messengers look like this when they expected to be punished for the words they carried.

The Wisp swallowed. His Adam's apple worked with difficulty, as if he were swallowing against a dry throat.

"Get him something to drink," Rugad said softly to Selia.

She nodded, stood, and left.

The Wisp took a deep breath, opened his eyes, and looked after her. Then he turned to Rugad. Their gazes met. Rugad had never spoken to this Wisp before. He would have remembered.

Very few Fey looked at him as if they were equals.

Perhaps the news made this Wisp so bold.

"Boteen is dead," the Wisp said.

And Rugad, who had been bracing himself for something, almost didn't catch the words. "Boteen?" he repeated. "How?"

"Murdered by a Red Cap."

That Rugad did not expect. One of their own people, a magickless one, murdering an Enchanter.

"Who?"

"One of the Failures, traveling with an Islander. They surprised Boteen and a Horse Rider. Slaughtered them both."

"How?" Rugad asked. He felt strangely calm, as if some part of him had expected this news.

The Fey rarely lost Enchanters to death. Usually Enchanters were lost to insanity.

"With their swords and knives," the Wisp said. "We heard it from a Scribe who recited the whole thing."

In tedious detail, Rugad thought. Well, there couldn't be a better witness than a Scribe. Scribes never lied. They couldn't. "Was Boteen affected by the wave this morning?"

"I don't know, sir," the Wisp said. "I assume so. The rest of us were."

Then Rugad nodded. That explained it, then. Boteen hadn't been able to fight back, his magick drained. The Red Cap had caught him at the opportune moment.

Rugad frowned. He had lost his Enchanter, and he had come

to rely on Boteen. He had been thinking that Boteen would help him take control of the Islander's power.

Perhaps that was what Boteen was thinking. Perhaps that was his plan. The previous Wisp, Ay'Le's Wisp, had said that Boteen was heading into the mountains. He had seen the Place of Power, even though he had not identified it as such to Rugad, and he was going to it.

"Where did this Red Cap find him?" Rugad asked.

"I do not know exactly," the Wisp said. "The Scribe said that he was hiding in an outcropping as he had been ordered by Boteen. Boteen and the Horse Rider had gone to investigate something, which was what they were returning from when the Red Cap attacked."

"The Red Cap followed them from the place they had investigated?"

"So it would seem," the Wisp said.

Rugad could sit no longer. Perhaps he wasn't as calm about the news as he thought. He stood, then wandered the room, touching the walls lightly. There were still marks on each wall from the shields and swords that had decorated it during King Nicholas's reign. All over the palace were tapestries and bits of Islander symbolism.

None of them showed the Place of Power.

"Sir?" the Wisp asked. "Would you like to hear the rest?"

Rugad held up a hand. Boteen dead. A Red Cap in the Place of Power.

He shuddered.

Red Caps knew nothing about such places. Very few Fey did any longer, at least the Fey who were raised away from the Eccrasian Mountains. The others knew but took no actions.

A Red Cap, who had to be with Nicholas, if Rugad's information was all correct.

And what did Nicholas know?

Perhaps the better question was, How much had he learned already? And how much more could he learn?

The key was that Place of Power, and now Rugad had no one to take it.

He could send Landre, but Spell Warders, for all their theory, had little to do with practice. The last thing he wanted to do was to send in Infantry or those with minor magicks.

Rugad had wandered far from the chairs. He stopped at the dais, now empty of the ornate throne that Nicholas had kept there, and he stared at the emptiness.

This, in some ways, was his fault.

He was ninety-two years old, and he had fought most of his life. Twenty years before, he had said to Rugar that once, just once, he wanted a worthy opponent.

It seemed he finally had one.

Rugad turned.

The Wisp was watching him closely. Selia had just returned with a large mug of water for the Wisp. The Wisp didn't look at her as she handed it to him, but he did drink like a dying man, spilling part of the liquid on his pointed chin.

"What else?" Rugad said. He was ready to hear it now.

"Licia sends her regards. She says that Ay'Le's message was hasty. Yes, the Fey have retreated from the initial attack, but she sees it not as a defeat, but as an opportunity."

Rugad suppressed a smile. A battle, then, between the Charmer diplomat and the Infantry leader. With Boteen gone, he wondered who would lead.

"Go on," Rugad said.

"She asks for reinforcements, all magickal. She wants Beast Riders and Foot Soldiers, anything that you can spare. She asks that the mind behind the assault on the Tabernacle join them in the Cliffs of Blood. She needs a fierce magickal leader. She says that Ay'Le is still lamenting her lack of opportunity to practice diplomacy."

Rugad looked at Selia and raised a single eyebrow in a question.

"Ay'Le can focus on herself a bit much," Selia said. "But her Charms are effective."

"Can she ruin Licia's command?"

"If she believes it necessary," Selia said.

"You don't like her," Rugad said.

Selia shrugged. "Charmers rarely like each other."

"But you don't respect her, and Charmers do respect each other, don't they?"

"Usually," Selia said.

"You did not oppose my sending her," Rugad said.

"I was not your advisor at the time," Selia said.

He took a deep breath. She had not been. Again, that had been Wisdom's error.

"You defended her earlier."

"You were criticizing her for trying to do what she had been sent to do."

"But you do not believe she is good at what she does."

"She has her strengths."

"Is she a good diplomat?"

"With non-Fey," Selia said, implying that Ay'Le did not handle Fey well. And Rugad had sent her with an Enchanter, the most difficult of all Fey.

Now dead.

He felt a twist in his heart. He and Boteen had worked together for decades. Then Rugad set the feeling aside. He had lost hundreds of friends and acquaintances over the years.

"Did you see Fey troops marching toward the Cliffs of Blood as you flew here?" he asked the Wisp.

The Wisp nodded. "They were only a quarter of the way. Their march seemed slow, but there were a lot of them."

So Kendrad was making as good time as she dared. "Selia," Rugad said, "Send a different Wisp to the Cliffs of Blood. Let the troops there know of Licia's request, and tell them that Licia is in charge. I would rather have my people led by someone who does not accept defeat than someone who does so easily. Send a second Wisp to Kendrad. Tell her that Licia's plan is sound. These Islanders must face the full magickal wrath of the Fey."

Which, of course, was impossible now that Boteen was dead.

But Rugad would still do his best.

"Then get me my Hawk Riders. I will catch up to Kendrad's troop."

"Sir!" Selia said. "You said you weren't going to go. You said—"

"I know what I said." He spoke curtly to her, not wanting to be contradicted. "But Licia has requested the person who thought up the attack on the Tabernacle. And that was me."

"Sir," Selia said, "Rugad." He could hear the shaking in her voice. She did not like to contradict him. "You could do that from here."

He shook his head. "I do not know the terrain, nor the type of magick they will use."

"We have maps."

"Useless," he said. "And worse."

"But you did not know the terrain of the Tabernacle when we attacked it."

"That was different," he said. "The Islanders did not even know the Fey had arrived. These people are prepared. They are willing to use their powers. I will go."

"Sir," she said and bowed her head. She did not approve. Even the Wisp looked shocked.

"It is a dangerous place, sir," he said.

"I know," Rugad said softly. "I've been to dangerous places before." He gave Selia his best, fiercest frown. "Go."

She nodded and backed out of the room, clearly frustrated. The Wisp still waited.

"You may go as well," Rugad said. "You are relieved for a few days. Go see Seger, my healer. She will help you feel better."

"Thank you, sir," he said.

Then Rugad focused on him. "What is your name, Wisp?"

"Chauncey."

Rugad felt a jolt of surprise at the name. The name was Nyeian, all pomps and frills and wasted air. Most Wisps had maintained the L'Nacin tradition of naming babies with a word, not a traditional name. But apparently, this Wisp's parents had been young enough to forgo that tradition. Chauncey was even younger than Rugad had initially thought. That explained the boy's stamina and his ability to stand after such an ordeal.

"Chauncey," Rugad said, "you are to be commended for your service."

"Thank you, sir," the Wisp said.

"Go now."

The Wisp did not need to be told twice. He bowed once, then left, his wings curled against his back, his legs trembling with strain.

As the door closed, Rugad let out a small sigh. What he couldn't tell Selia, what he could tell no one, was that there was a reason for his change of plans. Boteen's death meant no one could control the Place of Power, and the conversation with Landre had convinced Rugad of the need for that control.

It was the key he had been searching for.

He would be able to manipulate it.

After all, it was a different branch of his family—but still his family generations removed—who had first controlled the Place of Power in the Eccrasian Mountains. He would have to draw upon old knowledge, knowledge the Shamans had controlled for too long, to help him now.

He would have to be extremely careful. He knew the danger he was putting himself in. He would have to run the campaign like an old man instead of a warrior. He would have to remain at the rear of the action, perhaps even in camp, until he knew it was safe to go forward. And he would have to be guarded at all times.

The closeness to the battle would also bring him closer to his great-grandchildren. If they made any mistakes, any mistakes at all, he would be there to take advantage of them.

He would be taking a risk, yes. But no great victory was ever won without risks.

He smiled and touched a hand to his throat. The scar remained, jagged and lumpy.

It was time to make good King Nicholas pay for his treachery.

It was time to make Rugad's great-grandchildren worthy heirs to the Black Throne.

It was time to settle this matter of Blue Isle once and for all.

# FORTY-SEVEN

NICHOLAS opened his eyes. He felt weak and dizzy, shaking with a cold that seemed to come from inside instead of out. His back ached from the hard marble floor, and his hand, resting against the basin, was asleep. He let his hand drop, felt the stab of pins and needles through his arm.

The others huddled above him, all except Scavenger. Adrian was closest, his face so pale with worry that it was the same color as the marble. Tears floated in Arianna's eyes. She was leaning against Coulter for support. Coulter had his hands on Nicholas's shoulders, but Nicholas hadn't felt them until now.

Gift stood slightly apart, with his mother behind him. They were staring down at him as if they hadn't seen him before. Leen sat on the steps, watching from a distance, as if she were a bridge between the group on the floor and Scavenger, who had to be standing guard outside.

Nicholas opened his mouth to say something, then felt all that water he had drunk churn in his stomach. He rolled on his side almost too late. It spewed from him against the base of the fountain and, before he could recover enough to speak, seeped into the rock on the side.

It was as if the water had never been.

They had denied him the water's power.

They had even denied him its refreshment.

He rolled back over and wiped the back of his good hand across his lips. Unlike the other times he had retched in his life, his mouth did not taste foul.

There was no taste at all.

If he hadn't blacked out, if he hadn't awoken and lost all the water, he would have thought nothing had happened.

Coulter had removed his hands from Nicholas's shoulder.

"Daddy," Arianna asked softly, "are you all right?"

He nodded. His throat ached. That feeling, at least, was familiar.

He let them help him into a sitting position, and he placed his head between his knees to make the dizziness go away. He stayed that way longer than necessary.

He had to think, and he didn't want a hundred questions asked of him while he was asking a hundred of his own.

The fountain granted Feylike power. Nicholas's family had it, but had never used it. The second son's family had, and had gone insane. What had happened in those moments after the water was absorbed into them? Did they suddenly become like Coulter?

Would this give him the solution to the war with the Fey? Should he let Leen drink, and Scavenger—who would finally get his wish and become magical—and Adrian? Should he let Coulter try to enhance his own powers, even if it might kill him?

Or should he tell them nothing?

Was it his choice?

Or theirs?

He pulled his knees closer to his cheeks. The pain woke him up, made his thinking sharper, made him feel as if he could find the clarity he needed.

If he let them drink, then he would have to let them use the powers. And if they used the powers, they would eventually lose their minds.

Curious that he hadn't even thought of letting his children try. He knew that the creatures he had seen—the Powers, the Ancestors, the Right Hand of God—would have a choice: they would choose whether or not to enhance already existing powers. Powers being used.

Like his were not, apparently.

That's why the water had left him. Because something in it changed people. And the change happened not just in this generation, but in subsequent ones.

This had happened to the Fey, centuries ago, and all their people embraced it, choosing to use their powers in different ways.

Was this where their ruthlessness came from? This coldness at their very hearts? This mad desire to make war, to conquer the world no matter what the cost?

Even Jewel held to that. Even on the day she died, Nicholas wasn't sure if she would betray him for Fey conquest. They had talked about it just before entering the Coronation Hall.

And he knew she loved him.

That was the strangest part of all.

"Nicholas." Jewel was beside him now. He could feel her, her light touch on his back, so unlike any other. Her warmth. Something about this place brought her back to him. Something about this place had affected his whole life.

"Nicholas." There was concern in her voice.

"Daddy?"

He didn't want to move. The center of his decision was here. The center of it all.

What was he fighting for? He was fighting to keep control of his Isle, to stop the Fey forward march toward conquest, to save not just Blue Isle, but Leut and beyond.

But more than that.

He was fighting for his children. He wanted them to grow up in the Isle's image, not the Fey's. Their opportunities for that were nearly gone now, but he felt that he could revive it, after this war, after the Black King was dead.

He could teach his children compassion and warmth and the essence of being alive.

The Black King would teach them ruthlessness and conquest.

If Nicholas told anyone of the secret of the fountain, anyone at all, the others would know of it. Everyone would be tempted. He would lose everything he was striving for. The Islanders would become Fey, even without the Fey's conquest. The essence of the Isle would be lost.

His children had all the strengths of the Fey and only a few of their weaknesses. Those weaknesses counterbalanced his own. But if he let them drink, they would have all of the weaknesses of the Fey. They would lose themselves.

They would lose.

He let out a moan.

"Father?" Gift was beside him now.

"Nicholas?"

"Sire?"

"Daddy?"

It was the edge of panic in Arianna's voice that made him look up. The dizziness was gone. He felt heat in his cheeks from the pressure of his knees.

His daughter was crouching before him, her too-thin face drawn and haggard and filled with fear. He took her hand, and then took Gift's. He ignored the others.

"If I told you I know a way to win this thing," he said, unwilling to carry the entire burden alone, "if I told you that it would cost you your minds, your hearts, and your compassion, maybe even your life, would you do it?"

"What would we win?" Arianna asked.

"We would be able to defeat the Black King," Nicholas said. "Maybe."

"Not for certain?"

"Nothing is for certain," he said quietly.

"Who would run Blue Isle then?" Arianna asked.

"And who would lead the Fey?" Gift asked, his question quiet.

"I don't know," Nicholas said. "Maybe you. For a while. Maybe your children, but I couldn't guarantee their sanity or compassion either. Or that you would live long enough to have any."

"What did you learn?" Jewel asked, her voice sharp.

Nicholas ignored her. Gift glanced at her, but did not translate. He frowned at his father. "I thought the point was to keep the Black King from moving on."

"It is," Nicholas said.

"And letting it stop here," Gift said.

"It is."

"And keeping Blue Isle in our family."

The "our" warmed Nicholas. "It is."

"Then this method won't work," Gift said. "The risk is too great."

"You can't win a victory without great risk," Jewel said.

"Ari?" Nicholas said, looking at his daughter. She was frowning. She hadn't heard her mother; she didn't know that part of the argument. She didn't need to. Arianna always made up her own mind.

"Is there another way?" she asked.

"There might be," he said.

"Then maybe we shouldn't decide yet," she said. "Maybe we should wait, see how we do, and then if nothing else works, try this."

He hadn't thought of that. He wasn't sure he wanted to think of it. "Why?"

"Because," she said, "half a victory is better than none. If we keep the Isle, if we do live, if we have children, we have half a victory."

For a moment, he thought she sounded like her mother. And then he realized that she didn't. She sounded like him. He had made that very argument to his father, the day he decided to marry Jewel. It had been half a victory; it had given the Fey permanent access to Blue Isle. It meant they never went away. But they did not conquer it, and from that half victory, he had gained these two marvelous children.

And ended up here, in this cave, with the Black King owning most of the Isle.

"Half a victory is better than none," he said, almost to himself.

"This is about the fountain, isn't it?" Jewel said. "This is more than holy poison."

He sighed and turned to her. He would be careful in how he responded to her. He didn't want the others to know everything.

Gift started translating, but Nicholas held up a hand to silence him.

"This fountain can do something, can't it?" she asked. "It can grant great power."

He still didn't answer. He didn't know how.

"Nicholas, if you have something, if you have learned something, that gives you as much power as you said, then you must use it." She had her hands on her hips. "This is a Place of Power, and you've learned where the power comes from, haven't you?"

"I don't have to do anything," Nicholas said.

"You want to win this war, don't you?" Jewel asked.

He nodded.

"Then you must decide to win at all costs, or my grandfather will destroy you. He will find your weakness and attack you through it."

Nicholas frowned. "I thought we just discussed winning at all costs. It's not an acceptable solution."

"Nicholas, war is war. You must use every tool you have, especially against the Fey. You must take the risk."

"I am taking the risk," he said softly. "You of all people should understand that."

The others, the ones who couldn't hear Jewel, were shuffling slightly, confused by his responses.

"No, you're not," she said. "All this talk about hearts, minds, and compassion, settling for half a victory, is wrong, Nicholas. You must use everything, or you will lose."

"If I use everything, I will lose."

"You're wrong."

He shook his head. "You don't understand."

Gift was watching them, his blue eyes sharp. Nicholas wished the boy hadn't heard any of this.

"Make me understand," she said.

"I can't." The words hurt against his throat. "You're Fey."

Jewel took a step backwards. "That's never been a problem before."

"It's always been a problem between us, Jewel. It's just not always been tested."

"Nicholas," she said, "you risk everything by not taking advantage of your options."

"That's right," he said. "I risk everything."

She took a breath, about to speak, and then stopped. Apparently she heard something in his tone that startled her.

"And you said," he continued, "that you can't win a victory without great risk."

"That's not what I meant."

"It is," he said. "We just view our risks differently."

She shook her head and sighed. Then she crossed her arms in front of her chest. "Nicholas, if you have great power, you must use it."

"That's what you would do?" he asked.

"Yes," she said.

"Is that what your grandfather would do?"

She stopped, seeing the trap he had led her into.

"He knows we have a Place of Power, doesn't he?" Nicholas asked.

"If he doesn't now, he will," Jewel said.

"And if he had it, he would use all its tricks."

"Nicholas, this is like having a bow with no arrows. It is useless without its tricks."

"*All* its tricks," he said.

She stared at him.

"Wouldn't he?" Nicholas asked. "He would use all of them."

"Yes," she said.

"And that's the Fey expectation."

"Yes."

He took a deep breath and brushed a strand of hair out of his face. He was still tired from the experience, tired physically, and tired of fighting. "We cannot win this war by doing what the Fey expect. They have hundreds of years in battle and in magick. We cannot beat that sort of experience. Except with surprise."

"You have no surprise left," she said.

"I think I have some," he said. "I surprised you."

"By being foolish," she said.

"By making a choice that may make things more difficult in the short run and better in the long."

"There may not be a long run."

"There may not," he said. "But I'm gambling that there is."

"I hope you know what you're doing," she said.

He smiled. He was calmer than he had been. The argument had focused him, crystallized his emotions. He knew what he wanted, and he knew how to get there. "I do."

"I hope so," Jewel said, "because I think you're turning your back on your only chance for success."

She vanished. He watched her go, disliking this new aspect of their relationship. She could disappear whenever he upset her. And she could physically as well as emotionally withdraw her support.

But he could do this without her, if he had to.

He sighed and extended a hand. Adrian helped him up.

"What was that about?" Adrian asked.

Nicholas looked at him, imagined him trying to get used to a new power and at the same time fight with the Fey. It wouldn't work, no matter what Jewel said. No matter how much he wanted it to. It wouldn't work.

Gift was still watching him, as if waiting for Nicholas's response. As if Nicholas's response would determine his own.

"It was about tactics," Nicholas said. "Just tactics. Nothing more."

"Have you figured out a way to defeat the Black King?" Arianna asked.

"Yes," Nicholas said.

"Using this fountain?" she asked.

Gift bit his lower lip.

"No," Nicholas said.

"Is it holy water?" Arianna asked softly.

Nicholas sighed again. "It's dangerous," he said. "Too dangerous for us."

"It's what you and Mother were arguing about?"

Nicholas shook his head. "We were arguing about tactics."

"How, then, do you plan to defeat the Black King?" Adrian asked.

"By being Islanders," Nicholas said. He stood. He was a bit shaky, but he stood.

"We're not all Islanders," Leen said.

"I know," Nicholas said. "But I don't think we all have to be for this to work."

"For what to work?" Adrian asked.

"Our last stand," Nicholas said. "And our only hope."

# COUNTERATTACK
## [TWO DAYS LATER]

# FORTY-EIGHT

THE reinforcements threaded their way into the valley. The pass, approached from the west, was narrow, and only four Fey could march through it, shoulder to shoulder. Hundreds flew, of course, but getting the main body of the force through the pass had taken most of the night.

Licia wrapped a Domestic-spelled cloak around her shoulders, but even with it on, she was cold. The nights were frigid here, and probably worse on the mountainside, and the previous night had been the worst yet. Rain began pelting after the moon set, big fat drops that carried the chill of snow. She had ordered the wounded to be placed in shelters—she didn't have the strength or the magick to build a large Shadowlands—and she had let the rest make do as they could. She had been working on reviving their morale; the rain did not help her.

But the dawn was coming. She could see it, lightening the sky to the east. The mountains, as they always did, looked as if they were tinged with blood.

She ran a hand through her damp hair and turned to one of her assistants, ordering him to post new guards on the east side of the ridge.

The Islanders were proving dense in the art of war, and for that she was grateful. She had spent most of the previous day expecting an attack from the small town. When none had come, she wondered if it was all a ploy to make her complacent. She had redoubled her guards, and had some Owl Riders do a nighttime flyover. They reported that the Islanders appeared to be preparing for a siege.

That, at least, was a small blessing. So few of the Fey's adversaries ever attacked. Only the Nyeians had attacked, in one famous battle, and before that, the L'Nacin. There were others, she knew, but most dated beyond the memories of these soldiers. These soldiers were used to defenders who fought with their hearts and their bodies, but not with their minds—and certainly not with magick.

Her main goal in these days of quiet had been to remind her troops that the Fey had encountered magickal peoples before— although none as powerful as these Islanders. She also reminded them of the things the Black King had said before they left Nye, things he had repeated when they had arrived on Blue Isle just about a month before:

*Do not underestimate the Islanders.*

Now the reinforcements were coming in, and the numbers were larger than she had hoped. Obviously Rugad had thought this an important place to conquer. He had sent Kendrad, who was now directing the reinforcements into the lower parts of the valley. Kendrad also seemed frustrated at the slow progress of the troops, but could not see any other way to get them into the valley quicker.

She was worried, as was Licia, that the Islanders would see the troops and would mount an attack before the Fey were prepared.

But Licia had seen no evidence of Islander scouts. She had seen no normal procedures at all on the part of the Islanders. No counterattack, no scouts, no messengers sent for reinforcements.

It was as if this were the only enclave on the entire Island, and the Islanders would defend it to the death.

The thing she was most afraid of, though, the thing she wouldn't voice, was that the Islanders had another magickal response prepared, this one big enough to handle the entire Fey force.

She shivered in the cold. The sun still hadn't risen above the jagged edges of the Cliffs of Blood. Once it did, the air would warm a little.

She had hoped, when the reinforcements started to arrive, that they would be able to mount an attack by noon, but it was out of her hands. She was under Kendrad's command.

Licia felt no real relief in that. Kendrad had not come to her as any other commander would. Kendrad had not discussed the loss, nor the terrain, nor the unusual response of the Islanders. Kendrad had not acted like a commander coming into a new post.

Licia had not worked with Kendrad in years, but she could not imagine Kendrad forgetting the basics of command. Yet it seemed she had. Or perhaps she felt that Licia, who had ordered a rare retreat, was not worth consulting.

Someone tapped her shoulder. Licia turned. A woman, with the sharp features of youth and one of the most striking faces she had ever seen, bowed slightly to her.

The movement irritated her, and Licia suppressed a sigh.

Another Charmer.

"You are to come with me," the woman said.

Licia nodded, but said nothing. The woman led her through a small outcropping of boulders, past the impromptu hospital setup, and toward the new troops. The new troops, mostly Foot Soldiers and Beast Riders, were setting up a camp that had an efficiency she had forgotten in these last few days. A man stood in the center of them, tall and thin and familiar.

The Black King.

They had snuck him in without her knowing. No wonder Kendrad had not come to her. Kendrad was not leading this battle.

The Black King was.

He was wearing a cloak, much like hers, long and black and flowing. It covered his clothes. He had gloves on his large hands and custom-made boots that appeared to have no mud on them. Had he walked with the troop? She had seen no carriages come in.

Then she saw the Hawk Riders, milling around a contraption she had only seen once before, and then from a distance. She had seen it the day the ships had reached the Blue Isle. She had stood on deck and watched, hand shading her eyes, as the Hawk Riders had carried the Black King to a peak on the Isle's southwestern-most tip.

Now they were in the northeastern corner, as far from that spot as possible.

The woman leading Licia had gone to the Black King. He was surveying the air above them, obviously looking for a place to build a large Shadowlands.

"Rugad," the woman said. "I brought the commander."

"Thank you, Selia," he said. His voice was raspy and shallow, not at all as Licia had remembered. She had remembered a voice with such power that even a whisper would have shaken the rooftops.

Then he turned.

He was the man she remembered. His face, no longer handsome, was lined and weathered with age, as if his power had stamped his features in stone. He had a wide, jagged scar across his neck, a wound barely healed—the wound, apparently, that had nearly killed him. Small cuts dotted his skin. His eyes were dark and penetrating, and so full of intelligence that they seemed alive in and of themselves.

"You are Licia?" he asked. The raspy voice sounded almost as if it were not quite natural, somehow. It emerged from his mouth properly, but seemed to be a spell, made to transfer a voice from someone else's mouth to his. Apparently his own voice had been damaged by the Islander King, and this was what replaced it. It made her shiver, but not in the way she expected. She didn't shiver because of his voice's power, but because of its artificiality.

"Yes," she said. She had trouble speaking as well. She bowed her head slightly as she had been taught to do when she was in the presence of someone greater than she.

"You ordered a retreat three days ago."

"My Infantry was being slaughtered."

"By Islanders."

"By Islanders," she acknowledged. "They were using magick."

"So I was given to understand." Then he smiled. It startled her, the way it transformed his face, giving his features the same power as his eyes. "Fey are unused to the magick of others."

"Unfortunately," she said.

"You claimed you would get rid of this flaw in your troop, so that when we were ready for the second attack, everything would be better. Have you done so?"

She took a deep breath. "The battle will be the test."

"I won't send any reinforcements into battle with Failures," he said.

"They aren't Failures," she snapped.

His smile widened. He wanted to see her temper. Well, he had. "Not yet."

"Not ever," she said. "They are ready."

"To defeat the Islanders?"

"Is there anything else?" she asked.

His eyes met hers. She was startled by the power behind such a simple look. "You have killed Ay'Le."

"She interfered with my command."

"You could have demoted her."

"She Failed," Licia said. "In her attempt at diplomacy, in her attempt at leadership, she Failed."

"I authorize the death of Failures," he said.

"Except when they interfere with an ongoing campaign," Licia said. "She was turning the Beast Riders against me."

"If they could be turned, you were doing something wrong."

She straightened, no longer deferential. He wanted to be antagonistic. He wanted a reaction from her.

He would get one.

"I did nothing wrong. All my magickal Fey were injured by a wave of power that came through here. They were unfit for battle. I judged that the Infantry would do better."

"Were you right?"

She shrugged. "We were unprepared for the magickal counterattack. Perhaps the Beast Riders would have done better. I no longer know. It's not something that can be judged."

"You must judge it, to attack again."

"I have—had—a different attack planned this time. Fey-controlled, less formal, full magick. No Islander, even magickal ones, can withstand that."

"Never underestimate them," the Black King said.

She took a deep breath. "That was my mistake. I am ready to be punished for it if you deem it right."

Her heart was pounding, but she kept her expression impassive. She held herself as rigidly as he did. She wondered if he could see her increased heartbeat pulsing in a vein in her neck, or the fact that the tension was making her sweat slightly despite the cold.

She doubted he was the kind of man to miss those things.

"You are a courageous one," he said, not taking his gaze off her. "I had your record investigated. This is your first recorded loss."

"It is not a loss, sir," she said between clenched teeth. "The battle is not over."

"True enough." He nodded toward her. "And it is that knowledge which I like about you. Given what I understand of this battle, you were right to regroup. Your only mistake was in calling this a retreat. This section of the Isle is important, more important than I had initially realized. There are valuables here that Boteen discovered before his death. We will retrieve them."

"Yes, sir," she said. A trembling had begun in her hands. She clasped them together to hide it.

"You were right to ask for the reinforcements that you have."

"I did not expect you to come, sir."

He smiled again, this time the look was softer, almost tender. "You asked for me."

"No, sir, I—"

"You asked for the leader behind the destruction of the Tabernacle."

"I thought Onha, perhaps, or Kendrad—"

"It was my plan, and it worked."

"Yes, sir. It did."

"And this battle is even more important." He came closer to her and put a hand on her shoulder. His grip was tight, almost painful. "You will show me the ridge, sketch out your new plan, and we will see what we can come up with."

"Sir, I think Kendrad would serve you better."

"Kendrad arrived with me. She has not spent days here. She has not fought these Islanders. You will assist." He looked down at her. She wasn't used to being shorter than other Fey. "Have you problems with that?"

Her shaking had stopped, mercifully. "No," she said. "No problems."

"Good." He let her go. She had to move her right foot slightly apart from her left to keep her balance. "I have one task to complete here, and then we move to the ridge."

He turned his back on her. She wasn't certain if she should leave or not, so she waited. He cupped a hand, held it out in front of himself, and then flung it open.

A Circle Door appeared around his hand. A Shadowlands, created that fast, that expertly.

That was the difference between a Black Throne Visionary and a minor one like her. She didn't have the power to create a Shadowlands and leave her Vision open long enough to cover the battle. He could do it all without thought.

"I shall make another when we pass the wounded," he said. "We've brought extra Healers and Domestics."

"Good," she said, rather stunned. A command had never changed as quickly for her. It had gone from one leader to another, and she had never had a problem with that. But she had never been so close to the leader of the Fey Empire, so easily trusted as she was now.

She should thank the Mysteries and the Powers that he had agreed with her message, or it would be her body the Red Caps were carving now, in addition to Ay'Le's.

"Selia," he said to the Charmer, "people the Shadowlands for me."

"Yes, sir," she said.

He put his hand back on Licia's shoulder. She wasn't sure she liked the grip. "So tell me," he said as he led her toward the wounded, "do you believe we can win this fight?"

Everything rested on her answer. At least, everything for her: her command. Her life.

"Yes," she said.

"That is the answer I wanted," he said.

"I know."

"So I do not believe you."

She stopped, turned to him, and raised her chin slightly, "If I didn't think we could win this, I wouldn't have sent for reinforcements."

He smiled and slid his hand to the middle of her back, propelling her forward.

"Excellent," he said. "For I believe we can win this too."

# FORTY-NINE

THE city of Jahn looked empty.

Luke stood at the edge of what once had been a noble's land, and shivered. He was exhausted and hungry—their food had run out the day before—and now that they had reached the city, he wasn't sure how to proceed.

Con was standing beside him, staring as well.

The fires here had burned out long ago. The city was black ash and rubble. The Tabernacle still stood, but its walls were crumbling, its windows gone, its white sides covered in soot. On the other side of the river, the palace rose from the wreckage, looking as it had before all of this, as if nothing had touched it, or ever could.

"You think he's in there?" Luke asked.

"Where else would he be?" Con asked.

But Luke didn't answer that. Sebastian could be anywhere. He could be dead, if such creatures died. He could be with those Fey armies that had destroyed the countryside behind them.

Luke and Con had barely made it out. As they ran from field to field, from place to place, they encountered pockets of Fey everywhere, Fey bent on destroying the entire center of the Isle. Luke and Con managed to hide in fields and culverts, avoiding buildings because they were getting burned.

Yesterday morning, they had nearly walked into the full Fey force, coming down from Jahn, hundreds, maybe thousands of Fey, marching toward the barn that Luke had destroyed. Luke had said nothing then. His only thoughts were saving himself, saving Con. They had managed to hide; the Fey weren't really looking for two Islanders. Their orders seemed to be to demolish everything in their path.

More than once, a few Fey had seen them and noted the direction they were going. Con remarked that it seemed as if the Fey wanted some of the Islanders to escape, to report on what happened in the center of the Isle.

Probably to prevent any more internal dissent.

Luke closed his eyes. If he had known what would happen, he would never have planned that attack. His small action had caused hundreds of deaths and the destruction of everything important in the Isle. He knew, without going back, that his home was gone; the fields he had tended since he was a child were blackened ruins, just like the city before him was.

And he had caused that destruction.

"You ready?" Con asked.

Luke opened his eyes. He had to keep ahold of himself. Everything had changed, and he couldn't blame himself. Nothing would have changed if the Fey hadn't arrived on Blue Isle in the first place.

"The city looks undefended," he said.

Con nodded. "It didn't look that way when I left. There were soldiers everywhere."

"Do you think they sent the entire force south?" Luke's voice broke on that last.

Con shook his head, obviously ignoring Luke's reaction. "We didn't see enough Fey."

"They could be setting a trap here, then."

"For whom?" Con asked.

Luke didn't know. There was so much he didn't know. "Maybe

they tired of the city. Maybe they've found another place to make into their capital."

"Then it should be easy to discover," Con said.

"You want to check the palace, don't you?" Luke asked.

"I have to find Sebastian. He was my Charge."

Luke had heard about this over and over, mostly as they walked in the darkness of night. They had decided not to sleep—both of them felt that sleeping was dangerous—so they had talked to keep each other awake.

He knew that he couldn't dissuade Con from this course. He knew because he had tried. "All right," Luke said. "I think we can take the roads until we see Fey."

Con nodded. He had apparently come to the same conclusion.

"We need to reconnoiter the palace," Luke said. "We need to see if they're guarding it like they guarded . . ."

He let his voice trail off. He had almost said, "that barn." But Con hadn't been with him for that attack. Only Luke knew about it. He suspected the others who had been with him were now dead.

He cleared his throat. "Like they guard most anything."

"Do you think there are Islanders left in Jahn?" Con asked.

"Probably not a lot. If we get caught, we were fleeing the destruction of the countryside, and we hadn't heard what had happened in the city. Is that clear?"

Con nodded.

Luke glanced at him. The boy didn't look scared any more. The closer they had gotten to Jahn, the more determined Con seemed.

"I want you to do one other thing," Luke said.

"What?" Con asked.

"If it looks as if they're going to catch us, remove your necklace."

"I can't," Con said.

"You have to." Luke kept his voice soft. "If they kill us both, no one will rescue Sebastian. And they'll kill us if they see that religious symbol."

Con bit his lower lip. He swallowed so hard the movement was obvious. "All right," he said finally. "But I won't do it unless it looks as if they'll capture us."

"That's fine," Luke said. That was enough of a promise, for now. He was feeling a bit of hope. He hadn't expected them to get this far. They had done so on the strength of their cunning, on their good physical condition, and with something that Con called "God's Blessing."

Luke didn't know if he believed in God's Blessing, but he did believe that something had enabled them to slip through those troops, even if it was the Fey desire to let word of the destruction seep throughout the country. Whatever had allowed it, Luke would take it.

He had burned that barn for Blue Isle. Now he entered the destroyed city of Jahn for the same reason. Because Con was right. If they rescued Sebastian, whom the Islanders believed to be the King's son, they would give the Islanders hope. And sometimes, hope was all it took.

# FIFTY

IT was as if they were running a foundry for the Tabernacle.

Pausho walked through the streets of Constant, surveying the work. She hadn't slept in two days, but the mysterious weakness that had afflicted her was gone. Zak felt that she should take better care of herself, but she didn't have the time. They had too much work to do, and not enough people to do it. She didn't know when the Tall Ones would attack, but when they did, she wanted to be ready.

She was in the marketplace, which no longer looked like a marketplace. Special varin forges made of rocks and wood from the mountains were set up before the empty booths. Cold water, brought from designated mountain streams, sat in buckets, and was used sparingly, to temper the blades.

Zak had taught over a dozen Blooders how to make the swords, and they were working the six forges day and night to create as many as possible. The problem was, as Zak said, making these swords was delicate work—honing and rehoning the blade until it was so thin that it was barely as wide as a fingernail—and it usually took days to make just one. She needed dozens, hundreds if she could get them, and that was why she put the forges in the center of town. The work could continue while the fighting hap-

pened. She also put the oldest men in charge, figuring they would
be good for little else.

The oldest women worked the glass blowing, making globes
according to the specifications given to them by Matthias. He
had been here until the middle of the day yesterday, sharing the
Secrets the Tabernacle had once so jealously guarded. It felt odd
to hear the words from his mouth, knowing that even some of the
things he recited had been lost to her people.

She and he had tried to figure out several of the Secrets, but
the details were still lost, and they didn't have time to look
through the Vault to find them. He did send a group into the
mountains to pick ota leaves on the off-chance that the Tall Ones
would eat them, but she doubted that.

And she had forbidden him to use the Soul Repositories, although he claimed that might be the best weapon of all. They
scared her, made her think that the Roca's claim of demons was
true. Matthias had asked to bring the existing repositories up
from the Vault, and she had forbidden that as well. She had argued, falsely (although he didn't know that), that the Repositories could be used as a line of defense should the Tall Ones find
the Vault. But, in truth, she had just wanted to make sure that
they remained below, where no one could touch them.

Matthias was gone. He had taken the path inside the Vault
that led to the Roca's Cave. It was a mistake on his part, but she
couldn't convince him of that. Her words still carried little
weight with him. And why should they?

He had been right all along.

The three strange men who had traveled to the Cliffs with
Matthias were teaching her people how to fight with swords. They
were using sticks instead—she didn't want the varin swords used
for anything but the Tall Ones. Her people knew swordfighting,
but were unfamiliar with battle techniques. Matthias's strange
friends had fought the Tall Ones in Jahn, and in previous battles
that they refused to discuss, and they were doing well, teaching
her people a new form of ruthlessness.

She did not object to the ruthlessness. She objected to sharing
the Wise Ones' knowledge. She had spent her entire life in service of a moment that she had assumed wouldn't come. And now
that it had, it was nothing like what she had expected it to be.

Had the Roca expected this? Had he foreseen this?

And if he had, why had he insisted on destroying all that he
had discovered?

She knew the answer to that. She knew it in her heart and didn't want to think about it either. But it was in the Words. It was right at the beginning.

The Roca was a man. He was as fallible as she was. And he was the first, that she knew of, to discover his cave. When he had finally understood what he had brought upon his people, he had tried to destroy it, and it had been too late.

That was the beginning of the admonishments against Tall Ones; that was the beginning of the desire to keep the magick suppressed. That was even the foundation of much of what the Tabernacle considered to be a religion. They had taken the Roca's admonitions against a kind of people he had created, and they had turned those admonitions into a power that kept their own in charge.

It all seemed so clear now.

These new Tall Ones—these Tall Ones who had come across the ocean—were what her people could have become if they had been slightly different; if the Roca's desires hadn't kept the power underground, away from the majority of Islanders.

She made her way past the sword-makers to the group of younger women cooking ota leaves. The stench rose, thick and brackish. Ota leaves tasted wonderful, cooked or uncooked, but their odor was almost palpable. A table was laid out of the Feast of the Living, but like Matthias, she didn't see how that would be helpful.

There were only a few other things that could help. One was the chant like the ones she had used before. The other was a slightly different power that the Wise Ones had kept for themselves. She would use that only if she had to.

The other Wise Ones were in this main market area. She was keeping them close for two reasons. The first was that she didn't want to lose them; she needed their strength to fight this menace and their intelligence to come up with new plans should hers fail. The other reason was that she needed their powers to combine with hers. There was strength in their number.

She was even searching for Tri. She had banished him from the Wise Ones, but he still knew much of what they did. He would work with now; she was sure of it.

But using him required an apology, and she wasn't sure she was up to one. For once, he had been right and she had been wrong. He had known all along, it seemed, that Matthias wasn't someone to be feared. That Matthias would help them.

Matthias. She clenched a fist over her stomach. Her nausea returned at the thought of him, at the thought of that golden light bathing him. So few had the blood of the Roca in them, even with all these generations passed. So many of the Roca's line, the line from his second son, had died that they had almost succeeded in wiping the line out. But some remained.

Matthias remained.

She had told him she didn't want him to go to the Roca's Cave, but she was secretly glad he was gone. He had been right; her people would never have listened to him, and he would have pulled her in the wrong direction. She had barely been able to focus since they had come out of the Vault, but it would have been worse if he had stayed.

Even if he had been a fool to leave.

He had barely survived the mountain the second time. She doubted he would survive the third.

If she weren't so afraid of the Roca's Cave, she would have sent someone after him. The woman, Marly, perhaps—or perhaps not; she had shown real healing skill—or maybe her brother, Jakib, who seemed to have more compassion than his companion Yasep.

But Matthias had returned on his own once before. He might be able to do so again. If he did, he would bring the jewels, and increase the strength of the Blooders a hundredfold. If he failed, they would be no worse off than they were now.

She put a hand over her eyes and gazed at the ridge. There were troops moving up there. The troops had been there for two days, but they hadn't attacked.

Part of her wished they would.

Part of her wanted this started—and ended—now.

But another part, the sensible part, knew the longer those Tall Ones held off, the better off her people would be.

Better equipped, yes. Calmer, no. Her people were already getting restless. Everyone could see the troops above. The town knew an attack was coming. They just didn't know when.

The restlessness was deadly. She knew it, but didn't know how to stop it. She wondered if those Tall Ones were planning it that way.

She sighed and lowered her hand. So much to do, and she was not trained as a warrior.

At least she knew how to lead.

At least she knew how to defend.

She only hoped those two skills would be enough.

# FIFTY-ONE

NICHOLAS stood on a large flat rock he had half rolled, half dragged to the front of the cave. He was on his tiptoes, using a cloth he had ripped off his shirt to polish the jewels in the sword sticking horizontally out of the cave's mouth. He had cleaned a ruby near the edge of the blade, and then he had used a knife to get some of the grit off the next stone.

The grit came away cleanly, revealing an emerald. From the lumps in the sword's hilt, he figured he had four more stones to go. He suspected they were the remaining four stones in the cave. Only the stones on this sword's giant hilt were huge, about the size of Scavenger's fist, embedded in a hilt that was, unless Nicholas missed his guess, solid gold.

Who would make such a thing and then attach it to a cave door?

He sighed. The sun was just beginning to color the sky above him. He had been out here since light had turned gray. Sleep had eluded him since he had drunk the water from the fountain. He felt as if his brain had overloaded, as if he had to sort out the information he had received detail by detail, and somehow that made the process of sleep impossible.

Although Arianna caught him dozing more than once. She

said she had heard him snore. Perhaps he had, but he hadn't rested. His brain had continued processing, thinking, working the entire time.

The others slept in the cavern now. He let them. He had a feeling that this was the day.

He didn't know why.

But his feelings were stronger now, more than hunches, and he trusted them. For all the Powers or Ancestors or whatever they were had denied him, they had still given him something: a belief in himself where there had been none before.

He had always thought himself powerless, surrounded by the powerful: Jewel, Arianna, Gift, even Sebastian in his own halting way. All magickal creatures. All in some way greater than he was. He was simply an ordinary man born into an·extraordinary office.

And then he had learned that it was not true.

He was no more ordinary than they were. He had his own strengths—his familial strengths—just as Jewel did. His limitations were limitations imposed upon him by his family's choices centuries ago.

The talk of insanity and magick, death and magick, unnerved him on a very deep level. His daughter had a great deal of magick. And so did his son. And they were using it, at his request.

Even if he kept them from the water in the fountain, he was afraid he had already doomed them.

He put his knife in his hilt and removed the cloth, polishing the emerald. If the half-cleaned stone had reflected the light from the globe, focusing and steering it, cleaned jewels would do even more. He was thinking of taking the jewels from inside the cavern and bringing them out here, placing them at the very edge of the platform, as more protection.

The more protection they had, the better.

He had to be cunning and sharp, and willing to fight to the death. Even though he did have two strategies that would prevent his children's death, he hoped he wouldn't have to use them.

"Nicholas."

The voice belonged to Jewel. His heart bumped hard against his chest. He forced himself to keep working on the emerald.

Jewel had disappeared from his presence in anger two days before, and she had not returned. At first, he had thought it childish of her, disappearing because she disagreed with him. Then it had him questioning her entire existence. Was she the woman he had loved? The woman he had fought? Or was she something else entirely? Something like those blobs of mist he had seen after drinking from the fountain?

But that didn't stop his heart from leaping at the sound of her voice, his entire body from responding when he felt the warmth of her behind him. He wanted to turn and take her in his arms. But he didn't.

She had left him.

Again.

And she had had no right.

"Nicholas," she said, softly. "Please. It's important."

He stopped polishing the emerald and leaned his head against the dirt-covered hilt of the sword. The surface's roughness pressed against his skin.

He sighed.

And turned.

She was looking as beautiful as ever, as young as Gift, her hair in a single braid down her back. The woman he had fallen in love with. The woman he had hoped to spend the rest of his life with.

"You left," he said.

She shrugged. "You made me mad."

"I made *you* mad?" He braced a hand on the sword, and jumped off his rock. He stood a few inches from her. "You left us. You said you wouldn't."

"You said you wanted to win this at all costs."

"I said I wouldn't sacrifice my children," he said.

"And you think this new power of yours will?"

"Eventually," he said.

"Eventually doesn't matter," she said. "Now does."

He stared into her upslanted dark eyes. He knew how they looked in almost every mood, how they changed color slightly when he touched her, how black they got when she was angry.

He couldn't judge her mood now.

"Jewel, you can't believe that."

"They have to live through this first, Nicholas, and then pay whatever price comes."

"They'll live through it," he said. "It's the only thing your grandfather and I agree on. So price becomes important, even now."

She stared at him for a moment, then put a hand on his cheek. Her skin was warm. He leaned into her palm in spite of himself.

He didn't want to go through life without her. If he lived

through this, he would move the capitol from Jahn to here. He would spend the rest of his life with her.

The last two days had been sheer torture.

"Why were you gone so long?" he asked, suddenly not caring how vulnerable he sounded.

"I wanted to find out what that fountain is," she said. "Since you wouldn't tell me, I tried to get the Powers to."

"And?"

"They told me to ask you."

He sighed, then moved his cheek away from her touch. He shook his head slightly.

"Don't you trust me, Nicholas?"

He smiled slightly, hearing the echo of his thoughts from just a moment ago, all the doubts he carried, all the things he worried about when she was not there, were gone when she was. He could lie to himself all he wanted. He knew that this woman before him, this shade, this Mystery, was his wife.

He knew it with a knowledge so deep that it hurt.

"I trust you, Jewel," he said. "I've always trusted you. But my trust is this: that you'll act in your way, in your time. I can't always do that. I can't here. I know what you'll do. You've made it clear. And this time it's my decision. You won't trust me, and you need to. I'm right."

"Not if you know how to win against the Black King and you're turning your back on it."

Something in her voice stopped him. A panic, a tremor almost.

"What is it?" he asked.

Her eyes flattened somehow. The life left them. Jewel was afraid, and she was trying to hide it.

But she couldn't hide it from him. She could hide nothing of importance from him, no matter how hard she tried. "Jewel?"

"The Black King is here," she said.

"Already?"

She swept her arm toward the valley below. "He brought reinforcements."

Nicholas looked away from her. The morning light was growing. Everything was a golden red now. He moved away from the sword, headed across the cracked platform, to the edge overlooking the valley.

The river burbled below, blood red still because the sun had not yet touched it. Directly above the river, on the other side, was a slight ridge, and beyond that, a valley that he could barely see. To his left was the city of Constant, and to his right, the road leading to his home. To Jahn.

"How did we miss them coming in?"

She didn't answer him.

Of course.

He was too far away from the cave, the only place she could appear. He cursed slightly, took one more glance at the area below.

The river, so beautiful at dawn. The ridges, and the valley beyond, all green and brown and golden. The city, gray and forbidding. He might die here, in this cavern, above this place.

The place where it all began.

He ran a hand through his hair. If he did die here, he would do so for his children. For his Isle.

For the right reasons, no matter what.

Then he turned and walked back to the sword. Jewel was sitting just inside the cavern, watching him. "Why didn't we see them coming?" he asked softly.

She was behind him. He could feel her warmth. He wanted to lean into it, but didn't. "My grandfather is good."

"The road is directly across from us."

"Why take the road at this time of year?" she asked. "He only needed to do that in the passes."

He ran a hand through his hair, wincing as he felt the grime from his fingers scrape his scalp. "Why didn't you bring me here sooner? To have reinforcements meant he was traveling with a large company. Surely you would have thought that I wanted to know."

"I thought you might see them, Nicky," she said, moving even closer. Her breasts pressed against his back. Lightly. He thought for a moment that she was going to put an arm around him.

"You still haven't answered me."

She sighed, softly. "I was doing two things."

"Yes?" he said.

"I was trying to see if my grandfather was going to confide his battle plan in anyone."

"And?"

"He did not. I thought he might when he talked to the Infantry leader. But he didn't. Not really. Not anything I didn't already know." She leaned against him this time and did put her arms around him.

He wasn't ready. He still felt her by her absence, by her unwill-
ingness to help him. By the fact that she thought him a fool because he didn't fight the way she believed he should.

He stepped sideways, out of her grasp. She sighed and let her
hands fall.

"What else were you doing, Jewel?"

"Nicky—"

"Jewel." He made his tone harsh. She had been doing something she didn't want him to know.

He turned. She had moved away from him too. She was standing just inside the cavern, her hands clasped behind her back.
Her mouth was set in a straight line, and she looked older. Her
hair was up in its pearls, the pearls that had melted into her scalp
the day she died.

"Matthias," he whispered.

The flat look had returned to her eyes.

"You know where he is."

She said nothing.

"Jewel, the Shaman died for him."

"She made a mistake," Jewel said.

"She hadn't made one before."

"Don't argue for him!" Jewel snapped. "Don't!"

Nicholas took a step toward her. "I nearly killed him once myself, you know."

"I know," she said. She didn't move except to look at him out
of the corner of her eyes. There was a slight webbing of scars along
her forehead, as if the awful wounds had once been there and had
healed. But he knew they hadn't.

The fact that she couldn't come out of that cave proved that.

"But you didn't kill him," she said. "You didn't, and you
should have. Just like you should be using this new power you
found."

"The Shaman said—"

"That he's God." She spit the word out. "I don't believe in
your God and neither do you."

"But there's something here," Nicholas said.

"To believe that its God makes you as primitive as the people
who found this place," she said. "And Matthias can't be God.
He's an abomination."

"She said he'll prevent the Black Blood against Black Blood."

Jewel looked away from Nicholas. The pearls stood out whitely
against her black hair. She still wore her jerkin and pants, though.

She hadn't gone all the way with the reminder: no green dress, no pregnancy. The pearls were enough.

He remembered watching them melt into her as her skull dissolved away.

He felt vaguely queasy. He was defending the man who had killed her.

"The Shaman couldn't know that," Jewel said.

"Why?" Nicholas asked. "Because you don't?"

"We can't base our future on the words of a dead woman." But she sounded pleading.

"I'm not asking you to leave him alone," Nicholas said.

Jewel turned back to him. The pearls were gone. The braid had returned. He wondered if she did that consciously or if that were something else playing tricks with his mind. "Then what are you asking?"

"To wait," Nicholas said. "Wait until we know who wins this battle. Then do what you must."

She pursed her lips slightly, as if she were considering it. Then she frowned. "I don't know if I can, Nicky," she said. "I'm not as free as I'd like. My control came in my three choices. I'm bound to those choices now."

"What are you saying?" he asked.

She bowed her head. "I'm saying that if he shows up here, I might have to kill him. I might not have a choice."

"You don't know?"

She shook her head.

"Jewel, can you find out?"

"No," she said softly, and he realized, for the first time, that she had tried. "And I can't just absent myself until this is over. I went to the Powers. I asked. I *begged*." She took a breath. Jewel begging. He hadn't believed it possible.

She bowed her head. "I made my choice already, Nicky. I think there is only one way to stop me."

He moved closer, his heart pounding. He wasn't sure he was going to like this. "What is it, Jewel?"

"I think someone would have to destroy me."

"Is that possible?"

She closed her eyes and nodded.

His breath caught in his throat. She had given him a great gift, a gift of her trust. She had let him know that even in this form, she could be destroyed.

And he wouldn't do it. No matter what the Shaman said. No matter what the Shaman had done.

He wouldn't destroy Jewel.

He couldn't lose her a second time.

And he certainly wouldn't trade her for Matthias.

Again.

"How?" he asked, so that he knew, so that he would avoid the method at any cost.

"The tools are here, Nicky, in this place."

"I figured out that much, Jewel. I want to know so that we don't use them, just like we wouldn't do anything to harm Arianna and Gift."

She raised her head and smiled wanly. "There's a reason I absented myself when you were testing things. A good reason."

He waited.

She sighed. "And I can't say any more."

"So absent yourself during the fighting, Jewel."

She nodded. "I will. But if he shows up, I must also."

"Jewel—"

"It was my choice, Nicholas." She touched his face. "I never realized any of you would show up here. I didn't know. I thought I would be beside you, like I was for the last fifteen years, helping where I could, even though you couldn't see me. Helping you, helping Gift. Thwarting Matthias. I didn't know it would end up like this."

He took her into his arms. She was so warm and soft and alive. He couldn't lose her again.

"Isn't there anything we can do?" he whispered against her ear.

"All we can do, Nicky," she said, holding him as tightly as he was holding her, "is hope."

# FIFTY-TWO

ANOTHER fork in the tunnel.

Matthias sat on the stone bench carved out of the same marble that had been lining the walls. What an elaborate place this was, rather like a palace carved in the mountain. The Roca had spent the last years of his second life here, until something had happened to him, something he implied would happen to him, at the end of the Words.

The Words.

Matthias sighed. If only he had known all of that when the Fey had come the first time, before he had become Rocaan, before this entire mess had started. But if he had known, he never would have become Rocaan. The Tabernacle's system was based on false premises, and what had irked him the most was that the people who created that religion knew it and chose to ignore it.

He leaned his head against the wall and took a bite of an apple. It was sweet and fresh. He hadn't had fresh fruit in a long time. He had quite a bit of fruit in his pack, as well as water and tak. He also brought a knife, a sword, a globe, and one of the Soul Repositories. He had made sure the repository was empty. Pausho had been opposed to using them, but Matthias wasn't.

It might be the only thing that enabled him to go to the Roca's Cave and back.

He hadn't told Marly he was going. He hadn't told Marly anything at all. He couldn't face her, because he wasn't sure he was coming back.

He had found her working with the wounded from the battle, putting her healing skills to good use. He had kissed her and told her he would meet her after the next fight. She had been distracted by one man's cries of pain. She had kissed Matthias lightly, warned him to be careful, and gone back to work.

Then, as he was walking away, she had come to him, put her arms around him, and leaned her head against his back.

*Be careful*, she had said again. *I want you beside me.*

It was almost as if she had known.

He had patted her hands, turned in her embrace, and kissed her again, thoroughly this time, promising nothing.

He doubted he would ever see her again.

He took another bite of the apple, then set it on the bench, half-eaten. His appetite was suddenly gone. Pausho had been right; he was a fool to come here. But a wise fool, in his own way. If he survived this, if he survived Jewel, he would be able to help the Blooders below.

He would stop the Fey.

It took someone of the Roca's blood to make the Roca's weapons as potent as they needed to be. Once everyone else learned how to use them, then the leader was less important. Or that had been, at least, the Roca's theory. And who was he to question the Roca, even now?

Matthias sighed. He still didn't know what Jewel was, or how she had appeared to him, but he knew that she was a threat. And he had to trust in himself, in the powers he had just learned he had.

They had served him before.

He had to believe they would serve him again.

He could feel the power of that cave, the place Pausho called the Roca's Cave, pulling at him, even from here. He didn't know how long he had been in here; he had lost all sense of time when he had started down the corridors, but that pull let him know he was heading in the right direction.

The other corridors had different kinds of pulls, pulls he didn't really trust. He couldn't describe the feelings they gave him, except that they were colder or more frightening than any he'd experienced before.

Except here.

At this fork, he knew the direction to the cave, and yet he wanted to take the other path. He knew he didn't dare, that something was wrong in that way, something didn't fit, and yet he wanted to, with a longing so strong that it reminded him of the initial longing to get to the cave itself. He sat on the bench—it was not the first bench he'd encountered—and decided to wait a moment, until the feeling passed.

It wasn't passing.

It was growing stronger, and that made him even more uncomfortable. He didn't like the urge, especially when he knew it came from the outside.

He glanced at the second passageway. The main passage had its own interior light, like the Vault, as if the stone glowed from within. This passage was dark, and the darkness seemed *alive*, almost as if it were moving somehow.

He sighed. He didn't have time for the detour. He would have to do it on the way back.

If he came back.

He closed his eyes for a moment. Maybe the feeling he had, the strong compelling, was for a reason.

Maybe he was supposed to take the detour.

If he had gotten into the Roca's Cave without Jewel there, he would have discovered so much before going down to Constant. But if he had done that, he would have discovered those things without seeing the Vault, without seeing the Words.

He wouldn't have understood exactly what he was after.

He opened his eyes and slid to the very edge of the bench. It nearly went into the other passageway, and he could feel the passageway's presence. The live darkness had a texture to it, as if the air were thicker.

His hair stood on end.

At the very end of the tunnel, he could feel the presence of Fey. Not the Fey he knew, but other Fey, Fey who were looking back at him. They were at the other end, and yet so very far away.

It would take him days to reach them.

Years, maybe.

He shivered. His eyes were adjusting to the strange darkness. Beyond the Fey were others, people he'd never seen before. He couldn't sense where either group was. He had a feeling that if he knew exactly where the Fey were, he could find the other group, or vice versa. He felt as if this place held the secret to the others.

The Roca had mentioned this place. In the Words, he had called this a dream, a fantasy, a place where all points met.

Matthias shivered and slid back to the other end of the bench.

He felt as if he had just awakened from a long doze. He was groggy and disoriented, as if he'd slept, but he knew he hadn't.

He picked up the half-eaten apple and was about to take a bite when he looked at it. The end where he had bitten was brown and looked mushy, as if the apple had sat for an hour in the sun. He frowned at the walls. Had the strange light had an effect on his apple?

He didn't know.

He pushed at the brown stuff. The apple wasn't soft yet. Apples turned brown like that if they sat for a bit of time after the first bite had been taken out.

Had he been gone that long?

It had seemed like only a moment.

Yet the apple seemed to indicate it had been longer. A hundred times longer.

The Roca had called the place a dream, a fantasy, a place where all points met. He had also called that corridor a time-stealer.

The Roca was right: that corridor stole time.

And Matthias didn't have time to steal.

He finished the apple, then set its core on the other end of the bench, careful not to sit on that end himself. He would see what happened to the core by the time he came back—if he came back. Maybe it wouldn't be that much changed, or maybe it would be too greatly changed.

Or maybe something would eat it, some creature that lived here, that he hadn't sensed.

He tied his pack around his waist, and stood. He was shaking. That time loss had unnerved him more than he cared to think about.

He hoped it hadn't been too long.

He suspected they didn't have much time.

The corridor was slanted uphill. The incline was greater at some times than at others, but he felt the change in his calves, his thighs. He still hadn't recovered completely from the last trip; if he were honest, he hadn't recovered from his fall into the river and his fight with that Fey, let alone the attack by Jewel or the strange wave that had hit two mornings ago. That was one reason he didn't want to tell Marly where he was going. She would tell him he wasn't fit, worry about him unnecessarily, and make him feel guilty for leaving her.

He already felt guilty for leaving her.

All his life, he had hoped for someone to care about him. He hadn't realized, until too late, that the Fiftieth Rocaan had been fond of him, and had seen him better than he had thought, perhaps better than he saw himself. But that wasn't like this. What Marly felt for him, and what he felt for Marly, he had never hoped for. From the moment he had been allowed to join the Tabernacle as an honorary second son—he never knew who had bent the rules for him—he had thought he wouldn't be allowed romantic love.

And now that he had it, he didn't have the chance to enjoy it. His life, his duty, was keeping him away from Marly.

At least, if he died, he would know that he had seen both sides of life, the good and the bad.

He had seen both sides of life, and inflicted both sides.

He would hope that if he died tomorrow, God, or whatever took God's position in this world, would see that Matthias was doing his best to do good.

The incline had grown very steep now, and the carved roof of the corridor tightened down. Matthias still didn't have to bend, but the passageway felt a bit more claustrophobic than it had.

How strange that this place had no spiderwebs, no dirt, no dust. It was as if people used it all the time.

He didn't know how they could have, with the Vault on one end and the Cave so few people knew about on the other. But it felt that way, and he wasn't quite sure why.

It wasn't just the lack of dirt.

It was the feeling of presences, as if he were not alone.

But he was. He'd heard no footsteps, no breathing, no sounds but the ones he'd made. He knew he hadn't been followed into the Vault. He'd waited there, scanning the Words again, just to make sure.

Besides, Pausho had taken him down. She would have made certain that no one followed him.

Wouldn't she?

Of course. She would let no one into the Vault, and she couldn't spare the Wise Ones, no matter how little she trusted Matthias. What mattered was surviving the Fey. The differences between him and Pausho, between him and the other Islanders, could all wait until the Fey were vanquished.

And the only way that could happen was what he was doing now. He had to tap the powers that the Roca had left him, the powers that the Roca had either renounced or decided to use to destroy the ones who were just like him.

Matthias frowned. The Roca's plan had worked, to a point. He had destroyed most of those like him. But some had survived. They had had to, for Matthias to be alive.

It was the talk of insanity that disturbed him. Insanity in the second son, insanity that came with the use of the powers he had.

And another kind of insanity, one he dimly remembered studying back when he was in school with Alexander before he became King. Something about the early days of Rocaanism: how insanity was widespread.

Alexander had made a joke about it, saying there had even been some in his family, and he had been shushed by his instructor. It seemed it wouldn't do to have the King mention insanity in his family, even fifty generations removed.

Alexander never made that mistake again.

Matthias took a turn up the passageway. The incline grew even steeper. He didn't like it, but it was doing what he wanted. It was going up. Then there was another turn to the right—and before him, in semidarkness, were stairs.

The flight seemed to go on forever. The luminescence that filled this place apparently didn't cover the steps, only the walls and the flat floors. He wondered if it had been designed that way or if, somehow, the system had failed here.

He put his right foot on the first step, and heard laughter.

He froze.

The laughter faded as if it had never been.

He took his foot off the step.

Silence.

He put his foot back on the step.

Nothing.

He put his left foot on the next step.

Laughter.

Light, infectious laughter, as if someone were chuckling at a good joke.

He froze again.

And someone sighed.

"It'll take you forever to get up the stairs at this pace," a male voice said to him.

Matthias glanced behind him. The corridor was still well lit, and empty. He looked up the stairs. A light from the corridor behind him illuminated some of the darkness, and the light from the floor above did the same.

But they left a patch of black in the center of the stairway, and that seemed to be where the voice was coming from.

"Well? You going to stand there or turn back?"

Matthias's heart was pounding. "Who are you?"

"Not anyone you'd know. I don't know anyone anymore."

A male voice. Not Jewel. It couldn't be Jewel.

Could it?

Could she be deceiving him?

Matthias had promised himself that he wouldn't be afraid of her. He would face her, just as he would have if she were still alive.

He thought about a small flame on his right fingertip. One appeared, casting a thin light ahead of him.

"How very pitiful," the voice said. "Is this what our powers have come to in fifty generations?"

Almost without thinking, Matthias lit his remaining fingers. The flame illuminated the dark area.

It was empty.

"Who are you?" he asked.

"Why do you care?"

"Because you're taunting me."

"Taunting." The voice sounded faintly bored. "I wasn't *taunting*. I was conversing. Has conversation changed that much in fifty generations as well? Or am I using this confounded language wrong?"

Matthias felt a chill run down his back. "What language are you more comfortable speaking?"

"This language, in the original," the voice snapped. "Are you going to climb those stairs?"

"Yes," Matthias said in Ancient Islander.

"A learned man!" the voice said in the same language, sounding suddenly gleeful. "How wonderful! Say something else."

"Where are you?" Matthias asked in that language.

"Just climb the stairs," the voice said. "You'll see."

Matthias continued to climb. It felt awkward to hold his right hand out like a torch, but he did so. It still unnerved him to be able to call fire at will, to do so much with just a single thought.

"Your pronunciation is off, you know," the voice said. "You accent the wrong syllable. Apparently your supposedly modern language accents the second syllable. We used to accent the first."

"Makes for rather punctuated speech, doesn't it?" Matthias asked, not bothering to change his pronunciation. He had learned Ancient Islander one way, and he hadn't spoken it aloud since his school days. He wasn't willing to think in the language, attempt to speak it, and change his pronunciation all at the same time.

"Emphatic speech," the voice said. "Emphatic."

"That too," Matthias muttered. He reached the top of the stairs and let his fingers go out. The corridor was long and wide and well lit.

And empty.

"I thought you were here," he said, with a bit more bravado than he felt.

"I am," the voice said.

A mist formed against the ceiling. It stretched, then reshaped into a person, solidifying slowly until it became a recognizable as a man, although not one Matthias had ever seen before. If Matthias hadn't known a moment ago that the man had been mist, he wouldn't have believed it.

The man dropped all the way to the floor and landed on his feet. He was shorter than Matthias, and clearly Islander, although of a type that Matthias had never seen. The man was pale; his eyes were a light blue, his hair was white-blond, and his skin was so light as to be nearly translucent. He wore a white shirt tucked into dark pants and Fey boots.

Matthias stared at him.

As he did so, the man blushed and ran his hands over his clothes. "This is what you people wear now, isn't it?"

Matthias nodded, startled. He was dressed the same way. Couldn't the man see that?

"You were just staring at me so strangely. . . ." The man's voice had lost its mocking tone.

"I'd never seen a man form from mist before."

The man frowned. "Surely you're one of us. You look like one of us. You are probably one of Coulter's relations as well—"

"I'm Matthias. I don't know who my parents are, but I doubt I'm related to Coulter." That last felt like a lie. Coulter was the young burning man who taught Matthias that he had fire in his fingers. The way that Pausho spoke, the two of them—Matthias and Coulter—seemed to have a lot in common. Perhaps even family.

"You are not Matthias. I wish you were. Then I might have someone to talk to." The man put his hands on his hips and stared down the corridor as if he could see all the way past it. "Who taught you my language?"

"I learned it in school."

"So some people still speak it."

"Only a few of us," Matthias said. "Most of the others are gone now."

"Gone?"

"Dead." He didn't like to think of it; the loss of the Tabernacle, the loss of all that learning, all those traditions. Even if the Roca's Words had said all those traditions were being misused.

The man made a soft sound, like a cross between a laugh and a sob. "They are trying to teach me about this new place—"

"They?"

He waved a hand toward the ceiling, as if Matthias would understand. "They. And it's nearly impossible. Imagine trying to learn how fifty generations work. Fifty. It's something that will take years. Then they send me to you."

"To me?"

"Should we switch back to your ruined language? You. They sent me to you."

"Why?"

"They said you needed a guide." He laughed. "As if I could guide anyone. I barely know anything myself."

Matthias was cold, even though the temperature in the cavern hadn't changed. "Who said?"

"They." He waved his hand toward the ceiling again. "Especially the new one, the one who doesn't fit. The woman. They. I never thought there would be so many."

Matthias was shaking. "So many what?"

The man's eyes narrowed. "You ask too many questions. I should be asking questions of you. You say your name is Matthias, but you're not the Matthias I know."

Matthias didn't move. He had never shared his name with

anyone else before, and then in the last few days, he had heard it twice. "Who do you know that's named Matthias?"

The man sighed. "It doesn't matter. He's been dead nearly as long as I have."

Fifty generations. That Matthias would have been the Roca's son. His second son. The one who lost his mind.

"Who are you, then?" Matthias asked. His voice felt as if it had strangled in his throat. He wasn't certain he wanted to know the answer.

"I'm not who I used to be, that's for certain," the man said. He started down the corridor. He walked a slight distance, stopped, and looked at Matthias. "Are you coming or not?"

"I want to know who you are."

"And I want to be young again in a world I understand." The man put his hands on his hips. "Well?"

Matthias sighed softly and followed. He felt he had no choice. He had entered this strange realm for a reason. At the mouth of the Roca's Cave, he had nearly died at the hands of Jewel, the woman he had killed fifteen years ago. Down the stairs at the fork, he had nearly lost a great deal of time simply by looking in the other corridor. This man, this man made of mist, shouldn't have surprised him. If Matthias were smart, he would be expecting anything.

Anything at all.

After all, this is the place where the Roca claimed he gained his power, and, he had said, such power was always here, as if it were built into the rocks. Matthias should have known that the trip through these corridors wasn't going to be easy.

He should have known he wasn't going to be able to take the back entrance into the Roca's cave and find the jewels.

The Fiftieth Roca always said that God tested in subtle ways, but that God never gave a man more than he could handle.

Matthias hoped that was right.

He adjusted his pack and followed his new, nameless companion deeper into the mountain.

# FIFTY-THREE

It felt odd to walk through the streets of Jahn. There was still a Fey presence, but it was small. It felt as if Luke and Con were walking through the burned-out shell of a once-great place.

Luke noticed it most on Jahn Bridge. As he crossed the Cardidas River, morning sunlight sparkled on its surface, reflecting like diamonds. He had admired this view first as a small boy, when his father had brought him to the city after a very special harvest. Then he had admired it again after King Nicholas had pardoned him for trying to assassinate the Rocaan.

The bridge was made of stone and arched over the water as if it had always been there. Indeed, the Fey had not destroyed the bridge, and it, like the palace, was the only thing in the entire city that the Fey hadn't touched.

Con walked at his side. They had washed off the dirt and blood at the edge of the Cardidas before mounting the bridge so that they wouldn't look so suspicious. Now they were merely damp—the sun drying their hair. Con's was a very light blond, accenting the youthful beauty that Luke had noticed when they first met two mornings ago.

It seemed like a lifetime ago.

Con was watching everything warily. He wore his sword on his left hip but at Luke's insistence did not touch it. Luke didn't want to draw attention to the weapon. They were taking enough of risk walking in the open; he didn't want the Fey to notice any thing unusual about them.

But the Fey that they passed didn't seem to care. Most of th Fey that passed were Domestics, wearing their light woven gar ments that flowed about their legs. The rest were Red Caps, goin about their grisly business, their stench announcing their arriva Luke didn't know how Scavenger had spent most of his life i that work; he certainly understood why Scavenger left it.

The Fey seemed to be hurrying across the bridge on variou tasks. The Red Caps were on their way to take care of more bodie or, in the case of a female Cap, carrying pouches across the rive The Domestics carried medical bags or fabric or, in one case, foo The fact that Islanders were in their midst didn't seem to bothe any of them.

It bothered Luke. Every time he saw a Fey, he tensed. Con breath caught in his throat. They had spent days running from the Fey—killing the Fey—and now they walked among them as nothing had happened.

When they reached the top of the bridge, Con whispered "There's no soldiers."

Luke frowned. He hadn't seen a lot of Infantry in Jahn, bu then, he hadn't expected to. "The Infantry's in the countryside, he said softly.

Con shook his head. "I'm not just talking—"

A Fey woman passed closely by them, her features indistinc Luke couldn't remember what she looked like the instant she wa behind them. Con had stopped speaking. Luke hurried them for ward. Con glanced over his shoulder before continuing.

"I'm not just talking about Infantry," he whispered. He hardl moved his lips and he did not look at Luke as he spoke. "I mean any kind of fighting Fey."

A shiver ran through Luke. He had noticed that, but not con sciously. Since they had entered Jahn, several miles back, he ha seen a number of Fey, but none of them were the Fey that wen into the battlefield.

"You don't think they are all south of here?" Luke asked. H couldn't keep the tremor from his voice.

Con shook his head. "There weren't enough. This city wa overrun when I was here less than a week ago. Now there's hardl anyone. Something else is going on."

"That might make our task easier," Luke said, alluding to the plan to enter the palace.

"If Sebastian's still there," Con said.

"We won't know until we search." They started down the palace side of the bridge. Even here, closer to the palace, the Fey were few and far between.

Luke didn't like it. Things weren't the way he had expected, and that made him nervous. Something was happening, something besides the attack he had caused, and that worried him.

But he had to concentrate on the road ahead. The palace loomed before them, and in it was their first goal. If they found Sebastian, they would sneak him out.

And then there would be more consequences to pay.

# FIFTY-FOUR

HE could feel the magick currents the Wisps had mentioned.

Rugad clung to the fine strings of his harness. He glanced above him, following the strings. Their edges were looped around the talons of twenty-five Hawk Riders. The Riders flew toward the Cliffs of Blood, apparently oblivious to the currents around them. Rugad could feel the magick. It was almost as if he had been thrown into a river with an undertow that could overpower him if he stopped paying attention to it.

He had never felt anything like this, although his father had once described something like it—in the Eccrasian Mountains.

Despite himself, he felt some excitement. A Place of Power. The *second* Place of Power. Once it was his, he could find the third. He would be able to form the Triangle of Might, and all the power—all the magick—in the world would be his to command.

He smiled, and wrapped his fingers around the strings.

The Hawk Riders had taken him above the Cardidas River. This far east, it had taken on the color of the mountains. From his angle, it looked as if he and the Hawks were flying over a river of blood.

The idea intrigued him. He had seen rivers of blood in his day, real blood, created on the battlefield. But he had never seen a river like this, so red that it frothed pink.

He looked toward the Cliffs of Blood. Even though the Hawk Riders had taken him quite high off the valley floor so that the Islanders wouldn't see him and try to kill him with their bows and arrows, the mountains rose much higher. The peaks still grazed the sky above him. The air was cold here, colder than he had expected. Fortunately, he had worn the same clothes that he had worn when he had flown from his ship over the Snow Mountains to the south. Each item of clothing, from his cloak to his boots, were Domestic-spelled against cold and damp.

He wouldn't get injured by the chill, but he did worry about his Hawk Riders. He had insisted that the small Fey on the Hawks' backs wear clothing, and they had complained bitterly. It had delayed the start of the trip—the clothing had to be put on after the Rider changed into Hawk form—but he didn't want any of them to become frostbitten. Unlike the trip over the Snow Mountains, a simple flight to a landing place, this trip might take some time. He wanted to scout out the entire area around the Place of Power.

He wanted to know what Nicholas was doing, and what resources he had—if he had any—besides the Place of Power itself.

Kendrad had argued that Rugad should send scouts to fly over the area and report to him. She had said that it would be less conspicuous, less dangerous, and better, not just for him, but for the troops as well. He had listened to her advice, then had turned, and given an order that his Hawk Riders and harness should be brought to him.

Kendrad, who had known him a long time, had merely smiled. She knew that he would always do what he felt was best. She had learned long ago not to be tied to her opinion.

Licia, on the other hand, had looked startled when he mentioned he was going to scout the area around the mountain. She had opened her mouth—to argue with him, no doubt—and then shut it, as if she had thought the better of her own opinion. She wasn't used to him yet.

He smiled as he thought of her. She had the makings of one of the great commanders. He particularly liked the way she had gotten rid of her competition, the Charmer Ay'Le. He had heard the story several times now, from her and from several of the Beast Riders.

She knew how to command.

She might have more Vision than she gave herself credit for. Vision always grew with age. Hers might have started out small, but it might become bigger. He hoped so. He could always use good, new commanders. Her plan to conquer the small town of Constant was sharp and efficient. The modifications he had made came from his knowledge of the troops, not from his surveillance of the area. As he flew above now, he noted the positions below.

The Infantry still remained in the Valley, but the Beast Riders were already moving into position. Rat Riders had gone shortly after first light down paths he couldn't even see to infiltrate the town. Bird Riders—Eagles, what few Hawks he wasn't using, Gulls, and several others—were making temporary nests in trees and cliff sides, all so they could attack at their prescribed time. The Dream Riders were sneaking along rock faces and paths, their blackness like shadows on a sunny day. Rugad could see them the best from his angle above the river, black blobs skating across the landscape. But he also knew that no Islander would really notice them. In the few times he had had to destroy Fey Failures, they hadn't really noticed Dream Riders either.

If the Fey couldn't see them, the Islanders certainly wouldn't.

The Foot Soldiers were already in troop formation, although they wouldn't march for sometime yet. They were anxious. He could smell the blood lust on those who had been in the valley for the last attack; they were angry that they hadn't been involved and impatient for the new attack to take place.

He had warned Kendrad about them. She had nodded. She had note the same thing. Impatient Foot Soldiers often made for reckless fighting.

Then the Hawk Riders angled upward even more. The currents were mixing with the wind, buffeting him. They had no real effect on him, not like the magickal wave from several mornings ago, but it almost seemed as if they could. He didn't want to make a Shadowlands here; he didn't want to try to use his Vision in any way. To touch magick in this place was to play with something very dangerous, something so powerful that even he might not be able to control it.

The Riders were now following the mountainside. He glanced down. They were flying east, parallel to the mountains, heading toward Constant in the northeastern corner of the Isle.

Below he saw the rock quarry and a rabbit's warren of footpaths. The higher they rose, the thinner they got, and the harder they got to see. But he noted several resting places and, on one, three mutilated bodies, rotting in the sun. From his distance, he could tell what they were from the general shape.

A horse, a bird, and a man.

Threem the Horse Rider, Caw the Gull Rider, and Boteen.

Rugad felt his stomach lurch.

He tugged on the strings in a prearranged signal. The Hawk Riders flew over the area again, this time flying lower so that Rugad could see more clearly.

There was something else odd about the place.

The Scribe had described (at interminable length) the almost templelike area in which he had hid. Rugad saw that now—the stone columns, the flat rock above. The Scribe had thought the construction an accident of nature but Rugad wasn't so certain. From here, it didn't seem as if the flat rock above had been formed naturally. It looked as if it had been placed there.

It would have taken great power—a long, long time ago—to do that.

But that wasn't the oddity.

The oddity, to him, was the burned patches. The fire hadn't gone anywhere else. It seemed to have touched one area and not another.

It hadn't been a natural fire.

He wondered if Boteen had noted that, and if he had, what he had made of it. Probably nothing. Boteen had made a mistake somewhere, whether it was climbing the mountain in his weakened condition or misjudging the abilities of his opponents.

The Hawk Riders flew around the area several times. They too, apparently, noted the bodies. One Hawk let out a shrill cry, and he heard Fey voices shushing it.

So they were disturbed.

He hoped that Nicholas and his people weren't savvy enough to recognize the strangeness of the Hawk Rider's cry.

Not that it mattered. No matter what Nicholas and his people did at this moment, Rugad could outrun it. The Hawk Riders could get him across the river in the time it took Nicholas to notice him.

Rugad was certain of that.

He was not certain of other things.

Trails went up from the burned area. Rugad used the strings to direct the Hawk Riders above those trails. He could feel the Place of Power. All the magickal currents seemed to flow from it. He couldn't see it yet; he wasn't sure he would be able to see it as the old legends spoke of it, as a bit of light or as a jewel or as a darkness against the face of stone. He wasn't touching ground, and he knew what he was looking for.

Then he saw something he hadn't expected: a circle of light

rotating in the pale sunshine. Tiny dots flashing against the white-ness of the stone.

A Shadowlands.

Apparently made by his great-grandson.

He felt a flash of excitement in spite of himself. His great-grandson. His great-grandson had such talent at Vision, and if that talent grew, and he worked for the Fey Empire, and the Fey had created the Triangle of Might—

A movement below caught his eye. He signaled the Hawk Riders to go even lower, knowing it was a risk. They had an En-chanter and a Red Cap; he wasn't sure what other type of Fey was with them. The Wisp thought she had seen Infantry, but she wasn't certain. The Fey with them might have been a Bird Rider or some other form of magick user.

The currents around the Place of Power were extremely strong. The Hawk Riders flew into them, even though they didn't seem to consciously feel them. Beneath the Circle Door, he saw what was clearly a manmade platform with stones missing. Several ex-tremely large swords were standing point-down in the ground, studded with jewels.

Large jewels.

He frowned. Sometimes the Fey used things to focus their magick, although the most important thing they used was the skin, blood, and bone of their victims. But the Islanders seemed to use things almost exclusively to focus their power. The holy water was such a thing, and so was the sword. He wondered if the jewels were too. They were perfect for it; they caught the currents and pointed them in a direction. They were probably one of the reasons that the currents flowed in the manner they did. If it weren't for the jewels, the current would eddy here and create a vortex that would catch anyone with magickal powers, trapping them.

Rugad knew this Place of Power didn't do such a thing—the Wisp, the physically weakest of all the Fey, hadn't gotten caught in any sort of power current—although, she said, she had nearly fallen into one of the jewels.

Her grandmother had gotten her out.

Her dead grandmother.

Rugad peered below. Not only were there currents, and focal magicks, and the Place of Power itself, but the Mysteries could be made visible here, and the Powers liked to reveal themselves. That was how the Shamans had persuaded one of his ancestors to let them guard the Place of Power in the Eccrasian Mountains, by saying that someone needed to protect innocent Fey from the Powers.

Did Nicholas know that?

Had the Powers appeared to him?

Did he even know what they were?

The movement again. This time, he saw its source.

A single Fey stood near the mouth of the cave. She was examining the jewels. She was tall and slender—not a Red Cap—and carried herself like a soldier. She was also young.

Probably Infantry.

She examined the hilts of the swords, touching the jewels she could reach, and then walking across the platform to the edge. She did not look up. Her training had been poor.

She was one of the Failures.

He wondered why she couldn't hear the flapping of the Hawk Riders' wings, see the incredible movement they made. Fortunately, their giant shadow was west of her, but eventually, she should at least see that.

She peered over the edge.

She was watching his troops.

Nicholas had a perfect vantage from this height. He would be able to see anything coming toward him from any direction. It was an excellent defensive position, and, in the right hands, a perfect offensive one too. If Rugad had been trapped inside, he would have been able to hold this position—and perhaps improve it—for years.

Nicholas wasn't as good a warrior. He couldn't have been. He didn't have the training. If he had, his Failure soldier would have been looking up as well as down.

Rugad tugged on the strings. He wasn't in the best position himself at the moment. He would have loved to use the harness to look inside the Place of Power, but that wasn't a risk he dared take. He needed all his smarts to wage the war against Nicholas. Kendrad and Licia would be able to fight the city.

Rugad would take the cave.

As the Hawk Riders took him higher, he realized that his visit had given him some answers, but had also created some questions.

Why had young Gift built a Shadowlands? Weren't they staying in the Place of Power? The Failure didn't seem afraid of the mouth of the cave. Unless Rugad missed his guess, she had come from inside it.

So what was the point of a Shadowlands? Defense? A decoy? Protection?

Against what?

Him?

That would be the easiest way to let the Fey find someone—forming a Shadowlands. And this was the first one that young Gift had built on his travels.

That had to be no coincidence.

Rugad would tell his people to keep an eye on the Shadowlands, but not to attack it. They had to be careful, in this assault on the Place of Power. They couldn't kill any Fey—at least, any Fey that might be related to him. They would be able to take care of the Islanders only.

The Hawk Riders veered south, over the Cardidas and toward the valley where his Fey armies were preparing, and as the Riders turned, Rugad took one last look at the Place of Power, and as he looked, he wondered:

The Fey had a Place of Power.

The Islanders had a Place of Power.

They both had magickal abilities that obviously came from those places.

The Fey had a stricture of Blood against Blood.

Did the Islanders?

Was it as universal as the gaining of magickal abilities? Was that why the Islanders frowned upon fighting, made war nearly impossible, put down their own people using religion and a strict adherence to custom?

Had they, in their past, discovered, as the Fey had done, the awful power of the Blood?

And if so, did they remember it?

# FIFTY-FIVE

ARIANNA stood at the mouth of the cave, watching Leen check the jewels before heading to the edge of the platform to observe the troops. There was a lot to do, her father kept saying, but he would never let Arianna do any of it. He wouldn't let Gift either.

She felt like a prize people were fighting over, an object to be won.

She was getting restless, and she knew it, and that irritated her. It made her mother right. Her mother had said that the hardest part would be the waiting.

Arianna didn't think she would be able to wait weeks, even months, in this place. She couldn't touch most things, she couldn't work—not that she had ever wanted to work before—and she couldn't leave.

It was the not leaving that was the hardest.

Over the last few days, she had volunteered to fly over the Fey camp, to see what they were doing. She had volunteered to go to Constant and see what sort of plans they were making. Both times, her offer had been turned down. Her father and Coulter and, ostensibly, her mother, had worried that the Fey would find her and capture her.

Arianna was better than that. She was quicker than most birds and she could outwit them but, as her brother Gift had pointed out, the Fey had Bird Riders, and they were just as smart as she was.

She had felt as if the comment were an insult—after all, she had to be smarter than the average Bird Rider; she was the princess of two nations—and then she had realized that she was overreacting, as she often did to Gift. She tried to control her response, but it was getting harder. He was nice, he was trying, but he wasn't Sebastian.

And she missed Sebastian so.

She leaned against the door's edge, peering out carefully, just as she had promised her father she would. She made certain no one outside could see her, and she checked both the ground and the sky, something Leen and Coulter often forgot.

She would have to remind them, or tell her father to. He seemed preoccupied. Ever since they had found him on the ground after he had touched the water in the fountain, he had seemed different. Distant, as if something was making him think. As if he had looked into the darkness and seen something he didn't like. She had tried to get him to talk about it, but he hadn't said anything.

The slight conversation he had had after he awoke had been it. And that conversation, she had muddled over ever since.

Choices. That was what it all came down to.

Choices.

Her father had made a decision without really consulting any of them. He had to make a choice after that last incident, a choice none of the others—including her—had really understood.

She tucked a strand of hair behind her ear. These last few weeks on the road, and now, in this cavern, had taught her a lot about choice. It wasn't as easy as it seemed in the palace. From the day she thought she saw Sebastian die, she realized that the life she had had as a young girl was over. And that life had prepared her for very little. No wonder Solanda had gotten upset so often. No wonder Solanda had worried that Arianna hadn't learned how to be Fey.

She hadn't.

She had to learn it now, without losing her Islander heritage. She had to be tough and warlike and to make hard decisions, like her father—who wasn't Fey.

Arianna smiled. Maybe learning to be Fey was the wrong analogy. But all her life, she had thought the tough people in the world were Fey and the weaker ones were Islander. It even seemed that way in her home. Solanda was tough and volatile and emotional; her father seemed calmer, rational, rarely exerting himself.

Until the Black King arrived.

Now Solanda was dead, and her father wasn't.

She leaned her head against the stone. It was cool. Leen had moved past the jewels to the edge of the platform. A shadow crossed the stones behind her.

A large shadow.

Arianna frowned, looking at it. It was made up of several bird-like creatures, and a blob in the middle. She had never seen anything like it.

She took a step outside the cavern, even though she wasn't supposed to leave without her father's permission, and glanced up.

A dozen, maybe more, hawks flew in a tight square overhead. They were lifting a man in a wooden harness. He clung to the strings and was looking down.

She pressed herself against the cavern's mouth, hoping he wouldn't see her.

But she had to see him, to know who he was. He was Fey, that much was clear. And something about him was familiar.

"Leen!" she cried, but as softly as she could. "Leen!"

Leen didn't hear her. Arianna pressed herself against the mountainside, and edged onto the platform. The swords—the ones her father worried about—balanced above her. She had to ignore them.

"Leen!"

Leen was peering over the edge, completely oblivious to the flying Fey above her and the shadow behind her. She also didn't seem to hear Arianna.

"*Leen!*" This time, Arianna shouted louder. She was wagering that the man above couldn't hear her with the wind currents and all those flapping wings.

Leen looked back at her.

Arianna pointed up.

Leen followed the direction of her finger, and then started. The birds had moved away from the edge of the mountains now, over the river. They were turning. They would be heading directly away from Arianna, toward the valley where the Fey were amassing their army.

Leen cursed and waved a hand at Arianna. "Get inside. You're not supposed to be out here."

If she hadn't been outside, no one would have seen the Bird Riders. But Arianna bit back the retort. She squinted at the man in the center of all those birds.

How many middle-aged Fey men looked familiar to her?

The hair rose on the back of her neck.

That hadn't been just any Fey flying by. That had been her great-grandfather. He was scouting out the area.

He might have seen her.

She made herself take a deep breath.

If he had seen her, he would have come back for her. She was no match for all those Hawk Riders, and no match for him alone.

No. He was planning something.

She followed the rocks to the cave's mouth. She couldn't see anyone inside. They were all probably working, planning, trying to come up with yet another way to fight the Black King.

Arianna ran inside, and hurried down the stairs. Her father was sitting beside Coulter on the bottom step, and they were both looking in front of them. Gift was to the side. He was becoming nothing more than a glorified translator for his mother.

"Daddy!" she shouted.

Her father looked up.

"The Black King!" she said, and pointed.

Her father, Coulter and Gift all moved in unison, turning their heads so that they could see the top of the stairs.

"He just flew by. He was scouting this place."

"Are you sure it was the Black King?" Gift asked. She couldn't tell if he was asking for himself or for their invisible mother.

Arianna had learned, over the last month, to tell the truth as well as possible, even if it didn't reflect well on her. A few weeks ago, she would have said yes. This time, she took a deep breath and answered, "No. But I don't know many Fey his age, and this man looked familiar."

Her father turned away from her, nodded, and said, "You do that."

He had to have been speaking to her mother. Then he turned and saw Arianna's puzzled look.

"She's going to see if she can recognize who it is."

Coulter was watching her with those deep blue eyes of his. She could feel the pull from them. She smiled at him, a little uncertainly.

He didn't smile back.

"It's starting, isn't it?" he said

"It's been starting for days," Gift said, and this time Arianna knew it was him. He never spoke with such combined bitterness and affection when he was translating for their mother.

"No," Coulter said. "The real thing. He's going to come after you both."

"We always knew that."

"And this place."

Arianna nodded. Her heart was pounding hard. She didn't want to think about how right her mother had been. Arianna was ready to fight. More than ready, if the truth be told. She wanted the battle to start now, even though she knew, deep down inside, that nothing would ever be the same.

Some of them might even die.

She put her hand on Coulter's arm, feeling a jolt as she did so. She wanted to touch him more. It always took great control for her not to throw herself into his arms.

"We can't argue," she said. "We need to make plans."

"We'll wait for Jewel," her father said. "She'll be back in a moment."

Arianna nodded. Scavenger was hovering near the edge of the conversation, his hand on his sword. Leen was still outside. Adrian was sitting on the steps farthest from them. Apparently he had been up with the supplies, the things she couldn't touch.

She had never completely understood what she would do in a fight. She had once teased her father and said that her role, apparently, was to sit near the back of the cavern and look pretty. He had looked at her, quite seriously, and said, *That's exactly right.*

Arianna understood the necessity of being in the background. She realized that in some ways, she and Gift were the prizes. But she also knew that if someone entered the cave, someone who shouldn't be there, she would defend it. To do otherwise would go against everything that she was. And as hard as she was trying to change some aspects of herself that didn't seem to work here, she couldn't change everything.

"She's back," Gift said, looking at Arianna as he spoke. He often looked at Arianna when he translated, as if he felt guilty that she couldn't understand, that their mother had decided not to appear to her.

Gift was listening intently to the conversation that Ari couldn't hear. Coulter had moved closer to her. She knew—because he had once told her—that he was as frustrated as she was by not being able to see Ari's mother.

"Well?" Ari asked, unable to wait any longer.

Gift held up a hand. Her father was leaning in, that oddly soft look on his face, the one he always seemed to have when her mother was around. He looked younger and more vulnerable than Ari had ever seen him.

She didn't like that either.

"She says," Gift said slowly, as if he were waiting for her to finish, "that that was the Black King. She compliments you on your eyesight. She also says that the Fey have drawn up a complete battle plan that includes this mountainside and the town of Constant."

"Do they know?" her father was asking, even as Gift spoke. "Is there anything we can do to help them?"

"They've been planning for it," Gift said.

"What about here?" Arianna said. "What are they going to do here?"

"The Black King will lead the fighting," Gift said.

"He can't!" Coulter said. "I thought the Blood against Blood prevented that."

"Not if his goal is to get—ah—me and Arianna," Gift said. He always did that when he was translating. He always skipped over his own name and added "me." It made things a little more uncomfortable, somehow.

"He's going to have to be extremely careful," her father said.

"And so are we," Gift said. Arianna wasn't sure if he was speaking for himself or their mother. "At least, Ari and I are."

So he was speaking for himself.

Apparently their mother agreed, because she said nothing. She was quite vocal when she disagreed.

"That's how the battle is planned," her father said. He seemed to grow taller in that moment, as if he too had been waiting for this. "Well, then." He looked at Coulter. "Are you ready for stage one?"

Coulter swallowed. Of all of them, he seemed like the only one who wasn't happy that the waiting was over. "As ready as I'll ever be," he said.

"Adrian, you have first duty outside," her father said. Ari glanced at him. She didn't like this part of the plan. Only one of their number would be outside, but Coulter would duplicate that person, so that from a distance one person looked like an army. The duplication also made that person harder to kill. The copies wouldn't die unless the person did. It was, Ari's mother assured them, one of the safest ways to have a sentry.

"Scavenger," her father said, "tell Leen to rest for a few hours. She'll relieve Adrian after dark."

"Yes, sir."

"And what do we do?" Ari asked. "Gift and I?"

"You'll stay with me," her father said. "You'll learn that

commanders work behind the lines, and you'll get to know every aspect of this battle plan so that you can fight even if something happens to me."

"If you're back with us, how can something happen with you?" Ari asked.

Her father shook his head. "You never know in battle, Ari," he said softly. "You have to be prepared for anything."

Like invasion of her home.

Like the quick escape into the mountains.

Like the loss of Sebastian.

Her mouth went dry. She hadn't really realized, not deep down, that she could lose even more. Her newfound friends.

Coulter.

Her father.

Coulter must have seen something in her face, for he put his arm around her and pulled her close. She leaned against him, needing his support. He leaned back into her. His heart was pounding rapidly.

He was frightened. She put a hand over his. He had told her, the night before, that he didn't know how much more killing he could take. He had killed an entire troop of Fey on the way here, and it still haunted him.

He thought of himself as broken.

She thought of him as strong. Just like she had to be. Strong and sensible. That was what she had been training herself for, re-making herself for.

No one had told her not to go to the cave door again, but she wouldn't.

Not until this battle was over.

Or unless she had to.

# FIFTY-SIX

A rat scuttled across her path. It looked strange.

Pausho stopped and stared after it, not sure if she believed what she saw. A small naked person rode on its back.

A small naked person without legs.

She had been walking to the Meeting Hall, Tri beside her. They were going to check on Zak and the Wise Ones, who were removing the last of the stores from the Vault. Then they were going to lock it tight, despite the fact that Matthias had gone through it, so that they could protect the Words. Every few hours someone would go down to make sure Matthias hadn't come back.

Pausho was fairly certain he wouldn't make it.

Tri was certain he would.

But the rat bothered her. It was the second one she'd seen in the last few moments. And this one she'd seen up close.

They weren't far from the Meeting Hall. The cobblestone streets with their stone houses were as familiar to her as her own body. Yet she had never seen a rat in this area, let alone two.

Another watched her from a doorway. It stood on its hind legs, its front paws clutched together in a motion that seemed like supplication. Its whiskers twitched as it sniffed the air.

She couldn't see its back, couldn't see if anything rode on it.

She touched Tri's arm. "Do you see that?" she whispered and pointed to the rat.

"And that," he said, looking toward an alley. She turned in time to see a long pink tail disappear behind a pile of stones.

"Rats don't belong in this part of Constant," she said. The city had its trouble with rats, always had, but near the river, and the poorer areas. Not in the center. Not near the Meeting Hall.

"Is something driving them here?" Tri asked.

She shook her head, and felt her skin flush. She didn't want to tell him what she saw, but knew it would be better if she did. "I thought I saw a tiny person riding on one."

Tri frowned at her. "A tiny person?"

She nodded. She could feel the flush deepen.

"That's not possible," Tri said. And then he looked at her closely. "Is it?"

"Two days ago, I wouldn't have thought so," she said. "But now, I don't know."

"I wish Matthias were here," Tri said.

She did too, but she still couldn't admit it aloud. At least Matthias would know if the Tall Ones were driving the rats in from the river, or riding the rats as if they were horses. For all that he knew, for all that the Roca had written in the Words, she had never heard of anything like this. Her people couldn't shrink themselves. Could the Tall Ones?

"Keep an eye out for more," she said, and led Tri toward the Meeting Hall. The streets narrowed, all heading toward the central building, the one that kept the town running. The Hall.

She saw no more rats, and that felt wrong too. It was almost as if the rats had overheard her conversation, almost as if they knew that she was looking for them and had realized they were out of place.

All around her, she could hear the sounds of her people preparing for the upcoming battle. Metal rang as they practiced with their swords; voices rose in discussions; pounding echoed through the narrow streets as they built the items she had ordered.

She was preparing, but it no longer felt like enough.

"Something is wrong," she said to Tri.

He nodded.

She took his hand, suddenly and quickly, squeezing tighter than she should have. She hadn't trusted him either, in the beginning, and she didn't want to now. But this upcoming battle was forcing her to change.

"If something happens to me—"

"It won't," he said.

"If something does," she said. "Keep this going. Follow the Words."

"I didn't study them," he said.

"Then follow what I've been doing these last few days. Use whatever power you can. Fight hard. This place is our home. We can't let Tall Ones overrun it."

"The Fey," Tri said softly. "Matthias calls them the Fey. And he's tall."

She nodded, unwilling even now to make that concession. The jittery feeling she'd had since she saw the first rat was growing. "Go back to the market," she said. "We shouldn't be together."

"But you said that the Wise Ones and"—he grinned without humor—"former Wise Ones should remain together."

"I've changed my mind," she said. "If the Blooders lose us, they lose it all. Go back, please. And keep things moving. If the Tall Ones attack, follow the plan I've set up."

"I'm not the one who should be doing that," Tri said. "I have the least knowledge. Zak or one of the others, maybe, but not me."

"Go," Pausho said softly. She gave him a hard shove. "Now."

He shook his head slightly, but went back the way they came. She watched him for a moment, glancing all around him, and looking at his feet, as if he were searching for rats.

When he had turned a corner—and no rats followed him; no rats appeared at all—she climbed the steps to the Meeting Hall.

She pulled the door open and blinked at the sudden darkness. No one had bothered with candles. No one seemed to be around. The hall had no windows, by design, so that no one could see in when the Wise Ones had their meetings.

She stopped beside the door and picked up a candle, lighting it with the flint. It usually illuminated a large section of the room. But this time, the shadows seemed to have grown. She wondered if that were her imagination, if that reflected her state of mind. Nothing seemed out of place.

And maybe that was the problem.

The table still stretched across the middle, and the chairs were where they had been left days before.

It looked as if no one were here.

But she had sent most of the Wise Ones here. They still had to be in the Vault.

Then she saw a movement near the door to the Vault. Her heart started to pound hard. She took a step in that direction.

The darkness on that wall did not fade. It seemed to absorb the light, to steal it from her candle to make her feel smaller and less effective. Her breath was coming in small gasps now, and her hands were cold.

She clutched the candle tighter and then held it out as far as her arms would extend. It still didn't break the darkness.

But something moved again.

She made a small, involuntary noise at the back of her throat, and instantly wished she hadn't.

The movement was a hand, twitching against the floor. A hand, attached to nothing.

Except darkness.

She walked closer, holding her breath as she did so. The hand was attached to an arm, but the arm disappeared into blackness. The movement of the hand was jerky, twitchy, like she had sometimes seen in seriously injured people or very sound sleepers.

The darkness was something she had never seen before.

She crouched, holding the candle close, and the darkness detached itself. For a moment it formed into the shadow of a woman, and seemed to peer back at her. It had been covering Zak.

His face was pale, his eyes were closed, and if it weren't for his twitching hand, she would have thought him dead.

*"Begone,"* she whispered to the shadow. It continued to face

her for a moment, if something faceless could face a person, and then it lay back across Zak.

She braced herself, then reached for it, determined to pull it off. When she touched it, her skin crawled. It didn't feel like darkness should. It had a oily texture, thick, bouncy, resilient. It was slippery too, and her hands couldn't find purchase on it. There appeared to be no hard surfaces, no edges, nothing to grab onto.

Zak didn't seem to know what was happening to him. His hand twitched and twitched, and did nothing to help her. She shoved the candle at the darkness—

And felt something slam her from behind. She fell onto the slippery blackness covering Zak. The candle fell from her fingers and crashed against the floor, the flame blowing itself out.

She turned just as something black and heavy hit her face, latching onto it, clinging . . .

*She was on the mountain, a child in her hands, cradled against her chest. Her child. No, Matthias. No, a different little girl. It was her child, another woman's child, all the children she had ever carried to that mountainside, and it was squirming against her. She insisted on holding the babies—she knew, after the first time, that she alone might have the strength—and she set it down, naked in the snow.*

*They were above tree line and the snow was thick. It was winter, and the child was crying, screaming, knowing it was going to die—*

*That was wrong, that was wrong. She had done it in the past, but not now. Now she was struggling, struggling—*

*Like a child in the snow. She was getting colder and colder, watching the adult walk away, knowing she was going to die, as they had died.*

*She had killed them all. Only a few survived. Matthias. Coulter.*

*Only a few.*

*But not her little girl.*

*Not her child.*

*Then the despair hit her, the despair she had been burying for decades, deep and old and untapped. All those lives, all those innocent lives, lost.*

*Murdered.*

*By her.*

*Because someone long ago had misunderstood the Roca's words and she had followed that misunderstanding without question.*

*Without question.*

*She lay back against the frozen snow, feeling its coldness envelo*

er body. *This death wasn't enough, wasn't long enough, torturous*
*nough, horrible enough to repay her for her crimes.*

Only she wasn't on the mountain. She wasn't. She'd been
aching for Zak—

*And failing, as she had so often failed before.*

There was someone else in her mind. Someone who held her
own. A darkness, a blackness that infected her.

*Punished her, as no one had ever dared.*

And yet, it felt like a dream. A forced dream. A nightmare.

She didn't want to die.

*Neither did the babies. No one ever did. But she would die. And be-*
*re she did, she would remember everything.*

*All her crimes.*

*All the lives she had taken.*

*Starting with her own baby girl.*

*Who just happened to be the first.*

# FIFTY-SEVEN

HE Dream Riders, Beast Riders, and Bird Riders had already in-
ltrated. It hadn't taken them long. Licia had watched from the
dge above. It had seemed strange to see them fan out over the
ountryside—particularly the Dream Riders, who looked like gi-
nt shadows running across the land.

Their orders—from the Black King, not from her—were to
ait while one Dream Rider reached into the mind of a victim,
nd then to learn from that Dream Rider who the leaders were.
he Dream Riders would take out the leaders, would keep them
 a nightmare state until their fears or a Foot Soldier finally
lled them.

The Rat Riders would infiltrate as many buildings as they
ould, then hunt the inhabitants in packs. People usually weren't
lled by rats, but the Rat Riders often changed that. Licia never
derstood why many of the victims fled screaming into the
reet, only to be killed by Infantry.

She paced the edge of the ridge. Her Infantry were lining up getting ready to fight. The Foot Soldiers were still in the valle under the command of Kendrad. Licia glanced at the sky. Whe the sun was near its zenith, she was supposed to attack.

Time seemed to crawl by. Even the Bird Riders had landed i their assigned positions.

The Black King had returned from his scouting mission, look ing rather pleased with himself. Licia was glad he survived. Sh had felt that his travel to the side of the mountain bordered o foolishness, and she didn't like it. But she hadn't told him that.

She glanced at the sun again. It didn't seem to have move She went to her large flat rock, the one from which she had calle the retreat. From it, she could see in all directions. The Foot So diers hadn't left the valley yet, but Rugad's platoon had. The were crossing the ridge behind her, marching in lockstep towar the mountain.

Rugad was using few magickal Fey. He had some Beast Rider but he was mostly taking Infantry, for reasons she could not er tirely fathom. In fact, her troop was depleted. They would mere be decoys in the battle below, distractions to pull the Islanders a tention away from their own town.

She wiped her damp hands on her pants. She hadn't been th nervous before a battle in a long time. The retreat had affecte her too, even though she hadn't admitted it to anyone. She didn want to lose more soldiers, and she would.

No matter how quickly and efficiently the Fey attacked, would still result in loss of life.

She ran a hand through her hair and took a deep breath. N one had ever told her that such a loss would result in vacillatir emotions. She hadn't been prepared for that. She couldn't, fc the first time in years, shut down the doubts that kept arising i her mind.

And she had to. Her team, her troop, her Infantry, were th decoys. They were the ones the Islanders would attack, and proba bly defeat, thinking they were the main force of the Fey's troop Then the Beast Riders would attack from within, the Bird Ride would swoop down from the sky, and the Foot Soldiers would com in with their particularly nasty brand of combat.

The Islanders' leaders would be dead, and the Islande wouldn't know it immediately. They would fight, but they woul be disorganized.

And they would lose.

It was a solid plan. It was her plan, with ever so few changes,
and it would work.

She took a deep breath and glanced at the sky. The sun was in
position. She studied her troops. They were ready. If they had to
same momentary doubts she had just had, they weren't showing
. Amazing what the appearance of the Black King could do for
morale.

She glanced behind her, saw more Infantry heading toward
the mountains, saw the Foot Soldiers beginning to leave their potions in the valley.

Now was the time.

She raised her arm, and her first wave of troops stood at
attention.

Then she lowered her arm quickly, and the first wave ran off
the ridge.

This time the Islanders were ready. A small force of them
charged out of town to meet the Fey at the ridge line. Some car-
ied weapons—swords. Some started shooting arrows from the
buildings at the edge of town. And others stood in front of the
oads, holding out their hands and reciting a Compelling.

Her troops weren't immune to Compellings; no one was. They
stopped, unable to move forward, but this time they were pre-
ared. They didn't freeze like her troops had in the first battle.
They stood their ground and fought.

Not that it was doing them any good. The Islanders seemed to
e slicing them up.

She felt a flutter in her stomach, a nervousness that had first
shown itself when she had called the retreat. Still, the timing was
ight. She was supposed to send the second wave.

The blood was flowing below her, and it was Fey blood.

Decoys, she reminded herself. Decoys.

She raised her arm, and the second wave, good soldiers that
hey were, stood at attention. Then she lowered it, and they
charged down the ridge.

They seemed to meet the same resistance that the first group
ad met, but they joined into the fighting. She could barely see
hat was happening for all the sunlight reflecting off metal. But
he could hear the screams of pain mixed with the Fey battle
ries. A few victory shouts undulated in the morning air.

That was the sound she had been missing. Yes, the first wave
as a sacrifice, and they had probably known it. But the second
ave was doing better. The Islanders had sent out no more troops,

although the arrows were flying fast and thick. They didn't hav
the resources that the Fey did.

The Islanders were still killing more than their share of Fey
Their swords seemed to move faster than Fey swords, their aim
precise, their ability to injure uncanny. She could still see bloo
spurting, flowing, filling the field below.

It was a slaughter, just like the first time.

She frowned, wishing she could see into the village bette
than she could. She wanted to know if the Beast Riders wer
rising.

It didn't matter. Her job was to remain here, to send her troop
down to distract the Islanders.

She raised her arm for a third time. For the third time, her In
fantry stood at attention. And for the third time, she sent them t
their deaths.

She was doing it on faith.

Faith in herself.

Faith in her plan.

Faith in the Black King.

She had to believe that the Fey Empire would and could pre
vail. Otherwise everything that happened before was meaningless

Bodies littered the field below her, most of them Fey.

"Faith," she whispered to herself, and hoped she had enoug
of it.


# FIFTY-EIGHT


MARLY heard the battle cry from the makeshift hospital. Sh
shivered.

They had moved the hospital from the edge of town to a well
appointed house near the Meeting Hall just the night before
Several townspeople had carried wounded. Others had donate
their own beds. She brought in some of the elderly ladies to hel
with the care and to coordinate efforts all over town.

For the moment, though, she was alone except for the wounde
Many of her helpers were on the field. Others—most of them, i

fact—were reciting the spell that seemed to keep the Fey at bay. She didn't like being the only healthy one in the building.

When the battle cry echoed, she had been comforting one of the boys who had been wounded in the first attack. He had lost an arm—there was nothing she could do about it—and was disconsolate about that, about not fighting, about his future.

She wasn't sure he would have a future. She wasn't sure if any of them would. But she touched his remaining hand reassuringly, then made her way past the beds, many of them empty now—waiting, it seemed, for the new attack to begin—and went to the door.

She wasn't sure what to do. No one had given her instructions. Everyone was looking at her as the person in charge of the wounded. She hadn't planned it that way, but it had happened because of her gift for healing, a gift she had always had. Her brother Jakib had known sooner than she. He always brought his friends to her after they had been injured in some job, stealing something from some noble, breaking into a place they shouldn't have gone. He had been the one who first found Matthias, and who had brought him to her.

Matthias.

She stopped just before reaching the door, and wiped her hands on her skirt.

She tried not to think about him.

She had never met a man like him. Tall, powerful, and so completely insecure. She had fallen in love with him, much to the others' dismay, and she hadn't tried to hide it.

She had asked for nothing and he had given her nothing, except an empty promise that he would return safely. He had made that promise before and had nearly died on the mountain. This time, she was convinced he would die there.

She had known he was going back, even though he hadn't told her. It was in his eyes, in the way he carried himself, in the way he dodged the question every time she asked.

The feeling returned, low and strange and discordant. She didn't have time to think of Matthias right now. She didn't have time to moon after him and to worry about him even though he didn't worry about himself.

She had a hospital to prepare, and this feeling to examine.

The feeling bothered her.

She grabbed the door handle and pulled.

The pale sunlight surprised her—she had started work before dawn and now it was nearly midday. A creature, small, dark, quick, scurried past her feet so fast that she had a sense of the movement rather than seeing it.

She could hear the sounds of battle. Screams and cries and the strange ululation that had echoed through Jahn during the last battle. The ridge and the ground below were awash in bodies. Arrows, barely visible, flew through the air. Blades flashed in the sunlight. Her stomach turned, and she put a hand protectively over it.

So many more would die this day, and for what? A bit of ground? A different way to live life? Matthias believed the Fey were evil, but she didn't. She simply thought they were different. Life was about change, and the Fey brought change.

But there was more happening here than a battle on the ridge.

Something was happening in town.

She looked down. Rats were running by her. Rats with small naked people on their backs.

She suppressed a cry, and stood on the threshold, careful not to let her feet touch the cobblestones. The rats were ignoring her. They were running as fast as she had ever seen rats move, and they were heading to the Meeting Hall.

The doors stood open. Rats moved toward it like a furry river, laughing gleefully as they went inside. At the very edge of the door, she could see feet clad in Islander boots—feet that weren't moving.

And rats climbing over them.

She pressed her hand hard against her stomach, feeling nausea roll. She had seen this before. Rat creatures, Dog creatures, with Fey on their backs. They would show no mercy.

They would kill the living and eat the already dead.

The Wise Ones had been in there.

She hoped that Matthias had gone. For the first time, she hoped that he had made his way through the Vault and up the mountain, and she hoped that the path he had once described to her was a tunnel no one else could find.

She shuddered, but did not yet close the door. The rats were avoiding her, heading toward the Meeting Hall as if under orders. Then she saw all the birds flying over the town. Birds—

They were heading toward the very center of town, where the Blooders were working on the swords and the globes and the items that Matthias had sworn would save them.

Birds, flying with the same sense of purpose that the rats seemed to follow. She bet if she could see their backs, she would see tiny Fey on them as well.

Birds.

Rats.

Small creatures.

Creatures that could sneak into a town unnoticed by the untrained townspeople.

Another shudder ran through her. She wasn't really trained either. She had survived in Jahn only because of Yasep's planning, and then Matthias's insistence that they leave.

Yasep was in the center of town. Matthias was gone. She was working in the hospital alone.

She grabbed the door behind her, slipped around it and pulled it closed. So far, no creatures had entered here.

But they would.

She needed to find a way to protect herself. She took a deep breath and looked at the remaining wounded, all too weak to get out of their beds, most unable to defend themselves.

But they would do what they could. She had knives, a sword that Matthias had given her, swearing it would protect her, one of those globes brought by Jakib, who begged her not to touch it unless she needed it, and she had herself.

She clenched her fists and crossed her arms over her chest. Her mother, decades ago, had taught her a small protection charm. It had been secretly passed through the family for generations, her mother had said. Her mother had made Marly swear not to teach it to anyone but her own children and to use it only in the worst emergency.

Marly had never even tried it before.

But she tried it now.

She needed all the power she could summon, even if it was only the power of her own beliefs.

# FIFTY-NINE

HE was slipping in blood.

Denl held the sword in one hand, a knife in the other. He kept the knife out as balance, using it rarely. The sword was just as Matthias had said it would be: a magickal tool that sliced off anything it came into contact with.

Denl was using it to slice the Fey before him

Dozens and dozens of them, maybe hundreds of them, had poured off the ridge, running in a unit. Some were felled by arrows. Others stopped as soon as they heard the chanting.

He barely heard it anymore:

*Begone.*

*Begone.*

*Begone.*

And this time it wasn't directed at him or at Matthias. It was directed at the Fey. Blooders, behind him, standing in clusters set up by Pausho long before the fighting started, chanted softly, furiously, knowing that their words made as much difference as the swords Matthias had discovered or the arrows that some of the men had fashioned over the last few days.

The chant, though, was like a drumbeat in his head. He felt it more than heard it.

*Begone.*

*Begone.*

*Begone.*

It didn't turn the Fey away, not this time, but it kept them from coming forward. And this time, unlike the last, they kept fighting where they had stopped.

The Fey did learn from situations, and they did their best to change them.

Denl was standing on flat ground, about the area where the Fey had stopped before. He wasn't in the first line of defense—he had promised Matthias he wouldn't be—but he wasn't as far back as he had said he would be either.

Sweat was running down his face. His arms were getting tired. He was swinging, swinging, swinging his sword, and it was slicing, slicing, slicing. Fey after Fey was coming at him, and he no longer really saw them as people, only as parts to be cut. And while he did it, his mind was elsewhere, thinking about the goals, about the Blooders behind him.

If Denl concentrated on what he was doing, he would run, screaming, from the front lines.

The Blooders didn't really have enough fighters. And even though they had sent messages to the other villages lining the Cliffs of Blood, none of those villages had sent fighters.

Pausho didn't know if that was because they didn't believe there was a problem or because they weren't able to travel to Constant.

His feet were wet with blood. The Blooders beside him were

slicing too. They had practiced standing as far from each other as possible while still being able to maintain a line of defense. Not that it was needed. As long as the chanters could continue, the Fey would go no farther.

He swung and nearly lost his balance, putting out his knife hand to prevent his fall. He had to look then, at the ground in front of him. It wasn't just covered in blood, but in bodies and body parts, mostly arms. The Fey that had fallen were mostly still alive, but with limbs missing. They were bleeding to death.

His gorge rose, and he had to swallow to keep from losing the meager contents of his stomach.

He pushed himself up, the blood on his knife hand sticking to his skin. There was blood all over him—Fey blood—and he hadn't felt it until now.

Concentrate.

Concentrate.

He had to think of something else.

His arms moved as if by rote. He could still hear the chants, and as long as he did, he didn't have to worry about his back. No Fey could get around him. No Fey was even trying.

That was what was bothering him.

He raised his head, felt the sweat run into his eyes, stinging. A Fey got close, not even seeming to notice the bodies around Denl. She raised her sword, brought it down, and drew blood—his own—from his right wrist.

The pain slashed through him, and he muttered a blasphemy that he had once vowed he would never say. He raised his arm, slashed at her, and cut her stomach open. She opened her mouth, stared at him, then swung again, even as her intestines were falling out. This swing missed, and she dropped to her knees.

Because he suddenly saw her as a person, because he saw her at all, he couldn't bear her agony.

He took a step closer and, with his left hand, put his knife through her heart.

Another Fey approached, swinging at Denl's neck, and this time he dodged. He had to pay some kind of attention to the fighting. Thinking about it, seeing his victims, he actually couldn't fight as well.

He had to find that by-rote place, that nonfeeling place.

He swung and swung and felt the exhaustion thread through his muscles, the blood grow deeper around his wet feet. He was standing on something, on *someone* as he fought, and he didn't dare look down to see who.

It might have been the woman.

Beside him, one of the Blooders went down in a cry of pain. Arrows flew over him, but mostly he heard only the chant:

*Begone.*

*Begone.*

*Begone.*

And the ring of blade against blade. It wasn't steel against steel—this sword he held was made of varin, a material he didn't entirely understand. It could, if used right, break a Fey's blade in half. It was the most miraculous—the most terrible—thing he had ever seen.

More Fey were coming toward him. He didn't know how many. They still seemed to pour off the ridge. It made no sense to him. They had tried this before, and had to retreat. Why try it now? The Fey changed.

That was what he had been thinking about.

The Fey changed.

They learned from what they did.

So why hadn't they changed tactics now?

He felt something stir within him, something he hadn't felt all morning, not since the fighting started or even before.

Fear.

He had learned not to underestimate the Fey.

And this was stupid. They were sacrificing their people—and for what? To run up to a barrier that they couldn't get past?

He wished he could slow down, stop moving, wished he could take the time to look and contemplate. He was fighting another Fey now, and then another, and his wrist was bleeding, even though he couldn't really feel the pain. The blood wasn't bad, just enough to be noticeable, to make him wonder what really had been done.

He didn't have time to stop. How many Fey were there? There couldn't be an inexhaustible supply. But it felt that way.

His blade snapped another, a Fey blade, and then the Fey—a young man this time, very tall—managed to pull out a knife. Denl dodged, slipped on the blood, fell to his knees beside some of the bodies. The female Fey looked at him with empty eyes. The Fey above him stabbed at him, and Denl ducked, only to feel the knife graze his shoulder.

He wouldn't be worth much soon. Not all the magick swords in the world would change that.

The Fey stabbed again, but Denl brought up his own knife,

and stuck it into the Fey's knee. The man screamed and buckled and this time Denl used his precious sword—on the man's neck.

It was too easy. The head rolled, and so did Denl's stomach. This time he couldn't keep his breakfast down. He vomited, and felt the pain run through him from his shoulder to his wrist. Another Fey was above him, but he wasn't sure he could stand.

He swung anyway, hit a knee again—knees were so vulnerable—and the Fey fell.

Denl staggered to his feet, put the point of the sword at the Fey's throat—another young man; did they all look the same?—and screamed: "What're ye doin?"

The Fey looked at him, saying nothing, swallowing once and wincing as his adam's apple hit the sword tip. Another Fey saw the situation and started coming for Denl, but one of the Blooders got him, slicing through his rib cage as he hurried toward them.

"What're ye doin?" Denl asked again. He couldn't remember how to speak Nye. Surely these Fey could speak Islander. Surely they could understand him. This Fey wasn't talking because he was courageous and proud.

Or he had something to hide.

"What's yer plan?" Denl screamed.

The Fey closed his eyes, frowned, waited, it seemed, for the blade to end his life.

And in his frustration, Denl shoved. The blade went through, the Fey was dead, and the moment was gone.

But it had been enough. It had showed him what he needed to know, what he was afraid to know.

This wasn't the entire plan. The Fey were keeping the Blooders busy while doing something else.

But what?

What?

Denl started to turn, to shout back at the Blooders behind him, and then he saw more Fey heading toward him. He wasn't done yet. He couldn't turn his back on them.

If he did, he would die.

And then no one would understand.

No one would know.

All he could do was hang on—and hope he survived.

Hope that his body held on longer than the Fey reinforcements.

But he wasn't sure that would happen.

He wasn't sure at all.

# SIXTY

THE birds were the worst.

Jakib covered his head and dove behind the glass-blower's stall. The birds, pecking, poking, drilling into his skull. More than once, they'd drawn blood. He could feel its warmth running down his face. And the worst of it was, they were screaming in joy as they did it.

They weren't birds, but Fey birds, the kind that tiny Fey could ride. He didn't know what they were called, but he knew they existed. He had seen other such Fey creatures in Jahn. Bigger ones.

Although the birds could make short work of him if he weren't careful.

The delicate glass was falling all around him, breaking on the cobblestone. The Blooders were screaming too, only they were screaming in terror—they hadn't been prepared for this. Somewhere, somehow, he and Yasep and Matthias had forgotten to tell them of all the things the Fey could do.

How could they have forgotten the birds?

Something bit his calf and he yelped, slapping at it as he did so. He felt fur beneath his fingers, and then teeth again. He looked down, keeping one hand over his head in protection, and saw a rat.

A rat with a Fey on its back.

Oh, these creatures were clever. The trained fighters were in he field, preoccupied, while the real attack was happening in the illage. They were going to die.

They were all going to die.

He slammed the rat against the stone stall, killing its Fey rider, ut not it. The teeth were still latched onto his skin. He slammed gain and again, not caring how flat the body got, how bloody, ıst that it let go of him.

Finally it did and fell to the ground as another rat came toward :. That rat stopped at the body, and bit into it as a person would ite into a good meal. The Fey on the new rat's back screamed at :, and tried to urge it forward.

Jakib felt his skin crawl. Birds above him, rats below—there ⅴas nowhere to hide. No wonder the Fey had conquered half the ⅴorld.

He had no weapons here. He wasn't prepared. He wasn't ready t all. The rat Fey was still gnawing its companion, and the others ıadn't noticed him yet, but it would only be a matter of time.

The birds were cawing above him, and screeching, and diving t the booth. They couldn't get underneath it and still attack ım. For the moment, he was safe.

If only the globes hadn't broken. They must have been made ⅴrong. Pausho was sure they were unbreakable. Or maybe the un-•reakability came with time.

He didn't know. He wasn't able to think about it right now.

Another rat had come around the booth, its dark eyes glitter- ng, the Fey on its back smiling. She motioned at another, and it ppeared. Then another, and another. The birds were still hover- ng too.

He swallowed.

He would die here, unable to defend himself.

But he couldn't die here. He had promised Matthias he would ake care of Marly. He had to let the others know what he now ınderstood about the attack.

A dozen rats, maybe more, were watching him now.

And more were coming.

Fortunately, the stone behind him was built all the way into he cobblestone, so nothing could sneak up on him from that  irection.

He had to think.

The rat that was eating its companion was snout-deep in in- ʲstines, its paws resting on glass, its Fey still screaming at it, the ords too faint for Jakib to make out.

Something about that—

They could be distracted. The animal selves could distract the Fey selves.

And the glass . . .

He wrapped his shirt around his hand, picked up shards, and advanced on the rats. All it would take was blood. That's what he had seen with the other rat.

Blood.

He took the longest shard, and held it between his thumb and forefinger of his unprotected hand. He cupped the other shards, feeling their edges through the fabric. Then he advanced on the rats as if he were holding a spear.

The Fey on their backs were laughing at him. The sound was small, like laughter heard far away. A bird swooped at him, and he refused to cringe, knowing there wasn't enough room for the bird to hit him, then fly back up. He was gambling that the birds didn't like the rats.

It might have been an insane gamble, given that they were both Fey.

The rats didn't move. He watched them, and they watched him, as if they found his movement enticing. Then he stabbed the middle rat in the eye with the shard.

It screamed, and its rider grabbed it, trying to hold it in position. The rats nearest it backed away only for a moment, while the others rushed him.

There were too many to stab, too many to fight hand-to-hand. Birds swooped again, distracting him. He threw shards at the lot of them, hoping they'd hit their targets.

Some did, and he stabbed and stabbed and stabbed, feeling rat blood on his hands, feeling the beat of wings over his head, feeling, feeling, feeling—

And then he realized some of the rats had backed off. Like the other rat, they started attacking each other, driven crazy by the scent of blood.

He scooped up more shards, knowing he would have to run to the forge. He hoped there were still swords left, hoped that there were finished swords. Real weapons were his only chance.

He wouldn't be able to hold off these creatures forever.

He leapt over the pile of rats, and as he did so, he suddenly realized what he was facing.

Hundreds of rats.

And larger animals, cats, dogs, animals he didn't recognize, all with Fey on their backs, coming into the center of town.

The birds started swooping on him again, their beaks hitting [h]im this time, one bird getting caught in his hair.

He slapped at it with his shard and it squawked, letting go, but [it] was a small victory.

They were all small victories.

The forge was only a few booths away, but that looked like an [im]possible destination.

Blooders were lying between him and it, most of them still [al]ive, most of them covered with tiny animals, their faces being [m]auled by birds.

He thought he saw Yasep on his back, his stolen boots familiar [an]d untouched—and kicking.

Kicking.

A bird slammed Jakib in the face, and he winced.

He had to get to the forge, or he would die like all of the other [bl]ooders. He ran across the open space, across rats, across bodies, [a]cross living/dying Islanders. He ran, birds slamming into him [wi]th every step, creatures biting him as he went, blood running [d]own his face, his arms, his whole body.

He had almost reached the forge when the gull got past his [h]ands and buried its beak in his stomach. The pain was so intense [th]at he stopped moving.

The birds, sensing a weakness, hit him again and again.

He fell backwards, landing on something soft, on some-[on]e soft.

He had to get up, *had to*—

And he kept trying—

Even though he knew he would never succeed.

# SIXTY-ONE

[T]HE mysterious light grew redder the deeper he got into the [m]ountain.

Matthias pushed forward. He had lost track of whether it [w]as day or night. He stopped walking when he was tired and [na]pped—never really sleeping because he felt that he had only so

much time before all was lost. Usually, after his brief nap, h
would eat a little as well. But he was finding it harder and harde
to relax in the reddish glow of the walls and floor.

The stone felt the same. In fact, it felt cooler than other ston
He had thought it would be warmer the redder it got, like coa
or burning wood. But it still felt hard and smooth beneath h
fingers.

He had asked his strange companion about the stone, and th
man had smiled. *Don't they still call these mountains the Cliffs
Blood?* he had asked, this time in Islander.

Most of the time the two of them spoke Ancient Islande
which was quite a test for Matthias. Some words had not existe
then; apparently neither had some concepts. Every once in
while, Matthias would have to resort to using an Islander word–
a new one—when he spoke Ancient Islander, and his companio
would laugh.

"Your education lacks, boy," he would say, and move on, nev
answering the query or responding to Matthias's idea, as if n
longer wanting to acknowledge that fifty generations had passe

Matthias thought of little else when he looked at th
man. Sometimes the man looked as solid as Matthias, and some
times he would turn to mist. Every once in a while, he would b
come half mist, half man, mostly because he knew it unnerve
Matthias.

Sometimes Matthias thought it would be easier to walk throug
these tunnels alone, without someone who taunted him, wh
played with his mind, and forced him to speak an archaic versio
of the language.

Once, when he was tired of talking, Matthias had asked him
leave. The man had shaken his head. *They want me with you,* h
had said. *You'll see why.*

But Matthias didn't see. He didn't see anything.

He hated the color of the light, hated the reddish glow tha
covered everything, even his skin, and he hated the way the tur
nels had narrowed. The ceiling was lower here, the walls clos
in. He felt as if he were deep in the mountain now, and that ther
was no turning back. He wasn't encountering many forks any
more, and he seemed to be constantly walking uphill.

Worse was the sense of isolation, even with his mysteriou
companion at his side. He had too much time to think, to wonde
if he should have left Marly alone, or should have left Pausho i
charge, despite her knowledge of the area. Matthias understoc

ιε Fey, and he seemed to be the only one who knew what kind of
ιnning they were capable of, what kind of destructiveness.

Then he would have to reassure himself that he was doing the
ght thing. He hoped he would have enough time to get to the
ινern, to get the jewels, and get back before the Fey attacked.

"You've been quiet," his companion said, from a bend up front.
Ιatthias couldn't see him. The reddish light was darker than
ther light, and there were more shadows.

"I've been wondering what your name is," Matthias said.

His companion materialized completely, and Matthias felt
wave of annoyance. No wonder he hadn't been able to see
ιe guy.

"My name is not important," his companion said.

"It is to me. I don't have any way to refer to you."

"Except as 'you,' " the man said wryly.

"Not good enough," Matthias said.

"Who do you have to tell?" the man said. "There's me and
ιere's you. There's no one else."

"Not now."

"Maybe not ever. People might think you crazy."

Matthias smiled. "Some of them already do."

"I don't think it should matter to you anymore." The man's
ιne was rather lofty. He picked at lint on his shirt, as if it mat-
red, as if it were all real.

"Why not?" Matthias asked. The floor had gotten even steeper.
le could feel it in his calves. He was going up again. He could see
ιe slant in the floor, and he wished for stairs. There hadn't been
airs for a long time.

"Because," the man said. "Your people won't be there when
ιu get back."

Matthias stopped. It felt, for a moment, as if his heart had
opped too. As if everything about him had stopped.

The incline was too great for him to balance at that angle
ithout moving. His feet slipped from beneath him, and he
aught himself with his hands on the floor. He scraped his palms,
ιrsed lightly, and heard the man laugh.

"Such creative invective," he said. "I thought you'd men-
oned you were a man of God."

"Were," Matthias muttered. He had trouble getting his foot-
ιg, and it embarrassed him. He couldn't just turn into mist. He
ιuldn't see everything and lie about it.

"You don't use any of your powers, do you?" the man asked.

"What do you mean?" Matthias asked, bracing one han[d] against the wall.

"Make yourself a rope, create a series of stairs—you're not d[o]ing anything you can do. Is that part of this esthetic rejection [of] your abilities? More from your 'Roca'?"

"He's not mine," Matthias said, even though that wasn't real[ly] true. He was in ways Matthias didn't completely understand. Still, he heard what the man had said. He created a rop[e] and attached it to the wall. The rope seemed real enough, eve[n] though it had just appeared when he put his mind to it. Thinkin[g] that, though, made it thin and almost invisible—he couldn['t] use it.

"Concentrate!" the man said, and Matthias did. It reappeare[d] stronger.

A rope had done that to him once before: a rope of blood. H[e] had nearly drowned in the Cardidas, and a rope of his own bloo[d] had pulled him out.

He had made it. He hadn't realized it at the time. He had mad[e] that rope. And saved himself.

He got his footing back beneath him, and half pulled, ha[lf] walked to the place where the man was standing.

He was, perhaps intentionally, on the first flat surface Matthia[s] had seen in a long time. And ahead, stairs.

He leaned against the wall, still clutching his rope, his palm[s] burning from the scrapes. "What did you mean they won't b[e] there when I get back?"

The man raised his eyebrows as if he thought the questio[n] naive. Then he shrugged. "They won't."

"How do you know?"

"How do I become mist?"

Matthias grabbed him, expecting his fingers to go through th[e] man's shoulders. Instead, they found solid flesh and bone. Ma[t]thias grabbed as tightly as he could and shook. The man let hi[m] smiling the entire time.

"Tell me. Tell me what you know."

"Why?"

"Why?" Matthias repeated. He couldn't understand what h[e] had done to be saddled with this creature. This man who woul[d] not tell him what he knew, would not even tell him his name, an[d] who clearly had powers beyond any Matthias had ever seen. "I['m] here because of them. If they die, then I have no purpose in th[is] place."

The man laughed. "You're not here because of them. If yo[u]

ere doing things for them, you'd be in that pitiful excuse for a
illage, dying with them."

"Dying?" Matthias whispered. And he was here? He needed to
et back to them.

The man caught his arm. "Going back the way you came will
o nothing. They'll still be dead."

"The Fey attacked, didn't they?" Matthias asked. *"Didn't they?"*

"Of course," the man said. "And don't say you didn't know
ney would. You ran away."

"I did not! I came here for the jewels. They're supposed to fo-
us power."

"Focus magick," the man said.

"Whatever," Matthias said. "I came to get them to help in the
attle."

"When you knew what faced you in that cave? It nearly killed
ou the first time."

"So?" Matthias asked.

"You are drawn here. Every time you think of this place, you
eturn to it. Just like the rest of us."

"Us?" Matthias asked. "What are you?"

"What was I?" the man said. "A pathetic fool who was locked
way for centuries because of his beliefs. Because I could not resist
nis place any more than you could."

Matthias almost asked for clarification. Almost. He couldn't.
wasn't relevant. It had happened centuries ago. What mattered
ow were his friends.

"You don't care about anyone," the man went on. "All you
are about is your own impulses, your own drives. You could have
tayed below and used the powers you denied to help the ones you
oved."

"I planned to. When I returned, I planned—"

"Believe what you want," the man said. "It doesn't matter.
he woman you left in charge is dead, as are your minions. Your
raveling companions are dead or dying. And you don't care
bout the village itself, any more than it cares for you."

"Marly?" Matthias asked, his stomach turning. "Marly's dead?"

"Not yet," the man said. "But she will be, soon."

"No," Matthias said. "You can't let this happen. You have to
et me back there. You have to help me."

"I *am* helping you," the man said. "I am helping you get to the
ave."

"But my friends—I must go back to them."

"Didn't you hear me?" the man said. "They're dead. Or dying."

"How do you know?" Matthias asked. His voice rose as h[e] asked the question. He sounded like a child. He had told Mar[ly] he loved her. He had said he was coming back for her. She wa[s] worried about *him*; he hadn't been worried about her.

And he should have been. But the Fey had retreated. He ha[d] thought there would be time. "All those things I planned, a[ll] those things I showed Pausho—"

"She never got a chance to try," the man said. "Those 'Fe[y' outsmarted her."

"Why do you call them that? Why do you put that emphas[is] on the word?"

The man smiled. "You think they are different from us?"

"They come from another part of the world," Matthias sai[d.] "Their beliefs, their values aren't ours."

"But they could have been. If we had been smart, we could hav[e] done what they did. We had the same opportunity. It was you[r] Roca who stopped us." He smiled a bit sadly. "Who stopped me[."]

It was old history. "I don't care," Matthias said. "Get me bac[k] to my people. Get me to Marly."

"No," the man said. "Even if I had the power, which I do not,[ I] would not. Your purpose is ahead. However you were lured, yo[u] need to go on."

"To die?" Matthias asked. "That's what it is, isn't it? I'm sup[-] posed to be punished for killing Jewel and all the others."

The man stared at him, as if he couldn't believe what he wa[s] hearing. "You have a greater purpose than that, although I'm be[-] ginning to wonder why they chose you. That woman, that ne[w] woman, has faith in you. She sent me. She died for you."

The Shaman? The Fey's Shaman? "You come from the Fey?[" ] Matthias felt a chill. He hadn't even thought of the possibilit[y.] And he should have. He had been so focused—and the man ha[d] looked so Islander. He even spoke Ancient Islander. "You'r[e] Fey?"

"No," the man said. "Some day you will see there is more t[o] this place than Fey/Islander. There is more at stake. The woma[n] knows. She is using her power to guide me, since I had no desire[.] If I had died when I was supposed to, murdered, and my soul al[-] lowed to escape, I would have had the same choices as the woma[n] who tried to kill you."

"Jewel," Matthias said.

"But all my people are long dead. I am a rootless soul, not s[o-] phisticated enough to rise where the others have gone. I am yo[ur] guide only."

"You don't have to guide me," Matthias said. He turned and grabbed the rope he had made. He had powers. If he used them, he might get back in time. He might be able to correct the mistake he had made.

"Stop," the man said, grabbing Matthias's arm. "You have to go on."

"I won't," Matthias said. "My friends—"

"Are dead."

"Even Marly?"

"Not yet," the man said softly.

"Then save her," Matthias said. "Guarantee her a long and healthy life, and I will go on."

"What of the others?"

"Who still lives?" Matthias said. "You said they were dead."

"Denl lives."

"Then save him too. What of the others?"

"No others," the man said.

Matthias sat down. He sat before he had a chance to think about the movement. He sat before he could change his mind. It was as if his knees had buckled beneath him, as if they could no longer support him.

Jakib, Yasep—much as they had fought—Pausho.

"What of Tri?" he whispered.

"Still living," the man said. "But not for long."

"Then save him," Matthias said. "For godsakes, must I run through each name?"

"No," the man said. "Only three still live of the ones you know, and you named them."

"Can you save them? I'll go back if you can't."

The man disappeared. Matthias cursed, and used the rope to lever himself down the sharp incline. How could he have been so gullible? He had felt the power of this place the first time. He had known its danger. And still he had come, thinking he could help. Thinking the jewels were of importance.

He had left his friends alone.

And Marly.

The first person to have shown him love.

The man reappeared directly in front of him. "They will be protected."

He sounded as if he had authority now, as if it were true.

Matthias shook his head. "That's not good enough. You disappear, come back, and then say things will be fine. I don't believe you. What if I get home and they're not fine? What then?"

"Who says you will ever go back?" the man said.

Matthias felt cold. "What did you bring me here for?"

The man smiled. "Are you concerned for yourself? Or for them?"

"I can't be concerned for all of us?" Matthias snapped. He'd had enough of this mysteriousness, enough of the circular answers. "I can't be there and here. You tell me that if I go back, I won't get there in time. You tell me I may not survive this trip, that you lured me here—"

"I did not lure you," the man said. "I was brought in as your guide."

"You said I was lured."

"I said you were drawn," the man said.

"Then you said 'however I was lured.' Lured."

The man shrugged. "A figure of speech. Whatever is happening doesn't matter. You must go on."

"I need proof that they'll live beyond this, that they'll survive. Then I'll go on."

"You don't have that kind of magick."

"Give it to me anyway," Matthias said. He crossed his arms. The stone was cold beneath his legs.

"Or what?" the man said. "You'll leave here? You'll refuse to fulfill your destiny? You'll try to save those you have no hope of saving?"

Matthias said nothing. There was nothing he could say, nothing at all. He was simply refusing to play this man's games any more.

The man sighed, then looked up as if in supplication. "I can't guide him if he doesn't move."

Mist suddenly swirled around Matthias, so much mist that the cavern turned white with it, and chill. He felt presences in the mist, heard soft voices, felt the touch of the moisture, the dampness.

—*You chose this path*, one said.

—*Your family chose it, centuries ago.*

—*You must walk it.*

—*We promised your brother—*

—*cousin—*

—*relative—*

Those last three words all seemed to be one.

—*You must go to the cave.*

He said nothing. He simply sat, wondering if these voices,

these presences were a kind of madness that his mind had conjured up so deep in this mountainside. Perhaps the Roca's words were true, and anyone with Matthias's power lost his mind.

Perhaps.

—*Nicholas hates you, Matthias.*

That was a voice he recognized. It spoke Islander with a Fey accent. The chill around him grew worse.

The Shaman.

—*He blames you—rightly—for Jewel's death.*

Matthias wrapped his arms around himself tightly, now more as protection than in anger.

—*He blames you for the failure of his efforts to resolve the Islanders' differences with the Fey. He lays hundreds of deaths on your door. He is right in that too.*

"You're dead," Matthias said. "I watched you die."

—*And I became what my people call a Power. It only happens to those who die a noble death. I died protecting you.*

"It sounds like you should have let me die."

—*You have the power to right the wrongs you created. How many men get that?*

"I can bring Jewel back? Reverse time?"

—*No. But you can end this horrible war. And more than that. You can end the Fey desire for conquest, if you but go forward.*

"How?"

—*The future branches, Matthias. If you go back, you will not resolve anything. If you go forward, you have a dozen ways to help.*

"He"—and Matthias nodded toward the man, although he couldn't seen him any more. Nodded, then, toward the place where the man had been. "He said that I would die here."

—*You might.*

"Then how can I help anything?"

—*Sometimes death is a noble thing.*

"And sometimes it's stupid," Matthias said.

—*So is stubbornness.*

"I want to know my friends will live," Matthias said.

—*You cannot help them do that. You cannot go back and save them.*

"I want to know," he said.

—*If we show you, if we break the veil with an Open Vision, then you must believe it. You must go forward.*

"I will go forward."

"That's what you said when I told you I'd make sure your friends were protected," the man said, somewhat bitterly.

"I had no guarantee," Matthias said.

"Life doesn't provide guarantees," the man said.

"Except that we will die," Matthias said.

"Is that a guarantee?" the man asked. "Or just something we assume?"

"Please," Matthias said, unable to continue this conversation much longer. He would have to take action, whether it was to go forward, as these voices wanted, or to go back, as his heart urged them to do. "Please, just show me. Help me here."

—*You must have faith.*

That wasn't the Shaman this time. That voice belonged to the Fiftieth Rocaan, and Matthias wasn't sure if it came from his own memory or from the presences in the mist.

"I can't stake the lives of others on faith."

—*Why not?*

"Please," he said again, the desperation making him rise to his knees. "Please. I love them too much."

—*Love, Matthias? You have never spoken that word before.*

"Please," Matthias whispered.

The mist parted in a circle, and through it, he saw Marly leaning over a crib. Inside were two babies. Twins. She looked older, thinner—no, it wasn't age. It was sadness that lined her face, a sadness almost too great to bear. She was cooing at the children. Then the image faded, and another appeared. Tri at the door to the Vault, leaning on it as if he were protecting it, his face and hands marred by small white scars. They looked like bite marks.

Then that image faded, and he saw Denl sitting on the stoop to Matthias's own house, staring at the mountains. There were crutches beside him, and one pant leg was pinned up. He had lost a leg, but he was alive.

They were all alive.

Matthias took a deep breath. He felt a sadness, a reflection of the emotion he saw on Marly's face. What could he do if he went back?

The Roca had said there were things in this place that defied explanation.

He stood, without the help of his rope. The mist continued to swirl around him, but it did not rise as he did. As he stood above, he saw the eerie red light, and the tunnel extending before him—toward his destiny, maybe even toward his death.

He hadn't seen himself in any of those future visions.

But then, he hadn't asked to.

"All right," he said. "I'll go on."

A tendril of mist rose, touched his face, and then fell back into the swirl.

—*You won't regret this, my son.*

The Fiftieth Rocaan. Matthias's heart twisted. The old man was wrong. Matthias would regret this if he lived.

He already did.

# SIXTY-TWO

THEY had attacked him just before he reached the center of town. Tri had been hurrying, and he had seen no more rats. But he had seen birds. Hundreds of birds.

And then they swooped on him, pecking and squawking and screeching, going for his eyes, his face. He had his arms over his head, but it did no good. He could feel the blood running down his body, and he knew he would die.

Then he saw the rats. Felt them, really. They were climbing him, biting, and calling to each other in a language.

How could rats speak?

Tri resisted the urge to brush them away—he had to keep his eyes protected, his face. The beaks were in his hair, poking his scalp, tearing his cheeks. The pain was amazing. He had never felt anything like it. He shook his legs, but couldn't dislodge the rats. He started to run, tripped and fell, and then they were all over him.

He knew, at that moment, he was going to die, and it would be prolonged and ugly and painful, and he wished he had lived a better life, wished he had been the man he vowed to be, wished—

And then he realized that the pain he was feeling was an echoy pain, a lingering pain, not a new pain. Nothing was touching him. But he was still bleeding, still sore, injured almost everywhere there was exposed skin, and in some places there wasn't.

Slowly, carefully, he moved his arm away from his eyes, and saw nothing but whiteness.

They had blinded him, then, and it had been too awful for his brain to absorb. He still saw, but saw nothing.

Except his own bleeding arm.

The whiteness surrounded him, protected him, cocooned him, but it didn't soothe him. The pain was growing. There were no rats on him, and the birds, even though he could hear them screech, weren't touching him either.

He thought he heard voices in the coolness, whispering:

*With the Roca's Blessing.*

*Thank your friend Matthias.*

*You owe the future now.*

Some of the voices were not talking to him, but to each other.

*It is wrong to interfere.*

*We decided not to centuries ago.*

*And look what happened.*

He thought he would die from the pain alone. Each scratch, each wound throbbed. He couldn't move. The whiteness lifted him, bore his weight.

*But we were asked.*

*We were asked before.*

*We did not provide all we were asked this time.*

He was moving—he could feel it—but not upwards any longer. Sideways. He closed his eyes, and let the coolness take him.

*You cannot rest, Tri.*

He opened his eyes.

*If we save you, you will owe us forever.*

He wasn't sure he wanted to be saved. He wasn't sure he wanted to endure such pain for the rest of his life, or even for another day. But he could not open his mouth.

And in that instant, he realized how close to death he was.

*His life was not his bargain. We already have payment.*

*Matthias will pay.*

*It is not enough. He has brought us into this.*

*He did not. His brother—cousin—relative did.*

*As we should have been from the beginning.*

Matthias? Matthias bargained for him? With these voices? How did he find them? How did he know they would help?

Suddenly he heard a woman's voice, a familiar voice, and he was on a bed. She was speaking to him. Marly.

The cloud was gone, leaving him damp and chill, and slightly lonely.

A warm hand touched his face.

He closed his eyes, and knew that he was safe.

# SIXTY-THREE

RATS, possums, raccoons, all with little Fey on their backs, encircled the makeshift hospital. Several birds had come through the chimney and Marly had beaten them with a broom, throwing their carcasses outside. She had finally started a fire despite the warmth of the day, hoping the smoke would keep them out.

It had so far.

And her own protection, the charm her mother had taught her had kept the other creatures outside. But she knew it wouldn't last.

She would have to sleep sometime, maybe days from now, but she would have to sleep, and when she did, they would come inside.

A strange fog bank had built near the rear door. She had watched it, as she had watched the creatures, and she wondered what it was. She knew it couldn't be natural. She had never seen fog travel low like that, moving along a street as if it were a horse-drawn carriage.

As it got closer, she pulled the door closed and barred it, then barred the other door. She wished she could find a better way than the fire to block the chimney, but she didn't have it.

Her heart was pounding. The wounded were watching her as if she were their only salvation.

Strange animals surrounded the building, looking frustrated

that they couldn't get inside. The streets were filled with screams, and the skies with birds. From far away, she could hear the clangs and cries of battle, and she suspected that, no matter how hard her people fought, they had already lost.

The question wasn't whether she would die.

It was when.

She carried her broom like a sword and headed toward the front door, to see if any of her mother's other charms would have an effect on the animals outside, when she stopped.

The fog was coming in the space between the door and the floor. It seeped in like fingers, reached up and unbarred the door. As she watched, it pulled open.

"No!" she screeched and ran for the door. She reached into the fog, to try to grab the door handle, and fingers wrapped around her wrist.

*Stay, girl. We're friends.*

She continued to struggle, and the fingers gripped tighter.

*We come from your lover.*

Matthias.

Had he done this?

She felt a relief so profound that her knees wobbled. The fog enveloped her, and in its chill, she sensed a hundred presences. It was as if she had walked into a large room, into a meeting already in progress.

The voices whispered around her, but did not speak to her again. The hand held her in place as the fog filled the main area. One of her wounded cried out—and the cry stopped suddenly in the middle.

She wrenched free then. Had the voices lied to her? Had they really come from the Fey?

*Come here,* a different voice told her.

She went to it, was pulled to it, actually, by the hand gripping her. She was beside a bed, a bed where one of her sickest wounded had been before.

He was gone.

"Where is he?" she asked.

*In a better place,* a third voice said. *No matter what you did, he would not have healed. You have great powers, but not the power over death.*

She knew those words to be true. She had known he was going to die. She had just wanted to ease him into it, to be beside him as he breathed his last.

Not that that would have been possible. She probably would

have been too busy trying to defend this place, however futilely, to help him die.

"Where is he?" she asked again.

*We have exchanged him,* a fourth voice said. *We think you will be pleased with the change.*

The fog lifted, rose past her, and rested on the ceiling, where it broke up into bits of mist. She was frowning at it, and then her eyes caught movement on the bed.

She looked down and gasped.

Tri.

Only it barely looked like him. His lower face was covered with blood. His clothing was ripped and tattered, and every bit of exposed flesh was covered with blood or chewed skin. His breath was coming labored rasps.

She put a hand on his forehead, one of the few untouched parts of his body, and crouched beside him.

"Tri?" she asked. "Tri?"

He turned his gaze toward her—his eyes were untouched as well, and were the only recognizable part of him—but she wasn't entirely sure he saw her.

"Oh, God," she whispered. "What happened to you?"

But she knew. She knew as clearly as if she had seen it. Those birds, those creatures, they had attacked him. Just as they were attacking the others. Just as they had been trying to attack this house.

She turned toward the ceiling. The mist seemed to be in the form of people. Heads nodded toward her, as if in approval, then, one by one, the mist slipped under the door.

She wanted to stop them, to beg them, to ask them for help. But she didn't. Instead she went to the door herself, and opened it, thinking she would try the protection charm again.

The fog now surrounded the building. She couldn't see sky above her or ground below. The sounds of the battle were gone.

It was as if she now existed out of time, as if she were completely alone in the world, with only injured people for company.

She supposed it was supposed to make her feel safe—and it did, in its own way—but it made her wonder about Matthias. Would he be able to find her when he returned? And what of Jakib? Or Denl? Or Yasep?

How would they find her when they needed her?

Her heart twisted inside her chest. She put a hand into the fog, still not knowing what it was, but knowing that it had come to protect her.

To protect Tri.

"Thank you," she whispered.

*Thank Matthias*, someone said in response.

She turned toward the voice and saw no one.

"Is he alive?" she asked, and then wished she hadn't. She wasn't sure she was ready to know.

*He lives*, a different voice said.

And a third added, *For now*.

For now. She nodded, thanked them again, and backed inside. He lived. For now. Which meant he might not live later.

She couldn't tell, and she didn't want to ask. This time she knew she didn't want the answer.

She went back to Tri's bed, and crouched again. His eyes were glazed, and a small bloody bubble had formed on the side of his mouth. He was dying. He *would* die if she didn't act.

"You're safe now, Tri," she said, putting her hand on his forehead. His skin was hot. "Stay with me, and I'll do everything I can for you."

The mist had brought him to her for a reason. Because, it seemed, it believed in her skill. Tri was important. And she wouldn't let him die.

She couldn't.

He might be the only friend she had left.

# SIXTY-FOUR

HE had fallen in the mud and blood, slipping on the ground, and landing on something—someone—that he didn't want to identify. The battle raged around him. More Fey than he had ever seen were on the ground, fighting, fighting until they died.

But the onslaught was stopping. Fey were no longer coming down the ridge.

He was tired, so tired. He didn't know if he could fight much any more.

Denl still wielded his sword, but his damaged wrist kept seeping blood. Fortunately all who touched the blade were injured worse than he, but he kept making mistakes. Horrible mistakes. Opening his side to an enemy, nearly dropping his sword, dropping his knife once and managing to grab it before it sank in the muck forever.

The sun was high overhead and it heated him, making his sweat mingle with the blood on his body. The fact that the sun burned was the only blessing in this horrible day; if it had been raining he doubted he could have stood so long.

The Fey still hadn't gone past his back; he could still hear the chant:

*Begone.*

*Begone.*

*Begone.*

He hadn't been able to free himself from this battle, though, hadn't been able to tell anyone his suspicions, and it terrified him. Each moment he spent chopping, slashing, *fighting,* was a moment in which the Fey were able to continue their battle plan.

He pushed himself up with his knife hand. The muscles strained and pulled and popped as he moved. If he survived, he would feel this fight for weeks.

The Fey before him seemed to be getting the upper hand. There were more of them, suddenly, and his comrades seemed to be gone. He didn't know what that meant. Had the Fey simply better endurance?

Of course. They were fighters. The Blooders were miners and workers. Strong, but not used to war.

He wasn't used to war.

He was moving only by rote now, by instinct, defending, clashing, moving, trying not to give any ground, trying to slaughter the Fey that faced him before they slaughtered him.

*Begone.*

*Begone.*

*Be—*

The chant broke off mid-thrum. Denl felt it more than heard it. A strange silence followed, a silence that seemed to last forever, but which could have lasted for only a moment. Then he heard a scream, an unnatural scream, deep and eerie and completely terrified. It made the hair on the back of his neck stand up.

Everyone seemed frozen in place—him, the Fey, the other Islanders, everyone—listening to that scream.

Then it ended, as abruptly as it had started, and the spell seemed to break.

The Fey thrust forward, and instead of hitting the invisible barrier, as they had before, they continued. Denl turned, trying to stop them, knowing now that he had been right, that they had had a plan, and he had seen just enough of it to feel like a failure. He had been unable to stop them—he hadn't even had a chance to try—and now it was too late. They were heading into Constant, unprotected Constant, and it was too late.

They were ignoring the fighters now, rushing forward, with the Blooders rushing after them, shouting in futility. Denl joined them, screaming too, his blade and knife in his hands. He hurried, and Fey hurried past him, and he chopped at them as they went, managing to wound a few.

One Fey dropped before him, and Denl tripped, landing on his side in the dry grass. Amazing how it could be so blood-soaked in one place and dry in another. He rolled, but too late. Fey were running around him, over him, on him. He cowered and covered his head, and no one tried to kill him. No one tried to hurt him at all.

But the pressure of their boots, the weight of them landing on him, crushed him. He drew up as much as he could, holding himself together, but he was unable to draw up his left leg. They kept running on it, over it. He could hear the thud of their boots around him, and the strange yelping of their victory cry, and he knew, then, that all was lost.

He heard his bones snap as more and more weight ran over him. Pain shuddered through him, and once he thought he screamed.

There would be no end to this. He would die here, die, and no one would notice.

He kept his grip on his sword—he wouldn't die without a fight. He wouldn't—but he doubted he would have enough strength to use it.

The shouts were getting far away now, and no one was trampling him. He felt a coolness, a fog, fall over him, and he wondered how long he had lain on this field. The fog seemed to lift him, voices seemed to soothe him, tell him of Marly and Matthias and bargains, but he didn't understand them.

He didn't even try.

It was lost.

He was lost.

And there was nothing he could do.

# SIXTY-FIVE

FINALLY, they had broken through. Licia gave the signal and the Foot Soldiers started down the ridge, followed by Red Caps.

The Battle for Constant was hers.

She stood on the flat rock and watched her remaining Infantry hurry toward the town of Constant. They looked like small children running a race. They ran without symmetry, without the usual precision her armies were known for. They scattered as they reached the edges of town, and she knew without being there that the slaughter would continue.

The slaughter had been stunning, and harder to watch than she initially thought. Fey after Fey after Fey had died on the field. The Islanders' swords were powerful and deadly; she had never seen such accuracy, and such ease of cutting. It was almost as if the blades had a mind of their own.

Still, the Fey had given as good as they had taken. There were Islander dead on that field as well, hundreds of them, unless she missed her guess. Only a smattering of Islanders had followed her soldiers toward town. Only a smattering could.

The Foot Soldiers hurried down, as if watching the battle had infected them with a terrible blood lust. The Red Caps stopped the instant they reached the first bodies and began their grisly work. Rugad would be pleased about that as well; he had told her of the lost pouches in the center of the Isle. These would replace them.

She could head down now too. Her time of standing on this ridge was over. It would still take her troops a while to secure the town; but once secured, it would be theirs.

She put a hand over her eyes and glanced at the mountains. Rugad's troops had forded the river and were starting up the mountainside. Rugad was keeping toward the back, worried, it seemed, about the difficulties in sending an army against his own kin.

It made her nervous as well.

But she had a job to do. She climbed off the rock and scanned the area. The last of the Beast Riders were heading toward the mountain. Even though she had used a large troop to attack the town, Rugad was using an even larger one on that mountain.

And she wasn't quite sure why. From what she had learned, there wasn't an army stationed above, only a handful of people.

They had to have a lot of power.

She tucked a strand of hair behind her ear and started down the ridge. Ahead, she could hear the sounds of battle, the ringing of swords, the comforting tones of the Fey victory cry.

The ground was hard until she reached the edge of the fighting field. Then it squished beneath her boots. Red Caps were already bent over bodies, harvesting. They did not look at her as she passed.

Bodies were everywhere. They stretched from the river to the mountain, and all were concentrated in the small prescribed area where the fighting had been the heaviest, where the barrier existed, and then, thanks to the Beast Riders, had been brought down.

She hadn't been able to see that part, although she had known it was the plan. The Beast Riders had found the ones perpetuating the Compelling and killed them. Then the Fey had broken through the barrier as if someone had smashed a glass wall between them and the town.

But it had taken a long time, and that time was measured in bodies.

Faces of people she had known, of good young Infantry who hadn't yet come into their magick, stared sightlessly at the clear blue sky. She did not mourn them—she couldn't let herself yet— but she did acknowledge them, whispering their names as she passed.

Mixed with the Fey were Islanders. Their deaths seemed more gruesome, less sudden, as if the Fey had to fight harder to kill them than they had had to fight to kill Fey. A few still moved. She ignored them, and their grasping, seeking hands. They would die soon enough, and if they didn't die on their own, the Red Caps would kill them.

The stench of death was nearly overpowering. Blood mixed with the smell of soil, with the odor of bodies that had let loose before they died. She wasn't used to it—she would never get used to it—but she could tolerate it.

The Foot Soldiers had disappeared into the town. The real killing would start now, the horrid kind. The Foot Soldiers had waited through two battles—that was more than most of them could bear.

She had to pick her way carefully across the field now. The bodies were two and three deep. Beneath them, she could hear Islanders crying for help in their guttural language. She was a bit astonished that her people had not completed the job—had not killed them properly—but those swords, the ones she had heard about on the first attack, might have made it impossible. The swords seemed to kill or maim with a touch; her people, for all their skills, had nothing to compare with that.

The cries in town had grown less now. Her people were still caught up in the blood lust, but they were focused less on the conquest and more on the kill. This could go on for days if she let it, and she might. These Islanders were different from all the others. They had more magick, and hence more power. Usually the Fey method was to leave survivors alone, to get rid of the warriors, but to make sure there were enough people to carry on the mining or the farming or whatever the region was known for.

Here she might not do that.

Here it might be too much of a threat.

She would check with Rugad, of course, but until she could, she would let her troops release their pent-up rage on these Islanders.

She crossed over the invisible barrier. Here the grass was dry, and the bodies were gone, except for a few unlucky ones who had gotten trampled in the stampede toward the town. She began to run herself. She was tired of waiting, just like the Foot Soldiers had been. Tired of being outside the fighting, tired of leading, of watching, of feeling inadequate.

She put her hand on her own sword.

She would shed some blood herself.

And she would enjoy spilling each and every drop.

# SIXTY-SIX

THEY saw soldiers when they got close to the palace. Luke and Con ducked into an alley and watched from its edge.

The gate on the palace wall was open, but behind it were dozens of Fey Infantry, going through maneuvers. It was as if they were there to show anyone who approached that the palace was well guarded. But Luke had heard as he passed several Fey that the Black King was gone, fighting in the mountains somewhere, planning to capture King Nicholas.

Luke didn't know how much of that was speculation, but he guessed from the emptiness of Jahn that the Black King was gone. The question was, Had he taken Sebastian with him?

Con was watching the maneuvers with wide eyes. "If there are this many outside," he said, "how many are inside?"

"That's precisely what you were supposed to wonder," Luke said. "I would wager that there aren't a lot."

Con shook his head. "We can't go through that bunch."

"I wasn't expecting to walk through the front door."

Con glanced at him. "What were you expecting to do?"

"To see what we were up against and come up with a plan." Luke swallowed hard. "How many dead were there in those passages that you told me about?"

Con leaned against the building wall. It was as if Luke's question had taken everything out of him. "Hundreds. Maybe more."

"All Rocaanists?"

"Most," Con whispered.

Luke was silent. The Fey were probably harvesting down there then. Red Caps could work for days, sometimes weeks. "Most of the bodies were already decayed, right?"

Con closed his eyes. This wasn't pleasant for him, but Luke didn't have time to make it easy. He needed answers if they were going to come up with something.

"On the Tabernacle side they were," Con said. "Most died over here less than a week ago."

So there was still a good chance that there were Red Caps working the tunnels. However, if the Black King was fighting in the mountains, and the rest of the Fey army had gone south, then Red Caps had gone with them. They would take fresh dead over decaying dead any day.

"I think we need to get in those tunnels," Luke said.

"How?" Con asked. "We'll have to go back to the Tabernacle."

"Surely there are other ways in," Luke said.

"Yes, but I don't know what they are. I lost the map a long time ago."

The Infantry paced across the open gate. Their footsteps sounded like drumbeats on the hard ground.

"I think it's our only way in. Everything else I can think of will take too long. And it'll be too risky."

"Why did you ask me about the dead?" Con asked.

"I wanted to figure out how many Fey were in the tunnels."

Con was silent. Then a small shudder ran through him as he apparently understood Luke's thinking.

"You're guessing," Con said.

"Of course I am," Luke said. "But it's gotten us this far, hasn't it?"

Con didn't answer. He seemed dejected somehow, as if the idea of going back into those tunnels was a defeat for him.

"I thought you said the passages went past the dungeons," Luke said.

Con raised his head, as if the idea were his. "They do. Do you think Sebastian will be there?"

"I think that's the perfect place to start," Luke said. But he doubted Sebastian would be in the dungeons. He doubted anything could be that easy.

Nothing was ever easy when it came to the Fey.

# SIXTY-SEVEN

NICHOLAS went to the mouth of the cave. His nerves were raw, and he didn't want to admit it to anyone, not even Jewel. Arianna had seen the Black King outside this cave.

The time had come.

Adrian was already outside. He was standing, as Scavenger had initially instructed him, at attention. His movements would be copied by a hundred Adrians, and his goal was to make each one look real. It was almost as difficult a task as the one that Coulter had, the task of creating them.

Because if Adrian made only his own movements look real and not the movements of the duplicates, the Fey would find him easily and kill him in the Adrian horde, destroying all of them. But if he managed to make all—or even most—of their movements look real, then the illusion would survive as long as they needed it.

Adrian was their first line of defense. First, in that Nicholas hoped it would fool the Fey for a short time into believing there was more troops. Also, Jewel assured him that the duplicates would actually be able to hurt anyone who came in contact with their weapons. So if any Fey came up the mountainside, Adrian might be able to harm them simply by swinging wildly with his sword.

But he had to make the movements natural. And that seemed to worry them all.

Coulter had followed Nicholas up the stairs, and had stopped beside him. Arianna remained below with Gift. Nicholas had given Scavenger a subtle command to guard them both, to make sure they didn't forget who they were and attack their great-grandfather.

Coulter was staring at Adrian just as Nicholas was.

"Can you do this?" Nicholas asked Coulter.

Coulter nodded. His mouth was pinched, and for the first time since he'd known him, Nicholas felt an affection for the boy. Nicholas put a hand on his shoulder.

"Whatever happens," Nicholas said, "You have been a pillar of strength. We couldn't have done any of this without you."

Coulter glanced at him. The boy's blue eyes were wide with fear and something else, something that Nicholas couldn't quite identify.

"I can't do everything, you know," Coulter said. His voice was soft.

"I know," Nicholas said.

Coulter shook his head. "You don't. If this fails—"

"We'll act then."

Coulter swallowed hard. "Do you think this will fail?"

Nicholas shook his head. "If I thought that, I'd simply surrender. No sense risking all these wonderful people to a fruitless battle."

The fear seemed to disappear from Coulter's eyes, but the strange look remained. "You've been extremely courageous yourself, sir," Coulter said, and placed a hand briefly over Nicholas's. Then he stepped outside the cave. He went up to Adrian and spoke to him softly, so softly that Nicholas couldn't hear. Adrian locked the boy in a bear hug, and then shook his head.

It almost seemed as if Adrian were reassuring Coulter.

Then Coulter nodded, and the hug ended. Coulter placed his arms straight out, fists clenched. Adrian stood inside his arms, but did not lean against him. He stared straight ahead.

Coulter took a visible breath—it was as if he were taking the entire countryside into his body—and then he spread his fingers as wide as they went. As he did so, ten Adrians appeared, all standing in the same erect position he was in.

Coulter clenched his fists, then spread his fingers again.

Ten more Adrians.

Coulter did it again and again.

And each time, more Adrians. The groupings did not surround

him, but formed in different parts of the platform, some near the cave's mouth, some near the platform's edge, some near the broken stairs.

It made Nicholas dizzy just watching from behind. If he didn't know that the original Adrian stood inside Coulter's arms, but not touching him, he wouldn't have known where Adrian was.

It was dazzling, even if it was a trick.

Nicholas sighed. He turned back toward the interior of the cave, leaving Coulter outside. Coulter would have to be out there for a few more moments, establishing everything. Then the illusion could function on its own. Jewel had explained that such an illusion was like Shadowlands, a self-perpetuating magick. The Fey had hundreds of self-perpetuating magicks, most of them Domestic. But a few had purpose for warriors.

Leen was standing just inside the door, watching. Nicholas nodded to her. "You need to rest."

"I know," she said. "I wanted to see the procedure first."

Like a good soldier. Nicholas didn't have a large force, but as he had said before, he had a good one.

Before he had gone out, Adrian had started moving the jewels. They would be placed along the edge of the platform. Nicholas would complete the task—maybe with Coulter's help. Gift was standing at the bottom of the stairs. He and Nicholas had decided—independently of each other, it seemed—to build a Shadowlands there as well, so that Nicholas could use the weapons inside the cave without worrying about his children.

They would leave the other Shadowlands as a decoy.

Arianna was standing close to Gift, watching him work on the Shadowlands. Jewel was sitting on her favorite step, watching her children, a frown creasing her forehead.

Then she saw Nicholas, and she smiled. The look warmed him, just as it had from the first. He wanted this to be over; he wanted her to be able to leave this place with him, to go home with him, and to grow old with him. He wanted her at his side always.

He had never gotten over her loss, and he wasn't sure he would get over this either, this return, all these limitations. It was like he had a part of her, but not all of her, and it wasn't enough.

It would never be enough.

*—Will you have more children?* The mist had asked him while he was unconscious.

*No,* he had said, and meant it.

Because of Jewel. Because he couldn't be with anyone else, not forever, not in the same way.

She turned her head as if she heard a sound that startled her. Then she glanced at him, and her features were filled with fear.

Jewel—afraid.

That was new too.

He ran down the steps and took her outstretched hands.

"Nicholas," she said. "He's coming."

"Who?"

"Matthias." She could never say his name without the force of her hatred filling the word. "I know the Shaman saved him. I know that there is a reason, but Nicholas, I can't . . ."

He grabbed her hands tighter, as if he could hold her beside him.

"You have to," he said. "For all of us. The Black King first, then Matthias. You can wait, can't you, until we've dealt with your great-grandfather?"

"I want to." She pulled him closer to her. "Please, Nicky. Believe that. I want to."

He put her hands against his chest, leaned in to kiss her—

—and she vanished.

He stumbled forward, nearly fell, and cursed so loudly that Gift crumpled his Shadowlands. Arianna ran to him.

"Daddy?"

He let her take him down the remaining stairs, all the while staring at the fountain. The Shaman had died saving Matthias's life. She had felt it so important that she prevented Jewel from achieving one of her goals as a Mystery.

Maybe if he tried the fountain water again, he would be able to go after Jewel.

And what?

Stop her from killing Matthias?

Something Nicholas had nearly done once?

But the Shaman had never betrayed him. Not once, even though he thought she had.

She had died for this. She had believed it to be right.

"Daddy?" Arianna asked again.

He made himself look away from the fountain. He had made his decision and so had the creatures, whatever they were called. And so had the Shaman. Matthias had to know if he came back here that Jewel would be waiting for him.

It was his choice.

Nicholas would do nothing about it.

"Daddy?" Ari asked, her tone rising in panic.

"I'm fine," he said. But he wasn't. He had been counting on Jewel's help and she was gone.

Again.

"You don't look fine."

Nicholas made himself smile at his daughter. "I am." He had a battle to fight. For his children. For all he believed in.

"Go back and help Gift," Nicholas said.

"I want to do more," Ari said.

"You will," Nicholas said. "After we win. But we have to win first."

She stared at him for a moment, but she didn't argue with him. And that surprised him. She was learning, his daughter. She was learning how to make the hard decisions.

She touched his cheek lightly with her hand. "I love you, Daddy," she said. And he could hear it in her voice. She had spoken in case he didn't survive.

"I love you too," he said, and leaned his forehead to hers.

"We'll make it through this," he said.

"I know," she said, but she didn't sound convinced.

Maybe he hadn't either.

But he would give it everything he had.

# SIXTY-EIGHT

HE felt hollow inside, as if someone had taken his heart and put it away for safekeeping. Matthias kept moving forward, almost by rote, trying not to think of that emptiness, trying not to worry that the mist, the voices, had somehow lied to him.

Since he had left that steep incline, he had gone up three flights of stairs. They were crudely carved, and looked sinister in the red light. He had tripped on more than one, since they were uneven as well. But there was no dust here, just as there had been none in the other parts of the tunnels, and the air was warmer, almost comfortable. He didn't know how long he'd been traveling, but he had to be close.

The mountains didn't go on forever.

At the top of the third flight, the corridor widened, and toward the end of it the light paled. He saw that as a goal, a place to get to. He was tired of the redness, tired of the cramped feeling, tired of moving at all.

But he said nothing. His guide continued to float in front of him like a ghost, and more than once he had tried to converse with Matthias, but Matthias hadn't answered.

They had manipulated him here somehow, or he had fallen for it, or he had been lured, and all the while the people he cared about were fighting for their lives in the town he'd left behind.

He had failed them again, just as he had failed before. He had failed the Fiftieth Rocaan, he had failed *as* a Rocaan, and then he had failed the people who had saved him and the woman he loved.

And he did love Marly. He just hadn't known how to tell her. He had been reluctant to tell her. Why would she want to be with him, a strange broken man with a ruined face and an even more ruined soul? What had she seen in him? He wasn't sure he wanted to find out. He was afraid her answer would tell him that she hadn't seen him at all.

Ahead, he heard the trickle of water. He almost asked his guide what caused it—he could envision a mountain stream running across the corridors—but in the end, he said nothing. If there was a barrier, he would deal with it. If not, he would move on, just as he had been, feeling hollow. Feeling worried.

His guide stopped ahead of him and glanced over his shoulder at Matthias. The movement was furtive, almost frightened. Matthias was about to ask what was happening, when he saw a form in the light.

A woman's form.

His mouth went dry.

Jewel.

He glanced over his shoulder. There was nothing behind him. He could run.

But then what would happen to his friends? All the promises made, all the things the voices had told him, would they go away then? Would his friends die?

He clutched his small bag. He had come in here so blithely, believing that he could survive anything. Had that confidence been part of the trick too? If so, it was gone now, when he needed it the most.

"Matthias," she said with a mixture of scorn and loathing. "I should have thought you would never return."

He hadn't forgotten her voice. He could never forget her voice. Her Fey accent was as pronounced as ever, and it made him shudder.

Still, there was nowhere for him to go except directly toward her.

He glanced at his guide. Maybe that was why the voices had sent him. To protect Matthias.

Only the guide was doing nothing, nothing except watching. Waiting.

For what? Matthias's death? The end of it all? They had sent him here for a reason, they said. Was Jewel just another obstacle, or did she have some great purpose as well?

She walked toward him slowly, like a cat stalking her prey. He hadn't moved. He couldn't move. He didn't know what to do.

He said to his guide, "You have to help me."

Jewel laughed.

The guide shrugged. "I don't have to do anything."

And Matthias's entire body went cold.

"I thought you planned for this," the guide said.

"Sure, Matthias," Jewel said. "You planned for this. I guess you wanted to die."

"What are you?" he whispered to her. "A ghost?"

"I am a Mystery," she said. "Like your friend here." She turned toward the guide. "Who did you promise to kill? And why did you choose to protect this thing?"

"I didn't choose anything," the man said. "I am his guide, nothing more."

"A guide," Jewel said, as if it were the worst thing in the world. Then, while she was still looking at him, she lunged for Matthias, grabbing him, and shoving him onto the floor of the cave.

She was extremely strong. Her fingers bit into his skin, and he knew what she was going to do. She was going to grab his throat; she was going to throttle the life from him, like she tried to do before.

He had prepared. He had—

He grabbed his knife and slashed at her. The varin blade cut her, but she did not bleed. She slapped his arm away and crouched over him. He reached for her, and she hit his arms again, pushing them down. He squirmed, trying to kick her, but she sat on him hard. Then he bucked, shaking her off.

She fell onto her side and he rolled away from her. His guide was standing over them.

"Do something!" Matthias yelled.

"It's not my place," the guide said.

Jewel grabbed Matthias's ankle. He slashed at her with the knife, but she dodged out of the way. He twisted, trying to get away from her, and she threw herself on him.

His knife clattered on the stone, skittering away from him. She didn't try to grab for it. Instead she grabbed his throat, as he knew she would, and squeezed.

He wrapped his hands around her wrists and tried to pull her away from him. But he couldn't. She was too strong.

He would die here, just as Marly had predicted. Just as they had all warned him. He had lulled himself into a sense of safety, and he had been wrong.

He would die.

He could feel the warmth of Jewel's body against his back, feel the strength in her fingers as she cut off his air.

"I don't care what they say," she whispered into his ear. "You don't deserve to live."

And he knew she was right.

# SIXTY-NINE

RUGAD remained by the river. It was still chill here, and damp. He doubted it ever got really warm. Behind him the water gurgled. He was standing in muck, but it didn't touch his Domestic-spelled boots. He kept his cape around himself, and he wore a sword against one hip. He doubted he would see action that afternoon, but he didn't know. For the first time in a long time he wanted protection.

His troops were marching up the mountain. Licia had most of the Bird Riders, but he had the bulk of the others. He hoped there wouldn't be much of a fight—he knew that Nicholas had no troops with him—but Rugad couldn't count on it.

A Sparrow Rider had just finished giving him a report of

Constant. The Islanders were, for all intents and purposes, defeated. There were still pockets of resistance, but the attack he had devised from Licia's initial plan had worked even better than he expected. The foolish Islanders had been caught by surprise. While their so-called army was fighting the Infantry in the field, the rest of the Islanders were dying in their town. The army, even if it survived, would have nothing to defend.

The Isle was Rugad's now, all except for the Place of Power, which Nicholas held.

He scratched at his wounds. There was a great magick flowing through this place, even this far below it. It irritated the sores he had received from that Golem. He would need more treatment when he returned, a fact that annoyed him greatly. He only hoped that the itching would not turn into something worse.

Kendrad was farther up the mountain. She was supervising the trek toward the Place of Power. Rugad had given her leave to command the troops. If they killed one of his great-grandchildren accidentally, he didn't want it to be under his orders. Although he wasn't sure how much it mattered. The attack would happen because of him. It might make no difference at all.

It might make all the difference in the world.

He glanced at his Hawk Riders. They were in their Fey forms, wearing nothing. Their long feathered hair covered their bodies. They paced around the harness, waiting. They would take him to the top when the time came, but they were impatient about it. His Hawk Riders were the best fighters among all the Bird Riders, and he was keeping them at the lowest, most protected point. They didn't entirely understand.

They didn't have to. This was his battle, and he knew the risks. When his troops were lined up on the ridges below the Place of Power, and the Beast Riders covered the trails above, he would launch his attack. Nicholas, no matter how smart he was, couldn't fight numbers like that. And even if he could, Rugad had one more trick he would use.

He had figured out how to make the Islanders' power work for him.

He would launch himself with the Hawk Riders, and take all the magick he needed from the Place of Power. He would take care of Nicholas, take the Place of Power, and control his great-grandchildren all in one action.

If everything went according to plan.

He didn't expect it to—this was Blue Isle, after all—but even if it worked in part, he would be victorious. Nicholas had nothing now, although he probably didn't know it. Nothing except the Place of Power itself, and that would take generations to learn how to use.

Not even Rugad knew all its secrets. The Shamans had guarded the Fey's Place of Power too well. He wouldn't let a Shaman near this one. He would make it all his own.

Shadows fell across his camp. He looked up. Some of the Bird Riders from the Battle for Constant were arriving. Their beaks were bloodied and so were their small feet, but they looked victorious.

Apparently, they weren't needed any longer. They had come for fresh blood, and fresh blood was what he would give them.

He nodded, acknowledging them. As the day went on, more of the fighters from Constant would join him.

He glanced at the mountainside. It seemed alive with Fey. No Fey general had ever faced a force like this. Rugad doubted any of his best fighters could survive a battle like this. On force alone, he had won. But he knew better than to count that. Force alone would win nothing on Blue Isle.

As he stared at his people climbing the red mountainside, he knew that the difficulty wouldn't be in taking the Place of Power by force. The difficulty would be in restraining that force.

Because, if he wasn't careful, he would destroy the very thing he had come for: his great-grandchildren.

And then the whole world would be lost.

# SEVENTY

NICHOLAS could feel his body ready for battle. His heart was pounding harder, his senses seemed more focused, his hands were shaking slightly—not with fear, but with suppressed energy.

Everything was ready.

Coulter stood at the mouth of the cave. He had finished making extra Adrians, and he was outside, watching, waiting.

Nicholas was halfway up the stairs. He had just persuaded Arianna and Gift to go into the Shadowlands that Gift had built at the bottom of the stairs. Leen and Scavenger had joined them, and would stay until the early part of the fighting was over. Then Nicholas would need them, and they were willing to take risks.

Arianna and Gift couldn't take risks. Even Ari seemed to understand that. She had gone reluctantly, but she had gone. What she hadn't understood, and what he hadn't tried to tell her, was that she might have to be inside Shadowlands for days.

He had spoken to Gift, though, and persuaded him to wait until everything seemed safe before coming out. Gift had seemed to understand him. But Gift was an enigma too. The boy hadn't said much during the last few days. He seemed to be watching and waiting like the rest of them, but with a detachment that Nicholas had found very familiar.

It had taken him a while to realize that Gift's aloofness reminded him of Sebastian. And Sebastian hadn't been aloof. He had been quiet. The difference between the two moods was immense. And Nicholas didn't have time to explore those with his son. He had to make certain that they all survived. This was his last chance, his only chance, to keep Blue Isle away from the Black King, and he wasn't sure he could do it.

As Nicholas reached the top of the stairs, he saw Coulter's alertness. The attack was imminent, and Jewel hadn't come back. She had promised to lead this attack, but Nicholas doubted she would be able to. She was going after Matthias now, following that part of her that no longer lived, that part of her that was beyond Nicholas's understanding, no matter how hard he tried.

Nicholas went toward the wall and the shelves, wishing for the final time that he had more fighters. All those swords were going to go to waste, and he could have used them. He wished he understood more about Enchanter-magick, wished he knew if they were missing something, some opportunity that Coulter could help them with, but didn't know.

They had spread some of the jewels along the flat platform, and some remained where they were. Nicholas glanced at the cave mouth. Coulter hadn't moved, but his entire body was tense. Beyond him, Nicholas could see countless Adrians. It looked odd to see the same man in the same position, repeated over and over. Adrian had gone to it gamely, though. He didn't seem worried at all.

Nicholas admired his quiet courage. Not many would face the Fey alone like Adrian was doing. Adrian knew the risks he was taking. He knew that the Fey would eventually see through the duplication. But Adrian was close enough to the cave's entrance to try to escape inside when they did.

He had also told Nicholas that he would try to take out as many Fey as he could before they stopped him.

Nicholas started to turn back to the wall, but as he did, he caught a movement out of the corner of his eye. He whirled.

Adrian was giving the signal, a clenched fist drawn to his shoulder.

The Fey were on the move.

Nicholas felt a rush of energy and a bit of excitement. He glanced over his shoulder. Jewel had still not arrived. He would be doing this on his own.

"Coulter," he said, but the order was unnecessary. Coulter was ready.

Nicholas picked up one of the globes. Light flared as it had before. Then Nicholas tossed it to Coulter. The light faded as the globe flew through the air, then flared again, even more brilliantly, as Coulter touched it.

Nicholas was shaking slightly. He didn't know if he was wasting these first globes. He didn't know how far the light would reach and how far away someone had to be before the light no longer caused damage. He was afraid the Fey would have to be close. That was why they were using the jewels, to amplify the light if they could.

Coulter held the globe just outside the cavern, and as Nicholas watched, the light did strike the large jewels in the swords. It reflected, focused and grew stronger with each jewel it touched. The light flowed like sunlight, over the fake Adrians and down the mountainside.

Nicholas picked up another globe, and another, and carried them to Coulter, placing them behind the boy in case he needed them. No one knew how long the power in the globes would last. Their light had lasted for the entire time that Nicholas touched them, and then faded when he let go. Then he went back, grabbed two more, and joined Coulter.

Nicholas set one globe down, and held the other, and the light intensified. It grew so bright that he could see the bones in his hand and the skin surrounding them. He could see Coulter's bones as well, but not the bones of the fake Adrians. Only those of the real one.

He hoped this worked. If it didn't, he had just given the Fey a way to see through Coulter's illusion.

Nicholas's light struck the large jewels and flowed in a completely different direction. It too went down the mountainside, but it rode over Coulter's light, and did not mingle. The entire mountain seemed to be awash in light. It was as if they had taken part of the sun and made it their own.

Coulter glanced at him. There seemed to be no response, except for the concern in the boy's face. Adrian moved slightly, holding his sword at ready, and Nicholas felt his breath catch in his throat.

And then he heard the screaming. Long, drawn-out screams as if people were in extreme pain. He had never heard such heart-rending sounds.

"No," Coulter said, and started to put the globe down.

"Hold on to it," Nicholas snapped, a command in his voice that he had rarely used since he left the palace.

"I can't," Coulter said.

"You will, or we will all die," Nicholas said. His hands were growing hot. The power of the globe was fierce.

Then Coulter's went out.

The light diminished by half. It felt as if the world had been plunged into darkness, even though it was probably brighter than it had ever been.

"Pick up the next one," Nicholas said, knowing that if he didn't catch Coulter now, he never would. Nicholas had been warned about this, by Adrian, by Gift, by Coulter himself.

"*Now*," Nicholas ordered. "Pick it up now."

"No," Coulter said. "They're dying."

"That's the point," Nicholas snapped. "This is war."

But Coulter had frozen in position. Adrian started to turn—and all the Adrians turned with him—and he seemed to realize what he was doing. He looked back toward the mountainside.

"Coulter, if you don't do this," Nicholas said, "the Black King will get Arianna. She won't be the same. She'll become like him. Do you understand? He'll take my daughter and my son and make them into him."

"Oh, God," Coulter whispered. "I can't."

"You will," Nicholas said. The light in his own globe was fading. They would lose an advantage if there was darkness.

Then Coulter bent down and picked up another globe. It flared into life, its light bending a completely different way down the mountainside.

The screaming started anew.

Nicholas's globe went out. He grabbed a new one. Its light ricocheted through the cavern, and the jewels in the back flared for a brief moment. He caught his breath, hoped his children were safe in Gift's Shadowlands, and turned.

The light seemed to turn with him. This time it mingled with Coulter's light, and rose skyward.

Adrian's face had turned ashen, and the look was reflected in each counterfeit Adrian. Nicholas didn't know what he was seeing, but it had to be horrible.

Tears were running down Coulter's face, but he held his globe tightly. They needed more globes, and Nicholas was going to have to be the one to get them. He shoved his globe at Coulter, making him hold it, and hurried toward the side of the cavern.

There weren't as many globes as he thought, not given the length of time the power lasted. What he had estimated would hold off the Fey for days would only work for hours at most, and that was if each of the globes had power.

He couldn't think of that now. He grabbed two and carried them to the spot near the door. Then he grabbed two more, and placed them there. He picked up one and held it. The third light doubled the power again, and the screams below grew hideous.

"My God," Adrian whispered, and the sound echoed across the mountaintop, repeated on a hundred lips. Nicholas saw it rather than heard it, buried as it was under the screaming.

The tears continued to flow down Coulter's face, but he didn't move. He didn't seem to be able to.

Nicholas had to move for all of them. He had to be strong for all of them. This was his Isle, and these were his people, and his children hid behind him. He had to protect them all.

And he would, no matter how hideous the price.

He would.

# SEVENTY-ONE

IT was a slaughter.

The light flowed down the mountainside like water, into each member of Rugad's army, illuminating them from the inside. Then the screaming started. One by one, they fell to their knees, clutched their heads, and screamed.

Rugad could not see what, exactly, the light was doing to them. He was too far down the mountain. The light seemed to fill them and then move on, linking them all into a chain that glowed.

Then the light grew—almost doubled in intensity—and continued to come down the mountain. The screams grew, and he cursed softly.

He would lose again if he didn't act.

"Get Kendrad," he snapped at one of the Hawk Riders. The Rider glanced at the mountain with fear.

"If she's there—"

"Get her. Now." Then Rugad looked at another Hawk Rider. "Into the village with you, and get that Infantry leader. Licia. Bring her here."

He doubted the three of them would be enough, but it would ease the burden on him. The light rolled down another ridge, and the screaming increased. The Fey near the top, so far as he could tell from this distance, were not moving.

The light did not work like any light he had ever seen before. It traveled slowly and illuminated everything in its path. Buzzing started to grow in his head, and he realized that part of it—some part he couldn't measure—had reached him already.

Time was short.

He had no idea exactly how high the mountain was, how far away the Place of Power was. This had to be coming from Nicholas. And Rugad had to stop it.

He had to block the light.

He opened a fist and focused on the palm of his hand. A small Shadowlands formed there. He threw it up the mountain, using all the power he had, and spread it out as it went. He couldn't make it too big, for that would dilute it and maybe allow the light to go through it.

He expanded the Shadowlands, let it float for just a moment over some of his troops, then made the bottom level a Circle Door and brought it down hard, covering the troops, the mountainside and the ground. A few of them might have been crushed in the crash, but he didn't care.

The rest would live.

That part of the mountain looked as if it were enshrouded in grayness. The Shadowlands blocked the light. The buzzing eased in his head. He was getting a headache: that light went directly for his magick, for the controls. It would burn him out bit by bit.

How ingenious.

The Hawk Rider came down the mountain, tottering as he flew. He was half-formed, barely able to fly. His torso was too big, and his feet were Fey feet, not hawk feet. When he landed, Rugad heard the crunch of breaking bones.

"Found her," the Rider said, and tumbled forward. And from his tone, Rugad knew that she wasn't going to come down the mountain.

Nicholas had killed her.

He had learned how to use his Place of Power already. Or at least part of it. Enough of it.

Rugad cursed. His palm was out and it was shaking. He formed another Shadowlands on it, then sent it toward the mountain, stopping just beneath the last one. As he did, light came over the top of the first and buzzing began again. For a moment, the edges of the Shadowlands blurred.

They would be destroyed before he could save them all.

He concentrated. The Shadowlands expanded. The wide Circle Door formed, and then he dropped the Shadowlands on the mountainside just as he had before.

A quarter of the mountain was now shrouded in gray. A shadow flew over Rugad, and then landed beside him. The other Hawk Rider.

"She's coming," he said. "I found a Horse Rider to bring her."

That wouldn't be enough time, but Rugad said nothing. The second Hawk Rider crouched beside the injured one. "What happened?" he asked softly.

Rugad did not answer. The buzzing was growing greater. The pain was intense, burning. He was staring into that light, and he knew it was wrong.

With an effort, he wrenched his gaze away. The screaming was still continuing on the mountainside, but it came from the far side of the first Shadowlands. He had to make two, maybe three more. He had to hold on that long.

The light skipped across the second Shadowlands and down, hitting a group of troops who were just beginning to stand. They clutched their heads and fell again, moving in unison, screaming as they did. The buzz in his head had turned to pain. Immense pain. The light was boring into his eyes, into his brain, into his Sight—

He had time for only one more. He concentrated harder than he ever had in his life. Sweat rolled off his face. The Hawk Rider beside him had covered his own head, and started yelling. The scream seemed to be involuntary.

Slow, painful death, that's what this was. A slow, painful death.

Rugad focused on his palm. He could barely See at all, barely See the outlines of the Shadowlands, could hardly remember how to use his Vision. His knees were buckling. The pain was all in his head. He had to—

*focus*

—finish.

Using the last of his strength, he made the Shadowlands bigger, raised it up, and dropped it on the group around him. His group. The Hawk Riders, the leaders, the last of the Infantry.

The grayness blocked out the light, and for a moment, he thought himself blind, inside and out. Then he realized that his eyes—his real eyes—hadn't adjusted yet.

The screaming inside the Shadowlands had stopped, and all around him Fey stood, clutching their heads and looking bewildered.

He had never built a Shadowlands on the ground before. The walls and roof were gray, but the dirt remained beneath their feet, and behind them he heard the gurgle of the river. For that he felt a slight relief. Licia would not be able to cross. He hadn't, at least, invited her to her death.

Unlike Kendrad.

He had no time to think of it. He had to find a way to save the remaining troops, the ones he hadn't been able to touch. He would have to go back out there.

If he could.

# SEVENTY-TWO

JEWEL'S fingers tightened around Matthias's neck. She might break it before he strangled to death. Black spots began to dance before his eyes.

This had happened to him before, and before, he had passed out. He had nearly died, and the Shaman had saved him.

His guide refused to save him here, and if Matthias didn't do something, he would die. He couldn't pull her hands from his throat. No matter how hard he tried. She was stronger than he was. Stronger, smarter—

And dead.

Dead.

He let go of her wrists, letting his hands drop as if they had lost strength. She had been right when she had told him he didn't deserve to live, but that didn't stop him from wanting to live, or even needing to live.

He had made a bargain with the voices for Marly, and he didn't know if Jewel was their test. If he failed it, would Marly die with him? And Denl? And Tri?

Matthias couldn't risk it.

He found his pack, opening it with one hand. His heart was pounding, and it took all of his strength to hold back the panic. He had to move carefully so that Jewel suspected nothing.

Her fingers dug into his skin. The pressure on his lungs was severe. They were burning, burning, burning. He felt as if they would burst. His mouth was open and gasping. He couldn't control that, any more than he could control the muscles in his back, which were pushing him against her in a vain attempt to get free.

The fingers of his left hand found the repository. And he thought a prayer, thought it toward the heavens with the same fervor he used to feel as a young boy. He believed more now than he ever had. Ironic, since he had finally discovered the truth about his religion and it hadn't been pretty.

But he hoped it was accurate.

The pressure from his lungs had moved into his limbs. He could feel it, the urgent demand for air. It was flooding through him. Soon he wouldn't have control. Soon his body would take over and it would fight blindly, panicked, and he would lose.

He would lose.

Jewel was showing infinite patience, her strong fingers pressed into him, her warm body against his.

His fingers found the doll. The glass was cool in his hands. He had prepared for this. He had even followed the instructions for preparing the Soul Repository. Two drops of the Roca's blood lined the bottom. Two drops, enough to lure a curious soul once that soul was free.

He hoped hers was free.

The black spots were growing. He could feel the edge of oblivion moving closer. He worked the head off the doll with his fingers, holding it by the carved neck with one finger, and then easing it into the pack. He would reach for it when he needed to.

He would have to move fast.

He turned the body so that the neck faced Jewel, and then he shoved it against her hip.

She gasped, and her fingers flew off his neck. There was a wind around him, a wind like none he had ever felt before. He staggered, drawing in air as if it were water and he were dying of thirst. He felt dizzy with it, but he had to keep a hold on himself. He reached across his body, grabbed the pack and pulled the head out.

Then he turned.

Jewel was whirling around him, her body composed of wind and mist. She was fighting the pull—he could see it—flailing her arms as if she were in a water spout, trying to swim her way out. Her legs were gone, already in the Repository, and her torso was being pulled inside.

She was yelling at him, but the words were lost in the wind. The bottom half of the doll shook in his hand, and grew warm. He could see a brown mist inside as she went in.

She reached for him, cursing, her features contorted. Most of her torso was in now, and then her neck. Her head disappeared, and then her hands, fingers grasping.

He slammed the glass head on, and prayed he had lined the edge with enough blood. He had never done this before, ever, and he was terrified it would be a temporary thing.

The wind was gone, and he could hear nothing except the ragged sound of his own breathing. His neck felt as if it were on fire. The doll was hot too, and it shook. He looked at it closely. He could see Jewel inside, her features molding to the doll's, her hands pressing against its side.

Trapped. She was trapped, and he had her, just as the Words had promised.

He sank down slowly, the dizziness growing, and along with it nausea. He had nearly died again, and this time, the Roca's magick had saved him. Or he had saved himself.

"We need to move on," the guide said.

Matthias didn't respond. He clutched the Repository tightly in his left hand. He was still gasping. His whole body hurt. Couldn't the man see that Matthias had nearly died? That he needed to rest?

"You don't have time for this," the guide said. "Get up."

Matthias needed time for it. He needed to take care of himself. How many times could a man face death before it finally took him? How much importance did one life have?

"Get up," the guide repeated.

Matthias couldn't even curse him. He didn't have enough air in his lungs. But in his head, he used every curse he knew, good, bad, and vile. The guide hadn't helped him, hadn't shown any desire to help him, and now wanted only to make him move forward.

Still, he had made a bargain. He had Marly to think of. Marly . . .

Slowly he put the Soul Repository back in his pack. He had to be careful with it. The wrong kind of movement, and it would open, setting her free. But he couldn't leave it here. Even though he believed no one had been through these tunnels in a long time, it would be just his luck to have someone come through now, pick up the Repository, and free her.

Then she really would kill him.

He pulled the strings of the pack closed over the doll's head, and then he tied it to his waist. He put a hand on the stone floor and pushed himself up.

The dizziness was nearly overwhelming. He staggered toward the wall, put his hand there, and held himself for a moment.

"Have you forgotten everything?" the guide asked. "Take care of yourself."

Take care of himself? He didn't know what that meant, and didn't have the breath to ask. Take care of himself. He concentrated on breathing, on filling his lungs with clean cool air. The burning subsided and the air did fill him. He wasn't sure if that was because he wished it so, or if that was because he had waited long enough.

A thudding headache followed the air, but it was better than nearly dying, better than the nausea and the dizziness. He could handle the headache.

He clutched at his pack, careful to avoid the Jewel Repository, and found his water. He took a sip. The water was cool in his mouth, and soothed on the way down, until he had to swallow. Then the pain was stunning, sharp, and ferocious.

She had injured something, but he didn't know what. He didn't have time to find out. He had to keep moving, had to, and he wasn't sure why any more, except that it had to do with Marly and promises made.

He wiped his mouth with the back of his hand. His guide wa
watching him, blue eyes impassive. "Ready?"

Matthias nodded.

The guide went forward, bypassing a corridor that Matthia
hadn't realized was there. Matthias stumbled after him, the dizzi
ness returning. He had to remind himself to breathe, remind
himself to focus. He would recover soon enough.

He had to.

Ahead the sound of water grew. The strange light seemed al
most blinding in its whiteness. He was nearly there—he knew it
Then he would grab the jewels and run. Maybe he would be able
to return before the fighting was over below. Maybe the voice:
had lied to him.

But he doubted it. Something was waiting for him up ahead
something he was destined to do. He knew it; that was the only
reason he had survived all that was placed before him.

And it terrified him, more than he would ever care to admit.

# SEVENTY-THREE

RUGAD put a hand to his head, letting the silence calm him. I
was quiet and the air was still, and there was no light except the
natural familiar grayness of the Shadowlands itself.

A dead Hawk Rider lay near him, another crouching beside
him, mourning silently. Several of his troops were just sitting on
the ground, holding their heads as he was, allowing the Shadowlands to heal them.

Or maybe they hadn't even noticed yet. Maybe they didn't
know that he had protected them. Maybe they still thought they
were under attack.

He had never felt anything that painful. Which wasn't exactly
true. He had lived through a lot of pain, but none of it had ever
gone for his Vision before. The light seemed to be drilling a hole
in his brain. But it hadn't succeeded, at least not entirely. He had
made the Shadowlands and they were fine.

But he was boxed in.

Nicholas had won this first round. A brilliant ploy, brilliant. And now, if Rugad was not careful, he would be trapped in here. He leaned against the cool wall of the Shadowlands, the wall farthest north, closest to the Place of Power, and thought.

He was missing something. He knew it, but he hadn't had time to think before. He had only had a few moments in which to react. He hadn't saved his entire troop, but he had saved three-fifths of them. That was a start.

Some of the troops beside him moaned. They were coming round. This magick Nicholas had used had targeted Rugad's magick centers, yes, but it had also had an effect on his body as well. The troops up front had been Infantry who had not yet come into their magick. Somehow the light had found a way to get to them.

Just as the Islanders' holy poison had done. It had affected Fey, but not the Islanders themselves.

The Spell Warders on Nye had called it weapons magick, saying that it had been designed to target a specific group named when the initial user picked up the weapon. At first, they had thought the poison could be turned on the Islanders—a Fey could pick it up, target an Islander, and reverse the process. But it hadn't worked that way. Once started, the process couldn't be reversed. The change had to happen at the moment of the weapon's creation or the moment of its discovery. Sometimes, the Warders had said, the target could change if the weapon were altered in some small fashion.

What did he know of light?

Energy traveled on it—spirit energy, like his essence, traveling the Links, which were, essentially, light. It left a trail that Visionaries could see. And it had other properties, properties of its own, properties that made it so difficult to harness that only Enchanters and Visionaries could do so. And a few Warders, of course. Warders who needed it to explore Spells.

Enchanters, Visionaries, Warders. Shamans. All power eventually became light. Or came from light. And if Warders could use it, it could be harnessed.

The Islanders' magick was different, but it came from a Place of Power, just as the Feys' did. So there had to be similarities.

And then, as that thought crossed his mind, he raised his head and faced the Place of Power. Inside Shadowlands, he could no longer see it and he could no longer *feel* it. He was protected here from the magick currents that surrounded the place.

Magick currents that Nicholas had somehow gathered and used.

Only his use had been indiscriminate. The wave of light, the wave of power, had been undirected. Nicholas had been able to use it, but not to *focus* it.

He did not know all the tricks to the Place of Power yet.

Rugad let out a breath of air. There was still a chance. A slim chance, but a chance. He would be able to do what he had planned to do all along. He would be able to harness the energy from the Place of Power for himself.

But he would have to be very, very careful. If he made a mistake, he would lose his great-grandchildren.

He pressed a hand against the cool side of Shadowlands, and created a small Circle Door, keyed only to him. If he died out there, he did not want the others following. He wanted them safe until Nicholas tired, or believed he had won. There was no sense in wasting more lives.

Rugad took a deep breath and shut his eyes. With his Vision, he thought through all the angles of a Shadowlands, the pores, the membrane wall, the aspects that allowed Fey to survive within. He could eliminate those, and create a single side of Shadowlands. He would use it like a shield, only if he did it right, it would reflect the energy back the way it came. He could grab it and mold it and shoot it back with all its power, as if it were an arrow.

The magick would not work the same. It would not kill an Islander by touch alone. No. He would have to make a direct hit. He would have to aim for the heart.

And he couldn't aim for Nicholas's heart, since Nicholas would move. Nor could he try for any random person above.

He had another choice. The straw man Nicholas had used to create his army. That man and his constructs were all of a height. They all stood in the same position. If Rugad aimed the power back toward those men, he would hit them all in the heart. The constructs would absorb the energy, and the man himself would die.

The beam would have to be long, thin, and horizontal. It would have to rise up the ridge and hit all the constructs in the same place. He would have to make the beam into a thin board and level it across that ridge as if it were a freestanding table. The beam would cut through the constructs across their chests and burst the template's heart.

The problem would be in timing. Rugad could not let the power flow continue after the man was dead, and he had no real way of determining when that would happen. It would have to be guesswork—and trust.

He would have to trust that Nicholas had hid his children from this magickal onslaught. They too, after all, were Fey. If the power that Nicholas had harnessed had gone awry, they would have died.

Strange that Rugad had to trust his enemy in order to succeed. But he was beginning to get a firm sense of Nicholas. Nicholas had been a worthy husband to Jewel. Had he been born Fey, he would have been worthy of the Black Throne.

Rugad opened his eyes, focused, and built the single Shadowlands wall. Then he collapsed it into a square that could fit into his palm.

He had a few moments from the time he left this Shadowlands until he lost all control outside. He didn't dare go out with the shield before him—he didn't even know if the light was still flowing down the mountainside. Besides, he wouldn't be able to focus the light if he didn't see it one more time.

He walked through the Circle Door.

The light was still flowing down the mountainside, brighter than anything he had ever seen. Blinding light. Crippling light.

The screams were fainter now. Most of the Fey were dead.

He tossed the shield out of his hand, let it grow until it was bigger than he was, and felt the light bounce off of it. As it did, he felt the pressure recede. He used his Vision, allowing it to See through the Shadowlands shield, Saw the source of the light and grabbed it, turning it, focusing it as he had planned, and aimed at the plateau on the mountaintop.

The light flowed down like a wide stream, then hit the shield and bounced back toward the mountain in a fist-sized string. He flattened the string, formed it into the horizontal plane he had planned, keeping it within precise dimensions, and aimed it at the Place of Power. The power in light staggered even Rugad. He would not be able to control it long.

He only hoped he could control it long enough.

# SEVENTY-FOUR

THE screaming was fading. An occasional cry, cut off or choke
back, and that was all. Nicholas clutched two globes to his waist
His hands were hot and swollen, the skin beneath his shirt ho
as well.

Coulter hadn't moved except to receive more globes. Th
tears continued to roll down his face. The front of his shirt wa
wet, and that worried Nicholas. Not just for Coulter, who in thi
instance reminded him of Sebastian, unable to accept the loss o
life he was causing, but also because Nicholas was afraid that th
salty wetness would make the burning worse.

The Fey had stopped coming up the mountainside. Nichola
could tell that much from Adrian's expression. But Adrian's fac
had grown so pale as to be almost colorless. He seemed stunned b
what he saw.

Nicholas only hoped the globes would last long enough to de
stroy the entire army. They had used half of them now, an
Nicholas did not know how to make any more. But he woul
worry about that when he needed to.

The light flowed forward, a wide golden wall, sending its pro
tection away. He found a comfort in it. He was growing used to it
brilliance, to its—

"Sire!" Adrian turned, looking slightly alarmed, and as he did, a hundred other Adrians turned. "Something's changed."

But he didn't need to explain what. Light, as thin, hard, and concentrated as the long edge of a gigantic sword, soared over the ridge. It was as if someone had taken Nicholas's wall of light and compacted it into something finer, more precise. The light slashed through each and every Adrian, cut him through the chest. The light made no difference to the fake ones—they didn't even seem to notice—but when it hit the real one, he gasped in surprise.

His eyes widened—a hundred pairs of eyes widened—his mouth opened, and blood spewed out. The other Adrians replicated the motion for only an instant, and then they vanished—popped out of existence as if they were merely bubbles.

Adrian remained standing, his torso divided in half by the long flat beam, blood dripping from him. Then he toppled forward.

Coulter dropped his globe. It didn't shatter, but the light went out. He ran for Adrian, screaming his name.

The light flowing from the cave diminished by half. Then, a moment later, the light coming back diminished by half as well.

Nicholas dropped his globes as if they were killing Adrian—which they probably were. They hit the cave floor and rolled, the lights going out. The entire mountaintop seemed to plummet into darkness, although he could still see the sun.

The light from below, the wide flat beam, went out as well.

Coulter reached Adrian's side, and grabbed him, clutching him close and wailing as he did so. Nicholas had never heard Coulter make that broken sound before, but he didn't need to. He knew it.

Adrian was dead.

And Coulter would be too if Nicholas didn't get him back inside the cave. It seemed as if that light, that weapon, was related to the globes' lights, but he couldn't be certain. He was facing the Black King of all the Fey; he didn't dare underestimate him.

Nicholas hurried outside. There were bits of blood everywhere, as if the Adrians had had a bit of reality after all.

It didn't matter. Adrian was at the edge of the platform, right near the stairs. His legs were twisted at an odd angle no conscious man would ever allow, and his body was held by Coulter.

Coulter was sobbing so hard that his entire being vibrated. The boy had been on edge since the killing started; now he seemed to have crossed over. Nicholas cursed softly. He couldn't lose Coulter, not now. Coulter was as valuable to him—as valuable to their defense—as the cave itself.

Before he crouched beside Coulter, Nicholas glanced down the mountainside. There were gaps in his vision, as if part of the mountain had gone away. There were bodies just below, hideously burned, their faces nearly gone, and then there were two large patches of gray. He could barely see the river beyond them. Then there was another field of bodies, and another large patch of gray.

Was the grayness some kind of Shadowlands? Had the Black King mustered a defense that quickly?

He must have. And in that defense, he found a way to turn Nicholas's weapon against him.

So far, nothing was moving down there—at least that Nicholas could see. He remembered Arianna's admonition to look skyward as well, and he saw no strange birds, no contraptions carrying the leader of the Fey.

He went to Coulter's side. The boy held Adrian so close that Adrian's face wasn't visible. Nicholas put a hand on Coulter's shoulder. It shuddered with the force of his grief.

"Coulter," Nicholas said softly. "You must come with me."

Coulter did not respond. He didn't even seem to hear Nicholas. Nicholas glanced down the mountain again. Still nothing, but he didn't trust it.

"Coulter," Nicholas said, his mouth dry. He had to reach the boy somehow, and he couldn't use Arianna to do it. He didn't want her out of the Shadowlands. "We have to get Adrian into the cave."

"Why?" Coulter snapped. "He's dead."

That was more presence than Nicholas had expected from the boy. "We can't leave him here. You don't know what the Fey will do to him."

"Yes," Coulter said. "I do."

And he probably did. Coulter knew more about the Fey than most Islanders.

"Coulter, please," Nicholas said. "We have to get away from here."

"Why?"

Nicholas swallowed. He'd carry the boy if he had to. "Adrian died for you. The least you could do is preserve your own life."

"Adrian died for you," Coulter said, not moving. "He died for you and your silly cause, and your Isle, which you've already lost. And now you want the rest of us to die for you as well."

"No," Nicholas said.

"Yes," Coulter said. "Me, and Scavenger, and Leen. You want us all to die."

"And Gift? And Arianna?" Nicholas let his words hang. "You think I want to kill them too?"

With a moan, Coulter lowered his head.

Nicholas went to Adrian's feet and picked them up. "Let's get him inside," he said again.

Coulter stood, still cradling Adrian. The strange position made it difficult for Nicholas get a good grip, but he managed. Adrian's body was strangely light, as if everything that composed it had been blasted out through his mouth. He also smelled slightly charred, as if the light had burned him from within.

They struggled with him, got him into the cave, and set him near the globes. Coulter kicked one, and it bounced down the stairs. The glass was remarkably resilient. It clinked as it bounced, but did not break.

"We killed him," Coulter said, not facing Nicholas. "Us and your globes and that light. We killed him."

"The Black King killed him," Nicholas said.

"And we killed the others too."

"They would have killed us."

"Do you know how many people I've killed?" Coulter cried. "Do you know?"

"No," Nicholas said. He didn't want to think about it. He couldn't. The Black King would come up that mountainside at any moment.

"Neither do I," Coulter said in a very small voice.

Nicholas grabbed him by the arms, and turned him. "We have to get Leen and Scavenger. We need to try again."

"So that they can die too? I don't think so," Coulter said. "Besides, what you would have them do? Hold two swords against the Fey army?"

"The Fey army is in ruins."

"But not enough," Coulter said. "Didn't you see below? The Black King put a Shadowlands around them. Most of that army still lives. When they realize we're not using the globes, they'll come after us. And what do you plan to do then? Throw bowls at them? Send me out to them? Make me kill them? I won't! I can't!"

"Coulter—"

"No," Coulter said. "This is your war, not mine. I've lost my best friend, and now I've lost the only person who cared about me. I'm not going to do this any longer. Let them take this place, Nicholas. They've already won."

"And what of Arianna? What of Gift?"

"They're Fey, aren't they?" That last question was soft. Almost as if Coulter didn't want to voice it. "They'll be all right. It's just you who'll die. You and me, and maybe Scavenger and Leen. And that doesn't matter any more. Your line will continue. Mine was never meant to be. Who cares any more, Nicholas? Let them win."

Nicholas, the boy called him. Not Sire, not King. Nicholas. Was he right? Had the Fey won?

"I can't let them win," Nicholas said.

"Then you fight them by yourself," Coulter said, and dropped beside Adrian. He took Adrian's body in his arms, and made it clear that he wouldn't listen to anything more that Nicholas had to say.

Not that there was more to say. Coulter was right. The Black King would be coming up the mountain, and then what would Nicholas do? Try to kill him and the remaining troops with one sword?

The tapestries probably had an answer to his dilemma, but the he didn't have time to study them. It was too late to appeal to the creatures from the fountain. Coulter wouldn't help. Adrian was dead, and Nicholas didn't quite trust Leen and Scavenger enough to allow them near that kind of power.

He glanced behind him. The revolving circle of lights, no bigger than the crown he had worn during his coronation ceremony—when Jewel had died—were the only signs that his four Fey companions were with him.

Coulter was still rocking Adrian's body.

Nicholas was on his own. If he managed to somehow kill the Black King, then so be it. And if that caused the Blood against Blood, then he could do nothing about it. He didn't believe it would. All the theoretical arguments in the world hadn't quite proved it to him. Because, although his children were of the Black Throne, Nicholas was not.

He had to trust in that. The Black King obviously did.

Nicholas went to the wall of swords and took one. It felt light and comfortable in his hand, as if he had always held this sword.

He would hold it until he killed the Black King.

Or until he died, defending this place, defending this Isle, defending his children.

# SEVENTY-FIVE

THE burble of water grew incredibly loud. Matthias wondered if he was hearing it in his head or actually hearing it with his ears. The sound seemed to float around him like a live thing. The white light of the stone walls also seemed brighter.

He reached a fork in the corridor, thought he saw the outline of a body on the floor ahead of him, and then the guide turned. Matthias's gave followed him.

A fountain rose out of the stone, just as the Roca had described it in the Words. The fountain—the one that the Roca had once seen as a blessing and then saw as a curse. The fountain, the reason Matthias was what he was.

He stared at it for a moment. The air was cool around it, dappled with a slight mist caused by the continual motion of the water. It smelled fresh, like the mountains often did after an unexpected rain.

His guide touched his arm. "There's not much time."

"Time for what?" Matthias asked, but the man put his hand to his lips.

Matthias looked around. He saw no one. But he saw signs that people had been staying there. Cloaks on the marble floor, a makeshift bed near the stairs.

And above him, he heard a voice.

"Then you fight them by yourself."

The voice was young, bitter, so flat that it seemed as if the speaker no longer had hope of anything. A shudder ran down Matthias's back. He could remember feeling like that.

He kept toward the back of the cavern and took the stairs closest to the wall. The Words had said the jewels were stored near the back, so no one would find them easily. Matthias didn't know exactly where the "back" was, but it wasn't here, near the fountain, near the start of it all.

The stairs were shallower than he expected, and he nearly slipped once. He thought he heard a small clang coming from the area of the voice, but he couldn't be certain. He reached the top step, and saw the rows and rows of shelves, some empty and some still full. A few held globes. There were more holy water vials than he could count, and more bowls than he had ever seen before. In the corner were some full Soul Repositories. He carefully set Jewel's down beside them.

But he didn't see the jewels he had come for. The guide went ahead of him, stared at a wall of shelves, and cursed softly. A small handful of jewels glittered. But Matthias hadn't been expecting a handful. He had expected an entire wallful.

"They're gone, aren't they?" Matthias asked, forgetting to keep his voice down.

It echoed through the entire place, and he thought he heard a gasp. He turned.

Ahead of him, he could see the mouth of the cavern. Just inside it, a boy—the boy who had taught him fire—was cradling a man who seemed quite dead. Nicholas stood beside him, holding a sword.

Matthias hadn't seen Nicholas in fifteen years. He seemed taller somehow, and thinner. He wore pants and a loose shirt. They were filthy. His blond hair seemed less vibrant than it had, and it was matted against his head.

"Matthias," he said, and there was such sadness in his voice that Matthias winced. The sadness was not for him. It was for Jewel. It had always been for Jewel.

Did Nicholas know what Matthias had done? Did he know that Jewel was here, trapped in a glass doll?

"The Fey are attacking the town of Constant below," Matthias said. "People are dying. I've come for some weapons."

"You know how everything in here works, then?" Nicholas asked. He came toward Matthias, walking quickly. Matthias's heart started pounding hard. His throat still hurt from Jewel's attack, and he felt weaker than he wanted to.

He didn't even know where he could run.

"I know how most of them work," Matthias said.

"Good," Nicholas said. He came up beside Matthias and put his hand firmly on Matthias's arm. Matthias winced.

Nicholas saw it and grinned. It was not a pleasant expression. "I'm not going to kill you yet, Matthias," he said, his grip tight. "The Black King of the Fey is just outside, and I figure that, for once, your hatred will be useful."

"The Black King?" Matthias repeated stupidly.

"If we do away with him, we'll have our Isle back. Then we can worry about our differences."

"Differences?" Matthias's voice sounded weak to his own ears. This was Nicholas? The man who had pressed a knife in his back and threatened to kill him? His hair was shot with gray now, and his face had fine lines, but he looked the same.

He just didn't sound the same.

"You want my help?" Matthias asked, unable to believe what he was hearing.

"Do you see anyone else?" Nicholas asked.

Matthias looked at the boy on the floor. He appeared to be lost in his mourning. There was the dead man and on one else. Matthias frowned. He had thought there would be others here, like Nicholas's half-breed daughter.

But it was just Nicholas in the Roca's Cave.

With the Black King of the Fey outside.

"All right," Matthias said. It didn't matter what happened after the defeat of the Black King, if there was a defeat. What would matter was that he had tried.

This must have been the destiny the guide was talking about. This had to be the reason he had come, to work with Nicholas.

Matthias closed his eyes for a moment. To work with Nicholas, after killing Jewel a second time—or at least taking away her power. He couldn't tell Nicholas that. Not yet.

"Do you regret this already?" Nicholas asked.

"No." Matthias opened his eyes. He made himself stand to full height. "I will help you, Nicholas."

"Good." That voice came from behind them. The guide. Matthias wasn't certain what had happened to him in the last few moments.

Nicholas was staring at him, face pale. "You," he said.

The guide came up to them. He wasn't completely solid. He shrugged. "You didn't think I'd leave your forever, did you?"

"You know him?" Matthias asked.

"I freed him," Nicholas said. "And for that, he abandoned me."

"No," the guide said. "I went to my designated place. They sent me back here."

"I thought you came to help me," Matthias said.

"I came to undo Coulter's stupidity." The guide spoke bitterly.

Nicholas looked at the boy. "Coulter?"

"He means the Roca," Matthias said.

"Indeed," the guide said, and that was when Matthias realized the guide was no longer speaking Old Islander. "He felt he had cursed the generations. He guarded this place until he could be visible no longer. He created magick that, if used with the right intent, would destroy power instead of increase it. And he deliberately ruined the power that we had."

Nicholas took a step closer to the guide. "What do you mean?"

Matthias could feel the intensity of Nicholas's question.

"The swords outside," the guide said. "Haven't you wondered how they were to be used?"

"Of course," Nicholas said.

Matthias frowned. "The swords? I thought the Wise Ones put them there."

"Do you believe everything you're told?" the guide said. "Or did Coulter lie about this too in the silly letter he wrote?"

"He didn't mention it," Matthias said.

"What letter?" Nicholas asked.

Matthias shook his head. There wasn't time to explain.

"Do you want to know how to use the swords or not?" the guide asked.

"Yes," Nicholas said. "But you could have told me this when I freed you."

"No, I couldn't," the guide said. "You had to work with Matthias."

"Why?" Matthias asked.

"Because it takes the full blood of the Roca to make this work," the guide said. "You carry the blood of the second son, Matthias, and your friend here carries the blood of the eldest. This power was designed only for the Roca, or for his issue acting in concert."

Nicholas looked at Matthias. "You are truly the second son?"

"I guess," Matthias said.

"So you were the correct Rocaan."

Matthias shrugged. "The Fiftieth Rocaan apparently saw things that no one else did."

"We are related, then," Nicholas said.

"Distantly."

"And if I had killed you that day?"

"You would have brought your blood in contact with his blood over death," the guide said. "It would have created great chaos."

"Like the Fey," Nicholas said.

"Their blood is different from yours. It comes from a different fountain. You do not share their blood, although, I am told, your children do."

"Yes," Nicholas whispered. He looked pale and frightened, suddenly. Matthias wasn't quite sure what all of this meant, only that somehow the idea of blood and death and relationships terrified Nicholas.

"You will tell us the secret of those swords?" Matthias asked his guide.

"That's what I was sent for," the guide said, and then grinned at him. "Did you really think I was sent to protect you?"

Matthias flushed but said nothing.

"What do we have to do?" Nicholas asked.

The guide went to the shelves, took a bottle of Roca's blood, and held it out to them. "I'll tell you," he said.

# SEVENTY-SIX

RUGAD felt drained. The light had disappeared some time before—how long before, he wasn't entirely certain—and with it, the threat to his people.

But he wasn't going to remove the protective Shadowlands. Not yet. Nicholas was too cunning, and he would be regrouping. With luck, he would be using another kind of magick that Rugad could gain control of. Nicholas wouldn't know what Rugad could and couldn't do.

All power had lines. He simply had to follow those lines, gather them, and use them himself. Anything a nonmagickal person like Nicholas could use, Rugad could use better.

The thoughts sustained him, and he needed the sustenance. He had never been this exhausted in a campaign before. He had been physically tired, yes, but not so mentally drained. And he couldn't be. He needed to get control of himself, and to hold it rigidly. Blue Isle was worth the fight. The Place of Power was worth the fight, not to mention his great-grandchildren.

Ahead of him was a vast field of dead Fey. They lay where they had fallen, scattered along the mountainside, bodies sprawled. The stench was palpable; their flesh had burned from the inside out. His skin crawled at the thought. He had barely saved himself.

What he wanted to know, what he needed to know, was how many of his people were still alive. How many he could commandeer immediately. Then he would march up that mountain and kill Nicholas. And he would make the Place of Power his base.

No Shaman would ever get her toes inside the place. His family had been foolish to allow the Shamans inside the Place of Power in the Eccrasian Mountains. He would dislodge Nicholas's Shaman, and take the Place of Power for himself. Here, he would train his great-grandchildren. Here, he would unify the Fey. And from here, he would launch his next assault, on Leut.

Planning ahead. He needed a plan for the moment of his victory.

He still had Nicholas to contend with, and in all Rugad's years of fighting, Nicholas had proven to be his most worthy opponent.

Jewel had chosen well.

Rugad wished she were still alive so that he could congratulate her. But if she were still alive, his entire plan of attack would have had to be different—if he had attacked at all.

He set his solid Shadowlands shield on the ground outside the third Shadowlands he had built. Then he went through the Circle Door.

The moans of pain had stopped. The handful of Domestics who had been at the bottom of the mountain had somehow gathered the wounded and put them in one place. Then the Healers had started doing their jobs. That was good. It made Rugad's job easier.

He snapped his fingers. Selia came toward him. She had been near the river when the attack started. He had actually sent her back to camp just before the fighting started to get any remaining fighters and send them here. But she hadn't made it.

Her braids were coming undone, and a long streak of blood marred her left cheek. She didn't seem to notice. Her dark eyes looked hollow and pain-filled. Someone she cared about had been wounded, then. He thought it odd to know an adjunct of his had a life he knew nothing of.

She, of course, was professional enough not to mention it.

"How many are fit to fight?" he asked.

"In here?" She spoke, then seemed to realize how silly her question was. Of course he meant in here. How would she know the statistics for any other place? "Perhaps fifty."

"Then get me perhaps-fifty immediately. We are heading up the mountain."

"Sir?" she said, and in her tone, he could hear disapproval.

"You question me?" he asked.

She licked her lips. "You had said that I should tell you what I think."

He had. He had meant it at the time, too. "Quickly then."

"The morale—"

"Is immaterial to me. Anything else?"

"The weapons above—"

"Are constructs of the Place of Power. Have you anything relevant for me to consider?"

Her face flushed. She opened her mouth, closed it, then opened it again. "I guess not, sir."

"Good," he said. "Get me that perhaps-fifty. We have a very short window. Tell them they are expected to march double time."

She swallowed. He could see a struggle on her face. He would have watched it with amusement if he'd had the time.

He did not.

She seemed to sense it. "Do you . . ." Her voice halted, lost strength. Then she took a breath and seemed to gather herself. "Do you need someone with Charm, sir?"

So she understood part of it. He might have to negotiate. He might have to talk. But he wouldn't negotiate with Nicholas. The time for talking to that man was done.

"Charm doesn't work with Visionaries," he said.

"I didn't mean for your great-grandchildren, sir."

He smiled thinly. "They're the only ones I'll talk to," he said.

She nodded once, turned on her heel, and walked away. He saw her touch an Infantry man's shoulder, then another, speaking as she went. Maybe he did need her, in the other two Shadowlands up the mountain. The surviving Fey there had time to brood on what they would consider a disaster. They had time to feel fear. She might be able to calm his remaining troops so that they could walk beside him, a unified Fey force against the handful of people huddled in Nicholas's cave.

He touched his sword lightly, then checked his knife. Both were in place. He would take his Shadowlands shield as well. If Nicholas dared use the light again, Rugad would be able to deflect it. He might not be able to save some of the troops fighting beside him, but that didn't matter. What mattered was getting to that cavern. Once he was there, once he was within reach of the Place of Power, it would be his.

And once it was his, Blue Isle was his.

His great-grandchildren were his.

"Hurry up, Selia!" he snapped, and across Shadowlands, he could see her head bob in reaction. She touched a Foot Soldier, and he stood, speaking to other Foot Soldiers.

He could feel the Foot Soldiers' response, see it in their quick movements. They were ready. So was he.

Fifty here. Say another twenty-five or more in each of the remaining Shadowlands. Rugad would march into the Place of Power with a force a hundred strong.

It was a good start.

Rugad only hoped it would be enough.

# SEVENTY-SEVEN

"IT sounds risky to me," Nicolas said. He wasn't looking at the strange man. Instead he was watching Coulter, still huddled over Adrian's dead form. The boy was sobbing silently and making small magick with his fingers, as if he had the power to bring Adrian back. Nicholas had known that despair once. It had seemed like the only thing in the world.

But even then he had been able to reach out to his newly born daughter, to hold her, to care for her. Even then.

"You have a better idea?" Nicholas could hear the sneer in the guide's voice. The guide was standing slightly behind Matthias.

He was shorter than Matthias, and only partly visible, as if he were being viewed through a fog. Nicholas wished Jewel were here. She would know what the little man was exactly. She would know if he could be trusted.

The only thing Nicholas knew was that the man had come from the glass doll in the back of the cave. If Nicholas hadn't seen that, he wouldn't have trusted the man at all. He would have thrown him from the cave—if one could do that with a man made of mist.

"Well?" the strange man asked. "Do you have a better idea or not?"

Nicholas glanced one last time at Coulter. At Adrian. The man had sacrificed himself for all of this and had died a hideous death. "His son," Nicholas said, nodding his head in Adrian's direction, "burned the pouches filled with skin, blood, and bone that the Fey kept. There was quite a reaction, like a hole made in the magick fiber. Everyone seemed to feel it. It made the more powerful sick."

"So?" the guide asked.

Matthias frowned. "That's what that was?"

Nicholas ignored him. "So," he said, "you claim a lot of properties for those vials of the Roca's blood, and they're very similar to the properties the Fey claim for their harvest. Essentially, all the magick is conducted through that blood."

"Conducted, transmitted, stored, increased—" The little man would have gone on if Nicholas had not raised his hand.

"So if I destroy it, I will cause a reaction that will diminish the power of the Fey. Hours after Luke destroyed that barn, Scavenger was able to kill an Enchanter on the mountainside. I should be able to kill the Black King of the Fey immediately."

The man snorted. "You wouldn't survive. Setting off a reaction like that in here would destroy the mountains. It might even destroy the Isle. It might destroy the other two caves just like this plus anything near them for hundreds of miles. It would certainly destroy anything you were trying to save."

Nicholas's throat went dry. He had thought it a good idea. But he didn't know how many pouches Luke had destroyed, nor how close Luke had been. He also didn't know the damage done. Still, it had seemed more logical than the man's description of an unfamiliar magick.

Matthias said nothing. If he had stated an opinion in the argument, Nicholas would have been forced to judge it objectively. And while he knew he could put off his feelings about Matthias until the Black King was dead, he wasn't sure he could easily discuss things with the man.

The strange man shrugged. "It is your decision, of course. You hold the power in your two small hands to destroy things or rebuild them."

"Your plan rebuilds?"

"My plan only destroys whatever is standing between the mouth of this cave and the river. Yours destroys much, much more."

And could always be used if this man's plan was proven false. Nicholas swallowed, feeling pain in the dryness of his throat, and glanced at Matthias. "Are you willing to try this?"

"I read the Words," he said softly. "The real Words, hidden in a Vault below Constant. What he says explains some things that made no sense before."

Matthias looked down at the man. Nicholas noted Matthias's wariness with him as well, as if Matthias didn't know what to make of him either.

"You've done this before, haven't you?" Matthias asked.

The man smiled. His eyes danced with a pleasure that made Nicholas shiver, considering they were talking about a power that could kill a lot of people.

"Once," the man said.

"Once," Matthias repeated, and in it, Nicholas heard the tones of a man he hadn't heard for twenty years. The scholar who used to visit his father on rainy nights. The man who was supposed to teach Nicholas, young Nicholas, the ways of the religion. The man who had opinions about such esoteric things as ethics and morals.

Matthias didn't approve of the plan any more than Nicholas did. And he had even less reason to follow it. His children weren't hidden here. But he did know how to use the items in the cave. That might become a problem later.

"If we do this, you must start it," Nicholas said.

"But we have to follow through together," Matthias said. He looked at Nicholas. His eyes were slightly canted: the wounds on the side of his face pulled at his skin. Without those wounds, he had an ascetic's face, so thin that the bones were visible. His curls were mostly gray now, but he had a wiry strength that belied his age. He was older than Nicholas by more than twenty years. Once that had seemed like forever. Now they seemed to be of an age.

"Have you the courage to do this, Nicholas?"

And in Matthias's question, Nicholas heard his old teacher, and he heard something else: Nicholas hadn't had the courage to kill Matthias when Matthias had deserved it, shortly after Jewel died. Nicholas had said it would make him like Matthias—and perhaps that had been true—but there had also been a lack of ruthlessness in him. Matthias had never lacked for ruthlessness, not even in his scholarly days.

But Nicholas had grown a lot in fifteen years. In that time, he had learned that ruthlessness had a place in defending himself and his family. "Of course I have the courage. I'm not the one who has to live with the consequences of killing out of fear."

Matthias looked away. He nodded ever so slightly. It was almost as if he were ashamed of what he had done.

The man Matthias called guide was watching them. Was he truly helping them, or was something else involved?

The man noted Nicholas's scrutiny. "I was simply here to give you the information. Information you would not have had if you had not set me free."

Nicholas frowned.

The man smiled. "You are making the choices."

Nicholas took a deep breath. That was the fundamental part of all of this. He was still King, still the man in charge. And he had only one more chance to save everything he cared for. One more chance, and to do it, he needed the man who had killed his wife at his side.

"What of Coulter?" Nicholas asked. "Could he do this?"

Matthias froze as if the question bothered him. The guide's smile grew. "No," the guide said. "He is not of the Roca's blood. He is of mine."

"But his name," Matthias said. "It was the Roca's name. Was it yours too?"

"I was not called Coulter," the guide said.

"Then how could Coulter be of your blood?"

The guide looked away. "Don't men still name their children after the people they believe to be their closest friends?"

The question hung between them, revealing bits of a history Nicholas didn't have time to learn. He looked at Matthias.

"Are you ready?"

Matthias nodded, then walked toward the mouth of the cave. Coulter didn't even seem to notice as both men passed him. Nicholas realized that—as the guide had originally said—the best thing for Coulter was to remain where he was. Nicholas could do nothing to help him. At least, not yet.

Matthias stayed slightly inside the cave's mouth, as the guide had instructed. He looked at the five swords surrounding the entrance. Two were already in position, and Nicholas had ordered the jewels cleaned before that first attack. It was the other three that Matthias would have to move.

"I've never done anything like this before," he whispered.

"From what I understand," Nicholas said, "no one has, not for fifty generations."

He turned to the guide for confirmation, but the man was gone. A chill ran up Nicholas's spine. They were on their own now. The two of them, working together, as best they could.

Matthias raised his arms, and closed his eyes. A beam of light bright and hard, ran from him to the sword sticking horizontally out of the right side of the cave's mouth. The sword shivered as the light wrapped around it. Tiny rocks cascaded to the ground, sounding like a hard rain. Matthias's face was turning red with strain.

Nicholas bit his lip. It had to work. It had to. The only choices they had left were suicidal, things that no one would survive.

The sword kept vibrating. It made a slight sound as it did so, almost a musical tone. The dirt fell off the blade itself, and as the blade became visible, Nicholas could see that it matched the other swords inside the cavern. The light moved up the blade, wound itself around the hilt, and the dirt fell of there, too. Centuries of dirt and debris formed a large pile on the ground below. The sword, while still giant-sized, was smaller than it had initially seemed—an elegant weapon, not a clubby sword with no finesse.

Sweat ran down Matthias's face. Nicholas tasted blood and stopped biting his lip. He licked the wound he had created, not really thinking about it, concentrating instead on that sword as if, with his mind, he could help Matthias get it down.

The light around the hilt formed a hand. Its fingers polished the jewels to iridescent brightness. Its palm wrapped around the scrollwork as if made for it. The hand pulled and the sword came free.

It tottered in the air for a moment, bobbing as if in the grasp of a man who'd never held a weapon before.

Matthias opened his eyes. Tears were running from the corners. He moved his own hands, and the sword floated into a new position. Then he turned his hands palm down, and the sword went, almost instantly, from horizontal to vertical, landing point down in the ground.

It landed with such force the entire cavern shook. The accompanying sound was like an explosion. Some of the swords inside dislodged from the wall and toppled to the ground. A few narrowly missed Coulter. He still didn't move. Rocks fell from the ceiling. Nicholas looked up. A slight crack ran from the mouth toward the fountain.

The sword, though, was in place. Its hilt vibrated with the force of the fall, but the light was gone. Matthias staggered sideways, hands to his face.

"I can't do this again," he said.

"You must," Nicholas said. "Twice more."

"If I do, I'll have nothing left. I won't be able to finish." Matthias was speaking through his hands. His voice rose with panic.

Nicholas glanced at the three swords. The two up front were close together. The third was slightly behind them and to the right of the nearest sword. The fourth should go slightly behind and to the left of the other sword. The fifth should block the entrance completely.

"You can't give up now," Nicholas said.

Matthias was shaking his head. "Get Coulter to do it."

"Coulter can't," Nicholas said.

"Neither can I." Matthias's hands fell from his face, revealing skin paler than any Nicholas had ever seen.

Nicholas put his hands on Matthias's shoulders, reaching up to do so. Matthias was thin, almost as thin as Arianna. "This is our last chance," he snapped. "You will die at the hands of the Black King if you do not do this. You will die."

Matthias shook his head, eyes closed.

"I thought you said I was the one who lacked courage," Nicholas said.

"It's not courage," Matthias whispered. "It's strength."

"Have you nothing you care about?" Nicholas asked, shaking Matthias slightly. "Nothing that you want to protect? Because if you fail now, the Black King gets everything, including everything you love."

Matthias opened his eyes. There was a vulnerability in them that Nicholas had never seen before. "This could kill me," he whispered.

"This could," Nicholas said. "But the Black King *will*."

Matthias nodded. He pulled away from Nicholas, and returned to the mouth of the cave. Then he closed his eyes, extended his hands, and let the light envelop the second horizontal sword.

Nicholas let out a sigh of relief. He had gotten Matthias through this one, and maybe the third. But his real problem was still ahead. What if Matthias was right? What if he had nothing left when the time came to use the swords?

What then?

# SEVENTY-EIGHT

THE second thud shook Shadowlands so hard that Arianna bounced. This Shadowlands was smaller than the one outside, narrow and cramped. Her back leaned against one wall, her feet hit the wall across from her, and her head brushed the ceiling. She had asked Gift more than once what he had been thinking when he designed this Shadowlands, and he had not yet answered her.

She figured that was because he had no defense for not thinking at all.

At least it was long and narrow, and she didn't brush against anyone—until now. Until this jolting that shook her across the opaque floor and into her brother's side.

"What was that?" she asked in what she hoped was a reasonable tone of voice.

"I don't know," he said. He was staring at the Circle Door.

Scavenger was sitting close to it. He too was staring at the door. Leen had her legs pulled against her body, her arms wrapped around her knees. She had her eyes closed. She had been sleeping as per Arianna's father's orders, and not even this second rumble woke her.

"You don't know?" Arianna asked. "You don't *know*? I thought you said nothing from the outside could affect the inside of this place."

"I didn't think it could," Gift said.

"We're not touching the ground," Scavenger said, "or the ceiling of this place. So that couldn't be a ground tremor."

"Then what is it?" Arianna snapped. Her heart was racing.

Her father was out there. Coulter was out there. And she was sitting in here, waiting. Doing nothing.

"If I had to guess," Scavenger said, "I'd say it was a sound."

"A sound? How could a sound get in here?" Ari's voice rose. She knew she sounded petulant, but she was worried. Terrified, in fact. She didn't want something to happen to her father. For all her brave talk; she wasn't quite sure what to do.

"It wouldn't get in here at all," Scavenger said. "Sound makes things vibrate too, just like the ground can."

"It would have to be incredibly loud," Gift said.

Arianna took a deep breath. "What kind of sound could be that loud?"

"A weapon of some sort?" Gift asked.

"An explosion." Leen had lifted her head. Her eyes were bleary, as if the conversation had awakened her. "An explosion could be that loud."

If there had been an explosion, and it had been that loud, then her father was dead. Arianna reached for the Circle Door. Scavenger caught her wrist. His grip was tight, his hand leathery and tough.

"He said to wait until he sent for us."

"And what if they're all dead? What if they can't send for us?" There. She had finally voiced it, the fear she had been carrying all along.

"When we've all agreed that too much time has passed," Scavenger said slowly, as if he were talking to a child, "then I will go out and see what's happening. You will never leave here first, do you understand?"

"He's my father."

"And Gift's too," Scavenger said. "And you two are the reason this war is being fought."

"Don't put that on them," Leen said. "This war predates both of them. The Isle is what the Black King is after."

"If that were true," Scavenger said, "he'd have moved on to Leut by now."

Arianna swallowed. She knew there was truth to those words. But her father was her only family. She didn't know what had become of Sebastian, and Solanda was dead. Gift didn't count. She had met him only a few days ago. He was her brother, but he wasn't family. Not yet.

"I can Shift—"

"No," Scavenger said. "You'll stay here."

She took a deep breath. They were right. She knew it, but she didn't like it.

Gift took her other hand. His touch was soft, gentle, almost affectionate. "If they're not all right out there," he said, and she noted that he didn't say *If they're dead*, "then you and I will carry on the fight as best we can. We have weapons too. We can fight the Black King. We might even be able to get him off the Isle."

"And drown him in the Infrin Sea," she said, nearly spitting the words.

Scavenger smiled. "If you do that," he said, "then there's no Blood against Blood. Drownings are usually accidental."

"Maybe," Gift said, "we should plan for the worst while we wait. It will make the time go by, and it will also prepare us in case something goes wrong."

"I don't want to lose my father," Arianna said.

"He doesn't want to lose you either." Scavenger said that last, surprising her. He was rarely kind. Then she realized he wasn't being kind. He was stating the truth.

"He will do his best, won't he?" Arianna whispered.

Scavenger nodded. "Let's just hope it's good enough."

# SEVENTY-NINE

THE third and final Shadowlands was the worst. Rugad stepped inside, followed by the troop he had gathered from the previous two Shadowlands. The stench was horrible—burning flesh mingled with loosened bowels and too much blood. The smell of awful, sudden death.

If any soldiers lived in this place, they wouldn't be alive much longer. Rugad swallowed and pressed forward. He had hoped that he would get at least twenty out of this Shadowlands. He had gotten thirty mobile Infantry and Foot Soldiers out of the last Shadowlands, not to mention ten slightly injured Beast Riders. That, plus his troop from his first Shadowlands, ensured a force of nearly a hundred. And then they entered this place.

He hadn't realized how bad it would be. Nicholas had been moments away from destroying the entire army.

Now something else was going on. Those first two thuds that had rumbled down the mountainside had been ominous. Nicholas wasn't defeated yet. He still had another weapon.

But it would be a weapon that Rugad could turn. It had to be. There was no magick that Nicholas could use that Rugad couldn't.

Rugad crossed the body-strewn ground. The remnants of his army were lying across the well-worn path, and beside it, their broken and burned shells lying across rocks and boulders, on grass and the wispy beginnings of snow. The climb was steep here, and the Shadowlands reflected it, tilting to protect the ones inside against the elements.

As if the protection were necessary. It had been too late.

"Bring them," Rugad said over his shoulder to Selia. He watched her motion to the surviving troop with her hand, and then he continued, stepping over bodies, around them and on top of them where he had to.

His plan was simple. He would use his shield and his force and march into the Place of Power. If Nicholas attacked him, Rugad would repel the attack. There could only be a handful of people with Nicholas, and at least one was dead. Even if Nicholas tried to use another weapon, it would ultimately fail.

Nicholas would pay for each and every one of these deaths. The bodies did not discourage Rugad. Instead, they made him more and more determined. And they gave him a slight hope. If Nicholas had this ability, and Jewel had the same ability, then those two great-grandchildren were more than Visionaries and Shifters. They had inborn tactical genius. They were everything he could hope for the Black Throne and more.

They were worth all of this destruction.

His pace across the killing field was rapid. He glanced over his shoulder once more and saw Selia struggling to keep up, with the rest of the troop significantly behind her.

"March them double-time," he snapped. He didn't know what Nicholas was planning, but he wanted to get to the cave before Nicholas had a chance to start.

Rugad reached the wall of this last Shadowlands slightly before his troop. He created another Circle Door and left it open, since there were no survivors inside to protect. Ahead were more bodies. The Fey who had almost made it to the top, who had almost brought the Isle completely into the Empire.

They were scattered in the afternoon sunlight just as the Shadowlands bodies were, only the destruction here was even more terrible.

Rugad said nothing. He stepped onto the barren ground. It was colder here, and the stench wasn't as thick. Snow covered part of the path and seemed to rise higher. Rugad could see the broken steps leading to the platform, leading to the Place of Power itself.

His goal was just ahead.

He turned. The troop had caught up. "Nearly there," he said. "Be ready to avenge our fallen comrades."

That, more than Selia's simpering, put a light in the eyes of the Foot Soldiers. Rugad could feel the blood lust ignite in his troop. It would take little to get them to attack. If anything, he would have to remind them to be careful, to protect against killing his great-grandchildren.

The blood lust was rising in him as well. He was going to kill Nicholas himself, slice the man to the ribbons he deserved to be. Worthy enemy or not, the man had cost too many Fey lives to die a reasonable death.

Rugad put his Shadowlands shield before him, stretched it as wide and high as it would go to protect his troop, and began the final climb.

# EIGHTY

THE ground thudded as the last sword fell before the cave's mouth. A giant clap of thunder resounded as the sword vibrated to a stop.

Nicholas was breathing shallowly. Even Coulter noticed the noise this time. He had looked at Nicholas inquiringly, and for the first time since Adrian had died, Nicholas got a sense that the boy actually saw him.

"Move away," Nicholas said, but he hadn't been able to hear his own words in the last rumble of the thunder.

Apparently Coulter could read lips, for he caught Adrian in his arms and dragged him toward the back of the cave. At that moment, the light between Matthias and the final sword went out, and Matthias stumbled backwards.

He would have fallen if Nicholas hadn't caught him.

Matthias weighed less than Nicholas did, even though Matthias was taller. Matthias's entire body was drenched in sweat. The healing scars on his cheeks, near his eye, were livid; the bruises on his neck so dark as to be almost black.

"I can't," he whispered.

"You have to," Nicholas said.

The Black King had to have felt the concussions from those swords falling into place. No matter what the man did, no matter how he believed, he had to know that Nicholas was planning something new.

The Black King would have a counterattack planned.

"I can't," Matthias repeated.

Nicholas glanced at the swords. One stood in the very front of the cave's mouth. The center two were spread wide, and the first two were left where they were, with a smaller space between them. The jewels were aligned as the guide had told them.

And that guide was really and truly gone. Nicholas had been watching for him, and could not see him anywhere. Without him, and without Matthias, Nicholas had nothing.

"You will," Nicholas said. He eased Matthias to the ground and picked up the vial of Roca's blood the guide had given him. As per the guide's instruction, Nicholas poured the liquid all over his right hand.

The blood was thick and slimy. It smelled fresh, though, as if it had just been drawn from the Roca's veins instead of being fifty generations old.

He grabbed Matthias's left hand and poured the blood all over it. Matthias grimaced and protested softly, but Nicholas ignored him. He took Matthias's left hand with his right and pulled Matthias to his feet.

A tingling ran through Nicholas that he had never felt before. It wasn't a superficial tingle, like the tingle of frosty air on a chilly night. It was internal, as if his very blood were warming in response. He looked at his hand, joined with Matthias's, and saw a halo of red light rise from it. The light dripped, like blood would, into the stone beneath their feet, turning it red.

Like the mountain was red.

Matthias watched too. His exhaustion seemed to be forgotten. He met Nicholas's gaze. "I'm getting stronger," he said.

"I know." It was as if something were flowing from Nicholas

into Matthias through their joined hands, as if the common blood between them had found a Link and through it, Nicholas was able to give Matthias strength.

"We don't have much time," Nicholas said.

Matthias nodded. He held out his right hand, and flame sparked on his fingertips. "I hope this works," he said, and cupped his hand as if he were holding a ball. The flames from his fingers joined into one long stream. They hit the black jewel on the hilt of the first sword, and went through it. The jewel seemed to double the flame's strength, dividing the stream in half, and sending it toward the black jewels in the hilts of the next two swords.

Those jewels also doubled the strength of the flames, and they went through the remaining two swords. Again the flame streams grew, until they were thick as a man's torso. They came together again in front of the last two swords and started to arc down the hill.

"You're supposed to aim!" Matthias gasped.

Aim. As if Nicholas knew how. But the guide had said powers would flow between him and Matthias, so he took what he could of the tingle, and thought only of the Black King, of Rugad, his ancient hawk face arrogant, his voice strong and commanding, his body unbowed by nine decades of life.

Nicholas thought of him, and only him, as he watched the flame stream, now thick as a stone pillar, bend down the mountainside.

The tingling was flowing through him faster. He was growing warmer, and he was finally beginning to understand what Matthias had been saying about exhaustion. It was as if he were being consumed from within. It was not a matter of choice: if this didn't end soon, there would be nothing of him left.

Matthias looked at him. "We do it as long as we can," he said, and Nicholas didn't know if Matthias was speaking with Nicholas's strength or if Matthias had remembered how important it was.

Nicholas nodded.

As long as they could—and beyond. Until there was nothing left, except the Isle unencumbered by the Fey, and his children, growing up on their own.

He closed his eyes, thought of the Black King, and nothing else.

# EIGHTY-ONE

RUGAD had put his right foot on the broken stone step when he heard it. A roar like nothing he had ever heard before. It seemed as if all the air around him was being sucked away, and then he felt the prickle of an intense heat.

The cuts left by the Golem seem to rise from his skin, to emit a kind of sympathetic magick, as if they were hands pointing at him, saying that here was the target, here, here.

The shield felt heavy before him, and he knew something was wrong. Heat. Roar. Air being sucked away.

And then, the smell of smoke.

Fire.

But Nicholas couldn't control fire. No one could, except Warders and Enchanters.

Enchanters.

But Enchanters did not have the power to destroy a Shadowlands. Only a line attack, on a magick Link, could do that. How could fire run along a Link? What could create that?

He wanted to peer over the shield but knew he didn't dare. He could bring a Shadowlands down on himself, if there was time, but it didn't matter. Fire was not light. Fire went through things: it consumed things. It did not reflect. It went over, under, through.

"Get down!" he cried, but he knew it would do no good. He knew it, even as he extended the shield into a full Shadowlands, even as he brought it down on them.

He had a moment to debate—porous? closed?—and decided on closed. Porous would allow air through. The fire could travel with the air, and that was too much of a risk. Closed might make the fire skip over the Shadowlands as fire sometimes did over stone.

Without the air, they wouldn't have much time inside, and the heat might kill them, but the other way the smoke might.

He was on his hands and knees, the Shadowlands pressing against his back, his head, his feet, when he remembered the ground. He hadn't made the Shadowlands four-sided, and this time he needed to. He had started to construct a floor when the flames hit.

They seemed to target him. He could feel them slamming against the wall before him, heating it, burning through it.

He was going to die.

Rugad—the greatest warrior in the history of the Fey—was going to die at the hands of a man who had never conquered a country, a man with no magick, a man who was not Fey.

"No!" Rugad cried, and with his mind, he tried to grab the Link the fire traveled on, he tried to turn it, to bend it. But he couldn't. Somehow Nicholas had given the fire all the power of the cave above, all the magick in the area controlled that fire, and it had been aimed at Rugad.

The moment he touched the Link he knew.

The fire reared as if it were a horse startled in midgallop, and then it launched its attack like a Foot Soldier lusting for blood.

Rugad grabbed his own essence, and tried to travel across his Links, anywhere, to Bridge, his grandson on Nye, to Seger in Jahn, anywhere—

Too late did he realize that the fire consumed magick. It went for his Links as if they were tinder.

Using the last of his strength, he closed his Links so that no one else would die, and huddled down against the blood red mountain as he felt himself being burned alive.

# EIGHTY-TWO

NOTHING left. Nothing. Nicholas could barely get enough strength to breathe in or out. His legs wobbled beneath him, but they had been wobbling for so long that when they finally collapsed, he wasn't certain if it was because his legs gave out or because Matthias's did.

It didn't matter. The shock of the impact made him open his eyes.

The fire still streamed from them. Sweat was running down his face, but whether it was from the heat or the strain, he didn't know. The entire cave was an oven and he thought maybe he couldn't get his breath because the fire had stolen all the air.

He glanced at Matthias, whose hand still clutched his. Matthias's curls were plastered to his head, his body was drenched in sweat. The red glow still dripped from their joined hands into the floor below. The color spread like a bloodstain, and the once-white light of the cavern was turning red too.

"Nicholas," Matthias whispered, and Nicholas wasn't sure if he heard the words or felt them through their joined hands, through their whispering, suddenly shared blood.

He turned his gaze in the direction Matthias was looking, and saw something he had never seen before.

It was as if someone had punched a hole in the air to reveal another place. Only that place wasn't so far away—it was the mountainside below. The stream of fire had focused on a single spot in a long row of grayness, what was, apparently, a Shadowlands, but unlike those Gift had made. The fire had burned through the grayness and was consuming a man beneath. The man raised his head, and for a moment, even the fire seemed to clear.

Nicholas recognized the face.

The Black King.

And then the fire closed over the man's face. The man fell forward, and huddled as if he could protect himself. The flames ate his clothing, his skin, and he moved within the burn, but he did not scream. He did not utter a sound.

Some of the people around him were burning as well, but others were attempting to put out the fires. Still others were holding their throats and gasping as if they could not get air.

The hole remained until the Black King stopped moving. The fire continued to burn, past the skin, into the bones. By the time it was done, there would be nothing left of him.

And then the air in the cave returned as if nothing had happened. The vision was gone.

Matthias closed his fist, and the fire stream stopped. It took a moment for the effect to reach the jewels, but when it did, the fire disappeared completely.

Nicholas sat down, his heart pounding. He could still feel the flow between them, but it didn't seem draining any more. He glanced at their clenched hands.

"I think it's done," he said.

Matthias nodded and, in unison, they let go of each other.

As their hands parted, a small boom sounded throughout the cave, and something fell. It clattered on the red, glowing floor. With his shaking left hand, Nicholas picked it up.

He held a black jewel, as perfect as those he had placed outside, as large as those in the giant swords themselves.

"We did that?" Matthias asked. "What is it?"

It was, apparently, something their guide had forgotten to tell them. Something to ask the next time one or both of them encountered him. Nicholas did not let the jewel go.

Matthias did not ask him to.

Nicholas looked at his right hand. It no longer had blood on it, but it looked different. It was smaller than it had been.

He held it next to his left hand. Even with his left hand folded into a fist, it was clear.

His right hand had shrunk.

"My God," Matthias said, holding out his left hand.

They had been losing something. They had lost bits of themselves.

After a moment, Matthias stood. "Now they attack us, right? For killing their king?"

"No," Nicholas said. "Oh, no." But he couldn't remove his children from their hiding place, couldn't have them step forward, with Matthias still here.

Matthias's face went still. The shock and wonder and brightness that had filled it a moment before vanished. "I suppose we have something to settle."

He stood, shakily, but did not reach out for support. Nicholas didn't offer it.

Nicholas stood as well. He didn't feel quite the same way he had felt about Matthias. He was loath to resurrect those feelings, loath to change this moment. They had worked together, and together they had saved their Isle.

Nicholas couldn't kill him—not that he wanted to any longer—because they shared blood. Power traveled through the blood. To sever that Link was to tamper with something Nicholas didn't entirely understand. But he understood it better now.

"Jewel," he said softly, hearing the mourning in his voice, realizing that he was going to go through that agony all over again. He lost his wife—the same wife—twice to the same man, a man with whom he had to share himself in order to live.

"She's here," Matthias said. "She's not dead—if you can kill something like her. I'll tell you how to free her if you let me go first."

"Go?" Nicholas repeated. His brain wasn't as sharp as usual. It felt like it did when he awoke from a deep sleep.

"Nicholas, I want to trade my life for hers. I know it's not ethical. I know you don't owe me anything. But—"

"No." Nicholas waved his smaller right hand. "I don't owe you. I don't even think we're even yet. But if my wife can come back to me, then I'll let you go."

Matthias's eyes filled with tears. He blinked them back. "You are a greater man than I could ever hope to be," he whispered.

Nicholas said nothing. He wasn't a great man. He was a man who was tired of bloodshed, tired of conflict. Tired of *killing*. And he had limited time. He had to get his children outside to face the Fey, to let them know that the heirs to the Black Throne were here and ready to take over the Empire.

"Jewel," Nicholas said again.

"She's in a glass doll," Matthias said. "I put it down near the empty shelves beside the tapestries. To open it—"

"I know how to open it," Nicholas said. Trapped. Matthias had somehow trapped her as the guide had once been trapped. But if he hadn't, they wouldn't have defeated the Black King.

Together.

*He is your god*, the Shaman had said. But she had been wrong. Matthias wasn't God, any more than Nicholas was. He was the Roca of this generation. And together they had used the Roca's power, a power they couldn't have used separately.

That power had defeated the Black King.

"Go," Nicholas said. "You'll have to use the tunnels, and you'll have to go fast. She didn't notice you until you were nearly here."

"I know where that was," Matthias said. "It'll take me some time to get there."

"The Fey will determine how much time you have."

"What are you going to do?"

"Face them," Nicholas said. "Without you."

Matthias started down the stairs without a glance at Coulter or at the Circle Door not far from him. Halfway he stopped.

"And if we meet in the future?" he asked Nicholas. "What happens then?"

"I don't know," Nicholas said.

Matthias nodded, once, and then continued down, his head bent. He was a different man from the arrogant Rocaan who had murdered Jewel. That man had not listened to anyone, and it had seemed as if that man never would. This one had softened, just a bit. Not enough to trust—Nicholas never wanted him around his family—but a bit.

Matthias reached the bottom of the stairs and walked briskly toward the fountain. Nicholas knew, suddenly, that he would never see Matthias again.

"Matthias," he called.

Matthias stopped, looked up, and in a trick of the pale pinkish light, Nicholas saw the man he had known since he was a boy. His father's friend, the merciless teacher, the rigorous scholar, the man who had once demanded more of Nicholas than anyone else.

Nicholas swallowed hard. "Thank you."

Matthias smiled, just a little, then raised his left hand in a slight acknowledgment and turned away. He continued his walk past the fountain, into the darkness beyond.

Nicholas waited a long moment. Matthias's footsteps had disappeared beneath the burble of the fountain. Nicholas had been right. He hadn't had to sacrifice anyone to the awful power offered by this place. The fountain, and its temptations, were one secret he planned to keep.

Then he looked at Coulter. The boy was watching him with grief-haunted eyes.

"It was an open Vision," he said. "The Black King is dead."

Nicholas nodded.

"I didn't think—" Coulter's voice broke. "I mean, I—Adrian—"

"I know," Nicholas said. "It's all right."

And it was. Now. Now that it was over.

He walked past Coulter, past the body of Adrian, to the empty shelves, and the tapestries. There, just as Matthias had described, was a glass doll. It looked different from the ones farther back.

He crouched before it. Jewel was inside. He could see her small face pressed against the glass. He longed to touch it, but he had promised Matthias that he would have time to escape.

Nicholas would give him that time.

"Give me a moment, my love," he said. Then he smiled at her. She pounded on the glass insistently.

"After I free the children. After I deal with the remaining Fey."

*Now,* Jewel mouthed, but he shook his head. If she still had Matthias to kill, then she would remain here. He would have his wife. If he didn't prevent Matthias's death, Jewel might achieve her three objectives. She might disappear again.

He had nearly lost her a second time. He would do what he could to prevent it.

He blew her a kiss. She uttered a fairly graphic Fey curse that he could understood even without the benefit of sound.

Then he stood, and hurried down the steps.

Given the depth of his exhaustion during the magick, he was surprised at his energy now. It was as if the Black King's death had rejuvenated him somehow. He reached the bottom quickly, then extended his arm and shoved his fist in the Circle Door as Gift had shown him.

Arianna nearly tumbled out, but Scavenger caught her and held her back. He peered out, saw Nicholas, and grinned.

"Wasn't sure I'd see you again," he said.

"I wasn't either," Nicholas said. "Are my children all right?"

Instead of an answer, he had Arianna launch herself into his arms from the height of the door. He staggered beneath her weight, then hugged her.

Gift climbed out.

"The Black King is dead," Nicholas said.

"How?" Leen asked as she climbed out of Shadowlands.

"I'll tell you shortly. But first, my children need to face the Fey."

Arianna pulled out of his arms. "Why?"

"You rule them now, Ari," Nicholas said. "You and Gift. You are the heirs to the Black Throne."

Gift shook his head. "I can't do that."

"Why not?" Nicholas asked.

He opened his mouth, closed it, then looked at Ari. "You're the fierce one."

"And you're the firstborn."

"You were trained to rule."

"And you know the Fey."

"You'll go together," Nicholas said.

"No," Gift said. "I was thinking in there, and before. I'm not the kind of man who can lead an entire Empire. Arianna can. She's groomed for it. She has the temperament."

"You say that now," Ari said. "But you'll change your mind."

Gift shook his head. "We were talking about this, remember? Inside." He looked at Scavenger and Leen. They said nothing. Then he looked back at Nicholas. "My people always put a Shaman in the Place of Power, right? This one will have none. I want to be that Shaman. I don't want to go to war, or even to defend against one. I want to remain here, and live quietly."

"Somehow I doubt this place is quiet."

That voice came from above. Coulter. He was sitting on the top step, looking pale and ragged.

"Even so," Gift said.

Nicholas stared at him for a moment. Jewel had mentioned something about Gift's temperament. She had said that Nicholas would have to keep him away from the killing, that Gift's magick seemed almost Domestic. And the Shaman had said that Gift was like Nicholas's father, a man who hated the burdens of leadership, the burdens of war.

Nicholas's father could never have led a warlike people like the Fey.

"You're certain?" Nicholas asked.

Gift nodded.

"Arianna," Nicholas said. "Do you want the Black Throne?"

"No," she said. "But I'm more suited to it. Even though I'm reckless."

"Impulsive," Gift said.

"And I would need good advice."

"Not hard to get," Gift said, "even if you have to come to the edge of the Isle."

They looked at each other, and Nicholas frowned slightly. Something had happened while they were trapped in Shadowlands together. They had come to some sort of understanding.

He would ask them about it later. Now he needed to get one or both of his children before the Fey.

"This is not a decision to be made lightly," Nicholas said.

"I've tried to avoid leadership my whole life," Gift said. "It never worked. It might now."

"And you've trained me to rule," Arianna said to Nicholas.

"But not the Fey."

"Not the Fey," she repeated. "But I don't plan to be a warrior queen. The Empire building would stop here. At the Isle. Which is a place I'm familiar with."

It wasn't that simple. Arianna would have to learn so much more than she already knew. But that could happen in time. Nicholas took her arm.

"There are a bunch of wounded and confused Fey out there. They've just watched their king die. They need to know the hereditary line of the Fey will continue on the Black Throne. They know he came for you. Are you willing to stand before them and take command of their Empire?"

Arianna's large slanted eyes widened. Her skin flushed. "Where's my mother?" she asked.

"I can get her," Nicholas said. Matthias had to have had enough time by now.

"Please," Arianna said. "She'll know what to say to them. She'll know how to make them listen to me."

It was the right decision. It was the best decision she had ever made. Somehow it calmed Nicholas.

His wife would help his daughter with the intricacies of the Empire, and he would help her with the difficulties of being a ruler. He had his Isle back. He had his children. He had a world again, where a day before he had almost nothing at all.

"I thought you said we were in a hurry," Ari said, a tone of command in her voice that hadn't been present before. He smiled at her. He would have to remind her that she might rule the Fey Empire, but he was still King of Blue Isle. And her father.

But he would wait. All those details could wait.

He climbed the stairs, two at a time, and hurried to the glass doll. He grabbed a bottle of the Roca's blood, uncorked it, and then picked up the doll. Jewel frowned at him from inside. He took one of the glass arms and shoved it into the blood. Pink lines surged across the glass, as they had before, and this time, he shielded his face.

The glass shattered, and his wife surged out, yelling at him as she appeared.

Her eyes did not glaze. She did not look in the direction of the fountain. Nicholas had waited long enough for Matthias to get away.

She formed from mist into a solid woman, and as she did so, he grabbed her shoulders, pulled her toward him, and kissed her to shut her up.

She leaned into the kiss before remembering that she was angry at him. He knew her well enough to anticipate the reaction. He put a finger to her lips.

"We won," he said, and she smiled. He could feel the smile as well as see it, feel her relief as if it were a palpable thing. "We won."

# THE
# RESTORATION
## [ONE WEEK LATER]

# EIGHTY-THREE

MATTHIAS tamped down the dirt with the shovel, then set the shovel down. He glanced at Marly. She was leaning against a tree, her back braced against it, her body in the shade, her feet in the afternoon sun. Deep circles ran under her eyes.

She shouldn't have come here, but she had insisted. They had finally found Jakib's body, and it had been in terrible shape—the flesh was nearly gone, and what remained was rotting. Matthias had been able to identify him, barely, by his clothes, and his eyes, which had somehow remained.

Marly hadn't cried when she heard the news. She had already known. Matthias had told her when he came back. He hadn't told her much else—just that the Black King was dead and that the war was over. She seemed to already know that as well. The mist that had protected her, the mist he had sent, suddenly dissipated in the early evening of that terrible day, and all of the rat-Fey and the bird-Fey and the soldier-Fey had disappeared from the streets of Constant.

Marly hadn't had much time to reflect on the strange change, though. Blooders started to appear with their wounded and their dying, begging her to save them. She had been able to save some—not as many as she had hoped for, but some.

Matthias had found her the evening of the following day. She hadn't slept for a long time, and neither had he. He worked at her side for two more days before they both collapsed.

Then he went out to search among the dead for her brother.

They were burying Jakib in a small patch of ground behind Matthias's house. Jakib had never had a home, never had allegiances to any one place, except maybe Jahn itself. Marly had wanted him close, and Matthias had obliged.

She was still looking at him. It bothered him that she hadn't cried. She hadn't cried for any of it. She hadn't cried when she had to remove Denl's leg, or repair Tri's horribly damaged skin. She hadn't cried when she dealt with so many wounded, and she hadn't cried when Matthias returned.

The only time he saw tears glint was when he told her that the Fey were defeated, and she hadn't believed that until she saw the retreat.

The Fey were gone from Constant. They had left the nearby valleys and mountains as well. Somehow, Nicholas had gotten them to march back to Jahn. Somehow, Nicholas controlled them.

"Probably through his children," Marly had said, and hadn't added anything more.

Probably, which was why Nicholas had wanted Matthias out of there before facing the Fey. Nicholas had used Matthias's hatred to kill the Black King, but had been unwilling to risk unleashing that hatred on his children.

And who could blame him? Matthias had murdered Nicholas's wife.

Matthias sighed and went over to Marly. He crouched beside her and took her hands. "I would like to perform the burial ceremony, if you think it appropriate."

She freed her right hand and traced the scars on his cheek. They were healing, finally, and his bruises had faded. "If you don't, no one else will."

He bowed his head slightly. None of the Wise Ones were left. He had locked the door to the Vault, and he would guard its contents over time. He had explained its treasures to no one, and he wouldn't, not until the time came to choose a new guardian. He respected the Roca's wishes. After seeing the power that he and Nicholas had unleashed, he understood what the Roca had feared.

The Roca had seen the future. He had understood what that kind of power could do. It could turn its people into creatures that lived only for magick, and the dominance it gave over the nonmagickal.

It could turn its people into the Fey.

The Roca had prevented that, and Matthias would see to it that the Roca's wishes were preserved.

"Besides," Marly said, not quite understanding his hesitation. "You have the blood of the Roca, and you are the only living Rocaan. I think Jakib would be honored to have such an important person preside over his burial."

Matthias nodded, then picked up the herbs and the filigree sword he had brought with him. Then he went to the grave and crouched over it.

"Holy One," he said, in a reverberating voice he hadn't used since his days at the Tabernacle, "I am your most unworthy servant. But I beg you to overlook the messenger, and hear the message."

He held the sword over the grave. "Bless the Honored Dead. Treasure Jakib's being, and we will treasure his memory upon this land."

He bent and planted the edge of the filigreed sword in the soil, his hand scraping against the dirt. Then he reached into his pouch as he stood, and scattered the herbs across the ground.

"As the Roca honored God, so have you. As the Holy One has spoken to God, so have you. As God has loved us all, so have you. You return to the cycle of life, that in dying we might all live. It is with the Roca's highest blessing that I leave you so that the Holy One may absorb your soul."

He put his hand against the dirt, feeling the richness of the soil beneath his fingers and knowing, for the first time, how much he would miss Jakib's quiet strength. Then he felt warmth beside him. Marly had left her spot by the tree. She touched the dirt as well, her head bowed.

Tears dripped from her eyes to the ground below, mingling with the burial herbs and seeping into the grave. Matthias put his arm around her shoulder and she leaned into him, her body shuddering.

Nothing would be the same again. From the moment the Fey had arrived on Blue Isle over twenty years before, they had changed it. They had destroyed fifty generations of peace and created more turmoil—inner and outer—than the Islanders had experienced in generations.

Matthias put his face in Marly's soft hair. Yet somehow he had survived—all the things he had done, all the things that had been done to him—and he had this, another chance at life.

He would take it, and revel in it, and never forget the cost at which he had received it.

He kissed Marly's head and held her long after the sunset ignited the blood red mountains and reminded him of the power he and Nicholas shared. He held her until darkness fell across the land and the air grew chill.

Then he helped her up, dried her tears, and together they crossed the small yard to their tiny, precious home.

# EIGHTY-FOUR

GIFT found Coulter on the Tabernacle side of the Cardidas River, sitting in the grass near Jahn Bridge. They had been back in Jahn two days, and the place looked so different from the city Gift had left over a month before that he barely recognized it. When he walked through the streets, the Fey nodded to him, or bowed slightly. They all knew he was of Black Blood. His sister had made her formal announcement—she would take the Black Throne—but that didn't seem to make any difference. He was treated with complete deference by the Fey and by the Islanders as well. Being the King's son made a difference. Living in the palace made a difference too.

He supposed he would have gotten used to it in time, but he didn't have the time. He spoke to some of the Domestics and the Healers who still remained in the palace about becoming a Shaman, and they told him of the long and difficult process he would have to go through. He had convinced Seger, his great-grandfather's personal Healer, to speak to his father and sister about the procedure, and then he had fled.

He didn't need their permission, but he found he wanted it.

In the meantime, he had a few things to do. He wanted to return to the cave, but his father needed him here while the Islanders and Fey got used to the idea that they were all part of the same Empire now, an Empire ruled by a woman who considered herself more Islander than Fey. Very few people knew of the Place of Power, but those who did worried Gift's father. He had left guards there, and his mother had promised that the Mysteries and Powers would ensure that no one entered without Nicholas's permission.

Gift believed her. His father had too. Arianna had buried her skepticism. She owed her mother a lot, for her mother had told her how to calm the Fey soldiers on that mountainside and how to immediately establish dominance. Arianna had done so, and from that moment on, she was the Black Queen.

It startled Gift how quickly his great-grandfather's people had accepted Arianna, but his mother had merely laughed. *It is the way of our people*, she had said. *If they fight the new ruler, they risk losing everything. They simply move forward, as they have always done.*

He wished he could move forward as easily. He still hadn't mourned the loss of his family and friends when the Black King took Shadowlands, even though he had found his true family again and had made new friends. The loss of Adrian hit him harder than he wanted to admit, as well.

It had devastated Coulter.

Coulter hadn't spoken to Gift—or anyone except Scavenger—on the long trip back. Apparently Arianna had tried to talk with him, and he would keep his head bowed, listening, but not speaking. When they had arrived in Jahn, Coulter had kept to himself. This morning, Arianna had searched for him, to no avail. When Gift was leaving, she had asked him to see if he could find Coulter.

And so he found him on the other side of the bridge, the bridge where Cover had died less than a month before. Coulter was sitting with his legs stretched out before him, his hands buried in the tall grass, staring not at the burned-out Tabernacle but at the road leading past it.

The road to Adrian's house.

Gift approached, crunching grass loudly beneath his feet. Coulter did not turn. Gift sat beside him.

"I'm sorry for all the things I said." Gift spoke quietly. "And for the way I treated you. You were right. You wanted to protect me, and I didn't listen. I probably would have died if you hadn't closed my Links. Died or become something I didn't want to be. I didn't understand that until Ari and I were in Shadowlands, and I watched her try to protect our father, even though it was foolish. You were right, Coulter."

Coulter shrugged. That small movement gave Gift hope. It was more of a response than he had expected.

"I'm sorry too about Adrian. He was one of the best people I've ever known."

Coulter licked his lips. He continued staring forward. "They say everything is burned in the center of the Isle. They say all the farms are gone. Adrian's farm is gone."

"No word from Luke?"

"Your father's people found him hiding in the city. He'd been trying to get back to the palace."

"Have you seen him?"

Coulter shook his head. "How can I? I was holding the weapon that killed his father."

So that was it. The Black King had destroyed more than Adrian's life. He had destroyed Coulter's heart.

"You didn't turn it on him. You didn't use it against him."

"But I should have known," Coulter said.

"I'm the Visionary," Gift said, "and I didn't know."

"If I had only acted quicker—"

"He would have died anyway. He knew the risk."

"He only came along because of me."

"Do you think he regretted that?"

Coulter finally faced Gift. Coulter's pale blue eyes were clear for the first time in days. "No," he whispered.

"Then why do you?"

Coulter sighed and looked back at the road. "He was the only person who loved me."

"No," Gift said. "He wasn't. We're Bound, you and I, and will be forever."

"Another of my mistakes," Coulter said.

"A good mistake," Gift said. He put his hand on Coulter's back. He could feel the ridges of Coulter's spine. "Come on. Come home."

"I have no home," Coulter said. "It burned."

"My father wants you in the palace."

"To keep an eye on me."

"Because he sees you as family now. And because he's worried about you."

Coulter bowed his head and rested it on his knees. "I'm not made for this life, Gift," he said. "The power, the killing. Each time it has taken something from me."

"Ari isn't going on to Leut," Gift said. "The Fey Empire ends here. The fighting is over, Coulter."

"Do you know that?" Coulter asked. "Have you Seen it?"

"No," Gift said, "but it doesn't matter if I had. We've changed things. Some of my Visions did not come true."

"I hope you're right," Coulter said. And then he sighed and raised his head. "I'm sorry too. For acting quickly, for closing your Links without your permission, for hurting you. I'm sorry."

"You saved me." Gift stood. He couldn't say any more. He didn't want Coulter to apologize again. "I'm going back to the palace. Would you like to come with me?" Gift held out his hand. Coulter took it and pulled himself to his feet.

"Friends again?" Gift asked.

Coulter nodded. "Friends again," he said.

Then Gift looked at the river, the burned-out Tabernacle, the bridge behind them, and he smiled. "The Vision," he said.

"What Vision?"

"My mother—Niche—said there was an open Vision the day you Bound me. She described it as this. Then I saw it the day my father first routed the Fey."

"So this is an important moment," Coulter said.

"Isn't it?" Gift asked.

Coulter smiled and clasped Gift's hand. "Yeah," he said. "It is."

# EIGHTY-FIVE

THE garden was ruined. Arianna sat in her favorite spot, near the palace's stone wall, and stared at the remains of her favorite place.

Countless feet had trampled the flowers. The trees and shrubs were overgrown, branches torn and left hanging. Weeds grew everywhere. The birds were gone. It amazed her how much damage a place could suffer in such a short time.

The garden was her sanctuary, and it had been destroyed, just as Jahn had been destroyed, just as much of Blue Isle had been destroyed. Her father had come back to the palace, reluctantly leaving her mother, to heal the Isle. Arianna's job was to unify the Islanders and the Fey.

She wasn't sure she was up to it. For all her tough talk, she was not the strongest or the wisest person. Her mother had had to help her unify the Black King's soldiers after his death; her father was the one who devised the plan to get them away from the Place of Power.

Arianna had no idea how to be Black Queen of the Fey.

Her father told her she would learn. She hoped he was right. She had felt alone her entire life, but never like this. Suddenly she was alone and very powerful, and she wasn't sure how she would use that power.

She did know that she would end the Fey's march across the world. Her great-grandfather had conquered half the world. She would be content with that. Her father had talked with her about her responsibilities, and he had brought up the one thing that scared her the most: the Triangle of Might.

The Islanders now knew where two Places of Power were. With that knowledge, they could find the third, and once they had all three, they would be able to rule the world. Arianna did not want to rule the world. Her father seemed relieved by that and so, he said, did her mother. The small fighting force from the Place of Power were sworn to secrecy about it, but Arianna knew the word would get out. She knew it was her responsibility to protect that place, and the one in the Eccrasian Mountains. It was her responsibility to prevent anyone else from discovering—and using—the Triangle of Might.

She would. She had been raised in peace, and she had experienced war. She never wanted to experience it again.

"Arianna?"

She stiffened. The voice was male, uncertain, and so familiar. "Coulter?"

He was standing near the door to the garden. His blond hair shone in the sun, his cheekbones prominent and his eyes sunken. He had looked like that ever since Adrian died, and every time Arianna had tried to talk with him, he had moved away from her as if she had burned him.

"Gift said you wanted to see me."

She had asked Gift to find Coulter, but now that he was here, she didn't know how to proceed. She stared at him, hands clasped in her lap.

"I can come back," he said.

"No." She stood. She crossed the grass and stopped beside him. He looked down, but he didn't move away. She brought her hand up and, when he didn't flinch, caressed his cheek. His skin was cool.

"I—" her voice broke. "I wanted to let you know how sorry I am about Adrian."

"You've already mentioned that," he said. He wouldn't meet her gaze, but for the first time since the Black King died, he hadn't moved away from her either.

"I know," she said. "I just feel like we had become—friends— and I was hoping we could continue. Maybe I could help you like you helped me."

He leaned into her hand. "Arianna," he murmured. He turned his face and kissed her palm. Then he stepped away. "I can't."

"Why not?" she asked.

"Because," he said. "You're the Black Queen."

"That's not it," she said.

He finally brought his head up, finally met her gaze. His eyes were so sad that she could feel the sorrow as if it were her own. "I failed you," he whispered. "I told your father to forget fighting. I told him you and Gift would be safe because you were Fey."

"Adrian had just died."

"It doesn't matter," he said. "I'm not the man you deserve."

"You're the one I want."

He shook his head. "You're still young. We both are. Too young to make those decisions. You lead the Fey now. You have to do that on your own. You can't have me beside you. It'll give the wrong message."

"To whom? The Fey believe in female leaders."

"But Islanders don't. And one day, you'll rule them too."

Arianna swallowed. "Is this what's between us? Who I am?"

"And who I am," Coulter said. "I'll never be the kind of person you want."

"You already are," she said. "Please, Coulter. Stay with me."

She never asked. She never begged. They both knew that.

It seemed as if the sadness in his eyes increased. Finally, he bowed his head. "I love you, Ari."

"I love you, too," she said. "See? It'll—"

He put his fingers over her mouth. The movement turned into a caress, and for a moment, she thought he was going to kiss her. "No," he said. "We're not ready. You're not. You have to figure out what kind of ruler you'll be. What kind of person you'll be. And I need to heal. These last few weeks have nearly destroyed me, Ari."

"We can do this together," she said, but she knew he would disagree.

"I will always be here," he said. "Every Visionary needs an Enchanter at her side. I know that much about Fey. I'll be yours."

She was shaking. "And then what?"

"We'll give it some time," he said. "And maybe when I'm better and you're established, we can try again."

"I would like to try now," she said.

"You can't have everything you want, Ari," he said. "Sometimes it's better to wait."

She put a finger beneath his chin and held his head so that his gaze met hers. Then he leaned forward, and he kissed her. The kiss was slow and deep and lingering. His arms went around her and pulled her close. She put her arms around his neck and clung to him like she would never see him again.

Finally, he tilted his head back, breaking off the kiss. She still held him close. "You'll still be my friend?" she asked.

"I'll always be more than your friend," he said, and slipped out of her grasp.

# EIGHTY-SIX

THE palace looked different. The entire city looked different. It was filled with Fey, but they seemed a bit stunned, uncertain, as if they weren't quite sure where they fit and what they needed to do.

Luke still avoided them where he could. The King hadn't been back long enough to deal with all the disasters the invasion had created. But he had made an announcement that people should return to their homes. Any uninhabited house would first go to needy Islanders and then to Fey.

Luke and Con had taken over the small house where, Con said, he had stolen some Fey clothes before his trip south. They had remained together even after the announcement of the Black King's death and after that had tried, twice, to get into the palace. It proved just as hard with Islander guards as it had with Fey ones.

Con was beside Luke now, still carrying his sword and wearing the small filigree sword around his neck. Luke had brought him

even though King Nicholas had not asked for him. Luke felt that
the King needed to know what Con had done for the King's son.

The story was that there had been some confusion about the
King's children. Apparently he had three, not two. One son had
been raised by the Fey. That was young Gift, who was seen walking through Jahn on several occasions. His resemblance to his
sister, the Princess Arianna—now the Black Queen of the Fey—
was so startling that it seemed amazing no one had noticed him
before. And then, King Nicholas had another son, Sebastian, who
had been with Con.

No one had seen Sebastian since the King's return. Con
was worried that the Black King had done something irreparable
to him.

Luke was certain of it.

After Luke had given his name to one of the guards, he and
Con were asked to wait, while another guard fetched King
Nicholas and his children. The wait was long, but it gave both
Luke and Con a chance to get used to being in the palace.

Finally they were ushered into the audience hall. King Nicholas sat in an ornate throne on the dais. His daughter, the new
Black Queen, stood beside him, speaking to a rather wizened Fey
woman. The mixture of Fey and Islander in the palace had startled Luke; he would have thought that the King would get rid of
the Fey as quickly as possible.

But Nicholas was apparently true to his word. He had said, in
his first speech upon his return, that Fey and Islander needed to
work together to create a home here. He had also given anyone
who wanted it permission to leave the Isle, to go to Galinas. He
did not allow any ships to sail toward Leut.

Leaving the Isle, though, was still a bit of a problem. The
watchers of the Stone Guardians hadn't worked in over twenty
years, and many of them were dead. The currents had to be
mapped all over again for Jahn to work as a harbor. Now, if anyone wanted to leave, they had to do so via the remaining Fey
ships to the south.

When the King saw Luke, he smiled. They had met only once
before, when Luke had been Charmed by the Fey and had nearly
killed the Fifty-first Rocaan. The King looked older now, his hair
streaked with gray. He was thinner too. The weeks of exile had
given him a lean, strong look.

The Black Queen was almost too thin. When she turned,
Luke gasped. He hadn't realized how much she looked like her

mother. Luke still wasn't certain how he felt about Jewel; she had been the one who had ordered him Charmed and who had imprisoned his father. But she had also implanted a crush in him, a crush on her that he had never entirely overcome.

"Sire," Luke said, bowing at the waist. Con bowed beside him, sword scraping.

"Please stand." The King's voice was as strong as Luke remembered it, warm and kind as well. "I wanted to express in person my condolences on your father's death."

"And so did I," the Black Queen said. Her eyes were slightly swollen as if she had been crying. "Adrian was a great man."

Luke nodded, and swallowed hard. He had only received the news the day before. "What's happened to him?"

"His body is in the Cliffs of Blood," the King said. "We were unable to bring him home."

Luke's smile was small. "There is no home to bring him too. It burned."

The King nodded as if he had known about the fire.

"Your attack," he said, "was the first step in allowing us to defeat the Black King. I was hoping you would continue to work at my side, as one of the leaders of the new army."

"I thought we were done with fighting, sire," Luke said.

"I hope so," the King said. "But I think if we have learned anything from this, we have learned to be prepared for all contingencies."

Luke bowed again. "I would be honored." Then he rose. The King was looking at Con. The Fey woman had stepped behind the Black Queen and was watching from the shadows.

"Forgive my presumption, sire, at bringing a friend to this audience, but I felt you would like to meet him." Luke turned, put a hand on Con's back, and propelled him forward. "This is Con. He was an Aud. He had had a Charge from the Rocaan and—"

"You're Con?" The Black Queen's voice rose in excitement. She took a step off the dais. "Sebastian said you would know how to reassemble him."

Con looked around, his expression hopeful. "He's here?"

The Black Queen shook her head. "We don't know where he is. But I was wondering what I'd do when we found him."

"Sebastian?" the Fey woman spoke from the back of the dais. "The Prince's Golem?"

"Yes." This time, the King was the one who spoke. He turned slightly in his throne. "You know of him, Seger?"

"I have pieces of him in my room," she said. "I removed them from the Black King. The rest of the pieces were discarded."

"Discarded," the Black Queen said, and sat down. Luke had never heard such despair uttered in a single word before.

"It does not really matter," the Fey woman said, "as long as we have a part of him. I have made Golems before. If this young man can reassemble the pieces, then we can use extra stone to bring the Golem back to full size."

"You do know how to reassemble him, don't you?" the Black Queen asked Con. Her cheeks were flushed, her eyes bright.

"Yes." Con put a hand on the hilt of his sword.

"Get the pieces," the King said. Seger nodded, and hurried out of the audience chamber. The King smiled at his daughter. There was relief in his voice. "I thought we had lost Sebastian forever."

"We haven't reassembled him yet, Daddy," the Black Queen said.

Reassembled. Luke looked at all of them. The Fey had brought a myriad of changes to Blue Isle, and they were all evident in this room. An Aud who no longer dressed like an Aud, a King who allowed both Fey and Islander access to him equally, and a mixed-race Queen who outranked her father worldwide, but not in this tiny place, not in this Isle.

It would take Luke a long time to get used to the changes, but he would.

He had to.

They all did.

He leaned back and waited for the Fey healer to return.

# EIGHTY-SEVEN

NICHOLAS let Arianna talk to the young Aud and Adrian's son. He sat in silence while he waited.

No matter what Ari had said, no matter how the Domestics had reassured him, Nicholas had heard the story of Sebastian's pieces being discarded. He knew that no one had been able to capture his essence. Somehow, Nicholas had thought those facts meant that Sebastian was dead.

Nicholas had resigned himself to Sebastian's loss and had never thought to ask further.

How lucky it had been that Seger was still in the Audience Hall when Luke and young Con had arrived. She had insisted on speaking to Arianna, who had been hiding in the garden. Nicholas had sent for her, and while he waited, he let Seger talk. She had been trying to explain Gift's desire to become a Shaman. The training sounded too rigorous to Nicholas and rather boring. But Gift had seemed enthusiastic about it. The problem was that he would be gone from the Isle, gone from the family for a minimum of five years. And even then, his training would only be started. A Shaman didn't reach his full power until he was nearly the age the Black King was when he died. Nicholas's Shaman, whose body rested beside Adrian's in the Place of Power, had been considered a young Shaman, and she was old, older than Nicholas could ever hope to be.

But Gift was only one of his concerns. Nicholas suddenly had so many. He had to integrate the Fey into this culture. He had to rebuild the Isle itself, from the businesses in Jahn to the farms near Killeny's bridge. He had to teach Arianna how to rule, and he had to see Jewel, somehow, somewhere.

Jewel had promised him that she would be beside him when he needed her, but that wasn't quite the same thing. He could see her and touch her in the Place of Power. He was tempted to move the palace there, but that was a decision that could wait. He had more immediate things to take care of first.

Seger returned with another Fey following behind her. Nicholas recognized her as one of the Domestics he had let remain in the palace. He trusted them more than his assistants did. The Fey couldn't hurt him. He was the Black Queen's father and, as Jewel said, the Fey would do anything they could for the Black family. He had kept the Domestics and Healers here, sending the Infantry, Foot Soldiers, and Beast Riders away from the palace. The Spell Warders remained in their quarters as well. Nicholas hoped they could help with upcoming problems as more Islanders and Fey mated.

Seger was cupping several pieces of stone in her hand. She had a robe over her other arm. The Domestic carried a large rock in both hands.

"Where would you like this?" Seger asked.

"By Con," Nicholas said.

Seger set the stones down. Arianna crouched beside them as if she could already see her brother in them. The Domestic set the stone down as well.

"All right," Nicholas said to the young Aud. "Do whatever it is you do."

Con glanced at Luke, who nodded. "I think you might want to move, ma'am," he said to Arianna.

She looked at him, startled, and backed away. Con unsheathed his sword. The guards around the room put their hands on the hilts of theirs. Nicholas stayed them with a slight motion of his fingers.

Con set the sword on the rubble.

The room spun, and it felt as if all the air had suddenly left it. Thunder boomed, almost as loudly as it had when Matthias dropped the swords into the ground near the Place of Power.

Con and Luke slammed backwards as if they were pushed. Arianna and Seger stumbled slightly. The guards were pressed against the wall. Nicholas's throne bounced with the impact. The other Domestic held her place.

Then the air returned.

Nicholas looked down.

Sebastian sat in the middle of the room, totally naked. Seger went to him and put the robe around his shoulders. Arianna ran to him and put her arms around him. He held her and rocked her back and forth.

"I thought you would never find me," he said.

Arianna backed away from him as if she'd been burned. Nicholas stood up, heart pounding. Seger had a hand to her mouth.

That sentence didn't sound like Sebastian had spoken it. Nicholas had last heard that voice in this very room. The voice belonged to the Black King of the Fey.

"This can't be," Nicholas said.

Arianna's lower lip was trembling. "No," she whispered.

Sebastian was looking at all of them with an expression Nicholas hadn't realized he missed. The mixture of confusion and hurt, of desire to be accepted and worry that he would not.

Seger sighed. "Use your own voice, boy," she said.

"What . . . did . . . I . . . do?" he asked. "I . . . thought . . . it . . . would . . . be . . . easier . . . to . . . speak . . . that . . . way."

"Easier and more dangerous," Seger said. "If you use someone else's voice too much, you take on part of his soul."

Sebastian shuddered visibly. "I'll . . . get . . . rid . . . of . . . it."

"No." Arianna came up beside him and put her arms around him again. "Will it hurt him to keep it?" she asked Seger.

"Not if he doesn't use it very often."

"We might need it, Sebastian," Arianna said.

"Why?"

"We might need to convince some more Fey."

"Of . . . what?"

Ari smiled. "I'll explain later. There's so much to tell you."

"I . . . have . . . been . . . gone . . . a . . . long . . . time?"

"Yes." Con spoke. Sebastian reached out a hand to him, and Con took it. They had apparently become very close.

Nicholas couldn't wait any longer. He went down the three steps and crossed to his son. He wrapped Sebastian in his arms, feeling the rock solidity of him, the coolness of his skin.

"I thought we'd lost you forever, son," he said.

"You . . . can't . . . lose . . . me . . . , Dad," Sebastian said. "I . . . always . . . want . . . to . . . be . . . with . . . my . . . fam-i-ly."

"And we always want to be with you." Nicholas didn't want to let him go, but he did, allowing Ari to put her arm around Sebastian. The shadows under her eyes had disappeared as if by magick.

"Thank you, Sebastian," she said softly, "for saving me from the Black King."

"I . . . love . . . you . . . , Ari," he said.

"I love you too."

Nicholas stood back and watched them, two of his three children, and knew that the circle would be complete when Gift returned from his walk in the city. The three of them were his future. They were the country's future, the world's future, and he had no doubt they would do well in anything they tried.

He only wished Jewel were here to see them.

And then he remembered:

She was.

# VICTORY
## [ONE MONTH LATER]

# EIGHTY-EIGHT

SHE flew in the cool mountain air, wings spread. Arianna had never been a hawk before. It was freeing, majestic, and appropriate, somehow.

These mountains were smaller than the Cliffs of Blood, yet they were very imposing. Their gray sides held a lot of history as well, only she missed the faint redness in the stone. Still, the Snow Mountains were as much a part of her home as the Eyes of Roca. She simply had not seen the Snow Mountains before, and she had not seen them up close.

The Hawk Riders had just notified her that the climbers were near the plateau. She had thanked the Riders, and Shifted, startling them. The Fey, apparently, were not used to their Black Ruler Shifting into some other creature.

She had laughed at their startled expressions, and then she had said, "Aren't you going to join me?"

The Riders assumed their hawk forms and flew behind her. Two of them carried the robe she had insisted on between them like a ribbon.

Her father had wanted to come with her on this mission, but she had talked him out of it. The Fey were her problem now. When they resided on Blue Isle, they fell under his jurisdiction, but she always ruled them. He had agreed to her argument with only a hint of amusement.

She had asked Coulter to come, but he had said no. He had reminded her that she hadn't allowed her father to come, and had told her that she needed to learn how to rule alone.

There was still the attraction between them, but right now she was respecting his wishes and not acting on it. Still, she knew it was only a matter of time before their friendship returned to the intensity they had felt in the Place of Power.

She had never been to the plateau before, but the Riders said she would know it when she saw it—and she did.

She flew between the peaks as they instructed and there, in a long narrow crevice, was a simple plateau. The wind blew harsh through it, and she had to land carefully so that she wouldn't slam against the volcanic rock.

Her great-grandfather had stood here when he first arrived on Blue Isle. Some of the Hawk Riders with her had brought him, in a harness. She was proud of the fact that she needed no harness, and never would. She was proud of many things. She was most proud of the way the Islanders and the Fey were beginning to work together.

It was up to her to keep it that way.

She Shifted into her Fey form and shivered in the icy wind. Without even looking, she extended a hand for her robe, and one of the Riders gave it to her. They had transformed into their Fey forms as well, only they remained nude. Their long, feathery hair seemed to protect them from the cold.

She wrapped the robe around herself, wishing she had brought shoes as well. Then she realized it didn't matter. Her feet would be cold, but it was a small price to see this.

The fleet of ships her great-grandfather had ordered before he went to the Cliffs of Blood had arrived. Partway here, of course, they had received the messages she sent to Nye, proclaiming herself Black Queen, as her mother had told her—through Gift— how to do. Her mother doubted that her uncle Bridge would give her any trouble.

*He wouldn't dare*, her mother had said. *Blood against Blood applies to him as well.* Arianna was a bit amazed it hadn't applied at the Place of Power. After all, her father had killed the Black King. But, her mother had said, her father had wanted to. He had had reasons of his own. He was not doing it under Arianna's or Gift's orders.

And that made all the difference.

Arianna took one last step forward. She had never seen the Infrin Sea before. It was rough and rocky, gray and dark, not at all what she imagined. Whitecapped waves slammed up against the smooth ocean-side of the mountains, booming with a fierceness she hadn't thought possible. She wouldn't want to be in a ship on that ocean, and yet hundreds of Fey had been.

And they were climbing the rocks to get to Blue Isle, just as her great-grandfather's people had three months before. Hundreds of Fey scaled the mountainside, their bodies getting smaller the farther down she looked.

From this height, the ships were insignificant, barely able to hold their own against the waves. Lines trailed from the edge of the plateau here down to the ocean, and as she watched, the first of the new arrivals pulled himself to the plateau.

He was as old as her father, a Fey with a weather-worn face and a look of command. He used his arms to pull himself the rest of the way, and then stood before her. He was as tall as she was.

He stared at her, dark eyes wary.

Now it was time to do what she had come for, to establish herself once and for all as the daughter of King Nicholas the Fifth of Blue Isle and as the Black Queen of the Fey Empire.

She held out her hand, Islander fashion, to the Fey man before her. He stared at the hand for a moment, then took it.

She smiled at him.

"Welcome to Blue Isle," she said.

# ABOUT THE AUTHOR

Kristine Kathryn Rusch is an award-winning fiction writer. Her most recent sf novel for Bantam Books, *Alien Influences*, was a finalist for the prestigious Arthur C. Clarke Award. She has published four previous books of the Fey, as well as twenty other novels. Her novel, *Star Wars: The New Rebellion*, and several of her Star Trek novels have made the *USA Today* bestseller list. Her short fiction has been nominated for the Nebula, Hugo, World Fantasy, and Stoker awards. Her novella, *The Gallery of His Dreams*, won the *Locus Award* for best short fiction. Her body of fiction work won her the John W. Campbell Award, given in 1991 in Europe. *The Fey: Sacrifice* was chosen by *Science Fiction Chronicle* as one of the Best Fantasy Novels of 1995.

Until last year, she edited the *Magazine of Fantasy and Science Fiction*, a prestigious fiction magazine founded in 1949. In 1994, she won the Hugo award for her editing work. She started Pulphouse Publishing with her husband, Dean Wesley Smith, and they won a World Fantasy Award for their work on that press. Rusch and Smith edited *The SFWA Handbook: A Professional Writers Guide to Writing Professionally*, which won the *Locus Award* for Best Nonfiction. They have also written several novels under the pen name Sandy Schofield.

Her next books for Bantam are *The Black Throne Series*, which continue the story of Arianna, Gift, and Coulter.

Please visit her web site at www.horrornet.com/rusch.htm

# REALMS OF FANTASY

*The biggest, brightest stars from Bantam Spectra*

## Maggie Furey

**A** fiery-haired Mage with an equally incendiary temper must save her world and her friends from a pernicious evil, with the aid of four forgotten magical Artefacts.

AURIAN ___56525-7  $6.50

HARP OF WINDS ___56526-5  $6.99

SWORD OF FLAME ___56527-3  $6.99

DHIAMMARA ___57557-0  $6.50

## Katharine Kerr

**T**he mistress of Celtic fantasy presents her ever-popular Deverry series. Most recent titles:

DAYS OF BLOOD AND FIRE ___29012-6  $6.50/$8.99

DAYS OF AIR AND DARKNESS ___57262-8  $6.50/$8.99

THE RED WYVERN ___57264-4  $6.50/$8.99

- - - - - - - - - - - - - - - - - - - - - - - -

# REALMS OF FANTASY

*The biggest, brightest stars from Bantam Spectra*

## Robin Hobb

One of our newest and most exciting talents presents a tale of honor and subterfuge, loyalty and betrayal.

ASSASSIN'S APPRENTICE: Book One of the Farseer

_____57339-X    $6.99/$9.99 Canada

ROYAL ASSASSIN: Book Two of the Farseer

_____57341-1    $6.99/$9.99 Canada

ASSASSIN'S QUEST: Book Three of the Farseer

_____56569-9    $6.99/$9.99 Canada

## Michael A. Stackpole

High fantasy from the *New York Times* bestselling author:

ONCE A HERO _____56112-X    $5.99/$7.99

TALION: REVENANT _____57656-9    $5.99/$7.99

---

# REALMS OF FANTASY

*The biggest, brightest stars from Bantam Spectra*

## Paula Volsky

Rich tapestries of magic and revolution, romance and forbidden desires.

THE WHITE TRIBUNAL___57581-3   $6.50/$8.99

## Angus Wells

Epic fantasy in the grandest tradition of magic, dragons, and heroic quests. Most recent titles:

EXILE'S CHALLENGE: Book Two of the Exiles Saga
___57778-6   $5.99/$7.99
LORDS OF THE SKY
___57266-0   $5.99/$7.99

---

Ask for these books at your local bookstore or use this page to order.

Please send me the books I have checked above. I am enclosing $____ (add $2.50 to cover postage and handling). Send check or money order, no cash or C.O.D.'s, please.

Name _____

Address _____

City/State/Zip _____

Send order to: Bantam Books, Dept. SF 29, 2451 S. Wolf Rd., Des Plaines, IL 60018
Allow four to six weeks for delivery.
Prices and availability subject to change without notice.          SF 29 10/98